MAIA

AND THE

LEGEND OF TANSI

S. G. BASU

ISBN-13: 978-1-950350-04-9
ISBN-10: 1-950350-04-5
US Copyright number: TXu 2-341-381

For Saloni Jheelum

My bright-eyed little darling, the biggest fan Maia and the gang will ever have, and without whom this book would have taken two years to complete.

MAIA

AND THE

LEGEND OF TANSI

GALACTIC MAP

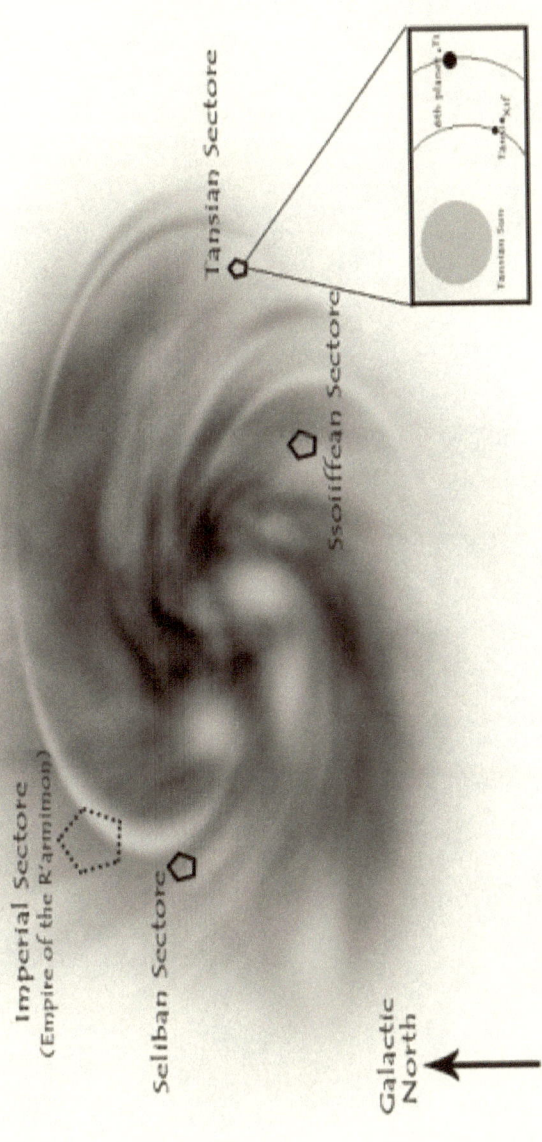

Imperial Sectore
(Empire of the R'armimon)

Seliban Sectore

Ssoliffean Sectore

Tansian Sectore

Tansian Sun

Tansia Klif

6th planet, ?!

Galactic
North

The Map of Tarsi

Coloni Aestei

The First Continent

The Fourth Continent

The Eastern Seas

ThulaSu ◎

Coloni Centrei

● Tra

Coloni Primei

Zagran ●

Miorie ◎

Shiloh ◎

Arpian ◎

Dorgashian Folds

The Third Continent

The Second Continent

Coloni Vestei

The Western Seas

Map Key

Jiord Settlement

◎ Solianese City

CHAPTER ONE

IN THE SHADOWS

The most venerated room in the R'armimon flagship was not its command center or the private suites of the heir-in-waiting. It was the Beholding Chamber. Although not large by the standards of the ship, it was by far the grandest. It was covered from ceiling to floor—velvet draperies, plush carpets, extensive murals—in violent shades of red. Light was minimal, an orb or two in the corners fighting valiantly to shed some brightness.

At the center of this room was a gigantic empty frame made of dull metal. Ornate carvings were etched into it, and every now and then, a flicker of red light coursed along those etchings. Before this frame, the heir-in-waiting, Crown Prince Aekken of the Empire R'armimon, paced relentlessly. Every few moments, he cast a nervous, worried look at the frame, then continued his pacing. Suddenly, the frame sputtered, startling Aekken. The Crown Prince rushed to the frame and placed himself carefully in front of it. He rearranged himself a little to make sure his posture was erect, every hair was in place, and his clothes were faultless.

The empty space within the frame swirled with smoke before clearing slowly, and a room, immense yet stark, came into view. Straight ahead was a platform, and on it stood a gigantic throne. Someone sat on it, but even though their form was visible, the face was shrouded in darkness.

Aekken bowed so low that his long tresses touched the floor. "Eternal respects, Emperor Glorious and Honorable of the Empire R'armimon," he said.

"Crown Prince Aekken, it is heartening to see you." The voice that emanated from the darkness around the throne exuded control. Every rise and fall, every nuance said the man was one in charge, aware of his power, and fearless about wielding it. It was not cold, but it was hard. It was not loud, but it was pervasive. "You have done well, Crown Prince Aekken," the emperor continued. "You have found the renegades after all. Your persistence is appreciated and will be rewarded aptly."

Aekken straightened himself and looked into the portal, his dark eyes still restless.

"Yet you seem unhappy," the emperor observed. "Are you frightened?"

"I am worried, Father," Aekken said. "That is why I requested this viewing with you."

There was an oppressive moment of silence before the emperor spoke, "What worries you?"

Aekken's fists curled, and his eyes narrowed as he stared fixedly at his feet. "I want to blast the deadwastes out of existence. I do not want to linger here one day longer than it takes to grind that planet to dust."

"That is what you must do, unfortunately," the emperor said, his voice betraying an undercurrent of amusement. "Blasting them would mean difficult times for Tansi. However, since Tansi is fortunate enough to host a living Nasfarii, you cannot lift a finger against them. That is the truth of the matter, is it not?"

"You know," Aekken said, looking up in surprise at the frame before hastily lowering his gaze.

"Yes. The seer has informed me."

Aekken gritted his teeth as he exhaled slowly. "It is settled, then? I cannot harm the Nasfarii."

"No. Never." The answer came swift and sharp. It made Aekken wince.

"What do I do, then? Wait here until she dies?"

Laughter, high-spirited and jeering, echoed across the chamber. Aekken's face fell, and his nervous eyes scanned back and forth on the floor as if he were seeking a place to hide.

"Crown Prince Aekken, this is good preparation for you for the time you hope to spend on this throne," the emperor said when his laughter had ebbed. "You need to learn to play the game. The Empire is not what it is because we take the cudgel to anyone who dares to oppose us. We only use force when absolutely necessary. Most times, we use a web of persuasion. Some call it deception, but that is simply another word. The essence of the matter is, we have to win, so we discover a way around problems."

"How?"

"Nasfarii are rare, Aekken. We have not been blessed with one in two generations. She could be of great use here in the heart of the Empire."

Aekken's eyes widened a little. "You wish me to bring her to you?" Then he shook his head. "She seems happy here. She will not leave willingly."

"Willingly? We are the Empire, Aekken. Someday, you hope to be the face of the R'armimon. We do not wait around hoping for people to willingly follow us, we *make* them. Nasfarii or otherwise, people will bend to your will. They must. All you have to do is outmaneuver them."

"Outmaneuver her?" Aekken looked up, and his eyes flashed. "That worthless traitor of a seer watches over her all the time, like a bird clucking over its hatchling. He has forgotten his vows to the Empire and become her protector. How can I—"

"Crown Prince Aekken" — the emperor cut him off coldly — "you *have* to find a path."

Another oppressive silence fell in the room until Aekken spoke again in a shaky voice. "What if she suspects what I am up to? I am fearful of a Nasfarii's wrath, Father. It is said that a Nasfarii wielding her full power has absolute control over not only the elements but also the universe, that they can bend space and time to their will. She could crush our fleet in an instant. She could even reach as far as the heart of the Empire if she —"

"Such are the tales about Princess Ataii. But this girl is not our lost princess, Aekken. Her powers are nothing in comparison. Nothing. I hear she can wield the light, but that is where the similarities end. Our seer has tried to train her, but I know he has made little progress. I think I know why."

"Why?"

"As I said, this is no Princess Ataii, Aekken. This is a mere child, a broken one from a broken home. Not only did her powers stay undiscovered until just a few years ago, she has had no true training since. She is weak, always fearful of losing what little she possesses, and always yearning for acceptance which no one wants to give her. Her heart is fragile, fractured. One careful blow and it will shatter."

"How do you know this?"

A throaty chuckle poured out of the darkness. "I am the ruler of the Empire R'armimon. I have my ways. And means."

"Please —"

"No, I shall not aid you in that, Crown Prince. You will need to find and acquire your own ways and means."

Aekken's head drooped lower. "I have failed you."

"No, you have not. You simply have more to learn." The emperor's reply made Aekken's downcast face brighten a little. "Know this, Aekken. This girl has potential, that is true. But she is in no position to withstand the full power of a Nasfarii. Our good Seer Ruche is well aware of that. He knows she does not have the strength to wield it, so he will not even try. Do you think he would have let you come near Tansi if he could use her?"

Aekken looked up, into the darkness inside the frame. "She is not strong enough?"

"No, I am certain of that. To ascend to the highest level of consciousness, to reach the state of Arotharan, she needs to be in a strong, content, peaceful state of mind. But right now, she is too weak, too damaged, too conflicted. She is not ready. I am certain the seer is trying to heal her, make her strong enough to get there. The seer will keep trying, but it will not be easy. The seer knows he cannot try it too soon, or she will die on her way to Arotharan." Aekken's dark eyes sparkled with hope and the emperor continued. "Your work is simple, Crown Prince. If she is weak, make her weaker. If she is broken, break her even more. Give her hopeless thoughts, Aekken, and show her a path that leads to you. Make her believe that the only place she has left to go is here, with us."

Aekken's lips twisted into a smile and his eyes gleamed. "That I can do," he whispered.

"I shall eagerly await your return, Crown Prince Aekken, with the Nasfarii by your side."

"I will not disappoint you, Father."

"I hope not," the emperor said, his voice momentarily sharp. "I will offer you one last thought, Aekken. Once the Nasfarii is removed, there will be no reason why you could not blast that planet to dust, just as they deserve."

Aekken bowed low as the scene within the frame faded and disappeared. When he straightened himself again, his pale face was luminous with hope and happiness, and his eyes gleamed. His hands curled into tight balls and a crooked smile tugged the corners of his mouth.

"I shall have what I want," he whispered. Then lifting his face toward the murals gazing down on him from the distant ceiling, he screamed, "I shall have what I want!"

CHAPTER TWO

AFTER THE STORM

A foggy day broke over ThulaSu the day after the R'armimon fleet arrived. The spaceship—one had shown up in the skies above ThulaSu, also—from the night before, or the "talon ship" as people had named the behemoth, was nowhere to be seen, and that was the one good thing about that morning. Maia feared it would reappear to hover over them forever, but nothing had come back since that first sighting.

Maia and her friends were huddled in the visitant chamber of the sanatorium, as they had been since the night before. They were waiting for news on Ori Pistado, who had been severely injured during the fight with the Jomral at the Trinity Caverns. The healers had been hard at work, and Maia kept praying that Ori would make it through. However, with every moment that slipped by, her hopes diminished. A steady stream of Black Phantoms and villagers came and went, but no one brought any news. The skies were starting to show a hint of light when Dorian walked over to Maia and her friends.

"You should get some rest," he said. "I will send you news as soon as I have any."

"But you're all here," Maia protested.

"You were there with him when we couldn't be. Now that we are here, you can take a break. Come back a little later. Your friends are tired too, and they won't leave unless you do."

He had a point. Maia looked askance at her friends. Everyone sported gashes of various sizes, bandages covering the bigger ones. Her own badly-scraped hands were wrapped in gauze. Their clothes were torn and blood-spattered. Dani looked the worst, her face dull and forlorn. The previous evening had taken a toll on her for sure. Causing Hilledunn's death had already left her battered, and now dreading that Ori had slipped through her hands must make it even worse. She surely needed to be away from here.

Ren, who had taken off for the Xifarian encampment at Frauz Point after making the second trip back from the Fourth, was the only one missing. *No, not just Ren*, Maia corrected herself. She could not find Miir either. As soon as they reached the sanatorium, he had blended into the huddle of Black Phantoms, and as she scanned the Phantoms now, she could not locate him.

"All right, we'll go. But please, send me word as soon as you hear anything. Anything at all."

"I promise."

No one said a word in protest when Maia asked, and they trudged in a morose pack out of the sanatorium. They were only halfway to the living quarters when Sana came rushing up to them.

"There you are," she said breathlessly, her face shadowing with worry as she saw their numerous wounds. "I went looking for you in your rooms. Ren just told me about last night."

As the rest of the group forged forward, Maia hung back a little with Sana.

"We were at the sanatorium."

"How is Ori?"

Maia shook her head. "Don't know. All we hear is they are trying to stabilize him, that he lost a lot of blood. And then . . . nothing."

Sana sighed. "If I hadn't told him how deceptive Hiso could be, he wouldn't —"

"Sana, don't." Maia cut her off forcefully. "Ori knew what Hiso is capable of, and he would have stayed anyway. Nothing you said made this happen. You know what did? Hiso and his cronies and their greed and dishonesty. So stop blaming yourself."

"I will try, Maia," Sana said in a low voice. "But the thought keeps coming back to me."

Maia knew exactly what Sana was talking about. Regrets never stopped coming. She should have done more, she should have decided sooner . . . should have . . . could have . . . they washed over her ceaselessly. Maia also knew she could not let them settle in her mind or she would drown. She had to help Sana, too. So, stiffening her spine, she said in a brave voice, "Don't let it get to you."

They walked in silence for a while before Sana spoke again, her voice a bit brighter. "Well, let's look at the silver lining. We have the stockade module master plan now, right? That's a big win."

"Yes, it is. Hans can move on with his project. Tansi will have a chance." They walked on in silence once more, until Maia remembered their other gain during the incident at the Trinity Caverns. "Oh, we also found the Shrine of the Settlers. It turns out that the stars on the ground were not Bikele's fantasy after all. They were real. Someone planted L'miere crystals all over the place. The entire forest floor glowed like the night sky."

Sana stopped and gasped. "I don't believe this. Really?"

"I still can't believe it myself," Maia admitted. "If we hadn't been running to find cover, we would probably never have found it at all. We could hardly even see the building. It's all covered in vines and undergrowth."

"What did you find there?"

"We didn't go inside. It was dark and we had no strength left to fight our way in. And I won't lie, that talon ship had me shaken. So the moment Ren sent word that he was near, I was ready to leave that place."

"Oh, don't remind me of that monster ship," Sana said, shuddering a little. "I'll have nightmares for ages. R'armimon, is it?"

"I think so," Maia said. "It was creepy, but it did help in a way. It scared off all the reinforcements Hiso had sent. The mouth of the caverns was completely clear. That was a blessing. I don't know if I could fight fifty more Jomral."

Sana slipped an arm around her shoulders and pointed at her bandages. "Are you badly hurt?"

"No. Nothing too bad."

"And you'll go back there to investigate the shrine, right?"

"Yes, of course. Shama has the spot marked, and I plan to head back there soon."

They had come to the entrance of the living quarters and Sana slowed. "You get some rest, Maia. I'll go to the sanatorium and stay there for a bit."

"Call me if you have news?"

"Of course."

Sana turned to leave and Maia had just stepped into the building when she suddenly remembered. "Hey, Sana," she called, turning back around. "What happened with Hiso?"

Sana's face puckered. "Don't ask. That piece of filth is now up in arms against the Solianese Council. Says it's a sacrilege that the caverns of the Nouvus could be treated so poorly. As soon as Ori gets better, Hiso is going to request punishment for everyone involved. Can you imagine?"

Maia's insides erupted in an inferno. The gall of that man.

"Once Ori gets better, huh?" she said, barely finding her voice. "And what if he doesn't?"

Sana looked away. "Then nothing, Maia. Nothing ever happens to people like Hiso. They get away with everything. Always. Even now, Hiso hasn't admitted that he is behind the takeover of the Nouvus. He knows no one can prove it, so . . ."

They stood for a moment in frustrated and thoughtful silence before going their own ways. Maia went to take a bath. The water was not as warm as she might have wished, but it was still refreshing. At least it washed away the constant reminders of the night's battle that clung to her skin.

"Take a quick nap, Maia," Rayan advised as she curled up in her own bed.

Perhaps Maia would have, but before she could towel her hair dry, the sound of running feet echoed along the corridor outside. Then came the pounding on the door. Maia knew what it would be even before she opened the door and saw Sana's tear-streaked face.

"We lost him, Maia," Sana said, panting. "Ori's gone."

Maia dashed out, forgetting Rayan, Bellator, and her dripping hair. She did not stop until she reached the sanatorium. The visitant room was full—Black Phantoms, villagers, and people from ThulaSu stood in grief-stricken huddles. A cloud of sorrow, thick and oppressive, had descended in the room and Maia realized, with a sudden, painful jolt, just how much people loved the chieftain. Maia headed straight to where Ori's wife Niyani sat sobbing, with Nahlo by her side. Her mind was in a daze as she knelt in front of Niyani, as was the custom when expressing condolences.

"I have no words," Maia said. "I wish—"

Niyani clutched her hand, making Maia forget the little she had prepared to say. "You were there for him, Maia. I'm grateful for that. I'm grateful that he was surrounded by true friends like you. May the stars bless you."

For a few moments, they stayed still, united in grief. Then, while the others took turns to speak with Niyani, Maia plodded out of the visitant chamber, her heart weighing like a boulder inside her. Then she saw Miir, a lonely statue on the side steps that led down from the circular stone porch surrounding the sanatorium, his vacant gaze fixed on the pathway ahead. As she walked up to him, Maia noticed spatters of red on the back of his hands.

Ori's blood!

He had not left the sanatorium for a moment. The bruises on the side of his face were untended. He had not even taken the time to salve them. Maia's heart wrenched at the sight and at the realization of how self-centered she had been. All the time since Ori fell, she had been wallowing in her own misery. Miir had consoled, comforted, and held her steady when she ran impulsively into the darkness. All the while he had been hurting. Had anyone felt the need to comfort him? She had not, that was for sure. Until now she had not even thought of how much Ori must have meant to him.

Slow, remorseful steps took Maia to his side, and she sat down on the steps beside him.

"Hey!" she called gently.

Miir gave her a sidelong glance, his faraway gaze never meeting hers.

"Hey!" His reply was just as distant, inattentive. He stayed quiet, and Maia let him be. This was his time to mourn, and silence was the best thing she could offer. The quiet stretched for a long time, but it did not for a moment feel tiring. Instead, it was soothing, like a calm, comforting patch on an exposed wound.

"You know" — Miir spoke up suddenly — "Ori took me in when I had nothing. I had lost faith in the world I knew, and the world in me. He had every reason to throw me out. But even after he heard who I was, and what I had done, he never judged me. Took me under his wing instead and . . ."

Miir's words faded and he fell silent. Once again, Maia waited.

"Many of the people closest to him did not want me in Walenveil, and I understood why. I was a Xifarian, their enemy through and through. I was one of those who attacked the fabled star child promised to them. They had every right to hate me, to doubt me. But not Ori. His decision about me never wavered. He really saved me, in more ways than one."

The pain in his voice, raw and searing, wafted through the air in a slow melancholy wave.

"Now I feel so empty," Miir said. "Almost makes me wish I had not known him."

"Don't say that. You are in too much pain now to think of it any other way, but . . . you had good times together, and those memories are important. Precious. I know they will come back to you and help you all your life, whenever you need them."

Miir turned to look at her, and Maia discovered with relief that the distant look in his eyes had faded a little. Somehow, her words had reached him. A wave of happiness, unexpected and intense, coursed through her and brought her the conviction to continue.

"He cared a lot about you," Maia said. "He valued your honesty, thought highly of your character. He respected you for who you are. He told me so."

Miir sighed deeply. It sounded as if his soul was crushed under the weight of Ori's death. "He liked telling me that a lot. As if I needed my head to get any bigger."

"That was not making your head bigger," Maia protested. "He built you up when you thought you'd lost everything. He showed you who you really are."

He looked at her again and turned away just as quickly. Then he spoke in a rush. "It is unkind of me to say it, but . . ." He stopped, and Maia saw the hesitation rippling across his face. She hoped he could continue, not simply because she wanted to know what he was thinking, but because she believed sharing it would help him heal. "I feel worse than when I lost my father. A hundred times worse."

Maia did not know much about the relationship between Miir and the late Xifarian Chancellor, but she knew it had been less than warm. There was understanding in the end, so Miir had said, but for most of their lives, they had probably been distant. Ori and his immense kindness had filled that void in Miir's life.

Maia wanted to put a hand on his shoulder to comfort him, but she held back. He looked so fragile, it almost felt as if he would shatter at the slightest touch.

"It is not unkind, not at all," she said instead, hoping her words would help him. "It would be unkind if you didn't acknowledge Ori for who he was and what he meant to you."

Neither of them spoke after that, but to Maia, it seemed some of the weight around them had lifted. It was too soon, and she knew grief took its own time to subside, but she wholeheartedly wished for things to get better for Miir. She prayed, not just for him but for all of them, hoping the gashes the previous night had left would start to heal someday soon.

Just then Maia heard a sweet, soul-curdling voice float out from the visitant room behind them, and all her hopes crashed to the ground.

CHAPTER THREE

WRATH UNCHAINED

Hiso's sweet voice, wrapped in fake niceness, hit Maia's tired nerves squarely and made her draw a sharp breath. She wanted to shut him out, not get riled up at a time like this, but every word Hiso said dug deeper into her.

"I am so grieved by this tragedy. You cannot imagine the depth of my sorrow," Hiso went on, perhaps speaking to Niyani. "We will surely get to the bottom of this situation, and bring the ones responsible to justice, swiftly and efficiently. I promise you. Hiso is at your service. Anything you need, anything at all, I am here."

Miir shot her a worried look as Maia took in another sharp breath. "Ignore him," he said.

"Believe me, I'm trying my best."

Hiso did not go on forever, thankfully. As soon as he stopped speaking, Maia sighed with relief. She would face him someday, but not now. Now was not the time or the place. But she had relaxed a little too soon.

"Oh, is that our fearless warrior girl I see?" Maia stiffened as

Hiso's voice drifted to her ears again.

He's not talking about me. Not about me.

Footsteps came closer and Maia quickly realized two things. First, Hiso *was* talking about her, and second, she had few options. The best choice was to stand up and talk to Hiso.

"What are you doing?" Miir whispered as she rose to her feet.

"I can't let Hiso come any closer. He mustn't see you," Maia said. "Don't worry, I've got this," she added.

Looking at Hiso's simpering face made Maia's skin crawl, but she managed to hold his gaze steadily. Two Jomral flanked Hiso. Behind them were Dorian and a few other Phantoms, their faces taut.

"Maia, dear," Hiso said in his sickeningly sweet tones. "Are you well?"

Why don't you just let me be?

"I'm fine," she replied.

Hiso's gaze swept across Maia and fell on Miir, who thankfully had not moved or turned around. "Making new friends?"

Maia did not like the way Hiso looked at Miir, as if he were reveling in the discovery of Maia speaking with someone. Maia could see the wheels in Hiso's head begin to turn, making connections and plans. Forcing a smile, she placed herself so as to block his view. She could tell by the way Hiso's lips twitched that he did not like that.

"Dear Maia, is it true what I hear?" Hiso asked next.

"Is what true?"

"That you went a little too wild at the Trinity Caverns. You need to restrain yourself, child. The rebels may have taken some liberties, but that's a sacred thing we house in there. You don't want it damaged, I'm sure."

Uncle Alasdair's haggard face appeared behind Hiso. Behind him were Steward Lok and all of her friends. Uncle Alasdair walked up to Hiso's side, his face grim, his eyes cold. "Commander Hiso," he said. "There will be time for this later, I'm sure. If you are done paying your respects, let's return to our conversation."

Hiso looked at Uncle Alasdair, his face full of contempt. "Our conversation? You need to speak with your darling niece first. We had some rules binding her here at ThulaSu, but I'm thinking she needs a few more. Imagine what would have happened if the caverns collapsed because of her fireworks."

Murmurs broke out around Hiso. Uncle Alasdair's face puckered and he shot a worried glance in Maia's direction. Hiso smiled again, his eyes turning to dark beads filled with malice. Maia shifted uneasily on her feet.

Why is he doing this? If I were him, I would have left already.

But of course. Hiso needed a scapegoat, and who better than her? She was the best way to deflect and dodge the allegations piling up against him. Now that Ori was dead, Hiso knew he was in trouble, and he needed something big to get out of it.

Now the question is, am I going to let him use me again?

Hiso continued in that cloying voice of his, spinning his web of spite. "I think you'll thank me for suggesting this, Maia. After all, you're such a kind girl. I'm sure you'd never forgive yourself if you damaged something so precious to our dear departed chieftain. So let me propose, right here in front of all concerned that—"

"He didn't give a darn."

All the murmurs stopped. Hiso's face turned from a shocked white to an enraged red as Maia's words sank in.

"What did you just say?"

"All Ori wanted was for all of us to be safe. He wanted me to get us out. He did not care if I destroyed the Nouvus in the process. That's the thing . . . the Ori I knew and the Ori I'll always remember cared more about his people than anything else. Ori would stand up for what was right no matter who he had to fight against. If he were here, I know he'd say that to your face."

Maia paused, not only to catch her breath but also to study the situation. She did not miss the blaze in Hiso's eyes. But more importantly, she saw the anger burning in the eyes of every Black Phantom in the crowd. Sensing their support, she continued.

"You know why Ori stopped caring about the Nouvus at the

end?" Maia asked. Hiso simply gave her a scornful look, so Maia continued. "Well, I do. That's because he realized that to the people who took over the Trinity Caverns, the Nouvus was just another object. They don't really believe it's sacred or respect it, they only put on a show to further their selfish plans. If they really respected the Nouvus, they wouldn't have unleashed the Jomral into the caverns. They just couldn't have."

Hiso looked furtively at the people around them. Maia did not know what he had expected, but she was happy to see glares on every face surrounding him.

"Are we done?" Hiso said impatiently. "I see you have quite the knack for lecturing but . . . we adults have work to do, you know? So —"

"No, I'm not done," Maia said. "You came to pay your respects to Ori and ended up seeking me out to punish me. I didn't run away when you called, although I never wanted to see your face or hear that sickening voice of yours again. I think as an adult you can at least return me the courtesy."

Hiso gritted his teeth. Once again he threw furtive glances at the crowd around him. Finding no solace in the grim faces, he crossed his arms and hissed at Maia. "All right, all right. Say what you have to say."

"It shouldn't have ended this way. The Nouvus was precious to Ori. He was so proud of it, so honored to have the task of tending to it. He and his Black Phantoms toiled on it for years, some for generations, even. For the last few months, they have been spending weeks at a stretch trying to get it back up, so some among us could survive the catastrophe that's coming. They weren't expecting to get a berth on it for their services, Ori wasn't looking out for his family. He was happy and proud to do his duty. Not you, though. You came here with a plan to take over the Nouvus, to have it all for yourself. Sharing the little we have was too much for your tiny heart. You had to take away Ori's pride and joy, and then your Jomral had to take his life too." Maia stopped to blink away the rush of emotions. "And after all that, you dare come here and pretend that you knew him? That you care about him?"

"You are overreacting, dear child," Hiso said with a nervous laugh. "I know you're distressed, so I will pardon you today. But this slander without proof is dangerous. You don't want to make a habit of it. One of these days you'll run into someone deadly and . . . we don't want you to make a fatal mistake."

The gall. He is standing here and threatening me.

"Don't worry. I won't make a fatal mistake," Maia said. "I can defend myself. You must have already heard this, but . . . I'll tell you again. I took down quite a few of your Jomral last night. Alone. By myself. You might want to think of improving their training regimen a little."

Someone giggled. Loudly. For a moment Maia could not believe that anyone could laugh when the tension was so thick that the weight might flatten a building. Then she spotted a little face. Nahlo, Ori's little boy, was grinning happily in a corner. As soon as she saw the boy's bright eyes, she broke into laughter herself.

"You made Ori's little one laugh, Commander Hiso. I guess your coming here helped after all."

"Your insolence is unbelievable," Hiso said through gritted teeth. He flashed an angry look at Uncle Alasdair. "You should get this girl under control quickly. I would, but I have to leave ThulaSu now."

"What?" Uncle Alasdair exclaimed. "Commander Hiso, you cannot leave. We have to finish our conversation first."

"There is no conversation to be had, Parliamentarian Avaroh. I'm finished here. I'm leaving ThulaSu." Hiso turned to leave.

"Oh no, you're not," Maia said.

Hiso whirled around, his eyes blazing. "What did you say?"

"I said you aren't leaving. Not before you give us some answers. We need to know whose greed claimed Ori's life. I need names, names of every one of your accomplices. After you've given us that, I won't hold you."

"How dare you? Who do you think you are?" Hiso spat the

words out at Maia. He looked angrily at Uncle Alasdair. "Aren't you going to say anything? She gets away with behaving like this?"

Uncle Alasdair shrugged. "What can I say? I offered you a civil conversation, and you didn't like it. Now you can deal with . . . what was that you called her . . . the tantrum-throwing freak of a teenager."

Hiso scowled and shook a finger at Maia. "I will not be spoken to this way. You can't stop me from leaving. No one can." He looked at the Jomral behind him and nodded. "What are you waiting for? Take her down."

The two Jomral exchanged a look, and Maia knew right away that they had heard about the debacle at the Trinity Caverns. They were not enthusiastic about taking her on. But their hesitation did not last long. Another glare from Hiso and the pair charged. They were just as fast as the others from the previous night, but all the Black Phantoms, Dorian included, were ready before they were. The two Jomral, fierce as they were, did not stand a chance against the twenty or more Phantoms, who tackled them to the ground in a heartbeat.

"Looks like no one is on your side today, Commander Hiso. Things are finally as they should be." Maia took another step closer to Hiso, her gaze locked with his nervous one. "I really don't want to hurt you. So please, help me keep my temper in check. Just the names."

"This is a grave misunderstanding," Hiso said, trying desperately to change tack, casting furtive looks around. "I have no names. I told Parliamentarian Avaroh, I don't know anything."

"*Yoteh*," Maia whispered. She felt the surge of the light inside her, but there was no warmth in it. It was a cold, vicious flow of wrath. It swirled out of her fingertips in delicate white wisps, a form that Maia had not seen before. They made Maia smile. She was still smiling as she advanced on Hiso, the pretty, smoky wisps coiling into thick braided whips in her hands.

Hiso looked from her hands to her face and back, nervousness congealing into fear in his eyes. He tried to back away, but there was nowhere to go with the Phantoms blocking his path. Maia extended an arm, letting the swirling, smoky tendril reach toward Hiso. He drew back as much as he could, his face white in terror.

"Just so you know, they can cut you to pieces before you can blink. Do you want that?"

"Stop it. Stop it right now," Hiso said frantically. "I will sit down with your uncle and we will talk. I'll help with the situation, you have my word."

"Too late to choose my uncle now, I'm afraid," Maia said, letting the tip of a tendril brush across his face. "Tell me who among the Solianese are with you. Leeam, I presume?"

"Yes, yes. This was Leeam's idea to begin with."

Maia moved her hand away a little. "And who else?"

"Sahiiraan Ronan of the House of the Sands." He went on to add some other names that Maia did not recognize, but Uncle Alasdair noted them all in a small notebook.

"You had Xifarians there too," Maia said when he paused. "And some Jjord. Who were they?"

"What? I don't know about that. I really don't know."

Before Maia could do anything, and she would have not hesitated to intimidate Hiso some more, Dorian's fist came crashing down on Hiso's shoulder and sent him sprawling to the ground.

Dorian loomed over the man and growled, "Out with it now, or it won't be Maia who cuts you to pieces," he said. "Now!"

"I don't know them all," Hiso wailed. "But Taillefei and Jarkko have been helping."

Maia bent down next to him. "Is the queen involved?"

Hiso shook his head. "No. It's just them and some of Phocluus's minions. There's a Lady Druuna. That's all I know."

"And the Jjord?"

Hiso looked from her face to Dorian's and with a resigned sigh, he closed his eyes.

"Aloysus and . . . Shone."

Maia could barely stop a gasp from escaping her mouth. "You don't mean Shone Arimann?"

"I do," Hiso wheezed. "How else would we get past their patrols?"

"Shone is the one in charge of the Jjord patrols?"

Maia's surprised reaction seemed to give Hiso immense pleasure. His mouth twisted into a crooked smile. "You have to be quite stupid not to think of that angle."

"You're right, I am," Maia admitted. How had she not thought of following up on who was in charge of the patrols? It was the clearest connection, and she had missed it. Shone Arimann had looked like a friend. CA Abebe trusted him. And once again, like a fool, she had fallen for the outward looks. Anger bristled inside her and the light crackled around her fingers. Maia let a whip coil around Hiso and waited until it was tight around his torso. "Abebe?"

"I have nothing to do with that witch."

Maia tightened the whip a notch. "The Premier?"

"No, no," Hiso screeched. "Those women don't even speak with me."

Maia let out a breath of relief. It was just as they had suspected. Even though the plot extended high into the hierarchies, the rot had not reached that far. Perhaps there was still room for hope, a chance for everyone to come together. She pulled the light back in, and Hiso went rolling backward as she tugged.

"Are you going to put me in prison now?" Hiso yelped, looking from Dorian's face to Maia's.

"Who am I to do that?" Maia pulled the light back in completely as she stared down at Hiso's pathetic form. "Maybe one of the councils will decide to put you in prison. I hope they do."

"Please don't destroy the Nouvus," Hiso begged. "I know you want to."

"The Nouvus . . . No, Hiso, I won't touch it. You see, I don't think the way you do. I want you to get it flying someday. It would make Ori happy."

The sound of running feet made Maia stiffen. Expecting a horde of Jomral, she almost pulled the light back out, but it turned out to be a large group of Kausakas instead. Their leader nodded at Steward Lok and pulled Hiso to his feet. Then they dragged Hiso and his Jomral away.

Uncle Alasdair rushed to Maia's side and slipped his arm around her shoulders. "Are you all right?"

Maia nodded. "I hope I didn't get you into too much trouble."

"Trouble? I'm grateful to you. I don't know how long we will be able to hold Hiso, but now we have some names. Now we know who among us needs to be weeded out. I couldn't have done that myself. No one could."

It was something. And it was good to be appreciated for a change. But even with her win over Hiso, Maia hardly felt joyful. The fact remained that Ori was gone. Forever.

"Hey, Maia." A tug on her shirt pulled Maia out of the misery. She found Nahlo, Ori's youngest, looking up at her. "That was awesome . . . the smoke and light and stuff. Think you can show me more sometime?"

Maia smiled and gently placed a hand on Nahlo's head. "Of course. I will, I promise."

His eyes sparkled for a moment and in that moment, Maia's heart lifted, far above her sorrows and the vileness of the treacherous world around her.

CHAPTER FOUR

SAYING GOODBYE

Ori's mourning day began shrouded in clouds, but by the time Maia and her friends—all except Kusha who had been summoned by Steward Lok earlier—started trooping toward Walenveil around midmorning, the sun broke through. Maia's spirits dipped at the sight of the black mourning flag, a grim reminder of the chieftain's passing. The village seemed deserted as the group trudged past the center, their hearts heavy.

Nafi stopped and sniffed the air just after they passed the clock tower. "Do you smell it?"

"Nafi, not today, please," Dani said in a gloomy voice.

Nafi quieted immediately. Even though everyone had smelled the aroma in the air, not another word was said. Maia glanced at Dani's pale face and stifled a sigh. There were dark circles under the girl's eyes, and over the previous two days she had hardly spoken to anyone. Even Kusha tiptoed around her, and as much as Maia hoped Dani would share her thoughts with them, it did not happen. She had tried to initiate a conversation a few times, but Dani steadfastly refused to speak.

However, as soon as they came up to Ori's house, Nafi could not hold it in anymore. "Am I seeing things?" she said.

Nafi's startled reaction was more than justified. What Maia stared at open-mouthed was not at all what they had expected. No somber groups of people walked about as they always did on mourning days, no one spoke in hushed voices or sported grave faces. The yard was filled with people chattering loudly, the aroma of food drifted in the air, and if Maia did not know, she could not have told this was a mourning day for anyone.

They would have stood there, speechless, a lot longer, but Niyani came up to them, arms outstretched. "There you are. I've been waiting for you to arrive." Her eyes were swollen but she smiled bravely. "Ori loved to throw a feast, you know. So I thought, why not celebrate his love today? Everyone came together and it looks like it will be a good one. Go on, have fun. He would've liked you to enjoy such a nice day."

"This is perfect," Maia said, lingering behind with Niyani, as the rest took off. "Ori surely would've been proud of this."

That was the truth. The yard was full of villagers as well as some people from ThulaSu, and everyone was running around busily. Slabs of meat were roasting at the far end, and a long row of tables nearby were laden with numerous other foods. A huge basket sat on one end of the row of tables, and seeing its contents brought a smile to Maia's face.

"Totos?"

"Yes, those were the first to arrive this morning." Niyani picked up a pack and held it out to Maia. Words were handwritten in large letters across the usual paper package.

Maia read out loud. "Dedicated to Ori, the fiercest chieftain on Tansi. Your inspiration will always be with us."

"Isn't that sweet?" Niyani said.

"It is." Maia smiled, her gaze misting as she spotted the Appian trio a distance away. "It is sweet of them."

After Niyani excused herself and walked away, Maia ambled around, finally finding a spot next to Dani at a table where the girl was shelling a huge pile of beans. Maia joined in. There were no words exchanged since Dani showed no interest in conversation, so Maia observed the goings-on as her fingers worked.

Dorian and a few other Phantoms were cleaning a bucketful of fish, and had attracted a good-sized crowd that seemed to be making wagers on who could clean them fastest. Nafi was the loudest among them, cheering on the cleaners. Rayan rewarded her every scream with a sharp nudge, but Nafi continued undaunted. Maia spotted Miir near the fire pits, Nahlo prancing about next to him. Ren was sprawled on the grass in the shade of a large tree in the far western corner, while Sana flitted about. The only person missing was Kusha, and Maia tensed a little each time she thought about him. The early-morning summons was odd, and Kusha's long and continued absence worried Maia even more. But since Dani was in no condition to bear any more anxiety, Maia kept her thoughts to herself.

It was close to midday when a group of people from ThulaSu—Sahiiraan Tsininio and Uncle Alasdair among them—came to pay their respects. Uncle Alasdair soon came over, followed by a little boy carrying a plate heaped high with food for him, and sat down next to Maia. This was the first she had seen of her uncle after the showdown with Hiso, and Maia was anxious to know what had transpired after Hiso's confession. It seemed that Uncle Alasdair was equally eager to tell her. He brought Hiso up right away.

"Hiso has been spilling his guts out, that scoundrel," he said, plunging his fork into a piece of meat with gusto. "He gave us more names, none as significant as the ones you've heard already but still, we have even more now."

"So what's going to happen?"

"Our Parliament has placed sanctions on the House of the Broken Seas and the House of the Sands. Their rights as representatives have been taken away. Not much will come of it, but at least they have been flagged. Now we know who is who."

"Did you share the information with the Jjord and the Xifarians?" Maia asked.

"Yes, of course."

"And?"

"Premier Oliena was furious. She had Shone arrested and Aloysus brought in for interrogation. They told her a lot more. Apparently, this plan had been in the works for months. They were simply waiting for the right moment to strike. All of the Jjord implicated have been isolated now, so we are safe there."

"And the Xifarians?"

Uncle Alasdair sighed. "The queen thanked us for the information, but hasn't said a word since. They work in mysterious ways, Maia. But no matter what, at least we know who is behind this."

"That is true." Still, Maia felt a tinge of sadness that nothing more had been done. A man had lost his life and . . . this was all. Then again, what more could be done?

"The Fourth is sealed off for now, so there's that," Uncle Alasdair continued. "I don't know what will happen to the Nouvus. We have a joint council with the Jjord coming up soon, and we might know by then."

Maia sat up with a start as her uncle's words sank in. "What do you mean the Fourth is sealed off?"

"No one is allowed to go there. They have evacuated the people inside the Chambers and closed the entrance back up. The Jjord are patrolling the shoreline around the clock now. I'm told no one can slip past this new routine."

"But . . . but I need to go there."

"To the Nouvus?"

"No, to this place I had been looking for. That building in Sophie's notebook . . . I . . . I might have found it. But I need to go there and look into it."

Uncle Alasdair patted her hand. "I can send word to the Jjord to let you in. I will let you know when I get approval. How will you get there?"

"I'm hoping Ren can fly us there."

Her uncle's face clouded for a moment. "You're not going alone, I hope."

"No, don't worry. I'll have friends." Miir would be with her, she was sure. And that would be enough.

Uncle Alasdair left a little after that. The day, brilliant and beautiful, continued in a calm, soothing cadence. Maia had joined her friends to help distribute food when Nahlo arrived, a bunch of his friends in tow.

He was nothing if not direct. "Hey, Maia. Can you show us some of your light tricks now?"

"Yes, I will. Of course."

Maia settled down with them under a tree, savoring the bright looks on their faces. She drew out the light and showed them the various formations she had learned over the years. She relished the looks of joy sweeping across the little faces, the astonished gasps that rose when she made a little exploding ball, or the squeals when she managed to shape the light into a pachyderm. The show went on for a long time and would have gone on longer if Niyani had not come over.

"All right, that's enough for today, Nahlo. Leave the girl alone now. She needs to eat." Nahlo was not shy about showing his displeasure, but Niyani would have none of it. "Come on, run along now."

As the kids dispersed, Niyani sat down next to Maia. "You must be famished. They tire you out?"

"Not at all. I was happy to show them. I think that was the best use of my crazy powers. I really enjoyed seeing them smile."

Niyani placed a hand on her head. "You're a kind girl, Maia. I can see why Ori liked you so much," she said. Her voice caught at the end and she hastily dabbed her eyes before forcing a smile. "I have something for you. Ori would've liked you to have this." Maia gasped when she saw the book Niyani held out. It was Ori's Book of Tunnels, the one she had returned after the falling-out with the Xifarian queen.

"But I can't . . . I let Ori down—"

"Yes, Ori was upset, but it did not last. Anger did not settle on Ori for too long, you know. He wanted to give this back to you the very next day. Then he thought it wouldn't be a good idea. He was worried that you'd stray into a tunnel, have an accident and hurt yourselves. So he kept up the show of being mad at you. But really, he wanted you to have this."

Maia did not need to hear any more. Her eager hands grabbed the book. Tears welled up in her eyes again as she clutched it to her chest. "I'm honored. I shall treasure this. Thank you."

Niyani patted Maia's shoulder. "No, thank *you*." She did not let the silence stretch too long. "Now come, you must eat. It's late and Nahlo kept you busy too long."

"It's all right," Maia reassured her once more. "I was happy to be with them."

Niyani tipped her head, looking at the far end of the yard. "Speaking of Nahlo, he's taken a sudden liking to our friend from Xif. I think hearing about the fight in the Trinity Caverns did something to him. He has always been dismissive of the young man, much to Ori's disappointment, but now . . . Look how Nahlo keeps following him around."

So it was not her random observation after all. She had seen the little boy tailing Miir all day, and wondered if something had changed. Seeing how eagerly Nahlo helped Miir and another man tend to a cooking pit brought a smile to Maia's face.

"Well, I should tell Nahlo that his new friend can show him some magic tricks too," she said, laughing.

"He knows already. But you should remind him." Niyani leaned over and whispered, "It will take some pressure off you."

After Niyani left, Maia joined her friends in one corner of the yard. Time passed at a steady, unhurried pace. Even though Maia's heart lingered on thoughts of Ori, the warm day and being surrounded by everyone she loved left her calm and soothed.

It was late afternoon when Kusha trudged in and slumped on the grass next to Dani. Maia noted he looked tired and distracted. For the moment, she chalked it up to the long walk from ThulaSu in the heat of the sun. But when Dani wrapped an arm around Kusha and peered at his face worriedly, Maia sat up.

"What's wrong, Kusha?" Dani asked.

"My parents."

"What happened to your parents?" Maia scampered to his side. "Are they sick?"

Kusha laughed in a tired sort of way. "No, they are fine. They're leaving."

"What do you mean, leaving?" Dani asked.

"They can't take all this anymore," Kusha said. He clutched Dani's hand as if he was afraid it would disappear if he let go. "So they're packing up and leaving ThulaSu."

"But they agreed to run ThulaSu in your stead until you came of age," Maia said. "And you don't come of age for another . . ."

"Five months," Dani finished for her.

"So it's five months too soon," Maia said. "Why are they leaving now?"

"Like I told you, they can't take all this anymore," Kusha replied. "They're tired of the fights and the deaths and . . . the R'armimon talon ship scared them off completely. They don't want to spend any more of their time here, doing things they don't like and . . . not doing things they want to do."

"So what's the plan?" Nafi burst out. She had been listening intently, her bright green eyes shining like beacons. "They go back to doing their circus thing again?"

"Yes," Kusha replied.

"What about here, then?" Dani asked. "Who runs ThulaSu?"

Kusha exhaled loudly. "Well, since I'm so close to official adulthood, the Solianese Council will assign me a counselor."

"So wait . . ." Ren sat up abruptly, abandoning his afternoon nap in the shade. "So you are officially taking on your duties as a Sahiiraan. I mean with an advisor, but still, it's the same thing, right?"

As Kusha sighed and nodded, Ren frowned. "What about the Initiative? Will you have time for that?"

"I don't know," Kusha said morosely. "I hope I will, but I really don't know."

"That's so, so selfish of them." Nafi stomped around with balled fists. "I mean, five more months . . . is that too much to ask? Can't take this anymore. . ." She continued to grumble. "As if this is fun for anyone. Running away like a bunch of chickens."

Even though Maia spared no effort to calm Nafi down, her own heart was in turmoil. Kusha's anxious face was hard to look at, but she was equally worried about the other situation—the Initiative. It was truly critical that they came out on top. Maia needed a win to acquire the legendary sword, Seigvard, which according to Ruche, was a necessary step to thwart the R'armimon. Yet now, it seemed quite likely that they would have to compete without Kusha. The competition was fierce already, and a win was far from assured. And the chances of scoring that win had just gone down another notch, since now they were one person short.

Chapter Five

Last One Standing

Kusha's news destroyed all hopes of ending the solemn day on a tranquil note. Even then, the gang spent as long as they could at Ori's, and stayed until late in the afternoon to help with the clean-up afterward. By the time they finally got back to their living quarters, Maia was looking forward to some rest.

Rayan gasped and jumped back as soon as she stepped into the room, and Maia knew right away that there would be no rest for her.

"Message from Ruche," Rayan announced, pointing her staff at the now familiar disc on the floor. "Hope he does not ask you to meet him today. Not at that faraway place, at least."

Maia hoped the same. On the one hand, she was eager to find out more about the talon ship and had been wishing for Ruche to show up. On the other hand, she wanted some time to slow down. She definitely did not look forward to trekking all the way to Northrock Expanse that very moment. As it turned out, Ruche did want to meet her, but at the bowers.

"I shall be there at sundown," Ruche's projection announced.

There was no time to lose since the skies were dimming already, so Maia ran back out right away. "Wait for me," Rayan called.

"No need," Maia said. "I have no intention of following the restrictions they put on me, Rayan. They can do what they want."

"Restrictions I do not care about," Rayan said, as she caught up with her. "But your safety is important."

There was not much left to argue about after that. They hurried up to the ramparts and while Rayan waited on a nearby bench, Maia ventured into the rose garden. She found Ruche pacing near the bowers.

"Sorry I'm late, Ruche. I was at Ori's all day."

"I know," Ruche said. He came up to her, placed his hands on her shoulders, and peered at her face. "How are you, Maia?"

"Alive."

Ruche sighed at her answer. "So it is *that* bad. I am truly sorry for your loss. You fought well, be proud of that."

"Not well enough, Ruche." Maia plodded to the nearest bench and slumped onto it. "This fight was not necessary, you know. That's what makes me so angry and sad. This did not have to be."

Ruche sat down next to her. "I hear there was quite a showdown with Commander Hiso."

"Too little, too late."

"It is something, Maia. A little something that *you* made possible." Ruche patted her back. "Don't lose sight of the bright side."

If only it were that easy. Maia tried, but her thoughts kept getting mired in regrets. If only she had confronted Hiso sooner, if only she had not been so afraid of being thrown out of ThulaSu. The little good she achieved kept getting lost behind the plentiful bad. Maia shook her head to drive the misery away. She needed a clear head, she needed to focus on other things.

"Ruche, we saw an enormous ship shaped like a talon. That's part of the R'armimon fleet, I guess."

Ruche nodded. "Those were a bunch of outrider craft. They came scouting, gathering information on Tansi. They must have been around Xif as well."

"Scouts? Where are the motherships?"

"A little distance away. The last I knew, they were planning to orbit the sixth planet."

"Why so far away? Why not here? The scouts came and went and . . . I was thinking they'd start blasting away at Xif."

"He will not. Not just yet, anyway. As I told you, you're an important symbol to the R'armimon. Aekken can't do anything that will harm you. Or so I hope." Ruche left the bench and paced around for a bit. "I've spoken to the emperor and I'm hopeful. Aekken is impulsive, but his father is quite the opposite. Powerful and egotistical, maybe, but sane. I don't think he would let Aekken go berserk on Xif. I still hope there can be some compromise."

"Compromise?"

"Perhaps the Empire will show mercy. If the Xifarian leaders show some remorse, ask for forgiveness."

Rahina Quemiila's prideful face flashed before Maia's eyes as Ruche said that, and she shook her head. "I don't think that will happen. Not in a thousand years."

"Well, we shall see," Ruche said, chuckling. "You may have a little time to sway Aekken. And the Xifarian queen."

"Sway the prince? And the queen? Me?"

"Do not underestimate your power, Maia. Or your importance," Ruche said. "Symbolic or not, you may be the last defense this planet has. And Xif too."

As Ruche paused, Maia's thoughts drifted. She—the last defense for not just Tansi but Xif as well. How things had changed!

Ever since the planet-spaceship of Xif had shown up next to Tansi three decades ago, the Xifarians had seemed all-powerful. Already divided into the feuding nations of the Solianese and the Jjord, the planet of Tansi had been easy prey for the newly-arrived, wily Xifarians. Soon, with its energy sources destroyed, Tansi found itself hostage to the energy laws they imposed. The Xifarians took what they wanted from the people on Tansi—laborers for their mines on Ti from the impoverished land-dwelling Solianese and technological know-how from the Jjord who lived under the Tansian oceans — in exchange for a heavily regulated supply of energy.

And now? The R'armimon, age-old enemies of the Xifarians from the far side of the galaxy where Xif originated, had finally caught up with them. Xif, stripped of the power to fly across galaxies, had nowhere to hide. As if that were not enough, the planet itself was falling apart.

And now, not only were the Xifarians seeking refuge on Tansi, but Maia, a lowly Solianese who they had hunted relentlessly in order to resurrect Xif's flying abilities, was the one standing between them and their immediate destruction.

Ruche's chuckles pulled her out of her reverie. "However, I will add a word of caution. Do not be overconfident either."

"Really? Do you realize you just contradicted yourself?"

"I know, I know. I'm getting old," he said. "One more thing, never ever meet Aekken alone. He will want you to, and you might be tempted to, but . . . no."

"Tempted? Of course not. Why would I want to meet him alone?"

"Well, you never know. Things change, circumstances change." He threw her a sidelong glance. "Remember my words, Maia, never alone. And don't show him emotion, particularly not your fear."

"You've said that before."

"I have?" Ruche shook his head and tapped his chin. "I'm becoming a caricature of a forgetful father figure. What a pitiful turn for a Seer of the Empire R'armimon."

The way he said it made Maia burst into laughter. "That's a bit over the top."

Ruche chuckled as he sat down next to her. "I shall tell you this, it is *not* easy raising a child."

Maia's eyes widened. "You're in a mood today. Now you think you're raising me?"

"Am I not?"

"All right, then. I'll be a good kid. Remember this moment,

Ruche, and never call me a difficult teenager who likes to keep secrets." Ruche had clearly not expected her to kick the dramatics up a notch, and his startled expression amused Maia no end. "So, I think we've found the place where Asiyaah spent her final days. It's on the Fourth and—"

"Do I really need to know the details?" Ruche interrupted with a groan. "I don't think I do."

"Isn't a father figure supposed to provide guidance?"

"Yes, but I also believe in nurturing independence, in letting the young ones soar on their own wings."

Maia shook her head. "You're just . . ."

"Annoying? I know. As I said, a bumbling, irritating father figure." Ruche laughed as he said that, but his face quickly turned serious. The lightness of moments ago ebbed away when he spoke. "I know my mannerisms frustrate you, but Maia, I've explained why I have to be that way. I do not want to steer you one way or another. You have to find your own path. I sometimes fear that I have already pushed you too much."

"I don't know, Ruche. I feel like I'm in a dark room, groping about hoping to find the way out, but all I do is keep going in circles. I wish you could give me something. At least tell me if I'm doing the right things."

Ruche smiled. "You're doing just fine. Almost everything you've done so far has taken you forward, I will tell you that."

That did not help much. Or at all. Here they were staring at complete annihilation, and even though Ruche could see the possible future, he refused to tell anything. Just a hint, that was all she was asking for.

Flustered, Maia got off the bench. She walked away a few paces and stared at the darkening valley beyond and the glowing tips of the ranges ahead. The quiet majesty of the scene calmed her a little. When she turned back around, her irritation had almost disappeared.

"You know, Ruche, I was thinking," she said. "About Seigvard and . . ."

"Yes, go on."

"Well, everyone looks up to you and trusts you now. And we're running out of time. So . . . wouldn't it be easier if you simply convened a council and asked for the sword yourself?"

Ruche fixed an amused stare on her face. "No. There are reasons why you, and you alone, should get it. Besides, if I were to ask for it, I'd have to tell them why. I'd have to tell them it is for Tansi's protection against the prince. But that would bring my stance against the prince out in the open, and that is not prudent."

There was not much left to argue about after that. "So what now? I wait for the prince?"

Ruche nodded. "You'll hear from me when it's time. For now, stay well and keep doing what you have been doing." He rose and arranged his cloak.

"Are you leaving already?"

"Yes. I came to check on you, see how you were holding up. You seem quite all right, so I have nothing else to do here."

Maia stifled a sigh and smiled. "Well, see you, then." She was almost halfway to the gate of the rose garden when Ruche called back.

"Maia, do you ever wonder?"

Maia turned around, her mind eager but prepared to be frustrated once more by the seer's riddles.

"What?"

"Do you wonder why the light didn't consume you like it did your mother?"

For a moment or two, Maia simply stood there, struck by the question. She *had* wondered about that many times. Each time, her thoughts had come to a dead end. She knew so little about everything. How was she supposed to know something so deep as the workings of a Nasfarii? It was not a topic she could look up in books, either, though she had tried. But other than the legends that told of an all-powerful star child, there was nothing to be found.

"I see you have thought about it," Ruche said. "Why do you think it is?"

"Perhaps she wasn't a true Nasfarii?" Maia muttered. "Or perhaps I'm even more of a freak than she was?"

Ruche groaned. "Aah, Maia . . . the words you use sometimes. Please, be respectful. If not to yourself, to my beliefs."

"So, am I right?"

Ruche took in a long breath and exhaled slowly before replying. "You are right. You are not your mother."

Obviously! But then what?

"Think about it, Maia. Think," Ruche said as he walked away into the deepening darkness of the rose garden behind him. "Sometimes it's not the question that matters, but the intent behind the question."

His words lingered in the cool evening air as Maia stood there, her mind buzzing with thoughts that went nowhere.

CHAPTER SIX

BACK TO THE FOURTH

Maia had hoped for some calm after the Nouvus incident, but she had never thought calm would be so hard to bear, especially when grief was so close and so raw.

A stillness had descended on ThulaSu. It was as if the whole place was holding its breath. During the seven days of mourning for the departed chieftain, all activity in ThulaSu came to a standstill. There was nothing to be done with the Nouvus, obviously. In addition, along with every other class in ThulaSu, the sessions for the Initiative were canceled as well. Monk Konnae suspended her training, and even the Xinhagyi only let Maia come in to train every two days. One thing that stayed constant was the grief, and following it, the nightmares.

Maia craved something, anything that would keep her busy and distracted. But nothing came, no message from Ruche, no breakthrough on the Initiative, nothing. Everyone kept to themselves, their feelings locked up inside them, their faces grim. What made the situation even grimmer was the departure of Kusha's family right before the mourning days ended. Maia and her friends paid a visit, but the frigid encounter with Steward Lok and his family only made their miserable existence worse.

It was not until a whole week after the fateful encounter at the Trinity Caverns that something worthwhile happened. Sana came running one evening, a piece of paper in hand.

"From dear Father," she said, as she handed it to Maia and threw herself onto Maia's bed.

Maia's heart leaped on reading its contents. "He's got permission. We can go to the Fourth."

"That's good news," Sana said. "Who's coming with you?"

Rayan, who had been polishing her staff with utmost attention, looked up. "I should go."

The Viperine did not have room for too many people. Maia knew Miir had to come, and that left space for two. However, she did not want anyone else at all. If it was indeed Asiyaah's tomb, Miir would need some time to himself, some privacy. She had a feeling he would not object even if she decided to bring all her friends along, but she also knew he would wish for a quiet moment or two. And she wanted to do the right thing by him.

Thankfully, as soon as she explained the situation, the two girls readily agreed. After that, it was all about preparing for the trip. At daybreak the following morning, Maia found herself sprinting down to the corner of the courtyard where the Viperine always stood. Ren was already there, and to Maia's surprise, Sana was with him. She flashed an awkward smile and walked up to Maia.

"Maia, I'm sorry. I didn't mean to be a bother. But Ren kept insisting and I . . . I'm too annoyed about everything to be selfless right now, so I accepted," she said in a stifled voice. "But I promise, I'll stay away from you guys. Miir will have his privacy. I won't—"

Maia laid a hand on Sana's to reassure her. "That's all right, Sana. But what's the matter?"

"That uncle of yours has enrolled me for classes at ThulaSu," she said in a grumpy voice. "He said I've had enough time off. It's either taking classes here or going back to dear Mother. And that I can't do."

"So what's the problem?" Maia genuinely did not understand. "ThulaSu is a great place to be. Rayan said Zaara wants Pai enrolled too." Sana put on an unimpressed face, so Maia continued trying to cheer the girl. "Oh, you might even be in the same class with Maks, Aman, and Nisa."

"Who cares who I'll be with? I needed some rest and relaxation, and his Highness won't let me have it. As if the private tutor wasn't punishment enough. I hate him."

"He's your father."

"So?" Sana made a face. She shook her head when Maia opened her mouth to protest. "Please don't argue. I'm not in the mood."

As if on cue, Ren swooped in and whirled Sana around. "Come on, Angel. My heart breaks when I see you sad," he said. "Laugh for me, please."

Sana did not laugh, but she smiled a little, and for that, Maia was happy. Sana was a happy-go-lucky sort of girl, always cheerful and bright, and when she stopped smiling, it dimmed everything. Miir arrived soon after, and by the time they got inside the Viperine, Ren had Sana giggling now and then.

"You don't mind if my angel sits up front with me, do you?" Ren asked as they clambered inside.

"No, not at all," Maia said. Miir shook his head too, but Maia could clearly see confusion in his eyes. He kept looking curiously at the front seats where Ren was showering plentiful attention on Sana.

"Are you all right?" Maia asked Miir as she strapped herself into one of the seats in the back.

"Are they . . ." He flushed and turned away for a moment before looking back at her. "Are they . . . you know . . . together?"

Maia chuckled, less at his question than at seeing how embarrassed he seemed about asking such a simple thing. "No, they're not," she said. "That's how they always act around each other."

"I see."

Maia did not find out if her explanation had put him at ease, because as soon as the Viperine's doors closed, memories of the last time they had been on the craft hit her like a hammer to the chest. Everything had been scrubbed clean, but the sight of Ori lying in a pool of blood, his life draining out of him, kept flashing before her eyes. It had to be hard for everyone, particularly Miir, she understood that, but understanding did not bring her the extra strength she wished for to comfort him. She was relieved when the Viperine took off. She kept her eyes on the view out the window and forced her mind away from the inside of the craft.

The scenery outside was beautiful. Lit up by the morning sun, Tansi glittered like a jewel. Mountain ranges tapered off into rolling coastlines that merged into sparkling seas. Soon they were hovering over the verdant greenness of the Fourth. Shama's directions were clear and precise. Ren landed the Viperine close to the shrine, so they did not have to trek all the way from the mouth of the caverns like the last time. It saved them time, but Maia was also relieved that she did not have to see the place where Ori fell. It would be hard to deal with right now.

"So all of this glows?" Sana asked as they walked along the pathway leading up to the shrine.

"Yes, it does," Maia said.

"And there are crystals under our feet?"

Maia nodded. "Very likely."

"You don't need to worry so much," Miir said, noting how Sana tiptoed across the grass, as if afraid to damage the crystals underneath. "L'miere crystals are basically rocks. You can walk on them without damaging them."

"Oh, good." Sana sighed in relief.

Ren had walked on ahead, and they found him glaring at the gates when they caught up.

"It's closed," he said. He grabbed a bar and shook it. "Won't open. We might have to climb over or dig our way in."

"But it was open when we left," Maia said. "How did it close back up again?"

"Let me, let me." Sana ran up and shook the gate. It did not budge. Miir gave it a tug next. That did not make any difference either.

Miir looked at Maia. "Your turn."

Maia had been observing from a distance all this time. After the ruckus she had created the last time, she did not plan to touch the gate, but now it seemed as if it had to be done. She still hesitated, the clanging noise from the other night ringing in her ears.

"What are you afraid of?" Ren said. "Come on, give it a try. It won't bite."

Maia flashed a sheepish smile. It was such a small thing, but the memory of that night after Ori fell, the sound of the rattling gate and the dread that they'd be found by Hiso's troops, was still fresh in her mind and made her insides tremble.

Miir walked up to her. "For all you know, it might not open at all," he said. "If it does, there are no vines holding it today, so I doubt there will be any noise. No one is chasing us either, so everything will be just fine."

His words helped. Her fears did not magically disappear, but his reasoning made them fade somewhat. Bracing herself, Maia strode up to the gate. Its rusted bars loomed over her, the Fatambian words — *no one who seeks shelter need go any farther* — now clearly visible in the morning light.

"Let me in, please," Maia whispered, her cold fingers wrapping around the worn-out metal gate.

For a breathless moment or two, nothing happened. Then, just like the night before, Maia felt the rumble. It coursed up the bars and spread through her bones. The gate swung open with a slight creak and a wobble.

Ren's fist shot up in the air. "All right, here we go."

While Ren marched in, Maia stayed frozen at the gates, still astonished by how the gate responded to her touch.

"How is this possible?" she asked Miir. She found him wearing a puzzled and distraught expression.

"This has been set up to work for you, and no one else," he said, his voice almost a whisper. "Someone . . . coded in a locking mechanism, to be opened by your imprint."

Maia took a moment to wrap her mind around his explanation. It made sense, but to have that happen here in this wilderness was unexpected, to say the least. Who could have done that? Asiyaah? Could she do that? Of course she could. She was Miizuken's daughter and the one who had figured out how to break the heart of the Sedara. This was nothing in comparison.

"We cannot be in here. Ren, get back," Miir yelled, tearing Maia out of her thoughts.

Ren, who had already hacked his way through some of the shrubbery, turned around with a disbelieving look on his face. "What? What do you mean?"

"This is a private bequest, Ren," Miir said. "The gates did not open for us. We are not supposed to be here."

"I don't see anything throwing us out," Ren argued. "Besides, we can't just let Maia walk into this wilderness alone."

Miir did not seem the slightest bit convinced. "We need to leave."

"Seriously?"

"I do not know how it works, Ren. But it is possible that our presence might damage something in there. There could be protective measures to keep it private," Miir explained. "Besides, this is wrong. We were not allowed in, and we should leave."

"But you're not sure," Ren continued to argue. "I think if something is meant to be private, it will only be visible to Maia. I don't think it will be destroyed just because someone broke in. I mean, anyone could have climbed that gate and walked in here in all these years."

"Maybe. You are probably right," Miir said. "It makes sense. But we are still trespassing."

Sana, who had been watching quietly all along, now walked up and thumped Miir on the shoulder. "You know, Miir, I get that you're all about honor and integrity and stuff. But stop being stuck on small things. Loosen up a little." She shook her head at both Miir and Ren. "Besides, this is not up to either of you to decide. If it is a bequest like you say, Miir, and I'm not doubting your wisdom at all, then per the bequest, this is all Maia's. Why don't you ask her what she wants? Maybe she wants us to be here with her. Maybe she'd like to have you by her side when she walks into that . . . a snake's den for all we know. And you, Ren. Can you get back here and wait until we've decided? That house isn't going to run away, is it?"

Sana's words had an immediate effect on both of them. Miir's outraged expression melted away and his shoulders relaxed. Ren walked back to the gate with a resigned look on his face. Maia did not wait for them to ask her. Miir's struggle was clear and while she understood it, she also realized he needed a hand in order to come out of that shell around him. And Ren? He was simply being himself.

"I would like your help," she said. "I don't think there's a snake's nest in there, but still. I want all of you to come with me."

"All right, done. Settled. I'm going in," Ren declared and started hacking a way through the shrubbery once more. "Sana, are you coming or not?"

Soon everyone joined in. It took a while, and Maia was dripping with sweat from clearing the bushes and crawling through them by the time they reached the building.

The *abayam* turned out to be smaller than Maia had imagined. It was also in immaculate shape, considering that no one had taken care of it in years. Its massive double doors, thick iron panels crisscrossing its body, stood closed. Ren gave it a tug, and once again, it did not move a smidge. This time, Maia did not wait until all of them had tried. She knew the answer already; the door was waiting for her. She walked up and grabbed the large ring pulls.

She did not even have to tug. The door creaked almost immediately. The handles slipped out and away from Maia's fingers as the door swung open. Maia held her breath as the room beyond slowly came into view. Then she frowned. She had expected it to be full of dirt and debris, broken furniture, knickknacks, and all that. Instead, a dusty but bare room stared back at her.

"This is strange," Ren said. "Quite clean for a deserted building. My room usually looks worse. But . . . but no snake's nest as far as I can see, Sana."

Sana scooted over to his side and peeked in. "All right, I'm satisfied."

"So hey! We'll go walk around while you two investigate here. We'll be back around midday," Ren announced. "That cool?"

"Yes, of course," Maia said.

Ren and Sana did not need to spend their time digging through the dusty interior. Besides, the quiet would be welcome. Miir, however, looked a little thoughtful as Ren and Sana traipsed away, all laughs and chatter.

"You look worried," Maia said. "Just so you know, you're not trampling on my privacy, I promise."

"I was not thinking about that." He nodded in the direction Ren and Sana had vanished. "Umm . . . are you sure those two are fine unchaperoned?"

Maia broke into laughter. It was funny to see Miir so flustered. That he was poles apart from Ren was not a new discovery. However, seeing that Ren's playful, if not openly flirtatious, behavior around Sana tipped the always courteous and reserved Miir into this protective mode, was utterly . . . endearing. She quickly realized that her laughter was only making his frown grow deeper.

"I'm sorry. I shouldn't laugh. But it's all right," she reassured him. "Ren likes to flirt with Sana, but his heart is in the right place. Besides, Sana knows how to take care of herself. You may think Sana is fragile, but she'll put Ren in his place if she needs to."

Miir frowned some more. "Why would I think Sana is fragile?"

"Oh, I didn't mean you in particular," Maia said and decided to explain further. "Since she's not the rough and tumble type, people generally assume she's easy to influence. But Sana's tough. Might sound strange, but I lean on her more than she does on me."

"I understand that," he said. "Toughness is not all about wielding a sword well. The fiercest of fighters are often the softest inside."

"That is true." She immediately thought of Ori, of how after all the disappointment with the Book of Tunnels, he had still wanted to give it to her. She stifled a sigh and blinked away her tears. Now was not the time to think of that. She had to get to work. "So, hey! Are you ready to go inside?"

As they stood at the threshold of that ancient building, Maia's hands trembled. She did not know what was awaiting her, but she suspected that whatever she discovered inside would change her life yet again. Whether for better or for worse remained to be seen.

Chapter Seven

Stringing the Past

Maia had not expected to find anything specific in the shrine, but she definitely hoped to find something. She had thought they would come across a clue right away that would confirm Asiyaah had been here. She had thought there would be some sort of memento, a notebook or a neurogenic interface like Sophie had left. However, as they looked around, it became clear as the daylight surrounding them that things were different.

This *abayam*, the Shrine of the Settlers, consisted of three main rooms—the entryway where the front doors opened and two other rooms on either side of it. A smaller door, possibly leading to the area behind the building, stood directly across from the entrance. Neither of the inner rooms had much left in them. No large furniture, no boxes, nothing to indicate anyone had ever lived there. There were smaller rooms for storage and refreshment attached to the two bigger ones, all equally empty. It made Maia wonder if coming here had been a complete waste of time.

She did not let the feeling settle on her. There had to be

something. This place *had* to be important. Why else would anyone have strewn L'miere crystals along the way? Why would the gate only open to her touch? There had to be something.

The more she thought about it, the more her conviction grew. This was important. Everything was so perfectly cleared out, with no sign of anyone having lived here, it must have been done purposefully. Bikele must have cleaned it out. And if he was the one behind it, every little thing he left here had to be there for a reason.

"Try this one first?" Maia pointed at the room to the right.

The room was bare. Maia's eyes took in the little that was there. A pair of boots standing in a corner. A glass tumbler on a shelf. A metal frame with wires sticking out of it sat next to it. Maia wondered if it had held a picture once. Perhaps of Asiyaah's family? A small stool, with a shell motif that spoke of Jjordic origins, stood in one corner. A pile of smooth river stones lay nearby. Maia poked and prodded everything, and Miir turned things over one at a time. But no matter how much they examined and for how long, nothing jumped out at them, nothing at all. It was hard to keep the disappointment from showing, and as much as Maia tried to keep it in, a sigh coursed out of her.

"Move on to the other room, then?" Miir asked after they had spent what seemed like an eternity turning over everything.

Maia was ready, even though doubts that the other room would yield anything had started creeping into her heart. Still, she hoped. Nothing extraordinary greeted her eyes when she walked in. Two sticks propped up in one corner. A LumTorch fallen over on its side. A large planter, empty now, had perhaps housed a plant once. It stood near the window next to a bare storage room. A couple of wooden spindles, wire coiled around them, were stacked to one side.

Maia slumped against the window, as the despair she had been trying so hard to keep at bay swamped her completely. There was nothing to find here. Miir, who had been fiddling with the spindles of wire, promptly looked up at her.

"We will find something, I am sure," he said, walking over to her side. "We cannot give up looking."

"What if this isn't what we think?"

"Not the end of the world," he said calmly. "Besides, it is too early to say that."

"You're right." Maia squared her shoulders and stiffened her spine. She could not give up so easily and so soon. She was just about to head back to inspect the plant pot when she noticed Miir's face. His eyes were narrowed as he stared out of the window at the overgrown garden outside. Following his gaze, Maia looked, only seeing clumps of shrubbery everywhere.

"There was a door to the back, right?" Miir asked, and Maia caught the hint of a tremor in his voice. "I need to check something."

"Yes, there is," she said eagerly, intrigued that something had piqued his interest.

Soon they had opened the back door and were in the courtyard outside. It was a small rectangular space and Maia could tell it had been a beautiful garden once upon a time. Now, however, nature had taken over and plants grew rampant. Miir headed to the left corner where a Jueyue drooped over a shady nook. Immediately, Maia sighed. How had she not noticed? This almost-circular nook had wild plants growing in it as well, but had a much tamer look to it, in part due to the layers of river rocks—they looked very similar to the ones she had found inside—covering the ground. Miir had already kneeled in front of it and started pulling out the weeds. As Maia drew closer, she saw the stack of rocks forming a column at the center of the circle. These were much darker, in stark contrast to the pale gray of the rocks making up the bed. Seeing the thoughtful expression on Miir's face, Maia was sure they were significant. She kneeled next to him, wondering what this meant. She did not have to wait for an answer.

"That looks like a Piraana, a memorial we make for our deceased," he whispered, pointing at the column of dark rocks. His hands moved swiftly and relentlessly, clearing the spot of weeds, and Maia soon joined in. It did not take long for the view of the memorial to be clear. Miir reached forward and ran a finger over the largest rock at the center of the column.

"She *was* here," he said, gasping under his breath. "This is my grandfather's honorary insignia."

Maia leaned forward to look. Although faded now, there was an etching for sure. It depicted a flaming torch with a spattering of stars above it. This was no coincidence. Someone took care to put that in place. No doubt remained. They were looking at Asiyaah's memorial.

"Thank you for finding her for me. And for letting me in here," Miir said.

His voice was barely audible. The depth of sincerity in it, and the clear and open gratitude that made it tremble, left Maia shaken for a moment. All she could manage was a nod in response. For how long they kneeled there, side by side in silence, Maia could not tell. An endless rush of thoughts crisscrossed her mind, yet there was a strange sense of peace in the moment. She could have sat there all day, not missing words, but Miir broke the silence.

"Your mother . . . where is she . . ." He stopped suddenly as if he had run out of words.

It took Maia a moment to realize he was talking about Sophie's memorial. She shook her head a little. "We don't make memorials. We are returned to the water," she said. "Water is your last cradle, memories of you, your shrine," Maia recited. Every last rite on Tansi ended with those words and the scattering of ashes in a body of water. "Dada took Sophie to the Eastern Seas."

"Ah, yes. They did the same for Ori."

Once again, silence fell between them. Peaceful. Gentle. Steady. Until Miir stirred.

"We should go back and start looking again," he said. "She *must* have left something."

So back indoors they went. Maia was ready to comb through the scant contents of the room once more. While Miir got down on the floor to check the wires, Maia fiddled with the LumTorch and then decided to investigate the plant pot.

The pot was large and an ultramarine blue, with little white painted flowers strewn across it. Maia kneeled next to it to take a closer look at the pretty design. It was filled to the brim with stones, the same kind she had seen in the other room. If there had been a plant in there once, it had died long ago. But then, there couldn't have been a plant growing in a pot full of stones. That thought made Maia frown. What was the point of a plant pot if no plant could be grown in it?

Curious, she moved a few stones, then a few more. She had taken out ten or so stones from the top when she noticed something reddish-brown underneath. Maia's heart beat faster, her fingers moving in a manic frenzy until she had removed another layer of stones. A clay lid stared back at her.

"Miir, I found something," she shouted, unable to tear her eyes away from her discovery.

He was next to her in a heartbeat, but by then Maia had lifted the lid. Under it was a large hole, and Maia realized with a start that she had uncovered the top of a clay pot. She peeked in, her heart leaping when she saw a sparkle inside. "There's something in it. It's shiny," she exclaimed and reached in.

"Stop." Miir grabbed her wrist and pulled her arm away.

"Wh-what did I do?" Maia stuttered as she almost fell over.

"Why would you put your hand inside a pot that has been sitting here for ages?" he said. "There could be anything in there."

Maia exhaled. She could not stop a chuckle from escaping her. "Like what? A nest of snakes?"

Miir let go of her wrist and frowned. "It is possible."

"Says the person who wanted me to walk in here alone because all this is supposedly just mine." Her words were said in simple jest, but from the way his eyes clouded, Maia instantly realized he had not taken them that way. She hurried to reassure him. "Hey, that was a joke. I know you meant well."

A flush spread across his face. "Meant well, but lost sight of what would actually help," he said with a wry chuckle. "Sana is right. I do get stuck on these notions sometimes."

"It's fine. We all have our quirks. I do rush into things sometimes," Maia said, nodding at the pot inside the planter. "So, what do we do now? We need to check what's in there."

"Well, it looks like a pot. Let's dig it out."

Although it took a while and removing a lot of the stones that were set carefully and tightly around the pot to keep it in place, they finally got it out. It was a regular clay pot, small and plain. Inside, Maia could clearly see now, were a bunch of shiny stones. She had no clue how a bunch of stones could be of any importance, but she had no doubt that they were.

She took a scarf out of her bag and spread it on the floor. "We can pour them out here."

The stones turned out to be glass marbles. They were of various shades, a mix of hues in all colors of the rainbow. A few of them had notches on the sides, but most were smooth all over. Useful or not, they were beautiful. Remembering an old pastime of hers, Maia picked one up, held it up to the light, and laughed.

"What is it?"

"I've always loved the way the light filters through marbles. I used to do this all the time when I was little. Didn't expect it'd look just as beautiful now." She offered it to him. "Try it."

Miir held it up in the sunlight, and slowly a smile broke over his face. "It is beautiful." Then his smile froze, and as if struck by lightning, he jumped to his feet. "I think I know what this is."

Maia simply sat and watched Miir rush out, into the other room, and rush back in. In his hands was the metal frame she had seen on the rack, the one she had assumed was a picture frame.

"This could be a projector," he whispered. "These marbles are . . . they might have messages coded into them."

His fingers deftly twisted wires into place so what looked like a pair of prongs hung from the two sides of the frame, their open ends close, but not quite touching. He scanned the heap of marbles once and then over again, before picking up an orange-red one. He slid it into the gap between the prongs. It fit perfectly. However, no projection miraculously appeared, nor did the frame show the tiniest change. Nothing happened.

Miir thought for a moment and rushed out once more. He came back with the stool from the other room and set it in the middle of a sunlit patch on the floor. He placed the frame on it and put the marble back in place. Yet again, there was nothing at all.

"Can I help?" Maia asked.

He looked at her in a distracted sort of way, and Maia could tell his mind was somewhere else. Then his gaze cleared and he whispered. "Of course." Pulling the marble out, he held it out to her. "This is yours. It won't work unless you do it."

Maia got down on her knees next to him.

"The ends of the prongs fit into the notches on the side of the marbles," Miir explained. "Just slide it in."

It sounded easy. Maia only hoped Miir's idea would work. There was little else to do if it did not. She was about to stick the marble in when Miir's hand shot out.

"Wait."

"What?"

"You will laugh at me but . . . are you sure you want to share this with me? This is clearly meant for you."

Maia stared at his earnest face in disbelief. Just a moment ago, he was rushing about, excited to solve the problem. He had to be dying to get a glimpse of his mother. Besides, after the many times they had talked about it, she had thought he was past this. Yet, even now . . .

Maia wanted to laugh it away. There was something about his offer, though, something peculiar yet sweet, funny yet moving, that drew out a somber response instead.

"I am sure, Miir. I'm absolutely sure I want to share this with you."

"Go ahead, then."

Maia held her breath as she prepared to set the marble in place, anticipation and fear making her fingers shake. She clasped the little ball of glass tightly in her palm and whispered a prayer. "Whatever you do, please don't disintegrate afterward."

"Disintegrate?" Miir looked curiously at her. "Why would it do that?"

"Long story," Maia said. "Along with my pendant, my mother left a neurogenic interface for me. She told me about all she had done, about the heart of the Sedara, about what could happen to me if anyone found out. That was the first time I had ever seen her, and other than that photograph I showed you, the only image of her I have ever seen." One sigh and then another wafted out of her, her eyes burning. "I wished I could keep it forever. But it fell apart right after she finished speaking. All for my safety, I guess. But I . . . I would give anything to get it back." Maia blinked back her tears, took a deep breath, and steadied herself. "So, anyway . . . I don't think these will show me Sophie, but it's still a thread that connects to her. And I hope I can hold on to these at least."

For a moment or two, there was stillness. Then Miir shook his head slowly. "It is not the same medium. This one will not disintegrate, I promise," he said. "Try it."

So she did. And just as Miir thought, this time it responded. There was an immediate sputter and a flash of light above the frame, but it died down just as suddenly as it had come.

"What happened?" Maia almost wailed

Miir had already bent down to look at the frame closely. "Something is wrong with either the reader or the projector circuit, I think. But at least we have something. We know what these are. That is good."

It surely was good. But Maia could not help but feel dismayed. They had come so close and this was a definite letdown. Miir was not one to give up so easily, however. He turned the frame over and straightened the corners, then untwisted the prongs and wiped them down before twisting them back in place again. "I think this will need some work. If you agree, I can take it back and—"

"Do what you need to," Maia said before he could finish.

He placed the frame back on the stool and nodded at Maia. "Give it one more try."

Miir's tinkering had definitely made a difference. Even before Maia put the marble in place, the prongs started quivering. And the moment it was all set, the frame shook. There was a squeal, a sputter, and finally a screech so loud that Maia's hands flew up to cover her ears. It was far from over. As the space above the frame filled with an explosion of light, Maia fell back and closed her eyes.

CHAPTER EIGHT

ASIYAAH

The noise stopped just as suddenly as it had started. A low, buzzing sound now filled the room. Maia opened her eyes, one at a time. A bright white beam of light hovered above the frame, flickering from time to time, but steady overall. Miir stared at the light, his face frozen in anticipation. For a while, however, not much seemed to happen beyond the beam. Then it started to quiver and vague shapes began to form within it.

Maia held her breath as a form slowly solidified. She recognized the face despite the graininess. Asiyaah, smiling, her reddish-brown hair loose on her back, sat on the outer steps of the Shrine of the Settlers. Maia stole a quick glance at Miir. His wide gaze was fixed on the projection, and Maia could see his eyes glistening. He must be so shaken, so moved right now. Yet not a word, not a sound escaped his lips. He sat rigid, holding his breath as if his whole being was intent on absorbing the vision quickly solidifying in front of his eyes.

"Maia, finally we meet."

Asiyaah's voice tinkled across the room and Maia blinked in

surprise. She had not had any clear conception of what Asiyaah would be like, but the light, breezy voice was startling. While Sophie had been quiet and soft, Asiyaah sounded full of life. Her face looked tired, but her eyes shone and her smile lit up the room.

"You are a young woman as you watch this, Maia, not the little baby I am thinking of and speaking to right now. For this day to have come, eighteen years must have passed and passed safely for you. I am happy. Even though I will never get to see you in person, knowing that you have had a safe life brings me relief."

As Asiyaah stopped to catch her breath and tucked a wayward strand of hair behind her ears, Maia sighed. Eighteen years had not passed, and the years had not passed safely at all. Such was the difference between hopes and reality.

In the projection, Asiyaah started speaking once more.

"I live with many regrets now. I know I destroyed many lives because I pursued this cause. Our brave Sophie is gone. Zaara lives, but her heart is lost forever. Raidyn . . . I wish we had been honest with him. I betrayed my family and placed a terrible burden on my baby. And then there's you . . . someone I never expected to be. My heart broke when I came to know of you. I have taken from you the person you need the most—your mother.

"I have had to leave my own children. They did not get to choose for themselves either, but they have a father, and they have safety. You will have to grow up with nothing and no one. How are you going to survive? Sophie's father is ill, and I know her brother has turned away. Even if my people never find out about you, you will still have to take on life all alone.

"Who will you run to now when you are afraid? Who will you share your secrets and dreams with? Who will comfort you when you are sad?

"The guilt eats me up every day. But then I think of the cause. And I come to the same conclusion always—even if I had known about you, I would not waver. Perhaps Sophie would, but not I. I do not mean that you are not important, Maia. But you see, when I think of the millions . . . billions that were waiting to be sacrificed by my people, I cannot . . . I do not think our individual lives matter anymore. Someone had to stop this slaughter. If not now, then when? If not us, then who?"

Asiyaah stopped and sighed.

"I hope you understand, Maia. I hope you are able to forgive. And most of all, I hope you are happy."

The light disappeared along with the buzzing, plunging the room into a breathless quiet. In Maia's mind, Asiyaah's image lingered, her words playing over and over again. She pored over every sentence. The regret in Asiyaah's voice was not new; she had heard it in Sophie's message also. It was understandable. Fighting for a cause greater than oneself, and sacrificing for it, seeing the toll it took on near and dear ones—that had to be a struggle to endure. Maia harbored no misgivings. She understood that saving Tansi was far more important than her having a normal childhood. To be honest, if Asiyaah had not decided to break the Sedara and Xif had left Tansi, she might not have had a life to begin with. So what was there to complain about?

"Are you all right?" Miir's voice jolted Maia out of her thoughts.

She nodded before looking up at his drawn face. "And you?"

"Fine," he said, but he sounded anything but. He was distracted, his face pale. "Do you want to try another one?" he asked, keeping his voice so meticulously even and steady that Maia could see the strain on his face.

Maia nodded again. He handed her another one, this one a bright blue. "If I am thinking right, this one should have been recorded much later. We shall find out."

He was trying to figure out the chronological arrangement of the marbles, but Maia's mind was hovering someplace else. "So, Miir, remember she talked about placing a burden on her baby? What was that about?"

Miir shrugged, his face thoughtful. "Maybe she meant that she left us behind. And it would be hard for us to grow up without a mother."

It might have been that simple, but the words stuck in Maia's mind. She was still thinking about it when she put the next marble in place.

Asiyaah's laughter brought her back to the present, and she squinted at the flickering vision. This time Asiyaah looked faded, and that was not because the projection kept sputtering. Her hair was shorter and paler, the tiredness on her face more pronounced — she looked like she had aged ten years between the previous message and this one. Maia realized this was indeed a recording from much later, when exposure to the Sedara's lighted core had taken a greater toll on Asiyaah. Her smile, however, was just as bright as before.

"Maia," Asiyaah called. The familiarity in that call made Maia smile. It was as if they had known each other for a lifetime.

"I hear you are quite a handful nowadays. My dear friend Bikele tells me so." She looked over to the side, as if at someone else. "You must already know him to be seeing this, but today, I'm going to introduce you to my friend."

The view of the projection swiveled around, and Maia recognized the room as the same room they were in now. It came to rest on a figure, a young man hunched over a large box he was unpacking.

"Bikele," Maia called out, forgetting where she was, that she was watching a moment long lost in time. For a fleeting moment, it felt as if she could simply reach out and touch Bikele. And she did. Her hand passed through, tearing the light, touching nothing but air. She drew her hand back immediately as realization dawned, swift and sharp, Miir's curious gaze making her flush in embarrassment. Asiyaah's voice in the background distracted and eased her a little.

"This, Maia, is the reason I am still alive. This is my friend, Bikele."

Bikele turned around, surprised. He held a hand up to hide his face. The projection swiveled back to show Asiyaah once more.

"Our friend is very shy, Maia. Of course, you must already know that. He made a promise to Sophie, and for that, he breaks a

Fundamental every few months and brings me supplies — food, water, medicines — and most important of all, his happy, smiling face."

All of a sudden, the projection dimmed and Maia had to squint harder to see Asiyaah. Asiyaah's voice was sad and morose when she spoke again.

"I do not know what I have done to deserve the care he gives, but I wish . . . no, I pray that I will not have to trouble him much longer."

"No, no." Bikele's voice drifted in. "I have told you before. That is no way to talk."

Asiyaah's eyes twinkled and she laughed a little, even though she looked exhausted.

"He reminds me of my father sometimes."

The projection flickered and faded once more. Maia could see the tears brimming in Asiyaah's eyes as she said the next words.

"I hope, as you watch this with Maia, you are happy, my friend. I hope after I am gone, the years pass peacefully for you. You stay safe, and you stay happy. May the stars bless you forever, Bikele. May you receive kindness —"

The light went out.

"What happened?" Maia cried.

Miir leaned over and tapped the frame a few times, but the projection did not come back. "I have no idea," he said. "I will have to look into it." He pulled the marble out of the prongs and handed it to Maia, not once looking up at her.

"Could you please collect all the marbles?" he asked as he hastily tucked the frame into his pack. He grabbed the stool and a spindle of wire and pointed at the door, his gaze never meeting Maia's. "I will wait outside. It is almost midday. Ren and Sana should be back soon. Then we can leave." He almost sounded as if he wanted to run away, far, far from here.

"Are you all right?"

"Yes. Just need some time to myself."

"Miir, what's wrong?"

"Just need some time to myself," Miir repeated.

Maia watched him lumber over to the group of boulders on one side of the yard and perch on one. She wished she could help, but after he so clearly expressed his need for time to deal with his thoughts, she had to give it to him. So she walked back to the corner and started cleaning up. She gathered the marbles into the pot and placed the pot carefully inside her bag. She had finished putting all the displaced stones back in the plant holder when she saw Sana outside and walked out to meet her.

"Where's Ren?" Maia asked.

Sana rolled her eyes. "Went to check on his darling Viperine. How did it go here? Find anything?"

"We found Asiyaah's memorial. And messages from her." Maia went on to explain how they had found the marbles and strung them into the frame to access the messages.

Sana peeked at the bagful of marbles and looked incredulously at Maia's face. "Those are recording devices? Those marbles?"

"Well, not all of them. Some are. We have to try them out one at a time."

"So, did you see anything at all? Anything worthwhile?"

"Bits and pieces. Nothing groundbreaking so far. The projection device stopped working before we could check out even two. Miir is taking it with him, to try to repair it."

"Well, it's something, right?"

"Sure is."

Sana looked over her shoulder at Miir still sitting on the boulder. "What's with him?"

Maia sighed. "He saw his mother after all these years. Couldn't have been easy. But I think he's most upset about Bikele. There was one log of him with Asiyaah. And that kind of threw him off."

Sana crossed her arms and frowned. "Did you talk to him?"

"I tried. Won't say a word. He's been sitting there ever since."

"All right, then. I'll have a chat."

Maia grabbed Sana's arm as she began to march away. "Sana, I don't think that's—"

Sana turned around and patted her cheek. "Don't worry. I won't hurt your Miir. I'll be very gentle."

It took Maia a moment or two to fix a glare on Sana. "Sana, he's not *my*—"

Sana placed a finger on her lips, her eyes wide and round. "Shhh . . . keep it down. I get it, all right?"

She did not get it at all, that was for sure. But clearly, there was no correcting her, either. Maia glared at Sana for a bit longer before walking back into the *abayam*. She strolled around aimlessly, cradling the bag of marbles, imagining Asiyaah's long, lonely life here. It must have been so difficult. Just thinking about it made Maia shudder. She was staring out at the wilderness behind the building, a melee of thoughts crisscrossing her mind, when someone walked in behind her.

"Hey." Ren stood at the door, smiling. "I hear you're all done here. Ready to leave?"

Maia was ready. She would have to come back here again someday, but now, it was time to go. She let her gaze trail over the empty room, taking in the scene around her—the dim sunlight that fell in patches across the open door, the lingering musty odor, and the distant cooing of a bird. She wanted to remember this, a slice of the life that had been Asiyaah's, the unknown and unthanked savior of her little planet, her home.

She took a long breath and nodded at Ren. "Yes, I'm ready. Let's go."

Miir and Sana had already started back, and Maia was both surprised and relieved to see them talking. Miir even had a smile on his face. The walk back to the Viperine seemed shorter than the way there, and Sana broke into excited chatter as they drew close to the craft.

"So this is why you took off, Ren?" she exclaimed.

It took a moment for Maia to notice what she was pointing at. A blanket was laid out on the grass below the Viperine, and on it was a scattering of food items.

Sana ran back to hug Ren. "You can be so sweet sometimes."

Ren placed a hand on his chest and put on a pained expression. "And she breaks my heart . . . again. When am I not sweet, Angel?"

It was definitely thoughtful of him. The food was badly needed since Maia's stomach started to growl at the sight of it. The sun rays were starting to pale when they finally finished their meal and were ready for the trip back.

"Want to fly the Viperine back, Miir?" Ren asked when everything was stowed away.

Miir's face lit up in an instant. As he nodded eagerly, Maia wondered how it had not struck her before. She had often thought of Miir missing his family, his home, and his friends. But she had forgotten one important thing, his love of flying, and his prized Onclioraptor, *Shadow*. The realization of how much he had left behind to make things right hit Maia squarely in the gut.

Much later, as they were flying back, Ren brought up *Shadow*. "You must miss *Shadow* a lot, huh?"

Miir did not reply right away, but a few moments later he sighed. "I cannot lie. I do."

"Then we should fetch it."

Once again, Miir took a few moments to reply. "Just walk in and walk out with *Shadow*? That should be easy."

Ren chuckled. "No, I didn't say it'd be that easy. But . . ."

"They will need my imprint to release *Shadow*. And—"

"You want *Shadow*, right?" Ren asked. "Yes or no?"

"Yes, I do," Miir replied with a sigh.

"Then you shall have it," Ren declared. "No reason to worry about it. Ren's on the case and we *shall* have a solution."

Maia had no idea what plan Ren would come up with. Knowing Ren, it would no doubt be an outrageous one. However, she knew this would be one scheme she would support without question. It was strange, but never in her life she had felt so desperate to fulfill someone else's wish as she did now.

CHAPTER NINE

THE CORRELATION CHALLENGE

A summons from the chief arbitrator arrived the night before ThulaSu opened up again. The final challenge was about to be announced at last. Maia found herself in a strange state of dissociation after reading the summons. On the one hand, she was eager to hear about the challenge, since winning it was the only viable path to getting Seigvard, the key to thwarting the R'armimon. On the other, she was almost afraid to believe that it was actually happening. Up until now, the Solianese phase had been paused, put on hold, threatened with cancelation, paused again, had lost its chief arbitrator, and then was paused once more. It seemed almost impossible that the final stage of the Initiative would ever be completed.

She woke up early and excited that morning, however, and after her training with the Xinhagyi, she freshened up quickly and rushed to the AR, where the team had decided to meet before breakfast and the trek to hear the announcement. Raucous cheers and a visibly excited Nafi greeted her when she entered.

"What's going on?" Maia asked, looking around tentatively.

Dani looked up at her but did not say a word. The grim expression she had worn since the incident at the Trinity Caverns had not changed. Ren, however, waved her in, and Nafi bobbed all the way across the room to her.

"Maia, we've found an awesome way to work the firestone communicators. This is just perfect."

The firestone wristbands Mahswa Tabrin had awarded the team during the Xifarian phase of the Initiative were excellent communicators, and the gang used them often. However, they were a bit tedious with setup processes and codes.

"Tell me," Maia said, sinking onto the couch next to Dani.

Nafi grabbed her own wristband. "So I'll try to connect with you, all right?"

"All right. What do I think about?" They always had to pick a common thought code for the channels to work.

Nafi's eyes twinkled. "We'll get to that later. Now, wait for it."

Maia had no idea what to expect, but she waited patiently. Suddenly, it came. A little pop in her head, like the bursting of a bubble. And again. And again.

She sat up and gasped. "Is that—"

"Now, try 'apple' for the code," Nafi directed.

As soon as Maia thought of a red, juicy apple, Nafi's voice came clearly into her head. *Helloooo, Maia.*

"Oh!" Maia gasped again. "But how?"

Ren shrugged. "No idea how. It's almost like the communicator decided to bless us or something. Anyway, it's pretty cool. Now we can connect with any of us whenever we want," he added. "We can do group communications just as easily."

"Yes, it is so easy. Watch." Nafi went on to demonstrate talking to the gathered group.

"All we need now is to pick a permanent thought code," Ren said and winced as soon as Nafi gave him a look. "No, Nafi. Not apple."

"How about Mahswa Tabrin?" Maia said. The Xifarian Tierremorphe was the one who had given them the wristbands, and she had been a confidante and a friend all through their journey in the Initiative.

"I like that," Ren said immediately. Dani and Nafi also readily agreed.

Soon after, they trooped out toward the refectory, their strides lively. A quick breakfast later, they headed to the Reception Gallery where the arbitrators usually met with the teams. When they reached it, the room was empty except for the huddle of team mentors.

A bright orange head bounded up to them as soon as they entered. "There you are, Core 21!" Hadeeyah's lopsided smile greeted them before turning into a frown. "Where's Kusha?"

"Umm . . . Kusha might not be joining us today," Dani said. "He has councils to attend. He has asked the arbitrators for permission to be excused."

Hadeeyah's frown had been growing deeper since Dani started to explain, and by the time she finished, the mentor's brow was in a ferocious knot.

"Might not be joining?" Hadeeyah's eyes widened in her rapidly-reddening face and she looked almost ready to explode. "This is the announcement of the challenge, and he . . ." Hadeeyah paused and zoomed around the stupefied group three times. "This is not good. Not good at all. All right, you guys sit down. I need to have a chat with Kusha. This is bad, very bad."

She circled them one last time and zoomed out of the room. The group simply stood there, watching her swiftly-disappearing form, until Nafi cleared her throat loudly.

"Well, I have nothing to say about that girl, but . . . I think we should sit down now."

The room slowly filled up. First came Monk Tessio, then Core 13 and Core 7. After that Master Kehorkjin and Supervisor Aerika arrived, followed by Core 34 and Core 10. Then, as Maia waited with bated breath for Zaara, in came a bright orange whirlwind dragging a sad-faced Kusha behind her.

Dani peered at Kusha's face as he slumped noisily next to her.

"Kusha, you said — "

Kusha did not let Dani finish. "That Hadeeyah is crazy. Pulled me out of a council. Wouldn't listen no matter how many times I said no."

"Oh well, now that you are here, no need to be grumpy," Nafi commented.

Kusha threw her a glare, but no words could be exchanged because the ominous thumping of booted feet made them forget everything else and sit up.

Zaara marched in, staff in hand. This time, although she still wore her cape, she was not covered head to foot in black. She nodded curtly at the arbitrators and Tessio before taking her stand on the dais. Maia did not know whether it was the presence of Kehorkjin or Aerika, or whether being at ThulaSu had a calming effect on Zaara, but the woman seemed less angry than the first time she had met the teams.

"Monk Tessio tells me you all have been working hard at the Glass House. That's excellent. Our environment, the ground we stand on, is important for our survival, and from the time this planet was settled, the importance of plants has been stressed many times in our fables and lore. Has anyone here heard of the *Fables of the Unsung*?"

Shaky hands crept upward one at a time. It seemed that a good many of the contestants knew of the fables, including all of Core 21.

"Perhaps you have heard of the part where Mindoza the Uniter heals the island of Hanuk Nai?" The only head that nodded was Nafi's, and Zaara's staff was pointed at her instantly. "You, girl, stand up. Tell us what you know."

Maia had never seen Nafi so nervous. She chewed her lips, blinked rapidly, and breathed like she was going through a panic attack before she uttered a word.

"Hanuk Nai's magical Jueyue had been struck by lightning and split in two. It was dying, and the island of Hanuk Nai along with it. Mindoza the Uniter was passing through with his band of warriors and he was touched by the hospitality of the people of Hanuk Nai who, even when they barely had enough to feed themselves, opened their homes to welcome Mindoza and his friends. Mindoza promised to heal the Jueyue. It was not an easy task. He flew across the skies to pluck out the heart of the moon and swam across the stormy seas to the Jueyue that sat on the sunken tip of Hanuk Nai. Then he tore the moon's heart and swathed the Jueyue's broken stem and—"

"And so it was healed. Hanuk Nai's grounds turned green once more, and its people prospered," Zaara completed the story for Nafi. "Thank you, girl. Sit." Zaara picked up some papers from the table behind her and handed them to the mentors. "Taking care of the environment we live in has always been important. We are nothing without what surrounds us. Understood?"

Heads nodded across the room.

"One of your tasks, as I have said a thousand times already, is to use the Spore and the fern to heal the soil. For now, you can experiment with the two samples in Monk Tessio's care in the Glass House, but as part of this challenge, you'll have to acquire your own specimens. For that, you will go to Korobieltes. Keep these maps, they will help. Master Kehorkjin and Supervisor Aerika are here to explain the other tasks of the Correlation Challenge."

Other tasks? Going to Korobieltes would be bad enough. What other tasks was she talking about?

Maia turned to look at Ren, who promptly shrugged and whispered, "No offense, but she's nuts."

Maia could barely keep from chuckling. It was so nice having Ren back, to not have to tiptoe around him, and to have some much-needed lightness in their conversations again. She was still smiling to herself when Master Kehorkjin started speaking.

"One of your tasks will be to extract Calbion from the mines in Ti." He handed out another set of papers to the mentors. "Study the mines marked on these maps, and pick the one you want to visit. Research the means of extracting the ore. You will be taken by craft from the base to the mine, a craft that you will choose and navigate by *yourself*. Two trips to Xif is what you get for the research on the mines and choosing appropriate vehicles to get to the mines." He stopped, and his gray-blue gaze swept the assembled faces twice. "Questions?"

Jiri's hand shot up.

Master Kehorkjin smiled. "Yes, Jiri."

"We have to actually go to Ti?" Maia thought she caught the hint of a tremor in Jiri's voice. "And extract Calbion? We need a lot of training for that, don't we?"

"Train yourself. You have time," Kehorkjin said calmly. "You are a top team, Jiri. After all that you have been through, nothing should scare you."

Aerika took center stage after that. "You have one more task on your list." She picked up another set of papers from the table and like the other arbitrators, handed them to the mentors. "I just handed out a map of a few Challowist farms off the coast of ThulaSu. This task will be similar to installing the hydrosol converters in the Roqowist farm during your stay in Zagran. Only, this will be a bit more complicated. To start with, you have to pick a type of equipment . . . any type from the choice of farms displayed here. During your first trip, you'll install its parts in the substrate to charge. Then you go back in a few months and bring it back here to use for the challenge."

Ren's arm shot up at this point and Aerika's brow furrowed. "What is it?"

"Do we get our aquatic partners back for this?"

"No, sadly, you don't." Ren looked crestfallen and Maia felt sad for him thinking of how deeply he had bonded with his partner, Chylomyhrra, a milk squid. Aerika flashed a sympathetic smile. "Anything else, Ren?"

"So we complete all these tasks and that's it? Or is there a connection?"

Aerika's thin lips curled into a ghost of a smile. "Perhaps. Perhaps not."

"Thank you," Ren said to Aerika. As soon as she looked away, Ren leaned toward Maia and whispered, "That's supposed to be an answer?"

Maia chuckled under her breath. "They *must* be connected. Zaara called it the Correlation Challenge and I wondered why. I'm sure it's because these tasks are somehow interlinked."

Ren frowned and let out a sigh. "Hmm."

Zaara continued. "You will be awarded points for successfully completing each task, as well as for the project plan you submit beforehand with all your research and a summary afterward." She paused and scanned the anxious faces around her. "You may also be awarded special points for exemplary behavior and effort, and penalized for misbehavior and disturbances. I do not like indiscipline, so watch your step, all of you."

Karhann raised his hand when Zaara paused.

"Will we have daily training sessions?"

Zaara frowned. "To do what? Hold your hand and teach you to walk?" Karhann flushed at the brusque response, but Zaara went on, "You are old enough now to find your own way. The Great Library is open to you. You have access to the specimens in Monk Tessio's Glass House. Besides, you get to visit Xif twice to plan for the trip to Ti. What else do you need?" Karhann did not reply and Zaara continued. "We will meet every few weeks and that will be all. It is time you grew up."

As the entire room drew sharp breaths, Kehorkjin's voice boomed. "Remember to keep on top of your combat skills. You never know when you might have to fight it out for a resource. And as always, fight only with your personal weapons and fight honorably."

As soon as the arbitrators and Monk Tessio left, the room erupted in animated discussions. Handing them the maps, which Nafi promptly slipped into her pack, Hadeeyah herded the team out and to a side.

"Now, Kusha" — their mentor fixed a worried look on Kusha — "as you can clearly see, the challenges are not easy. You don't even know if they go together or not, whether this is all you have to do or not. So . . . your sitting out is not an option. We have to solve this problem about you."

"Well, Hadeeyah, I can't be here all the time," Kusha said emphatically. "Believe me, I want to work on the Initiative full time and not be buried out there under mountains of chores. But I cannot quit my duties. I've spoken to the Arbitration Committee and they have agreed to excuse my absence. So we are fine."

"Can't quit your duties?" Hadeeyah glared. "Isn't the Initiative your duty too?"

"It is. But there are four awesome people who I know can manage in my absence. I will join them from time to time and do as much as I can. That I promise," Kusha said in a calm, stoic voice. "But I can't give up ThulaSu. There is no one I trust enough to look after it for me. Especially with our clock ticking and planning for evacuations to do. I just can't."

"Hey, Hadeeyah, it's fine," Ren chimed in. "We'll work harder and Kusha will join in whenever he can. It'll all be fine."

Around him, heads nodded eagerly.

Their reassurances did not seem to inspire any confidence in their mentor. Her mouth twisted into a disapproving scowl. "Well, it's not the best solution, but we have to work with what we have." She clapped her hands. "So, make it work, people. I'll come by every evening to check on your progress. I don't want to see any slacking, understood? Now go on . . . off to the libraries you go."

They went, hurried away by Hadeeyah, in some vague direction away from the room they had gathered in. Kusha left soon after, assuring them one more time that he would be with them as much as possible. Although everyone in the team understood his situation and bore no grudges, that did not make the weight of their task any lighter. The reality was—they were practically one person down for this final challenge. That, when the stakes were so high, was not a happy situation.

Maia trudged along listlessly with Ren and the girls, Nafi leading the way, along the meandering pathways that led to the Great Library. She kept forcing herself to think in more positive terms. A win was still possible. They only had to plan better and work harder. But however much she thought, her shoulders kept slumping.

"Hey! Isn't that Sana?" Nafi's surprised voice pulled Maia out of the endless loops in her head. "Looks like she has a boyfriend."

Nafi was not mistaken. It was indeed Sana, and she looked quite happy and cozy, laughing as she leaned on the shoulder of a striking boy who looked familiar.

"One of her new classmates, I'm guessing," Nafi said. "Not even a day into her classes and she's already found a beau. I just have no words."

"I know that boy," Maia blurted, recognition suddenly flooding her. Jez—she remembered his name. He had laughed and jeered when the Viperine was vandalized, and had finally stopped when Maks threatened to file a complaint. She wondered, with a sinking heart, if Ren too had recognized him.

"Thought she had better sense than that." Ren's wry comment answered her unasked question.

Nafi cocked her head at him. "Hmm . . . do I smell jealousy?"

Ren scoffed. "I don't do jealous, Nafi. It's totally uncool."

"What is it, then?" Nafi asked. "I see why she might like the boy. He's cute."

"Guess that's all it takes," Ren said. "Well, I just remembered I need to be at Frauz Point. Catch you guys later."

"Hey, wait! What about the library?" Nafi asked, but Ren had already turned around and left. Nafi watched him disappear, then turned toward the two girls. "He's touchy, isn't he?"

"He has reason to be, Nafi," Maia said. She went on to explain how she knew Jez. When she was done telling them everything, Nafi's eyes flashed.

"What a despicable character," she said angrily. "Of all the people Sana could find, she had to pick *him*?"

Maia had to admit it was quite an unfortunate choice. "I will talk to her."

"I don't think you should be meddling, Maia," Dani said in a low, calm voice. She hardly spoke these days and her voice always had an undercurrent of sadness. This time was no different. It did not lack conviction, however. "If Ren has a problem with it, he should talk to

Sana himself. It's not as if he doesn't know her, or he's shy about expressing his opinions."

That was quite true. But it was not Ren Maia was thinking about, but herself. The idea of Sana with Jez did not sit well with her. That Sana could be with such a spiteful person—even if not seriously—bothered her.

There was not much time to think about it at that moment. The rest of the day passed busily, wrangling books at the Great Library. The always gracious librarian, Monk Atriss, was a huge help as usual, and soon the girls had found heaps of material on the plants and also on many of Mindoza's tales. Time passed swiftly. Taking notes and poring through books all day left their backs aching by the time they trooped back to the living quarters.

Maia found Sana in her room, lounging with Rayan. The thoughts of Jez she had pushed aside came rushing back once more. Maia knew she was clueless and inept as far as relationships went, and Sana was anything but. However, a sense of responsibility gnawed at her heart. Knowing what she knew of Jez, she believed she had to tell Sana her opinion. Maia decided to tackle the topic as the duo was walking to the refectory for dinner that evening.

"Sana, are you seeing Jez?" she asked bluntly.

Sana arched a shapely brow at her. "You know already? News sure travels fast in this place."

"Well, we saw you out on the terrace. How did you even . . ." Maia's voice trailed off, her mind unable to find words for a moment. She resumed only with difficulty. "You barely know him, Sana. It has not even been a day since you met him."

"He's cute and fun." Sana seemed to have plenty of confidence in her reasoning. Then she noticed Maia's frown. "You don't approve?"

"No, I don't." Maia told her about the incident a few weeks ago when the Viperine was vandalized, and how Jez had laughed at the Xifarians. "I know you can take care of yourself, but that boy is not—"

"Don't worry, Maia. It's just fun to have someone to hang around with. It's not like I'm engaged to be married to him." Sana laughed and linked an arm through hers. "Speaking of marriage and stuff, Ren told me Miir was engaged to this girl on Xif. Did you know?"

"Sana, we're talking about you and Jez," Maia said. "Who Miir is engaged to is none of our business."

"Well, guess what?" Sana's eyebrows danced. "I asked him. Asked him what their status is."

"Sana—"

"He gave me this cryptic answer before shutting me down. Told me that chapter of his life is over and closed for good. What do you make of that? I think he broke it off with her around the same time he left the SDS. What do you think?"

Maia stopped and turned to face her cousin. "I don't care. As I said, none of our business." Sana seemed to find her answer amusing, which was completely aggravating, but Maia ignored it and continued. "But you, Sana, I care about. And you should rethink this thing with Jez. He's really not—"

"All right, Maia, I get it," Sana said, cutting her off once again. "I'll take it slow with Jez. Now let's go eat. I'm hungry."

What 'taking it slow' meant in Sana's dictionary, Maia had no idea. But she sincerely hoped that her advice had achieved something.

CHAPTER TEN

THE DIE IS CAST

A spell of happy, warm days had descended on ThulaSu, and spirits were high everywhere. The students gathered on the ramparts and in the rose garden, the Sun Temple grounds were unusually full during combat practice every evening, and even Core 21 — Hadeeyah's stressful prodding notwithstanding — were in a joyful mood.

The challenge — weirdly disparate puzzle pieces flung at them — looked forbidding, no doubt, yet the weather lifted their glum spirits in no time. Sana planned a small picnic in the bowers, Ren took them all out in the Viperine one day, and on yet another bright and shiny off day, the group trekked up and down the trails behind Kusha's house.

Maia returned to her room smiling gaily after their walk in the mountains, but as soon as she opened the door, her heart sank. Sitting on the ground was a disc, Ruche's calling card. His message was short and succinct.

Need to see you tomorrow. The bowers at sunrise. Bring no one else.

"You can't go alone. No," Rayan declared right away. "I am coming."

It would have been one thing—difficult but not inconceivable—to convince Rayan otherwise, but when the rest of her friends sided with Rayan, Maia realized the task was completely impossible.

"Guys, Ruche specifically asked me not to bring anyone. He's never asked that before. So it's important that I follow his instructions."

"And walk into a trap?" Rayan asked. "The seer is not the only R'armimon around anymore. Their whole fleet is here now."

"I agree," Nafi said. "Who knows what's going on in those crooked heads?"

In the end, however, the gang relented. It was decided that they would escort Maia to the rose garden and only stay until Ruche arrived.

The following morning was frigid, and Maia had to put on a thick hooded jacket to ward off the chill. All of her teammates, along with Rayan and Sana, walked in silence while the skies were just showing a hint of pink. They only managed to troop as far as the entrance of the rose garden before finding they could go no further. A pair of Faceless seemed to appear out of thin air as soon as they stepped inside the gates, their arms outstretched to stop the procession.

Before Maia could think of what to do next, Ruche appeared behind them, and his eyebrows came together as soon as he saw the big huddle.

"Did I forget to ask you to come alone?" he asked Maia, his voice unusually grim and severe.

Maia had known Ruche for a while and talked to him a lot, but this was the first time he had ever scolded her like that. It was odd how it made her eyes burn and her gaze drop.

"I didn't mean to—"

"Hey! You can't expect her to walk around alone this time of the morning." Ren's sharp voice cut off Maia's apology and made Ruche's eyes narrow to slits. Without a moment of hesitation, Ren continued.

"If you were a friend, you'd understand."

Maia was a little surprised at Ren's combative tone. She also realized this was the first time Ruche and Ren had met. Perhaps the brusqueness was due to Ren's prejudice against the R'armimon.

"You have a robust spirit," Ruche said after a short, tight bout of silence, his voice even colder than the morning air. "However, there are some things, Ren, that you shouldn't tangle with. Some things are just too dangerous for someone as young as you."

If Ren was at all surprised when Ruche called him by name, Maia could not tell, but the way he crossed his arms and met the seer's frosty gaze made it clear Ren was in no mood to back down.

"Calling me a child, are you, Ruche?" His eyes flashed, even in that dim light. "You should know, though, I tangle with whoever I want, whenever I want. It's just that simple."

Maia had no idea what had come over Ren, but she had had enough. Ruche was their friend and the only person who Maia believed could help Tansi. He was the last person they needed to antagonize. She turned to stop Ren, but Dani was faster. Grabbing Ren by the arm, she dragged him away.

"Come on, everyone," she said. "Let's leave Maia alone for a bit. Come on."

No one else objected, thankfully. As Maia walked toward Ruche, she was a little anxious about the way Ruche's frigid stare stayed fixed on Ren's back. The seer was clearly disturbed, and a pensive frown hovered on his face. It melted away quickly, however, and Ruche led her further into the garden, past the bowers, close to the edge of the mountain.

"Maia, Prince Aekken will be here to meet with you shortly," he said, once again in a gruff, almost hostile tone. "Follow my lead and you will be fine." Maia breathed in deeply and braced herself. It was not as if she had not expected this meeting, but still, it was unnerving and simply . . . scary that it was happening at all. Ruche let out a long sigh. "Remember, Maia, keep your emotions in check."

A circle of fire had been lit near the edge of the hill. Ruche stood there, waiting, Maia next to him. The skies had lightened just a bit when Maia felt it. It started with a slight tremor in the air around them, and then as she scanned the area, she noticed the shimmer. And then, they formed out of air.

The prince of the R'armimon was just as striking in person as he had been in the portal. Truth be told, Maia found his presence even more commanding than she had thought. He looked older than he had seemed then. Maia guessed he was at least ten years older than Hans, if not more. His mottled-gray eyes were sharp and his nose sharper. Thick, black hair hung in tight curls a little above his shoulders. As he stood tall, flamboyant in a long blood-red coat, flanked by five of his own Faceless in red bodysuits, Maia thought how incongruous he looked in the rose garden.

Then he smiled and lowered his head. "Nasfarii of Tansi, honored to finally meet you."

Maia lowered her head a little in response, her insides shaking with trepidation. Aekken took a step closer, his hand outstretched, and Maia noticed how Ruche took a step forward as well, his fists tight.

"Seer Ruche, I hope you will permit this." On the prince's upturned palm was a small glass ball. Inside it, a flame flickered, bright and shiny.

"Prince Aekken." Ruche sounded outraged. "Did you *have* to?"

"Please," Aekken insisted in a sharp, cold voice.

Ruche took the ball from the prince's hand, his face hard as he turned toward Maia. "The Crown Prince demands proof of your abilities, Maia," he said. "Please oblige him by accepting this."

Maia looked from Ruche's annoyed face to Aekken's smug one before she stretched her hand out to receive the ball. She had no idea of how this test was being conducted, but she relished the cold, smooth touch of the sphere on her palms. It lasted only a moment. As Maia stared in shock, the ball burst into flames and then disintegrated in her hands, finally dissolving into the air.

Ruche's hands wrapped around Maia's trembling ones as he

snapped toward Aekken. "Satisfied, Prince Aekken?"

Aekken bowed low. "My apologies, Nasfarii, for startling you. But protocol demanded that I follow through and confirm the extent of your powers. Now I have."

"What did you find out?" Maia asked, trying her best to keep her voice even.

"You are, as our seer always says, special."

His words made Maia flush. Seeing how the prince's eyes gleamed as he picked it up, she immediately wished she had not.

"You seem anxious. Why is that?" Aekken said.

The sudden question startled Maia. "Anxious?" She forced a laugh. She thought of lying, telling him he had guessed wrong. Then as she noticed Aekken's gaze scanning her face, she realized what a wasted effort that would be. Not much could escape those eyes, not when her face was like a mirror to her soul, as Dada always liked to say. So after a moment's hesitation, Maia went with the truth. "I have been thinking of our last conversation, of the blood and tears you spoke about. I worry about the future of my world. Perhaps that's why you find me anxious."

"Oh no, please do not fret because of what I might have said before." Aekken seemed to be in a rush to reassure her. "No matter what the need is and what vengeance my soul seeks, I shall not harm the Nasfarii's home world." He looked around at the garden surrounding them. "Yours is a beautiful world, Nasfarii of Tansi."

He turned and walked to the far edge before coming back toward Maia and Ruche.

"I cannot, however, simply forgive those renegades. Even if I wished to, the Empire would not let me," he said with a telling glance at Ruche. "Their crimes are enormous, and suitable justice has to be meted out." His gaze flitted over Maia's face once more, a small smile hovering on his lips. "I, too, have been thinking of what you said at our last meeting, Nasfarii. Your suggestion of punishing only those responsible is a commendable one. Perhaps we can start with the one that started it all — that most despicable of the deadwastes, Veiles."

"Veiles? But he's dead."

Aekken laughed a little. "Yes, of course. He is fortunate to have died before I found them. However, his descendants must still be around." His eyes glinted with joy as he said the next words. "We could plan an unforgettable punishment for everyone to see and remember."

"What is their crime? Being born into Veiles's family?" Maia asked. Seeing Aekken's eyes still, she continued. "Isn't it enough that their planet has been stripped of its powers to fly? Isn't it enough knowing they will never kill another star?"

The prince's eyes narrowed. "You are too kind, Nasfarii. Why do you speak for the people who do nothing for you in return except try to take your life? I hear those deadwastes have tried, many times, to kill you. The Chairman Phocluus, for instance, keeps coming back to harm you. That is an outrage, and I shall not stand for it." He tilted his head and looked into Maia's eyes. "How would you like a public execution of that filth?"

It would be so easy to let herself be carried away by his promise of vengeance, and even a year ago, Maia would have been happy at the prince's fiery offer. But that morning, Maia found no pleasure in his words.

"I'm touched by your kindness for me, Prince Acldken. But all I really hope for is peace. At least for the next six months. I will be forever grateful if you can grant me that."

"Six months? For what?"

"It's a simple thing," Maia said. "A little contest I have been participating in. It will be over in six months." She forced herself to hold his dark gaze. "I understand your need for justice, but I wish it might wait until the contest is complete."

Aekken's expression went from wide-eyed incredulity to amused and indulgent as Maia spoke.

"Just that? All you wish for is to complete this contest?" He lowered his head as soon as Maia nodded. "Of course, Nasfarii. Your wish is my command." He placed a hand over his heart and bowed to

Maia. "I sincerely hope you become the champion, Nasfarii of Tansi. And I promise I will cause no distractions."

"Thank you." Maia bowed back, unable to believe that the prince had so easily and quickly accepted her request.

Aekken turned toward Ruche, his eyebrows furrowed in curiosity. "I am intrigued by this contest. Seer Ruche, I need to hear all about this."

He turned back toward Maia, the flowing hem of his long coat swishing over the frozen ground.

"I do have a wish of my own, and I hope you will bestow your consent," Aekken said, a playful smile hovering on his lips. "I shall be eternally obliged if the Nasfarii would grant me audience from time to time."

Maia looked sideways at Ruche and seeing his blink of approval, she nodded. "Yes, certainly."

Aekken's face brightened and he smiled broadly. "I am honored, Nasfarii." He extended his hand toward her. On his open palm sat a small metallic disc with a jeweled button on top. "Any time you need me, I will be here. All you need to do is press that button."

Ruche blinked again, so Maia picked up the communicator gingerly from the prince's hand. Aekken smiled again, his face even brighter this time.

For a moment, Maia wondered about that joyful look on his face. Was he truly happy that she had agreed, or was it just for show? Was it possible that the prince had a kind corner somewhere deep within his heart? She did not get to think about it any further, since Aekken spoke again.

"I would like a council with the leaders of the Nasfarii's home world, Seer," he said next. "Would you please arrange for that?"

As soon as Ruche nodded, Aekken's gaze returned to Maia. He smiled once again and bowed. "Until the next time, Nasfarii of Tansi."

As soon as the prince shimmered away along with his guards, Maia let out a sigh of relief. Ruche seemed to feel the same way. He sank onto the nearest bench and exhaled loudly.

"That wasn't as bad as I thought it'd be," he said after a while. Maia was happy to note that his voice had now lost its edge, and sounded almost normal.

Maia sat down next to the seer, her heart beating along happily at his words. "That's good."

"Well, I'm a little worried, to be honest," Ruche confessed. "Any time Aekken behaves nicely, I worry. He's a schemer through and through, Maia. A schemer with an ugly heart. Nothing he does is without reason. Every step is to further a plot of some kind. The one thing . . . the only thing he truly cares for is his goal of securing the throne." Ruche stopped and stared for a while at the glistening vista beyond the ledge. "Besides, Aekken is prone to changing his mind. His word is no guarantee of any sort."

The joy of achievement Maia had felt just moments ago trickled steadily out of her as Ruche spoke.

"Sorry I made you glum, Maia." Ruche placed a hand on her shoulder. "Let's be happy with small accomplishments. This meeting went well, and he has promised you six months of peace. Now let's hope his council with your leaders goes just as well." Ruche gave her a warning before leaving. "I let you keep that communicator to make Aekken happy, but do not use it. Store it somewhere, but away from your person. I will arrange for these audiences he seeks, not you."

Maia left the rose garden after Ruche departed, and found her friends waiting for her on the ramparts. They lingered there that morning, ignoring the cold, the bright rays of the sun warming their backs as they talked about the prince of the R'armimon.

CHAPTER ELEVEN

RULES OF ENGAGEMENT

Everyone had hoped for the warm days to linger forever, but the weather grew progressively chillier. Maia, and all else who heard about it from her, eased a little at hearing the lease on life they had received, even though, according to Ruche, the prince's mind was prone to rapid changes.

A few days after the meeting with Prince Aekken, Maia received another summons from Ruche. She found him pacing in the rose garden that morning.

"Aekken will be meeting with the Tansian Council five days from now," he announced without a preamble. "Please be prepared."

"Prepared? Me? What for?" Maia was genuinely surprised.

"Well, you need to be there, obviously. You're why he's meeting them here. Actually, I should say you're why he's meeting them at all."

"I have to be there? To do what?"

"Did you hear me, Maia? You are the reason the prince is coming. So you have to play the part of the host."

Maia's eyes almost popped out. "The host? Do you have any idea what the council will think of me?" Maia shook her head at Ruche's curious look. "They'll brand me an accomplice, that's what. And I'm tired of—"

"Do you have to care about what those ignorant fools think of you?" Ruche continued after a considerable pause. "After all this time, all you've been through, you fear *them*?"

Maia stifled a sigh. She had to admit that Ruche was right. She had no reason to care. All the councils had done was heap scorn on her, torment her with insults. Yet, why did she find that hesitation in one corner of her mind? Wasn't it time she accepted that they would always treat her as a rogue outsider? No matter what she did, she would always be a monstrosity they abhorred.

"Fine. I'll play host, whatever that means. Will you be there?"

"Of course, Maia. I will be there," Ruche said with a loud chuckle. "We can't have the Crown Prince frolic about unchaperoned, can we?" Whatever mirth Ruche's comment about the prince brought was wiped away by his next announcement. "I will have to see you every two days from now on, Maia. You need to train."

"But I train with the Xinhagyi every day," Maia protested. "Why do I—"

Ruche's eyebrow shot up. "Am I *that* annoying?" As Maia fidgeted in embarrassment, he smiled and explained. "The Xinhagyi's training is invaluable. But he cannot help you the way I can. After your power came out, the Xinhagyi was the perfect teacher. He helped you learn to accept the light. Now that it is a part of you, you are ready to take the next step. It's about time you did, since we only have a few months until an inevitable confrontation with Aekken. You'll need to be prepared."

Ruche left soon after, but his last words lingered in Maia's mind as she walked back to her room with Rayan. An inevitable confrontation . . . it made Maia shudder. She wondered how, if at all, she would be able to face the threat that was the R'armimon fleet.

* * *

The day the R'armimon prince met with the Tansian Council was cold and cloudy. Maia had to drag herself out of bed, wishing someone would tell her the meeting was canceled. However, nothing of the sort occurred, and she found herself trudging toward the Gathering House where the meeting was to be, with all her friends in tow. Everyone was remarkably quiet. It was unsettling, and Maia almost wished they would chatter as usual and keep her distracted. By the time they reached the building, Maia's heart was thudding like a hammer in her chest.

The doors of the Gathering House were wide open when they arrived and the Kausakas standing guard nodded sharply as Kusha led them inside.

"You will have to be inside the circle when he comes, Maia," Kusha explained as they walked through the rows of seats. Although Kusha was not a part of this council, he had been involved in the planning. "But that's after Ruche arrives. Wait here with us until then."

'Until then' turned out to be a long, difficult time. The Gathering House was not teeming with people, but was not empty either. Most of the people there ignored Maia's presence, which was exactly what she hoped for, but some stared and shot suspicious looks at her. The huddle of her friends around her was the best possible wall and Maia was thankful for their presence. The inner circle where the council was about to happen was empty except for the ten Kausakas who ringed it, their hands on the hilt of their swords.

A group of Black Phantoms entered and while most of them gathered at the other side of the chamber, one of them walked over to Maia and her friends. Maia was happy to find it was Dorian, the newly elected chieftain of Walenveil and the new leader of the Phantoms.

"Why are you so glum?" he asked Maia.

Nafi huffed. "How can she not be? She's why this is happening in the first place, and all those idiots can do is look at her like she's a curse or something."

"Nafi, stop saying such things," Dani chided gently.

Dorian thumped Maia's back. "Listen, kid. All them people and what they think don't matter. You know what does? What you think of yourself. And I think you should be mighty proud." Seeing her unsmiling face, he thumped her again. "Come on now. Chin up. We'll be on the other side there, cheering you on."

Maia had just thanked him for the support when people started trickling into the inner circle. A group of parliamentarians, including Uncle Alasdair, some of the House leaders, Sahiiraan Tsininio and Goren among them, as well as Premier Oliena and four other Jjord took their seats in the semicircle of ten chairs. Even from that distance, Oliena shot a smile at Maia, as did Tsininio. Soon Ruche arrived, and Maia stood—fingers cold and numb—next to the record keeper's desk, waiting for the prince to make his appearance. Ruche did not speak; he hardly looked anywhere other than the space at the center of the council floor.

It was not long before Maia felt the tremor in the atmosphere, a sign that the prince was about to teleport, and as she expected, the air shimmered. Prince Aekken's striking figure formed at the center of the circle, along with five faceless guards surrounding him. As soon as they materialized, the faceless guards scattered in a spiral around the ring. The Kausakas drew their swords equally swiftly and stepped forward to counter them. About two arms' length was the closest they could come to Aekken's guards. Something, an invisible barrier, Maia deduced, stopped them from getting any nearer.

Ruche stepped forward quickly, arms outstretched to calm everyone. "We mean no harm," he said hastily. A breathless moment or two passed before Sahiiraan Tsininio nodded at the Kausakas, gesturing them to sheath their swords.

"Crown Prince Aekken of the Empire R'armimon," Ruche announced.

Aekken, resplendent in his flowing red cape, nodded curtly at the council and then at the audience. His curious gaze swept across the room, over the members of the council, and finally came to rest on Maia's pensive face. A small smile played on his lips as their eyes locked, and he lowered his head just a little in acknowledgment.

Sahiiraan Tsininio rose from his seat first. "Welcome to Tansi, Crown Prince. I am Sahiiraan—"

"I do not wish to get acquainted with any of you. I am simply here because the Nasfarii of Tansi"—Aekken turned around and lowered his head to Maia once more, making her flush in embarrassment as every pair of eyes were instantly drawn to her, then turned back again—"made a wish and I cannot refuse her."

Maia shifted her feet uncomfortably as Sahiiraan Tsininio took a step backward, his face a bright shade of crimson. Aekken did not seem to notice and simply continued his speech.

"You know why I am here, and I will not linger long on those matters. Let me simply say I find it unfortunate that your beautiful planet is caught in the middle of our war with your renegade neighbor. The Empire will not relent in its pursuit of justice, and sadly, you will have to bear the brunt of our conflict. However . . . I cannot harm the Nasfarii of Tansi. Fortunately for you, you have in her a shield."

He stopped for a moment and nodded at Maia for the third time.

"There is a contest the Nasfarii wishes to finish in peace, and I have promised her I will not cause disruptions in the meantime. So, people of Tansi, you have been gifted six more months to make yourselves safer."

As a wave of murmurs broke across the room, Premier Oliena lowered her head a little. "Thank you, Crown Prince. We are grateful for this time."

Aekken nodded, just a little. "As happy as I am to oblige the Nasfarii, I still have some expectations of you, leader of Tansi. I will not harm your planet because it is innocent of the crimes of the renegades. If you, however, proceed to aid and assist those criminals, then you will be innocent no more. That you do not want."

"What do you wish us to do?" Sahiiraan Tsininio asked. Maia held her breath. This was new, and she had no idea what he might ask.

"You will have to adhere to some stipulations. I understand you have allowed the renegades refuge on this planet. That has to end now. I am not asking you to send back the ones already here, but no more should be allowed in. I also ask that they be kept inside their shelters and not allowed free access outside them."

"You mean we should corral them in these camps," a parliamentarian with a shock of white hair asked.

"Yes, you should," Aekken replied.

"But we have given them our word," the man said again.

"Your word or your life, leader of Tansi? I believe the choice is not difficult."

As the man slumped back into his chair, Aekken chuckled. "You will also sever all communications with them, starting now."

Oliena frowned and shook her head. "Much of this we cannot do, Crown Prince. We have an agreement, and even if we wanted to renege on our word, we cannot. That's because the Xifarians are helping us build shelters in return for refuge. Refusing them altogether, cutting off communication is not just dishonorable, it would also be disastrous for our survival plans. We cannot—"

"Would you prefer to be enemy of the R'armimon, then?"

As Oliena's face clouded, Maia fidgeted. This was not going well, not for the Xifarians whose environment was collapsing rapidly, and not for Tansi. Tansi needed Xifarian technology, and the Xifarians surely needed refuge. The nascent collaboration could not end. Maia's mind scrambled for something, anything to foil Aekken's plan.

Her thoughts came to an abrupt halt as the reality of the situation sank in. What was she thinking? She was just a young girl, a child, really, compared to the seasoned leaders of the council. The fact that Aekken had given her six months was a lucky break. How could she expect any more? She had to let it go, and leave the decision-making to the leaders. It was not her place to interrupt.

She turned away, forcing her gaze from Aekken's gloating face and Oliena's downcast one. Her eyes skimmed over the gathered crowd, desperately seeking her friends. Her heart sank as soon as she found them. Ren was staring at Aekken with hopeless rage. Another face, heartbreaking in its desolation, flashed in her mind. She remembered what Miir had said . . . *all of a sudden, we are stripped of our home, threatened with destruction, struggling to accept the difficult reality of our murderous history* . . . his voice, on the verge of breaking, rang in her ears.

Maia's fists curled. She *had* to try to stop Aekken. What was the worst that could happen? He would refuse, humiliate her perhaps. But that was a small price to pay for the happiness of her friends.

"Crown Prince Aekken," she blurted, and immediately sensed Ruche's worried frown on her. "May I say something?"

Aekken whirled around, an amused smile etched on his face. "Nasfarii of Tansi" — he lowered his head — "how may I please you?"

Maia drew a breath as Aekken's cold gaze bored into her. "I do not mean to impose on you, but breaking a treaty now would hardly be the peace I hoped for, the peace you promised. Could you please consider more lenient clauses? I sincerely hope you can."

His face twisted into a grudging smile. "If you so wish, Nasfarii," he said after a prolonged pause. He turned back toward Oliena, his shoulders stiff, the lines of his face hard.

"The Nasfarii's request I cannot ignore," Aekken said, sighing. "I will not put a complete stop to the arrangement you have, but you will reduce the transports to half of what they have been so far." Aekken looked back to catch Maia's gaze. "Is that acceptable, Nasfarii of Tansi?"

Maia did not know what to say. It was an improvement over what Aekken had initially proposed, but she was no leader in a council to decide such matters. Then again, she was the one he was listening to, so why not?

Maia stiffened her spine and returned a firm nod.

"So be it," the prince said. He flicked his hair and strode closer to the leaders until he loomed over them. "Tell your neighbors of the updated terms to follow, until such time when all terms end." He ignored the profuse thanks that erupted from the leaders and stared into the distance, his eyes gleaming, perhaps with a vision of Xif exploding in a million pieces. "The Execution Fleet will remain at a distance until it is time, but the Imperial Battlecruiser will orbit the renegades. I will be watching."

With a swish of his cape, he spun around and walked over to where Maia stood with Ruche. Maia could see the frustration in Aekken's eyes as he drew closer. He had accepted her request, but not happily. And that could not be a good thing.

"You have a heart of gold, Nasfarii," Aekken whispered, his gaze a pit of darkness. "But do you not see that your affection is wasted on those deadwastes? All you get from them is contempt, and yet you fight for them? Do you hope they will learn to respect you? Or be grateful?" He shook his head, a scornful smile on his face. "You will never be cherished, here or there. To all of these people, you will always be the traitor's daughter, to be spat upon, to be reviled."

"Crown Prince Aekken." Ruche's voice was sharp. "Perhaps you have something else to say to the Tansian Council?"

Aekken started at Ruche's interruption and hurriedly shook his head. "No, it is time to leave."

As soon as the prince left, Ruche went over to the huddle that was the Tansian Council. Maia headed back to her friends, Aekken's final words a whirlwind of stormy clouds in her head. The prince was right. She would always be the traitor's daughter, here and there. She would always be spat upon and trampled and —

"Hey!" A familiar voice made Maia stop and turn.

"Miir?" She had not noticed him among the Black Phantoms that arrived with Dorian, nor had she seen him walk over to her.

Miir's eyes shone with concern as they scanned her somber face. "Are you all right?"

"Not really but . . . I'll be fine." Maia tried to put on a brave voice. She was far from fine in reality. That abyss in her heart had been split open once again, and once again, she found herself staring at the endless pit, her mind —

"You were very brave." Miir's voice pulled her back from the brink. "It could not have been easy talking to that man. You surely did not need to. Yet you did."

At least someone understood how hard it was. Strength surged back into Maia, replacing the swirling misery inside her. "Easy it wasn't, but I couldn't simply stand by knowing I could do something about it."

"Well, my people will probably never have the courage or the decency to acknowledge your effort, let alone express gratitude. So even though it does not mean much, I would like to thank you . . . for standing up for my nation."

And just like that, in an instant, the abyss vanished. All that remained were words, kind and gentle, and a grateful smile that washed away the hurt clawing her insides to shreds. Then, as her friends rushed up, and Ren slipped an arm around her shoulders, nothing remained but a vague memory of the pain.

CHAPTER TWELVE

BACK TO THE ROOTS

After the R'armimon prince's council in ThulaSu, matters calmed down. Councils were called with the Xifarians to discuss the prince's ultimatums. Kusha stopped by once in a while to update Maia and her teammates about how the Xifarians had accepted, albeit resentfully, the new terms. Meanwhile, the Initiative was back in focus for the contestants, and ThulaSu's students, including Sana and Pai, returned to their routines. Maia was surprised to return from Monk Tessio's session one day to find Premier Oliena waiting at the AR, along with Uncle Alasdair and Kusha.

"Maia, I'm leaving soon for Zagran, but I had to come and thank you before I left," the premier said as soon as greetings had been exchanged. "Your courageous intervention the other day saved our treaty with the Xifarians. It is still an unfair situation, but given the circumstances, I couldn't be happier. At least we have the transport channels open and some more people can be brought out of Xif. We have to be very careful about how much we interact with them, but we are working that out." She placed a hand on Maia's shoulder. "All because of you. I told your uncle he should be very proud of you."

"And I am," Uncle Alasdair said. "She's every bit like her mother . . . my sister, Sophie."

So many times Dada had told her how much Uncle Alasdair loved Sophie, how proud he was of his sister. But never until now had Maia felt that in her uncle. Now as his voice rippled with emotion, Maia knew Dada was right. Maia's heart was full of happiness that day, and a smile lingered on her lips long after Oliena and Uncle Alasdair left.

That day, the Solianese parliamentarians and the House leaders departed, and the Jjordic delegates left as well. After that, it was back to the grind.

And what a grind it turned out to be. They were supposed to assemble at the Glass House one morning. As soon as Maia entered with her teammates, she knew what they were in for that day. Rows of heavy bodysuits hung along one wall of the Glass House. They were almost exactly like the suit she had worn when Zaara took her into Korobieltes. There could be only one reason for them to be here — it was time to handle the Spore.

Tessio confirmed her suspicions as soon as all the teams had arrived. "Today we are planting the plants," he said, chuckling as he pointed to the row of suits. "You'll have to put on armor. Those will protect you. I will also give you masks. However, armored or not, you still have to be very careful around the Spore. If even a small amount seeps into you, it will be dangerous. So, be very serious and pay utmost attention. Yes?"

Heads nodded all over the room.

"Now, I need a few volunteers who are not afraid of handling a little dirt. They will be the ones setting the plants into the holes you have all dug." Tessio tapped the tips of his fingers and looked around. "Volunteers?"

No one seemed to be interested. It was not difficult to understand the hesitation. Getting in the mud was bad enough for most people, and getting into the mud with a deadly plant was certainly not an attractive proposition. Someone had to do it, however. So up went Maia's hand, slow but unwavering.

"Maia." A big grin broke out on Tessio's face as he clapped. "Very nice, very brave. I need another. I hope a boy can show a bit of courage."

Jiri's hand shot up on the other side of the room even before Tessio had finished speaking.

Once again, Tessio clapped. "Very, very nice, Jiri. I will award extra points to your teams. Now dress up and come over to me for masks. Go, go."

Soon they were wrestling with the unwieldy suits, heat, suffocating face masks, whines and complaints, dirt and mud, and a poisonous plant almost as tall as they were. The Silverblood fern went in first, into one of the large holes dug in the prior weeks. Maia and Jiri were covered in mud by the time the plant had been lowered, its roots relaxed, soil poured in, and water administered in five stages as per Monk Tessio's directive.

"Good job, everyone." Tessio clapped from the side as Maia and Jiri slapped the final bit of soil in place. The fern looked happy, the silver-striped veins on its dark leaves glittering in the sunlight.

The easier of the two plantings completed, Maia braced for the more difficult task at hand. The Spore looked angry and unfriendly as always, its faded green leaves showing blood-red stripes, the barbed branches ending in transparent spheres that shielded the seeds. The specimen was huge, and it was going to be tricky to get the plant into the hole.

They started out slowly and carefully, everyone helping to get the Spore out of its container. Then as gently as they could, and taking care that the seed pods were not disturbed, Maia and Jiri carried the Spore toward the large hole at the center of the mound next to the Silverblood fern. They soon found it was quite impossible to slip the plant down into the hole without dropping it. That they could not do, since any violent movement could shake the seed pods and release the poisonous seeds.

"I can get inside the hole," Maia offered as the youngsters fretted to find a solution. "Then Jiri can lower the plant in. Once we have it halfway down, I'll get out from under."

No one objected to the idea right away, not even Tessio who had been observing from the side. Dani, however, clutched at Maia's arm. "Maia, that's too dangerous. What if you get trapped underneath?"

"Don't worry, Dani. I'll be fine. What's the worst that can happen? My hair will get a little muddy, that's all."

It began well. Maia slid into the hole, and Jiri followed to give her a hand. From the surface, Luem and Anja eased the Spore down into their waiting hands. Maia had scarcely grabbed the rootball when she heard someone giggle. And then things went wrong one after another. There was a commotion up top, water spilled from a bucket someone was holding, dirt went flying and someone shrieked. Then Maia saw the Spore start to topple.

There was no time to move. And even if there was time, there was not enough space to get out from under it. So Maia watched as the poisonous plant, its angry leaves with their deadly extremities, swung toward her. She forgot to breathe or blink. Frozen with panic, she simply stared.

Just an arm's length separated the nearest seed pod from Maia's face when a large, sturdy shovel flew in. It embedded itself in the edge of the mound and held the Spore in place.

Maia released the breath she had been holding and realized she was trembling like a leaf.

"Help them out," Tessio screamed.

Hands grabbed her and dragged her out. Maia soon found herself on the other side of the room, Jiri next to her, surrounded by worried faces. Tessio poured a bitter liquid down her throat. This was followed up with an even bitterer pill that she was ordered to chew.

Things became clearer once the fog of panic subsided. Loriine had been the one to start the ruckus. A joke with Baecca, giggles, and a toppled bucket of water might have been easy to handle, but Loriine also had to kick the bucket away to keep her boots from getting too muddy. The bucket hit Luem on the shoulder, his grip slipped, and then there was no going back. Karhann's quick thinking had saved the day. The Spore would have surely hit Maia and Jiri in the face had he not grabbed a shovel and wedged it in place.

Monk Tessio, who Maia had never seen without a smile, wore a very grim look from then on. Loriine and Baecca were given a stern talking to, but from the smug expressions on their faces, the duo had no remorse about the dangerous situation they had brought about. That everyone pitched in after that to get the Spore planted was the one good outcome of the incident.

Soon both plants were well settled, an enclosure erected around them, and new tasks assigned to everyone. Tessio had Maia and Jiri seated and resting on one side while the rest of the contestants prepared plant food on the other side of the Glass House. Dani kept coming back to check on them, and no amount of reassurance that they were both feeling fine could keep her away for long.

"This is almost like punishment. I feel like a clown in a circus," Maia grumbled after Dani made her hundredth round to check on them. "Nothing really happened, and Tessio gave us antidotes too."

"I know, but" — Jiri flashed a grin that Maia would have called evil had she not known how good-natured Jiri was — "sometimes it's good to have a little break, don't you think? Besides, we're not clowns. We're the audience. The circus is out there."

After that, Maia stopped feeling silly sitting on the sidelines. Time passed in a joyful rhythm as they watched little spurts of drama erupt among the contestants. Someone dropped too many foul-smelling horse dung pellets and caused an uproar, Kenan made the side of the mound collapse and received an unending barrage of angry mutterings. Junko, a boy in the all-Jjord team, did the worst by spilling two buckets of water over the mound. That generated more mud, more wails, and more mess.

Maia and Jiri had been giggling to their heart's content, watching Tessio try and commandeer teams into cleaning up the muddy floor, when the sound of thundering boots made Maia stop and sit up.

Zaara, her eyes blazing, marched inside. "Who in the name of hell's pit-fires is Loriine?" she yelled.

How Zaara had found out about the incident so quickly, given no one had left the room since, was a question Maia would have loved to know the answer to. But she was busy being stunned. If everyone in the room had been holding their breath, now they looked ready to run for their lives. A terrifying silence hovered in the room and no one, not even Monk Tessio, said a word.

"Well, who is it?" Zaara roared. "Is someone going to tell me or do I have to thrash it out of you?"

"Come on, Loriine," Tessio finally said. "The Chief Arbitrator wants to speak with you. Come out here, please."

Loriine sauntered forward, flicking her shiny brown hair airily. Zaara's staff was pointed at Loriine's chest before Maia could blink.

"You," Zaara hissed. "You think the Spore is a joke? Or maybe you think getting people hurt or killed is a joke?"

Loriine did not say a word, which Maia counted as a good thing. Knowing Zaara, a challenge now would have severe repercussions. But good things rarely last long, and Loriine broke the silence far too soon.

"It was an accident," she said.

"Accident?" Zaara hissed. "You call being inattentive and silly during a serious operation an accident?"

"It was what it was," Loriine snapped back.

Zaara's staff flicked up and Loriine scrambled back. She moved too fast for the muddy surface. Her feet skidded and amid gasps, Loriine came down on the muddy floor with a resounding thud and a splash. Mud splattered everywhere—on her clothes, her hair, and her face. As everyone stared, she broke into loud sobs. Zaara loomed over the bawling Loriine and placed the tip of the staff on her chest.

"You have the nerve to talk back and hurl excuses at me? All that after endangering two people? Have you ever heard of an apology? Try looking that up in a dictionary, that is if you can spell it right." She paused for a moment, still glowering at Loriine. "I would have disqualified your team for sure. The fact that one of your teammates helped save those lives you so carelessly endangered is the only thing that holds me back. But I still need that apology."

Loriine continued to bawl.

"Now!"

"Sorry. I'm sorry," Loriine shrieked through her tears.

Zaara's staff swung in the direction of Maia and Jiri.

"Say it to them."

Loriine did not need to be asked again. "Sorry, Maia. Sorry, Jiri. I'll be careful from now on. I'm sorry."

Zaara exhaled loudly. "Good. You remember that from now on."

Everyone heaved a sigh of relief as Zaara grounded her staff. Loriine made no effort whatsoever to get up. Things could easily have ended there, had it not been for the foolhardy Baecca. Maia had never considered Baecca to be particularly bright, but that day she realized Baecca must be completely devoid of intelligence.

The girl jumped forward, fists curled, and, scowling fiercely, matched glares with Zaara.

"This is abuse. You think you can get away with this just because you are an arbitrator?" Baecca yelled. "I will file a complaint. You will be punished. You will be the one thrown out of the Initiative."

If the Spore had released a single seed at that moment, it would have sounded like a drumbeat, such was the silence that fell. Then Zaara's face crinkled and she chuckled, softly at first, before it grew into loud guffaws. Baecca gulped, wilting in fear as she stared teary-eyed and pouty-mouthed at a laughing Zaara. It took a while for Zaara to stop. Then she wiped the corners of her eyes and peered at Baecca.

"Guess I should thank you. I haven't laughed that much in ages. But your stupidity is just . . . it's the most hilarious thing I have seen in years." Zaara paused and shook her head, chuckling again. "Well, I don't care if you complain. I don't care to be here at all. So do what you want to do, foolish girl. But while I'm still an arbitrator I will do this. I will make you clean up this mess."

As Baecca's expression turned from scared to surprised, and finally settled on horror, Zaara turned toward Tessio. "Monk Tessio, please dismiss the rest. This girl alone is responsible for all the mopping and cleaning."

"Alone?" Baecca howled. "I'll have to work all night to get this done."

"Yes, you will work through the night. I will come by to check tomorrow morning. I want to see everything neat and tidy by then. I will ask the refectory to have your meals delivered here tonight." Zaara peered at Baecca's downcast face for a while. "Well, come to think of it, I shouldn't be so hard on you. Let's see . . . since you stood up for your silly friend, you could ask her . . . only her . . . to assist you."

The look on Loriine's face as Zaara spoke was a treat to see. Clearly, she had no intention of helping Baecca, and Zaara had put her in quite a spot.

Zaara chuckled. "Let's find out how deep your friendship runs, eh?"

With a curt nod at Monk Tessio and barely a passing glance at Maia and Jiri, Zaara left the room. Tessio soon dismissed them all. Nafi was in the highest of spirits and could not stop talking about how wonderful Loriine looked caked in mud. As Maia — grimy from head to toe, tired, and still a little stressed — trooped back with the rest of her team, her steps were lively. Zaara, even though she did not seem to care, had stood up for something. That was reason enough to be happy.

CHAPTER THIRTEEN

DOWN IN FLAMES

Miir had been working on the frame Asiyaah had left behind, and Maia helped him with it from time to time on the off days. It was on one such day that Nafi—her satchel full of reading material on Ti—came along with her to visit Miir. Nafi had also invited the rest of the team, but Dani, still barely speaking with anyone, refused politely. Kucha was hardly ever around anyway. He seemed to be drawn deeper into administrative work every day, and that day was no exception. Ren had to go to Frauz Point yet again, but he promised to join the girls as soon as he got back.

Nafi's agenda became clear as soon as they arrived.

"So, Miir"—she began in a sweet voice, diligently scratching a speck of dust off a post—"we need help with combat training for the challenge and I was thinking . . . maybe . . . perhaps . . ."

"You want me to train you?"

Nafi's face broke into a sunny smile. "Will you? Please?"

Miir sighed. "Well, that should be permissible per the clauses. But you should still—"

"I will check with Master K, promise," Nafi pledged solemnly, hand placed firmly over her heart.

"All right, then."

As soon as Miir agreed, Nafi ran off to the back of the yard to scout for a suitable sparring ground.

"I have other news," Miir said when Nafi was out of sight. "I got information about my mother's Connaissance. She was indeed a Tierremorphe and she refused to serve. It almost caused a scandal. Apparently, my grandfather had to go into a lot of trouble to hush it up."

Maia let out the breath she had been holding. So what Kehorkjin had said was indeed true. Now there was little doubt left that Asiyaah must have been the one who broke the chalice. The information had barely sunk in when Maia found herself confronting another question.

"How did you find out?" she asked. "Don't tell me you went to Xif again."

Miir looked up at her, squinting. "Thought I promised you I would not."

Warmth trickled to the tips of Maia's ears. That was the wrong thing to ask Miir. He was not one who handed out promises on a whim.

"Sorry. I'm sorry," she said hastily.

"No need to be so sorry," he replied just as quickly. "No offense taken. I was simply teasing you."

That was a relief to know. Put at ease, Maia's curiosity multiplied. "How, then?"

"Karhann."

Of course. Karhann was Miir's cousin, and the easiest way to communicate with his mother, Asiyaah's younger sister, was through him. However, while that made sense, it also meant that Karhann now knew of Miir's presence in ThulaSu.

Miir must have noticed her clouded face, since he chuckled a little. "Nothing to worry about. Karhann is completely trustworthy."

He had to be if Miir thought so, but still, a worry persisted. As she helped set up the tools for repair, fear for Miir's safety kept raising its head. Nafi sprinted back just in time to distract her, wildly excited about the perfect clearing she had located right behind the Darkwoods. Soon they settled down to their respective tasks.

The day was peaceful and in a refreshing change, it was warmer than usual. A cool breeze blew every now and then. The weather took away the worries, and also much of the frustration Maia felt about the job at hand. Miir diligently tried various options to rectify the reader module in the prongs. Even after a long time and many trials, nothing worked. Every now and then, Maia had to stifle a sigh or gulp down an angry mutter out of respect for Miir's quiet dedication. How he managed to keep on tinkering without a single frown on his face was beyond Maia's understanding.

Nafi sat on the porch steps, surrounded by notes and books, poring over the handouts Aerika and Kehorkjin had passed out. From time to time, she grumbled. "Where is that Ren? He was supposed to be here."

"He will come, Nafi," Maia replied.

"He'll come? When? Tomorrow?"

Maia sighed. "Be patient," she said, not just to Nafi but also as a reminder to herself.

Some time passed, mostly in silence, until Nafi piped up.

"Hey, Miir! Tell me something. Why do you guys need so much Calbion? You aren't building a space fleet or anything, so what do you use it for?"

Miir did not answer right away. Lips pursed, he fiddled distractedly with the circuits he was working on, then dropped them and exhaled loudly.

"Well, we have been stockpiling it," he said. "Not to build spacecraft but . . . to reinforce the interior of Xif. The Tierremorphes used to be the ones who would repair and reinforce any weak spots. But that was when we had a lot of them and their powers were strong. Since we started losing the Tierremorphes, we have had to rely on Calbion for repair work to stop the planet from collapsing."

It was startling to know the reason behind the Xifarians' rush to get to Ti. It did not justify their cruel methods, but knowing they needed it to survive and did not simply profit from the mining made something, somewhere in Maia's mind ease a little. Nafi, she noted, also had a calmer expression when she looked away. However, the girl chirped loudly not too long after.

"Apparently, the Molligessian Seam has the biggest deposit clusters. Master K said we should pick one of them. I think we should go for one of the less popular ones. What do you think?"

"It's a good idea," Maia said. "We might have less competition if we choose an obscure spot. I'll have to look into it, though."

Some more time passed. Maia had just managed to fasten a tiny wire into the side of the frame when Nafi cleared her throat loudly.

"They can't seriously expect us to extract a whole bucket full of Calbion. I mean, can you imagine how long that would take? And there has to be a better way than scraping it out by hand." She stayed silent for a moment. "Maia?"

Maia returned a shrug. "I don't know, Nafi. All I've ever heard is that Calbion can only be taken out by hand. That's the whole reason the miners were needed. So . . ."

"There has to be something else. Something we are missing. Something they're not telling us."

Miir sighed and Nafi went back to taking notes. She was not quiet for long, however.

"Can't imagine how we'll survive the flight. It's all ice everywhere, and some random person will be flying."

"A random person will be fine," Maia tried to reassure her. "They fly on Ti all the time. We'll have time to practice with the equipment until then, too."

"And that Ren is stuck on picking a Raptor. I think we should take a smaller craft." She fiddled with her notes a bit before looking up at Maia. "What do you think, Maia?"

At this point, Miir turned around and gave Nafi a look. "Do you really think I do not understand what you are trying to do?"

Nafi stared back, wide-eyed and innocent. "What? What am I trying to do?"

Miir exhaled loudly. "You are trying to get me to comment." Nafi was about to protest, but Miir shook a finger sternly. "No, do not try to convince me otherwise. I see it clearly."

Nafi rolled her eyes. "You see too much sometimes. I didn't even ask a direct question and . . ." She threw a beseeching look at Maia as Miir's frown deepened. "Maia, back me up here."

Between Miir's frown and Nafi's indignation, there was little room to maneuver. "Sorry, Nafi. I have to agree with Miir."

"Really, Maia? That's the path you choose? Whatever happened to supporting your teammate?" Nafi said, glaring.

"Well, you need to work on your persuasion skills, particularly on subtlety."

Nafi let out a snicker, clearly placated by the answer. Miir, however, stared at Maia. "You just *had* to encourage her."

It was Maia's turn to look wide-eyed and innocent. "Encourage? Not at all. I was simply advising her."

Miir sighed. "Tell me why I should not evict both of you from here right now."

"Because that's not even an option, Miir," Nafi replied. "Could you ever be so heartless to a couple of poor, innocent girls?"

As Maia broke into giggles, Miir shook his head. "Poor, innocent girls . . . indeed. You two better be silent or be gone."

His severe tone and solemn face were hard to ignore completely, and things went quiet for a while after that. One circuit Miir was working on seemed to function correctly and that grabbed Maia's attention. Nafi gave up on her persuasion project and did not speak to anyone. It was close to noon and the girls were about to leave for lunch when Nafi jumped suddenly.

"Really, Ren? Now?" she said, angrily. "Where are you, anyway? Pampering those fan club airheads?"

Maia put down the parts she had been working on and looked at Nafi, whose face quickly changed from outrage to anxiety and then to fear, and finally to dejection.

"No," Nafi whispered. By then, Maia had scooted to the girl's side, worriedly studying Nafi's face as she finished her conversation with Ren.

"What happened?" Maia asked as soon as Nafi looked up.

"Bad stuff," Nafi said, her eyes restless with agitation as she looked from Maia to Miir and back again. "That stupid R'armimon prince . . . he attacked Xif."

"What?" Miir's shocked whisper cut through the peaceful air of the morning and left it shaken. "Why?"

"Because he can?" Nafi said in a morose voice. "Ren thinks they attacked just to show their power. A mothership showed up and released about a thousand fighter craft. They bombarded some sort of outpost in Quad 6."

"Kantralls Hold?" Miir asked. Maia could not help but notice how his face had paled.

Nafi nodded. "That's it."

"Kantralls Hold out of Aperture 15 is our main military base," Miir explained. "What happened after they attacked?"

"Your people fought back, but . . ." Nafi's words trailed off, and her gaze dropped. Clearly, the Xifarians did not have much luck against the R'armimon. "Ren said he'll come back soon with information, but he said many have died."

Miir slumped on the bench and lowered his head into his hands. A strange emptiness swamped Maia. It was not just the news of the unprovoked attack and the unnecessary deaths, but also seeing Miir so visibly distressed.

Her fists curled. This was not supposed to happen. Aekken had promised. He had given her his word that if his demands were met, he would not harm Tansi or Xif. Not while the Initiative was going on, at least.

She suddenly remembered the little communicator Aekken had given her, the one she had promptly put away as Ruche had directed. Ruche had asked her not to call the prince, and she had had no intention of doing so. Until now . . .

"I'm going to speak with Aekken," she announced, picking up her satchel.

"Wait, what?" Nafi dropped her books and sat up.

"I'm going to speak with Aekken," Maia repeated. "He promised if his demands were met, he'd hold off on his plans while the Initiative was on. All his demands have been met and still . . . this? It's not right."

"Maia, I don't think that's a good idea," Nafi mumbled. "He might act like a friend, but in reality, he's a creepy lunatic. You can't just go and speak with him like that." Seeing the unconvinced look on Maia's face she added, "Even Ruche asked you not to talk to him on your own. And you shouldn't."

"And let people die?" Maia rushed down the stairs. "Anyway, I'll try to reach Ruche too."

"Maia, pl—"

Maia did not wait for Nafi to finish. She had to dig out that communicator and get in touch with Aekken. She had to remind him of his promise and . . .

Grabbing Ruche's ring, Maia focused her thoughts and called for the seer as she dashed out. She had just left the little house behind when she heard the sound of running feet behind her. "Hey! Stop!"

Maia did not have to turn around to know that Miir had run out after her.

"Don't have time," Maia said.

"Stop!" he yelled.

Reluctantly, she turned around. "Why?"

"Because you need to slow down."

"I need to speak with Aekken. He promised me—"

He pointed at the front porch. "Sit down."

"What?"

He walked over to the steps, sat down, and pointed to the space next to him. "Come here. Sit."

With a resigned sigh, Maia walked to the steps and slumped

down next to Miir. "We're wasting time. I should be talking to him now."

"And then what? Is he going to listen? How much do you even know him?" Miir leaned forward to peer at her face. "He has already broken his promise. What do you expect him to do now?"

"I can remind him so he doesn't break it again."

"Remind him? You really believe he has forgotten?" Miir asked. "Do you realize this could be a deliberate ploy?"

She had thought of that. But the fact remained, she had some power to change the situation and it felt bad to not even try.

"What about Ruche?" Miir asked next. "When you call Aekken, will he know?"

"No. I've called him already, but he might not arrive in time. He doesn't have the fancy teleportation tools Aekken has."

"You think it is sensible to meet the prince on your own?" Maia already knew it was far from sensible. Sighing, she shook her head. Miir stayed quiet for a while. "I know you want to help. But rushing into it might only make things more complicated," Miir said. "You did more than your part when you intervened at the council the other day. You should not put yourself at risk anymore." He stared at his hands for a bit and let out a wry chuckle. "You know how strongly I feel about my nation. You could call me shamelessly, absurdly devoted, and it would still not be close. Yet I do not want you tangling with this man. He is not someone you trifle with unless you are well prepared. And even then . . ."

Maia's shoulders sagged. "So I do nothing now?"

"You can plan. Make a strategy. Talk to Ruche, perhaps."

A long sigh came from Maia. "What if he attacks again? By that time so many will have already died."

"Believe me, I want to go up there and help right now. I really do. But my rushing out will not solve anything. So I have to wait and do my part when the time is right."

"What if the time is never right?"

He turned sharply toward her and laughed. "Now you are

making me depressed."

Maia hunched in embarrassment at the realization of how disheartened she had to sound, which was far from her original intention. "Sorry, I didn't mean to."

He picked up a pebble and toyed with it. "The R'armimon prince has shown you respect. I understand that. It is a good thing, a great thing. But you should not underestimate his strength. One mothership alone has many fighter craft, and he probably has many more such ships parked near the sixth planet. Can you imagine what they have all together?"

Maia recalled Ruche's words. The Execution Fleet had been ten motherships strong when it left the Empire. Even half that number would be bad enough.

Next to her, Miir continued in a subdued voice. "We are completely helpless against his firepower. Completely. Xif does not have anything to match it, and obviously, Tansi does not. All we really have is Ruche, his plan, and . . . you. You cannot go about risking that."

There was no debating what Miir said. Ruche had said that many times already. And Nafi was right, too. Maia knew she could not see Aekken alone, and not while she was agitated. He would see too much of her.

"That prince has come all this way for vengeance," Miir went on. "He has so much power. His word has no value. I was about to say that you simply do not know him well enough, but the truth is, you do know. He is *not* to be trusted."

"You're right. I will wait for Ruche."

"Good. I am glad you agree."

They sat there for a long time. The cool breeze came and went, and Maia's thoughts ebbed and flowed with it. Hope was not present, and fear abounded, yet somehow it felt peaceful, just sitting there, staring at the path through the Darkwoods. Maia would have forgotten all about getting back to ThulaSu before lunch, had it not been for a loud voice that made her jump.

"Helloooo!" Nafi yelled. "Hey, you two! Are you there? Anywhere? Has everyone forgotten about this poor little defenseless girl?"

Miir shook his head and sighed. "Aah. The poor little defenseless girl."

Maia rose to her feet, chuckling. "We're right here, Nafi. No one's forgotten about you."

The girls were soon on their way. Their steps were far from lively, their hearts leaden. All the way back to ThulaSu, Maia hoped and prayed that Ruche would come soon, and with a plan that could stop the unnecessary bloodshed.

Chapter Fourteen

Shattered Beliefs

Maia headed straight to the rose garden to wait for Ruche, while Nafi went back to her room. The garden looked rather bare, since except for the few Darkwoods, the plants were leafless. In the winter, the rose garden was barely visited, even when the weather was as mild as it had been this year. While it was cold, ThulaSu had not had a single day of snow, much to the disappointment of the students eagerly awaiting the snowy days. Maia also wished for snow. The previous winter had been a haze; she had just discovered the light inside her, and the agony of losing her family had been closer and nearly unbearable. She had not had the ability to see, let alone feel the world around her. Days of snow had come and gone like a fading dream, and now Maia wished she could see it once more, to really remember it.

Maia had just reached the garden gates when she saw Kusha rush out and head in the direction of the Garaha Gates. His head was bowed, his face downcast.

"Kusha," Maia called and bounded up to the boy. "What's the

matter?"

Kusha sighed and shook his head morosely.

"More news about the R'armimon siege of Xif?" Maia asked.

"What?" Kusha looked baffled. "What are you talking about? What siege?"

Maia quickly told him what they had heard from Ren before worriedly looking at the open gates behind him. "So you didn't know of the siege. What are you so glum about, then?"

Kusha let out an enormous sigh. "It's Dani."

Maia's heart dropped to the pit of her stomach. What did that mean? Was Dani sick? Or did the duo break up?

"What about her?" she barely found the strength to whisper.

"She's so upset," Kusha said. He fell back against the wall of the ramparts and pulling off his red headband, started running his hands through his hair. The helpless look on his face made Maia's heart twitch. "She doesn't even want to speak with me. I-I don't know what to do."

Maia laid a hand on Kusha's arm, hoping to calm him down. "Where is Dani now?" she asked.

Kusha jabbed his thumb in the direction of the garden. "In the bowers."

"I'll try to talk to her. Don't worry, Kusha, she'll come around."

Her reassurances did not seem to reach Kusha. He vaguely nodded, muttered something about a council, and trudged away.

Maia walked into the rose garden looking for Dani. It was not hard to locate the girl; the sound of soft sobs told Maia exactly where to find her. Dani was hunched over, her head on her knees, shuddering as sobs tore through her, when Maia kneeled at the entrance of the bower.

"Dani—"

"Please, Maia, I don't want to talk."

"I won't talk," Maia said. "Can I just . . . sit with you?"

Dani did not protest, so Maia ventured inside and sat down next to the girl. A cool breeze blew now and then, riffling and rustling through the fallen leaves. Other than their breathing and Dani's sniffles, that was all Maia could hear. She sat patiently, waiting for Dani to speak, to show the slightest sign of opening up. It was a long time before Dani raised her head and sighed.

"I'm so useless. So, so . . . useless." The words sputtered out of the girl, along with another sob. Maia wanted to throw an arm around her friend but stopped herself. Dani needed some air right now, and although it was hard not to rush to comfort her, Maia kept her words and her hands to herself and let Dani speak. "All I've ever wanted to do is to help people. And all I ever do is fail at it."

Maia let a silent moment or two pass by before she said a word. "That's not true, Dani. You always help. You are the most . . . selflessly helpful person I've ever known. I mean it."

"What's the point of wanting to help, Maia?" Dani whimpered. "I'm no good at it. I couldn't do anything for Ohimet. And not for Ori either."

"Dani!" Maia scooted closer. "You helped them both. I do wish we hadn't lost them. But I also think of how much comfort you gave them when they were hurt. They would both have suffered so much more had it not been for your care. You know that, Dani. You must know that."

Dani did not reply. Her eyes stayed unfocused, sobs shaking her every now and then. Once again, Maia waited. This time, however, she did not have to wait long.

"I took a life I didn't create. I had no right," Dani said sullenly. Maia had just opened her mouth to reply when Dani looked up at her, eyes flashing. "Please don't tell me Hilledunn was a bad man, so his life didn't matter. Every life is sacred. It's not for you or me to take. Hilledunn's included."

Maia was taken aback by the glimpse of anger. Dani was always soft and sweet. She was also by no means devoid of character or opinion, that Maia knew from experience. But this flash was unexpected. Then she realized it was not surprising at all. That Hilledunn was a bad man, and she was justified in taking his life, was all Dani had been hearing. And she did not want to hear that. So Maia deliberated and picked her next words with care.

"Dani, I won't say a word about Hilledunn. But I will say this—I am and will be forever grateful that you fought for me that night. You are suffering for it and it will stay a load on your heart for a long time, perhaps forever. But knowing that you chose this painful path for yourself so I could live . . . I can't even tell you how thankful I will always be to you."

Maia paused a moment as her thoughts flew to that night in the Trinity Caverns, and the hallucinations Hilledunn had induced in her. She had found herself at the edge of a deadly drainage pit. A few more moments and she would have . . .

"I survived that night because of you, and only because of you. Because you fought for me. Perhaps I'm selfish to think my life is more important than Hilledunn's, but I'm so glad that even though you consider it a mistake now, at that moment, you thought so too."

"Maia!" Dani flung herself on her and held her arm tightly. "Please don't compare yourself to Hilledunn. There could never be a question about who I would choose if I had to choose again. I just wish—"

"You just wish you didn't have to make the choice at all." The voice made both of them jump. Ruche came into view a moment later, as he sat down on the bench across from the entrance of the bower.

"Yes, I do wish that," Dani said.

"Don't we all, Dani," Ruche replied, sighing. "Sadly, life is not so easy. We often pick one thing over another, even weigh the importance of one life against another. Not fair, never easy, but . . . such is the way." He leaned to peer at Dani's face. "You may not want to hear this now, Dani, and it might take time for you to accept it. But this is what I will say—never let a vile man's death cast a shadow on your heart."

Dani's sigh wafted through the air and left Maia's heart heavy. "It's not just that, Ruche," Dani blurted. "I'm . . . why do I always fail? I try so hard. Ori . . . he would've lived if I could have stopped the bleeding. I knew what to use and what to do, but—"

"Were you afraid to use it?" Ruche asked.

"No. I just didn't have the right things with me. The Viperine had basic first aid, but I needed a blood coagulator that wasn't there. If I just . . . he would've lived."

Ruche left the bench and sat down at the doorway of the bower. "This coagulator . . . is it a big machine?"

Dani shook her head. "We have tiny injectors filled with coagulators down in the colonies. They're very small, and they're part of every aid pack. I wish I'd had one of those packs with me."

"And what's stopping you from keeping one such pack on you?" Ruche asked. "Seeing how much trouble you people always get into, it'd be a wise thing to carry your own aid pack. Why don't you put one together? Gather the best things you know of and be ready to fight your war."

Dani took time to nod, but when she did, the dimness in her eyes had cleared a little. "I will. I definitely will. Thank you, Seer Ruche."

Ruche patted Dani's shoulder and smiled. "You're very welcome." He turned toward Maia and twinkled. "Looks like I'm raising multiples now."

Maia let out a soft chuckle, but then she noticed Ruche's face and stopped. There was an angry red welt across the left side of his face.

"Ruche!" she exclaimed. "What happened to your face?"

Dani looked up as well, her eyes dimming once more as she saw the bruise. "You're hurt," she said. "Did someone hit you?"

"Aah, I'm fine. This is nothing." Ruche waved their concerns away. "Hazards of the job."

"Aekken?"

Ruche nodded gravely. "We got into an altercation over this morning's fireworks. He wasn't happy that I reached out to his father. Not that the emperor said much, at least not as much as I had hoped. But Aekken's ego was bruised and he . . . threw a little tantrum."

"Why did he attack Xif all of a sudden?" Maia asked. "Another tantrum?"

"At-tack Xif?" Dani stuttered. "When did *that* happen?"

Maia shared how she had come to know of the siege and Dani slumped once more. "I thought he promised to hold his fire until the Initiative was over."

Ruche pursed his lips and sighed. "Aekken's promises mean nothing. Every day that passes without an attack is a miracle. He tires quickly and he's itching to get his revenge. Today's attack was a warning, a show of his power. I think he was simply having fun."

"Is he mad?" Dani asked.

"Mad and evil," Ruche replied in a grim tone. "It's a bad combination." He fiddled with a broken twig for a moment before looking at Maia. "This is why, Maia, you are never to see him on your own. I don't know what is brewing in that head of his, but I'm sure it's nothing good."

Maia stifled a sigh, thinking how she had been about to do just that.

"Why the long face?" Ruche asked, his sharp eyes not missing her drooping gaze. "You were planning to meet him, is that it?"

"Well, I didn't in the end," Maia said. "I-I was upset by the news. He made me a promise and—"

"Maia, Aekken is not a friend. You need to understand that," Ruche said. "I'm glad you decided against it."

"My friends stopped me," Maia admitted, thinking of how Nafi and then Miir had hurried to stop her.

"Happy to know that the company you keep has wisdom." Ruche smiled a little, but Maia could see the tiredness under it. "Aekken will be calm for a while. I think. So don't worry."

After more assurances and words of advice, Ruche left. As they walked back to the living quarters, Maia was glad to note that Dani's face was not as cloudy as it had been since the incident at the Trinity Caverns. And things got progressively better. Nafi was in the AR, working on her information gathering for their upcoming trip to the Challowist farms, and Dani joined her eagerly. They worked together until lunch, and then they trooped out. The boys soon joined them, and seeing a happier Dani as well as hearing about Ruche's assurances cheered both Kusha and Ren. Although the unprovoked attack on Xif weighed on their minds, Maia could feel a distinct sense of relief in the air. Everyone was happier for sure—and it was surely because Dani spoke more freely, actually ate something rather than pick at her food, and even let a smile or two slip out. This was what mattered most, Maia thought to herself, that her little family of friends was happy.

CHAPTER FIFTEEN

FROZEN DEPTHS

Two days before the trip to the Challowist farms, a massive snowstorm hit ThulaSu. It was the first real snow of the year, and likely the last as well, so the excitement was palpable. Classes at ThulaSu were suspended for three days, and the students were ecstatic. However, there were no changes to the schedule for the trip underwater, and that left the contestants of the Initiative in a grumpy mood. Not only did that mean they would have to slog through their research and keep working on their project reports while all of ThulaSu frolicked in the snow, but it also meant they would have to trudge through waist-deep snow to the western shore for the challenge. Even though Monk Tessio promised them calorfine to counter the cold, it would still be a hard journey.

Nafi was in a foul mood on the morning before. Hadeeyah had just made her daily rounds, and she was most displeased to hear that Core 21 had not yet decided what equipment to pick from the Challowist farms.

"All the other teams have submitted their choices," she said, circling the table at the center of the AR at a frantic pace. "You are the last ones. What's taking so long? Get it done, get it done."

Now they were all hunkered down at the AR, still trying to decide what item they should pick from the Challowist. Ren, very wisely, and according to Nafi, conveniently, left the decision to Dani. He lounged on one side, flicking through a databank on Ti as Dani went through her reasoning for picking a simple energy generator.

"I think a generator is the best. It is a power source that can feed anything we need," Dani said. "If we pick a specific piece of equipment, on the other hand, it'll only serve a specific purpose."

Maia was perched on the arm of the couch next to Dani. "I agree, that would limit its usefulness," she added.

"I don't know, guys." Nafi did not seem convinced. "I keep thinking these are plants and they'll need light to grow. So perhaps it's best to get a light source."

"Yes, but Nafi, we can easily fashion a light source if we have the generator."

"Hmm . . . but—" Nafi had barely opened her mouth to respond when the door of the AR flew open and Sana zoomed in.

"Are you people crazy?" she exclaimed. "All that glorious white stuff is piled up out there and you're all locked in this gray room, reading? Come on, get out there, all of you. It's time to enjoy the beauty of mother nature."

Ren was on his feet in an instant. "Finally, a voice of reason," he muttered before rushing out to get dressed.

Maia and Dani did not take much convincing either. Maia had been hoping they would find some time to go outside. Nafi was the last one to trudge out. Sana, however, would not let Nafi's grumpy face deter her. She herded the gang—everyone except Kusha, who was away at his house as was usual nowadays, and Rayan and Pai, who had been summoned by Zaara—out of the living quarters as soon as they had armed themselves with parkas, boots, gloves, and the like.

The air was frigid, but the sun was bright and the skies blue. The snow was deep and the temple grounds would have been a perfect place to be, if not for—

"Looks like all of ThulaSu is here," Ren said. Indeed, the courtyard of the Sun Temple looked busier than a fairground. People of all ages walked, jumped, and pranced around.

"So?" Sana raised an eyebrow. "There's still plenty of space, and we'll find a spot."

"And do what?" Nafi demanded, scowling. "It's cold, and I don't like cold."

"Oh, come on, Nafi." Dani patted the girl on the shoulder. "It'll be fun. We can have snowball fights, build a snowman, and even—"

"All of that involves handling the stupid cold snow," Nafi said, pouting. "Besides, has anyone thought what'll happen if Hadeeyah spots us out here, playing?"

Ren's face fell immediately and Maia had to admit, the prospect of their mentor finding them was not a cheerful thought.

"You'll be fine," Sana said. "Besides, everyone looks the same in snow gear. What's the chance anyone will recognize you guys in this crowd?"

That was a point but still, Hadeeyah was—

"Hey! Maia!" Maia almost jumped at the voice. Then she spotted Maks. He came running toward them along the ramparts, grinning from ear to ear. "You're on my team."

"Umm . . . what?"

"We're building a snow fort out here. We're going to have the most epic snow battle."

Maia could not find a single word to say, but—

"We're going on a research walk, Maks," Ren butted in. "You get started, and we'll join you later." Grabbing Maia by the elbow, Ren steered her toward the end of the ramparts away from the rose garden.

Maia had no complaints at Ren's maneuvering, but Nafi objected immediately. "Why did you do that? We could've joined them. Now we have to walk through the snow . . . and where are you taking us, anyway?"

"Join them? Did you see Maia's face?" Ren said. "As to where we're going . . . I know a place."

"What place?"

"You'll see."

Ren led them westward along the ramparts, beyond the residential buildings. This portion of the ramparts was not as well tended, and no one came this way much. Maia had not either. She remembered Ori and his Black Phantoms walking up from the western end once, and that was it. So as Ren led them down a staircase that descended into a grove of Darkwoods, the thrill of discovery made Maia's spine tingle. There was surely a path through the Darkwoods, now covered in snow. Ren marched forward. Nafi grumbled from time to time, but the rest quietly followed. They did not have to go too far. The place—a gem of a place, although in sore need of polish—turned out to be an abandoned building. Its grounds were large and most importantly, empty.

Ren gestured flamboyantly at the view before them. "I give you our own paradise."

Sana squealed and Maia's face broke into a wide grin, but Nafi had an unending set of questions. "What is this place, Ren? It must be empty for a reason. And how do you know about this place anyway?"

"Well . . ."

Ren was just about to reply when Nafi held up her hands. "No, stop. I don't want to know."

"It's safe, right?" Dani asked.

"Well, I come here all the time and I've never gotten into trouble, so . . ."

That was all Maia needed to know. It was a perfect place, and just as Ren said, their own paradise. Time passed in an exciting and happy, albeit noisy rhythm. They had snowball fights where Maia discovered her aim was lousy, built snow forts which turned out to be her special talent, slipped and skidded across the snow on planks Ren and Sana retrieved from a wood pile nearby, and had even erected a sizable snowman when they heard voices. There was no time to hush before a pair of figures clad in hooded parkas came into view.

As they neared, one of them marched up and exclaimed loudly. "Seriously, you guys!"

"Kusha!" Dani squealed.

"Come and join us, Kusha," Nafi yelled. "It's cold, but sort of fun."

"I'm not here to play, Nafi. This is an abandoned building. It's not safe. You all have to leave," Kusha said grumpily. Crossing his arms, he glared at them. "Of all the places you could be, this is where you had to come. I got a complaint from one of the guards. At least he recognized you and was kind enough to call me. You could be sent to the Safety Council otherwise."

Ren chortled. "Sahiiraan Kusha has come personally to cover up our trespass. This is so cool."

Kusha glared some more. "Nothing cool about it, Ren. Let's get out now. Hurry up. This place is abandoned for a reason. It's unsafe."

"Oh, come on, Kusha." Ren laughed as he scooped up some snow and busily fashioned a snowball. "We've survived worse places. Remember that old building at the XDA? That was ready to collapse around us, and here we're not even inside."

The other person who had come with Kusha and stood at the gates watching suddenly strode forward. "Hold on a moment. What building at the XDA are you talking about?"

Nafi's eyes grew wide. "Miir? How did you get here?"

"Dorian and I were meeting with Kusha when . . . that is not the point. What is this building—"

SPLAT!

"Hey!" Miir exclaimed as the snowball Ren threw exploded on him. "That is—"

SPLAT!

Sana's snowball landed right in the middle of his face. Maia was rolling on the ground laughing when a shower of snow descended on her. "Hey! Not fair. I didn't even hit you," she yelled at Miir, who had casually dumped a pile of snow on her before heading toward Ren and Sana.

"You were laughing when I was under siege," he shot back. "That is the mark of an enemy."

"No, Miir, not you too," Kusha almost wailed.

"What?" Miir asked. "You expect me to take this ambush quietly?"

No one took any ambushes quietly after that, and soon the grounds erupted in shrieks and laughter. After a while, Kusha too, thanks in part to Dani's cajoling, joined in.

They did sober up eventually and trooped back to their rooms, tired but happy. Nafi hopped and skipped all the way, and Maia, exhausted as she was, did not mind joining Maks and his army for a while in what was indeed an epic battle of snowballs.

* * *

The biggest Aqumob Maia had ever seen picked them up the next morning from the western shores of ThulaSu. The trek down to the coast had been tedious, even with calorfine from Tessio. It had left everyone grumpy, but as the Aqumob sailed northward and Aerika's assistants showed them to two large tables laden with food, almost all of the frowns melted away. Maia served herself a deep cup of soup and before long, the chill in her bones disappeared.

"Feels like we are on a luxury vacation," Nafi said, as she chomped on a sandwich with a filling of puréed shellfish. A plate full of them rested on her knees. "Mmmm . . . good."

"Seriously, Nafi" — Kusha shook his head — "you lose it when you see food. What's wrong with you?"

"I'm hungry. You have a problem with that?"

"How can you always be hungry? We had breakfast right before we left."

The discussion would have continued had it not been for the appearance of Supervisor "Bones" Aerika. She clip-clopped her way in, her sharp gaze scanning the faces around her, and then settled into one of the chairs the assistants placed at the center of the cabin.

"So, off we go to the Challowist. Everyone ready?" Aerika asked. If she was expecting eager nods, she was disappointed. Aerika's brows crinkled. "If I were you, I'd focus on this task. This is by far the easiest of the three and the best place to build up some leads."

Everyone sat a little straighter at Aerika's words, including Maia and her teammates. She had not thought of the task that way, but Aerika had a good point. The Challowist farms were not only the easiest environment they would have to deal with, it was also one they had visited before. They needed a win in this phase to acquire the legendary sword Seigvard—a key to combating the R'armimon—and establishing a lead in this task would be the perfect first step.

"Now, let's look at what each team has chosen," Aerika said as she scrolled through the screen of a data bank. "Core 7, you have a LumTorch, 101 Paras. A light source, I see. Excellent." Loriine beamed and Karhann nodded when Aerika glanced at them. "You have Site 44." An assistant handed out a box that contained the equipment. "That's your piece. When you get to the site, you'll find an open area marked for you. Set your equipment up for charging and get back here. Questions?"

No one had any questions so Aerika flipped through the screen some more. "Next, Core 13. You also have a LumTorch. 202 Paras."

Aerika's eyes widened a little at the brightness specifications of the device and someone sniggered, as if on cue. The supervisor frowned and she snapped toward Core 7.

"You find something humorous here, Bakhari?"

The newest member of Core 7, who barely ever spoke, shrugged airily. "It's strong enough to burn down a forest, so . . ."

"We can always tone down the power if we need to," Luem angrily defended their choice. "Can't turn it up as easily."

"Just don't set the Glass House on fire," Bakhari retorted.

Something about the new boy unnerved Maia. He had an odd voice—frigid and harsh—and a disdainful way of speaking. Luem sounded so innocent next to him, so unmatched. She did not like the dismissive look Bakhari shot at Luem, and was relieved when Aerika interrupted.

"I'm not here to host a debate club, boys," she said coldly. "Site 53 for you, Core 13. On to Core 21, you have . . ." Maia's heart sank to the pit of her stomach as she noted the disbelieving look on Aerika's face. Something was wrong, she was sure. Aerika's next words confirmed that. "You picked a Taikorov generator?"

"Um . . . yes," Dani replied, flushing brightly as the rest of the team stared at her. "It holds a good amount of charge for a while and you can power anything with it, so I thought — "

"Well, it's a good thought, but I think you forgot something about the Taikorov," Aerika said, squinting at Dani. "The Taikorov comes in three parts — "

Dani gasped. "The sub-chargers are separate from the main. Oh no!"

Maia had no idea what Dani was talking about or why her face fell, but Aerika explained. "Yes, they will be in two different sites. What is more unfortunate is that the sites for the sub and main chargers are not co-located. You have 11 and 24."

The implications were clear. If this task was timed, and there was no reason why it would not be, Core 21 would come in last because they would take the longest to get to both sites and back. This task was as good as lost.

"Oh no, no, no," Dani kept muttering. Although Kusha and Ren both tried to comfort her, she did not seem to hear. Even more than the certainty of losing this task, Dani's ashen face made Maia's heart sink. The girl had barely recovered from the Trinity Caverns incident, and now —

"Supervisor Aerika," Maia blurted as a sudden thought came to her. "Can our team split and go two different ways?"

Aerika, who had just read out site assignments for Core 34, who had also chosen a generator, but of a different kind, stared at her for a moment. Nafi had not said a word since the Taikorov situation exploded on them. Now she marched up to Maia's side and looked pleadingly at Aerika as the woman pondered.

"You bring up a good point, Maia. I don't think there is a clause that prohibits that, but I shall have to check," Aerika said. "Then I have to confer with the other arbitrators as well. We will look into it."

"That's not fair!"

Loriine screamed so loudly that not only Maia and the other contestants nearby, but also Aerika jumped a little.

"Not fair," Loriine said again, just as loudly as before. "You can't change the rules for them." Karhann and the pasty-faced boy tried to placate Loriine, but in vain. The fact that Baecca and Bakhari glared just as spitefully as Loriine only made matters worse. Loriine shrieked again. "You're all in this together. You're all trying to help them win."

Maia expected Aerika to snap at Loriine. But the supervisor simply stared at the girl for a long moment before shaking her head. Then she spoke, in a voice that was as calm as it was cold.

"I heard you got in trouble with the chief arbitrator just a few days ago, Loriine. And now this?" Aerika tapped her chin a few times. "Are you desperate to get yourself thrown out? Or are you looking to get your whole team disqualified? Which one is it?"

"Please, Supervisor Aerika," Karhann said. "Please excuse us. This won't happen again. I apologize."

Aerika gave him a curt nod and addressed the final team while Maia and Nafi trudged back to their corner where Dani sat with her face in her hands.

"Dani, come on," Maia said. "There's a chance we'll be able to split into two groups. Even if that doesn't work, there are two more tasks. We'll find a way."

Ren nudged Dani's arm. "I agree with Maia. This doesn't mean we're out altogether."

"You have to focus and set up the parts for charging now, Dani," Kusha said. "No time to give up."

"We should've just picked a simple LumTorch," Nafi said with a sigh. As everyone else glared at her, Nafi simply shrugged. "What? That's the truth."

Someone sniggered behind them and Nafi whirled around. "Shut it, Loriine, or else . . ."

Loriine cackled some more, bumped fists with Baecca, and crooned, "Now we'll see how deep *your* friendship runs."

It was a good thing that Aerika called the teams over just then to prepare to get into the water, or matters would have surely gotten out of hand. Loriine's jeering voice stayed with Maia for a long time, however. Even the little torpedo-shaped crafts called Propettes that they boarded to get close to the Challowist farms and set up their units did not lift her sagging shoulders. Seeing the distance between the two sites they were assigned made them droop even more. It took a long time—the longest among all the teams—to get the main charger and the sub-chargers set up in the two sites. The setup was not timed, which made the situation a little bearable. It was clear, however, that if the team was not allowed a split, they were definitely slated for the last spot.

But the worst part was the fear that there could be, once again, a falling-out in the team. Maia hoped and prayed that it would not be so, that they would weather this storm together, as a family.

CHAPTER SIXTEEN

THE SHIELD

It took a while for Core 21 to regain its spirits after the Challowist setback. Even though there was no discussion on the matter, Maia kept fearing an outburst from Nafi. Everyone trod lightly, and all of them spoke less for a bit. Frequent lectures from Rayan, Miir, Hadeeyah, and even Sana came their way but helped only a little. What shook them out of their misery was the announcement of the Tansian shield project. The work on it started in earnest a week or so after the teams returned from their first trip to the Challowist farms. Other than hearing the news of its initiation from Kusha — engineers and scientists from all three nations were to come together for the work — Maia and her friends did not know much about it until Hans visited them late one night.

"We're making great progress," he said once the team — all except Kusha — as well as Rayan and Sana had gathered in the AR, where Hans had decided to crash for the night. Maia noticed that even though Hans looked tired, his eyes sparkled with excitement. Seeing that made her hopeful in turn. "We have come up with a solid design for a shield, thanks to everyone's hard work and . . . advice," he added, with a quick, grateful look at Rayan.

"How will it work?" Maia asked. "You need a power source, right?"

"Well, the primary hub will be in Zagran and the secondary in Reifnor in Coloni Vestei. We are rerouting all the energy we can find to hold up the shield. Then we have to build the Prop Points." He continued after taking a bite of an apple Nafi had handed him. "Here's the idea. Think of the shield as an enormous umbrella covering Tansi. The big umbrella is basically made of smaller umbrellas, and each of those needs to be propped up and held in place. So we build pillars . . . not physical structures, of course, just control stations that deploy the sheath and hold it up."

"These pillars will be all over Tansi, then," Maia said.

"Yes. We will need twenty-eight of these . . . Prop Points or PPs. We have identified the locations for them. Now we get to build them."

Nafi had been sitting next to Sana, on the arm of the large couch. She hopped off her perch and scooted over to Hans's side. "Please tell me ThulaSu is one of the locations."

Hans chuckled loudly before replying. "Yes, it is."

As Nafi whirled around in excitement, Ren shook his head. "Seriously, Nafi. What are you going to do about it? We have to work on the Initiative. Hadeeyah is clocking us."

"Well, we're counting on volunteers, because this needs to happen quickly," Hans said. "So, if you can spare any time at all—"

"Of course," Nafi declared. "We're all volunteering." She turned around and glared at Ren. "That includes you, Prince of Laziness."

"You're calling me lazy?" Ren glowered back. "All you do nowadays is hunt for apples."

"At least I—"

"Hold it, guys." Maia cut their debate short so she could ask Hans some more questions. "So you're here to set up the Prop Point?"

"No, not really. Vin is in charge of the ThulaSu Prop Site. He's setting up shop as we speak. Kusha found us the perfect building behind the Gathering House," Hans informed them. "I came because . . . I just . . . missed you guys."

Nafi's eyebrows shot up. "Missed us? How about just saying you missed Rayan? How hard is that?"

Hans flushed, stared at her for a moment, then sighed. "All right. All right. I missed Rayan. Happy?"

"Much better," Nafi said, grinning widely. Then she put on a stern look and wagged her finger at Hans. "I better not see any more of this too-shy-to-say-it-out-loud business."

As Hans fell back on the couch, rolled his eyes, and shook his head, the room erupted in laughter. Nafi strutted back to her original perch with a look of fulfillment on her face and bumped fists with Sana.

"Well, I also came to take Miir to Zagran," Hans announced next. "With the future of the Nouvus on hold, I figured he has time to spare. So —"

Nafi's bright face dimmed. "You're not taking him for good, are you?"

Hans laughed. "For good? I can't take anyone away for good. Who do you think I am?" He shook his head and laughed again. "No, but I did hope he might spend the next few months in Zagran. He could be of immense help. But apparently, he has duties at Walenveil. Chief Dorian put his foot down and absolutely refused to let him go for too long. So . . . Miir will be shuttling back and forth between here and Zagran. When he's here, he'll work on the Prop Point."

"Oh, that's better," Nafi said, sounding relieved.

Although Maia did not say it out loud, and she hoped she did not show it either, she too was relieved that Miir was not going away for very long. It was funny how she had become used to having him close by and seeing him every now and then. The idea of that changing stirred up an odd restlessness. The feeling was unexpected and utterly unnerving, so Maia was happy when Hans got off the couch and walked up to Rayan, drawing everyone's attention.

"Want to go for a walk?" he asked, and Rayan promptly nodded.

"There you go," Nafi exclaimed. "So much better than the fidgety, angst-ridden—" Nafi stopped and stared wide-eyed and open-mouthed at Rayan's staff hovering in front of her nose.

"Behave," Rayan growled, before walking out of the room with Hans.

As everyone else started laughing, Nafi grumbled, "Seriously! Some people are so needlessly touchy."

* * *

The next day, being a rest day, seemed to be a good time to check out the ThulaSu Prop Site. Hans left in the morning, and after breakfast, Maia trooped out with the rest of the group toward the Gathering House. The building was not hard to find since a bunch of people had already gathered there, among them Maks and his friends. They waved and walked up to Maia and her teammates.

"Hey! We just signed up for the shield business. Are you volunteering too?"

Everyone nodded except Ren, who gave Nafi a look. "I had no intention of volunteering, but seems like I don't have a choice."

"What's wrong with you?" Nafi said. "Everyone's helping and you don't want to?"

"I have work, Nafi," Ren said.

"What work?"

"Can't tell, so don't ask," Ren said as he strode up to the door. "All right, now hurry up. I don't have all day."

Nafi followed, shaking her head. As the rest of the group walked in, Maks pulled Maia aside.

"Hey, Maia. Is everything all right between you and . . . his Princeliness?"

Maia put a hand on Maks's arm to reassure him, chuckling a little at the name he gave Ren. She remembered how Maks and Aman had seen Ren raging at her after the Viperine was vandalized. Maks and Aman had helped defuse the situation and defended her as well. "Yes.

We talked, and everything's fine now," she said, grateful for Maks's friendship. "Thank you for checking."

After the Appian gang left, Maia walked inside the building. She found her friends talking to a young Jjord man.

"I've heard a lot about you from Hans," he was saying as Maia joined the group. "So . . . I have all your names. I'll add them to the roster. I'll have the schedules set up by tonight and put it up outside by tomorrow morning."

"Thank you, Vin. I'll see you soon, then," Sana said, almost singing the words.

"I'm looking forward to seeing you too," Vin replied with a striking smile and Maia realized why Sana was melting into a puddle. Sana was not alone. Some other girls, mostly students of ThulaSu, were giggling together on one side. As much as Sana would have loved to stay, the group soon headed out.

"What's wrong with you, Ren?" Nafi demanded as soon as they stepped outside. "You put your name on and then took it off. You really don't want to contribute?"

"Realized my time will be better spent on other things," Ren replied gruffly. "Besides, I don't think there's any shortage of contributors. Sana will skip classes to volunteer, I'm sure."

Sana had a dazed look on her face. "You know me so well, Ren. I'd love to, actually."

"There you go," Ren said.

Nafi was about to retort when Rayan cleared her throat decisively. "I have a session with Monk Konnae," she said and left right away, with Pai in tow.

"We should head back and do some research on Ti, don't you think?" Maia said.

While Nafi nodded and Ren did not seem to care one way or another, Dani clearly hesitated. "Well, I was planning to check on Kusha, so . . . you guys carry on."

Maia jumped at the idea of spending some time with Kusha. They had not seen much of Kusha since his parents left. The boy only joined them occasionally nowadays. Maia missed him, and she was sure everyone else did too.

"We will come too," Maia said, and immediately realized her mistake. She rushed to correct herself. "Unless you want to be alone with him, of course. I'm sorry, I didn't mean to intrude." Kusha and Dani had been together for so long that they all tended to take it for granted. Maia often did not even remember the depth of their closeness. Reflecting on her thoughtlessness made Maia shrink with embarrassment.

Dani blushed and shook her head. "It's not like that at all. I'm just worried. I don't see him very often since his family left and . . . he's alone and overwhelmed, I'm sure." She linked her arm through Maia's and smiled. "I'd love it if you all came. I know Kusha would, too."

So they trooped along, all the way up to the north end of town where the mansion of the House of the Sun nestled between two walls of a cliff face. A solemn man in uniform—Maia assumed he was an attendant—opened the door as soon as they knocked. He was about to seat them in a large waiting room when they heard Kusha's voice.

"Enzo, who is it?"

Dani sprang up and dashed out, and the rest of the group followed. They found Kusha on the staircase, dressed in official garb. He looked tired and thinner than usual, but his face lit up as soon as he saw all of them.

"It's you guys." He laughed happily as Dani rushed up and hugged him. "Come on up. The place is a mess, though."

They followed him up the stairs but as soon as they reached the top, they stopped in horror and gawked at the room in front of them. 'Mess' was an understatement. It was a battlefield. Maia remembered the last time she had seen it, when every little thread was in place. Now, there was barely space on the floor to walk to the window on the opposite end of the room. Books, trinkets, plates, spoons, pieces of fabric were strewn all over. The massive table, sitting below the equally massive sun-shaped chandelier was filled with dust and debris of all kinds. Parts of the chandelier were broken and hung precariously. It looked like a tornado had swept through.

"Kusha, what happened here?" Dani's shocked voice brought Maia out of her daze. "What is going on? Are you all right? Did you do this?"

"Yes, I did. But I'm fine. This is just—"

"I knew I should've come to check on you more often." Dani broke into a sob. "I've been so selfish, all wrapped up in my misery. I forgot all about you."

Kusha turned toward Dani to explain, his face shadowing as he saw her teary eyes. "Dani, I'm fine." He cupped her face in his hands and peered at her. "I haven't gone crazy or anything. I'm not hurt, either."

That explanation clearly did not help much, since a few tears had already rolled down Dani's cheeks. Kusha slipped an arm around her shoulders and pulled her close. "Dani, I really am fine."

Ren flipped over what had once been part of the chandelier with his foot. "This isn't fine."

"I was practicing with the chakra last week, and things got a bit out of control. That's all."

"Umm . . . so . . . practicing with the chakra inside the house?" Ren said. "Is that safe? Doesn't look like it."

Kusha shot him a displeased look. "Not helping, Ren."

Ren did not seem to have any interest in helping. He picked up a shredded book from the table and turned it back and forth. "This is tragic," he said. "Please tell me you've improved."

Kusha beamed. "Oh, I have." He pulled the chakra out from under his shirt and untied it from its string. "I've got this pesky thing under my thumb now."

"Are you sure?" Dani asked.

"Quite sure, Dani," Kusha said. "I wouldn't lie to you or put you in danger. Let me show you."

Ren spread out his arms protectively. "All right, everyone, get back."

"Hey! I want to see," Sana protested as Ren pushed everyone except Kusha to the edge of the staircase.

Ren shrugged. "Just trying to keep you safe."

"I can keep myself safe just fine. Move over," Sana said and elbowed her way back to the front.

Kusha set the chakra in motion, and Maia noticed a difference immediately. The Xinhagyi had trained them together for months, and Kusha had always seemed nervous and unwilling to use the weapon. Now his face looked open. He looked happy wielding it.

The chakra whirred about the room once and then circled the chandelier. It hovered over every spike in the sun sculpture, executing tight spirals yet never touching them. Dani gasped as it circled around Kusha once. Then it slowed down and dipped to the floor. Maia held her breath as it gently scooped up what looked like a broken piece of a knickknack, and she marveled at Kusha's fine control over the weapon's motion.

The chakra zoomed toward them, slowing down in front of Dani. Everyone broke into smiles when they realized what the red thing at the center of the chakra was—a tiny red flower of hardened clay.

Dani laughed. "Is that a rose?"

"Go on. Take it," Kusha said.

Dani reached for it, her fingers trembling a little. As soon as she took hold of the rose, the chakra sped back to Kusha and settled down on his upturned palm.

Sana started clapping. "That's unbelievable, Kusha," she exclaimed.

It was indeed. Maia was breathless. Having seen Kusha's unwillingness to embrace the weapon not very long ago, she found it particularly astonishing.

Kusha smiled bashfully as he walked over to them. "After my family left, I was really upset about everything for a while. I did not want any of this, you know. I did not plan to run a city full of people. Not yet anyway. I did not want the chakra either. Every time I took it out, it reminded me of the sage and . . . how, in a way, I was responsible for his death. Everyone told me how lucky I was to have been given the chakra, to be a Sahiiraan, when in reality, they were burdens to me."

Suddenly, Maia understood Kusha's reluctance to engage during his practice sessions with the chakra. As Kusha stayed quiet for a while and ran a hand through his unruly mop of hair, Maia wished she had tried harder to find out about his struggles.

Kusha flashed a shy grin at Dani and continued. "One day I thought I'd give it all up and run away. And then I realized, that'd make me no different from my parents. I could not do that. I had to try harder. Instead of moping about being overwhelmed with responsibility, I should try to get back in control of my life. That's the best I can do, right?" He reached for Dani's hand. "I had to put in time and effort to learn stuff, including the chakra. So I started and I kept on trying." He flushed a little. "Messed up this room, but—"

"It's nothing that can't be cleaned up," Dani said. "I'm proud of you."

Kusha grinned like he had won the biggest wager ever. Maia found herself smiling, her heart flitting like a cloud in the bright blue sky as she looked at his radiant face.

"All right, good job," Nafi said, speaking for the first time since they had arrived at Kusha's. "All this spectacle has made me hungry. What have you got, Kusha? And please don't tell me you've wrecked the kitchen as well."

Kusha smiled sheepishly. "No, the kitchen is just fine. Go find yourself something."

"I will. I hope you have better things than Totos in your pantry," Nafi said. She grabbed Dani by the arm. "Come on. You need some refreshments too. Let's find some lunch."

While Dani and Nafi went off to hunt for food, and Ren goaded Kusha into showing off some more skills with Sana cheering him on, Maia ambled over to the bookshelves in the next room. She picked out a book on farming practices in ThulaSu and settled down on a large couch. She had just begun to flip through the pages when Sana flopped down next to her.

"Done with rallying the troops?" Maia asked.

"Kusha is doing great, and Ren is actually giving good advice. So the cheerleading squad is not essential anymore," she said.

Her matter-of-fact statement made Maia laugh. Sana looked at her curiously.

"I like this," she said. "You're not all clouds and rain."

Maia raised an eyebrow. "Clouds and rain? I'm not always like that. Maybe sometimes when I'm stressed—"

"You're laughing a lot these days. Even with that crazy R'armimon hovering over us. And I like seeing you happy. Reminds me of you in Miorie." She gave Maia a quick hug. "I never thought I'd find that Maia again. So whatever it is that's making you smile, I pray it lasts forever."

Sana was right. Looking inward, Maia found lightness in her heart too. Perhaps it had to do with Ren being back with them, or maybe it was because the nations were finally coming together against the threat of the R'armimon. Maia felt content, hopeful, and indeed . . . happy.

Chapter Seventeen

A Heart So Cold

Work on the planetary shield picked up and intensified for weeks on end. Maia and her teammates, every other team in the Initiative, and students in ThulaSu old enough to work pitched in, along with every available adult. Building a scaled-up model of the Orekemino box was exhausting work. It started with putting together small parts to form the larger modules, which then fit together to make the final system. Tiny tweezers and pliers were needed to work on the smaller parts, and then everything had to be soldered on. Overall, it took a lot of attention and quickly drained everyone of energy.

Maia and her teammates were lucky enough to get a morning slot on the roster every day. That was much easier than the evenings, since their minds were fresh. Although that meant when it was time to work extra hours on the challenge, they were all understandably tuckered out. But they managed to pull through, taking turns to get everything done. All in all, things worked out fine.

Maia was in an upbeat mood as she wrapped up her tasks early one cold, bright day. Her part was complete, and not only did the lead engineer, Vin, flash that smile that made every girl's heart flip, he even patted her back in appreciation.

Nafi, who had also finished and had been waiting for Maia, frowned as Maia packed up. "Why are you grinning to yourself like that?" she demanded.

"Um . . . nothing."

"Don't tell me you're gushing over something Vin said," Nafi commented. She noted Maia's startled expression and shook her head in displeasure. "You are! Seriously, Maia? You too?"

"What's wrong with being happy about something someone said?" Maia shot back and walked away, shrugging. She kept walking at a brisk pace, hoping to keep Nafi and her comments at arm's length.

"Nothing. Nothing at all, but wait—" Nafi stopped abruptly and pointed at a figure a few paces ahead of them. "Hey, isn't that Miir?"

Before Maia could decide if it was indeed Miir, let alone answer Nafi's question, Nafi had bounded ahead.

"What are you up to?" Nafi asked Miir as Maia caught up with the duo.

"Just completed my shift here. Heading home." He looked back and tilted his chin up at Maia, "Hey!"

"Great, we're walking that way too," Nafi said. "Me and Princess Airhead."

"Nafi!" Maia protested vehemently at the name.

Nafi, however, in typical Nafi fashion, ignored her protests. Even more annoying was the amused expression on Miir's face.

"Princess Airhead? How is that?"

"Don't ask. Apparently, Vin said something nice to her," Nafi informed him, loudly enough for the entire neighborhood to hear. "You know the lead engineer Vin, yes? He's cute and whatnot. All the girls keep making googly eyes at him. And today, our dear Maia decided to join Team Airheads."

Maia shot a glare at Nafi's back. "Stop it already, Nafi," she yelled.

Nafi stopped and turned around. "You know, if you like him, you should ask him out on a stroll," she suggested wisely. "What do you think, Miir?"

"You have a point," Miir said, his tone brimming with wisdom, just like Nafi.

Maia flushed a violent shade of red, and embarrassment turned into anger as Nafi smirked. Pushing the two aside, Maia stomped ahead, grumbling. "You are just too much sometimes, Nafi."

"Hey, what did I say wrong?" Nafi called from behind. "I didn't say marry him or anything. Just said try him out. I do like Vin better than that creepy R'armimon prince trying to woo you."

Maia spun around, fists curled. "Wooing me? Where did you get that crazy idea?"

Nafi rolled her eyes. "Seriously, Maia. The way he looks at you? I knew it that very first day he came to meet you. It was — "

"Wait! What first day? You weren't even there."

"Oh, come on! We were watching, of course."

"How? Ruche set up a perimeter and everything."

"Where there's a will, Maia. Or maybe I should say, where there's a Ren and a Sana." Nafi laughed. "Anyway, so Miir, tell me this . . . isn't Vin better than that creepy Aekken?"

"Nafi, stop! You are bad enough. You don't need to add *him* to this."

Nafi crossed her arms and cocked her head. "Why ever not?"

"Because . . . because . . ."

There were so many things to say, so many points to counter with, it was weird that Maia could find no words all of a sudden. As she stood there, flushed and flustered, Nafi found a brand-new distraction.

"Speaking of boyfriends, there's Maia's last one," Nafi announced. Once again, before Maia had even spotted Maks, Aman, and Nisa outside a spice shop across the street, Nafi dashed away toward them.

"Where are you going now?" Maia called.

"I have business with them. Goods to collect," Nafi shouted back. "I'll catch you later."

Within a few moments, after the trio from Appian had waved at Maia, the group disappeared around a corner while Maia gawked after them.

"She is a storm today," Miir said.

"I'm not talking to you," Maia snapped and strode away.

Miir followed, chuckling. "What did *I* do?"

"You encouraged her. And now you're laughing. It's not funny."

"Well—"

"Aekken is *not* wooing me and I'm *not* interested in Vin. End of story."

For a few moments, there was only the sound of their boots on the stone.

"You know, you are not helping yourself. The more annoyed you get, the more she will tease you."

He had a point. But Maia was not in the mood to acknowledge that. She kept walking, keeping her eyes to the front, her mind trying to recapture a fleeting realization she just could not pin down. Thankfully, Miir did not continue the conversation about Nafi's teasing or say anything at all, so along they went, walking in quiet tandem until the path turned toward the Sun Temple. A figure clad in black, a long staff in hand, was striding across the courtyard toward them. As soon as Maia realized who it was, she slowed.

"What is it?" Miir had caught her pensive gaze.

"Zaara."

"That is Zaara?"

"Yes. It is."

"I would like to speak with her," he said next, surprising Maia. "Can we do that?"

"We could, but . . ." She took a moment to arrange her thoughts. "She can be harsh. I've known her for a while, and her words are still hard on me sometimes."

"I can handle it."

Maia was not so sure. But Miir wanted to speak to the woman and Maia thought that like her, he too wanted to know the one person from the group of four who was still around. She assumed he was looking to retrieve a memory of his mother through Zaara, so even though her heart told her this was not a good idea, she did not object.

They found Zaara near the corner of the courtyard as she headed northward toward the visitor residences.

"Zaara," Maia called.

Zaara whirled around, her vivid green eyes flashing through her veil. "You stupid, stupid girl," she said, raising her staff menacingly at Maia. "Do not use my name out in the open like that, you understand?"

The severe response left Maia holding her breath. She had not expected a smile or a greeting in return, but she had not expected such a violent rebuke either.

"Sorry," she mumbled.

Zaara lowered her staff and looked into the distance. "Why are you prancing about ThulaSu? Your project work does not start until later. You should be in your room."

"I was working on the shield and—"

"Aah! Another useless venture. Didn't you learn enough from the Nouvus debacle? After all that, you're wasting time on the mindless shield project. Stop making decisions with your heart, girl. Think with your head."

"You mean we shouldn't even try to get the shield up?"

Zaara shook her head. "It won't work. There isn't enough time to put it all together the right way."

"So we give up and do nothing. Just wait to die. That's what you're saying."

"Why not? We all die sometime anyway. It's time we let the R'armimon cleanse this planet once and for all. There's too much malice in the air, too much."

She looked around suspiciously, searching the corners and staring at the shrubbery as if she expected assassins to jump out and accost her. It was then that she noticed Miir. Her eyes widened in an instant and her face froze. Maia was about to introduce them when Zaara lifted her veil and strode up to Miir.

"You are . . ." She jumped back as forcefully as she had approached him. She held her staff defensively across her body, almost as if she was afraid of his presence. "You're Asiyaah's spawn," she hissed.

Maia's insides shriveled at the scornful name. She had heard Zaara use the moniker before, but it was utterly embarrassing and painful hearing it used to Miir's face. She looked at him for signs of resentment and found none. But obvious or not, he had to be vexed.

Zaara, however, either oblivious or uncaring of the discomfort she had caused, continued her scathing appraisal. "You're the little one, aren't you?" she said. Maia thought Zaara's eyes softened just a little as she looked Miir up and down. "I hear your parents are both dead. Good riddance, I say. Is your —"

"Zaara," Maia almost shouted. "Can you not be so cruel, just for once?"

Zaara looked at her strangely, her wide eyes narrowing to slits as she scanned Maia's face.

"He doesn't seem to mind. What's *your* problem?" She turned back to Miir. "Do you mind, Spawn?"

"He has a name, Zaara. That's no way to —"

"Silence." Zaara did not turn, but the end of her staff hovered between Maia's eyebrows.

As Maia held her breath, Miir raised his hands and looked from Zaara's face to Maia's. "Please, please. I am fine. You can call me anything."

Staff pointed at her head or not, Maia was about to protest again when she saw Miir's pleading look. Angry as she was with Zaara, she took a step back.

"You were about to ask me something," Miir said.

"Yes, I was," Zaara replied, lowering her staff again. "Is that rascal brother of yours still alive?"

"As far as I know, Remii is fine."

"As far as you know . . . I assume he's still a scoundrel of a brother, that one." Miir did not reply, but he did not have to. The way his eyes shadowed made plain the answer to that. Zaara shook her head. "Used to torment you all the time, that idiot. Hated me because I always put him in his place." Zaara sighed and looked into the distance, her eyes glazed, her mind lost in memories.

She snapped back toward Miir shortly. "But what are you doing here in ThulaSu, Spawn?" Before Miir could reply, Zaara took a step closer to him, her gaze narrow and piercing on his face. "You're in hiding, aren't you? Did you *really* murder that useless father of yours?"

"I certainly did not harm my father."

"They framed you, then?" Zaara's mouth slowly curled into a mocking smile. "Asiyaah's darling baby turned fugitive. Now, that's a treat to watch."

How Miir could listen to all that and hold Zaara's gaze calmly, Maia could not fathom. She stood quietly, her fists curled, teeth gritted, only because of his request. But there was only so much she could tolerate.

"May I ask *you* something?" Miir asked after a spell of silence.

"Yes. Doesn't mean I'll answer."

"What do you know about Raidyn?"

Zaara's face hardened in an instant and her eyes flashed again. "Hate him. Hate him. He was the first one who took Sophie away from me. Raidyn's not so bad, Zaara, she'd tell me. Not so bad. I didn't see him come to help you when you were in trouble, Sophie."

Maia saw a curtain descend in Zaara's eyes, as if her heart was being sucked away into a vortex of painful memories.

Miir however, continued calmly. "Did you ever meet his parents?"

"No. I didn't care anyway. He looked rich and he was well-spoken, must have been from a noble family. That's all I know." Zaara stopped and squinted at Miir. "Why are you asking these questions about Raidyn?"

"Just curious."

"No one's curious simply for its own sake. What are you up to, Asiyaah's spawn?"

"Of the four of you, he is the one I hear of the least, so—"

"Like I said. He was a selfish coward, not a friend to Sophie. He must be living a nice life out there somewhere." Zaara thumped the stone pathway with her staff. "My Sophie, always so trusting, always ready to give. Your mother used her and threw her away when the work was done. Never looked back at my Sophie."

"My mother suffered too," Miir said in a quiet voice. "She had to give up her family. She died alone."

Zaara scoffed. "You think . . . you dare to think your mother suffered the same as my Sophie?" She raised the staff again to point at Maia. "Look at that girl. You think she suffered the same as you?" Miir's face wilted in an instant, but Zaara did not pause. "You people think you are the best, that you deserve the best. That we are scum, we are not worthy of happiness. We exist to serve you and your selfish needs. That your pain is the worst, your sacrifice is the noblest that can be. Selfish, arrogant vermin you are!"

Zaara spun away from Miir and glowered at Maia. "And you . . . you're just like your mother." She pointed accusingly at Miir. "You think he's a friend? Well, think again. With your head this time, if you have one."

The intensity of Zaara's words left Maia shaken. Every painful memory she had, every agony she suffered emerged from the darkest recesses of her mind and engulfed her heart. Anger, fear, and every other desolate emotion she had ever known swamped her.

"Open your eyes, Maia. They are all out to get you. All they want to do is use you. That's what they always do."

"That's enough. Stop it," Maia shouted, covering her ears to shut out Zaara's voice. "I don't want to hear any more."

"Truth hurts, doesn't it?"

Maia spun around and started walking away from Zaara. Truth or not, Zaara's words did not help. They wanted to push her into a dark abyss of fear and suspicion and leave her there. Stranded forever. She could not let that happen. She could not listen to Zaara. She could not stay stuck in that pit of hopeless and unending loneliness.

Maia had not gone ten paces when she stopped, suddenly realizing Miir was not with her. She turned around to look. He still stood transfixed in front of Zaara.

Maia's fists curled. She was not about to leave anyone else stranded in that abyss either. Not if she could help it. She strode over and grabbed Miir by the wrist.

"Come on, you're leaving too."

She pulled him away and kept on going.

Zaara's voice surged after them. "Nothing good ever comes of being friends with their kind. Remember that, girl."

Maia just kept walking. One step after another. And another.

CHAPTER EIGHTEEN

A SEASON TO HEAL

Maia kept on going because she had to. She had to get Zaara's words out of her head before they engulfed her soul. The best way to fight them was to keep on walking. She immersed herself in the rhythm of her shoes.

Click-clack! Click-clack! Click-clack!

Nothing good comes of being friends with their kind, girl!

Click-clack! Click-clack! Click-clack!

They are all out to get you. All they want to do is use you. That's what they always do.

Click-clack! Click-clack! Click-clack!

"Think we have come far enough now?"

Miir's voice, clear and startling, tore through the fog in Maia's mind and made her slow down. She blinked rapidly in a desperate attempt to ground herself. They were close to the ramparts, not far from her living quarters. She had not realized they had come so far.

She looked back at Miir and flushed immediately. She still had him by the wrist and the thought that she had practically dragged him all the way from one corner of the courtyard to the other made her flush even deeper. She stopped and let go of his arm before shrinking away in embarrassment.

"Sorry. I'm so sorry. I didn't realize—"

"Sorry? Why?" Miir asked, peering at her. "Because you dragged me away? Or dragged me this far?"

He was clearly trying to make light of the matter, but Maia shriveled some more. Retreating to the closest bench, she slumped onto it and lowered her head into her hands.

"I can't," she whispered. "I won't. I have to keep on going. I have to."

Miir sat down next to her. "What is it? What bothers you so much?"

"Her words. They are so . . . they drown me."

"You know she is harsh. You said it yourself. You should not take her words to heart."

"I know. But they still get to me." Maia sighed. "I don't want to end up like her. I don't. She's so unforgiving . . . immovable. So miserable. I can't be like her."

"Why do you think you will be? You are nothing like her."

"Because I've done it. I've been like her before," Maia confessed in a voice so low that she had trouble hearing it herself.

As her mind flew back to that evening in Miorie when she had overheard Uncle Alasdair's accusations against Sophie, she realized she had not spoken of it to anyone. No one other than Dada, Herc, and Emmy had known that what had happened that night made a bubbly, carefree little girl withdraw so tightly into a shell. Until now.

She let it pour out of her. Starting from that fateful evening in Miorie to her time in Appian, she told Miir every little detail of her heartbreak so many, many years ago.

"So I closed myself off," Maia said when she had finished. "I should have rejoiced at finding my family, my mother. Instead, I shut Sophie out. All thoughts of her. Not that there was a lot to begin with. Dada didn't talk about her much. He didn't even have a picture of her in the house, nothing to tell that she existed. I understood later that it was because he needed to protect me. There couldn't be anything linking me to her. But even that wasn't enough for me. I decided to go further. I stopped talking about her, thinking about her. I couldn't be anything like Sophie, I promised. You know, I used to love flying. Gave it up because I couldn't . . . I wouldn't let myself turn into Sophie." Maia stopped and breathed deeply to fill her insides. It hardly helped. "Going to Xif had changed her, Uncle Alasdair said. So I had to shun Xif and everything related to it. I wouldn't think about Xif or know about it. I wouldn't even mention the name. I would go to ThulaSu and I would be everything Sophie wasn't."

"Oh! So that is why."

Maia looked up at Miir's curious response. "What do you mean?"

"Well, I finally understand why you were so upset when Principal Pomewege went to invite you to the Initiative. I have always wondered."

Maia let out a sad chuckle. "My carefully built-up world collapsed around me that night. I even considered running away from home. But I couldn't. I couldn't be that selfish and make Dada face the consequences. Or maybe I wasn't brave enough to do it."

"Whatever the reason, I am glad you did not."

"So am I," Maia said, "Surely, my life changed a lot, and it brought me a lot of pain that I'd rather not have. But it brought me a lot of good things too. There are many things I would change if I could, but I wouldn't change that night Principal Pomewege called." She drifted back into her thoughts for a moment. "Since I'm being so honest, I should say this too. I hated you for a long time for spotting me in Kusha's glider. But now I'm glad you did. If you hadn't, I'd still be stuck in that world of lies I created around myself."

"Happy to hear that my first sin has been forgiven." His voice was light, and it lifted Maia's spirits a little.

"So you see, I have a habit of building walls around me."

"You know, you cannot hold that against yourself. You were a child, hurt, shocked. It may seem foolish to you now, but that reaction was only natural."

"Thank you for trying to cheer me up, but . . . that wasn't the only time," Maia said, slipping back into her memories again. This was one she did not want to dredge out, but she forced herself. She slowly recounted how blind her rage had been when she had met Zaara for the first time. Zaara's words had brought out all the fears that her intense grief had brought on. "When I struck you down on that cliff, I did not give you any chance to explain. All I thought was that you were my enemy, you had to go down. You had to pay for all the pain I had endured. It was so . . . wrong."

Miir had been fidgeting while she spoke. Now he burst out, "You cannot blame yourself for that. To be honest, I was cruel and arrogant. After all you had been through, after all that my people . . . myself included . . . brought upon you, I did not even apologize. Instead of comforting you, I . . . I chastised you, mocked you." He paused and drew a sharp breath. "You had every right to lash out against me."

"No. I had no right. Revenge is not a right." Maia pulled her knees up to her chest and hugged them tight. "You came to help me. And I attacked you without questioning. Because I couldn't see past the hate. I had heard of a Raptor taking off from Appian, but that didn't mean anything. I decided it was *Shadow*. For all I knew then, you might not have been at Appian at all that night."

"But it was *Shadow*. I *was* there. I am responsible, even if not fully, for what happened at Appian that night."

"Well then, so am I." Maia had never thought she would tell anyone this, her deepest, most shameful secret. But it only felt right to tell Miir now. "That evening in Shiloh, I saw Remii before he saw me. I knew who he was, and after all that happened in Zagran, I could guess what had brought Remii to Shiloh. I should have run. I should have come back home and taken Dada and Herc and Emmy and . . . run. Do you know what I did instead? I stood there and when he saw me, I challenged him. I felt so invincible, so spectacularly capable that like a brainless idiot, I challenged him." An enormous sigh coursed out of Maia, leaving her empty and weak. Her next words drained her of the last bit of energy. "I might as well have set that fire myself."

Maia lowered her head to her knees and gasped for air. She felt Miir's hand on her shoulder.

"Hey! You did not mean it. You could not have known what would happen."

"And you did?"

He pulled his hand away and sighed. "No, but—"

"Don't you see? You made a mistake. So did I. It hurts. And I'll regret it always. But I can't be stuck in that moment blaming myself, wishing I could undo the moment, fearing that I'll do something else just as stupid." Her hands tightened around her knees. "I can't be stuck hating you for every mistake you made, either. Not when I can see how much you regret making them."

Maia could not tell if Miir accepted her reasoning. He stayed silent for a long time. And Maia went back to Appian, to memories she never wanted to revisit again. She knew she had to face them someday, and now felt like the right time.

"That morning before I left for Shiloh, I hurt them all. I said the cruelest things. Thought I was being so smart. Never thought that would be the last time I'd see them. Never thought I'd never be able to tell them how sorry I was, or how much I loved them." A sob choked her and she buried her face in her knees. "Never knew how much I'd miss that little house, that even if I had the whole universe, it still wouldn't be enough to fill that hole in my heart." A cold breeze blew past. "But I can't . . . still can't lose myself." Maia's fingers curled into determined fists. She wiped away her tears and sat up straight. "Dada always said, our past molds us but it does not define us. Back then, I didn't understand what he meant. Now I think I do. I know I have to move forward with an open mind, starting with forgiving myself."

Quiet crept in once again. Maia's thoughts drifted.

"I'm sorry for the way Zaara spoke about your family. That was no way to talk," she said after a while. "You've probably figured, she's very fond of Remii," she added with a chuckle. "She goes on and on about him every chance she gets."

"That part I really did not mind at all," Miir said. "Hearing about Remii was not shocking. He has hated me all his life. He would have me dead if it were up to him."

Maia frowned, surprised at his words. That he was at odds with Remii was nothing new to her, but she had not known the extent of the animosity between them.

"That can't be true," she said. "I mean, I understand how different you are, but he can't be wishing you harm. You're his brother, after all."

"A brother he would rather not have," Miir said. He fell back on the bench and his troubled gaze scanned the skies. "He has resented me all his life. Why did my grandfather leave his memories for me? Why was I good at everything he wanted to be good at? Why did everyone like to spend more time with me than with him? Why? Why? Why? It has gone on for as long as I can remember. I never asked for those things he was jealous about, but to him, it was all my fault.

"There was this one time, I was about six or seven, when we had come down-planet. I do not remember where we were on Tansi, but I know it was the first time I had seen an ocean. Water . . . so much water . . . blue as far as I could see. It was unbelievable."

Miir's eyes took on a dreamy sheen as he recalled the moment, and Maia could only imagine the wonder he must have felt at seeing the ocean for the first time. She had been stunned when she first saw the Eastern Seas. But it had to be a thousand times more astonishing for Miir, since Xif had no open water.

"Remii and I played all day on the shore," Miir continued. "Then we went into the water. I must have waded in too deep at one point. I found myself struggling to get back on my feet. The more I tried to fight, the more the water pulled me down. Remii stood next to me, watching me flail with a gleam in his eyes. 'Not so perfect after all, are you?' Remii said. 'Now you are going to drown and die, all because you were too lazy to learn to swim.' I forget how I managed to get back up, but I remember that Remii never offered a hand."

A chill sped up Maia's spine and made her shudder. For a while she simply stared in utter disbelief at his cloudy face. Then she blurted, "Did you tell your father?"

"Tell my father? No." His voice held the hint of a tremor. "I have told no one about this."

"But your father needed to know."

"After our mother left, our father became distant. We hardly saw him anymore. The few times we crossed paths, I could tell he did not hear me when I spoke. After a few years, I stopped trying to reach him." He let out a small sigh and distractedly scratched the surface of the bench. "I decided I could not tell anyone. Besides, it was my fault. It had to be. I should have known how to swim. How could I have not learned?"

"It wasn't your fault at all," Maia protested with vehemence. "How could you think that?"

"I was a child. I was foolish, I guess," he said with a small laugh. "I did learn to be careful around Remii after that." He paused as if to gather his strength. "But anyway, it is good to know he was bad to me even before our mother passed me her sword. I always thought that was what really angered him."

"Your mother's sword?"

"Yes, this one," Miir said, pulling the dark blade halfway out of its scabbard. Maia fell back a little at the sight of it. She had seen it many times before — it was a magnificent double-edged sword, the blade an intense, burnished black, its guard shaped like a crescent moon and engraved with a two-tailed dragon. The dark blade was decorated with the same design and its sharp edge glinted in the sunlight. "Fury was my mother's before it was mine."

As Maia stared at Fury, she felt a strange dissonance. As much as she admired the way it looked, she also found herself pulling away from it. Perhaps it brought back memories of every time Miir had wielded it against her, of every subsequent loss she had had in her battles with him. She remembered his furious swordplay, she remembered how it even cut through her light. The thoughts left her dazed and she was relieved when Miir sheathed it.

"If Remii could, he would steal it away from me," Miir said. "To him, it was the best sword that could ever be. The sword that should have been his. I got everything easily, he said, even this. He never saw how I struggled to get used to its heaviness, how difficult it was to wield. He just . . ."

His words trailed off and Maia stared into the distance, trying to process everything she had heard. Remii had always come across as cruel and spiteful, but what Miir said spoke of a heart truly dark. *How do people get that way,* she wondered. Or maybe they did not. Maybe people like Remii were born with no love and no kindness in them. Maia was so deep in thought that she almost jumped when Miir started speaking again.

"We should get going now," he said. "If Zaara comes to check on you and finds us here, this will be the last day of my life."

Maia laughed. It sounded silly, but it was probably not too far from the truth. Except she also knew Zaara well enough.

"Don't worry. Zaara won't come to check on me. She doesn't check on anyone," Maia said. "But I do need to go. Have a bunch of reading to catch up on."

They got up and started walking again.

"I'm curious," Maia asked as they neared the ramparts. "Why did you ask Zaara about Raidyn?"

Miir shrugged. "There is something about him. He looks familiar, but I cannot tell what it is. I just feel as if I have seen him before."

"Maybe you know him as someone else? He might be going by a different name now," Maia said. "After the situation with the Sedara, I wouldn't be surprised if he wanted to put some distance between himself and his time with Sophie."

"I had thought of that, but no one springs to mind. I will have to keep thinking."

"Maia! Hey, Maia!"

Maia turned around at the loud shouts. Nafi had appeared in the distance, a big sack on her back.

"What is this?" Miir asked when they walked back to help the girl.

"Stuff," Nafi answered.

"Tell me you didn't get more apples," Maia wailed. Thanks to Nafi, eating apples had become an everyday task. Maia did not mind them, and they were mostly quite tasty, but Nafi's obsession with the fruit had gone on for a bit too long in Maia's opinion.

"It's a new variety, Maia," Nafi said, her eyes bright. She opened the mouth of the sack and pulled one out. "Try it. It's really crunchy and tart."

"It is good," Maia admitted after a bite. "But don't you think it's time for you to try a different fruit?"

"Why? I love what I love. I don't give a darn about what else is out there." She handed one to Miir and settled down on a bench with another. "Mmmmm . . . good. They make me so happy. Why in the stars would I want to try anything else?"

Guess that is that. We're all stuck with apples for life.

"So Maks gave you these?" Maia asked. "Is he into selling apples now?"

Nafi shook her head. "He doesn't sell, he facilitates. He introduced me to a woman who has this great little orchard. The last person was all right, but this woman *really* knows her stuff."

"Facilitates, huh? Did he take a commission, too?"

"Nothing too bad. An apple for each of them."

"Maks the Facilitator . . . who knew."

"I think he'll do well. Maks knows stuff, Maia. He knows everything there is to know about ThulaSu," Nafi said. "He is a gem. You know, you might want to reconsider your decision about—"

This time Maia was ready to cut her off. "You say one more word, Nafi—" she said in the sharpest voice she could muster, "—and I'll chuck this bag of apples right off the cliff. I mean it."

That did the trick. They spent the rest of the time munching apples without getting into contentious topics.

Chapter Nineteen

Shooting for Ti

Training sessions with Ruche always left Maia oddly shaken. At the end of every session, an anxious emptiness settled on her and she found herself in a state of melancholy mixed with fear and rage. It almost felt like she became a different person after these meetings with Ruche. That was why she had wanted to avoid seeing him on the day they were set to go to Xif to research the future trip to Ti. Getting this task done in the best possible way was important, so she needed to think and see clearly.

But Ruche . . . Ruche always had his way. And so Maia sat, pouting and fidgeting, facing Ruche on the southern ledge of the rose garden. A beautiful dawn was breaking over the valleys below, but Maia was too annoyed to enjoy it.

"Maia, you are not here," Ruche said, poking her knee with a twig before waving it in front of her face. Maia sighed loudly and Ruche's face crinkled into a smile. "What is it that you dislike so much? All you have to do is recite the words I tell you and meditate. The intent is for you to embrace the power inside you more fully. It's not like I'm making you run around the way the Xinhagyi does."

What the Xinhagyi made her do was tiring but easy. Who knew handling the physical manifestation of the light would be effortless compared to these . . . feeling and understanding exercises Ruche sprang on her?

"I'm not myself after I do these, Ruche. I turn into someone else. Someone I don't recognize."

"What kind of someone?"

"Someone who's angry, vengeful, ready to kill . . . I've . . ." Maia's words trailed away as exhaustion swept in. Even thinking about that other side of her did not feel good. It tired her and reminded her of the moments in her life she did not want to think about. That side of her had taken over when she had thrown Miir off the cliff, and again when she had attacked Lex. She had felt strong, powerful at the moment, but once the moment of vengeance passed, she had nothing but regrets left to cling to, and . . . she did not want to be that person.

Ruche fell into a thoughtful reverie as she told him all that, and shook his head when she finished. "I will let you go now, Maia. Winning the Initiative and acquiring Seigvard is indeed a top priority. This trip to Xif is an important step toward that and I can't jeopardize it. So you're excused for today."

"Thank you," Maia exclaimed. She wanted to hug Ruche, but the thought of offending the seer kept her from throwing herself at him.

Ruche's eyes twinkled for a moment before he put on a somber face. "However, we have to continue these exercises. I believe it is necessary. We need to bridge the divide between the regular you and the one you see when you try to reach the light."

"So you think these emotions I feel are mine? Somehow they come out from time to time?"

Ruche got to his feet and smoothed out his cape. "It could be. We . . . all of us always have repressed thoughts and feelings. It could be that. Or it could be the spirit of the light itself. It is a powerful entity, Maia. And it could have urges of its own." He fell silent as they walked to the entrance of the garden side by side. "Although I imagined this power would be benevolent and peaceful. I can't imagine why . . ." He left his thought unfinished and did not speak until Maia had walked past the gate. "I have told you this before, Maia, and I will say it again. It is important that you be in control of your powers and not the other way around. That means we have to keep trying until you are completely comfortable with them. So . . . I will see you again in a few days."

The skies were bright when Maia walked back to her room, relieved and happy. Even though she knew that she would have to face this again soon, at least at the moment she was spared. And for that she was thankful. She needed all her attention on the planning for Ti. Anything else could wait.

* * *

Maia was rushing to get ready for their trek down to Frauz Point, where their shuttle was to depart for Xif, when she heard a ruckus in the corridor outside. Voices she did not recognize—mostly girls, but a few boys too—were creating quite an uproar. Maia exchanged a look with Rayan before she opened her door and peeked out. She immediately wished she had not.

Two doors down, a crowd—four girls and two boys—were engaged in a fiercely animated discussion with Ren. The door to Nafi's room was open as well, and Nafi stood, arms crossed, glowering at the huddle. Sana was next to Nafi, tittering. As soon as Maia peeked out, Nafi marched over and into her room, Sana following.

"I can't take this stupidity anymore," Nafi growled as she slumped onto Maia's bed. "I just can't. I'm going to hurl things at them one of these days."

"What is going on?" Rayan asked in a calm voice.

"Ren and his fan club action is going on," Nafi informed, sarcasm dripping from her voice. "He better finish up with this drama quickly or we'll be late."

"What do they want?" Maia asked.

Nafi simply made an exasperated face but Sana happily explained. "Time on his schedule, apparently. From what I understand, some of his slots were overbooked and . . . some people are angry."

"He has a schedule for them all?" Rayan sounded flabbergasted.

Nafi's nose wrinkled in disdain. "I wouldn't mind that if he also had a schedule for work on the Initiative. Most of the time he's running to Frauz Point for the stars know what, and then this." Nafi stopped and glared at Sana who burst into fresh giggles. "What's so funny?"

"Did you hear? One of those girls wants to work on her poetry writing with Ren," Sana said, almost choking with laughter. "Ren and poetry, who knew."

"I'm a man of many talents, often beyond the understanding of simple folk." No one had noticed Ren walking up to the open door. Sana sobered immediately and Nafi was about to retort when Kusha peeked over Ren's shoulder.

"Come on, people. You're making us late," he said. "You can gossip when we get back. Come on."

"Now *we* are making us late," Nafi grumbled but otherwise did not say much.

It was indeed getting late. They rushed down to the rose garden and toward the entrance to the tunnel under the ramparts. Maia had heard that the tunnel had been made into an official thoroughfare between ThulaSu and Frauz Point, but it was her first time seeing it since their misadventure in the Xifarian camp. It looked like an entirely different place. Lights had been put up all along it, the path cleaned and paved, and at the end of it, stairs carved down to the floor of the canyon. A pair of guards stood at the end of the stairs, and they quickly verified the group's credentials before pointing them toward a small buggy waiting to the side. Soon they were settled inside a medium-sized transport craft at the landing site.

The rest of the way to Arpasgula and then through the tunnel through Xif went as usual, but Maia sat up when their craft emerged from the hole in the sky. Always, up until the last time she had visited, the Xifarian cities had sparkled beneath a vibrant Sedara. Now an unending swath of buildings still stretched to the horizon, but they were dark and grayed under a Sedara that barely shone at all. The sight was not unexpected. Yet seeing Xif like this was unsettling. Maia held her breath, as did every person in the craft.

"This is bad." Nafi's whisper trickled into Maia's ear and shook her out of her stupor. "Really, really bad."

"I'm so sorry, Ren," Dani said.

Ren simply shrugged in response but his listless face made Maia's heart twitch. She knew it was not easy for him to see and endure this. Miir's words, his plaintive voice rang in her ears once again. She could not help but think that Sophie . . . and thus in a way she, was responsible for the situation. There was no doubt that the Sedara's heart needed to be broken, but that might have brought this about as well. And as sure as Maia was that Sophie did not wish for this to happen, there was no denying the fact that it had happened.

"Don't worry." Ren's spirited voice pulled Maia out of her thoughts. "We'll fix this."

There was not much discussion after that since Master Kehorkjin, an assistant in tow, walked up the aisle and started speaking. "May I have your attention, please? As you have heard and now see, the atmosphere inside Xif has changed a lot. The air quality is not optimum, so for your protection, you will have to wear masks when you are outside of the XDA." The assistant started handing out conical silver-gray contraptions to everyone when the master paused. "Thankfully, there is no reason for you to venture out of the XDA on this trip," he said, throwing a long and pointed glance at Maia and her teammates before continuing, "so for the most part there will be no need of these masks. We will spend most of our time in the library, with the data vaults. Make good use of your time. Am I clear?"

Things could not be clearer. Perhaps it was seeing the Sedara and those masks being handed out, or perhaps it was the master's grim tone, that no one smiled anymore. The craft deposited them at the XDA, and the almost empty building was a stark reminder of the forbidding times. There were hardly any students around and barely any activity. Maia's heart was heavy, and it would have stayed that way if it were not for a flamboyant figure that came sashaying down the main stairs at the entrance and greeted them brightly.

"Welcome, welcome, finalists of the Alliance Initiative," he said, raising his hands in the air in a regal pose. Maia blinked in surprise at Master Geir-Sei, Vice Principal of the XDA. It had been a while since she saw him last, but he looked just the same as he had all those years ago when he had met them at Arpasgula during the first phase of the Initiative. He looked just as poised in his impeccable Gambrill. The goatee, the perfectly coifed hair arranged in sculptured waves on his head, and the white stone studs dazzling in his ears—everything was just the same. As was his smile, a little too wide and lasting a little too long.

Next to Maia, Nafi groaned. "Someone please, please tell me Smiles won't be with us all day," she said under her breath.

No one told Nafi anything, but Geir-Sei walked down the stairs, perfect smile firmly in place, and twinkled at the group.

"It is a privilege to see you, the best of the best, the bravest, and the most talented." He continued after a deep bow. "The XDA is honored to open its vaults to you today." He bowed again and made a sweeping gesture with his arms. "Go and shape the future of our universe, statespersons of tomorrow."

Maia had stared, stupefied as always at Master Geir-Sei. However, when he ended his speech, instead of the feeling of annoyance that his shows always brought her, Maia found herself smiling happily. Perhaps it was the familiarity of his performance, or perhaps the spontaneous joy in it, that lifted her sagging heart. Her steps were livelier after that and the deserted hallways did not upset her so much anymore. She even relished the quiet and appreciated that given the lack of crowds, accessing the data vaults at the library was definitely easier.

The entire day, except for mealtimes, was spent looking at maps of Ti, reading the specifications of various craft they could use on Ti to fly from the base to the mines, and choosing the sites for Calbion extraction.

Around midday, Master Kehorkjin arrived with Flight Master Demissie. "Master Demissie is here to advise you on your craft picks for Ti. He has arranged for prototype craft, or maybe even real ones, to be brought over to Xif and then transported to ThulaSu for practice. Remember, you will have to write a summary of your research on your craft choice. That's a prerequisite for your trip to Ti."

Master Demissie made his rounds, stopping at the desks of each team. He had a big smile on his face when he came over to meet Core 21.

"Good to see you all again," he said, as he laid out a map display of Ti on their table. "I will explain simply for you. Your task starts with picking the mine you want to go to. That you decide based on how much Calbion deposit there is. Then, based on what the surrounding topography looks like, you pick a craft that's best suited for landing in the area. There are differences not only in topography but also in the environment, such as wind direction and pressure.

"Once you pick a craft from this list here"—Demissie tapped a list of craft he had pulled out—"you chart a path to the mines." He chuckled at the worried faces around him. "Well, this will not be as difficult as the Seliban Challenge. But pay attention to the details, because every moment you save or lose will add up eventually."

The enormity of the task ahead of them made everyone's shoulders sag. They had to accomplish a lot, and that was even before getting into the mine and extracting the Calbion. Heads leaned closer to the data vaults, hands jotted down every available detail. Maia's fingers hurt and her head ached, but she carried on, finding as much as she could, as fast as possible. It was quite late in the evening and Maia had just finished scanning through an enormous resource on the mines when shouts and yells made her jump up and look around.

The unlikeliest of pairs—Bakhari and Jiri—were glaring at each other, their faces scowling, hands fisted. Master Kehorkjin, who had been lounging in the teachers' corner to the side, walked up, his face grim, a deep frown etched on his forehead. "What is the reason for this spectacle?"

"He refuses to give back a document I found, Master Kehorkjin," Bakhari said.

"No, I found it first," Jiri retorted. "You tried to snatch it away. I'm not giving it to you until we're done with it."

Master Kehorkjin's sharp gaze scanned their faces, three times over. Then he extended his hand toward Jiri. "Give it to me."

"But Master Kehorkjin, I'm telling the truth. I—"

"Jiri, now."

Bakhari grinned slyly as Jiri reluctantly handed over the long data slide. Kehorkjin flipped it back and forth and then gestured at the two boys. "Follow me."

They headed over to the teachers' corner. Though everyone else continued to work silently, every mind was occupied by the huddle in that corner. The two boys returned shortly after, with Bakhari sulking and Jiri with a big grin on his face.

"The master asked us both questions about the contents of the document," Jiri shared much later. "Obviously that idiot could not answer them correctly, since he did not know half of what was in there. So Master K gave it back to me. Warned Bakhari, too."

All the teams worked late into the night, returning to the library after dinner. Maia was tired but content when she finally got into her bed in the wee hours of the morning. They had made good use of the time they had been given.

The trip back to ThulaSu the next morning was calm and smooth. Maia spent some time poring over her notes and soon got bored. Dani and Kusha were in deep conversation and Maia did not have the heart to disrupt their privacy. Ren was yapping away with Kenan and his mates. Nafi had been sitting to one side, furiously scribbling in her notebook since they got back into the transport, so Maia decided to check on her. She half expected Nafi to close her notebook on seeing her, but the girl flashed a smile instead.

"I spoke to Kehorkjin today and filed for a modification of my personal weapon," she said, surprising Maia with her unusual candor.

"Why? Is something wrong with your daggers?"

"No, nothing's wrong. I love them. But they are too short sometimes," Nafi said with a sigh. "Sometimes I wish I had more space in a fight. Then I found these." She held out the notebook. In it were drawings of daggers on chains and a person wielding one like a whip. "The Palonkians used these things called the latsore-kaha, basically a dagger on a chain. I want to mount mine on chains too."

"Cool, I approve." Maia had not noticed Ren walking up behind them, but he seemed to be quite impressed by Nafi's illustrations. "So Master K's fine with a mod?"

"He said he sees no reason to disapprove since they're still my daggers," Nafi said. "He'll have to confer with Zaara, of course. So that's that."

"I think Zaara will agree if Kehorkjin recommends it," Ren said. "I can't wait to see you fight with these."

"Not so fast, Ren," Nafi said in a morose voice. "I don't actually know how to use these. I have to practice first. And the saddest part is, I've been trying to find a trainer, but no one will train me."

"How about Monk Konnae?" Maia asked.

"She has no time."

"Oh, I know"—Maia sat up with excitement as she recalled—"the Xinhagyi could help. He knows a lot of Palonkian techniques."

Nafi grimaced and shook her head. "I asked him already. He refused, says he doesn't know enough about the latsore-kaha."

Maia's shoulders slumped. "But you'd *have* to train before you actually use these, or you might end up hurting yourself."

"I know," Nafi said. "Well, I spoke to Miir and he said he'd read up on the technique. And if he can find enough information, he'll think of a way to train me."

"I'm sure he can. Guess what I'm doing with him now?" Ren wiggled his eyebrows. As the two girls looked at him blankly, he smiled. "I'm learning to fight TEK waves."

Nafi's eyes grew wide. "What? How? Can you see TEK waves now?"

"No. And that's the fun part. He's teaching me how to sense them," Ren said. "So, Nafi, if anyone can help you, it's him."

"I sure hope so," Nafi said. "I really want to start using these. I think we'll have a fierce fight over these tasks. It'll be brutal, and we have to be more than prepared."

Nafi was right. Everyone was on edge, no one willing to allow a moment's slack. When even the kind Jiri did not think twice about fighting Bakhari to hold on to that resource about Ti, the fact was clear — things were shaping up into a perfect storm.

Chapter Twenty

Evil Intentions

ThulaSu was covered in snow for the second time that winter. It was far from the knee-deep snow that stopped everything, but still fun. The grounds turned white and pretty overnight, and blue skies appeared with a blazing sun the following day. Much to the disappointment of the students of ThulaSu, however, nothing closed down. Classes were on as usual, and Sana sported a long face as she came out of the refectory that morning.

Maia was happy she did not have to sit through classes, even though her day was not entirely free of chores. A few days ago, Nafi had read of a new way to improve the health of the Silverblood fern, and Monk Tessio had been quite impressed when she told him about it. So impressed that he awarded sole upkeep responsibilities for the Silverblood to Core 21, much to the disappointment of the other teams. Core 21, with the exception of Nafi, of course, found no joy in the work, but since it freed them from handling the Spore, they did not grumble much.

The real problem revealed itself later. Ren and Kusha stomped into the AR a day or two after the team took over the upkeep of the fern.

"Where do you get these bright ideas from, Nafi?" Ren yelled.

Behind him, a frowning Kusha shook his head. "We've looked all over and found three rainbow grub shells. Just three. I don't know what sort of fertilizer you'd make out of these tiny things."

Rainbow grub was the popular name for the grub of the Limata beetle. Natives of the First Continent, the grubs shed their rainbow-hued summer shells in the dead of winter. These shells, ground up and mixed with dried potato peels, were supposedly the best nourishment for the ferns. Only, as the boys had just discovered, there were no grub shells to be found.

Nafi's face puckered. "Oh, come on. How useless can you boys be? They're supposed to be all over ThulaSu in the wintertime. And you found only three?"

Ren threw himself on the couch, put his legs up on one of the armrests, and yawned. "We found what we found. That's it. There's no more."

Since then, a good part of each day had been spent hunting grub shells, without success. Frustration mounted steadily until Hadeeyah, who stopped by one evening to drop off a list of libraries—big and small, public and private—in and around ThulaSu, and found the team slouched around their empty buckets, shared a sanity-saving bit of information.

"I've never studied Limata beetles, but grub shells always show up on snow days," Hadeeyah said.

What a valuable tip that turned out to be. After a dusty adventure into another pile of books, Nafi confirmed that the grubs preferred to shed their shells in the snow. A lot of arguments about the feasibility of the enterprise erupted at that point, and the dire situation was explained to Monk Tessio. Monk Tessio peered at their faces, listened to their quandary, tapped his fingers together, and finally laughed. Then he upped the ante by promising them extra credit if they managed to deliver the grub shells. No one could refuse that offer.

After that, there was an endless wait for the snow that refused to visit ThulaSu. There were cold days, blustery days, frozen days, and icy days. But no snow. And now that snow had finally arrived, the team had to run out, buckets in hand, in search of the rainbow shells.

Nafi and the boys took off right after breakfast, toward the eastern part of town. Maia and Dani had to finish up a report on the Spore, so they went out a little later, planning to head north from the Sun Temple. The girls stopped in their tracks as soon as they came out of their living quarters. A black craft sat at one corner of the temple grounds, its dark shape standing out in sharp contrast to the whiteness of the snow.

"Never seen anything like that," Dani said. Maia had not, either. The pitch-black craft was half the size of the Viperine and had a curved silhouette that reminded Maia of a talon ready to capture prey. Next to her, Dani shuddered a little. "It looks very . . . mean."

Maia had to agree. The craft had a look of cruel efficiency about it. "Wonder who came in that?" She stopped and pointed at the symbol—a silver circle enclosing two crossed swords—on its wings. "Never seen that emblem before, either."

"Looks familiar," Dani said, squinting at it. "Can't quite place it, though."

The two girls walked along until they reached the corner of the temple grounds where the pathways split in different directions—north toward the visitor residences, east toward the Garaha Gates, and a third to the west toward the pavilion and classrooms. A nearby grove of trees was the first place they wanted to check for grub shells. As soon as Maia bent down to look, she forgot all about the craft and her questions about it. Scattered all over the ground, like colorful pieces of glass, were shells the color of the rainbow. With an excited squeal, Maia fell to her knees, Dani following. They picked the shells up gingerly, one at a time, and placed them in their buckets. People walked by, but Maia and Dani worked on, oblivious of curious stares thrown their way, happy that their long wait had finally borne fruit.

Their buckets were filled almost to the brim and the entire grove cleared of shells when Maia heard the crunch of boots. It was unusual, different from the lighter sound made by ThulaSuian soft soles. It made Maia look up in the direction of the sound. Her heart stilled for a moment.

A group—two men and a woman clad in the black uniforms of the SDS—strode down the pathway toward them, and immediately Maia knew who had arrived in that strange craft on the temple grounds. As Maia recognized the man in front, a chill sped up her spine. It was Remii, Miir's brother and an agent of the SDS. He was Phocluus's right-hand man, the one who had murdered her family in Appian and led the team that captured Bikele.

For a moment, Maia deliberated whether to acknowledge his presence or let him pass by. There were people around, and it was not the place or the time for a confrontation. So even though Maia wanted to ask Remii about that night in Appian, she turned away, head bent in search of shells. Some situations, however, are destined to be, as Maia soon discovered.

"I think we've cleared this spot of shells," Dani chirped gaily from the other side of the grove. "Should we head further up now? Maia?"

From where she sat hunched on the ground, Dani could not have seen the SDS trio and there was no way Maia could have warned her, but the harm, unintentional as it was, was done. Immediately, the crunch of boots stopped. Maia felt Remii's gaze on her and heard him walk closer, his steps slow. There was no point pretending, and she could not sit with her back to an enemy, so Maia turned in his direction.

"Hello, hello," Remii said, his voice just as bitter as she remembered. "Haven't seen you in a long time, Maia. How have you been?"

Maia could not simply ignore him, so she looked up. Remii's crooked smile greeted her. He spread his arms wide and cocked his head. "What? You aren't going to say hello to me anymore? What have I ever done to you?"

Maia slowly rose to her feet and met his gaze. "You killed my family, in case you've forgotten," she said, her voice even, her insides burning with anger.

"Oh, let bygones be bygones, Maia," he said, taking another step closer. "Besides, that wouldn't have happened if you had cooperated with us. So you have a hand in that tragedy too."

Maia tried hard to keep her temper under control. Her fingers curled and her nails dug deep into her palms. The pain was the only thing that kept her from unleashing the tempest of fire that Remii so richly deserved. But she could not. A fight here would risk many innocents, and that could not be.

Patience! There will be a time, a better time, a better place to get back at Remii.

Maia breathed in deeply. The chilly air settled inside her, the anger within ebbing a trifle. "Sure, it's all my fault," she said caustically. "What are you here for, anyway?"

"I had heard a lot about this place, so I came to check it out," Remii said. "Better than most places on this planet but . . . it could use a little cleaning up. And some good taste would make it look a little less wretched." He stopped and peered at her face. "You don't mind my visiting, do you?"

"Why would I? ThulaSu doesn't belong to me, so—"

"Thank you. You're gracious as always," Remii said. His eyes, glinting with malice, scoured her face. "Maybe you can do me one more favor and tell me where I can find my brother."

His words struck Maia like a hammer and made her heart race. A wave of terror—sharp and intense—made her fingers go numb.

They know Miir is in ThulaSu, and they have come to take him away.

Knowing how bad she was at masking her emotions, and knowing Remii would pick up on any little mistake she made, Maia hastily forced laughter. She would have to make a pretense of incredulity, the best one she could manage.

"Shouldn't you know?" she replied, her tone scathing. "He's your brother, not mine."

"A very willful and wild brother, unfortunately. One that neither listens to good advice nor has any good sense. I haven't heard from him in a while, so I thought . . ." Remii chuckled. The grating sound wriggled through Maia's ears and left her feeling sick.

"So you thought of asking me?" Maia shot back. "You expect *me* to know where he is?"

Remii's gaze narrowed on her face. "Shouldn't I?" he asked. Behind him, the other agents drew closer.

"No, you shouldn't. Wish I could, but I don't keep track of every person that has wronged me," Maia said. "Besides, I can't imagine *your* brother being in a place so wretched."

Remii broke into loud, raucous laughter. "You are right. I couldn't imagine him in this hovel either. But I keep hearing reports of him being seen around here. His tastes must have deteriorated considerably to tolerate a dump like this for even a day." His lips curled with scorn as he shook his head. "Not the brother I knew. Have to say I'm disappointed."

"Maybe those reports are wrong."

"You think so?" Remii sneered, stepping nearer, the other agents close behind him.

Maia took quick stock of the situation. He was barely three steps away from her. They would not dare attack her in ThulaSu, but she was not taking any chances. Maia reached inside and stoked the light. In an instant it flowed, smooth and warm and comforting, up from the core of her being to the tip of her fingers, pliant and ready as it waited for her command.

As they stared at each other, waiting for the other to make the next move, Maia was suddenly aware of a change around her. A ring of Kausakas was slowly forming around them. Dani had something to do with their swift and silent arrival, she was sure. Remii saw them as well. His smugness rapidly faded away, and frustration took its place.

"Well, if you happen to come across my illustrious sibling, do pass on a message. We miss him at the SDS and . . . we'll find him sooner or later. *Later* would not work out in his favor, so . . . if he values his life and his freedom, now is the time to repent and return.

This is the last time we're asking." His lips twisted into a crooked smile as his eyes once more scanned the ring of Kausakas around them. "So long, Maia. We shall meet again. Very soon, I hope."

He gestured at the other agents behind him, and they strode away toward the Sun Temple. Some of the Kausakas followed them at a distance.

Dani was next to Maia in a heartbeat, an arm hooked through hers. "Can't imagine having a brother like Remii," she whispered, her voice trembling. "What Miir must've endured, growing up with a creature as horrid as that."

Dani's words brought back a memory and Maia shuddered, remembering the incident with Remii that Miir had told her about. She had no doubt, none whatsoever, that Remii had wanted his little brother dead, drowned, and lost in the ocean that day.

As soon as Remii and his agents disappeared from view, Maia clutched Dani's arm. "We have to warn Miir, right now."

They had just placed their buckets safely in a nearby corner and were prepared to hurry off when they heard a scream. It was the voice of a young child, and for a moment, Maia's heart stilled. Then it came again. Along with Dani and a few Kausakas, Maia ran toward the sound. Her mind was empty and fear made her unable to feel her limbs. She ran, unthinking, unfeeling toward the scream that now came repeatedly.

They found a little boy hunched near a bush close to the visitors' residences. As Maia drew close, her heart thudding incessantly, she saw two bodies sprawled beside the pavement. They were small, a boy and a girl, and even before Maia saw the girl's face she knew who she was from the large brown cloth lizard lying next to her.

"Lonnie," she whispered as she took slow, fearful steps forward.

Dani was already bent over them. "They're alive, just unconscious. Someone get the healers," she yelled. "Now!"

A Kausaka dashed away toward the sanatorium. Maia kneeled next to Dani to look at the kids. There was a livid bruise on the side of Lonnie's face, and a similar one was clearly visible on the boy's neck.

"TEK waves," Maia said, slowly, almost unable to believe what she was saying. "Remii . . . Remii attacked them."

Dani had pulled out some med patches from the belt pack she always wore now, containing the emergency supplies Ruche had suggested. Her shocked eyes snapped up to Maia. "Why did he have to hurt little kids?"

"I don't know. Maybe they got in the way?" Maia muttered. But . . . got in the way of what?

She looked around, her eyes seeking clues, her heart pounding relentlessly in some unknown fear. She looked up along the pathways and the surrounding buildings until she spotted one across from the bushes where they were crouched. Immediately, the connection became clear.

"Dani, come with me," she whispered.

She ran, Dani behind her, and did not stop until she reached a door she had entered before, one to Master Kehorkjin's room. She grabbed the doorknob with icy hands, and with a prayer on her lips, she pushed the door open.

A gasp escaped Maia. Master Kehorkjin lay on the floor, his eyes closed, at the center of a pool of red. A sword, likely his own, lay beside him, its blade smeared with blood. The wound it had created in the master's abdomen left a huge, bloody splotch on his shirt.

Dani was next to him in a heartbeat, pulling out items from her belt pack in a frenzied rush. "He's alive," she said. "Maia, get help. Call the healers."

Maia's legs wanted to give way, but she forced herself back to the staircase. "This way," she screamed at the cluster of healers tending to Lonnie and the boy. "Need help here, please."

As the healers rushed up the stairs and ran into Kehorkjin's room, Maia sank to the floor of the verandah, exhausted, her mind reeling. How could Remii injure the master so badly? What could have Kehorkjin done to him? And then, after grievously wounding him, Remii had simply walked away, not caring, not even pausing to think as a man bled to death. He had even blasted a pair of innocent little kids on the way out.

A parade of healers streamed up and down the stairs as Maia watched. Soon they had Master Kehorkjin moved to the sanatorium. Maia and Dani waited in the visitant chamber, and a healer came out to speak with them after what seemed like an eternity.

"He is stable. Luckily, the sword missed most of the vital organs." He gave Dani a curious look. "Are you the one who administered the blood coagulator?" He smiled as Dani nodded hesitantly. "You might have just saved his life. We will do our best, but I wish we had better equipment here. It is a terrible wound."

As soon as he left, Dani pulled out her Urso and started sending messages frantically. It was not long before Vin, the young man leading the construction of the Prop Point at ThulaSu, rushed in. "Dani, I just got some messages from Hans about the master. How is he now?"

Dani hurriedly explained the situation.

"Hans has made arrangements for the master at the HCH. And I have a transport waiting to get him to Zagran right away."

Soon the healers at ThulaSu had prepared the master for his journey. They took him away in a stretcher, Vin leading the way. Maia and Dani followed them to the mouth of the tunnel leading to the shore.

"I hope he recovers, Maia," Dani whispered as the party disappeared from sight.

Maia hooked an arm around Dani's. "I'm sure he will. And it will all be because of you. If you hadn't stabilized him right away . . ."

"You're the one who thought of him. If he'd lain there unattended for much longer, it'd be too late," Dani said. "I can't believe Remii could hurt him so badly."

They stood there for a bit, trying to calm their thoughts, until Maia remembered. "Have to warn Miir. He's probably next on their list."

The girls hurried off, and soon they were walking along the faint path down to the tiny house among the Darkwoods, Maia's heart thrashing violently all the way. She heard the chatter of voices even before she reached the place. It took her a moment to recognize them, and immediately breathed in relief.

It was Nahlo. That meant . . . Miir was safe.

Nahlo's little head peeked out after a moment, more little heads lined up behind him. Then Miir came out, his face creasing into a worried frown as his eyes fell on their bloodstained clothes.

"What happened?"

By the time they had told him of Remii's visit, his attack on Master Kehorkjin, how Maia and Dani had found the master, and how Dani's timely intervention had likely saved his life, Miir's face was ashen.

"He's stable now. The healers here were quite satisfied with his condition," Dani said. "Luckily, Vin had a transport leaving for Zagran and Hans got permission to get the master transferred to the HCH. He's on his way there now."

"Remii is just . . ." Miir paced back and forth. "He's gone crazy. What did he want from Master Kehorkjin anyway?"

"He wants you," Maia blurted. "Asked me quite a few questions too. Told me to let you know this is the last time they'd ask you to come back."

Miir scoffed, his jaw hard and hands fisted. "They just do not get it. I did not leave them only to go back now."

There was a fretful silence, and then Dani spoke. "Miir, perhaps you should live in ThulaSu. Or even somewhere inside Walenveil. This place . . . is not safe."

Maia was glad Dani brought up the thought that had been at the top of her mind. She had hesitated to voice it, knowing how much Miir loved the house. But the truth was, it was far from anything or anyone.

Miir exhaled loudly. "I will be fine, Dani. I will set up some perimeter alerts. And —"

"And we'll be on guard too," Nahlo chimed in, his little face furrowed with determination. "This morning we saw a bunch of mean-looking *wahris* near the stairs up to ThulaSu and we got them all messed up real quick." Giggles and chitters rose from his gang. For once, Maia did not wince at the name Nahlo called Remii and his agents; she only relished the joy of seeing how confidently Nahlo spoke. "We watch the village, especially my father's special friends. Now we'll patrol this side even more."

"Your father would be very proud of you, Nahlo," was all Maia could say.

"But still . . ." Dani was far from satisfied. "Remii is dangerous, and the way he talked to Maia today . . . I don't know, Miir. I think you should find another place."

Miir sat down next to Dani and put a hand on her shoulder. "I will be fine, Dani. Besides, I am hardly ever here nowadays. I spend half of my time in Zagran."

"Don't worry, we'll keep an eye out," Nahlo reassured him. He gestured at his troopers. "Come on, let's go. We have work to do."

The gang of little people were barely out of sight when new voices sounded far down the path. It did not take anyone long to identify Nafi. Soon, the entire gang was scattered around the porch, getting caught up with the events of the morning, while Nafi stomped up and down the yard.

"You need to take this seriously," Nafi said for the umpteenth time. "Get a dog, maybe?"

Miir exhaled loudly. "You all are making too big a deal of this. I am not a fair maiden in need of a protective detail."

Sana pinned him with a glare. "Hey! I resent that comparison. Ever consider it can be hard work being a fair maiden? She can't do everything by herself and she's smart enough to realize that. So she employs bodyguards."

"Umm . . . sorry, never thought of it that way," Miir mumbled.

"Well, think, then," Sana snapped. "I'm with Nafi. Get a guard dog."

"How did they even find out?" Nafi grumbled on. "No one got a whiff of you all this time. Did you talk to anyone other than the people you usually do?"

Miir shrugged. "I have started going to Zagran lately, so that is new. And—"

He stopped abruptly and Nafi stomped up to him in a heartbeat. "And?"

"I spoke to Karhann a while ago, but—"

"You spoke to Karhann?" Nafi burst out. "Of all the people here, you had to find that stupid Karhann to chat with?"

"Nafi, I needed to speak with him. Besides, he is my cousin and I have known him for a long time now. I trust him. He could never have . . ."

Ren had been sitting silently at one corner of the porch, away from everyone, his face grim. He sprang up suddenly and strode over to the rest.

"Nafi, you may have a thing against Karhann and I will not comment on that," he said sternly. "But please don't accuse him of betraying Miir. He wouldn't. He just wouldn't."

Nafi crossed her arms and rolled her eyes. "Well, fine. Your friend is golden. But someone must have ratted. And I bet it's someone on his team. Karhann has some stellar teammates, that you have to admit."

No one objected to that idea. No one even blinked. It was likely — no, more like a certainty — that Loriine or Baecca found out something and passed it on to their higher-ups.

Ren broke the bout of oppressive silence that had fallen. "Hey, guys. I'll see you later."

"Where are you off to?" Nafi demanded.

"Stuff. I have stuff to do."

"What stuff?" Nafi asked. Ren did not reply; he did not even look back at her. He hurried off, leaving everyone open-mouthed behind him.

Ren's sudden, odd departure left discontent in its wake. Once Miir had given them enough promises to be careful, the rest of the gang trooped back up to ThulaSu. They had to. There were classes to attend, reports to prepare, and grub shells to grind up. Ren, however, was missing all day and did not show up for dinner either.

It was very late that night, and Maia had already crawled into bed when there was a knock at the door. As soon as Rayan opened it, Ren walked in and, ignoring Rayan's disapproving glare, deposited himself on Maia's bed. He looked tired, but Maia could also tell by his smile that he was genuinely happy.

"Where were you all day?" Maia asked.

"Lots of places," he replied with an inscrutable smile. "But the news is . . . Remii is taken care of."

Maia frowned. Perched on the edge of her bed, Rayan frowned even more. "Explain," she said.

"Well, our queen is quite embarrassed after hearing of Remii's accomplishments today. So she has banned the SDS from any activity outside the encampments."

Rayan's frown eased a little. "That is good. But will they listen to her?"

"I think so," Ren said. "Their flight plans will be monitored from now on. And they'll think twice before attacking people so openly. That's for sure."

That was indeed some relief. It was a miracle that Master Kehorkjin had survived and the little kids were not hurt too badly. Remii was dangerous and ruthless, and ThulaSu was not equipped to handle such a menace.

"Have you eaten anything all day?" Rayan asked suddenly.

Ren returned a casual shrug, and Rayan took off immediately to retrieve some food from her stash. The moment she turned away, Ren leaned closer to Maia. "Listen, don't worry about Miir, all right? They won't be looking for him anymore."

"What do you mean?" Maia's brow creased once more. "How?"

"Well, don't ask for details, I can't tell," he replied with a sheepish grin. "But trust me. I've got this covered."

They spent a long time talking after that. How Rayan managed to produce a full dinner for Ren, Maia had no idea, but by the time Ren had cleaned his plate, he looked contented. Then after profuse thanks and a mighty hug that left Rayan dazed, Ren left.

Maia had thought she would have a difficult time getting to sleep that night, since worrisome thoughts had paraded through her mind all day, but Ren's information, cryptic as it was, had clearly helped. As soon as Rayan turned the lights out, Maia drifted into a deep slumber.

CHAPTER TWENTY-ONE

A FUTURE WITH YOU

Maia had thought matters could not get any worse after that terrible encounter with Remii, and for a while, that seemed true. To everyone's relief, Lonnie and her friend, who Maia visited every day at the sanatorium, recovered quickly. Dani brought news from the HCH of Master Kehorkjin's condition improving. One day soon after the attack, Uncle Alasdair came by to share a letter of apology from the Xifarian queen that confirmed what Ren had already told them—she had prohibited the SDS from any activity outside the encampments. All in all, things were looking up. Then Ruche brought the proposal of a visit from Aekken, and Maia's shoulders drooped like never before.

"You should refuse if it bothers you so much," Nafi said, stomping across the length of the AR with a scowl on her face.

"Come on, Nafi. It isn't that easy," Dani chimed in. "Millions of lives are in his hands. He has no integrity and he's clearly prone to mood swings. He's the last person you want to anger by refusing."

Nafi stomped some more. "Don't like that stupid prince."

"Who will be there with you, Maia?" Sana asked, poking

furiously at an embroidered flower on her dress.

"Just Ruche and me. Probably a few guards."

"The rose garden again? At dawn?"

Maia nodded grumpily. It was annoying, no . . . downright aggravating to have to wake up so early to meet with someone you did not wish to spend a single moment with. Yet she had to.

Maia retired early that night. The next morning, the skies had started to show a hint of pink when she walked to the rose garden with Rayan. Ruche, who was waiting at the gates, led her in.

"I don't know what he wants, Maia," he said in a low voice as he walked her in. "Just keep up a conversation."

"Can I ask him about the attack on Xif?"

Ruche let out a long sigh and Maia braced herself for a refusal, but surprisingly, he nodded. Aekken and four guards shimmered into view soon after.

"Nasfarii of Tansi, it is delightful to see you again," Aekken said, lowering his head a little, and Maia returned the gesture. "I hope I am not troubling you with my sudden visit, Nasfarii."

"Not at all," Maia lied and smiled. "It's a pleasure."

Red cape swishing, Aekken paced about for a few moments before he spoke. "I realized that ours was not a pleasant introduction. We met under such strained circumstances. We only spoke about our nations and barely talked about ourselves. In a way, we never really got acquainted with each other."

The last thing Maia wanted was to get acquainted with *him*. But Aekken seemed determined. He went on and on with stories of Ragamallor, the capital city of the R'armimon Empire where he was born. He spoke of his time growing up as the Crown Prince, his dreams of someday inheriting the throne and becoming the emperor after his father. By the time he finished, the skies had lightened considerably.

"Ragamallor is an extraordinary place, Nasfarii. I wish I could take you there someday," he said wistfully, as he put up a projection of various images from the city. Although the visuals were stunning, and the city larger than any place she had seen in her life, Maia could summon no interest in Ragamallor. She watched the projections and praised them as was expected, wishing only for the display to end quickly. She was relieved when Aekken put away the tiny projector. "I have spoken much and not given you a chance to speak at all. My deepest apologies, Nasfarii."

Maia had been itching to ask him one question, and she jumped at the chance. "May I ask you something, Crown Prince Aekken?"

"Of course, Nasfarii. You need not ask my permission."

"You promised me peace for the next six months," she said, keeping her gaze locked with his. Aekken's face grew stiffer with every word she uttered. "Yet you attacked Xif. I had hoped—"

Aekken did not let her finish. "That was a mistake, Nasfarii. One of my commanders got the wrong idea and he thought he could impress me with his bravado. He has been dealt with and I assure you this will never happen again."

All the time Aekken spoke, Maia kept looking at his face for cues. She knew he was lying. There was no way this man would allow a commander to carry out an attack that large without knowing about it himself. But not a single muscle on Aekken's face twitched and there was not a trace of emotion in those flat eyes of his. This man, she realized, was a liar through and through.

"Thank you, Crown Prince Aekken."

"I hope you can keep your faith in my promise, Nasfarii."

Maia had no faith whatsoever. But she could not say that to his face, so she smiled and lied. "Certainly."

"I call you Nasfarii, but it sounds very strange," Aekken said suddenly.

That was a weird statement, and also unexpected. Maia did not care what he called her, but Aekken seemed to be fixated on the matter even after she reassured him.

"Will you allow me the use of a term of endearment, Nasfarii?"

Term of endearment? What for? Maia shot Ruche a panicked look, but the seer seemed to have found something interesting in the tree branches above them.

"I'm perfectly fine with Nasfarii," Maia blurted in desperation.

"No, I insist. These walls of formality do us no favors." Aekken either did not see her open and obvious discomfort, or ignored it completely. "From here on, you are my starlight."

Maia cringed, and she was sure her dismay and horror were plain on her face.

"Do you approve, my starlight?"

She did not. But what could she tell him when he refused to listen?

A loud crackling noise in the shrubbery brought an abrupt but much-wished-for end to the painful interaction. Aekken's guards sprang into action and Maia was struck speechless when Ren and Karhann ambled out from behind the bowers, apparently oblivious to the commotion they had caused. What the two boys were doing in the rose garden at this hour was beyond Maia's understanding, and she had no time to think about it.

"Ren! Karhann!" Maia exclaimed, realizing Aekken's guards had rushed toward them, weapons drawn. "They're friends, Prince Aekken. Not threats. Please call your guards back."

It was far too late to call them back, and Aekken did not even try. Eyes narrowed to slits, his face hard as a rock, the prince stared coldly as his Faceless grabbed both boys, twisted their arms behind them, and held swords against their throats.

"No, stop," Maia shouted, forgetting Ruche's advice to keep her emotions in check. "Please, don't hurt them."

Moments of stunned silence trickled by before Ren croaked. "Hello there, your Highness. We didn't mean to intrude."

"Please, Prince Aekken," Maia pleaded. "They don't mean any harm. Please let them go."

Maia held her breath until the rigid lines on Aekken's face relaxed a little. Then he nodded at his guards. As soon as the guards removed their swords from the boys' throats, Karhann, most sensibly, slunk away toward the entrance. Ren, however, bounded up to the prince, arms outstretched, ignoring the menacing poses of the guards.

"I have heard so much about you, your Highness." Ren bowed so low that Maia thought he would topple over. "I am so fortunate to make your acquaintance." He fell to his knees in front of Aekken and bowed once again. "My eternal respects, Crown Prince of the Empire R'armimon."

"Ren!" Ruche roared. Maia had been too busy worrying about the guards and Ren's crazy antics to pay attention to Ruche, and only now she noticed the scowl that made his face look like a desiccated plum. "This is no time to—"

Ren, however, cut him off. "Seer Ruche, you're interrupting my homage to Crown Prince Aekken."

Ruche's face flamed and Maia's mouth fell open. Aekken's eyes narrowed, however, and an unexpected smile curled his lips.

"Rise," he said to Ren, waving his hand with regal flamboyance. "What is it you want?"

"He wants to leave now," Ruche said, striding up to Ren and glaring. "Now, Ren."

Ren did not seem to hear Ruche at all. He scrambled to his feet and bowed to Aekken again, just as low as the last time. Then in typical Ren fashion, he shook his head casually at the seer. "Can you not be so overbearing all the time?"

Maia held her breath, expecting the guards to pounce on Ren and shove him out of the garden. She could not believe it when the smile on Aekken's face grew.

"That is our seer's special charm, young man. So you are my starlight's friend?"

"Yes, your Highness. Humble fan here is Ren. I'm a great admirer of your perseverance and ambition. I hear it's a long way from the Empire to here."

Aekken chuckled a little. "Yes, a long way indeed."

"Well, Ren is at your service." He bowed once again. "Anything you need to make your life a little more tolerable in this arduous venture of yours, I can make it happen. I have a lot to offer, your

CHAPTER TWENTY-ONE

Highness."

Aekken crossed his arms and looked curiously at Ren. "Why would you do that?"

Ren did not even blink. "Because you have given my friend the respect she rightfully deserves. I wish people around here did half as much. I'm grateful to you for that. And also because I'm curious about your amazing technology. I mean . . . I'm stunned by this teleportation magic I hear about. It is—"

"Ren"—Maia held her breath as Aekken cut him off—"you interest me. The next time I am here to meet with my starlight, I would like to speak with you. Perhaps you *can* make my life a little more tolerable."

Before Maia could even fathom what had just happened, Ren had bowed three more times and expressed eternal gratitude far too many times to count. Maia did not understand why Aekken suddenly seemed much more interested in Ren than in her. Although she had no complaints about being relieved of the prince's attention, she also did not like the odd gleam in Aekken's eyes as he observed Ren. The prince and his entourage promptly took their leave, promising another meeting soon.

"What in the stars are you up to?" Ruche snarled at Ren the moment the prince shimmered away.

"Making new friends," Ren said with a shrug. "Anything wrong with that?"

"That man is not your friend," Ruche said. "He is dangerous. Not to be trifled with."

Ren shrugged again. "You worry too much, Seer. You need a vacation or something."

Ruche opened his mouth to speak, then closed it. He drew a deep breath and nodded at Maia. "I will see you soon, Maia." With that, he left.

Maia cornered Ren as soon as Ruche disappeared into the far end of the rose garden. "Ren, what are you doing? Where did you come from? Were you spying on us?"

"We were just walking back from Frauz Point when we happened to hear some interesting conversation and—"

"And you decided to eavesdrop," Maia completed the sentence for him. "But Ren . . . Ruche is right. Aekken is not a joke. Besides, have you forgotten he has a vendetta against Xifarians?"

Ren flung an arm around her shoulders and leaned his head on hers. "Don't worry, Maia. I'll be fine. As long as I'm of use to him, he won't hurt me. And I think . . . I think I've caught his interest."

"But why? Why do you need him to be interested in you?"

"I need to keep an eye on this prince character, that's all."

"Why, Ren?"

"Ah, curiosity," Ren said before arching an eyebrow at her. "You're his starlight now, huh?"

Maia winced. "Please, Ren. I have to put up with these stupid conversations so we get a few months of peace, so we can get more people to safety. I couldn't care less about what he calls me. And I could certainly do without your teasing."

"Sorry. Didn't mean to upset you." Ren flashed a regretful smile. "Anyway, I have a training session with Miir now. Want to come?"

"Training? Now? Isn't it too early?"

"He leaves for Zagran today and since it's an off day for us, I thought I'd sneak in some time with him. I'm really liking the TEK sensing exercises, honestly."

"Well, I don't have much to do, so . . ."

Maia found herself accompanying Ren down to Walenveil, quite happily. Miir was waiting for Ren in the clearing behind his house, at the large ring they had marked a few weeks ago that had been serving as their sparring grounds. The training started almost as soon as they arrived. As Maia watched the duo spar, she quickly realized Ren had made quite a bit of progress in sensing TEK waves. Even though he was a Xifarian, and although he was fascinated with TEK, Ren did not possess the ability to see TEK waves. Now, he fended off quite a few formations with his sword, some of them as complex as a triple helix. When the session was over, Maia rushed to Ren's side, applauding loudly.

"You were awesome, Ren," she said. "You managed so well without seeing. I can't believe it."

Ren flushed a little. "Well, Miir taught me to sense the dips in the surrounding air. It takes a lot of concentration, though, and I don't think I'd be any good if this were real combat."

"You will get there," Miir said. "If you keep practicing, it will be a habit soon, just like your reflexes in regular sparring. And you will be able to sense the changes even in real combat. So practice. Ask Karhann to help."

"I agree, Ren," Maia joined in. "You're so good already. To be honest, I couldn't tackle half of those formations even though I can see them."

Miir frowned. "And why do you sound so proud about that?"

Maia blinked in surprise. How did she become the point of the conversation?

"Umm . . . p-proud?" she stuttered. "I'm not. I'm just—"

Miir's frown did not ease in the slightest at her feeble attempt to explain. "Maybe not proud, but you feel no shame at your incompetence. That is most painful to hear." He nodded at the practice ground they had just left. "Get in there. We need to have a look at your swordplay."

"What? It's not my turn today. I'm not—"

"Come on. I have to leave soon, there is no time for debate," he said, his sword already unsheathed as he strode back to the center of the ring. Maia had to draw Bellator and follow. As she cast a worried look at Miir's sword, Fury, which almost literally turned into fire in his hands, Miir's eyebrows shot up. "What is it?"

She could not say that seeing him with that sword in his hand brought back too many harsh memories and unnerved her. She simply shook her head and assumed her stance. Maia expected Miir to spring to the attack immediately like he always did. She was surprised when he did not, and instead gave her an understanding smile.

"Practicing with your powers is good, but during the challenges, you are only allowed to use your sword. But the Initiative aside, no one will ask you for permission before they attack you. They will not ask you what sort of weapon you prefer, either. You have to fight with what you have."

He knew. He must have noticed her discomfort. Ever since Nafi set up the sparring sessions, Maia had quite diligently avoided this scenario. Usually, she spent every turn she got with him practicing countering TEK with the light. This was the first time she would actually cross swords with him. He had surely noted that avoidance as well. Miir peered at her face.

"You know what really matters?" he asked, but did not wait for her to answer. "Not the weapon you fight with, but the intent that drives you. You can defeat me. You only have to believe."

If only believing were that easy. It had been a while since the last time they had fought like this, that fateful night on the shores of Lupitiali. Maia forced that memory away and squared her shoulders, gripping Bellator tight.

"Ready when you are," she said.

"Start the timer, Ren."

In the next instant, she was swallowed by the fire of his fearsome swordplay. He was fast, like always. She could barely see him. She only felt the incoming blows, swift and hard. Maia stepped back and sideways, ducked and dodged, over and over again, trying to evade the black blade. It took Maia a while to get used to the dance of Fury around her. It took her a bit longer to fight back, her senses becoming accustomed to Miir's lightning-fast moves. She struck and she parried, and she pushed and she lunged. Sweat coursed down her face, and she panted for breath as she countered every blow fearlessly.

"And time's up," Ren yelled.

Maia fell back and wiped her brow. She was exhausted. Miir's swordplay was relentless. But she could not lie, sparring with him was as oddly satisfying as it was tiring. Maia looked forward to these sessions with him, and even though today started differently and she had to face that sword, it felt good to have made it through. She was glad he forced her into a sword fight. Her fear of it was now distant, almost forgotten. Maia had just pulled herself out of her musings when she noted the curious smile on Miir's face.

"What?" she asked, still trying to catch her breath. "Something wrong?"

"Look where you are," he said, calmly sheathing his sword.

Maia looked around and found the center of the circle right next to them. "Almost where I started?"

Miir nodded.

"That's great, right?" Maia had not forgotten the very first time they sparred at the XDA, where she had found herself with her back to the wall. Miir had, quite unceremoniously, highlighted her utter lack of aggression. This time, though, even with a shaky start, she had stood her ground.

"I would not go as far as 'great'," Miir said, "but you have picked up some aggression. So . . . good."

It was weird how her heart flipped on hearing that, weirder still that she felt happier knowing he had remembered that flaw than at hearing the praise itself. The weirdest part was how long and hard she had to struggle to keep from smiling to herself like a silly ten-year-old.

Maia did not get to spend much time musing. As soon as she had caught her breath and got herself a drink, she and Ren were called up to duel again. Maia protested vehemently, as did Ren, but apart from being called lazy and threatened with ending all training sessions if they did not stop arguing right away, they did not achieve much. This time, Miir used TEK while both Maia and Ren used their swords to counter.

It ended up being an excellent round. A while later, after Miir announced plans of training everyone on the team to sense TEK, Maia trekked back with Ren. She was happy with how much she had learned that day and how much all of them were improving with this training. Better yet, the cringe-worthy morning spent with the Crown Prince was now a distant memory.

CHAPTER TWENTY-TWO

A PROMISE OF HARMONY

About a week after the creepy prince's visit, the gang found themselves trooping down to the newly-built pier on the western shores, escorted by a pair of Black Phantoms. Their destination was Zagran, and everyone was looking forward to watching a propitious event in the history of Tansi—the signing of a treaty between the three nations. The Trinational Pact, as it was called, was to be completed in Zagran, and Hans had managed to get viewing passes for the gang. Kusha, as part of the Solianese delegation, had already left the day before.

"Hadeeyah is going to kill us for this," Ren said, as they made their way from Walenveil to the edge of the forest. "Kusha had to leave early, and now we will be gone for two days."

"So?" Nafi said.

Ren exhaled loudly. "I'm afraid of annoying that girl. She is . . . scary."

Hadeeyah was indeed the strictest mentor they had ever had. She kept tabs on their day-to-day progress, chided them profusely if they were late with their tasks, and even assigned work lists for the off days.

"Why are you so afraid of her?" Nafi asked. "She's just a little strung up, that's all."

"That's why," Ren replied. "I don't like her bobbing up and down in circles around me telling me everything I need to catch up on. Just thinking of it makes me dizzy."

"She *is* strung up," Dani commented. "I never thought anyone could be tougher than Miir, but . . ."

"Doesn't mean we can't rest a little on off days," Nafi countered. "That's too much. And it's not like we do this every week."

Maia had been walking ahead of the group with Sana, with only half her attention on the conversation, her eyes scanning for the pier that had been built on the western shore to facilitate transport between Zagran and ThulaSu. Now, as they reached the final line of Darkwoods and she saw the gleaming structure and a row of watercraft next to it, she squealed in excitement and rushed forward.

It did not take them long to get on board. Soon they were speeding across the blue depths of the ocean, and then down the enormous funnel that was the gateway to the Jjordic colony. Before long, they were in Zagran, walking up to a beaming Hans who led everyone down to the government sector where they usually stayed.

"The rooms are not as awesome this time," he said, pointing at the puny windows with barely any view of the waters outside. "Many delegates are visiting for the Trinational Pact and the demand for rooms is high. But . . . there is one great thing." Hans unlocked the girls' room, ushered everyone in, then strode up to a door on the left wall and threw it open. "Behold our private dining area."

The dining room, with a long table in the middle and benches along the sides, was not huge or spectacular, but it was cozy and brought an instant smile to Maia's face. Hans was not done yet. He walked to the far end of the dining room and opened another door.

"And on the other side here, we have the boys' room."

"Oh cool! Good job, Hans," Ren said and nudged Sana's arm.

"Hey, Angel, we can hang out all night if we want."

Hans seemed to be at a loss for words at Ren's comment, but Rayan's staff was on Ren's back in an instant. "This is for dining, not for hanging out all night. Go to your room."

"All right, then. Rayan and I will go get food for all of us," Hans announced.

"Behave yourselves until we get back," Rayan added in a stern voice.

There was not enough time to freshen up, let alone *misbehave*, before Hans and Rayan returned with bags of food. Soon they were settled around the dining table, devouring a lovely platter of stuffed rolls and skewered fruit bits. They talked about the progress of the shield, the upcoming pact, and the status of relations between the nations. Hans sounded quite elated about the state of affairs, Maia noted, her own heart joyful at seeing his cheer.

"Isn't Miir here in Zagran?" Nafi asked when they were halfway through the meal. As soon as Hans nodded, Nafi asked more. "Isn't he coming with us?

"Yes, he is. He should have been here by now. Said he'd join us for lunch."

Miir did not show up until a while later. By the time he joined them, everyone else had almost finished with lunch, and conversation had moved to the big event. Hans talked about the special seating section he had reserved for them.

"The council starts in the evening, so you'll have some free time during the day," Hans said. "Any plans?"

Ren stretched and yawned. "I'm just going to rest."

"No. All of you go out," Rayan said sternly. She looked around the table. "No hanging out here and no excuses."

"Don't worry, Rayan," Dani said. "I will take everyone for a walk, have some pops and stuff. Ren will come and he'll like it. Right, Ren?"

Ren rolled his eyes and put on a bored expression, but the resolve on Dani's face did not waver.

"You will have to excuse me, Dani," Miir said. "I need to visit

Master Kehorkjin at the hospital. They said he can have visitors now. I have the rest of the day off, so it works out."

"Oh yes, I got a note too," Dani said, smiling giddily. "I'm so relieved. Please tell him I'll say hello over the viewing channel."

"See you later at the council then, Miir?" Hans asked.

"Yes."

The time passed pleasantly. Dani described the various pop-shops in the area and their specialties. Everyone enthusiastically voted for their favorites while Ren's yawns kept getting bigger and bigger. A winner was picked and the group hurried to clear the table so they could go on their excursion. Maia walked up to Miir before they left to get ready.

"Happy to hear Master Kehorkjin is better now," she said.

"So am I. When I visited two days ago, they did not allow me inside. Since they called me back now, I am sure he is more stable. Perhaps he will be able to speak."

Maia wished she could see the master too, but promptly banished the thought from her mind. Given his delicate condition, it was not sensible for too many people to visit. Miir was the one who really needed to see him. Besides, they needed privacy.

"Please say hello to him for me," Maia said, making a mental note to ask Dani if she could join her on the viewing channel. "And tell him we miss him at the Initiative."

"Would you like to visit?" he asked just as she was about to walk away.

The question was unexpected and Maia fumbled with the answer. "Um . . . I wouldn't want to intrude. You need your time with him. Besides, he's too sick to—"

Miir picked up on her confusion and chuckled. "Just asking what *you* want."

Maia did not expect him to keep asking, so for a moment or two, she could not answer even though the answer was clear in her mind. It was more complicated than a simple wish, wasn't it?

"I can't just . . ." Maia stopped and rearranged her thoughts. He had asked twice already and he deserved a clear answer, whatever it was. "Yes, I do."

"Finally. Was it that difficult?"

"Well, maybe not. But you don't understand. I—"

"I understand. You think it will be an intrusion, but I know it will not. I am sure Master Kehorkjin will be happy to see you."

"And you?"

He chuckled before replying. "Why would I even ask if I did not want you there?"

Maia felt warmth rush up to the tip of her ears. Why, indeed? *Leave it to me to ask the silliest question,* Maia thought. It was a relief that Miir turned away to look at the table where Rayan and Hans were still talking. "I guess you need to get permission from Rayan first. Not sure I can help you with that."

As it turned out, Rayan was not an issue at all. She did not even let Maia finish before saying, "Yes, go."

They all headed off in different directions. The bigger group led by Dani left first. Hans wanted to show Rayan his first school in Zagran, so they went another way. Maia soon found herself walking into the HCH with Miir. The hospital looked just as impressive as the last time she had seen it, and Maia was relieved to find that Master Kehorkjin was in a section less grim than where Mahswa Tabrin had been.

The master was far from well, however. Tubes and monitoring wires still snaked into his body from all directions, and he looked frail and withered, but he opened his eyes and smiled as soon as they walked in. "Ah, so good to see you both. Tell me, how are things?"

They drew up chairs next to his bedside and Miir explained the upcoming ratification council for the Trinational Pact.

"That's good progress. Wish I could see it," Kehorkjin said.

"I am sorry—" Miir had barely started but the master cut him off.

"You have no reason to be sorry," Kehorkjin said forcefully. He stopped briefly to catch his breath. "Miir, I don't know what it is, but Remii wants something from you."

CHAPTER TWENTY-TWO

"Wants to arrest me for a crime I did not commit?"

"No, it's not that. Remii wouldn't say, but . . ." he stopped and took a long breath. "He said he needs to find you. And kept muttering . . . 'why didn't I think of it before? He has had it all along'."

Miir looked confused. "Had it all along?"

"Yes."

"But I have had many things . . . what does he mean?"

"I don't know. But he sounded desperate to find you. When I said I didn't know where you were, he was angry. Or should I say enraged?"

"When is he not?"

Master Kehorkjin chuckled. "Maybe so, but be careful, please." He closed his eyes and rested a little. "You too, Maia. Don't forget Chairman Phocluus. He does not give up so easily."

"I will be careful, Master Kehorkjin," Maia said. "I promise."

"Good." He stopped and breathed for a while. The effort of talking seemed to have exhausted him. "Thank you for coming to my aid the other day. And Dani, please thank her. I wouldn't have survived if she hadn't helped."

"I will. She said she will speak to you soon. She has been very happy that she could help."

"Tell her she should be proud of her abilities," the master said. "Now, Maia, tell me how things are going with the Initiative," Master Kehorkjin said.

Other than Principal Pomewege taking over in Kehorkjin's stead, not much had happened since the incident. Maia told him all about their plans for the various tasks. The master's countenance did not give much indication of whether they were on the right track, but he seemed happy to listen to her chatter. Presently an attendant came over and declared that it was time for the patient to rest.

They said goodbyes and left his room. Miir had been exceedingly quiet for a while. He did not seem to be in a mood to talk, his forceful strides eager to maintain some distance between them. Maia let him be for a while, but once they left the hospital, she was anxious to break the silence. "The council will have started by now, don't you think?"

"Yes, it will," Miir said curtly. "We have to get to Elevator Bank C."

He did not say a word after that, nor glance in her direction as they walked along the corridor toward the elevator bank C. Under the cap with a long visor he had put on as soon as they walked out of the hospital, his face was all hard lines, his gaze distant. She did not miss how he found the corner farthest from her to stand in the elevator. He had withdrawn into his shell, and although Maia wished to break the quiet, she could not find anything to say.

The silence around them grew suffocating as the elevator zoomed up toward their destination. Maia was not one who talked all the time, but being so suddenly shut out left her lost. Miir seemed so unreachable, and she so hopelessly unequipped. It was as if she had been exiled, with every access to the outer world snatched from her. She could barely look at his grim face. Memories, of all the times they had fought each other to the bitter end, of every unscalable wall of misunderstanding, flooded her mind.

Close to a hundred floors had gone past when Maia clenched her fists. She could not bear the quiet anymore.

"Do you *have* to be so silent?" Maia asked. "If something is bothering you so much, you could tell me about it." Maia's hopes surged a little when Miir looked up at her. But he went back to staring at the corner without another glance at her face. Maia wrapped her arms around herself. Words, a confession she did not think would ever escape her, left her mouth in a whisper. "You scare me when you're like this."

Miir looked up at her with a start. He strode up to her in the next moment and peered at her downcast face.

"I am sorry." Maia could hear the regret and anguish in his voice but she still could not look up at him as he sighed. "I am so sorry. I . . . I have this habit of closing myself up when I am upset. I try not to, but I just get sucked in before I know it."

The elevator slowed and the door opened with a low hum.

"It's all right." Maia hastened out, keen to leave the confines of the elevator. The directions took them along a long empty corridor, and this time Maia led the way, finding herself eager to stay ahead of Miir. Sadness kept smothering her thoughts.

"Now you are silent," Miir said after they had walked a few paces.

"If you can, why can't I?"

"Because it is not something worth emulating," he said. "But of course, you could. You could never speak with me if you choose not to."

Maia kept walking, the sad lump inside her shrinking rapidly with each step. "I don't like fighting with you," she said, wincing as yet another unplanned confession slipped out.

"Neither do I."

Maia stopped and turned around to face him. "Can I help with whatever's making you sad?" she asked with an earnest desire to help. "It's fine if you can't tell me. I can talk about our crazy new mentor and that will cheer you up."

"Hadeeyah? So you hate her more than you hated me?"

"I don't hate her." Maia thought a little and added, "And no, she doesn't compare to you."

"Dooon't compare to me?" Miir's eyes widened. "Is that a good thing? Do I even want to know?"

Maia shrugged and giggled. "Nafi calls Hadeeyah a hyperactive bunny, and at our first meeting she shows up with—"

"I do not need to hear about bunny girl," Miir said. "I will tell you what made me upset. It was seeing Master Kehorkjin. He is so badly injured, and I kept thinking, this would not have happened if not for me."

Maia crossed her arms and frowned at him. "So that's it? You're blaming yourself for what those despicable thugs did to him?" She sighed on seeing his dimmed eyes. "Oh, great! Here I am hanging on to the wisdom of not being responsible for anything other than my own actions, while the one who preached it to me has conveniently forgotten all about it. What do you think I should do now? Discard the advice or heckle the advisor?"

Miir pursed his lips and stared for a moment before breaking into a chuckle. "All right, you have made your point," he said. "You do not need to do either. I will remember."

"All right, then." With a smile on her face, Maia resumed walking. "Now back to bunny girl."

"What? I still have to hear about her?"

"Why not? She's funny."

There was no more silence for the rest of the way to the council room. One of the guards at the entrance checked their passes and escorted them inside, then up to their seating section.

"There you are," Hans said as soon as they arrived. "I was getting a bit worried."

Sana grabbed Maia's arm and pulled her aside. "You took your time." She leaned closer to whisper, "I almost thought you had eloped with your Miir."

Maia glowered. "Sana, enough already."

Nafi turned back with a frown and a finger on her lips. "Shhhh . . . It's about to begin. Be quiet now."

Maia focused her attention on the floor of the council. This room, like the first one they had seen such a council take place in years ago, had a sunken oval center. But it was a much smaller space, and instead of the hundreds of chairs that fit into the other one, there were only about fifteen. They were arranged into three clearly marked sections — occupied by representatives from the Solianese, the Jjord, and the Xifarians.

Maia recognized Sahiiraan Tsininio, Sahiiraan Goren, and Kusha from the Solianese. There were two others that Nafi informed her were representatives from some other Houses. There was also a trio of parliamentarians.

"Sahiiraan Goren will be sealing the pact on the Solianese side. He's the leader of the Solianese delegation," Nafi said. "Our Kusha looks dapper," she added, nudging Dani.

Premier Oliena and CA Abebe sat in the Jjord section, along with some other people Maia did not recognize. Finally, on the Xifarian side, there was Rahina Quemiila, her advisor Lowanabe and Statesman Taillefei, along with some others Maia did not know. It was quite frustrating to see that Taillefei, one of the people Hiso had identified as being part of the plot to take over the Nouvus, was not only unpunished but given a place of importance. But then, life was unfair that way, so Maia had learned over the years. With a sigh, she looked away from Taillefei to Lowanabe, whose sharp gaze and dignified air drew instant attention. Had Maia not heard about him from Ren, she could never have guessed this man was a Gnelexian. She stole a quick look at Ren and was relieved to find him unbothered by his stepfather's presence.

The proceedings soon started. It was nothing like the tumultuous session of the previous council Maia had witnessed in Zagran. A woman in the white uniform of the Jjord walked in with a large scroll and began to read the various agreements.

There were many things described in it, but a few — the sharing of Calbion by the Xifarians to reinforce the shelters, the continuing collaboration between the nations to complete and launch the shield of Orekemino, and finally the joint enterprise to revive the Nouvus project — stood out to Maia.

"So they will go back to rebuilding the Nouvus," Nafi said. "Hey, Miir! Are the Phantoms going back too?"

"No, we are not. Walenveil refuses to take any part in it."

It made sense that the coalition was restarting work on the Nouvus. It was a valuable tool to ensure the survival of some people, and no matter what had happened before, it was not wise to simply discard that option. However, Maia understood why Walenveil declined to participate, and she wholeheartedly supported their stand.

In the central oval, the scroll bearer had finished reading through every detail. She passed the scroll around, starting with the Solianese, and representatives of each of the nations took turns placing their seals on it. Once everyone had finished, the woman looked through it and held it up for the audience to see.

"The Trinational Pact is now ratified," the scroll bearer announced.

The room erupted in applause and Maia, along with her friends, was on her feet, cheering. Soon the council was dissolved and the gang trooped back to their rooms, their strides happy, their voices ringing with joy.

The excitement continued during dinner, with debates over various new possibilities the coalition could bring. Maia was entrenched in thought through it all. Even after almost everyone had left the table, she sat there fiddling with the last pieces of crumb cake on her plate. She hardly noticed when Miir walked up.

"Hey! You have been awfully silent," he said, sitting down on the bench next to her. "Something wrong?"

"Oh no! Nothing's wrong, just been thinking. We could have done this years ago and helped each other. But no, it took all this to get everyone together."

"Getting over age-old divisions is not that easy."

Maia sighed. "Yes, I should know that. I'm kind of silly wishing for instant friendships when I couldn't reach out across divisions myself. No one can. Well, except Dani."

She looked around for her friend, remembering how Dani had not waited a moment to walk up to Kusha and her in that pod to Arpasgula. It must have taken so much love in her heart and openness in her mind to want a pair of bumbling Solianese kids as friends. Maia's eyes welled with tears of gratitude. She drew a breath and blinked away the happy tears before smiling brightly at Miir.

"But I'm happy we have come this far. I really am. I hope we stay this way forever."

CHAPTER TWENTY-THREE

BEST FRIENDS FOREVER

The gang woke up early the next morning. Even Sana was up without complaints and sped through breakfast, thanks to the promise of a big surprise Hans had made the previous night. Their steps were sprightly and everyone's eyes sparkled with excitement as they trooped into a special shuttle Hans had hired.

"Where are you taking us?" Nafi was the first to blurt out as the shuttle made its way slowly across Zagran.

"Patience, Nafi," was all Hans would say.

However, as soon as the shuttle took a particular turn toward the right, Dani jumped.

"Hans, are we going to Discovery Cove?" she shrieked. She barely waited for Hans's shocked face to reveal her guess was correct before sharing every detail of their destination. "Oh, it's a wonderful place. An amusement park like no other. They have habitats of various marine creatures, lots of games, and lots of activities of all kinds. We'll have so much fun."

"I hope they have good food," Nafi said as soon as Dani paused.

"All right. Since the secret's out," Hans said, giving Dani a telling look that did not seem to bother his sister in the least, "I got really lucky to get tickets for all of us to Discovery Cove. They keep the visitor count strictly limited, and given the little time I had — "

"You're very influential, Hans," Sana observed.

Hans flushed a little and shook his head. "I wouldn't say that. Kindra from the Premier's Office has been extremely helpful. Anyway, I need you all to be on your best behavior. Understood?"

"Why are you looking at me like that?" Nafi protested as soon as Hans paused. "I have never misbehaved in public."

Hans sighed. "Good, then. Let's keep it that way."

"Not fair. I don't like this bias," Nafi continued to grumble. However, her anger was short-lived since the shuttle soon arrived at their destination.

The supposed entrance of Discovery Cove did not look like an entrance at all. A pair of nondescript ticketing buildings flanked an equally nondescript gate. Maia had expected large crowds, but other than a few employees, the place was empty. The only impressive part was the grandiose name of the park — Discovery Cove: Aquatic Conservancy, Animal Sanctuary, and Activity Center. Hans led the gang to one of the buildings where everyone received an arm tag, five tokens each to cover food and other purchases, and waterproof clothes to change into. Soon they were all dressed and ready to enter.

"Let's go," Dani chirped. Just a few paces from the booths and a few turns later, the path ended at a giant waterfall over which was a massive stone arch with the name *Discovery Cove*.

"No more than two at a time," Hans reminded them.

"Two at a time? Why's that?" Maia asked.

"Come on, Maia," Dani said and tugged her by the arm. "Through the waterfall, we go."

"Waterfal — " Maia's question remained unspoken. She was busy catching her breath instead as first, the waterfall soaked her, and then the ground swallowed her. They fell a long way — Dani shrieking in delight and Maia screaming from the shock — and landed on something soft that turned out to be a raft. It sped forward with them, spinning like a top through a bright blue cave and then through another wall of water. Maia blinked and then blinked again in surprise. They had emerged on a lake surrounded by a massive complex of colorful buildings.

"We've arrived," Dani declared. "You had fun getting in, right?"

"Yes, I kind of did," Maia said, grinning. Now that they were on a placid lake floating around peacefully, and her heart had a chance to calm down, the entry did seem fun.

"You know . . . when I was little, I always wanted to visit here. All my friends were always talking about it, so . . ." Dani let out a small sigh. "But we weren't allowed much money and we never had enough for tickets to come here. So the day Hans earned his first pay, he bought us tickets to Discovery Cove. The fun we had that day!" She linked her arm through Maia's and squeezed it. "And we'll have even more fun today."

It did not take long to start having fun. Soon they were racing Aqumobs; Ren won every race, much to Nafi's annoyance. There were various other things to look at and do, but Maia's favorite was the Slingshot. She loved streaking through the water, catapulted out at a tremendous speed from the slingshot machine. She could have spent all day at that attraction, but Dani had other ideas.

"Hans, Hans!" Dani rushed up to her brother, her eyes sparkling. "We should have a rollerbubble smackdown. There are so many of us, it'll be perfect."

"All right," Hans replied, grinning. Maia saw a glint in his eyes that she would call evil if she had not known him. "Let's do it."

"What is this smackdown business?" Nafi demanded.

The business was clear when a short walk later, the group stood staring through the glass walls of an enormous pool. Inside, huge transparent balls of various hues floated like massive droplets of water.

"It's simple," Dani said. "We get inside those balls and then we try to get the others."

Nafi wrinkled her nose. "What? I didn't understand a word of that. Explain again, Dani."

"Each of us gets inside a ball. Then we try to push each other out of the way. Whenever anyone bumps against the walls, they're out. The last one remaining becomes the smackdown champ."

"Bump against the wall?" Kusha ran his hands worriedly through his hair. "I don't want to break my head."

Dani laughed. "Don't worry, Kusha. The walls are soft. The bubbles have thick insulation, too. You'll be fine."

"How do the balls move?" Ren asked.

"You have to move inside to make the bubble move. Use your weight to change direction."

"That sounds like too much trouble," Sana announced. "Not risking chipping a nail. Sorry, I'm sitting this out."

"Come on, Angel," Ren begged. "Maybe you and I can share one."

Rayan doused Ren in an icy glare. "No. That is *not* happening."

"Relax, Rayan," Hans said with a chuckle. "That's against the rules anyway."

Everyone except Sana was soon assigned bubbles of various colors and Maia was happy to get a golden yellow. A brief training session was announced in a smaller pool but Hans gathered everyone before they filed in for training.

"Anyone up for a wager?" he asked, his eyes twinkling.

"Sure," Ren replied in a heartbeat.

"No, Hans," Dani protested. "Not fair."

"Why isn't it fair?" Nafi cocked an eyebrow.

"Hans always wins the smackdown, that's why."

"Oh, I'm in," Ren declared. "I'll smack him down. What's the wager?"

"Not much," Hans said. "The champ gets one token from every player." He looked at Dani and grinned. "That's fair, right?"

Everyone agreed heartily and that was that. As soon as she got inside her bubble, Maia realized it was terribly difficult to simply stay upright in that wobbly sphere. She fell—on her face, on her back, and sideways too—countless times. Moving forward was another challenge. She had no idea how the motion of her feet was converted into motion for the bubble since the direction she went felt completely random. The good part was, apart from Dani and obviously, Hans, no one else seemed to be doing any better.

Sana walked over and leaned close when they were transferring to the real pool for the smackdown. "You still have time to quit, you know."

"Was I *that* pathetic in practice?" Maia asked.

Sana pursed her lips and flicked her eyebrows. "Well . . . you're all equally pathetic, but I care about you the most so I'm trying to save you from embarrassment."

Maia looked around, her gaze coming to rest on Hans's smug face. She could not walk away now and be teased about it forever. Maia squared her shoulders. Since there would be embarrassment either way, she was going to take this head-on. "Nope. I'm doing this."

The moments right after the starting whistle blew for the smackdown were downright chaotic. They rolled and bumped into each other, mostly clueless and without control. Pai was the first to be eliminated, thanks to Nafi who did not seem to intend it. As Maia tried to scramble out of Nafi's path, she discovered a valuable clue— balance came much easier when she did not stand still. So, Maia ran. And her bubble took off, slowly at first, and then zoomed into Nafi's bubble and crashed it against the wall.

This is good, Maia thought. *Maybe I can go faster.*

At the far end of the pool, Hans was causing a ruckus, plowing through whoever was near him. Rayan, Maia noted, was closest to her and also near a wall. That meant she was a good target. Rayan had no idea what hit her. She had been staring at the commotion Hans was creating and her eyes went wide when Maia slammed her straight into the wall.

Content with getting Rayan, Maia grinned. Passing a hand over her brow to wipe off the sweat, she took in the rest of the field. Dani was still in, as was Ren. And of course, there was Hans. With the king of rollerbubble smackdown staring menacingly at them, neither Ren nor Dani was looking at her. That was an opportunity and Maia planned to make full use of it.

She sped forward just as Hans went after Ren, swerving around Dani as she backed up to put some space between herself and the boys. Maia noticed the stunned look on Dani's face as she went careening past and crashed into Hans. Her timing was perfect. Hans had just smashed Ren against the wall, and he did not have time to refocus his attention. Besides, he had probably never expected Maia to bump into him with such ferocity. His stupefied expression as he bounced against the wall was a treat to see, but as much as she enjoyed it, Maia did not linger. She had one last opponent to take care of first.

Dani turned out to be quite a tough adversary. She was as smart as she was skilled. Not once did she take Maia lightly, not once did her gaze slip from Maia's bubble. For every step Maia took forward, Dani went back one calculated step. If Maia moved to one side, Dani moved to another. For a while they kept up the defensive choreography, each mirroring the other's movement. Then Maia decided to make a change. There was no guarantee it would work, particularly since Dani was experienced at this, but she was going to try to take Dani by surprise.

She sped up and went around Dani in a spiral. Faster and faster she went, tightening the circles. Dani tried to get out by ducking under her, but it did not work. Next Dani tried to run out of the whirlpool Maia had created. She was almost successful. But something had come over Maia that day, and she zoomed in and slammed against Dani's bubble like lightning. Dani flipped backward and drifted away some distance. As Maia prepared for the final bump, Dani recovered.

"Oh no, you don't," Maia muttered to herself as Dani sat up.

Teeth gritted, she charged. The golden bubble streaked through the water, leaving a trail of churning foam behind it. With a war cry, Maia barreled into Dani. They crashed into the wall one after another, but Dani was first.

"Yes!" Maia screamed and forgetting where she was, jumped in excitement. And fell face first on the bottom of her bubble. That did not reduce her joy the slightest, the grin on her face wide and unwavering until she came back outside to join the rest of the gang.

"By the stars, Maia," Dani exclaimed. "You were on a rampage."

Nafi stopped massaging her arms and gave Dani a look. "I know, she was out to destroy. Did you see that look she had on her face?" She turned toward Maia next and shook her head. "Now I'm happy that you broke up with Maks. That sweet boy has nothing to counter this evil streak."

"Evil streak?" Maia rolled her eyes. "Come on, Nafi. That's too much drama even for you."

"I have to side with Nafi on this, Maia. You did have a look about you," Sana said. "But, seriously, Nafi. Maia and Maks? I'd fear for that boy's life."

Maia shook her head and sighed. "You two make me sound like a witch or something."

Ren sauntered in, slipped an arm around Maia's shoulders, and pulled her away. "Don't pay any mind to them, Maia. These girls are sore losers."

"Hey! Who are you calling a loser? I wasn't even in the game," Sana protested.

"Even worse," Ren shot back. He bumped fists with Maia as they walked away. "You killed it, girl."

"It was fun."

It was even more fun getting tokens from everyone, and a particularly happy moment when Hans handed over two of his own. "Here, you earned it," he said, patting her head and making Maia beam.

"Time for lunch," Hans said next. "We have two options. One's a pop-shop that Dani loves, the other's my favorite, a CYOM. That stands for Cook Your Own Meal. Obviously, you have to put together your food at the CYOM, but it's fun. I—"

"Pop-shop for me," Sana declared. "Not interested in cooking."

"I'm hungry," Rayan said. "I need food right now."

"What a bunch of lazy spoilsports," Hans said. But if he had hoped his comment would change the girls' minds, he was mistaken. Rayan and Sana took off almost immediately with Dani's directions.

"I'll try the CYOM," Kusha said. All of the boys quickly rallied behind Hans while Maia and Nafi stuck with Dani.

"All right, I'll stop by the pop-shop once we're done," Hans said.

That settled, the girls marched down the main street, stopping briefly to look at various attractions. They were only three storefronts away from Dani's favorite pop-shop when Maia came to a halt, her eyes glued on the display in a toy shop. The shop was like many others in the park, stuffed to the brim with toys of various kinds and with a game in front that one needed to win to get any of those toys. This one had a ring toss, the target being a large hook going in circles on the far wall.

"Come on, Maia," Nafi said crankily. "I'm hungry."

"Wait a moment." Maia drifted toward the shop, her eyes scanning the wall of toys. A face peeked out from the array of cloth animals, one that left her heart pining. It was an ink-blue dolphin with cheeky black eyes, that transported Maia back to a moment years ago when they were assigned aquatic partners during the Jjordic phase. "It looks just like Keiki."

"It does," Dani said.

For a moment or two, memories of the moment she had lost Keiki drowned Maia with sadness. She shuddered as she recalled how the Timiti attacked when they were on the way to the Karnilian Caves. Keiki had tried to dodge the massive whale, but—

"Are you going to try for her?" Dani asked.

"I want to." Keiki would never come back but this would be something to keep her memory alive forever. "Yes, I absolutely will."

"Come on, Dani," Nafi wailed. "I need food."

"Go on," Maia said. "I'll join you in a bit."

Maia strode up to the shop brimming with confidence. But it did not take her long to discover a couple of unhappy truths. The hook moved way faster than it seemed to, and she was quite hopeless at aiming rings onto spinning hooks. One went flying to the side, the second bumped against the wall, and the shop owner had to duck out of the way of the third. Just like that, Maia had exhausted all three of her first set of tries. *It will work better the second time,* she thought. But the second round went just as badly as the first. Maia looked up at Keiki peeking at her, trying to decide whether to try one more time. She knew her aim would not miraculously get better, but that face . . .

She pulled out her tokens and counted them. She had been rich in tokens just a few moments before, thanks to her rollerbubble win, but after her lousy attempts at ring tossing, she was close to being poor again. She had nine tokens left, most of which she'd need to buy herself lunch. But the way the adorable ink-blue dolphin stared back at her with adorable little black eyes . . .

One more time, Maia thought.

The proprietor of the shop smiled at Maia as she held out three tokens. "Again?"

"Yes. The third try is always lucky."

"Well, all the best," he said before handing her the three rings.

Maia grabbed the rings tight and breathed in deep.

"Come on, Maia," she muttered to herself. "You can do it. All you need is one good shot."

Balancing herself on the balls of her feet, her eyes glued on the hook in the middle, Maia threw the first ring. It flew from her hand and . . .

Thwack! Splat!

The ring bumped against the hook and settled on the floor. Maia's spirits dipped. This was not going well at all. Sure enough, the next two tosses ended up the same way, far from the target. Maia sighed. So much for luck on the third try.

"Sorry," the shop owner said. "Want to try again?"

Maia shook her head. "No. I want to, but . . . I can't."

She gave the Keiki toy one final, longing glance before turning away. She almost jumped when she found Miir standing behind her with an amused look on his face.

"The fearsome rollerbubble champion has the lousiest of aims. Who would have thought?"

Maia flushed to the tip of her ears. "Yes, I'm horrible at this. Zero out of *nine* tries. Can you believe it?"

His eyes widened. "Nine tries? What is it you want so badly?"

Maia jerked her thumb backward. "There's an ink-blue dolphin in there. Reminds me of Keiki, the partner I was assigned to during the Jjordic phase. I lost her in the end."

"Oh, I see her," Miir said. He peered curiously at Maia's face. "Why are you looking the other way?"

"Because I don't want to see her anymore. She'll make me want to try again, even when I know it'll be a useless effort. I'll only lose and end up being even sadder. So . . ."

"You think in strange ways," he said, chuckling. "So hey! Would you mind if I try to get her for you?"

Maia spun toward him, her heart jumping in excitement. "You would?" She could barely keep herself from bobbing up and down in joy when he nodded. "You're good at this, right?"

"That we shall soon find out."

Maia pulled out three tokens but Miir shook his head firmly. "I got this."

"But . . . you shouldn't be wasting your tokens on something I want. That's —"

"Something friends do for each other?"

There was nothing Maia could say to that, so she did the next best thing as Miir walked up to the proprietor. Still looking away from the shop, she clasped her hands and prayed.

Thwack!

Holding her breath, Maia spun around. The ring was on the wall, perfectly settled on the hook. Maia's arms shot up in the air, and she twirled round and round, squealing.

"All right. Calm down," Miir said, laughing. "I still have two more tries to go. You might end up with more than one dolphin on your hands." He squinted and sighed. "Or maybe not. The wheel is going faster now."

It did not matter how many more tries he had or how fast the wheel spun. It did not matter if he failed the next time. One win—that was all Maia needed. She had Keiki and that was enough. Eyes closed and grinning from ear to ear, Maia skipped and flitted about a few more times.

Thwack!

Thwack!

Maia opened her eyes and stared incredulously at the three rings, all piled on top of each other. Miir was good . . . no . . . awesome at this after all.

"Three in a row," the proprietor exclaimed. "That's impressive, young man. You qualify for a special prize."

"Thank you, but we do not need a special prize," Miir replied. "We just need that blue dolphin, please."

"Aah, don't worry," the shop owner said. "She'll be happy when she sees what I have."

The man was right. Maia shrieked with joy when he emerged from a room in the back of his shop, carrying an ink-blue dolphin three times bigger than the one on display.

Maia could not remember the last time she had been as happy as that moment when Miir handed her the replica of Keiki. Her arms went around it protectively, the memory of the first time she had dived into the waters with the real Keiki flooding her mind and bringing tears to her eyes.

"I'll always love you, Keiki," she whispered into the soft plushy folds as she clutched it tightly to her chest. Nothing could bring Keiki back again, but this was something that would keep her close forever.

Blinking back her tears, she smiled at Miir and threw an arm around his neck for a quick hug.

"Thank you," she said as she let go. "Have to show this to Dani now. See you later." She ran toward the pop-shop as fast as her legs would carry her, Keiki firmly clutched under her arm.

She found the girls seated around a large table. As soon as Dani saw Maia with Keiki in her arms, she smiled brightly and rushed over. Sana, who had been collecting food for herself, strolled over as well.

"You got Keiki!" Dani squealed just as loudly as Maia had.

"Well, Miir got her for me," Maia said, grinning. "But yes, I have Keiki."

"Keiki's cute, and your Miir is quite capable. Good for you," Sana commented wisely before sauntering away.

Maia was just about to retort when Dani giggled and tugged her on. "Let's get you something to eat. You must be pretty hungry with all the Keiki scoring business."

A timely pang of hunger made its presence known right then and Maia happily tagged along as Sana explained the various foods to her. Soon they joined the rest of the girls, and a good time was spent eating and laughing. Nafi was back to being happy after devouring a huge plate of fried fish rolls on sticks. Not long after, Hans came by.

"We're done with lunch," he said. "And if you girls are finished here, we can check out a few more things."

They trooped out of the pop-shop in a happy mood and ambled lazily from one attraction to another. They tried out a few chutes, from most of which Ren, Nafi, and Pai had to be dragged away kicking and screaming. Maia spent some time in a whirlpool along with Sana while the rest tried swimming along the reef, and they all trekked through a wonderful habitat of gulls. It was almost time to leave when Hans herded the group to a pop-shop near the exit. Although this one was nothing compared to the one they had visited for lunch, the crispy rice puffs were good.

"What is that thing?" Nafi pointed at a large enclosure next to the shop that was surrounded by a ring of heavy canvas panels.

"That's where they house visiting animals from time to time," Hans explained. "They're probably expecting someone new, so they've covered it up while they prepare."

Ren pointed at some employees on a platform inside the barricade. "Wonder what they're doing up there." He walked up to a gap in the barricades and peeked in.

"Looks like they're feeding a . . . squid? Hey, is that—" Ren stopped midway, his face frozen in a look of surprise and wonder.

That was enough to prompt Maia and Dani to walk up beside him. The water in the immense pool beyond was churning, and in the middle was a hurricane of waving tentacles.

"Could that be Chylomyhrra?" Ren whispered.

"It's a milk squid for sure," Dani said.

"Chylomyhrra," Ren yelled. The tentacles froze in midair. Then the dark shape of the enormous milk squid streaked toward them. "It *is* Chylomyhrra," Ren said.

"Ren? Ren, stop!" Dani shouted.

It was far too late to stop Ren. He had pushed aside the barricades and dashed in. He ran toward the platform as if his life depended on it. Maia's heart yearned. Memories—the mad sprint toward the Karnilian Caves, the terrifying attack of the Timiti, the rush of fear and then hope as Chylomyhrra's tentacles wrapped around her, saving her from certain death—drew her in. A determined smile curled Maia's lips as she watched Ren dodge the workers and dive into the pool. She thrust Keiki into Dani's arms and broke into a run herself.

"Maia, what are you doing? No!"

The shocked and screaming workers did not notice Maia until she reached the platform. They turned to stop her but they were too late. One woman rushed at her but it only took a little effort—a sidestep and then ducking past the woman's outstretched arm—and Maia was flying through the air. The cold surface of the water broke below her and a tentacle wrapped around her possessively before she could blink.

She was swishing through the water in the next moment, then over the surface. Holding Maia and Ren like a pair of dolls, Chylomyhrra twirled and spun and sped about gleefully. Ren tried his somersaults and Chylomyhrra followed. She tossed Maia up in the air like a ball and rolled over with them both. It was a blissful interlude, and Maia enjoyed every bit of it, oblivious to the outraged screams and shouts of the workers on the platform and the scandalized looks on the faces of her friends watching from the far edge.

The joy only lasted so long. Soon the overseer arrived with his troops. Maia and Ren were dragged out of the pool, with little time to say a proper goodbye to the milk squid. They were marched to the overseer's office, and Hans and Dani were summoned as well. A lengthy scolding followed—how such behavior was unheard of in the history of the park, how dangerous such antics were for the animals and the visitors, and how this was truly outrageous coming from a group led by someone with Hans's credentials.

After what seemed like forever, the overseer let them out of his office. But his assistants were lying in wait outside and they pounced as soon as the group emerged. They dismissed Maia and Ren, and continued to lecture Hans and Dani about appropriate behavior.

As brother and sister listened to the assistants' tirades with their heads hung low, the other girls—mostly Nafi—cornered Ren and showered him with rebukes. Seeing no one was paying attention to her, Maia slunk away to a nearby bench. Burying her face in Keiki's soft belly, she let her thoughts float away.

What a day it has been! What a wonderful, happy day!

Maia was giggling to herself when she heard footsteps. Kusha, Pai, and Miir walked over, their faces somber. Kusha plunked himself on the bench next to her and held out a bowl of cheese-dipped rice fritters.

"Nafi and gang let you escape?" he asked, frowning as he crunched.

Maia grabbed a fritter and shrugged. "They're more interested in Ren, so . . ."

"Seriously, Maia. You could've hurt yourselves. You had no breathing apparatus on and—"

"But Kusha, it was Chylomyhrra. She knew what we had. She

always knows," Maia chirped gaily. "She was so fast. It was just like the times we practiced at the reef. Remember how—"

"Could you consider putting on a serious face for a little bit?" Miir interrupted. "For Hans's sake? Poor guy is getting raked over the coals out there."

"Nothing Hans can't handle," Maia said.

"But do you *have* to look so happy?"

The shield of happiness around her was so impenetrable that the answer bubbled out without hesitation.

"But I am," Maia said without a shred of regret. "I *am* happy."

Miir sat down on her other side and sighed. "Sometimes you just leave me speechless."

Soon they all boarded the shuttle for the trip back. Hans did not speak or look at anyone. No one else spoke either. The quiet got unbearable after a while. Since no one seemed to be interested in breaking the silence, Maia decided to give it a try.

"Hans, I'm sorry you got yelled at," she said. "Didn't mean for that to happen."

Hans raised an eyebrow. "So you're sorry that I got yelled at but not sorry you did what you did?"

Ren, who had been sprawled on the seat across from Maia, sat up. "Come on, Hans. It was my girl Chylomyhrra. I couldn't just leave without saying hello to her. And can you blame Maia for her excitement? I mean, it's Chylomyhrra. Maia wouldn't have survived that Timiti if it weren't for her."

A resigned look came over Hans's face and his frown mostly disappeared.

Nafi cleared her throat loudly. "For the record, let it be noted that Nafi wasn't the one who misbehaved in public. Nafi is sweet and nice and *mostly* law-abiding. And on the rare occasion that she does make a mistake, she's apologetic, unlike some—"

Hans broke into chuckles. "All right, Nafi. Let's leave it at you're nice and sweet." He sighed and looked from Maia to Ren. "Just so you know, you two are banned from Discovery Cove for life."

"Aah . . . it's fine," Maia said. "I've had the best day of my life. Couldn't ask for more. I'm just relieved no one else was penalized on our account."

Ren jumped to Maia's side, slipped an arm around her shoulders, and leaned his head on hers. "It was totally worth it, right?"

A lot of head-shaking and frustrated sighs followed. Rayan even turned to glare at the duo.

"You know, Hans. Not that I approve of these shenanigans, but it's not all bad," Sana said.

"All right. Let's hear your wisdom too," Hans said.

"Well, this is practice for when you have a family of your own. Your kids couldn't possibly be any worse than this lot. So . . ."

The shuttle erupted in a wave of giggles and laughter. Soon they were chatting happily once again, all the way to the living quarters.

Much later that night, Maia walked into the dining room for a glass of water and found Miir staring out of the small porthole-sized window. He smiled a little as she entered, but Maia could tell his mind was far away.

Glass in hand, she walked over to his side and peeked out the window. The waters were dim and dark outside and other than some distant city lights, nothing could be seen.

"What are you looking at?" she asked curiously.

"Nothing really," he replied. He turned abruptly to face her and blurted, "I am sorry. I did not know how you lost Keiki or how Chylomyhrra saved you. You had every reason to be excited and . . . to be happy without care. I should not have said—"

"That's all right. Really." Maia did not let him finish. "I didn't think anything of it. I had the best time of my life today, and much of it was because of you. I'll never forget how you got me Keiki. So, thank you."

"Maia!" Sana's voice came through the half-open door to the girls' room. "What's taking you so long?"

Maia sighed. "I have to go or I'll get in trouble. But, please, don't worry about it."

She did not know if her words helped him, but she sincerely hoped they did. She had not exaggerated one bit. This day would forever be a treasured memory, in no small part due to Miir.

Chapter Twenty-Four

Leave No One

After the uplifting visit to Zagran, the gang had to hunker down and get to work on the Initiative. Amid the drudgery, two things brought them joy and hope. First, Nafi's weapon modification request came through. Miir found some information on the latsore-kaha and the Palonkian techniques that went with it. He put together an exercise regimen, and Nafi worked hard on it.

Then, when the team had almost given up, the request to split their team for the Challowist task was approved as well. Even though they were still at a disadvantage, Core 21 was hopeful. This meant there was a chance, however slight, to finish the task without ending up in last place. Even Hadeeyah, who had been completely devastated by the Challowist situation, grinned at the news.

"That doesn't mean you slack off," she warned them, wagging a finger severely. "It's looking better, but still no guarantee of anything. So work on your other tasks. You've been taking too much time off lately. Now focus. There's no time to lose."

With the second and final visit to Xif to select their aircraft for Ti coming up quickly, there was indeed no time to lose. For the next few weeks, everyone pored through countless books and made endless calculations to decide on the best path for them. The team had a long discussion about choosing a mine, with Hadeeyah presiding. Maia and Kusha, who were leading the effort to research the mines, had narrowed their choices down to two—the smaller Builliganes Narrows and the giant Molligessian Seam.

"Explain your choices," Hadeeyah demanded. Their mentor was not taking any chances this time around and firmly inserted herself into the decision-making.

"Well, there are very few open mines that show enough remaining deposits, so I had to pick from those," Maia said. "The Builliganes is a smaller place, and there is a chance no one else will choose it. However, if someone does, we will probably have to fight it out. On the other hand, the Molligessian is a big place, and chances are there will be other teams in there. But there will still be plenty of Calbion to go around, from what I can see."

"The only problem with the Molligessian is access," Kusha chimed in. "The wind vortices around it are fierce. And the entrances are practically in the middle of the ice floes. The eastern entrance, in particular, is not very . . . friendly."

"So . . . what's the choice?" Hadeeyah asked.

They went around the room. Everyone seemed to favor the Molligessian Seam, the guarantee of Calbion being the most important factor. Hadeeyah did not disagree.

The next step was picking out a suitable craft. That did not come together half as easily as choosing a mine. Ren, Dani, and Nafi were in charge of that, and the trio—Ren and Nafi in particular—were at loggerheads over the choices. There were discussions and there were debates, and even with Hadeeyah's constant involvement and just a few days to go, they had not yet settled on a craft—although most votes were for some kind of Raptor—let alone the upgrades it would need.

Two days before the trip to Xif, Maia had just returned to her room after a quick lunch with the team. She was in charge of the big report on their choices, which was due before the trip to Ti. Much remained to be completed and Maia was working hard on an explanation of flight paths and trajectories when a loud rap sounded at the door. She jumped a little and frowned, annoyed at being interrupted when she was so close to finishing. The knock sounded again before she could complete the sentence she was working on, louder this time.

"Maia, open up," came Ren's voice.

Maia pushed everything aside and shot to the door. "What is it?" she asked, her eyes scouring Ren's flushed face. It was weird how every time she heard urgency in a voice, she assumed the worst.

"Come on, let's go," Ren said simply.

"Go where?"

"Miir's." Ren turned and started walking away.

Maia had to hurry to catch up to him after grabbing her coat and Bellator. "What's going on? What's the rush? Is he all right?"

"Don't worry. He's fine." Ren leaned over to whisper. "I have a plan to get *Shadow* out. Thought you might be interested."

"All right. That." Maia exhaled in relief. No one had been attacked or killed, and that was good. At Ren's curious stare, Maia explained. "I'm always jittery nowadays. Every time someone knocks on my door, I hold my breath for the bad news."

Ren's arm slipped around her shoulders and he leaned his head lightly against hers. "No one's coming to take Miir away. Told you, I've taken care of that."

"How?"

"Oh, Maia. Can't tell, so don't ask."

There it was again. Those same words — *can't tell, don't ask.*

"Ren—" Maia was about to question him further when they ran into Nafi and Dani walking up the front staircase, each carrying a stack of books.

"Where do you think you two are going?" Nafi glowered, mostly at Ren. "We're supposed to make final cuts today. We should be in there," she said, pointing at the building behind them, "going over our calculations."

"We're going to Miir's. Want to come?"

Nafi's frown vanished in an instant. "Sure."

"I thought we were supposed to go over our calculations," Dani said, shaking her head. "Guys, our trip is in two days, and the final choice has to be submitted by tomorrow. The report is due soon, too."

Ren grabbed Dani by the shoulders and turned her around. "We don't need to spend all day there, Dani. There'll be plenty of time in the evening to hash out the calculations. Besides, we all know what our pick will be—the Raptor 2XC."

"Why 2XC?" Nafi asked. "I don't like its extended wingspan. 3YB is much better."

"No, it's not. The wingspan is why . . ."

They debated and discussed all the way across ThulaSu, down the staircase, and through Walenveil. Soon they were trooping into the cottage nestled in the Darkwoods.

They found Miir on the back porch, hunched over a table strewn with tools and supplies. Asiyaah's frame projector sat in the middle of it all.

"Hello," he said with a smile as they marched in.

Nafi stomped up to him, arms crossed and frowning. "What's the meaning of this?" she demanded. "You're sitting with your back to the road, just letting random people walk in? They were combing ThulaSu for you just a few weeks ago. Shouldn't you be more careful?"

Miir's eyes widened at her forceful scolding, but he smiled indulgently when she finished. "Nothing to worry about. I am very well protected. Nahlo and his troopers make their rounds every now and then. I have sensors set up all around the place so I know if random people come by. As for you, sensors are not needed. I could hear *your* voice all the way from the village."

The last bit made Ren guffaw. Nafi flushed and scowled and grumbled. As Dani tried to calm the duo down, Maia slipped onto the bench across the table from Miir to look at the repairs.

"Any progress here?" she asked. She had been waiting eagerly for the rest of the recordings, but knowing how diligently Miir had been working on it, she was determined to be patient.

Miir sighed. "A little. Not as much as I hoped." He looked up at her and grimaced. "Sorry. I wish I could give you better news."

"You're trying, and there's some progress," Maia said. "That's good enough news."

He smiled a little before sighing again. "It is more complex than I thought," he said. "I am afraid to take it all apart. What if I cannot put it back together?"

Ren sat down with a thump next to Maia. "Are you joking? You and not putting it back together?"

"I think you should give it a try. I think you will do just fine." Maia meant every word. She truly believed there was no risk at all, not in his hands.

"Need supplies? Tools?" Ren asked. "I can get you anything you need."

Miir shook his head. "No. Most of this is Jjord-made, and I want to keep it that way. I picked up everything I needed in Zagran, so I am fine there. The complexity of the design is the troublesome part."

"Well, I can help if you need it," Ren said.

"I can too," Dani chimed in.

"I got this. You have your Initiative to finish," Miir said. "Speaking of the Initiative, you have a deadline coming up, right? What are you doing here?"

Nafi, who had settled down on one end of the porch with her books, raised an eyebrow. "You keeping tabs on our tasks?"

Ren chuckled. "Once a mentor, always a mentor."

Nafi jumped up and scooted close to Miir. "Still a mentor, huh?" she asked, looking up hopefully at his face. "Any words of advice on the craft we should choose for Ti? I'm sure you already know that we're going to the Molligessian Seam."

Miir patted her head and pushed her back a little. "Nice try. But I do not approve of cheating. Go pick your own craft." As Nafi exhaled loudly and slunk back to her end of the porch, Miir looked from Dani's face to Ren's, and then at Maia's. "So back to . . . why are you here?"

"Well." Ren eyed the ceiling for a bit. Then he sat up, his eyes shining. "I have a plan to get *Shadow* out." Miir's face tightened as Ren continued. "I just found out that we will be in the main hangar during our next trip up-planet. They'll demonstrate our practice aircraft before they bring them here. That's where *Shadow* is too, right?"

Miir nodded. "Last I checked."

"And since our dear prince probably won't allow another transport as big as this, our people are using the chance to bring out additional craft. So I figured this is the perfect opportunity. We'll get *Shadow* added to the list and no one will notice."

"Sounds easy. Too easy," Miir said. "Anyway, I have to get it released first."

"Yes, you can take the same transport we'll be on to check out our craft. You go in, do your thing, release it to a friend of mine and he will hand it over to the Tokii. You can take our transport back here. My friend will pick *Shadow* up once it lands, and then hand it over to you. And that's it, *Shadow* is back with you."

"This friend is reliable?"

Ren closed his eyes and nodded. "Absolutely. I'd trust Adienos with my life."

"The same Adienos?" Maia remembered the swarthy Xifarian, an associate of Ren's, who had helped them twice, once to scale the fence of the Sanctuary of the Stars and next to get into the Chancery.

"Yes, the same. He was good, right? We broke in perfectly both times."

Miir exhaled, quite loudly and clearly on purpose.

"He's good, Miir. Trust me," Ren said. "Adienos gets things done. You'll have your Raptor here in two days. All you have to worry about now is finding a place to keep *Shadow*."

"Miir also has to get in and out of Xif," Maia said.

Nafi glared over at them. "That's a stupid idea, Ren. It's not safe for Miir to go back there. Not after what that stupid Remii did to the K. How can you even—"

"Nafi, you're too chicken," Ren said. "Miir can get in and out of Xif in his sleep."

Nafi snorted and looked away in a huff, clearly in disagreement. Ren, however, was very casual about it.

Maia fidgeted. "But Ren, seriously. This is risky. They are looking for Miir and—"

"Oh, come on, Maia," Ren said, waving away her concerns. "I told you what I told you, right? Trust me." Ren obviously meant his earlier reassurance about getting Remii off Miir's back. All Maia could do was sigh. Ren continued, "Besides, it's not as if Miir has never sneaked into Xif before. As if those fools could catch *him*."

After all of Kehorkjin's warnings . . . this. She had promised the master to stop Miir and now . . . this. Sure, Ren had assured her time and again that the SDS had been diverted. Doubting him would be hurtful. But . . .

Then again, how could she oppose this plan, knowing how much Miir wanted *Shadow*? Maia was happy when Dani asked the other question on her mind.

"So Adienos would just walk away with *Shadow* and no one would stop him?" Dani asked. "What if the SDS is tracking *Shadow*?"

"They're not," Ren said, stifling a yawn before sprawling on the floor.

"But Ren, even if they don't notice right away, they'll surely notice once *Shadow* is here. They can easily track—"

"No, Dani, they won't. Adienos will fudge *Shadow's* matrix and that'll camouflage it," Ren said.

"I thought *Shadow* had special colors and stuff?" Maia asked.

"Told you . . . the matrix will take care of that. Besides, once it's here, it's here. The SDS is banned from operating outside the encampments. They wouldn't dare go against the queen's directive and come here again."

Maia had no idea how the camouflaging worked, but since Miir did not question Ren's plan, it likely made sense. She had doubts about the SDS, however.

"But they could come after him in Xif," Maia said.

"No one will expect Miir there," Ren said. "No one would imagine he'd do anything that crazy."

That was a good point. This plan was just as brash as Ren; nothing about it sounded like Miir. But still . . .

"The Tokii are in charge of transports," Ren continued. "Once they have the release and their money, they won't object. Adienos will sweeten the pot for them a little, so . . . it's all set, my friends." He yawned again, stretched, and then propped himself up on his elbows. "Miir, we're all set, right?"

"And what about afterward?" Nafi interjected, glowering at Miir. "Where are you going to keep *Shadow*? It's not like a Raptor is a toy you can hide under your bed. Everyone will notice. You might as well scream from the rooftops that you're here."

"That's after," Ren snapped. "We'll figure something out once we have it."

"Well, I still don't approve," Nafi said grumpily.

Ren dismissed her with a shake of his head. "Miir?"

"I am sorry, Ren. I do not think this is the time for—"

"Oh, come on, Miir," Ren burst out, almost wailing. "This is a solid plan. I've worked really hard on setting it all up."

Maia expected Ren's pleas to go nowhere. She watched in disbelief as the determined look in Miir's eyes slowly turned hesitant. Just a few years ago, little could ever persuade him to change his opinions. Now he could not seem to resist Ren's disappointed face. And Ren's pained look was just as unbelievable. The Ren she knew did not take dismissals to heart. But this time, he did not even attempt to casually wave it away. He truly cared about getting *Shadow* out.

How things had changed.

Regardless, there was an extended pause before Miir nodded, and Maia could tell his heart was not in it. "All right, I am fine," he said in a quiet voice.

Maia's thoughts were disrupted by a clattering sound. Nafi, she discovered, was rummaging through some cans stacked on a table along the wall.

"Nafi, what are you doing?" Dani exclaimed.

"Sorry. I'm stressed. And I'm hungry. I need a snack."

"You can't just go through people's stuff like that," Dani chided.

"Oh, come on, Dani," Nafi retorted. "Miir's not *people*. And it's not like I'm going through his personal journal or anything. This is a pantry. It's made for rummaging. I'm hungry."

Ren shot up. "Hey, I'm hungry too. What have you got there?"

"Ren!"

No amount of scolding from Dani seemed to have any effect on Ren and Nafi, who continued to riffle through the cans in storage.

"Let them, Dani," Miir said.

That did not ease Dani's indignation one bit and she continued to fume at the duo. "Seriously, you two."

Any other time, Maia would have joined in, but now she found herself staring with concern at Miir's clouded face.

"You don't look happy. Or excited."

Miir did not look up. "I am more worried than anything else."

"Worried?" Maia could not help teasing him a little. "It's not as if you've never sneaked into Xif before," she said, quoting Ren. Miir grimaced and Maia realized things were not as usual. She also saw a great opportunity to back out of the plan without hurting Ren. "Are you seriously worried about getting caught? You shouldn't do it if you're worried. You'll be nervous and make mistakes and . . . I think we should abort."

"I am not nervous and I will not make mistakes," he said in a heartbeat. "They cannot catch me. That is not why."

Maia's curiosity was piqued. "Then what is? You've done this before. I mean, not this exact thing, but—"

"That was different."

"Really? How so? You were alone then. If you got caught no one would even know. How is that better?"

"Alone is always better. I only had myself to think about. Now it is . . ."

Maia peered at his face as his words trailed off. "Now it's what?"

He pursed his lips and fiddled distractedly with some tools. Maia was not about to give up. "Hello. Thought I asked a question."

"You should not, because you might not like the answer."

Maia crossed her arms and peered at his solemn face. "Try me."

Miir looked at her, his gaze scouring her face as if to gauge her. He let out a sigh before replying. "A plan with too many people who act on impulse. Far too many things out of my control."

"I see," Maia said, tapping her chin and nodding wisely. "Acting on impulse. That'd be Ren, Nafi, and . . . me?"

Miir did not reply.

"All right. I admit I rush into things. Sometimes."

Miir did not respond, his gaze fixed on a bag of shiny bolts he was fiddling with.

"Fine, I do it most of the time," Maia conceded. "But have you considered that you might . . . sometimes . . . overthink things?" Miir looked up, his glance sharp. For a moment, Maia thought he would retort. But he did not, so she continued. "Honestly, I don't like the idea of your going to Xif again after the Remii incident, and after all of Master Kehorkjin's cautions. But Ren's plan might work perfectly, even with us crazies around. Your *Shadow* might make it to you safe and sound."

"I am not worried about *Shadow*."

"Then . . . you're worried about us?" He did not reply, but his grim face gave her enough of an answer. "We will be fine. We've made it through tougher situations, and this is not even a situation. Besides, we're just props. You're the only one who'll be doing anything. You're the only one who'll be in any danger."

He had just started to say something when Nafi careened over, a can in hand. "You think we could pop these kernels?" she asked Miir, grinning as if she had found a pot of gold.

"Yes, you may."

Nafi's grin grew wider still. She whirled over to Maia and tugged her to her feet. "Come on, come on. Let's do this."

Much time was spent popping kernels and feasting on them. Miir did not seem as glum as before, and thinking that her words might have lifted his spirits made Maia absurdly content. There was a lot to be done—the craft for Ti to be chosen, decisions to be submitted, and trips to be made—and Maia knew there would be tiring days ahead. Her heart was light, however. There was much to look forward to.

The sun was not as fierce in the sky when Kusha arrived, to the surprise of everyone but Ren. "Sorry I'm late," he said, slumping onto a bench. He looked tired, and for once Nafi did not pounce on him with her sharp comments.

Dani sat down next to him and held out a bowl of popped kernels. "Everything all right?"

Kusha gave a little nod. "Who knew being a Sahiiraan meant there would be so many documents to go through every day? It's—"

"You're doing a great job, Kusha," Dani said. "Really."

"And we're all proud of you," Nafi piped up. "So much that I don't even give you any grief on how much of your slack we have to take up at the Initiative," she added.

"Thank you, Your Graciousness. I'll be forever grateful," Kusha said, placing a hand over his heart. Nafi smirked and Kusha turned toward Ren. "So, hey! Why did you call me here?"

Very quickly, he was told all about the plans and he agreed readily. "That's awesome. I'm in."

"Nafi?" Ren cocked an eyebrow.

Nafi returned a grudging smile. "Well . . . since everyone else is fine with it . . . I'm in, I guess."

"All right then. Time for our thing." Ren held his fist at the center of their huddle. "Go on, Maia. Say it."

Leave it to Ren to remember the fun touches, Maia thought. She placed her fist on his. "Together we're stronger than we'll ever be alone," she said, grinning happily.

CHAPTER TWENTY-FOUR

Ren chuckled. "Together."

"Together." Kusha's fist flew in.

"Together," Nafi and Dani followed in unison.

They all looked up expectantly at Miir who stood watching, a curious expression on his face. Then with a laugh and a little shake of his head, he placed his fist on their pile.

"Together."

Maia's heart soared with happiness, and looking at the bright faces of her teammates, she had no doubt they were just as ecstatic as she was. Finally, years after Mahswa Tabrin had tied them all together in a Craedonnen with the firestone wristbands, their circle of trust was truly complete.

CHAPTER TWENTY-FIVE

INTO THE FIRE

The trip to Xif started early on a cool, crisp morning two days later. Maia and her teammates were extra anxious that day because of the plan with *Shadow*. Principal Pomewege, who was now the Xifarian arbitrator in Kehorkjin's place, greeted them at the Frauz Point landing site. Their transport—an enormous shuttle that was almost empty—took off as soon as they boarded, and before long they were in Arpasgula. Another transport—this one smaller, but also quite empty—took them through the hole in the sky to the northeastern corner of the capital city, Armezai, where the hangars were located.

The structure that housed the central hangars was nondescript, rather ugly compared to the XDA buildings. It was basically an enormous gray block in the middle of an enormous gray patch.

Flight Master Demissie met the teams at the entrance, his smile warm and welcoming. There were no personnel there, only a few automated checking stations where Master Demissie logged their particulars. As soon as they were cleared for entry, he led them inside.

A long corridor stretched all the way across the building. To each side of it were doors that Maia assumed were entrances to the hangars. Every few hangars, a corridor ran perpendicular to the main one, essentially splitting the area into blocks. The entire place was dimly lit and that, along with its deserted look, made it quite unnerving. As they walked in, the lights in the corridor brightened around them, dimming as soon as they had passed.

"We are going to Hangar 14, down that way." Master Demissie pointed to the far end of the corridor. "Good work on your selections, by the way," he said as they walked. "Core 7, I am very impressed with those upgrades you chose. Keeping things light, are we?"

Karhann beamed, Loriine and Baecca exchanged prideful glances, and next to Maia, Nafi snorted.

"We'll see how fast you go," she muttered under her breath. "Light, my foot."

Ren nudged her playfully. "Relax, Nafi. No need to get so stressed out right now. We have a long way to go."

Nafi snorted again. She stayed silent for a while before elbowing Ren. "Hey! Any news on the . . . other thing?"

Ren frowned. "Nafi, we're not going to talk about this every other moment, all right?" His voice had dipped a notch when he spoke again. "He's in."

"Last question. Please," Nafi tugged Ren's shirt and put on a pleading look. "Where's the . . . you know . . . the thing housed?"

"Hangar 22," Ren said in a tired voice. "No more questions. None. Or I'll stop telling you anything at all."

Ren looked exhausted. He had reason to be. Since the beginning of the trip, Nafi had been peppering him with questions, demanding every minute detail about *Shadow's* extraction plan. Maia understood she was worried about Miir's safety—they all were to various degrees—but Nafi had been fretting, sulking, and being tedious in the way only she could be. Ren quite wisely had set a special code for the communicator between Miir and him, and Maia was thankful for that. She could not imagine how much anxiety it would cause if Nafi was part of that conversation. Nafi, however, sulked even more at being left out. In the end, it was not just Ren—they were all tired of it.

Nafi quieted for the moment, and as Master Demissie opened the door to Hangar 14 and led them in, Maia had no attention to spare for anything else. What the building lacked in exterior looks, it more than made up for inside. It was beyond imagination. Maia remembered seeing the Dyosican Hangar at the XDA and how completely overwhelmed she had been by its immensity. The Dyosican was nothing compared to Hangar 14. Maia could barely imagine the combined size of all the hangars in the building. Then again, according to Ren, this place was built to house the aircraft of all the Xifarians in the sector, so it had to be big.

Hangar 14 was a rectangle, enormous columns the only structures punctuating the seemingly endless expanse. Among them, at a distance from each other, were the five aircraft the final five teams had picked.

"Gather around, everyone," Master Demissie called as soon as they stepped in. "These are practice prototypes of the craft you will be using on Ti, and you should find all the equipment matching the ones you've picked. Make sure you have everything. These craft will be sent down to ThulaSu for you to practice on, and once they're out of here, we won't be able to add anything to them. So make sure the equipment is what you wanted." He paused to look at the anxious faces around him. "Now, go on. Find your craft and climb in. No funny business and no loitering. You'll be penalized if I find you doing anything other than what you're here for. Understood?"

The teams dispersed in a heartbeat. Every team with the exception of Core 10 had chosen an Onclioraptor, and from the outside, all of them looked the same. Large plaques set up outside the aircraft spelled out the details, and Maia and her teammates found their 2XC right next to the entrance. They had already distributed the various sections among themselves. Maia had only started to investigate the landing gear when Master Demissie strode in, assistant in tow. While the assistant deposited a carton of food packs on one side, the master went about checking everyone's work. He soon left, looking satisfied with their progress.

"I will be at the transfer station if you should need me. Otherwise, I will be back at the end of the day. Carry on. Use your time well."

Things went smoothly. Dani and Ren busied themselves with the navigation unit near the pilot's section. Nafi and Kusha worked on the topology mapper. Maia worked diligently on the landing and extraction equipment near the back of the craft. She was in the hold, testing out the various exit options and being all kinds of awkward, when Ren peeked in. "Hey! It's all going well on the other side. *It* has been released. Adienos has the clearance already."

Nafi ran over to them. "Where's *he*? Is he out yet?"

"No, he's still here. He's waiting for the right time. There's some unexpected movement in the upper hangars, apparently."

Nafi frowned. "I don't like this," she said.

Ren patted her on the back. "He can take care of himself, Nafi. You need to calm down and do your thing here."

Nafi went on with her work but Maia could tell she was anything but calm. She fidgeted constantly. She fretted and she frowned. And as soon as Ren came over to announce their work on the navigation unit was complete, Nafi pounced.

"Is he out yet?"

Ren exhaled loudly. "No, Nafi. He's not."

"I don't understand. What is he waiting for?"

"The path's not clear," Ren said impatiently. "For the hundredth time, Nafi, quit worrying. He knows these places better than any of us. Far better than even me. He'll be fine. Even if he misses our transport, he'll find a way out."

That did not seem to placate Nafi in the least. Maia had to admit, she felt a little anxious too. But there was nothing she could do to help, given how little she knew of anything inside Xif. No matter how that lump of fear inside her sputtered constantly, the best option was to be calm and let Miir do his thing.

"Everything will be fine," she whispered to herself, and forced her attention back to the grabber tools she was working on.

It was a while before Maia finished the study of her section. She wrapped up everything and clambered out of the gear room. She found Kusha hunched over a table, taking copious notes. Nafi was nowhere to be seen.

"Hey, Kusha. Where's Nafi?"

Kusha looked around and frowned. "Don't know. She was just here."

"Maybe she's up front," Maia said. "I'll check."

Nafi was not there either. Head clouded with worry, Maia was walking back to Kusha when she spotted Nafi through one of the windows. She was outside the Raptor, looking around in a suspicious manner.

"What are you doing?" Maia muttered to herself.

As she watched, Nafi threw furtive glances around and scampered to the entrance of the hangar. Suddenly Maia realized what was about to happen.

"No, no, no. Nafi, don't you go out," Maia whispered.

But her hopes and wishes did not reach Nafi.

Maia watched with a sinking heart as the girl slipped out of the hangar. Dani was in the section closest to her, so Maia dashed over.

Dani's eyes grew large as soon as she heard. "Nafi did what?"

"I'll fetch her back," Maia said, rushing toward the exit.

"But, Maia, you can't go."

"We can't have her straying, either. She can't have gone far, Dani. I'll be right back."

She sprinted out of the Raptor and after making sure Master Demissie was not around, she tiptoed to the entrance and slunk out. The thick door of the hangar closed with a light thud behind her as Maia walked out into the corridor and looked up and down. She spotted Nafi's shadowy form about four doors further down from the entrance.

"Nafi," Maia called. The girl was already some distance away, but she heard nonetheless. She stopped and turned around. "What are you doing?" Maia asked, walking in her direction. "Get back in there right now."

"I'm just—"

Before Nafi could finish, a blur of motion swept her out. Nafi went flying, further away from Maia and further into the dimness. Then, with a resounding thud, she crashed to the ground.

"Nafi!" Maia screamed and ran into the darkness. She had barely run five paces when she realized her mistake and stopped. She turned back, but it was already too late. A pair of figures, a woman and a man, emerged from the junction she had just passed. Clad in dark, body-hugging suits and dark masks with slits for the eyes, swords drawn, they steadily approached like a pair of bogeymen from a nightmare.

The first thing Maia tried was the communicator. One by one she called her teammates, desperate to find someone. Nothing happened. No one answered. There was not even a hint of a presence in her mind. Other than Nafi's fallen form in the distance and the two dark figures, the corridors were deserted. The doors to the hangars were thick, so screaming would not help either.

What then?

Maia threw a quick glance behind her. Nafi lay on the floor, likely unconscious. The path ahead was blocked by the sword-wielding figures. She could not get past them and back to Hangar 14, and she could not leave Nafi behind, so Maia fell back, one step at a time until she reached Nafi.

"Nafi," she called. Other than a muffled groan, she received no response.

Maia yanked out Bellator and debated whether she should call the light. She had no idea who these people were, but they were not friends, that much was clear.

"Maia." Nafi sat up groggily when the two figures, their continuing silence menacing and deathly, were no more than four paces away.

"Get up, Nafi. Get up if you can. We're in trouble."

The male figure chuckled throatily. "That you are. We were hoping you would stray. All that patience paid off, finally."

"What do you want?" Maia said. She kept hoping, praying that these were not Phocluus's goons.

Next to Maia, Nafi rose to a shaky stand. "You can't attack us like this," she said, wheezing. "We are protected under the clause of the Initiative."

"Well, the Initiative does not grant you trespassing rights, little one," the man replied. "What business did you have anywhere outside of Hangar 14?"

"So you are going to throw us in prison for trespassing?" Nafi asked. "Don't you have anything better to do? Who the heck are you, anyway?"

"That one's a pocket-sized firecracker." The man guffawed. "You were right, Amanii. These don't back down so easily, do they?"

"Amanii?" A shocked whisper escaped Maia's mouth. So these were Phocluus's goons after all. This was quickly turning into a real nightmare.

The woman pulled her face cover down and smiled. Maia would recognize her anywhere. Those eyes, that flawless face framed perfectly by the vibrant red hair. The beautiful, dazzling Amanii—Statesman Taillefei's daughter, Miir's fiancée, and an apprentice at SDS—was an unforgettable presence.

"Hello, Maia. Happy to see me?"

Amanii . . . the name left a trail of fire inside Maia. Her perfect face hid a hideous heart. Amanii . . . one of the two who had walked into a home in Appian. By the time she walked out, Maia had lost her family.

"No, Amanii, I'm not," Maia said. "Are you?"

"Seeing you is always a joy," Amanii said and her mouth twisted into a smile. "But you break my heart, Maia. Not happy to see me? Why ever not?"

Maia did not reply but Nafi snapped. "You killed her grandfather, or have you conveniently forgotten that?"

CHAPTER TWENTY-FIVE

"Did I?" Amanii laughed. "And what are you going to do about that, Maia?"

Maia's fists curled. Even before she called to the light, it trickled out of her and flowed to Bellator.

"Ooh! Will you use your special powers on us?" Amanii crooned.

Her companion chuckled. "That's even better. Try it. Let's see what you can do."

Maia was about to raise her hand to blast the two to oblivion. But something stopped her and she pondered a moment. Something was not right. The way they kept talking and talking—it felt like . . . they were biding their time. They were likely waiting for reinforcements. Or were they waiting for her to make a mistake? Maybe. The way they were goading her could only mean that using her powers here would be a mistake. She did not know how yet, but it seemed like a possibility.

No, no matter how angry she was, she was not going to step into another trap. Maia pulled the light back in, and her fingers tightened around Bellator's hilt. She would fight them the regular way.

"Sorry, I'm not in the mood to put on a show for you today," Maia said, letting a smile curl her mouth. "Come get me if you want."

What they had planned, Maia had no idea, but she saw them frown at her words. Bellator raised steadily in her hand, Maia was ready to fight to the bitter end, as was Nafi next to her. Then a door opened behind them and someone walked out. Maia froze, her heart sinking to the pit of her stomach. It had to be more agents of the SDS.

There was no escape. They were trapped.

CHAPTER TWENTY-SIX

TIES AND BONDS

The grimness of the situation stared Maia in the face. She did not dare move a muscle or take her eyes off Amanii and her companion, who stood ready and poised to strike. She did not know how much of a match she would be for the two of them if it came to a fight. The SDS always hired the best from the XDA, so it followed that Amanii's companion was a TEKist just like Amanii. While Maia could see TEK waves, Nafi was blind to them and would be of no help against a TEK attack. For all practical purposes, Maia was on her own. And then there was the issue of whoever had emerged from the door behind them.

Maia braced herself for an attack, watching Amanii's hands curl up to unleash a TEK wave. When she heard approaching footsteps behind her, she froze, her mind racing, her heart racing faster. Next to her, Nafi gasped. Amanii's eyes widened, and her hands fell slowly to her sides.

"I knew it," Amanii hissed. "I had hoped you had chosen a better path, but . . . no. Look at you . . . look how far you've fallen."

For a moment, Maia was bewildered. Then she realized with a start who Amanii was talking to. She felt Miir's presence, collected and steady as always, beside her. She did not have to look at him to know how his eyes had narrowed, his gaze turned sharp and focused, every muscle taut and ready for battle.

"Get behind me," he whispered to Maia, his eyes never slipping off Amanii and her companion. "And keep moving back, slowly, until you reach Hangar 22."

Maia did not waste a moment, or think. She fell back behind Miir, and Nafi followed. One step at a time, they walked back. One step at a time, Amanii and her companion came toward them.

"What now?" Amanii's voice was steely, caustic. "You're going to fight me?"

"Only if you force me to."

"So it has come to this, Miir? You're opposing the ones who are trying to put our world . . . *your* world back together? All to protect the daughter of a traitor who tore it all apart? Do you know what that makes you? It makes you a traitor too."

Miir did not reply. He did not even twitch.

Amanii went on. "When you chose to not participate in the hunt, I thought I understood. You took pity on the girl. But this? Taking up her cause and fighting *for* her? I didn't think that was possible."

Once again, Miir returned nothing but silence. He was stalling, Maia realized, just as they were. Miir was not going to fight the SDS duo until they reached Hangar 22. Or unless he had to defend himself. He kept moving backward, in tandem with every step Maia and Nafi took. Amanii strode forward, her companion in lockstep, the distance between the groups staying the same. It was a strange choreography and had the situation not been so dire, Maia could have chuckled.

"You had a future, Miir. You still do if you choose," Amanii continued. "You can still come back, you know."

"Really? You would let me?" Miir said, his voice unbelievably light.

"Of course. You are our own. Your place is with us, not with *them*.

You should be by my side, not standing against me," Amanii said. "I don't want to fight you, Miir. I don't want to fight the friend I grew up with, the one I've loved all my life. Our friendship, our bond was special, still is to me." She extended her hand toward Miir. "Come back to me."

"You can walk away yourself, Amanii," Miir said. "I told you years ago that all you have to do is leave. You could have left with me. I asked you. I asked you many times."

Amanii laughed, but there was no mirth in it, only derision, anger, and spite.

"Leave with you? And do what? Become the protector of the filth of the world?" She spat the words out with a vehemence that made Maia shudder.

"Mind your tongue, Amanii," Miir snapped, his voice icy.

"Oh, really? Does it hurt when I call her filth?" Amanii sounded vicious, her words designed to hurt. "But see, that's the truth. That's who you left me for. You are so blind. Swept away from the moment you set eyes on her, you fell for her lies and her fake righteousness. That girl . . . destroyed our perfect future."

Amanii tilted her head to look at Maia, a scornful smile pasted on her lips. Maia braced herself. Amanii's nonsensical rants were not new. She had heard them before when they confronted each other at the Chancery. But it sounded worse now, even more hateful, even more bitter.

"Are you happy, Maia?" Amanii crooned. "You should be. All your carefully laid schemes of deceit worked after all. Must feel really good when you hold him in your arms."

"Enough, Amanii," Miir said, his voice sharp and menacing. "Tell me whatever you like, but leave *her* out of this. She has nothing to do with what happened to us. No one has anything to do with it, but us. I had to choose between you and the values I hold dear. It is as simple as that." He paused and let out a wry chuckle. "And stop telling yourself these lies. We never had a future, let alone a perfect one. We were worlds apart long before any of this happened. A bond, you say?

If we had anything at all, you would know better than to question my loyalty to you. You should have known I could not be dishonest if I tried."

"That's a lie, that's a horrid lie. You didn't have to be *with* her, she got into your head and possessed you anyway," Amanii yelled. "What do you see in her? She is nothing, a nobody."

Miir sighed. "Please, Amanii. For the sake of the friendship we once had, one that you just called special, stop spewing this nastiness." He turned, ever so slightly, toward Maia and Nafi behind him. "How far?"

"Almost there," Maia whispered.

"I'm nasty now?" Amanii strode up closer, faster. "I'll show you, Miir," she said, in an intense, irate voice. "I'll tell you what I'll do. I'll do everything, anything to restore what belonged to our nation, I will fight to get back what's ours. I won't rest until that girl gives back what her mother stole from us. I don't care if you stand in the way, I will fight through you and I will end you if I need to."

There was a moment of silence. Then Miir chuckled. "Well, good, we are all square, then. We stopped being friends a long time ago. Now we can finally stop pretending and call each other enemies."

"Sounds just fine to me, Miir," Amanii said through gritted teeth. "You think anyone respectable would want to call you a friend anymore? You know what you are? You're an oathbreaker, a liar, a cheat through and through. If you had any integrity, you would not have turned on our nation or left me."

"I have not turned on my nation. I have only left people like you who *think* they know the meaning of integrity. I would be a fool and a coward if I hung on to promises I was tricked into pledging when I did not know any better."

One more step . . .

"We're there," Maia said.

"Then get inside," Miir replied. "Now!"

Nafi made a mad dash for the door of the hangar. Maia followed, barely catching a glimpse of what was happening behind them. She saw Miir raise his hands, and the space folded in a series of waves. Amanii and her companion returned formations almost as big, but they were a moment too late. The TEK waves collided in an explosion of energy. Maia could sense the ripples flowing through until Miir hurtled inside the hangar and slammed the door shut behind them. His fingers flew across a panel embedded in the door, lights flashing in response.

"Safe for the moment," he muttered.

"You locked them out," Nafi said, grinning. The girl seemed to have forgotten that their troubles were far from over. They had to get back to Hangar 14. And their path — possibly the only one — back there was blocked by the SDS duo who were still outside, likely getting reinforcements.

"For now. They will eventually override the lock." Miir moved to another panel on the wall. Nafi tagged along, wide-eyed, as he pressed some more buttons.

Maia did not forget their looming troubles. But her mind kept returning to Amanii's words. The anger in them, the hatred, and the derision were savage and visceral. And even though Amanii's absurd words did not mean much to her, they had to have hurt Miir. Maia stared at his unflappable face, still unable to believe how calmly he took Amanii's abusive tirades and unfounded allegations. Once again she marveled at his courage. It could not have been easy tearing his way out of the pressures and the enticement, and yet he did. He had done all that, obviously not out of any personal attachment to her as Amanii wanted to believe, but no doubt with her plight in mind. As Maia thought through all that, a wave of gratitude toward Miir swept her with an intensity she had never thought was possible.

A muted flash of light spreading across the room brought Maia back to the present.

"What was that?" Nafi chirped.

"Enabled structural reinforcements inside here."

"Structural what now?"

"Reinforcements. The damage will be minimal if . . . in case they bring in the cavalry."

"How do you know so much?"

"This is my hangar," he replied calmly as he clipped the panel shut.

Nafi's eyes bulged out of her head. "This whole hangar as in . . . Hangar 22 . . . is yours? All of it?"

"Yes."

"But it's empty. What do you do with an empty hangar?"

"Those are irrelevant questions," he snapped and Nafi shrank back a little. "What I would like to know is why you two were loitering outside Hangar 14. Did you have a task to complete out there? Or maybe Master Demissie asked you to patrol the corridor?"

"Thought you were in trouble," Nafi said in a voice almost inaudible. "Thought you might need a hand."

"I said I would be fine," he hissed at Nafi before glowering at Maia. "And you! Do you have a death wish? Have you forgotten where you are? This is Xif. The chairman of the SDS wants you dead. And you still walk out of your safe zone and right into a trap. What do you think you are? Invincible?"

It was weird, Maia thought. She did not feel a shred of resentment at his outrage. Perhaps because there was no denying that she had acted rashly. Her intent was to help her team, and Nafi in particular, but still, her action could have benefitted from a little more thought. But most of all, she kept thinking how Miir had just stood up for her against everything he had known and loved and grown up with. That, she figured, earned him some indulgence when he was angry, even if somewhat unfairly.

Miir looked away at the wall for a moment and there was quiet. But the respite did not last long and his glare was pinned back on Maia. "You wanted to know why I worried? This is why. Not for *Shadow*, or myself, but because *you* do not seem to learn to think rationally. Keeping you safe is an impossible task. Do you know why? Because you are *so* intent on endangering yourself. You get half a chance and you are off doing needless heroics. It will get you killed one day. Do you even care?"

Next to Maia, Nafi had been fidgeting since Miir began to chide. Now she burst out.

"Stop yelling at Maia," Nafi wailed. "It's not her fault. She only came out to call me back. I'm the stupid one who came out looking. And they got me before I knew it. I'm sorry, so sorry. I should have done better, I shouldn't have freaked out so badly. But none of this is Maia's fault. So shout at me if you have to, I'm the one who really deserves it."

Nafi stood, her eyes brimming with tears, as Miir stared wordlessly. Moments of silence trickled past, until with a sob, Nafi took off. She dashed away to the far end of the room and crouched in a corner. With a sigh, Miir turned away. He pulled out some white wedges from a cabinet and started sliding them up against the door. Maia stood frozen, looking from Nafi's sobbing figure in the distance to Miir intently setting the blocks in place. Safety came first, she reasoned, and forcing her attention away from Nafi, she kneeled next to Miir.

"May I help?"

He passed a stack to her as if he had been waiting for her to ask. "Push them in as hard as you can," he said. "It is not much use, but might buy us some time."

They worked side by side in silence. Maia shot a glance back at Nafi from time to time, but the girl had not moved.

"Have to find a way to get you out," Miir said when all of the wedges were in place. "I am afraid the main door might be the only way. Or we might get to the grounds outside, but that will activate the security system. We do not want that unless we absolutely have to." He scanned the room a few times, finally pointing at a row of silver mesh-like structures on the wall. "Those are air vents. I am not sure, but if we could get one open we might —"

He strode off to the nearest one and fiddled with the clamps holding it in place. Maia followed, hoping to help.

"The clamps come off this way," he explained.

CHAPTER TWENTY-SIX

"Got it."

Miir stopped midway between trying the third and the fourth clamp and turned to face her. "I am sorry for losing my temper. That was thoughtless and completely . . . disgraceful. I should have heard you out before I—"

"I didn't mind. I know you meant well. Besides, I'm not really faultless. Rushing out like that was the wrong thing to do. So . . . it's fine."

He fiddled needlessly with a corner of the vent. "Also . . . about everything Amanii said—"

"I know. It's all nonsense," Maia rushed to reassure him. "Don't worry. I've heard it before." Miir nodded. Maia hardly noticed his unconvinced expression; her mind had drifted somewhere else. She looked back at the corner where Nafi was still crouched with her head on her knees. "Nafi didn't mean to cause this. She was worried. She cares a lot about you. She lost her sister—"

"I know about Sejya. She told me."

"Maybe you could go and talk to her."

Miir exhaled loudly and his voice was hard when he replied. "Maybe she needs some time alone to understand how much of a mess she has created. Someone needs to teach her to control her impulses. She has to think with her head and not with her heart."

Maia's insides twitched at his response. Miir was frustrated and angry, and he had a right to be. But Nafi needed a kind word or two right now. The girl had made a mistake, one she understood had landed them all in deep trouble, one she clearly regretted. To forget that her mistake came out of deep concern was wrong. Nafi did not need a lesson right now, she needed a hand. And Maia suddenly knew the vents had to wait.

"Where are you off to?" Miir asked as she turned to leave.

"I'm going to talk to Nafi."

"How is that going to help *this* situation?" he asked, fixing a cold stare on her face. "Helping me access a vent might help you get back. Do you want to get back at all?"

"You don't know if we can use these vents to get back, you said so yourself. So trying these is taking a chance. But over there, my friend is hurting. Alone. And I know if I sit down with her, it will surely, definitely help her. So I will." Maia's voice was resolute and so was her decision. "I'm not asking you to come. You can keep trying the vents all you want."

She turned away, but that was all she could do. Miir's hand clasped her wrist before she took one step.

"I will go," he said, sighing. "You keep checking the vents. And if you see the slightest movement at the door, fall back."

Maia watched as Miir walked up to Nafi. When he kneeled next to the girl and put a hand on her shoulder, a rush of joy filled Maia's insides. At that moment, she forgot the troubles facing them, her spirits lifting in happiness for her friend. Maia was still smiling as she tried the vents and their clamps one after another, although with no success. She was down to the fifth vent when a pop went off in her head and a cacophony of voices sounded on the communicator.

"Dani?" Maia whispered.

"Maia, where are you?"

"What in the stars, Maia?" Ren sounded irate. "What if Demissie comes in to check and you two are missing? Where are you?"

"Stuck in Hangar 22," Maia said with a sigh. "We'll be back, don't worry."

"Hangar 22?" Ren burst out. "That Nafi—"

"You'll be back? As in when?"

"What's the trouble? We'll come."

"No, no, we'll be fine. Miir's here," Maia said. "You just wait there. Hide our absence in case Demissie comes by."

"But . . ."

Maia did not get to hear what Ren said next since her eyes were drawn to the panel above the door. It had started flashing. Maia's heart thrashed and she skittered backward with a shout. "Miir!"

He was already on his feet. He pointed at a column situated almost at the center of the room. "We stay behind here for now."

For now. For now, they were safe. But Maia had a feeling it was going to get bad very soon. Maia whispered a quick prayer as the door of the hangar fell open with a thud.

CHAPTER TWENTY-SEVEN

CLAIMING MY SOUL

P eople marched into the hangar. It was not an army, as far as Maia could tell from the intensity of footfalls, but it had to be at least five people. From the sounds, they were arranging themselves near the entrance. The thud of heavy boots drifted in, likely from the corridor. A grimace spread across Miir's face.

"Remii," he said. He listened to the continuous rise and fall of the sound for a while, then frowned. "Odd that he is not coming in yet." He was lost in thought for a moment or two. "They are waiting for something," he muttered.

"What?" Maia asked.

"Not sure." Taking a long, deep breath, he looked at Maia and Nafi. "All right, time to make a plan."

He turned toward Nafi first. "You need to stay here, hidden, no matter what happens out there. You cannot go out and fight them. They will use TEK, and I have a feeling they will not hesitate to kill. So please—"

"I won't. I promise," Nafi said earnestly.

"What about me?" Maia asked.

"You can come out, but only if absolutely necessary." He stopped. "If I am incapacitated."

The thought of Miir being incapacitated, and particularly the somber way he said it, shook Maia and left her feeling hollow. "You can beat Remii, I'm sure of it," she said, in a desperate bid to drive the thought from her mind.

"Remii, yes. But Remii and five more?" A smile, light-hearted yet somewhat melancholy, played on his face. "Not sure what you think of me, but I am not all-powerful."

"You don't have to be all-powerful," Nafi piped up. "But please don't be dead."

Miir chuckled. "I will try my best."

"Can I use the light?" Maia asked, bracing herself for the worst possibilities.

"Yes, in here you can. The reinforcements are on, and they should withstand—"

"Sorry, irrelevant question but . . . why would anyone put reinforcements on a hangar?" Nafi asked, clearly halfway back to her usual self.

"I have no idea," Miir said with a shrug. "This used to be my grandfather's hangar. He passed it on to me along with many of his other possessions. It came empty, though. But since I got *Shadow*, I have kept it here."

"Aah . . ." said Nafi, as if the universe's deepest mysteries had come to light. "Well, maybe your grandfather envisioned this day."

Maia was too entrenched in her thoughts to take notice of Nafi's enlightenment. She turned to Miir as soon as Nafi paused. "I might be wrong, but in the corridor, it felt as if . . . as if Amanii and that guy wanted me to use the light."

"Of course they did," Miir said. "If you made the hangar collapse and people died in the process, there would be no need for this hide and seek anymore. They could brand you a fugitive and hunt you down openly."

Nafi shook her head. "I don't get it. What's the point? With the R'armimon here now, isn't it in everyone's best interests to help Maia? Why are they still hunting her? Are they stupid or something?"

"Vendettas are not easy to get rid of. This has been Phocluus's goal for so long, that—" The sound of machinery being rolled in stopped Miir mid-sentence. An expression of fear came over his face, a look so unusual for him that Maia's heart sank a little. She wondered what had shaken him so, and the explanation came quickly. "They are bringing in Dampers. They are machines that create disruption in the air that makes it really hard to use TEK." He stood with his eyes closed for a little while. When he opened them again, the determined look had returned. He nodded at Maia. "All right, change of plans. You will *have* to be out there. I will need you."

It felt good to be needed, but it would have felt far better if the situation had not been so frightful. Maia grabbed Bellator tightly, took a deep breath, and stiffened her spine, bracing herself for what was to come. It was not a moment too soon. A low hum of machines rose behind them, and in came the sound of heavy boots, echoing through the empty space. Then came Remii's voice.

"Hello, hello," Remii said. "Where are you, Chichi?" Miir gritted his teeth, his face twisting into a scowl. Maia and Nafi exchanged a look, utterly surprised by the name Remii called Miir. "Now, come on out, baby brother, come on out. All this time, I thought I'd never see you again. I couldn't believe my luck when I heard you are well and you're here. Oh, I've missed you."

Miir did not move or reply.

"You're hurting my feelings now," Remii said. The fake niceness was starting to wear off already, the bitterness that always marked his voice showing underneath. "I came all this way to see you and you won't even say hello. You don't want me to come and find you, do you?" Maia could see the hesitation on Miir's face, the unease and the tension rippling through his narrowed eyes. Remii continued, his tone growing sharper by the moment. "I don't think you want to find me with your friends, Chichi. And especially not that tiny one who has nothing but some itty-bitty pieces of metal to defend herself with. You don't want her to get hurt."

Maia chuckled wryly to herself. From missing his dear brother to threatening Nafi, that came down quite fast. And here he was, the real Remii.

"I am going out," Miir said. He shot a quick glance at Maia. "Wait as long as you can."

Maia held her breath as he walked out from behind the safety of the column. After an endless, breathless moment, she heard Miir's voice again.

"Hello, Remii."

"Aah, there you are, Chichi. Hangar 22. Of all the places in the world" — Remii guffawed — "to find you here, brother of mine. It had to be Hangar 22, didn't it? Our beloved grandfather's bequest to his favorite grandchild. You always got everything and I still can't figure out why. And then, you had the gall to walk out on the best that life offered you and only you. You know . . . you are one entitled brat."

"Thought you would be happy to see me."

"I am. Can't you tell? Now, where's our dear friend, the apple of our eyes? Where did you hide her?" Maia held her breath, realizing he was talking about her. "I need to see her too. Oh, Maia. Please don't be shy. If you want your little friend to be safe, you'll come out now. You know her chances if — "

Clammy hands tightening around Bellator's hilt, her mouth as dry as the black sands of Korobieltes, Maia stepped out. There were not five, but six people, including Amanii, all dressed in black bodysuits. In between them were three large, bulbous machines with transparent tops, which Maia deduced were the Dampers. Remii stood at the center, in the regular black uniform of the SDS, his sallow face filled with spite. Maia did not miss the fiendish gleam in his eyes as her gaze met his. A smile, if one could call that a smile, twisted Remii's lips.

"Hello, Maia. Told you we'd meet again soon." He crossed his arms and cocked an eyebrow. "So . . . you did know where my brother was. Not what you told me the last time we met." He shook his head a little, his face filled with mockery. "Did your darling grandfather forget to teach you that good girls don't lie?"

Maia had to breathe hard and fast to keep her rage in check. It was difficult. Faces flashed in her mind—Dada, Herc, Emmy, Bikele—in an unending loop. Their voices, their laughter tinkled in her ears. Then Remii spoke again and tore everything apart.

"This is my lucky day," Remii mused, looking from Maia's face to his brother's and back. "I didn't expect to catch two birds today. This is . . . incredible. Amanii surely deserves a special honor, don't you think, Chichi? Waiting here was her idea, after all. And now we have you both."

"You have nothing," Miir said. "You will have nothing."

"Oh, really? Let's see how you get out of here." He nodded at the Dampers behind him. "You know you are useless with these around." He flicked a finger and the machines swiveled around, their transparent tops now pointing in Miir's direction. From the corner of her eyes, Maia saw Miir's face grow pale, as his eyes narrowed to slits.

"What are you waiting for?" Miir asked. "Get on with it."

"What's the rush?" Remii said. "Aren't you happy to see your brother?"

"The chairman. You must be waiting for him."

Remii sighed. "Ah, yes. He wanted to say hello to Maia one last time. But don't feel left out, he wants to see you too. You see, he has a special place in his heart for traitors. But, kind and forgiving as he always is, he's ready to welcome you back. He hopes you'll return home today."

Remii took a few steps forward and Maia saw Miir's hand stretch. He was preparing for a TEK wave. But with the Dampers pointed at him, how much could he do?

"I have no patience for you, though," Remii continued bitterly, his gaze sweeping over Miir and settling on the dark sword he held. "All that pampering and look where that got you. You were always their favorite, always. Getting everything . . . this hangar, that sword . . . everything one could wish for."

"I did not wish for any of these."

Remii tilted his head, scorn shining in his eyes. "Aah. My dear, selfless brother. Why don't you hand that sword over to me, then? Let's see how little you care."

Miir fell back a step as soon as Remii advanced, arms extended.

"There you go." Remii jeered. "Not as generous as you like to pretend, are you? You're selfish, always ready to take everything. You even had to take our father's life because he objected to your lousy choices."

Miir shifted on his feet. "That is a lie. He never objected. You know that. You also know I would never think of harming him. I could not and I had no reason to."

Remii scoffed. "Prove your innocence, then."

"I was not even on Xif when it happened. You can check the logs."

"The logs prove nothing. They won't tell you're here right now, will they?" Remii roared with laughter as Miir's gaze wavered. "You killed him," he shouted. "That is the truth I know, and that will be the truth forever. Murderer!"

Their hands went up at the same instant, and the air between them rippled and crumbled. But it moved in Remii's favor. Significantly, totally in his favor. The air rushed, dissipating in a fine web from Remii's hand and hitting Miir. Maia winced as Miir fell backward, his body slamming against the column behind him. She forced her eyes away from his face, unable to watch as he writhed in pain. As Maia struggled to get her mind back in focus, she noticed Amanii and her smug, satisfied smile. The pleasure on her face at seeing Miir in pain stunned Maia. To Amanii now, Miir was a traitor and an enemy. But she had loved him once. How could she derive such joy from the pain of someone she had cared for so much?

Maia's attention did not stay on Amanii for very long. Remii turned toward her, his mocking gaze sweeping over her face.

"Distressed, are we?" he sniggered. "Don't worry, Chichi will live. He has survived worse fights growing up." Maia shuddered, thinking what that meant—nothing good, she assumed. Remii, who had been watching her intently, shook his head. "Ah, to see you two being friends. You know, Maia, when we hunted down your grandfather and those idiotic companions of his, my dear brother was just as keen on getting justice for our nation as we were. Now he's your friend. But I wonder, how could you forgive him? Didn't you want to avenge your poor sick grandfather?"

Maia's insides bristled at Remii's attempt to poison her mind. What did he think she was? There was a time she might have been naive enough to step into his trap, but she was no naive young kid anymore. She knew her friends from her enemies, and she had no doubt which side Miir was on. But Maia was annoyed enough to want to taunt Remii a little, just as he was taunting her. It was more than a simple payback; she needed to get Miir time to catch his breath.

"You aren't very bright, are you, Remii?" Maia asked, in a tone as caustic as she could make it. The way Remii's face changed color was a treat to watch. "Don't you think your brother would have already told me that? Did you really think he'd wait all this time so *you* could tell me? But then again, how would you know? Integrity is not something you'd understand."

Remii's fists curled, and he smiled through gritted teeth. "No, I wouldn't. I do enjoy crushing vermin, though. Like those I found in that pitiful little village you call Appian." Maia's insides caught fire in an instant. "Wretched little people in a wretched little house. You should have seen the look on that old man's face when I told him you drowned in the lake." Remii laughed, shredding Maia's senses. She felt the light swirl up inside her like a tempest. It coiled up her bones and flowed into her blood. "You know, he was just short of begging me to kill him. I did him that favor. Don't I deserve some thanks for that?"

The fire shot out of her hands like a pair of meteors on chains. They came to life on their own, fluid agents of death, eager for destruction. One swept across the room in a blazing arc that cut the dampers in half and scattered the black-clad agents of the SDS, while the other swirled around Remii. It wound around his neck and threw him to the floor. Remii thrashed, his eyes bulging, his face a violent shade of red as the fire coiled tighter around his throat and held him in a vise-like grip.

"How do you like this for thanks?" Maia could hardly recognize the voice speaking those words. It was the same voice she had heard when she threw Miir off the cliff. It was ruthless and vicious, and it promised death. A fiery fog descended on Maia's senses, and it demanded vengeance. Cruel, savage, merciless revenge.

Kill him. He deserves to die. You have the power to make him pay for his crimes. Do it.

"P-please," Remii gasped.

"Are you begging me to kill you?" Maia asked, walking up to Remii as he squirmed on the floor hopelessly.

"P-please."

"I'll grant you your wish, then," she hissed. "Prepare to die."

Maia tightened her grip, happiness flooding her insides as she watched Remii's skin burn. She laughed, gleefully, just as gleefully as Remii had mere moments ago, in a voice that did not belong to her.

Recognition of the acute similarity jolted Maia and threw her off balance. No, she could not be that. She could *not* be Remii. The Xinhagyi's words flew through her mind.

Let go of your anger. Those who have left us cannot be brought back by acts of revenge.

But Remii deserved punishment. He tortured and killed Dada. And poor Herc and Emmy. And now he was bragging about it. How dare he?

Maia's grip tightened once more. Remii's eyes widened, his flesh burned raw, his open mouth gasping for breath. Now he was going to die. Finally, the scores would be settled.

Maia was about to yank on the fiery chain when she heard it. Through the mists of fire floating in her mind came a voice, a kind voice.

Every life is sacred. And it's not for you or me to take.

The voice sliced through the haze in her head and left Maia cold and empty. Her grip loosened and in an instant, the fire slipped back inside her. Before Maia could catch her breath, and before she could regain her clarity, the air twisted and lunged at her, a searing pain tore through her arm, and in the next moment, she was hurtling backward. Maia crashed to the ground, momentarily stunned by the impact, breathless, reeling from the pain. Someone grabbed her by the arms, pulled her to her feet, and dragged her behind the safety of a column. Maia blinked hard, desperate to figure out what had just happened. She found herself staring at Miir's concerned face. If it had not been for his hands that held her up by the shoulders and kept her standing, she would have crumpled to the floor.

He grimaced at the long bruise on her arm. "I should have moved quicker. Remii attacked the moment you let him go."

"I let go?" A disbelieving whisper slipped out of Maia. "Why did I let go?"

She knew why. Something stopped her, something deep inside her threw her off her path of revenge. A voice that said life was sacred. But Remii . . . that despicable man who had tortured Dada . . . how could his life be sacred? It could not be. He was evil and he deserved to die. How could she let him go?

Maia looked at her trembling hands, tears trickling down her face as the realization of her failure set in. "I couldn't. I . . . Why did I let him go? How could I?"

Remii's sniveling face flashed before her eyes. His gloating smile, his jeering voice, and his cruel words burned a hole in her mind. She should have ended him. She had been so close. And then she let go.

She clutched Miir's arm, desperately seeking support, as the pain of failure swept through her and left her shaking. "I couldn't avenge my Dada. I wanted to. I did want to." Maia gasped for air, but no matter how much she breathed, her insides stayed empty. "I'm so useless. Pathetic."

Miir's arms wrapped around her and held her as she sobbed into his shoulder. "You are not pathetic," he whispered. "You stopped because you are not Remii. You are not a murderer."

She looked up in hopes of finding strength. Miir's face was blurred in the mist of her tears, but the kindness in his eyes still shone through. Every venomous word, every cruel and false accusation Remii had hurled at him came back to her, making her wonder where he got the strength to bear it without so much as a twitch of his face, and thinking of his pain brought more tears to her eyes.

"And neither are you," Maia said.

Wordless moments, trembling with unexpected tenderness and understanding, stretched between them, uniting them in an ephemeral bond that startled Maia with its intensity. Never had a battlefield felt so tranquil, and never had she felt so utterly and completely safe. The little time felt like an eternity, filled to the brim with hope and promise. And even though Maia could not quite fathom what she yearned for so desperately, she wished that moment would last forever.

It only lasted until Miir spoke. "We have no time to lose," he said, his voice gentle but urgent. "They are scattered at the moment, trying to regroup. This is our chance to strike. Once the chairman gets here . . . he will surely have more people with him and possibly more equipment. And it will be too late."

He was right. There was no time to lose. Maia wiped away her tears and squared her shoulders. They had to get out now, or —

There was no *or*. This had to be done. Now.

"I'm ready."

Miir peered at her. "Are you sure?"

"Yes, let's do this. What's the plan?"

Maia's fists tightened. She might not have killed Remii, but she was not going to be killed either. She was going to fight her way out of this.

CHAPTER TWENTY-EIGHT

SYNCHRONY

The plan was simple—get out there and take out Remii and the SDS agents. It sounded easy, but Maia knew it would be anything but. Remii had yet to recover from her chokehold; his continuing wheezing and coughing were clear indications of that. He was not in top form anymore, which was a good thing. But there were six others to reckon with, and they were going to be tough.

"You take the right, I will go for the left," Miir said as they went over their plans. "Remii may be down, but he is not out yet. So—"

"I'll keep him in mind, don't worry."

"Good," he said, flexing his hands. "Ready?"

They swung out from behind the massive column. All six agents were still in the hangar, but only two saw them right away. They came rushing forward, and as they clashed with Miir, the left side of the room turned into a churning vat of energy.

"Yoteh."

Maia coiled the light up Bellator and took in the rest of the scene. Pieces of the Dampers were strewn across the floor. Two of the agents on the right were trying to patch up one of the Dampers. Remii sat near the door, hands clutching his throat, his eyes bulging as he wheezed. Amanii and another agent were at his side. They jumped up and pulled their weapons out as soon as they noticed Maia, and Remii's hands shot up.

Maia saw a vortex—colossal, fierce, and designed to hurt—rushing at her. Her heart sped up. She planted her feet and rearranged the light around her hands. The TEK formation, as massive as it was, was no match for the shield of light she placed in its path. Even so, she skidded back a few steps from the impact as the vortex slammed against her shield and disintegrated with a violent crackle.

"Get her," Remii screamed.

Maia's mind raced to formulate a plan as the agents advanced. Four of them and Remii—she could not take them all in one-on-one combat. So the whip formation was out of the question. She had to do something else. She decided on balls of fire, but she was a moment too late. The projectiles blasted out of her hands, but a knife-like formation had already swept out of Amanii's hands. It ruthlessly shredded the light. The other three joined Amanii, two with shields and the other with a formation that mirrored Amanii's.

Maia tried again, making the light as big as she could. This time the knives could not shred it, but that did not make much difference either. The light that reached the agents seemed to be deflected before it touched their bodies.

Amanii cackled as Maia skidded back a few steps, trying to ward off a stream of boulders she unleashed. "Not so easy anymore, is it, Maia? Our new suits are made to resist your powers. They're just as special as you are. Like them?"

No wonder all of the agents had these suits on and not the usual black uniforms of the SDS. No wonder the light was not reaching them.

Maia changed her plans again. She willed the light into spears that would pass through the wall of knives. They went one after another, in a rapid, fiery storm from her hands. It was not perfect, but it worked better. A few caught the man on the right and pushed him backward. Just as Maia had expected, Amanii and the other one wielding the knife formation had to work harder to counter the bombardment.

Maia was just thinking she would keep this up when the man nearest to the door unleashed a simple but massive wave formation. It plowed through the shower of light spears and swept them away, and once again, Maia had to retreat and search for a new way.

Every new blow she conjured up, the agents blocked with flawless efficiency. If one of them fell, another took their place. If one missed, another stepped in. Sweat trickled down Maia's brow, her confidence sagged, and her legs grew sluggish under her. The ball of fear grew bigger inside her with every passing moment and the window of opportunity shrank. Maia did not give up. She kept volleying fireballs, or sweeping across them with whips, but no matter what she did, they kept inching closer.

All of a sudden Maia realized she was defending more than she was attacking. One moment she put up a shield to hold off a shower of spikes, the next she was cutting up a gigantic avalanche that threatened to crush her. The SDS squad was fast, and keeping up with them was not easy. As energy slowly dripped out of her, she backed up, one step at a time. They kept coming, their arms moving in unison, their onslaught unrelenting.

Maia had just pushed them back a few steps with a wave of light, hoping for a moment to catch her breath before she brought up the formation, when Amanii screamed.

"Together!"

All of the agents raised their arms and the air collapsed into a rainstorm of pellets. It caught Maia off guard and the sheer force of the incoming mass pushed her backward. Hard as she tried, she could not form a full shield. Raising her arm to cover herself, Maia braced for impact. This was it, she thought as the first rush of pellets gashed her arms and threw her to the floor. A tormented gasp escaped her. Frozen in fear, her eyes wide, she watched a million particles impinge on her, ready to tear her apart. A TEK shield slammed into place above her before they could touch her.

It took Maia a moment to realize it was Miir. "Thank you," she wheezed, scrambling back to her feet, grateful for the moment's reprieve.

Amanii's jeering voice cut through the din. "Ah, the damsel in distress waiting to be saved. So that's how you endear yourself." One of her companions guffawed.

Rage, intense and sharp, made Maia's fists curl. The light emerged in her favorite form, a pair of whips. She had to think of something new, something that would cut through the solid wall of attack the SDS squad put up.

She strode forward a few steps, brought her hands together, and pulled them apart just as Amanii and her companions sent a deluge of boulders her way. The top whip of light tore through the formation, and the bottom sliced across their legs. It could not touch them, but the force was enough to make them unsteady. Two of them fell like toy soldiers, and Amanii barely managed to keep standing.

Maia took the opportunity to advance some more. For a while, it seemed like she would hold her ground. But the squad was formidable, and untouchable in those suits. Soon Maia found herself falling back again, pushed back by their fierce, relentless attack. One step at a time she retreated, until once again, she felt Miir's presence behind her. He too, Maia realized, had not gained ground. Things were not going well.

They fought back to back, arms weaving through the air as they made one form, then another, and yet another to stop the advance of the SDS squad. Once in a while, Maia sent one flying or Miir pushed one back to the wall. But it was never enough, and the ring around them kept getting tighter and smaller.

Maia's arms throbbed, and her legs were not as stable anymore. This could not go on for very long. They needed a new plan, a better plan.

"It's not working," she said to Miir. "They keep coming closer."

"I know."

"What do we do?"

All she received was silence and Maia's heart beat in a panicked frenzy. If Miir did not know either, what then? What else could they do? Break out to the grounds behind, even at the risk of creating a bigger mess?

"Together," Miir said suddenly.

"What?"

"We have to go together. Remember how it worked outside the Trinity Caverns?"

A smile flooded Maia's face as she recalled. The blast that had brought down the mound of dirt at the caverns was an accidental but wondrous fusion of the light with a TEK wave. She did not know whether it would work again, but if it did, it would be just the miracle they needed now.

"I'm ready when you are," she said, her heart surging with hope.

"All right then. Make me a really, really big ball of fire. Aim it at the center," Miir said. "Now!"

Maia had no idea she could create a formation so big. The light came out of her palms in a massive, brilliant, scorching sphere. It hovered on her cradling hands for a moment; then as Maia pushed it out, it shot forward, burning its way through the hangar toward the entrance. Maia saw their eyes widen. She saw them scamper to create counterattacking formations. Then Miir raised his hands and the air broke. It fractured into a million pieces, connected in a massive web. It surged forward, hitting the light from behind, lifting it for a moment. They fused together, the light spreading out in a gigantic web of brilliance across the room, and sweeping forward in a blazing wave.

Maia only had time to notice Remii's horrified face before Miir pushed her to the ground and threw up a TEK shield around them where they crouched. Then the room flooded with a blinding light and Maia closed her eyes. She did not open them until the tremors had ebbed.

"Nafi, come on out," Miir yelled even before Maia got back on her feet. "We have to leave. Now."

Maia looked around as she dashed to the door. The agents were scattered all over the room, like broken twigs after a storm. They groaned and whimpered, but no one moved. Amanii had fallen in a heap near the door. Remii was sprawled out on the other side. Maia could tell they were breathing, but she could also tell they would be in no shape to fight for a while.

Miir rushed to the door and yanked it open. He slipped outside and froze immediately. Maia and Nafi had followed in his footsteps, and Maia's heart dropped to the pit of her stomach as she realized why Miir had stopped in his tracks. A man, clad in a black body suit, stood just outside the door holding an enormous blaster in his arms, his hand firmly on the trigger. The weapon's menacing open end was pointed directly at the trio, and all Maia could do was hold her breath, for there was no way out of this.

Breathless moments trickled by. Maia's heart thundered. Then she blinked in disbelief as the man lowered the blaster.

He pulled down the mask covering his face and Maia recognized him right away. He was one of Miir's classmates at the XDA, one who had the dubious honor of breaking up a fistfight between her team and another during the first phase of the Initiative.

Maia exhaled as he smiled brightly. "Never thought I'd see you again, brother," he said to Miir.

"Damone." Miir's face lit up just as much as Damone's. "Good seeing you."

They clasped hands and embraced before Damone's eyes narrowed on Maia. "So this is why they needed all this. It is awful," he muttered before jabbing his thumb in the direction of the main entrance. "You two should be in 14, right? Go on. Get in there before the next unit hits the scene. They're almost here." He turned toward Miir. "Upstairs, chute from 54B is clean." He took a peek into the hangar and shook his head. "I better get to work. This'll be some incident report."

"Hey, Damone," Miir called as Damone was striding into Hangar

22. "Get out if you can," Miir said.

Damone gave him a look and sighed. "Don't think I have your guts, but . . . you never know. You stay safe."

As soon as the door of Hangar 22 closed behind Damone, Miir nodded at Maia and Nafi. "Hurry up. Get back in."

They sprinted across the corridor, down to Hangar 14, and then back into their Raptor, much to the boisterous relief of their teammates. A whole lot of time was spent discussing everything that happened and trying to cover up the biggest bruises. Maia stayed on tenterhooks, jumping at the slightest of sounds, worrying that an army of the SDS would burst in through the doors any moment.

"Relax, Maia," Dani reassured over and over. "No one will come here. The sanctity of the Initiative is above everything and that is a promise no one has broken. You know that."

She knew that, of course. Time and again, she had been told that. And no one had ever attacked her while she was within the domain of the Initiative. But this time, it was close. And the fear refused to leave.

"Besides, they wouldn't dare," Ren added. "After Remii's capers at ThulaSu, the SDS has fallen out of favor with the queen. So unless they can frame you as a threat to public safety, they will not risk coming after you openly."

Turned out, her teammates were correct. No one burst through the doors to grab her and other than frowning once at Maia's now slightly disheveled look, Master Demissie left them alone.

However, Maia breathed freely only after they had boarded the transporter for Tansi. The trip back was uneventful. Nafi sat by herself, in a seat some distance away from the rest of them. She was quiet, far too quiet for comfort, so Maia walked over and slipped into the seat next to her.

"I'm really sorry for all the trouble, Maia. Thank you for coming after me and for . . . understanding," Nafi said right away as if she were waiting for Maia to join her.

Maia patted her hand. "It's all right, Nafi. We made it out just fine, so . . ."

"I promise, I'll work on my fears." Nafi stayed silent for a while before she flashed a brilliant smile. "But you know, now that we're all out safely, I have to say this. That was a fight I'll never forget. You two were good together. Wait, no . . . you were great together. Just the two of you against the seven of them and those horrid machines." Nafi paused and tittered happily. "The way those people went flying. That stupid Amanii smashed like a boiled potato." Maia frowned at the girl. "Wait. How did you know? Did you peek?"

Nafi shrugged. "Well, I had to from time to time. How else would I know if you were still alive?" She giggled merrily. "Oh, I'd pay to watch that fight again."

Maia chuckled at Nafi's words. Paying for it was an exaggeration for sure, and the day had been quite an ordeal, but it was true — the fight was, in hindsight, a thrill. She had fought alongside Miir at the Trinity Caverns, but not this way, not really together. And together felt good, the camaraderie and the synergy satisfying.

However, more than the fight, Maia's mind lingered on Remii and Amanii's cruel words, mostly on the ones they heaped on Miir. She found herself marveling again at Miir's quiet strength. She had always thought of his life as perfect. He had everything one could hope for. In reality, he did not have the one thing that mattered most, someone to lean on. He had lost his mother, his father he could never reach, and his brother was no brother at all. Except for Damone, she had yet to see him with a good friend. He always wore that stoic expression, one Maia had always read as coldness and arrogance. The reality was, hidden under that cold indifference was a whole lot of pain. And loneliness. She wished she had tried to understand, to know him better instead of tearing into him out of blind, prejudiced anger the way she had done for years. She sincerely hoped she would get a chance to make up for some of it. That evening, Maia did what little she could at that moment — prayed over and over that Miir could find happiness, and that someday, his heart could heal.

Chapter Twenty-Nine

Unexpected Turns

The team was in an upbeat mood the day after their return from Xif. The craft details had been submitted. Zaara had pored through every detail in the preliminary summary reports as well as Master Demissie's comments. She added her own opinions for every team, and Core 21 was happy that other than a thoughtful nod or two, she had nothing to add to theirs.

After that, she announced the upcoming trips. "It's time for your next two steps. Both will be timed, so prepare well. First comes your trip to the Challowist, and then Korobieltes."

Someone drew a sharp breath, and most faces fell. Maia was no exception. There was no doubt that their times for the Challowist trip would be bad, so their hopes rested on Korobieltes and Ti. However, both of those were tough. Both had brutal environments and both were unknown. Winning those would be difficult.

From the dais, Zaara waved some papers. "Your task in Korobieltes is to extract two specimens of each plant per group. I have maps with areas allocated for each team. Some of them overlap. You'll find out which teams overlap once you get there. You'll either have to fight or collaborate to get your share." She stopped and grimaced. "Obviously, with some teams, collaboration will not be an option. So prepare for combat." She looked amused as she took in the grim faces in front of her. "You'll be timed, of course, and you'll also be running against a clock. Take too long and you're out, even if you were the fastest of them all. Understood?"

A roomful of heads nodded.

Aerika walked up to the dais next. "There isn't much I need to tell you about your Challowist trip. You have already set your parts up, and now you need to pick them up. You will be timed as usual and . . . that's it. Questions?"

Jiri's hand shot up as expected. "Will we run against a clock there too?"

"No, you won't. Take all day if you like, Jiri," Aerika said. Her skinny fingers tap-danced on the table behind her before she spoke again. "As I said before, the Challowist is probably the simplest of the three tasks you've been assigned, so do your best there and grab some easy points."

Maia stifled a sigh. Grabbing 'some easy points' . . . that was clearly the case for every other team. However, for them, Challowist was as good as lost. They had to focus on the other tasks.

Zaara dismissed them, and after spending some time with Teooio at the Glass House, the group dispersed. Ren headed to Frauz Point after lunch and the rest of the team—Kusha had some free time on his hands and joined as well—gathered in the AR. The impending trips were all they could talk about.

"It's going to be brutal," Kusha said. "Remember the heat in Korobieltes? And this time we have to run around in the sun, wearing those suits, fighting for these specimens. I'm not looking forward to this."

"Looking forward or not, we have to time well there," Maia said.

Dani let out a huge sigh. "Sorry, guys. It's all my fault. I should have thought through the generator some more. The Challowist might be in play if I hadn't picked the Taikorov."

"Nothing we can't handle, Dani," Maia said. "Besides, now that we're splitting two ways, there's still a chance. We might not win, but we won't have to come in last."

Even though Maia meant every word she said, Dani did not seem much cheered by them. Nafi stomped up and flopped on the couch next to Dani. "All right. You want me to say sorry for being annoyed at you the other day? I'm sorry. Happy?"

"What?" Dani looked befuddled. "Why would I—"

"Because other than my . . . spectacular performance that day, you shouldn't be upset over picking the Taikorov. It was the best choice, as you explained to Aerika. When we need it, I'm sure it'll make a difference. So what if we have the worst times? I call it an investment. Now move on."

A smile flooded Dani's face and Maia's heart flipped with joy. There was no doubt about how deep friendships ran in this circle. Loriine could laugh as much as she wanted, or win as much as she wanted, she could never dream of having friends like these.

"All right. Now that Miss Niceness has apologized and ordered people to move on, let's plan." Kusha laid out the maps on the table and gestured at them to join him. "We *have* to get the best time at Korobieltes. But even at the Challowist, we can't give up. So Dani, tell us how."

Heads gathered to analyze every little detail of the Challowist farm and the best possible strategies to secure the parts in the least possible time. They discussed and debated for a long time. They would have continued longer, but the sound of running feet in the corridor outside made them pause. The door to the AR flew open and a red-faced, scruffy-looking Ren dashed in. While the other four stared dumbfounded, he slumped into the nearest chair, panting.

Dani was the first to walk up to Ren, a glass of water in hand. "Want this?" she asked.

Ren gulped down the water, grabbed Dani's hand, and planted a kiss on her fingers. "You are a lifesaver, Dani. Thank you."

Dani flushed a vivid pink and Nafi marched over to Ren's side.

"All right, your life is saved now, Prince Charming," she said, tapping her foot impatiently. "What's the matter? Why are you stomping around like a pachy on the loose?"

"Stomping around?" Ren glowered. "Just wanted to find you guys as soon as I got the news."

"What news?" Nafi demanded.

"*Shadow*," Ren said with a loud sigh. "They blocked the release and sent it back up to Xif."

"What?" Nafi just about exploded. "Why?"

Ren shook his head. "The Tokii wouldn't tell Adienos anything except it was blocked."

"Phocluus," Maia whispered. "He must have got it stopped. He must have been really mad that Remii and his troops got beaten so badly."

Ren nodded. "You're right. I'm sure he did. He couldn't get you so he hit back the only way he could."

Maia drew a long breath to fill the sudden emptiness inside her. This was all because she had stupidly stepped right into Phocluus's trap.

"It's my fault," Nafi said, slumping into a chair. "If I hadn't—"

"Not you, Nafi." Maia cut her off. "Me, it was me. If I hadn't run out there, they'd have let you wander around and nothing would've happened. They were looking for me, waiting for me. I should have known. I should've been more careful. It's not like I don't know they're after me."

"Maia, you went to look for Nafi," Dani said. "And Nafi was just worried about Miir. This is no one's fault."

"Well, fault or not, our plan failed." Ren walked over to the window and stared out with a hopeless look on his face. "We were so close."

"Does Miir know yet?" Kusha asked.

Ren shook his head. "I'm going over now to tell him. Anyone wants to come?"

Everyone was on their feet instantly.

Except for Maia. She could not. She just could not face Miir and tell him that she had lost the one thing he wanted. It was not shame she felt, nor fear. It was a pain so acute that it tore her insides into pieces, over and over. The pain of knowing she had destroyed a dream he held so dear. Just the thought of him finding out his hopes were all for naught, thinking of that look on his face when they told him—

"I'll pass," Maia said.

Ren frowned. "What? Why?"

"I have a headache," Maia lied. "It's all right. I'll talk to him when I see him later. Sometime."

She had just walked out of the AR when Dani rushed over to her side. "Maia, don't take it so hard. It's not like *Shadow* was destroyed. It's safe and undamaged. It's just not here right now. It's all fine."

"I know," Maia said. "I just . . . my head . . . I need some rest, Dani. Please?"

"All right." Dani's arm slipped out of hers.

Maia trudged back to her room and threw herself onto her bed.

Miir must have found a spot to keep *Shadow*. He must have made plans to fly it around. And now—

Dusty who had been curled up on the windowsill, marched up to the bed and settled near her face, purring loudly and distracting Maia for a bit. As she stroked the calico's smooth coat, Maia's thoughts drifted again.

How could she have let this happen? All she had to do was keep herself in check, and keep an eye on Nafi. And she could not even do that. She knew this was important to someone she cared about, she knew that she would never be off Phocluus's mind, and yet . . .

The cat jumped away, perhaps sensing her absentmindedness.

Maia pulled the blanket over her head and curled up underneath. The warmth of her cocoon brought a little comfort and a few bracing thoughts. Dani was right. It was not as if *Shadow* was destroyed. It would all be fine. Miir would get *Shadow* back, one way or another.

Why did it hurt so much, then? Why did it feel like she had lost something of her own? Why were her insides twisted into an aching lump, ready to burst into a barrage of tears?

* * *

Maia woke up to a gentle nudge. It was dark outside and Rayan was bent over her. Maia turned over and slipped further under the blanket.

"I'm tired, Rayan. I want to sleep."

"Someone is here for you," Rayan said. "Should I ask him to leave?"

Maia sighed. Couldn't she have just one evening to herself?

"Is it urgent?"

"Not sure. Says he wants to speak to you."

Maia turned around. "Who is it?"

"Miir."

Maia froze, her heart and mind racing. What was he here for?

"Could tell him to leave. Should I?" Rayan asked.

"No. No, I'll come."

She had to face this, no matter how weirdly shaken she was. Maia crawled out from under the covers and grabbed Bellator. By the time Maia had buckled her belt in place, Rayan was ready with her jacket.

"He is at the entrance," Rayan said as Maia walked out of the room.

Maia stopped a few paces down, suddenly realizing Rayan was not following. "Aren't you coming too?" she asked. "I mean, it's dark and I thought you didn't like me being alone with—"

Rayan shrugged. "I know what I need to know. Go."

Sluggish steps took Maia down the stairs to the entrance. Seeing Miir perched on one of the sidewalls next to the front stairs made her heart skip a beat, embarrassment turning her fingers cold.

He turned around and smiled as soon as she walked out. "Hey!"

Maia returned a nod and a half-smile, all without looking up at his face.

"All your friends came to see me." They did, of course. And she was the only one missing. After being the one who messed it all up. How highly Miir must think of her now. "They said you were not feeling well. I came to check."

"It was . . . nothing." The smile she forced came out awkward. "I'm fine now."

"Good." He tilted his head toward the ramparts. "You up for a walk?"

A walk? To what end? All she needed to do now was say sorry. If only she could make her mouth say it. But the words refused to come out. How was a walk going to solve that?

"We could stand here and talk if that is what you want," Miir said.

Talk about what? Just thinking of bringing up *Shadow* made her cringe. It felt as if broaching the topic would swallow her from the inside out. This odd situation would take some time to handle. She could not just stand here all that while. People would come and go. And Miir . . . his gaze would be burning her face as it was at the moment.

"No, I'd like to walk."

She did walk, in silence, all the way up to the gate of the rose garden. Fists curled with determination, Maia thought of a million possible ways to bring up *Shadow*, but . . . her mouth would not budge. It was just plain absurd.

"End of the world, is it?" Miir asked suddenly.

"What?" Maia looked up at him, startled. "What do you mean?"

"That face you have on," he said. "As if the prince of the R'armimon were pointing a blaster at us right now."

"I'm upset," Maia blurted.

"I know. Why do you think I am here?"

Maia stopped and looked up at his face. And suddenly, those runaway words she had been hunting for appeared out of nowhere and gushed out of her like water from a broken pot.

"Why *are* you here? You lost *Shadow* because of me. I should've been the one to come to you and say I was sorry. Even if that wouldn't fix anything." She looked away for a moment, her eyes darting over the soft glowing contours of the Sun Temple behind them. "And I didn't. I couldn't face you. After all my lectures about you overthinking . . . I was the one who messed up. And I can't even bring it up and say I'm sorry." She turned away and stared blankly at the dark shadows of the rose garden, anguish gnawing at her heart and making her eyes burn. "What is wrong with me?"

He walked around to stand in front of her. "Nothing. Nothing is wrong with you. Sometimes, when we are too upset, we cannot find words. We think we should do something, but find ourselves frozen. It happens to all of us." His voice was kind and soothing. The silence when he paused momentarily was unbearable. "Yesterday, when I was angry with Nafi, I froze too. Then you made me realize talking to her was important, and the only thing of consequence I could do at that moment. Reaching out does not come very easily to me, especially when I am upset. You helped."

Maia looked at his face. His earnest eyes shone back at her.

"Shall we?" Miir nodded at the road. He started walking again and Maia fell into step with him.

"When I did not see you today, I knew you were very upset. And I thought I should come by. See if *you* needed a hand." He chuckled a little. "Looks like you do. Even though I still see no reason for this world-ending unhappiness."

"No reason?" The question fell out of Maia in a pitiful whimper. "If I had not gone looking for Nafi, then—"

He squinted hard at her. "You would rather let Nafi go wandering about wherever so I could have *Shadow*?"

"No, absolutely not. That's not it. But I should have done something right. Maybe stopped her sooner or talked to her so this wouldn't happen at all. All would have gone as planned and . . ."

"Sometimes, plans do not go the way we wish them to. Sometimes, you find yourself standing on a road you never expected to be on. You know that."

She *did* know that. But it did not change the fact that Miir did not have his Raptor. And he was so close to having it, too.

"I just . . ." Her voice trailed off, words lost in a rush of thoughts. "I really hoped you could have *Shadow*. I know you miss it and—"

He did not let Maia finish. "Yes, I do. But really, the world does not end if I do not have *Shadow* here today. I mean it."

"Even so, having it would've made you happy."

He stared at her for a moment, his eyes glowing with characteristic Xifarian incandescence, his face frozen for an instant as if something she had said had shaken him. It passed in a blink and he laughed.

"Yes, but you know, you can make me even happier if you wish to."

Maia was thankful for the darkness so he did not see how ludicrously she flushed, and she hoped he did not hear the odd quiver in her voice. "How so?"

"Just smile a little."

She did not have to try. A smile, small but effortless, broke out.

"I like that. Thank you," he said, laughing. They walked a few more paces quietly before Miir spoke again. "I want to tell you something. But you have to keep it a secret from everyone, Ren in particular. Can you?"

It was weird how her heart flitted all over the place, and as hard as she tried, Maia could not pin down why. Was it just silly, childish glee at being chosen to keep a secret, or was it an anticipation of what he wanted to share?

"Yes, of course," she said hastily, realizing too many silent moments had trickled past. "I promise."

"Well, in a way"—he slowed and nodded to a pair of Kausakas on patrol—"I am relieved that Ren's plan did not succeed." He quickly explained, perhaps seeing Maia's wide, uncomprehending gaze. "I am not saying that I do not miss *Shadow*. I do, very much. But . . ."

Miir fell silent, and Maia's mind spun as her eyes darted between the hulking shape of the Garaha Gates in the distance and Miir's thoughtful face. A realization hit her suddenly and she blurted. "You can tell me. I won't be hurt or offended, if that's what you're thinking."

Miir chuckled a little. "Well, the plan was a little reckless and . . . shortsighted. I am grateful that Ren took so much trouble arranging it, just to make me happy, and that is why I could not refuse when I knew I should have."

Maia remembered seeing the hesitation on his face.

"So I went along, hoping nothing would go wrong."

"And of course, it did," Maia said sighing.

"But see, that is the point," he replied before she could say any more. "Even if we had *Shadow* here, what could I do with it? I could not fly about ThulaSu whenever I wanted. People would notice. And, regardless of the ban Rahina Quemiila put on the SDS, it would only be a matter of time before someone came investigating. So, really, it was a—"

"Stupid plan?"

Miir sighed and shook his head. "It would be cruel to call a selfless idea that. But even if we went to great lengths to make it work after *Shadow* arrived, it would only barely work. *Shadow* would, for all practical purposes, simply stay parked at Frauz Point or hidden at Northrock Expanse."

Maia groaned inwardly. Although she had thought of some of these issues before, it had been hard to push back against Ren's enthusiasm.

"Ren can be a little . . ."

"Overly enthusiastic? Needlessly daring?"

Maia had to laugh at the descriptions, each of which was perfectly apt. Ren was just . . . Ren. As much as she wished Ren's plan had succeeded, after hearing Miir's thoughts, she too was relieved that they failed to retrieve *Shadow*. She now wished they had not tried for it at all; she could have done without that frightful encounter with the

SDS.

"Can *I* tell you something?" Maia asked and continued as he nodded. "If you felt this would not work, you should have said no. You see . . . we are not that sensitive to hearing no. We often have crazy ideas and we often argue over them."

"So I have noticed."

Maia chuckled a little. That they debated a lot was hard to miss. "Next time, please don't feel like we'll be all broken up if you go against our opinions. You'll probably get an earful, but we'll be just fine. And we'll still be friends afterward."

"All right, duly noted," Miir said. "Now I need one more thing from you."

It had been an evening of surprises, albeit pleasant ones. Maia looked at Miir, curious to find out what else he had in mind.

"What is it?"

"I have been dying to know about this Adienos person. Ren refuses to tell me much at all, so I am hoping to get some straight answers from you. Where did he help you break in?"

"Adienos, huh? It's a long story."

"Since the world is no longer about to end, we have some time on our hands," Miir said. "Tell me."

Maia began, her thoughts flying back to the very first phase of the Alliance Initiative. Miir obviously knew parts of it, but there was so much he did not. It was fun seeing him surprised at the many things that happened during their stay at the XDA. They talked and laughed and talked for hours. Maia felt she could have talked all night and not run out of things to say, and if she did run out of things to say, she could be content with the silence. How time flew by, she had no idea. They walked all the way to the Garaha Gates and back in what seemed like a heartbeat.

After they said goodbye, as Maia stood at the entrance of the living quarters watching Miir vanish into the dark, a strange wistfulness enveloped her heart. Her thoughts were a convoluted, puzzling mess as she walked up to her room. She stopped at the threshold, her hand frozen on the doorknob. *How weird,* she thought. They had only just parted, and she already missed him.

Chapter Thirty

One Step Closer

The day of their second and final trip to the Challowist was balmy, quite a contrast from the snowy morning when they had made the first trip. Tensions were running high and when the large Aqumob pulled away from the shore that morning, there was hardly a word spoken, even within the teams. The arbitrators were all on board, and Pomewege in particular was in the best of spirits. He made the rounds, stopping to speak with every team, and reminding them to try the wonderful food that had been laid out. Most of them were too anxious to be hungry. Even Nafi only picked up the tiniest creamed oyster sandwich, and only because the principal spoke so highly of it.

Core 21 would split in two. Dani and the boys were headed to Site 11 to pick up the sub-chargers, while Maia and Nafi were to fetch the main charger from Site 24. Dani went over the map a few times, and although it seemed easy when they studied it, Maia knew it would not be that easy to actually collect the parts. Indeed, Aerika had a long list of cautions for the teams.

"Gather around, everyone," she called them to the center of the main deck. "You have already used the Propettes, so that is nothing new. You will take them again to the allocated sites. You will pick out the part you have installed and one extra of the same type, as a substitute just in case. The substitute will be flagged with the same marker as the one you set up." She pointed at a pile of boxes on a table. "Those are the cases you'll put the parts in. So pick them up, put them in the container, seal them, and then bring them back. Is that clear?"

Everyone nodded solemnly.

"You will be timed from the moment you leave this craft to the point you hand the parts over to me . . . all the parts you've collected," Aerika continued. "However, be careful when you take the parts from the substrate layer. If you are too hasty, you might damage the connectors and end up with faulty equipment. That you do not want."

They had to be quick but careful—not an easy task in a race, and submerged in frigid waters. They all donned water suits and took last looks at the maps. The Aqumob stopped at the release point, a location equidistant from all the assigned sites. Then one by one, the teams took off.

Maia and Nafi shot off toward Site 24 at a furious pace. The water was cold and even though the suits provided some insulation, it still numbed their bones. Thousands of parts were hung on the substrate base where the continental shelf formed a long wall. Finding the site was not hard, although locating the part they had installed during their last trip took some time. What was really difficult was pulling it out from the substrate layer below while balancing on the Propette. It took some delicate finagling to get both the main part and a substitute, one by one. They took turns prying them out, Nafi working on the first with Maia assisting, and the other way around for the second. While the first came out relatively quickly, the duo faced trouble with the second.

The second, or the substitute, was at a spot slightly removed from the first, possibly to make sure there was some variation in the underlying substrate between them. The variation would ensure at least one working unit. However, it also made for a trickier extraction. They had chosen a particularly open, calm location for the first, but the second — either by design or by coincidence — was not as easy.

The currents that swept across the Challowist were different at different spots. At the location where the substitute hung, it pressed a little too close to the wall. Maia set her Propette on hovering mode next to the part and reached for it. But barely halfway through, she was pushed flat against the wall by the force of the current. She tried again, and although this time the push was expected, it still disturbed the smoothness needed to pry the piece out. It did not help that the substitute was at a sharp point, and being slammed against a pointy rock wall was not a pleasant experience.

"I'm going to hang upside down, Nafi," Maia declared after she had tried three times and failed. "The force up top is much less, and there are fewer chances of being thrashed around, I think."

Nafi nodded, but slowly. "Be careful, Maia. If you slip off the Propette, it'll be a mess."

It would be for sure. And the stars knew, they did not need any more troubles on their plates at the moment. But however risky it was, it had to be done to get their parts out undamaged.

She slowly maneuvered the Propette until she was suspended right above the unit she had to take out. Her calculations were correct and the current only nudged her slightly. Holding her breath and gripping the Propette as steadily as she could, Maia worked with her tools. One by one, the hooks came off the substrate, and soon the tubular main charger came free.

"Done," Maia announced happily.

Nafi was waiting eagerly to bag it. Parts secured and sealed in the boxes, the girls hurried back to the Aqumob.

Aerika greeted them warmly when they reached the vessel. "You are the first to arrive. Good work."

As good as that was, it did not mean much, since their time could only be noted once their entire team returned with all the parts they were assigned to retrieve. They waited patiently at first. Then, as time passed, Nafi started fidgeting. Soon Maia started getting antsy, especially when Core 10—the all-Jjord team—arrived to claim first place.

"Come on, come on," Nafi kept muttering. "Dani, where are you?"

Dani and the boys did not show up until much later. In between, Core 7 arrived, cheering as Aerika logged them in second place. Maia and Nafi were slumped hopelessly side by side, their fists curled and faces despairing, when Maia heard Ren's voice. She jumped up and ran to the outer deck. Dani, Kusha, and Ren had arrived barely a moment before Core 13.

Maia's fists went up in the air and Nafi screamed. No sooner had Aerika logged their times than they were in a huddle, shouting in jubilation. To make third place when they had expected to be last was a feat just as sweet as coming in first, if not sweeter.

"I'm happy," Maia said. "We may not be in the lead here, but we're still in a position to make up and win in the end."

Everyone heartily agreed, their faces shining with hope. They *had* to win, Ruche was counting on them to get the prize—Mahswa Tabrin's sword, Seigvard—to resolve the threat of the R'armimon. So the fate of the two planets, and the millions on them, rested on them winning the Initiative.

"Given the situation, we did good," Nafi said, beaming as they trooped back to the main deck. "I'm proud of us."

"Proud bunch of cheaters, that's what you are." Loriine's biting drawl made them all jump.

Core 7 stood behind them, Loriine in front, flanked by Baecca and Bakhari. Before anyone could take stock of the situation, Nafi scoffed.

"Shut up, Loriine. We always play fair, unlike you."

"Fair my foot," Loriine hissed. "If you didn't get so much support from all of the arbitrators, you'd be out of the Initiative by now. You're the most useless bunch. You make mistakes yet come in third. What a joke."

"Why don't you take it up with the arbitrators then, Loriine?" Nafi snapped, thankfully in a low voice. Maia's hand clamped on her wrist and the rest of Core 21 moved in as well. As annoying as Loriine's comment was, no one needed an argument or a falling-out now.

Loriine, however, was not in a mood to relent. "You know what? I will. I will take it up with Aerika right now."

"Yes, we will," Baecca parroted. Bakhari looked just as supportive of Loriine's idea.

But before Loriine could stomp off, Karhann and the pasty-faced boy stepped in her way. If Maia and her teammates were surprised, it was nothing compared to the stunned expressions of Loriine and her backers. Loriine's mouth fell open and she spent a while gawking wordlessly before she finally sputtered to life.

She crossed her arms and glowered. "What? What do you two want?"

"You're not going to say a word to Aerika," the pasty-faced boy said.

Maia's eyes almost popped out of her head, and she was sure everyone else felt the same way at seeing the pasty-faced boy speak up so stridently. He was always quiet, so quiet that Maia did not even know what his name was. Yet now he looked fearless standing next to Karhann, matching Loriine's scowl.

"You, Adi?" Loriine squawked.

So . . . that was his name . . . Adi. As Maia wondered why she could not remember such a simple name, Loriine went on.

"You're going against me? Do you know what your mother will say about that? It—"

"What you're doing is stupid, Loriine," Adi, the pasty-faced boy, interrupted. "We're just a few steps away from the final prize, and you're messing it all up. Stop and think for a moment before you go ranting against the arbitrators, will you?"

"I'm not listening to a lecture from the likes of *you*," Loriine hissed. "I will do what I want."

"You're going to drop the issue. Right now." Karhann had never sounded more decisive.

Loriine's gaze wavered and she drew a sharp breath. Her voice trembled but she fought back regardless. "Why? You have a thing for that girl?"

"Can you ever think past me having a 'thing' for someone?" Karhann snapped back.

"Then why are you two taking *their* side?"

"We're not taking their side. We're trying to stop you from sabotaging us." Karhann looked livid as he stared Loriine down. "You were this close to getting thrown out just a few weeks ago, and yet you keep on pulling the same petty stuff over and over. Your silly behavior is only helping the other teams."

Loriine stayed quiet for a while before her mouth puckered. "I'm only trying to help us."

"Well, it's not helping. It's making things worse."

Before Loriine could react to Karhann's last words, Aerika marched in.

"We are almost back, so get ready to disembark, everyone. All the equipment you have collected will be delivered to you soon. Good work today."

Soon they were all on the long trek back to ThulaSu. Core 21 chirped excitedly all the way back, their mood lifted by the joy of their accomplishment. Kusha went his way on reaching ThulaSu, while the rest continued toward their living quarters. As soon as they turned onto the pathway bordering the Sun Temple, they ran into Sana. She was looking particularly enchanting in a blue-and-yellow dress, and Maia had to admit she made a pretty picture with the handsome Jez by her side. When she spotted the group, Sana rushed over to Maia.

"How did it go?" she asked eagerly.

"Great," Nafi replied, grinning. "We came in third."

Jez, who had also walked over, quirked an eyebrow. "Coming third is a great thing now? Is that the new fashion?"

It was clearly a joke, but Maia's insides bristled. It was not funny, but downright annoying coming from someone like Jez who they hardly knew. Sana clearly understood the situation. She flushed and waved at the boy. "It's a long story, Jez. I'll explain it to you later." She peered at Maia and her teammates. "I can tell him, right?"

Maia's insides clenched for a moment remembering how Ren had been around Maks, always guarded. She almost expected him, or Nafi, to snap. However, before any of her teammates could say a word, Jez spoke.

"Yes, make sure you get permission from everyone, Sana. Don't spill state secrets just to make me happy," he said, smirking. "You know what, I don't even want to know. No need to stress that pretty head of yours."

They were simple statements, but something about them irked Maia. Perhaps it was the teasing tone. It felt like he was putting Sana down, or perhaps it was her own prejudice against the boy. Maia could not find an appropriate response. For a few embarrassing moments, they all stood tongue-tied and staring.

"I'm sure Sana knows what's secret and what's not." Ren broke the awkward silence. "She's just as smart as she's pretty."

That should have ended the matter, and yet, for reasons Maia could not fathom, the atmosphere grew even more tense. Then Jez slipped an arm around Sana's shoulders and pulled her close.

"For a *wahri*, you sure know a whole lot about my Sana."

A fire lit in Maia's head and her fists curled. She did not care if Jez was special to Sana. There was no excuse for that kind of foul language. "Jez—"

She got no further, because both Ren and Sana interrupted at the same time.

"Let's go," Ren said to Nafi and Dani. "I'm tired as heck. Need a nap."

Sana peeled Jez's arm off her shoulder. "I'll see you again later, all right? Need to speak with Maia now."

Another moment of silence and the huddle fell apart as if it had exploded. Ren, along with Nafi and Dani, continued toward the living quarters, Jez went the opposite way, and Maia and Sana were left alone at the corner of the Sun Temple courtyard.

Sana exhaled loudly and slumped onto the nearest bench. "That was super awkward. Jez can be so dumb sometimes."

'Dumb' was putting it nicely. Maia had no doubt that Jez had used that word on purpose. It was meant to hurt. That Ren had decided to not take offense was surprising and saved them from a brawl, but Maia was no less angered by the situation.

"I'm sorry, Maia," Sana said. "I know you despise that word and—"

"What do you see in him, Sana?" Maia asked, a bit more sharply than she intended. "Why is he so special?"

"He's not special," Sana replied in a heartbeat. "He simply happened to be around when I was looking for a fun person to be friends with."

"You have friends. We might not be fun all the time, but you have us."

Sana stared at her for a moment before sighing. "I don't know how to say this, Maia, but . . ." She studied her immaculately painted nails for a while before starting again. "Don't get me wrong. I know you guys always try to make me feel like one of you, but . . ."

Maia held her breath. There was that *but* again.

"There's something about the five of you," Sana said slowly as if she were measuring every word. "You are so tight, so close . . . you share every memory, you can predict each other's every step. You're like branches of the same tree. And that's a great thing . . . for you. But everyone else . . . we're on the outside. Seeing you together makes me feel like an outsider. No matter how hard I try, I can't ever get that close, and it leaves me wanting something of my own. Something I know just as well." Sana's worried gaze scanned Maia's face. "I don't mean to blame you for anything or want you to lose your friendship. It's just that seeing you, I feel inadequate. So . . . as much as I value you as friends, you are not enough. I need something of my own."

Maia sat down next to Sana, trying to fathom what Sana had just said. She had never heard this before, but when she thought about it, she saw Sana's point quite clearly.

"I'm sorry we make you feel that way," she said. "I never thought about it."

"It's all right." Sana placed a hand on hers. "It doesn't excuse Jez. I know he's terrible."

"What can we do differently, Sana? You know we all care a lot about you."

"Nothing, Maia. Don't worry about it," Sana reassured her. "It's nothing you do. It's just the way you are after all you have been through together." She patted Maia's hand. "I used to think it was my fault, maybe I was jealous or something. But then I noticed Miir. He has known you all the longest, but I see a lost look in his eyes when you all start chirping. I realized that's exactly how I feel. Lost. There's a familiarity about you that no one else can relate to as easily."

They sat together in silence. Maia felt a little small on hearing how they had made people feel excluded, however inadvertently. If Sana was right, and Miir felt that way too, that was sadder still. He was supposed to be part of them, and yet . . .

Right then, Maia decided she had to make a change. She could not make Sana part of their past memories, but she could make her part of them going forward. She hooked her arm through Sana's and tugged at her. "Come on. We have a lot to tell you about our trip today."

It was great seeing Sana's face break into a smile. A circle of friendship, however strong, was no good if it threw up walls and intimidated everyone else. What she and her teammates had was a thing to be cherished, but one person's treasure could not be a source of hurt for another. Maia's fingers tightened into balls. She had to try harder to make everyone feel welcome. They all had to.

CHAPTER THIRTY-ONE

HUNTER'S CREED

Less than two weeks remained until their trip to Korobieltes and things were getting stressful. Maia and Dani pored over maps of the fallen capital of the Solianese every day to pick out the minutest details. They would be timed on this challenge, so every moment they could save by finding shortcuts would add to their score. Nafi had dug up a number of books on the history of the city, some of which also contained details of architectural layout, and Maia was flipping slowly through the pages for any relevant information.

"Nafi has been gone for a while, hasn't she?" Dani said suddenly.

Nafi had left earlier that morning to secure permission from Zaara to access all available libraries in ThulaSu. Maia had been engrossed in the books and not noticed the delay, but now she fidgeted.

"I should've gone with her. Hope Zaara did not get annoyed and punish her."

"Well, let's wait a little longer, and then we should go look for her," Dani said, to which Maia heartily agreed.

Together they pored over a particular map of Korobieltes that showed the layout near the plant sites. Dani tapped on a pair of roads that cut diagonally through the grid crisscrossing the area. "These roads, if they still exist, of course, could be shortcuts between the sites, Maia. The map Zaara gave us highlighted the grids, but there is no rule that says we *have* to take those."

It was a good idea, and getting to the farthest sites faster would help create a lead Core 21 needed so desperately. "It could work," Maia said. "The thing is, these roads may just be a pile of ruins now. We can only check it out once we get there."

Dani nodded, her face grim. Deciphering Korobieltes was far from simple. Without access to current maps, this task was like trying to run in the dark. Once again they sank into their respective books, hoping to find clues. Time passed slowly, tediously.

"Maia!" Nafi's scream boomed across the corridor and made both girls jump. Dani was the first to rush to the door. She was just in time. Nafi careened in, her eyes as big as saucers, sweat trickling down her brow. "Maia, come quick. Hurry!"

They were out of the building in the blink of an eye. Along the pathways Nafi ran, Maia and Dani behind her. "What is it, Nafi?" Maia shouted, panting to catch her breath. "Where are you taking us?"

"Aekken," Nafi said. "He came and attacked the Solianese Council."

"What?" Dani yelped. "Why?"

"He thinks we're allowing in too many refugees from Xif, and he's mad," Nafi said. "Says he'll kill everyone."

"Where's Kusha?" Dani asked.

"They're all at the Gathering House."

A sizable crowd had grown in front of the building by the time the three girls reached it. The main door was closed, and a few Kausakas and other people huddled in front of it. A group of healers were tending to a couple of wounded Kausakas. Maia also spotted Enzo, the attendant Maia had met a few times at Kusha's house, sporting a large bandage on his head. Maia ran up to the Kausakas near the front door.

"What's going on?" she asked.

"The R'armimon prince and his soldiers got in. They drove us out and locked the door," one of the Kausakas explained. "The whole council is inside. The prince said he'd kill everyone if we tried to get in."

Maia's heart beat in a frenzy. Questions bombarded her mind. What was Aekken up to? Did Ruche know about this? What could she do to help defuse the situation?

Calm down, she told herself. *Think!*

Grabbing Ruche's ring, Maia called for help. She knew Ruche would come, but she could not wait for him to arrive. Aekken might do anything, and Kusha was in there. There was no time to lose.

"Help!" A scream drifted out and made every face fall. Maia recognized the voice. It was Sahiiraan Tsininio. "I don't know," he screamed, clearly in pain.

Maia decided. She had to get in, one way or another. She asked the Kausakas to clear the doorway and took a step backward. Planting her feet and stiffening her spine, she reached inside.

"*Yoteh.*"

The light surged out of her, strong and intense. Maia released it and in the blink of an eye, it spread over the door and devoured it. Maia walked in while the fire was still blazing around the frame, her fists balled, her muscles taut and ready for battle.

Maia quickly scanned the area. A group of eight faceless guards clad in red stood on the other side of the door, ready to fight back. Maia was prepared to take them on, but they let her pass. The council and Aekken were all in the center of the room. Maia's heart thrashed in her chest at the sight of a bloodied heap on the ground. Who was that? Tsininio? Goren sat next to him, a deep gash on his forehead. Maia jumped when Aekken grabbed Kusha, and she could barely keep from screaming when she saw the strange metal attachment on his hand. It was a gauntlet, only this one had clawed fingers.

"Tell me, who among you authorized this trickery," Aekken hissed. "Was it you?"

"I don't know what you're talking about," Kusha yelled. "I don't know of any trickery."

"You lie!" Aekken's claws dug into Kusha's shoulder, and blood spurted out of the wound.

"Aekken!" Maia shouted. "Stop. Right now." She let the light coil out of her hands and trail on the floor as she approached. "Let him go."

Aekken let go of Kusha and shoved him away. He pulled off the bloodied claw-like attachment from his hand and threw it to one of his faceless soldiers. Then, smiling, he walked up to Maia. "My starlight, why are you breaking down doors? Why so enraged?"

"You hurt my friend," Maia said, barely able to contain her fury. She remembered Ruche's words — *never show him your emotions* — and tried desperately to keep her voice calm. But anger seeped out nonetheless. "We had an agreement. You promised me six months. And now you're hurting innocent people."

"No, my starlight, no." Aekken shook his head vigorously. "You do not understand. I did not break any promise." He raised an accusing finger at the council members. "They did. I told them to stop allowing too many deadwastes in, and they agreed. But I am seeing the people in these camps swell like floodwater. So tell me, my starlight, what am I to do?"

He sighed and took another step closer. "I could destroy one of these deadwaste camps if you prefer," he said, a malicious grin twisting his lips. "Would you like that, my starlight?"

Maia breathed in deeply. She had to get this situation under control. Kusha was hurt and bleeding, Tsininio was probably dead, and Goren was injured. They needed attention from the healers as soon as possible. But Aekken's Faceless were guarding the door and she had a feeling that Aekken would not allow anyone in until she stood down.

"No, I wouldn't. I would prefer if there was no blood spilled at all."

"As you wish, my starlight." Aekken bowed his head in mock submission before looking pointedly at the tendrils of light swirling around her hands. "I hoped you would spare me the fire now."

"Ask your guards to move away from the door. The council members need healers."

"Done," Aekken said, clapping his hands. The guards moved away from the door in an instant. "The healers can come in," Aekken said next.

Maia pulled in the light as the healers streamed in. Aekken gently nudged her elbow and turned her away.

"Let us forget about this misunderstanding," he said. "Let us enjoy the beautiful weather instead. It is a good day for walking, my starlight. Come with me."

Maia looked back at the bloody scene behind them. She wanted no walks with the despicable prince, beautiful day or otherwise. Her resolve to turn down Aekken's proposal did not last long, however.

"I think your friends will fare better if I leave," Aekken said, his touch on her elbow far from gentle anymore. "The healers can work better without me staring down at them. Half of their mind would be worrying if I might attack again. I do not blame them—they would be right to worry. After all, there is no predicting *my* mood." Maia suppressed a shiver as he chuckled under his breath, his inky gaze locked with hers. "You'd like me to give them some room to breathe, right? Then you should accompany me out, my starlight."

That was a threat, pure and simple, disguised by gentle words and a calm voice.

"Yes," Maia said. "Let's go."

The crowd outside parted to make room as Maia walked out with Aekken, his guards following. She spotted Nafi and Dani in the crowd, bewildered looks on their faces. Maia flashed them a tiny reassuring smile, although she was hardly sure herself if it was the right thing to do. Ruche had told her many times to not be around Aekken alone. And here she was, walking out with him. But what else could she do? The council members needed immediate help.

Every step was a chore, every moment a punishment as Maia walked down the central avenue toward the Garaha Gates with Aekken. His troop of faceless guards followed a few paces behind them.

"I get upset when people break agreements. Your friend and every other member of that council are guilty of breaking the promise they made to me." Aekken's voice reminded Maia of the bitter north winds that blew across Appian in the dead of winter. It promised to leave nothing standing in its wake. "I spared your friend and the rest only because you requested it, my starlight. I need you to remember that. No one in that room would have escaped otherwise."

Maia fought to keep the chill at the base of her spine from rushing up and making her shudder. She wished she could pull her elbow out of Aekken's grasp.

"But I need this treachery to stop, my starlight," Aekken said. "I cannot have this uncontrolled flow of those deadwastes. If that continues, it will make me want to do one of two things—destroy one or two of these shelters and kill a few of the deadwastes to balance things, or take offense against the people of this planet." Aekken paused and peered at her face. "I do not want to do either, least of all attack the innocents of your home world. Do you understand?"

Something about his voice told Maia that he would enjoy doing both, even though he said otherwise. Maia nodded. "I will speak with them. I promise."

Aekken placed a fist over his heart and bowed a little. "You have always been kind and fair, my starlight," he said. "I promise you my eternal gratitude and loyalty. Shall we continue our walk now?"

Maia forced a smile and nodded, bracing herself for the continued torment of being with him.

"How is your competition—"

Aekken stopped midway because of a commotion that rose behind them. He spun around, a vicious scowl on his face, and Maia's heart dropped to the pit of her stomach when she looked back. Ren, his arms flying, was engaged in a vigorous altercation with Aekken's guards.

No, Ren! Not you too, please. I couldn't bear all of you being hurt.

She was just about to tell Ren to go away when he waved at Aekken. "Hey, Crown Prince! I have something important for you, but these idiots won't let me by."

Aekken sighed and gestured at the guards to let Ren pass. "Your friend annoys me," he said, as Ren ran up to them. "He has been useful so far, but . . . . . . he tests my patience."

"Crown Prince Aekken!" Ren grinned and bowed low when he reached them. "Your flunkeys need training. Seriously, they do."

"Yes, Ren. You had some news. What is it?"

"Oh, that!" Ren grinned sheepishly. "Well, I have something you'll be very happy with, I'm sure."

"I will?"

"This is from our mutual friend." Ren pulled out a small vial from his pocket and held it out to Aekken.

Aekken's face brightened, and he grabbed the vial greedily. "If this is true—"

Ren cut him off. "It is. Have some faith in Ren's abilities, Crown Prince Aekken." He bowed again. "You should get it analyzed right away. Tell me what you find."

Aekken nodded. He turned toward Maia and bowed a little. "Please pardon my sudden departure, my starlight. This requires my immediate attention. But I promise I will make up for this discourtesy."

Maia smiled back, hoping he would stop talking and leave so she could go back to the Gathering House and check on Kusha. She also hoped there would be no chance to 'make up'. Talking with the prince was always unnerving, but lately, it downright creeped her out. The last thing she wanted to do was talk with him again.

As soon as Aekken and his troops walked aside and disappeared with a shimmer, Maia turned toward Ren. "What did you give Aekken? What was in that vial?"

Ren winked. "Stuff."

Maia strode up and grabbed his arm as he sashayed away. "What stuff?"

Ren sighed. "It's information on Phocluus, all right?"

Maia stopped in her tracks, too stunned by his answer to fathom what it could mean. For a moment or two, she could find no words. "W-what information? Why?"

Ren slipped an arm around her shoulders and pulled her along. "Trust me, Maia." He leaned to look at her face. "Aren't you happy Aekken left?"

"Yes, I am. Thank you for rescuing me. But Aekken is dangerous and—"

"Always at your service," Ren said. "Now let's forget about me and check on Kusha. That dastardly R'armimon hurt him pretty bad. I hope he can hold up in Korobieltes with that wound."

Maia hurried with Ren toward the Gathering House with worries weighing her down. The troubles just kept coming. As if the challenge was not complicated enough, and as if Kusha did not already have enough on his plate, now Aekken had to mess up the situation even more.

She forced herself to look on the bright side. Things could have been much worse. At least bringing down the door had been the right decision, and thankfully, Aekken had relented. It was not the best of situations, but she was grateful for a little relief.

CHAPTER THIRTY-TWO

ARMORED AND READY

Almost two months after their last trip to Zagran, the gang returned to the Jjordic capital to watch the launching of the Orekemino shield around Tansi.

It was a welcome break after Aekken's ruthless attack on the Solianese Council that left many wounded, some grievously. Sahiiraan Tsininio had survived, but his eyesight was severely damaged. Worse was the injury to his spine, which according to the healers would keep him bedridden for months. Kusha's wound — it was a miracle Aekken's clawed gauntlet had missed major blood vessels — was deep enough to keep him at the sanatorium for a week. Sahiiraan Goren sported a huge bandage on his head. Quite a few Kausakas on guard duty that day, as well as attendants and other workers, including Enzo, were left with injuries large and small.

Since then, not just Maia and her teammates, but the entire population of ThulaSu spent their days and weeks on tenterhooks, fearing more attacks from the mad prince. Even Ruche, who was at first incensed with Maia for having seen the prince alone, was shaken by the magnitude of the injuries. Days passed in a slow, nervous rhythm. However, thankfully, nothing else happened.

And then, when they were tired of holding their breath and tiptoeing around, Hans came to invite them to Zagran. That Hans had forgiven their past shenanigans was not a surprise to Maia, but she had not expected him to get them passes to the launch gallery of the Mission Control Center, or MCC as Hans called it. It was just the kind of lift the gang's spirits needed at that moment.

On the morning of the launch, Hans herded everyone aside near the entrance of the gallery and turned to look all of them in the eye. "Please, please, no disruptions today. Promise?"

Ren's hand shot out and gripped Hans's arm. "Promise. I will not even breathe in there."

Hans chuckled. "I did not ask that. But—"

"I swear, Hans," Maia chimed in. "Not a peep."

"Thank you," Hans said with a relieved smile. "There will be a lot of important people in there, watching. So we need to be extra quiet."

Indeed, there were important people inside. From the Jjord premier Oliena to CA Abebe, many Jjord leaders Maia had seen before were present, as well as many Solianese house leaders. They were all in a seating section far removed from the gang, but that did not lessen the burden of responsibility much. However, for once, and possibly because the event did not take long, Maia and her friends did not have much trouble staying on their best behavior all through.

The viewing gallery overlooked a massive control center where Jjord engineers and scientists worked at the numerous portals in the room. A gigantic screen across the front of the room showed the twenty-eight Prop Points across Tansi as well as the two main hubs at Reifnor and Zagran. Maia marveled at how quickly this had come together. It almost felt like she was witnessing a miracle as the PPs lit up one by one. Then, as everyone held their breath, the net of Orekemino unfurled from the hubs and zigzagged its way from one PP to another, covering Tansi completely.

The control room erupted in cheers. The viewing gallery broke into loud applause. The gang was still chattering excitedly among themselves when Hans escorted them outside.

"So, Hans, this means Tansi's safe now, right?" Kusha asked as they trooped down to the main lobby.

"We have the basics in place, but I won't say we are free of issues. We still have to strengthen the structure." He sighed and smiled a little. "But yes, we have some armor now."

"Wish Xif had something similar in place," Dani said in a pensive tone.

"Well—" Ren started and stopped abruptly. Then he threw a cautious look around and lowered his voice before saying more. "I've heard our engineers are working on deploying our deflection shields. Although the main power source is the Sedara, and that as you know is being a little moody. So who knows how long it'll hold up against serious bombardment?"

"But that's still something," Dani said, her face lit with a smile. "Better than having nothing at all. This is good news."

Maia let out a breath of relief. This was not just good, it was great. But then again . . . Maia's heart sank as she remembered Aekken. Seeing Xif resisting in some way would probably drive him into a fit of rage, and that was not good. Not good at all. The reality was that nothing could ever be good with the crazy prince around.

"Hey, Hans!"

Maia spun around when she heard Miir's voice, and her eyes went wide. He was dressed in the kind of Jjord uniform Hans usually wore, and he looked so—

"You look different in that uniform," Ren exclaimed before Maia could pin down her thoughts.

Miir raised an eyebrow. "Different? How so?"

"Umm . . ." Ren scratched his head.

"You look great." Dani came to Ren's rescue. "You almost always wear black. So seeing you in white is . . . refreshing."

Dani was right, but it was more than that. It brought a lightness to him. It made the deep amber of his eyes so clear and . . . striking. Maia flashed a hasty smile when Miir glanced in her direction, embarrassed that he found her staring.

"Glad you guys approve," Hans said. "Miir has been working so hard with us, the team decided he should be made an honorary member, complete with his own uniform. So . . . he is one of us now."

"Thank you. I am grateful for the honor," Miir said to Hans. "I came over to say, I will be late joining you tonight. The western PPs are not behaving. Since I am heading back up tomorrow, I think I should spend some more time here now."

"All right. We'll start for T'ra without you," Hans said. "But try to be there by dinner time. I have an announcement to make. Need all of you there."

"We're going to T'ra?" Nafi bobbed up and down with excitement.

Hans had just nodded when a shout tore through the humdrum of the lobby. "Oh my goodness, can't believe it's you," said the voice. "My little munchkins!"

"Oh dear lord of the stars," Nafi exclaimed, her eyes as wide as saucers. "This isn't happening."

A girl in a white uniform, her honey-colored curls a summer cloud haloing her head, rushed toward them, grinning from ear to ear.

"Joolsae?" Maia stared incredulously at their bubbly mentor from the second phase of the Initiative.

Kusha gasped and Dani grimaced.

"Oh, no! Nafi, hide!" Ren chortled.

"Hello, Joolsae," Hans greeted the girl with his usual pleasantness. "Good to see you. It's been a while."

Joolsae blushed to the tips of her ears. "Good to see you too, Hans. You look great." She looked around at Maia and her teammates. "Look at you guys. All so grown up and . . ." She dabbed the corners of her eyes. "You were teeny tiny babies when I first saw you." As Maia and her friends winced at her words, Joolsae's gaze turned to Nafi. "Nafi . . . you're still so cute and little."

Joolsae's hand shot out toward Nafi's head. In a blur of motion,

Nafi skidded backward and placed herself in between Hans and Miir. She flashed a smile and waved from her newfound safety. "Hello, Joolsae."

"Awww . . . shy little Nafi," Joolsae gushed. She went on and on about the wonderful time she had spent with the team, how proud she was to have worked with them, and how she missed them every day. After being introduced to those in the party she did not know, and after a long story about her new position at the UAAS as an Associate Trainer, Joolsae finally decided to say goodbye.

"Bye-bye, munchkins," she said, smiling sweetly. "See you around, Hans." She waved as she flitted away.

As soon as Joolsae disappeared into the crowd, Nafi triumphantly marched out of her hiding place and announced, "Can't believe she still has a crush on you, Hans."

Hans sighed and shook his head at Nafi. "Now you emerge, all courage and cheek."

"Seriously, that Joolsae," Dani grumbled. "Best time of my life . . . what a liar."

"I thought that painful conversation would never end," Maia said with a sigh of relief.

"How was that even a conversation?" Ren scoffed. "It was just her talking. We did not say more than two words."

"I really didn't even want to talk to her," Kusha added gruffly. "I'm glad she kept the chatter to herself, by herself."

"Tell me something," Hans said thoughtfully. "Why do you always have such . . . stormy relationships with your mentors? No one is ever good enough." He turned toward Miir and chuckled. "No offense, Miir."

"None taken," Miir said. "After all I have been through with them, you could not offend me if you tried."

Nafi crossed her arms and frowned at Miir. "Hey! That's not fair. What have I ever done to you? Besides, you were plenty weird at times," she declared.

Miir nodded at Hans and smirked. "See what I mean?"

"You're so touchy sometimes." Nafi waved Miir away. "As for Joolsae, she was just useless. Other than patting my head, she did nothing."

"And remember, in the end, she had the gall to ask for a note of recommendation," Kusha added.

"Happy with your current mentor, I hope?" Hans asked.

Ren sighed. "Hadeeyah's fine. Just hyperactive. Makes me dizzy."

"Makes *you* dizzy. That's quite a feat." Hans chuckled loudly. "So this one's not perfect either. Ever consider that something might be wrong with *you* people?"

Nafi turned up her nose at Hans. "No. You heard Joolsae. We are adorable little munchkins. End of story."

And that was that. Soon they were marching up into the Aquiccela to T'ra. Nafi tried to cajole Hans into revealing what his big announcement was about, without much success. The way Dani giggled every time Hans refused to answer Nafi's questions, Maia was sure she knew what her brother was about to share. Before long, they were in Hans and Dani's beautiful apartment, enjoying the peaceful view of the reef outside.

Dinner was finished in a hurry that evening, since everyone was excited about the announcement Hans promised. But Miir had not arrived from Zagran yet, and restless as the gang was, they had to resign themselves to waiting. At first, they gathered on the balcony, but then Nafi started lecturing about balanced diets and, as she put it, 'the historical impact of apples on society as we know it.' When Kusha and Ren started arguing with her, Maia slunk away. Soon Sana and Dani joined her in the living room, eager to avoid the contentious discussion. Dani pulled out a photo archive and together they flipped through Hans and Dani's many memories. Rayan joined them when they were halfway through, and they had almost scrolled through it all when Miir finally arrived.

Rayan immediately went off to get some food ready for him while Sana walked up to Miir, arms crossed. "You are *very* late. You were supposed to be here by dinner time. Where were you?"

"I was working on some adjustments for the shield," Miir replied, looking bewildered at the sudden interrogation.

Sana tapped her chin. "Took that long to adjust stuff, huh?"

"Yes, it is complicated. Takes time."

"We were thinking you were working on a girlfriend."

Miir frowned. "What? Why would you even think—"

"Hans said you have quite a fan following, so we thought you might be out with a special someone."

Who was this *we* Sana kept referring to, Maia had no idea, but Sana carried on nonchalantly.

"There is no special someone," Miir said resolutely. "And fans do not interest me."

At that point, Rayan handed Miir a plate of food and he promptly left the room, while Rayan turned to glare at Sana. "Stop bothering people."

Sana simply twirled away and flopped down next to Maia with a smug smile on her face. "Not interested in fans," she said. "Intriguing."

How and why it was *intriguing*, Maia had no clue. Neither was she interested in finding out.

Dani chuckled. "You like messing with Miir, don't you, Sana?"

"He's so easy to mess with," Sana replied with an evil smile. "Hope you don't mind, Maia."

Maia did not venture a comment, lest she be teased about it. Besides, what was there to comment about? That was a typical interaction between the two. Sana had a different vibe with Miir, always verbally poking and prodding him. Miir always took it in stride. Responding to Sana's remark with a casual shrug, Maia started flipping through Hans and Dani's archives again.

Hans soon gathered everyone in the living area. While they were taking their places, a communicator buzzed. Hans pulled out his Urso and grinned. "Here's more good news. It seems the Nouvus will be ready to take off in a couple of months. That's some more people safe."

Nafi's fist shot up in the air. "Woohoo!"

"Nothing to get excited about," Ren said in a grim voice. "Now there'll be a bloodbath as people fight for seats."

"Will it be a random lottery for spots, Hans?" Dani asked.

"So I heard," Hans replied. "They might set aside some for—"

"Special people like you," Ren said. "They'll need smart ones like you to help them resettle Tansi after the simple folk are all dead."

Hans stared at Ren for a moment or two, his eyes narrowed as if he were trying to guess the intent behind Ren's brusque words and sharp tone. Then he sighed. "Well, maybe. But I'm not going anywhere."

A silence, tight and suffocating, fell over them. Maia wished she could say a word or two in praise of Hans's courage, but the idea that the end for Tansi was so near and so inevitable hit her like a sack of bricks. For a while, she simply had no words.

Ren, however, crossed his arms and peered at Hans. "Sounds like you've already turned down an invitation." He sat down with a thump on a couch. "I don't know what to say. If it were me, I'd be out of here the first chance I got."

Dani frowned at the boy. "No, you wouldn't, Ren. Stop acting like you don't care."

Maia's mind had whirled away far from the room. "So, Hans, how are they going to contact and gather all these people in a month or two? I mean . . . there are villages out there that—" She stopped abruptly, seeing the look on Hans's face. She knew what those lightless eyes meant. "They're not even trying to reach everyone on Tansi, are they?"

Maia's words were a whisper, but they seemed to echo endlessly around the silent room. Gazes came her way, all kind and understanding, but nothing could fill the emptiness that tore through Maia's heart. The Solianese did not stand a chance. A village like Appian was remote enough; the minuscule land settlements further west on the Second Continent probably did not figure on anyone's list. A tear dripped from her eye, a burning droplet on her arm, a startling reminder of reality. There was nothing she could do to help, except to win the Initiative. Blinking away her hurt, Maia smiled.

"I'm sorry, Hans. I got carried away. It's not fair to ask you all this," she said, smiling as brightly as she could.

Hans exhaled loudly. "It's all right, Maia. I wish I had better answers myself, but . . . I'm sorry. I really can't do much."

Eager to lift the dejected mood, Maia hurried to change the subject. "Anyway, that wasn't why you gathered us all here, did you?"

"Oh no, not at all," Hans said. "I wanted to share a piece of very personal news with all the people I consider special." He paused and ran a hand through his hair before continuing. "So . . . three years ago when Dani wanted to join the Initiative, I didn't like it at all. There was nothing worthwhile outside of our colonies, that was my opinion. Nothing worth getting out and fighting for anyway. Dani, however, would not give in. That was probably the first time ever that she went completely against my judgment. Well, I'm happy that she did. Turns out, my little sister is smarter than I am. If she hadn't put her foot down and fought me all the way to get into the Initiative, I wouldn't have what I have now — all of you. I wouldn't have found family.

"And" — he walked up to Rayan and took her hand — "I wouldn't have found you." They held hands and gazed at each other for a blissful moment before walking to the center of the room together.

"Rayan and I have decided to get married," Hans said, grinning. He exchanged a glance with Rayan before adding, "It'll be next month, at ThulaSu."

For a moment there was silence. Then Ren shouted.

"Awright! Now that's real good news."

The room erupted in cheers and laughter and hugs and chatter. Dani looked happiest of all, laughing louder than Hans and blushing more than Rayan. As Maia celebrated the news with Hans and Rayan and all her friends, she realized this was the first wedding she would ever see. She could not wait.

Nafi soon drove the boys off the balcony. "Go away," she said, shaking a fist at Ren. "The balcony is ours. The bride-to-be needs her space."

Ren was in no mood to give up without a fight, and he quickly brought up the rights of the groom-to-be, but Kusha dragged him away. The girls settled down, giggling and chattering. Maia was simply ecstatic for Hans, Rayan, and Dani, and quietly enjoyed the excitement and the conversation. Sana detailed everything that needed to be accomplished before the wedding ceremony, and it was quite an exhausting list. On top of the agenda for Sana was scoring a new dress for the occasion, while Nafi had some serious thoughts about the food service.

Maia stepped away for a moment to get blankets for everyone, and found Miir and Kusha in the kitchen, gathering popped kernels into a large bowl while a kettle whistled merrily in the background.

"What? You're hungry already?" Maia asked, peeking in.

Kusha shot her a sheepish grin and hurried away with the bowl, but Miir, who was watching the kettle, lingered. His concerned gaze soon came to rest on Maia's face.

"Are you all right?"

It took Maia a moment to realize that he was alluding to her distress over the Nouvus situation. She slowly nodded. She had accepted it for the reality that it was, and Hans and Rayan's announcement had distracted her for the moment. "Yes, I think so."

"You do not look so."

"Well . . . I keep thinking of all the little places out there. The people . . . some probably won't even know of the situation until it's too late. That's . . ."

Sadness did not let Maia continue, and they stood for a while in silence. Maia was glad when Miir broke it.

"It is unfair and . . . unfortunate," he said. "This whole situation is distressing. But I have realized something. When I start thinking of what is about to be lost, the magnitude of the calamity that is coming, I feel so helpless and upset that I can barely function. And that does not help anyone. So I try to keep my eye on my tasks, and my goals.

Little they may be, but I figure if I keep at them, those little things will add up to something in the end."

Maia let out a sigh. That was certainly the right approach. But it was not easy to keep dreadful thoughts from barging in.

"You cannot do everything," Miir continued. "All you can do is your part. And *you* are more than doing your part."

All her friends had said more or less the same thing, but somehow, hearing it from Miir made her spirits lift far more than they had before. Maia relished the peace and fortitude his words brought, thankful that she had run into him.

"I am boring you with my lectures," Miir said suddenly, nodding in the direction of the balcony as he took some cups out of a cabinet, "and you must be missing the chatter out there."

"No, I'm not," Maia replied. "I'm not missing anything. And your lecture isn't boring." She stopped, flushing profusely. "I mean . . . I don't think it's a lecture at all. It helped. Thank you."

Miir peered at her and flashed a playful smile. "You encourage me and my lectures at your own peril."

Maia countered his teasing with a defiant frown. "You can't scare me. I'm not afraid of you anymore."

"Anymore?" His brow crinkled. "As if you ever were."

"I was too," Maia protested. "You were very . . . daunting. And every time I saw you, I was *quite* afraid."

Miir walked out of the kitchen, cups in one hand, kettle in the other. He stopped and fixed a curious gaze on her face. "I do not care who or what you are. I will not sit back while you disrespect my Dada," he said. As she stared, wide-eyed, on realizing that Miir had quoted almost exactly the very first words she had ever spoken to him, he continued. "Saying that to a Xifarian who is not shy about displaying hostility — you call that fear?"

Maia's arms tightened around the stack of blankets she was cradling while she thought up a fitting reply. "I call that being brave." She released a small sigh before letting out a confession. "And maybe a little reckless."

A moment of silence fell between them before Miir lowered his head just a little. "I admire that in you." As Maia's heart skipped a beat, he hastily added, "I mean the bravery, *not* the recklessness."

They parted laughing. When Maia returned to the girls, Sana was perched on the arm of Rayan's chair, her eyes sparkling. An engrossing conversation seemed to be in progress. Maia put the blankets down on a stool, then stood at the doorway of the balcony and just watched.

"How did you know Hans was the one?" Sana asked.

Rayan, reserved as usual, simply shrugged. "You just know. It feels different from anything else."

Sana sighed. "See, I don't understand that. Every boy seems different in the beginning. Fun. Exciting. And then, after a month or two, I've run out of things to talk about and I'm bored. I don't get how one person could be so special that you'd want to spend more than a few months with them, let alone marry."

As Sana looked around the room for someone to enlighten her, Nafi shook her head. "Don't look at me. I can tell when people fall for someone because they start acting all crazy and stupid. But I don't get why people do it. To me, boys are boys, mostly silly and useless and annoying. You should ask Dani . . . she's the most experienced in these matters."

Sana, taking Nafi's advice to heart, immediately turned toward Dani. "All right, Dani. Tell me. I don't need an essay about what makes relationships work . . . you know, respect, trust, honesty, and all that. Mother Dearest has lectured me on those about a million times. I just need to find that someone special. How do I even know?"

"Well, I think respect, trust, honesty, and the rest have to be there to make you really like someone," Dani said. "I couldn't consider someone special if they didn't respect me or if I couldn't trust them or if I knew they were dishonest."

Maia smiled, remembering the big fight Kusha and Dani had in Zagran over Kusha's heritage. That, she now realized, was all about trust and honesty, and not just between friends. It had not taken long for the duo to get together after that mess was cleared up.

Sana chirped on. "I get that. I don't think I could either," she said. "But tell me, how did you know you liked Kusha differently from say . . . Ren?"

Dani snuggled into her blanket and laughed. "Well, I don't know about anyone else, but I realized something was different when I started wanting to be with Kusha all the time. You know . . . we'd just have spent an entire evening wrangling maps for a project and yet, the moment we'd part, I'd . . . miss him. It was weird."

Maia's heart thudded. That . . . that could not be right. How could it be? Just the other day, she had felt that way about Miir and —

No! It's just a silly coincidence, that's all.

"And then there were little things all the time," Dani continued. "Everything Kusha did or said, good or bad, affected me a lot. A careless word from him would make me want to cry; a casual smile would make my heart flip. Every word he said mattered so much more."

Maia backed away from the door, one step at a time, her heart thumping nervously with each word Dani said.

No! No, no!

Dani went on, her voice tinkling softly but clearly in the quiet of the apartment. "Seeing him in pain upset me more than if I were hurt myself. Seeing him happy made me feel like I was soaring with the clouds."

Maia spun away as she recognized every feeling Dani described, the realization shaking her insides. Her eyes scanned the dark living room, looking around at everything and nothing in particular, her mind rushing through a maze of confusion as her heart thudded.

No! This isn't true. Miir is a friend . . . just a friend.

"Even if a room was filled with people, he'd be the one I'd notice first," Dani said. "His voice would always sound the clearest." She paused and chuckled a little. "He was so easy to talk to, and with him, I'd never run out of things to talk about."

Maia teetered onto a couch and lowered her head into her hands, breathing desperately to calm her thundering heart.

Dani, stop! Why do you have to keep pointing out things that I never thought of as special?

Voices . . . distant, faded . . . floated out from the balcony.

"So, Sana," Nafi asked. "Ever felt like that with any of your boys?"

"Nope. And Jez is over. That's for sure."

"Good riddance," Nafi said.

A roll of laughter rose.

"Hey, where's Maia?" someone asked.

Maia rushed to the safety of her room. She almost made it, but the door to the boys' room opened just as she grabbed the handle to hers, and Hans walked out grinning.

"Maia!" he exclaimed. "Just the person I was thinking about. We need an arbitrator to settle this argument. Come on in—"

"No, no I can't," Maia blurted. She could not go into that room. She could not face Miir. Not now. She would surely make a fool of herself if she did. She had to sort out this mess in her head first. "Have to go. Sorry."

Hans stared incredulously as she dashed into the girls' room and shut the door behind her. She stood with her back to the closed door, her eyes shut tightly, her lips muttering over and over, "No! This can't be!"

A few moments later, when her heart had calmed a little, she trudged to her bed and crept under the covers, a million questions making her head swim.

What if it is true?

How? When had this happened? With Miir, there was so much to remember. So many memories, so many words between them. The numerous hurtful moments, yet the brightness of the happy times washed away all the shadows. When had she started caring so much? For a long time, she had struggled to forgive him, to move past the wrongs, and appreciate his effort to make it right. In all that time she had slowly come to trust him again. And then? There had been moments when she had felt a pang, a yearning for something she did not quite understand. Was this—

No!

Why did it have to happen? Why now? It was best left unknown.

Maia did not know when she drifted to sleep that night. But the last thing she remembered was her own anguished whisper.

"I didn't mean for this to happen."

Chapter Thirty-Three

The Scars You Leave

Maia woke up very early the next morning. Any other time, she would have rushed to the balcony and spent the quiet time staring at the view of the reef, but on this day, she did not dare. Fear of running into Miir and creating some kind of silly spectacle turned her fingers numb and made her burrow deeper under the covers. Dani's words from the previous night kept ringing in her ears, and even though she wanted to write off every feeling she recognized as an accidental coincidence, she also knew that hearing them changed the way she thought of things. She would be awkward around Miir, and then . . . someone would notice.

No! Maia turned over and pressed her face into her pillow. She could not let this—whatever it was, true or not—come out. It could ruin everything. The friendships and the camaraderie in the team could all be jolted out of balance. And that was not even considering what Miir would think if he found out.

Maia turned over again, unable to breathe as a series of heart-numbing possibilities tore through her mind. She had just found a quiet equilibrium with him, a friendship that comforted and healed. He might very well consider this a betrayal of his trust, and he might even hate her for disrupting what they had built. The friendship she cherished so much would be lost.

No! I can't risk what I have. I'm not letting this happen.

She would put a lid on it, pretend to be normal, and go about doing things just as before. Her fists clenched, and her resolve forced the last wayward thoughts into submission. She stayed in bed, feigning sleep until everyone else had left the room, then lingered even longer repeating her resolution many times over.

Act normal. Act normal. Act normal!

Sana flitted in as Maia was packing up her bedroll. "You're finally up," she said, perching on the edge of a chair. "You left so suddenly last night. We were worried. What happened?"

Maia shrugged calmly. "Nothing happened. I was tired. Thought I'd lie down for a little bit. Don't know when I dozed off." Trying to look as normal as she could, Maia forced a smile and some extra cheer into her voice. "Did I miss anything?"

"Not much," Sana replied. "We were just talking about relationships and true love and stuff that wouldn't interest you anyway." She stopped and sighed. "I realized I have to break up with Jez. He's clearly not the one."

Maia laughed in relief. "I'm happy that he isn't. I've never liked Jez, and it'd be a pain if—"

The door flew open behind them and Dani rushed in. "Girls, come on. We have to get going if we want to catch our shuttle to ThulaSu."

Sana grimaced. "I wouldn't mind missing the shuttle."

"But you would mind Ren going berserk. He's already stressed about annoying Hadeeyah if we're late," Dani said. "So hurry up. We're leaving soon."

Maia finally tiptoed out of the room and found her way into the crowd. She smiled, laughed, and only talked about utterly commonplace things—the spread on the sandwiches, the color of the plates, how long it would take to get back to ThulaSu. She even said a casual word or two to Miir, without a hint of awkwardness, or so she hoped.

A giant of an Aqumob with three decks was waiting for them when they arrived at the docks. There were no passengers other than the gang, and that surprised everyone, including Hans.

The captain soon explained when he met them at the entrance. "You're lucky! The shield project's wrapping up at ThulaSu, so we need to pick up some equipment from there on the way to Zagran." He smiled indulgently at the group. "You can have the entire top deck to yourselves."

"Cool!" Ren exclaimed and took off immediately. "We have our private luxury yacht. Party time!"

Nafi rushed behind him, and Pai giggled and followed. "Ren, please," Hans started, when Rayan placed a hand on his arm.

"I got this," she said. "I'll keep an eye on him."

"I'll see you soon, then," Hans said to Rayan. As he pulled her close and kissed her, Maia and Dani hurried away to give the couple some privacy.

Dani squeezed Maia's arm as they headed up the stairs. "I'm so happy, Maia," she said. "I can't believe this is really happening. It seems too good to be true."

"I'm truly happy for you, Dani," Maia said. "If anyone deserves such happiness, it's you. I mean it."

The top deck was beautiful. Glass windows along the sides provided unrestricted views of the outside. The aisles were wide and laid with plush carpet, and the seats were plump and inviting. It was indeed a luxury yacht.

Soon they were on their way. Even with Rayan keeping a strict watch, things got a bit noisy. Maia tired quickly. Mostly because of the quandary she was in, even when she knew there was safety in numbers, she yearned for some time alone. While everyone kept talking about everything and anything, she walked away, the quiet at the far end of the shuttle beckoning her exhausted mind.

She soon settled down at the back of the deck. She decided to take her mind off the distractions and pulled out the scroll she had been studying the week before. It was an ancient treatise on Tansian plants, and many of the notes were in old Eatambian, so Maia also had to pull out the translation sheet. Slowly she worked through the pages, writing down anything that seemed important in her notebook.

Shouts filled the air every now and then. Rayan tried her best to calm everyone down, but Ren had worked out a complicated game of hoopball that seemed to catch everyone's fancy. Soon people were running amuck. And screaming.

"Maia, want to play?" Ren landed with a thud across from her.

"No, I'm a bit tired," Maia replied. "Also I promised Hadeeyah I'd work on this translation, so I better finish at least one page."

Nafi flew in and swooped on Ren. "Let her be, Ren. She's working. And over there" —she grabbed Ren by his shirt and dragged him away—"we're down by one point. You better get us back on track. I'm not losing to your angel."

Maia chuckled as the duo rushed away, then forced her mind back to translating one particular note she was stuck on. Her determination to crack it did not lead her anywhere except into a headache. Maia closed her notebook and stared out the window for a while, watching the bright blue waters sweep past. From the color of the light, she could tell they were close to the surface, which meant they were nearing ThulaSu. She had been in an Aqumob so many times now that it felt like she had known it forever. It was incredible how much she had learned in the past few years, and how much that little pigtailed girl from Appian had changed.

The sound of footsteps pulled Maia out of her thoughts.

Miir slipped into the seat across from her and smiled warmly. "Hey!"

Maia's heart almost jumped out of her chest. She blinked, then blinked again. As if that were not enough, the confounded pen she had been holding decided to slip out of her hand.

So much for keeping things normal.

As Miir's hand shot out to grab the runaway pen, his eyes narrowed. "Sorry. Did I scare you?"

Maia could barely hear him over the thunder of her heart.

"Yes. I mean, no—" Maia stopped, her fingers curling around the pen, her senses acutely aware of his concerned gaze on her face. She breathed in, struggling to gather her thoughts. "I was reading," she finally muttered.

"Yes, I see." His voice was gentle. "Do you want me to leave?"

"No! I am not." Whatever did she mean by that? Maia felt warmth flood her face and spread to the tip of her ears.

Stop blathering. Stop blushing like an idiot. He'll notice and he'll know. Get your act together.

"I mean, I'm not reading right now. I was just thinking . . ." At least something coherent came out this time. Miir stared expectantly at her, so Maia had to find something to finish her sentence. "I was thinking of what to wear for Hans and Rayan's wedding."

His eyes narrowed once more. "Really? You were designing a death trap for yourself?" He sounded incredulous, and rightly so, since that thought figured nowhere in Maia's mind. "Are you feeling well?"

I'll be fine if you just leave me alone. Of all the space in this humongous yacht, is this the one spot you have to be?

"Maybe I like dresses now," she blurted. "Can't I change my mind?"

"Of course you can. You should do whatever makes you happy."

What makes me happy . . . I don't know anymore.

Her thoughts strayed all over the place, turning her head into a jumbled mess. Maia did not know where to look. She did not know what to say. The only thing she could think of was Miir's gaze that coursed over her face and left it burning. She could not find a single thing to talk about. Thankfully, Miir broke the awkward and protracted silence.

"Oh, look at me. I forgot to say what I came to say. I picked up some more supplies in Zagran to fix the frame. I think I can get it to work this time."

"Great," Maia squeaked. "Good luck."

"Are you sure nothing is bothering you?" he asked, leaning forward to peer at her face. "Anything I can help with?"

You're the last person I can ask for help with this.

"We've arrived!" Ren's shout tore through the awkward pause. Sana careened in just in time, saving Maia the necessity of finding an answer to Miir's impossible question.

"Maia! Pack up. Can't believe you spent all this time with your notes. Sometimes, you just—" She stopped abruptly, noticing Miir on the other side of the booth. "Oops, sorry! Didn't see you. Didn't mean to disrupt your privacy, Maia."

"You're not disrupting anything," Maia said, hurriedly packing up her scrolls. She slipped out of her seat, flashing a quick smile at Miir, who stared at her with a baffled look on his face. "Let me know when the frame's done."

The rest of the gang was already out of the Aqumob when Maia and Sana reached the exit. Bright sunshine shone down on the Darkwoods, and a soft breeze caressed Maia's face as soon as they walked out. It lifted Maia's spirits immediately. She was about to break into a run to catch up with the group ahead when Sana's hand clamped on her arm and they stopped.

"No. Please, no," Sana whispered. Her face was drained of color, and her eyes, wide with terror, were fixed on the pier next to theirs. Maia only caught a glimpse of what Sana was looking at—a woman stood on the shore, her silk gown shining—before Sana dragged her backward.

"Sana, what—"

"Get back in, Maia," Sana whispered urgently. She hurtled back into the Aqumob and crashed right into Miir, who was walking out behind them. They would have toppled off the stairs if he had not grabbed them both by the arm.

"Careful," he said.

Maia was so startled by Sana's strange behavior that she barely noticed how close he stood or how his hand stayed on her arm long after he had let Sana go. Maia's eyes were fixed on Sana's pallid face.

"Sana, what's going on?" she asked.

"That woman is here," Sana replied. Closing her eyes, she fell back against the railing.

It took a while for Maia to understand who Sana was talking about. "You mean Aunt Rowyena?"

"I can't go out there. I have to hide," Sana said.

"But, Sana—"

"You cannot stay in here forever," Miir said, his voice gentle but clear. "You *have* to get outside. There is no other way." Seeing the wild look in Sana's eyes, he added, "We will walk with you."

"Hey, Maia!" Ren's boisterous voice floated in. "Sana, angel, what's taking you so long?"

Sana gritted her teeth. "Why is he calling me that? Stop it, Ren."

"Sana, he always calls you that," Maia said.

"Not in front of her ladyship, he can't."

"He doesn't know that, Sana." Maia grabbed Sana's hand and held it tightly. "Calm down, everything will be fine."

Sana did walk outside calmly. She did stride along the pier right up to Aunt Rowyena who stood on the shore, resplendent in her purple silk gown, her jewelry dazzling in the sunlight. Uncle Alasdair stood to one side. Behind him, standing guard over a pair of traveling cases, was the bespectacled maid, Iriana. They must have just arrived from Miorie, Maia deduced.

"Sana," Aunt Rowyena said, smiling.

"Mother," Sana replied curtly.

Aunt Rowyena's eyes skimmed over Maia's face, and other than the smallest nod, there was no acknowledgment of her presence.

"Good that we found you right here, Sana. You need to come with us."

"Come where? Why?"

"To our boat." Aunt Rowyena nodded at the gleaming Aqumob at the next pier. "We need to have a conversation."

"About what?

"About your future."

Sana's fists curled. "I'm not going," she said. Maia could hear her voice tremble.

"Sana." Aunt Rowyena's voice had grown sharp.

"You heard me. There's nothing I need to talk to you about. I don't want to and you can't make me."

"You're my daughter." Aunt Rowyena fixed a cold glare on Sana's face. "And you are not an adult yet. So like it or not, you *have* to listen to me." She snapped back toward Uncle Alasdair who stood quietly with a grim look on his face. "Alasdair, please talk to her. Tell her."

"I don't care *who* tells me. I'm *not* coming with you," Sana yelled.

"Sana, you are making a scene," Aunt Rowyena said in a cold, steely voice. She nodded meaningfully at the rest of the gang who now stood in a huddle to Aunt Rowyena's left, watching Sana and her mother's incensed discussion. "This is not how you behave in front of strangers. If you have an argument to make, you can make it in private."

"They are *not* strangers," Sana snapped. "They're my friends. I don't need privacy from them. If you do, that's your problem and I can't help you." She stopped a moment and breathed heavily. "For the last time, I'm not coming home with you. Please, leave me alone."

"It's not about going back home, Sana," Uncle Alasdair finally spoke. "Your mother . . . we have been offered seats on the ark. Preparations have started and your mother has come to take you there with her."

Maia could hardly believe what she was hearing. Only yesterday they had heard about the Nouvus being ready, and Aunt Rowyena had already secured seats. She did not know if she was supposed to be happy knowing things were progressing so quickly, or worry about the fairness of the selection process. In the end, she felt happy. Sana would be safe, and that was great news. But before Maia could congratulate Sana, the girl shook her head vehemently.

"You think I will leave Maia behind and run into the ark with you? Well, hear this." Sana's voice was cold, just as harsh as Aunt Rowyena's had been. "I won't. I'm not letting you separate us again. You can't make me go. If you try, I will kill myself and that'll be the end of it."

The silence that fell was deafening. Aunt Rowyena's eyes flashed, her face hardened, and her lips thinned to a hard line. She stood there, gaze locked with Sana, for long moments. Then she turned toward Maia and advanced on her in a cold rage.

"You ruined everything," she hissed. "You destroyed my daughter, our lives. I thought I was done with you eight years ago, but you keep coming back into our lives, bringing misery every time."

Every word went like a dagger through Maia's heart, sucking strength from her. Hatred spilled from Aunt Rowyena's eyes and the intensity of it stunned Maia into silence.

"You took my daughter, my only child, away from me," her aunt continued in a bitter, scathing voice. "I lost her because of you. I will—"

Things were a blur after that. Aunt Rowyena rushed forward suddenly, eyes glinting with rage. Unbridled fury and a promise of suffering danced in her eyes.

"Rowyena," Uncle Alasdair yelled.

Heart thrashing, Maia stumbled backward, her knees wobbly and weak, her mind barely fathoming what was happening or what could happen. Miir stepped in front of her, blocking Aunt Rowyena's path just as Sana threw herself at her mother, grabbing her arm and pushing her away.

"Get away from Maia. It's not *her* fault you lost me. You lost me because you never tried to understand what made me happy!" Sana screamed. Every word that came out of her seemed to exhaust her. "All you ever wanted was to drive Dada away from Miorie, so I wouldn't be able to see Maia anymore. Every time I visited them, you threw a fit. And I remember how you celebrated the day they left. You were so busy being happy that you didn't see your daughter, your only child, cry for weeks because she missed her best friend." Sana stopped and gasped for air. Then she looked at Uncle Alasdair beseechingly. "I know you were sad when Dada left. I saw you sitting alone in your dark library every evening while she threw parties. Yet you never said a word. Even when Maia came back to us, homeless and helpless, you did not dare to let her stay. You drove her away in the middle of the night because you were too afraid to stand up for her. Why do you always have to be so afraid?"

For a few moments, Sana's tortured breathing was all that could be heard. Then Uncle Alasdair spoke.

"Sana, I couldn't have let Maia stay," he said. "I knew she wouldn't be safe in our house. You know why. So I found her the safest place I could think of, in the hands of Aihnswothe Feirah, the most trustworthy person I knew." He stopped and took a few steps toward Sana. "Why do you think I'm here all the time? Not because I have to be. It's because I want to be around Maia, even though I know there's only so much I can do to help."

Sana seemed to relent a bit at Uncle Alasdair's words, if only for a little while.

"So . . . when are *you* leaving to prepare for the ark?" she asked, her voice subdued.

"Who said I am?" Uncle Alasdair said in an equally quiet voice. Maia noticed how Aunt Rowyena's nostrils flared. "I had decided to refuse the offer anyway. You won't believe me, I know, but I can't leave Maia behind. However, now that *you* want to stay, it makes the decision even easier."

Aunt Rowyena shook her head. "Alasdair, you disappoint me," she said and started walking back to her Aqumob, Iriana following with the cases.

"Sana, go with your friends," Uncle Alasdair said before he hurried off after Aunt Rowyena. "Rowyena, wait."

Maia flew toward Sana, her arms wrapped protectively around her cousin. They had barely walked into the Darkwoods when Sana sank on a fallen log and broke into sobs. Sana was always a happy girl; seeing her cry was painful enough. But when Maia thought of what that lonely little nine-year-old had endured in that shadowy house in Miorie, she shuddered. Maia figured the best she could do to help was to let Sana cry away years of hurt. She sat next to her cousin, her arm wrapped around Sana's shoulders, and let her weep. The rest of the group stood waiting in silence, until after a while, Sana looked up.

She started to speak, her voice a pitiful whimper. "One day we were playing and the next, you were gone. They wouldn't tell me anything. Why Dada left, where he went . . . nothing. I didn't ask them to take me to you, I just wanted to know where you were. Even that was too much. Why couldn't they tell me?" Sana ran a hand over her face to wipe away the tears that kept on coming. "I used to have nightmares of you being dead."

She stopped and grabbed Maia's hands, clasping them tightly.

"Remember, Maia, how we used to play with swords Herc made for us?" Sana said. "We used to have so much fun. We'd pretend to be warrior princesses. Remember?" Maia nodded. How could she forget? Those were some of the best days of her life. Sana sighed and continued. "I burned the last one we played with. Never wanted to touch a sword again. Never wanted to do anything I used to do with you."

Maia suppressed a sigh. She had shunned fancy dresses and twirling like a princess since she left Miorie. She never imagined Sana had given up her sword. It was funny, in a sad sort of way, that they had both given up the parts the other liked the most.

"We'd always dream of coming to ThulaSu, remember?" Sana said between sniffles. "I thought if I could come here, maybe I'd find you. She must have guessed why I wanted to go to ThulaSu. So she wouldn't let me. Nothing but the fanciest school in town would do for her daughter. I was supposed to strengthen ties, someday marry into a family that was as renowned as hers and improve the bloodlines. I didn't care about the posh school or the scions of the principal families who went there. All I wanted was to go to ThulaSu. She didn't care."

Sana lowered her head into her hands and sighed.

"Then, one day, I was done crying and begging and hoping things would change. If a mother could care so little about her child, why couldn't I hit back? So I hung around with those fancy boys from those fancy families she so admired, partied through the night, every night. What do you know? She didn't like that either. How she worried and fretted and frowned. I told her I was making connections. She wanted me to, didn't she? So she had to deal with my ways, however abhorrent they were."

Maia remembered how surprised she had been to see the changes in Sana when she came to Miorie after she lost Dada. Now she knew why. A wave of guilt coursed through her. She should have asked, but she never took the time.

"I could not stand that prison of a house or the people in it," Sana continued. "So I stayed away as much as I could. Some days, I would not return home at all. Some days, I'd sneak out in the middle of the night."

"That was neither wise nor safe," Rayan said suddenly.

"I know. I know. I was always careful but . . . I'm lucky that I never got into trouble. I could have." Sana stopped and shrugged. "I didn't care. Guess I was tempting fate." She looked up at Maia and smiled. "Everything changed again when you came back. I suddenly had a new goal. I decided that if you survived and somehow reached a safe place, I would find a way to you. When I heard you were here, I knew exactly what to do. I told that woman I really liked this rich older guy whose wife had just left him, that he might make a good husband. That freaked her out completely and just like that, ThulaSu became the best place for me." Sana shook her head and let out an enormous sigh. "You know . . . I hate having to do things like that to get what I want."

Ren had been fidgeting, and now he plopped down next to Sana and bumped shoulders with her.

"Hey! You're done with that now. You've found Maia, you're in ThulaSu, and you refused to go with your mother. You won. Time to stop being sad, don't you think?"

Sana simply stared back at him, but Maia agreed. The miserable times Sana had had to bear alone were now over. She squeezed her cousin's arm.

"He's right, you know," she said softly. "You've made it past everything. Time to smile now."

Ren grabbed Sana's wrist and pulled her up. "Come on, warrior princess. You're back on weapons practice, starting today."

"What?" Sana gawked. "I have to go to the dressmakers today."

"Oh no, you don't. Not today," Ren said emphatically as he tugged her away. "Warrior comes first, then comes the princess. Don't even try to convince me otherwise." He turned around to look at the stupefied faces looking back at him. "What are you guys staring at me for? She has to catch up on years of practice, so everyone pitch in with the training. You, Maia. You go first."

"No, she trains with me first," Miir declared.

"What? No," Sana protested. "No way I'm training with *you*."

A teasing smile immediately formed on Miir's face. "Scared, are we?"

Sana crossed her arms and glared through her tears. "I'm not scared of anything."

"Looks like you are," Miir said, and started up the trail through the Darkwoods.

"I am not!" Sana shouted at his back.

"See you at the house, then," Miir shouted back. "I like my trainees to be on time, by the way."

Nafi skipped forward happily. "This, I have to watch."

"Watch? What is this?" Sana yelled. "A circus?"

Ren smirked. "Well, training with Miir always is. Now walk fast. Don't keep people waiting for the first show." Then he sprinted away.

Maia linked an arm through Sana's as they started walking. "Come on. You'll have fun."

Sana let out a sigh before a smile lit up her face. "Maybe I will." She grumpily added, "I have to say, though, I'm not happy with your

Miir right now. Something tells me—"

"He is going to give you a very hard time," Rayan, who was bringing up the rear, commented wryly. "I like that. You deserve some payback for all the grief you give him."

Sana grimaced and Maia giggled. That day, walking through the Darkwoods with all her friends and Sana, Maia felt thankful. They had endured a lot, and it was a miracle that they made it through. And it was certainly a miracle that they had found each other in the end.

CHAPTER THIRTY-FOUR

DEAD HEAT

The dreaded trip to Korobieltes arrived sooner than anyone had expected. As if to foreshadow how badly things were about to go, everything started to fall apart for Core 21 before that.

Two days prior to the trip, Nafi caught a cold. She promptly visited the sanatorium and started on medicines and a regimen of herb-infused soups. They did not help much, and the day before the trip, Nafi was running a fever. She refused to give up on the trip, even though on hearing the news, Zaara had excused her.

"We can't be one person down," Nafi declared. "Not when we need to come out on top with this task."

"But, Nafi"—Dani was not about to give up either—"if your condition gets worse in Korobieltes, it will do us more harm."

"I know, Dani," Nafi retorted. "I know how important it is for us to win the Initiative. I know Maia needs Seigvard. I know Tansi's future depends on it. And that is why I can't give up."

"But you're quite sick," Dani protested.

"I will be fine," Nafi reassured, her voice groggy. "Not like I'm collapsing every other step I take."

"But Korobieltes is bad, Nafi," Maia said. "The heat—"

"I've lived my whole life on the Third Continent, Maia," Nafi snapped back. "I can deal with a little heat. I'll do just fine in Korobieltes. And now I'd like some peace, please."

Nafi slipped back under the covers. Maia and Dani had to respect her wishes and leave her room.

Nafi's fever was no better the next day, and gloom descended on the team. As far as Maia could tell, things could only go one of two ways. Nafi would have to drop out of the Korobieltes task voluntarily, or Zaara would make her. Knowing Nafi and how badly she wanted to take part, Maia feared the moment of that decision.

"I'm going to Miir's for some sparring practice," Ren announced after they had aimlessly lingered in the AR half the morning.

"Practice today?" Maia asked, a little incredulous.

"Why not?" Ren shot back. "We don't leave until late afternoon, and we have nothing to do right now other than sulk. So it's the perfect time to practice."

Any other time Maia would have jumped at the chance. But anything to do with Miir had stopped being easy since—

"So who's coming?" Ren's loud voice disrupted her thoughts.

Everyone in the room, Sana included, jumped to their feet. For a moment, Maia thought of sitting it out with the excuse of keeping an eye on Nafi. However, Nafi was asleep and needed no checking, and her sudden reluctance would look weird, so Maia followed the rest of the team.

The practice started well, and Maia had to admit that even with her nervousness about sparring with Miir, the workout lifted her out of her worries about the upcoming task. Each took their turn, and Maia was happy when she completed hers without making any sort of foolish mistake. Miir seemed quite content with everyone's level of prowess, which lifted spirits even more.

Perhaps buoyed by Miir's praise of his footwork, and probably hoping to delay facing the decision on Nafi, Ren decided to go for a second bout after each of them had taken a turn. That was when it all went horribly wrong.

It was a simple parry-and-strike sequence that Maia had seen them do many times over. Nothing seemed out of the ordinary until Ren slipped and fell. No one expected Miir to let up on the attack just because his opponent had fallen, and he did not. He brought his sword down and Ren blocked his strike. But before the smirk on Ren's face could widen into a smug grin, his sword snapped in half.

Had it been anyone other than Miir, things would have ended worse and with bloodshed. How he managed to regain his balance and keep his sword from striking Ren and injuring him was beyond Maia's understanding. The audience was up on their feet gasping by the time the sparring duo caught their breath. Dani was the first to reach them.

"Ren, are you all right?" she asked. "What happened?"

Ren dusted his clothes off and shook his head with annoyance at his sword that now lay in two pieces. "My stupid sword just had to break today of all days. Now, what will I take to Korobieltes?"

"That's not important," Dani said. "Be thankful that you were not hurt." She walked Ren away from the sparring ground, Sana following. "Rest a little now. Drink some water."

Maia was about to join the girls when she noticed Miir and Kusha. They were both hunched over the broken sword. She decided to join them instead.

"How could it break like that?" Miir was saying, studying the broken pieces intently.

"Maybe it was worn out," Maia suggested.

"No, Maia," Kusha replied. "Swords don't suddenly snap like that. Not during an exercise when no one is really fighting for their lives. Besides, this sword is far thicker and sturdier than Miir's."

"I don't see anything odd about it," Miir muttered. "But this is strange."

Miir spent some more time looking at the pieces, while Kusha and

Maia watched. But there was nothing to be found, so after a while, they picked up the broken pieces and walked back to the house. Ren sat on the porch steps, looking glum. Dani sat next to him while Sana paced, both their faces clouded.

"Did you lend your sword to anyone recently, Ren?" Miir asked as soon as they joined the rest of the group.

Ren shook his head firmly.

"Does anyone else have easy access to it?"

"No. Of course not."

Miir did not look satisfied with the answers.

"Why do you ask, Miir?" Dani inquired. "You think someone messed with Ren's sword?"

"I do. The way this happened is not . . . normal," Miir replied. "Hand me your weapons. I have to check all of them."

He went on to inspect each of their weapons one by one while Ren fidgeted.

"No one tampered with our weapons, Miir," Ren said when Miir was done. "That's not the problem. The issue is I don't have a weapon for Korobieltes. I'd have to return to Xif to get a replacement, but there's no time. We're leaving this evening and —"

"Take mine," Sana offered, pulling her own sword out. "I can get by for a day without one."

Ren's face brightened for a moment, but as soon as he held Sana's sword, it dimmed once more.

"It won't work," he said. "This is too light compared to mine. It'd take me a while to get used to this."

"We could search the armory at ThulaSu," Kusha suggested. "I'm sure we'll find something satisfactory."

They all sprang to their feet, but Miir shook his head grimly. "It won't work." His voice was just as stony. "That was a special sword, infused with metals from the Draegen-Mor. That is the reason for its weight. Nothing you find here will match it."

Shoulders slumped once more.

"Try mine," Miir offered suddenly. His words were so

unexpected that everyone simply stared wordlessly. Miir, however, calmly drew Fury from its sheath and held it out for Ren. "Come on."

Maia doubted if anyone else knew Fury was his mother's before him, but seeing the way Ren hesitated to even hold the weapon, and the looks on the faces of the rest, the offer had clearly astounded everyone.

"It feels fine," Ren said after he had given it a few twirls. "But this is yours and I couldn't—"

Miir swiftly cut Ren off. "I am not giving it away forever. Just for now. If it works, you can keep it until the Initiative is over."

"But . . ."

Miir placed a hand on Ren's shoulder. "It is just a sword. I will be fine without it."

"I will get you some replacements from the armory," Kusha said. "For while Ren has it."

"There you go," Miir said. "I will get the binding set up now."

It was unbelievable how casually he said it. The smile on his face never wavered, but Maia could see the sorrow in his eyes. The sword was his mother's last gift to him. How could he not be sad?

Forgetting all her fears of awkward conversations, Maia rushed up to Miir as he headed into the house.

"Miir, you can't," she said as soon as he turned around at the threshold. "I'm sure we can find Ren a substitute from the armory. You shouldn't have to do this."

"I broke his sword. So in a way . . . I am responsible for restoring it," he said. Noting her distraught expression, he chuckled. "It is just a sword that I am giving away for a little while."

"But it's not just any sword. It's your mother's."

Miir smiled, but there was no brightness in it. Clearly, he was hurting and desperate to not let it show. "The Initiative is at stake here. I think my mother would want you to win it." He sighed and tapped the wall absentmindedly before looking back at her again. "I will be fine."

The binding process did not take very long. Although Miir held on to his stoic expression, Ren looked completely heartbroken.

"Stop being so miserable," Miir said once he had handed Fury to Ren. "Your focus should be on this task. Nothing else." He looked at Ren's dismal face and shook his head. "Do I get a win tomorrow or what?" He looked around at all the faces surrounding him. "I am talking to all of you."

Heads nodded in unison, and smiles were forced. Soon they trudged back up to the living quarters. Nothing could cheer them up that afternoon. Maia's heart stayed leaden. She could not forget how calmly Miir had given away his most beloved possession and a memento of his mother. She had seen the anguish behind that imperturbable facade and wished she could do something to comfort him. But nothing could be done at the moment other than prepare for the mammoth task ahead of them, so remembering the promise they had made to Miir, Maia steeled herself and soldiered on.

* * *

Not much was known of the task until the teams—dressed in the tight rubbery suits and masks that needed to be worn in Korobieltes—faced Zaara the morning of their trek to retrieve the plant samples. They had arrived in Zaara's own Inception Colony #4 the evening before. A Raptor had dropped off the teams and the arbitrators near the entrance after sundown. Even though the sun was down and the temperatures were bearable, everyone reeled from the short exposure to the harsh conditions on the Third. Faces stayed worried and drawn all through mealtime, and Maia knew why. Everyone was anxious about how things would be during the day, and it was not a happy thought. She had been out there in the heat of midday, and the idea of braving it again made her shudder. It would not be easy for anyone.

"Attention, all of you." Zaara's sharp voice made Maia jump. "Before I hand out the zone assignments, I will say it one last time. The heat out there is not a laughing matter, and the air is not healthy. Make sure your suits are tight and your masks fit you well. For as long as you are out there, they will keep you alive. But do not think these suits make you invincible. The spores, particularly if you happen to brush against a clump, can burn right through them. So be careful."

Faces fell all around Zaara. Maia drew a breath and held it for as long as she could to brace herself as Zaara continued.

"If you planned it well, you should not have to be outside for too long. You will carry with you two packs to get your specimens back. Make sure you seal them well. We do not want poisonous spores inside our colonies, and if I see carelessness, you will be penalized or disqualified altogether. Understood?"

Heads nodded rapidly.

"Be creative. You can split your teams however you want. All that matters is getting back here with your collection before that"—she pointed at five large sand clocks filled with the characteristic black sand of the Third Continent—"runs out. Remember, two specimens per plant. No more, no less. And that is it."

She turned toward Pomewege and Aerika. "Would you like to add anything more?"

Aerika shook her head, but Principal Pomewege smiled and walked up to the teams. "Always keep in mind the principles of the Initiative. Collaboration is key. But if you *have* to fight, do it with honor."

After that, Zaara called up the teams one by one, per core number. As soon as a team was handed a map, a member of the Desert's Watch led them away and Zaara turned a sand clock. One at a time, the teams left. Core 21 was fourth in line and they rushed up eagerly when Zaara beckoned.

"You feeling up to it, girl?" she asked Nafi first.

Nafi nodded vigorously. Her fever had subsided since the previous evening, and although she looked a little pale and worn out, there was no shortage of spirit.

"All right then, try not to die out there," Zaara said. She held out five copies of a map—Maia recognized it as the same master map she had shared earlier — with their core number marked on two spots, one close to the exit of the colony, the other some distance away. "These are your assigned sections." She tapped at the near section first. "Site A has your Spores, and here" — she tapped the distant spot — "at Site B, you'll find your ferns."

"I see overlaps in both areas," Maia said, squinting at the dashed lines crisscrossing them. "Who are we sharing with?"

Zaara scoffed. "Find out for yourself. At this rate, you'll ask me to collect your plants for you next." She nodded at a pair of swarthy men waiting on one side. "Hozzy and Kam will take you to the exit now. Good luck."

At that curt dismissal, Hozzy and Kam marched the team away. As the group walked down the long corridors leading to the exit, they made plans amongst themselves.

"I think the girls should take Site A and we should tackle Site B," Kusha said.

"Why?" Nafi demanded. "You think us girls are too fragile to go that far?"

"What if we are stronger?" Ren said casually. "What's the harm in admitting that?"

"Because you're not," Nafi snapped back. "I'll beat you in a sparring session any day."

Kusha held up his hands. "All right, gang. I didn't mean to call anyone strong or weak. I was simply strategizing."

"Please let Kusha explain, Nafi," Maia chimed in.

"Well, Nafi, you've just recovered from a fever. And this is not the last task, so we need you to keep getting better and not worse. So, the best option for the team is to keep you closest." Nafi drew a sharp breath but did not say a word when Kusha paused. Visibly relieved, Kusha continued. "Also Site B has the Spore, and that will need precise handling. Dani is the best at the finer operations, so I think she should be at Site B as well."

"All right, fine," Nafi said in a flat voice. "Agreed so far. Why do we need Maia?"

"Because you'll be handling the Spores," Kusha replied. "If we had more people, I would have four of them working on the Spores. You need as many hands as you can get. Besides, Maia is the only one who has any experience with these spores in the wild, so she should be with you."

"Sounds like a good plan to me," Dani said. "What do you think, Nafi?"

Nafi barely had time to return a halfhearted nod before their escorts opened the large reinforced door at the end of the corridor. One by one, they stepped into the scorching heat. The sight outside shook Maia just as much as it had done the first time she had seen it.

Broken buildings surrounded them, giants as tall as the sky, their charred frames grotesque as the skeletons of monsters baring their fangs. Heaps of twisted metal and stone formed mounds at the feet of the burned-out buildings, and wreckage was strewn all over. Spores grew everywhere, from the open frames of the structures, on the rubble-strewn path, and everywhere in between. They looked as unfriendly as ever, with their faded green leaves with blood-red stripes, their barbed branches ending in the venomous seedpods. The air was hot, almost scalding. The stuffy, stale odor made Maia dizzy.

Maia remembered what Zaara had told her the last time she was here. "Breathe," she said to her friends. "Breathing will help."

It surely helped. The dazed looks slowly dissipated and soon they were back to discussing their plans.

Ren pointed at the rubble-strewn path to the left. "We should be heading that way."

"Yes, let's take the highway Dani found. It'll save us some time," Kusha added.

The boys promptly took off and the three girls started on their way to Site A. Maia was worried about Nafi, but the girl was tough. Even with the stifling heat and the weight of their heavy suits, the trio made it to their destination without so much as a hiccup. The joy of making it there disappeared as soon as they approached the designated clump of Spores.

"I don't believe this. Of all people . . ." Nafi's exasperated whisper summed it all up.

Hunched around the clump were familiar figures—Nafi's cousin Loriine and her teammates, Baecca and Karhann. As soon as Loriine saw the trio approach, she drew her weapon and assumed a stance.

"This is all ours. You'll have to fight to get your hands on any of them."

"Oh, come on, Loriine," Karhann said. "There are more than ten plants here. There's no need to fight over it."

Loriine scoffed. "Seriously? I don't believe you."

"Get back to work, Loriine," Karhann said. "I need help bagging this."

Loriine sheathed her sword, albeit grudgingly, and went to help Karhann. Maia and her teammates picked out two Spores on the other side of the clump and started digging them out. Things went quietly for a good while, and soon Core 7 had packed their plants. Maia breathed in relief as the trio prepared to leave. They would finish the task without any trouble, after all. But she had thought wrong.

"Say, how is that loony mother of yours doing, dear cousin?" Loriine drawled as they wrapped up.

Nafi said nothing, but Maia's fists curled. "Shut up, Loriine," she spat. "Go away."

Loriine however, had no intention of leaving just yet. "Really, though, I don't see any reason for the drama," she went on. "She should have celebrated. My father did your mother a favor by taking that half-dead girl off her hands."

Karhann gasped at the heartless words Loriine casually and needlessly flung at Nafi, but Baecca giggled. Nafi had been quiet all along, but now she looked up at Loriine, eyes flashing.

"What a pathetic life you must have, Loriine," Nafi said, in a voice that could cut through stone. "It must be so hard to find anything good in that father of yours when all he has ever achieved is getting drunk and killing little kids. But then, he must be your role model, seeing all you're good at is losing too."

Loriine's eyes grew wider and her mouth twisted into a scowl as Nafi's words sank in.

"I'm good at losing?" she hissed. "I'll show you. I'll make you lose right now."

It happened in the blink of an eye. Loriine drew her sword and struck at the clump of Spores on which Core 21 was working.

"No," Maia screamed.

But it was already too late. Loriine's strike barely made a dent on the Spore she hit, but the seedpods swung and burst free. Maia ducked and pulled Nafi out of the way. Loriine struck again and again. Shouts and screams rose around her, but the girl seemed to be possessed. Shaking Maia's hands off her shoulders, Nafi sprang up and dashed toward Loriine, daggers and chains flying. Just her stance distracted Loriine enough to stop her frenzied strikes at the Spores. The girls clashed. Nafi's daggers were a blur of motion on chains, glinting menacingly in the pitiless sunlight, whirring incessantly around Loriine. Even though Maia knew Nafi was far from well and could use her help, she could not just jump into the fight and violate the honor code of duels. So she watched, holding her breath, as Nafi battled Loriine's frenetic swipes.

Then she heard Karhann gasp and Baecca shriek. Maia turned and froze in panic as she took in the scene on her other side. A bunch of seedpods had landed on Karhann's left arm and shoulder, and he was swiping frantically at them. Two of the pods fell off, while the third burst open and released its spores. They spread all over his mask in a hellish cloud of purple and gray. As Karhann swatted them, they seemed to adhere more tightly to the rubbery surface. Dani sprang forward before anyone could make another sound.

"Karhann, hold still," she said. Pulling out a pair of tweezers from her medical aid pack, Dani started pulling out the rice-grain-sized spores one by one. Maia watched in horror as pockmarks formed on Karhann's mask. Just as Zaara had warned them, the spores were eating into it. Dani worked furiously, but Maia noticed Karhann's eyes dilate.

CHAPTER THIRTY-FOUR

"Help," she screamed. "Somebody help."

Baecca joined her, running up to the nearest mound and yelling.

The struggle seemed to go on forever. Loriine and Nafi kept fighting. Dani kept working on the spores on Karhann's face. And Maia and Baecca kept shouting for help.

For a bit, it seemed like a lost cause. Then suddenly things changed for the better. Nafi subdued Loriine; who stripped of her sword and bound in Nafi's chains, howled hysterically. A pair of dark figures, clad in the uniform of the Desert's Watch, appeared among the ruins. Even before Maia had fully explained the situation, they set off a flare. Almost instantaneously, more people appeared, and soon after, they put some kind of salve on Karhann's mask and put him on a stretcher.

"I should go with them," Dani said, "to explain what happened."

"Yes, you should," Nafi replied.

Maia nodded. "We'll be fine here. Go."

Even though most of the party left—Karhann, his team including Loriine who was still bound in chains, and Dani—a few of the Desert's Watch stayed at the site. Maia and Nafi worked silently until they had collected their specimens. They found Kusha and Ren waiting for them at the gate.

"How's Karhann?" Maia asked.

"Barely conscious," Ren said with a grimace.

Nafi peered at Ren's face. "He'll be all right, yes?"

"Dani thinks so," Ren said. He reached out to pat Nafi's shoulder. "Great work subduing Loriine. Would be worse if she kept up her rampage. You all could've died."

Nafi beamed. "Glad I got into the latsore-kaha. That helped." She sighed as they walked to the collection center where an assistant was in charge of collecting the specimens. "We have probably come in last, though."

"You're in fourth place," the assistant said curtly as Maia handed her the collection bag.

Kusha slipped an arm around Nafi's drooping shoulders. "It's all right, Nafi. We'll make up for it during the last task. We're just happy you were not hurt. Nothing is more important than that."

He was right, but his words could only do so much to lift spirits as they sat and discussed Loriine's terrible outburst. Other contestants came to inquire after them, including Adi, the pasty-faced boy from Core 7.

After the last team arrived with their specimens, the assistant dismissed everyone. News of the situation with Karhann spread like wildfire and when the contestants gathered shortly for their afternoon meal, the room buzzed with conversation. Zaara walked in around the time they finished eating. The crowd hushed immediately.

"All caught up on the gossip?" Zaara said, her lips twisting into a mocking smile. "Follow me. We have some serious matters to discuss."

She led them into a dimly lit room, and Maia and her teammates huddled near the back of it.

"Sit down," Zaara said as soon as the contestants had all gathered. There were no chairs in the room, so there was some confusion until Zaara thundered. "Are you all royalty? Never sat on the ground before? It's too lowly for you?"

Maia had never seen confusion clear as quickly as it did. Silence fell once again as Pomewege walked in with Loriine. Aerika followed behind them along with Dani and Baecca, who rushed over to their respective teams. Zaara waited until everyone took their places and then started.

"Today, we completed a dangerous task. Every team bagged the specimens they were required to obtain. Good work," Zaara said. There were a few smiles around the room. "However, a terrible incident also happened and we almost lost a young life. Thankfully, he is expected to make a full recovery."

Sighs of relief rose around the room at Zaara's words.

"This was not the result of an accident. It was not carelessness or stupidity either. Pure malicious intent led to this catastrophe." She stopped and pointed at Loriine, who stood with her gaze fixed at her feet. "Let's applaud this fine young lady for her achievement, shall we?"

No one moved. It seemed to Maia that no one even breathed.

"Oh, imagine that," Zaara said, smirking at Loriine. "No one seems to appreciate your grand accomplishment today. Not even your teammates. Sad, isn't it?" Loriine's gaze drooped even more. Zaara waved in the direction of Core 21. "One group's quick thinking saved lives today. This team had the chance to do better at the task, but instead, they aided an opponent and made sure he lived. A silly sentiment some would say, but some would call it heroic."

Anything else Zaara might have said was drowned out by a burst of applause. When the clapping quieted, Zaara shook her head at Loriine. "If it were up to me, I would have this girl thrown out of this contest, but sadly, it is not up to me. So I have decided to ask for advice from my fellow arbitrators. What do you think, Principal Pomewege? Supervisor Aerika?"

Pomewege and Aerika exchanged a look before the principal spoke.

"What happened today was so despicable and so beneath the moral codes we hold dear at the XDA, that I have no words," he said. Maia could tell he was distressed and disappointed. "Karhann is doing well, that is the saving grace. But for one of my own students to have displayed such a reckless disregard for another life makes me think I have failed as an educator and as principal." He looked at Loriine and let out a long sigh. "Anyway, we have decided not to punish you."

Loriine looked up at Pomewege, her face bright. Maia and everyone around her held their breath until Pomewege spoke again. "We have heard whispers of accusations against the arbitrators. Our fairness has been questioned. So we have decided to put your fate up for a vote among your peers."

Loriine's face dimmed in an instant. She had reason to be worried. Right from the beginning of the Initiative, she had hardly endeared herself to her fellow contestants. Maia remembered how everyone had backed Ren when Loriine had been cruel to Chylomyhrra in Zagran. And even after that, she had made no effort to change. Now the results showed. Other than the members of Core 7, every contestant raised their hand in favor of her disqualification.

Principal Pomewege looked around and nodded gravely. "Well, Loriine, your peers have spoken. I hope you consider this fair enough."

Seeing Loriine's scowl, Maia doubted if she considered the sentence fair, but it definitely was.

"Shameless creature," Nafi whispered. "If I were Loriine, I'd volunteer to drop out."

Maia wholeheartedly agreed.

"We also have another issue to decide on," Aerika said as a sniffling Loriine walked over to her teammates. "As you heard, Core 21 ruined their standing to tend to an opponent. Do you think they deserve bonus points for their selfless action? Raise your hand if you do."

Jiri's arm shot up before Aerika had finished. Almost everyone in the room followed. Maia's eyes filled with tears of joy as she looked at the ring of hands surrounding them. At that moment she did not care if they got a hundred bonus points or none. It was fulfilling to know that doing the right thing still mattered.

CHAPTER THIRTY-FIVE

FARE YOU WELL

Ripples from the horrendous visit to Korobieltes took a while to die down. Anxiety hung in the air for weeks, but as Karhann's condition steadily improved, a slow, peaceful rhythm settled in. Perhaps that was the wrong way to put it. It was slow and peaceful apart from matters of the Initiative. At the Initiative, things were worse than hectic and moods were worse than foul. The Raptor training sessions were terrible, if not terrifying. Ren and Dani had been selected as copilot and navigator respectively, and while they were doing well, things were far from stable. One day they would almost crash on landing, on another they would plummet and nosedive. The good news was the short distance they were required to fly—it was not far from the base to the Molligessian Seam. However, everyone had doubts if they would survive even that short a flight.

Then there was Hadeeyah. She had been furious and distraught about the happenings at Korobieltes, and now she went berserk. Every day she arrived with comparative statistics on flight practice, and if by chance any other group performed better than Core 21 by even a hundredth of a point, there were energetic lectures. The only saving grace was that her lectures, even if overly spirited and tiring, were not condescending. The other good thing was that other than Core 7, no one was in a good position. Even in Core 7, since Karhann was still recovering and Loriine was gone, the performance timings were far from stellar.

Then again, flying to the Molligessian Seam was only the first part of the work on Ti. They would then have to descend into the mines, locate a pocket of Calbion, extract it, and return to the surface, all while making the best time to ensure a win. Reading about how to do that kept the team working through the nights.

Then there was the matter of the upcoming wedding. It would be a small, intimate ceremony, so Hans and Rayan had repeatedly said. But that did not mean it did not need attention. Sana certainly made sure it got plenty.

"It's the biggest event of your lives," she lectured the couple in a serious tone. "I understand 'small', but I don't understand why it shouldn't be special. I won't let you skimp on things."

And so she went about in a frenzy, planning, arranging, and going spectacularly crazy.

Aunt Rowyena had returned to Miorie and other than Uncle Alasdair saying, "She's your mother, Sana. She does care about you," not much was said about it. It was surprising, however, when Uncle Alasdair brought over a large package a week after Aunt Rowyena left. It contained two dresses — both in beautiful shades of orange, one for Sana and the other for Maia — and a note.

Dear Sana,

Thought these would suit you and Maia. Might need some alterations.

Love, your mother.

Sana sat in a stupor for half a morning, packet in hand, until Maia decided to have a talk with her. And finally, after the rest of the morning was spent discussing the need to move past grievances, Sana accepted the gift, although somewhat grudgingly.

One morning, about two weeks before Hans and Rayan's big day, Sana was hunched over putting the finishing touches on their dresses, and Maia was buried up to her neck in reading material on Ti, when a loud rap sounded on the door. Sana grunted loudly in displeasure, so Maia extracted herself from her pile to check.

Ori's son, Nahlo, and four of his troopers stood in the corridor. Nahlo held out a note.

"For you," he said simply.

Two short sentences were written on it in a familiar, neat hand.

It is fixed. Ready whenever you are.

"Sana, Miir fixed the frame," Maia said, giddy with excitement. It had taken a long time, but in the end —

"That's great," Sana replied, not even sparing her a glance. "Go take a look."

Maia turned toward Nahlo. "Is he home now?"

Nahlo rolled his eyes. "Of course. How long are you gonna make us wait?"

Maia chuckled a little at Nahlo's disapproving expression. "All right, give me a moment."

She tucked the note into a drawer and picked up Bellator. Then, grabbing her satchel with the all-important marbles that were Asiyaah's recordings, Maia set off with Nahlo and his troopers. Her little protectors kept up a constant chatter that distracted Maia during the long walk, but she could not completely ignore the increasing thump of her heart with every step she took toward Miir's house.

Some time had passed since Maia had come to face her changing feelings for him. And since returning from T'ra, she had constantly analyzed and reanalyzed her thoughts. For a while, she had been determined to push it all away, bottle it up, and hide it somewhere until it faded. It would fade away, she was confident. Then she realized things were far worse than that. Thoughts of Miir came to her countless times a day. Everything she did, every step she took, every word she spoke, her mind rushed to draw a connection to him. Her heart yearned to share the smallest things—thoughts, laughter, and most of all, frustrations—with him. She also realized this was nothing new. Things had been that way for a while. The only recent development was her discovering it. Finally, she came to accept her feelings. Whatever they were, they were not about to fade as she had hoped. They only grew stronger and clearer with each passing day.

Time had normalized things somewhat, and thankfully so. The joint training sessions she and Sana had with Miir had calmed Maia's jittery nerves as well. Conversations were close to being easy once more. Maia hoped she could keep things that way while quietly holding on to her secret. However, the idea of being alone with him now put her a bit on edge.

"She's here," Nahlo shouted when they reached the little house among the Darkwoods, and soon the troopers left.

"You look tired," Miir observed as they walked inside. "The Initiative bothering you much?"

Maia huffed. "That Molligessian Seam is a horrid place. It should be banned from existence. If it were up to me—"

"You'd design a challenge in the rose garden of ThulaSu."

"Hey! Don't underestimate the rose garden. Or me." He had clearly meant it as a joke, but Maia could not give in without a protest. She also figured that talking had brought back normalcy. It was a relief that even though she realized the difference in her feelings for him every moment they spent together, she was not the bumbling idiot she had been during the trip back from T'ra. Maia deduced that keeping up a conversation was necessary as the best antidote to that awkwardness.

Seeing the frame on the table, she took the jar of marbles from her satchel. "Oh, Sana says she's not training next week."

"What's the excuse? Wedding planning?"

Maia nodded. "Yes, that. She's also reworking the dresses Aunt Rowyena sent. I offered to help, but she told me to stick to my weapons of bloodshed. Guess my needlework isn't as stellar as I thought."

"So you have another death trap to handle," Miir said, chuckling. He turned somber in the next instant. "Curious that you accepted your aunt's gift after all that she said to you, about you. You forgive her?"

"What else can I do? Close my heart to her? Never speak to her or of her again?"

Miir did not answer, simply stood with a thoughtful expression on his face. As always happened lately with him, Maia's thoughts poured out freely, without fear. It was a strange need, an intense one, to tell him her deepest secrets.

"I know Aunt Rowyena doesn't like me. She never did. My company and any association with me threaten her child's future. All she wants is to protect Sana. She's selfish, perhaps, but she's within her rights to want to protect someone she cares about." Maia paused to draw in as much air as she could. "I know what I represent. My mother with her past so questionable, my father . . . unknown. I know to my aunt I am . . . unacceptable." Her fists clenched, and Maia blinked hard to keep her tears at bay. "I won't go asking for her acceptance. But if she reaches out with sincerity, I can't look away. If I do that, it'll only show how small a heart I have." She stopped, overcome by sudden exhaustion. "Besides, Sana needs to heal. She needs to move forward. And if I cling to my aunt's unkind words, she will too. Even more than I do. I can't let that happen." Maia smiled as brightly as she could. "So that's why the death traps stayed. Word of caution though, they're orange, so they may burn your eyes."

"That last part, I do not agree with," Miir replied, laughing. "Your aunt may not be a nice person, but she would not send anything that might question her refinement. So I think my eyes are safe."

Miir had a point, as always. The dresses Aunt Rowyena sent were a testament to her impeccable taste. Maia even wondered how she managed to pick a color that could so nicely complement both her coloring and Sana's, given that they looked so different.

Maia gave in with a grudging grin and they were soon settled down on two sides of the table, the frame between them. Miir picked out the marbles with notches on their sides and set them in a line. He picked up the blue one they had been watching at the abayam when the frame failed.

"We have to rewatch this," he said.

Miir had fixed the frame perfectly—there was no sputtering, no loud noises, and no ear-splitting wails when Maia placed the marble in between the prongs. Once again, Asiyaah and then Bikele came into view, making Maia smile. However, there was nothing much beyond the point where the recording had been cut off at the last viewing, and soon it was time to move on to a new one.

"That one is next," he said, pointing at the yellow marble on the left.

As soon as Maia put it in place, the space above the frame flickered and the form of a woman rapidly took shape.

"Hello again, Maia. Ready to hear about it all?"

Asiyaah smiled out of the grainy projection, her face just as bright as it had been in the previous recordings. Maia could not help but think how solemn Miir was compared to his mother. She wondered if he had always been like this, or if over all these years of loneliness, he had simply forgotten how to be happy and laugh.

In the projection, Asiyaah began to speak.

"I discovered the Origin Scrolls by accident. I was eighteen. Xif had just arrived in the Tansian system, and there was plenty of work to be done. My father had not been well after our transition to Tansi, and I found myself assisting him on one project or another. One day I was in the Chancery Archives with my father, digging for a master plan of something. The data vaults had been opened wide for us, and I looked at places I was not supposed to. Not in my wildest dreams had I expected to find this—the Origin Scrolls.

"I read, not believing. For weeks, I stayed in a stupor, unable to fathom the depth of the disclosure, or should I say, unwilling to accept the implications. Slowly I realized I could not wish away my knowledge or the truth.

"I did not yet trust the statements, however. I started looking for proof, trying to ascertain the veracity of the Origin Scrolls, hoping I would be proved wrong. But the more I looked and thought, the surer I grew of the terrifying reality. My glorious nation had its hands soaked in the blood of billions. There was no way to look past it. Ours was an appalling history, and I decided I would not let it repeat itself.

"I knew my destiny. I could not be a loyal servant to my nation. I would be a traitor. And I did not mind. I refused my Connaissance. Shocked as he was, my always-indulgent father accepted my decision. He hushed it up, letting my secret be. It took a toll on him, though, and I could see the worry in his eyes. It was as if he knew what was in my heart. But if he feared constantly, he never stopped me, never asked me a question. I took his silence as his approval.

"After that, my life was all about finding a solution. I searched far and wide. I dug into books and scrolls and data vaults. I spoke with people who would know. One answer kept coming back to me—break the mechanism that makes Xif's flight possible, break the heart of the Sedara.

"It would not be an easy task. It was not beyond the realm of possibility, however. The heart was a core of light wrapped in a chalice of fortified Calbion, and all of it accessible only to a few through the Foundation Chamber. Getting to the Foundation Chamber would be easy, since my father had unrestricted access. I was a Tierremorphe, so I could tear apart the chalice. But who would handle the light inside? I needed a Shimugien."

Asiyaah threw her head backward and laughed, her eyes sparkling as they caught the sunlight.

"As if finding a Shimugien was as easy as going to the market and picking one up. It was the hardest task of all. No one on Xif would advertise their ability to possess the light, and no one on Tansi would even know what it meant to possess the light. So what was I to do? I figured I would go looking and scour our planet and our neighboring one. But that would take time, time that I did not have.

"After much thinking, I joined the XDA. As with every passage, our assimilation of the host population was about to begin. We were luring the best minds the host planet had to offer, as we always had in every system we visited. A Shimugien, I deduced, would be talented enough to find her way to the XDA. I waited, and I waited. I almost thought it was useless, almost thought I had failed. Until after about four years of waiting, I came across this slip of a girl. Her bright blue eyes were so kind and curious, her smile so shy and sweet. She seemed . . . different.

"I found her one day at the Sakoro groves, happily chatting with another girl. 'I'm Sophia. Everyone calls me Sophie,' she said. "This is my friend, Zaara.' She did not know I had a tiny L'miere crystal in my palm when she clasped my hand, she did not even sense its disappearance. But I knew right then that I had found what I was looking for, my path to end the centuries-long bloodshed. It would be a long time before I told her anything, but I knew my plan was no longer as impossible as it had been."

It was oddly unsettling to hear about Asiyaah's plan, knowing how it would go about changing destinies. It would touch not only the lives of Asiyaah and her peers but also those of the next generation. Thinking of the future that had unfolded since brought on a feeling of utter vulnerability, and Maia shuddered a little when the projection vanished.

"Are you all right?" Miir asked as he handed her the next marble, one the color of the Darkwoods.

Had it not been for the annoying awkwardness that had descended between them, Maia would have hopped over to Miir's side of the table and sat closer to him. Now, however, even thinking about it made her flush. So although she yearned for the comfort of his proximity, she simply smiled.

"I'm fine," she whispered bravely.

"Wait," Miir said and disappeared into the house. He came back shortly and handed Maia a wrap. "Here. This might help," he said.

It helped. Even though the day was warm and the sun shone

brightly, fear left Maia cold. Why she was so shaken, Maia did not know, but there was no denying it. Thanking Miir silently, Maia pulled the wrap close around her and slipped the green marble between the prongs. In the next instant, Asiyaah's smiling face formed above the frame.

"Can you believe it took us eight whole years to prepare and plan for the day? Sophie turned out to be a most eager accomplice, her heart bigger and stouter than I ever expected. Not once did she dither, not once did she fear the consequences. Who knew there was so much strength in that slip of a girl?

"There were so many things to be considered, so much to be learned, so many steps to be taken before we could strike. Plans kept changing right up to the end. My father, who I counted upon as the key to our entry into the Foundation Chamber, suddenly retired due to illness, renouncing all his privileges. So we had to devise a new plan. It was one that neither of us was happy about, but we went along because it had to be done.

"Then there was the constant change in timing. One day we were rushing because Xif was about to leave the system. The next, we heard that enormous deposits of Calbion had been discovered on Ti, and Xif would stay for another few years. Then things changed again. And again. In the end, we decided we would go ahead as soon as we could. Time or not, we had to finish what we had started.

"We worried still, right until the last moment. Would we manage to get inside the Foundation Chamber? Would I be able to take apart the chalice? What if Sophie could not handle the immense power of the lighted core? There were so many risks, so many questions, but one thing was clear—one step into the Foundation Chamber and our lives would change forever. And we were fine with that.

"Xif was celebrating the commemoration of First Passage when we walked in, ready to strike at the heart of the beauty that was the Sedara. All went well—the Foundation Chamber opened its gates to us, and I pulled out the Verto-balancer Capsule. The chalice fell apart as I had hoped and Sophie extracted the core. And then . . . everything went wrong."

Asiyaah's face looked haggard, and Maia knew from her distant gaze that she was drawn back to the moment when they took apart the heart of the Sedara. Asiyaah glanced away as if trying to gather the strength to say the next part. And even though Maia had pieced together what had happened from then on, her heart trembled and shook like a leaf in a storm. She pulled the wrap closer, desperate for some warmth to counter the intense cold within her.

"Our plan fell to pieces right after we had torn apart the heart. Sophie could not split the Afterlight. We had planned to break it into five shards, and then scatter them far and wide. We had the vessels prepared, but as much as Sophie tried, they refused to come to life. I knew right then something was terribly wrong. There was something I did not foresee, something that fate had sprung on us. But there was no time to investigate. They would discover the imbalance in the Sedara soon, and we had to flee before they came. So we fled.

"We went separate ways, Sophie and I. She carried the light with her, and I took the chalice. We did not tell each other what we were going to do with them. That was the best way. If we were discovered, there would be nothing to tell them about the other half. I went back home. Sophie was to leave for Tansi after she had met with her husband."

"Sophie never left Xif that night."

A whimper came out of Maia so suddenly that it startled her. The projection vanished instantly, and as Maia blinked to clear the fog of grief sweeping through her, she realized that Miir had yanked out the marble. His gaze, intense and worried, scoured her face and after a moment's hesitation, he came over to her side of the bench.

"We can watch this some other time," he said, placing a hand on her back. His touch was comforting, and it soothed and strengthened Maia's frayed insides.

"No, I'm fine," Maia reassured him, even though half of her still wanted to flee. She knew, sooner or later, she would have to face it. She would rather do it sooner. "I want to do this now."

CHAPTER THIRTY-FIVE

Maia slipped the marble back on and Asiyaah spoke once more.

"They caught Sophie the next morning at the XDA. She was waiting to meet her husband in the Hall of Spires, where they had first met. They never saw each other again.

"I had an elaborate plan to hide the chalice, a way that would ensure no one would ever be able to resurrect it. But the moment I heard they had found Sophie, I knew my time was short. I abandoned my original plan and devised a new one that was full of risks. I am glad I did it because Phocluus soon came to visit me. He told me he knew everything, that out of respect for my father, he would not take me away while he was alive, but my days with my family were numbered, and my movements were always watched. They came for me two days after my father passed away."

For a while, Asiyaah sat with her head hung low. When she looked up again, her eyes were glistening.

"I long to see my baby boy so much. I wish I could speak to him, or leave him a message. I know I cannot. He is safer not knowing anything about this. But I so desperately long to see him again, to hold him, to look into those wide and trusting eyes and tell him all will be well one day. I am sorry I could not be there for you, and for the burden you will carry all your life because of me."

Miir's eyes were brimming with tears when Asiyaah's projection faded. He kept staring at the empty space for a long time before exhaling. Then he sat up with a start.

"She did not say what she did with the chalice," he said. "What happened to it?"

While Maia understood Asiyaah could not have plainly stated the location of the chalice, it was indeed strange how abruptly her tone changed at the end. However, Maia was happy that at least a small part of the message was just for Miir. He would treasure it, she knew, the way she treasured the memory of Sophie's message to her.

"The burden . . . that's the second time she mentions it," she said, pondering Asiyaah's words.

"I do not understand." Miir shook his head slowly. A silent

moment or two passed before he handed Maia the next marble, one with blue-green striations. Asiyaah reappeared, and her bright smile returned once again.

"I came to Tansi because of Sophie. Right before the agents of the SDS caught her, she managed to hand off a few of her belongings to Zaara, along with a note to help me if I needed it. Zaara . . . her heart is full of hate for me, for having destroyed her friend's life. I do not blame her for thinking that way. It is true. Sophie would have spent a peaceful life, oblivious of the truth, had it not been for me. I did not force her into it, but it was my plan, after all. I destroyed us, sacrificed us all.

"After I was banished from Xif, I reached out to Zaara. She would have nothing to do with me, so she sent Bikele. Bikele . . . Sophie's loyal friend, became my friend also. Time and again, he risked his safety, his life, to help me.

"When he told me about you, Maia, I finally understood why Sophie could not split the Afterlight. It was because she did not possess it anymore. It belonged to you. I knew what that meant. It meant you were not just a Shimugien, you were more than that. And thinking about it, I realized why that could be. It made perfect sense.

"Sophie had left a message for you. She wanted you to know a little about her when you turned thirteen. I knew I had to leave something for you also, explaining everything. I had to tell you of the light you carry within yourself. The Afterlight would be benign, and you will probably never feel any different for it, but you had to know.

"I could not let you know of this until you were older, much older. I would rather you not know of me while you are a curious child with a pliant heart. You might even expect to form a connection with the family I leave behind, thinking there is a bond you share. But that cannot be. You see, there has to be a separation between the family I leave behind and you. I do not worry about Zaara. I know she will have nothing but hatred for me to share with you. But I fear Bikele and his soft heart. I have told him not to cast me in a favorable light until you are ready to see this. I hope my friend will stay strong.

"Now that you know what has been, I hope you find some comfort in the truth. All these years have passed peacefully, so there is no reason to fear anymore. You can live a free life now.

"There is only one thing I ask—do not seek out my family. It is for your safety that I ask you this: stay away from my sons and their father. If you come across any of them, and I think you might, do not reveal Sophie's connection to you. Immense harm may come to you if you do not heed my words. So please, remember my words of caution."

Silence fell, and Maia's mind reeled. This explained why Bikele had used words about Asiyaah that planted suspicion. Asiyaah had wanted it that way. Immense harm . . . Maia's thoughts stayed stuck on those words. Did Asiyaah know that Remii would turn out the way he had? Probably she feared that her husband, being the chancellor and having known Sophie, would come after Maia if he knew her identity.

"Looks like this is the last one," Miir said. He had picked up a purple marble.

Maia's mind had been drawn into the words of Asiyaah's last message, and she had forgotten about everything around her. Suddenly, as Miir returned to the other side of the table, the stiffness in his voice hit her. It was strange. Even stranger was the look on his face—distant, withdrawn. His eyes seemed lightless, as if a curtain had dropped over his heart. Maia had no chance to ask him what was bothering him, because Asiyaah's face formed on the screen once again as she plugged in the final marble.

"Here I am again. This will be the last time I speak with you, Maia, and I miss speaking with you already. It is strange, this unexpected kinship I feel with you. You hear the thoughts no one else has heard, you see my soul. I burden you, perhaps, but being able to tell this to someone relieves me.

"I have enjoyed making these memories for you. These were something I looked forward to. Building the projector, finding a way to record these, and plotting with our mutual friend about ways to hide them. Now I have nothing else to do, except wait . . ."

A sad, resigned look came over Asiyaah's haggard face. But it was only fleeting. The bright smile that never failed to lift Maia's heart came back momentarily.

"Our lives were broken, and our dreams stayed unfulfilled because of a cause that demanded sacrifice. I hope that our pain has brought the world peace, and given you a chance at a better future.

"Maia, I wish you a happy life, a full life, a life filled with love, and a life free of fear. May your future be different from ours."

Asiyaah paused. Her eyes looked tired, and for the first time, Maia saw the effort that went into the smile that came next. It was a bright smile nonetheless.

"May all your dreams come true, Maia. Fare you well."

It was indeed strange, she too felt a connection with Asiyaah. Now that the last message was complete, an emptiness engulfed her insides. She stared at the open space above the frame, yearning for more, wishing to see that luminous smile again.

Miir broke the silence. "Thank you for sharing these with me." He extracted the last marble and placed it back in Maia's jar with the rest. He set the frame near her satchel. "Here, all yours."

The way he said it was odd. The way he hurried away from the table and sat down on the steps, staring into the distance, was odder still. Maia quickly packed up the frame and the jar of marbles before walking over to his side.

"What's wrong?" she asked, squinting at his hard, darkened face. She was sure he was pondering Asiyaah's words, thinking of her ominous warnings for Maia. She decided to ask, if only to break the shell he had withdrawn into. "Is it because of what your mother said?"

He sighed a little. "Yes, her warnings were very clear. I am worried."

"Miir, you can't think like that. Next, you're going to tell me I can't talk to you because your mother said I should stay away from her family."

Not only did he stay silent, he did not even look up at her. Fists clenched, Maia stared in disbelief. *He is thinking exactly that!*

She suppressed a sigh and sat down next to him. His gaze was fixed on the Darkwoods, a frown deeply etched on his brow. Maia wished she could lay a hand on his tight fists, or wrap an arm around him, but she hesitated. Things were no longer simple between them. They could not be easy and spontaneous as long as she kept secret the feelings in her heart. The situation would not change until she had shared her secret with him. An annoying wall of nervousness had grown between them, and even though she desperately wished to breach it, Maia finally gave in to the distance it created.

Words, that's all I have right now. So she went with them, forming her sentences with careful deliberation.

"When your mother made these recordings, she had a different idea of the world she was leaving behind. She did not foresee everything that has actually happened." She paused a moment to scan his face, looking for light in his eyes, but found none. "In the future she saw, I have come of age, and I'm viewing her messages with Bikele. In that future, you're not here with me; you're in Xif, with your father and your brother. So what she says doesn't apply. You *have* to understand that."

"You are telling me we should ignore what she said?"

"No. I'm telling you that you can't accept everything as is."

Once again, she received no reply. What else could she do? She could only hope that he would see the truth with time.

"You should get back to ThulaSu. You have work to finish." Miir suddenly broke the silence, his voice still distant, his manner frigid. "Let me walk you back."

The oppressive silence clawed at Maia's heart as they walked out. Miir remained aloof, his face rigid, his gaze fixed on the path ahead. Maia knew it was going to be a long, quiet walk. They had just passed the front of the house when a sweet fragrance hit her nose and she stopped abruptly.

"Wait! That smells like . . . but it's not possible." She turned around, her eyes desperately scanning the surroundings.

"Hansa flowers?" Miir asked in a quiet voice. He pointed casually toward the far corner of the house, at a shady nook near the Darkwoods. "Over there."

Maia rushed over as fast as her legs would take her. A familiar-looking bush, small and rounded, its dark green leaves shining, greeted her. A lone white flower shone on one side. Its fragrance took Maia to Appian in an instant, to those sultry summer days and calm evenings. They would sit on the porch, Dada and she, immersed in the smell of the Hansa.

"You could take it if you want."

"What? No, I can't. That's the only flower it has," Maia said. "There are plenty more buds, though. I may take one once those bloom."

"Yes, of course." There was no life in his voice, Maia noted. Asiyaah's words . . . he was still stuck on them. They had snuffed out a flame inside. "We should go now," he reminded her stiffly.

"It's unusual for the Hansa to grow here," Maia kept up the conversation as they resumed the walk back. "It's so cold in ThulaSu. It's a miracle it survived the winters. Back in Appian, they grew everywhere. Their fragrance will always remind me of summer, I guess."

There was no reply, only silence and disappointment.

Maia decided to try again. She had to be more direct to draw him into a conversation. "How do you know about the Hansa?"

"Nahlo."

"They are said to be very auspicious," Maia chirped on. "I wish there were more of them so we could have some at Hans and Rayan's wedding."

A nod was all Maia received in return. That walk back was the quietest she had had in a long while. Every word Asiyaah had said weighed heavily on Maia's heart, but that was nothing compared to Miir's continued silence. The absolutely miserable part was—Maia felt completely helpless and inadequate to fix the situation.

CHAPTER THIRTY-SIX

A MEETING OF HANDS

Hans and Rayan's wedding day arrived sooner than seemed possible. A beautiful morning broke upon ThulaSu that day, the skies were blue with flitting clouds, the air was cool, a light breeze came and went, and all was perfect.

No one would have suspected how crazy things had been leading up to that day. Sana had gone berserk for a while putting together Rayan's wardrobe, and every day Rayan grew progressively more nervous. Maia would never have believed that Rayan of all people could be so anxious, but Sana and the situation had managed to do just that. At one point it seemed as if Rayan would just abandon the preparations, and Sana would lose her mind trying to do innumerable things by herself.

Although they wanted to, Maia and the rest of the gang could offer hardly any help because of the Initiative. A boatload of work and Hadeeyah's constant supervision left them with no time.

"You barely scraped through in Korobieltes," Hadeeyah pronounced as she paced in circles around them, "so now you need to get the best time on Ti. Weddings will come and go, but the Initiative won't happen again. So get to work."

Even Nafi did not utter a peep in protest. Hadeeyah's prodding or not, everyone knew the absolute seriousness of the task ahead of them. It was the last chance they had to win the Initiative and acquire Seigvard, and thus, gain an upper hand against the R'armimon prince. The group was hunched over, every day, from morning until late in the evening, working out details on the upcoming trip to Ti. And every day, Hadeeyah reviewed their notes and kept track of their progress.

Sana gave up on getting any help from them, and for a while, she also gave up on half of her plans for the wedding. At last, her desperate search for assistance bore fruit when Niyani, Ori's widow, made an appearance. Niyani—'the lifesaver', as Sana liked to call her—fixed it all. Sana was relieved to have her support, which was abundantly clear from the way she kept repeating, "This is how a mother should be," or sometimes, "Why can't all mothers be like Niyani?"

Niyani, along with her sons Nahsemi and Nahlo, as well as a group of villagers from Walenveil, jumped into the preparations. Soon all was back in order, Rayan's wedding outfit, the menu for the banquet afterward, and everything else, all the way down to the timing of every little step.

"Get up, Maia." Sana's vigorous shaking made Maia roll out of bed that morning. "Hurry up and get dressed. I'm leaving with Rayan now."

The door slammed shut and Maia groaned as she left the warmth of her bed. She was tired. The previous night had been hectic, with not only a lot of work planning for Ti but also trying on their outfits and listening to Sana's lectures about how everything needed to be perfect and how they all needed to work on their smiles.

By the time Maia had dressed and replicated to a decent degree the hairstyle Sana had diligently taught her over the past few weeks, everyone except Nafi had left for the venue.

"Sana has lost it. Do this, do that, don't do this, don't do that." Nafi grumbled all the way to the pavilion where the wedding was to take place. "Can you imagine how crazy she'll be at her own wedding? I pity the guy who marries her."

"Let's get through this one first, Nafi," Maia said. "We're late and—"

"We're as good as dead if Sana sees us walking in now." Nafi looked up, her eyes fearful for a moment. "Hey, let's cut through the annex. That way she won't see us come in. We can sneak in . . . sort of."

That sounded like an excellent idea. Maia happily followed Nafi along a side walkway, across the annex where countless boxes—all presumably supplies for the wedding—lay scattered, and then up the stairs and along the short pathway that led to the back of the pavilion. They ran into Dorian hauling boxes. He frowned on seeing them.

"Aren't you a little late?" he asked.

"We know, we know," Nafi said in a rush. "But we're here now."

As they were speaking with Dorian, Nahsemi and Miir appeared at the top of the second flight of stairs, laughing as they carried more boxes. The first thing Maia noted was how carefree Miir looked, and her own spirits lifted immediately. The last time she had seen him, he had been worried about his mother's warning for her, and her repeated assurances had failed to do anything. Now, however, his face was bright again and when he nodded at them, his smile was as normal as could be.

"You are late," Miir said. "Sana has been looking for you, Nafi. You are supposed to read something."

"Oh, no!" Nafi let out a howl. "I forgot. The marriage oath, I was supposed to help them practice . . ." The words were lost as Nafi ran like a meteor across the pathway up to the pavilion.

"Slow down," Dorian called out, but Maia doubted if Nafi heard him.

Maia was just about to hurry after Nafi when Miir stopped her. "Can you wait just a bit? I have something for you."

Maia ambled away from the stairs as she waited, toward the side of the pavilion where two long tables had been set up for the banquet after the ceremony. She let her fingers trace the tiny blue and pink flowers embroidered along the sides of the butter-yellow fabric. So beautiful, so perfect. A breeze wafted through and it took Maia far away in an instant.

What was it like during Sophie's wedding, she wondered. No one knew who she had married, no one. Was she all alone? Did she even have a ceremony or a celebration? Had she wished for one?

I'll never know.

Maia blinked at the sudden rush of tears. No. She could not cry today, not on Hans and Rayan's special and perfect day. Today was meant for laughter, for joy. Maia brought herself back to the dainty vines that wove through the flowers on the tablecloth, but it did not take long for her thoughts to drift once more.

Will I ever have a day like this? Can I even hope —

"Hey!"

Maia's heart almost leapt out of her chest. Unexpectedly and unreasonably shaken by Miir's voice, she scooted back a few steps, bumped into the bench behind her, and almost fell over it. She caught her balance somehow and composed herself swiftly, but her reaction had already had an effect.

"I scared you. Again?" Miir's gaze was sharp on her face as if he was trying to solve a problem.

"No, I was just . . . no." Maia flushed, her words coming out in a jumble, her thoughts rushing too fast to make sense. Thankfully, he looked away from her face.

"I brought these." He held out a small bowl. Maia's heart leaped when she looked inside the container. A cluster of Hansa flowers sat inside it, looking so pretty.

"Thank you, thank you," she exclaimed. She wanted to hug him, but obviously that could not be. So she thanked him once more. Or maybe ten times over, Maia could not remember.

"It was perfect timing. So many bloomed this morning," Miir

said.

She reached out, smiling happily as her fingers wrapped around the bowl. He moved his hand at the same instant, and for a heart-stopping moment or two, they stayed on top of Maia's.

How a casual, accidental, and totally random touch could make her heart jump, send a bolt of lightning through her senses, and make her oh-so-ludicrously snatch her hand away and let go of the container was beyond Maia's understanding. It was nothing short of a miracle that Miir's hand shot out and grabbed the falling bowl just in time.

"Careful," he said.

"I'm so, so sorry," Maia whispered. Warmth flooded her face and rushed up to the tip of her ears. "I-I just . . ." Her thoughts disappeared midway.

What are you doing? You almost ruined those flowers. Get a grip on yourself before you spoil everything.

She found him looking, clearly reading every expression that crossed her face. There was a distinct tightness about him and a look of . . . worry . . . fear? Maia's mind searched frantically for an explanation she could give for her clumsiness, but he did not say another word about it.

"Here you go." He placed the bowl on the table and slowly walked backward a few steps, as if he were afraid that any sudden movement would cause her to jump again. His eyes stayed locked with Maia's until there was space between them. Then he turned and hurried away. All the while, Maia simply stared back in silence, unable to find a single word to say, though she knew something needed to be said or done.

"Maia!" Nafi's shout stopped her from doing anything at all. Maia tore her eyes away from Miir's disappearing form. Seeing Nafi's distressed waving, she grabbed the bowl and walked over to Nafi on the other end of the pavilion.

"What is it?"

"A disaster," Nafi declared. "Zaara was here. Rayan asked for her blessing and she refused. Now Rayan has locked herself in the dressing room and won't come out. I doubt the wedding is going to happen at all."

They ran across the pavilion. Maia found most of her friends huddled on a bench outside the dressing rooms. Dani had clearly been crying, Sana sat next to her with a woebegone face, and Kusha was pacing up and down in front of them. Maia saw Niyani near the door of the dressing room, possibly trying to comfort Rayan.

Sana shook her head when she saw Maia. "Zaara just came by and said some nasty things. And now Rayan refuses to come out. Won't talk to anyone. Even refused to speak with Hans, and that got Hans rattled as well."

"Zaara's very important to Rayan," Nafi said. "She's obviously upset."

Maia's fists curled. She would not let this fall apart. Not without a fight. She was going to talk to Zaara about it.

"Hold this." She placed the bowl of flowers in Sana's hands. "I'll be back. I need to talk with Zaara."

Maia ran toward the front gates of the pavilion, hoping to catch Zaara, with Nafi a few paces behind her. She saw Zaara's upright form as soon as she stepped outside the gates.

"Zaara," she called. "Zaara, wait!"

Zaara froze. Then she spun around, eyes flashing, her staff raised at Maia. "How many times have I told you to not use my name out in the open? Do you not listen, girl?"

Sure, she had said it plenty of times, but Maia did not care. Not now, anyway. With a defiant glare, she strode up to the woman.

"Do you ever listen to yourself, Zaara?" she said.

Zaara's eyes narrowed. "What is this? Are you here to lecture me?"

"Yes, I am." Maia's nails dug into her palms as she held Zaara's fiery gaze. "You refused to bless Rayan. You upset her on a day she should be nothing but happy. You upset her so much that she could very well call this off. Why?"

"Because calling it off would be the most sensible thing to do." Zaara thumped her staff on the stone walkway. "I'm done watching unhappy endings, and here's another one in the making. That girl, marrying *that* boy . . . you think any good will come of it? She'll be miserable the rest of her life, and I can't—"

"She will be happy the rest of her life," Maia shouted. "Hans loves her, and she loves him back. They can *never* be miserable."

Zaara scoffed. "They love each other. Indeed. Can't you see how different they are? Are you blind?" She broke into laughter that made Maia shudder. "He has no respect for her. He can't have any respect for a girl who has nothing, who comes from nothing. That's the truth, Maia. The sooner you realize that, the better. Or you too will have a miserable ending like your mother before you."

"Stop it," Maia retorted. "My mother may have died in pain, but her ending was just what she wanted it to be. She died knowing she finished what she set out to do. She succeeded, she knew that." Maia stopped, out of breath and suddenly tired. "You know, Zaara, every ending has its happiness. You just have to find a way to look at it right. Sophie's ending is happy despite all the pain she endured. That's because we're all alive, because Tansi lives, and because now Hans and Rayan have a future together."

For a while, no one spoke. Only Zaara's eyes blazed and burned on Maia's face. Then the woman's face twisted into a scowl.

"You've learned how to lecture, that's for sure," Zaara said, her jeering tone searing Maia's insides. "Anyway, this is not your fight. What are you here for?"

"This is very much my fight," Maia said, pushing aside the hurt that choked her throat. "Hans and Rayan's happiness together is my dream too. Every moment they have together is worth fighting for, and I will. And you have to come back and bless Rayan. You mean the world to her, and now is when you should be by her side."

"Every bit like your foolish mother you are," Zaara said. "I will see who comes to fight for you, girl. Remember this, no one cares for the real you, no one. You are just a means to an end. Mark my words."

She whirled away and then turned back again. "I won't bless that stupid girl for making the stupidest mistake of her life. I won't. Not now, not ever."

With that, Zaara strode away, every thump of her staff on the stones hitting Maia like a hammer in the chest. She vaguely felt Nafi's cold fingers on her wrist, a tug.

"Maia, you tried," Nafi whispered. "Don't let her words get to you. She's crazy."

"I don't care what she says to me, Nafi. But if Rayan can't get over this—"

"Maia! Nafi!" Dani streaked out toward them, screaming, and Maia had no chance to finish her sentence. All she saw was Dani's smiling face. "Guess what?" Dani said, completely out of breath. "Rayan says . . . she doesn't care what Zaara thinks. So . . . everything is good."

Nafi screeched in delight, Maia jumped, and they all squealed together. It was all smiles and laughter after that. The arrangements came together wonderfully, the guests arrived, and the Xinhagyi came to officiate the ceremony. Rayan looked radiant in a pale pink Anaka—the traditional wedding attire of the Solianese. Hans looked dashing in blue and white and despite Dani's persistent cajoling that quickly turned into threats, refused to undo his ponytail.

"That is who I am, Dani," was his reply. "I'm not going to pretend to be someone else just to look appropriate for a ceremony."

Maia and Nafi were giggling at their squabble when Sana rushed over and hugged Maia. "Thank you for the Hansa flowers. I'll put them on the altar. They are just perfect. What a blessing." She flitted away just as quickly as she had arrived.

"Where did you get the Hansa?" Nafi asked. "I didn't know they even grew here."

"I know, I didn't think so either." Maia went on to tell Nafi how she had spotted them outside of Miir's cottage, and how he had remembered to bring some for Hans and Rayan's ceremony. She leaned her head on Nafi's shoulder as they watched the Xinhagyi build the ceremonial altar. "Everything's coming together just perfectly today. I'm so happy."

Soon the ceremony began. The couple stood on two sides of the small altar with the spiritual witnesses to the union—a square mound of soil signified strength, a circular moat of water representing life, and the burning fire in the middle that stood for eternity. The Xinhagyi tied a silken thread over and around their clasped hands as they recited the oath, and after a long, entrancing chant, ancient and mellifluous, he blessed them on behalf of the stars and declared them husband and wife.

The pavilion erupted in laughter and cheers and greetings. Maia saw the blissful look on both Hans and Rayan's faces, and she thought of how far from reality Zaara was. There was nothing but happiness in this couple's future. There was no difference they could not overcome. Zaara was wrong, completely and indisputably wrong.

Maia had been immersed in the wedding until now. But as the party dispersed and mixed and mingled, with innumerable words exchanged and just as many photographs captured, Maia quickly sensed the weirdest thing. She had spoken with almost everyone in the party, her own friends, friends of Hans and Rayan who had arrived from Zagran and Korobieltes, and even every villager from Walenvell, yet she had never, not even once, come face to face with Miir. Her eyes searched him out, but oddly, he never met her gaze, and odder still, she always found him at the farthest corner from her. Always. It was a strange choreography, keeping the maximum distance between them, and no matter how Maia tried to change it, the gap stayed firmly in place. Always.

Soon after the sumptuous meal—fluffed rice grain, pickled greens, sea fowl braised to golden perfection, and steamed sweet yogurt—all planned by Dorian with assistance from Nafi, the couple left for the Sun Temple with the Xinhagyi. That was the final part of the marriage, collecting the blessings of the stars and the ancestors who came before. Hans and Rayan planned to travel after that, first to Korobieltes and then to T'ra to pay their respects to their families.

The guests soon dispersed, and after helping Dorian and his crew with the clean-up, Maia and her friends clustered near the gates of the pavilion. Sana, content with how successful the wedding was, had a blissful, faraway look on her face as she lounged on a bench. The rest were scattered around her. They were all chatting away, subjects ranging from nothing to everything. The Appian trio, who had been handing out Totos to the guests as a parting snack—their secret was out now, and they were no longer the anonymous vendors of a few months ago—walked up.

"Hey, guys." Maks grinned happily. "Great party, Sana. And thanks for letting us hand out Totos, Nafi."

"No need to thank me," Nafi said, a little more grumpily than necessary. "Totos had to be added due to popular demand. Nahlo and his troops were relentless."

Maks bumped elbows with Aman and Nisa, all of them grinning from ear to ear. "Well, thanks anyway. By the way, we've been allowed a space in the refectory to make Totos. It's quite a nice setup now, almost like a factory," Maks said to loud cheers and hearty compliments. "Want to come by to take a look? Maia?"

Maia barely heard what Maks had been saying, and even the parts she heard barely registered in her brain. Her eyes had been following Nahsemi and the others from Walenveil, specifically Miir. Not once, she noted with a growing ache in her heart, did he glance their way. This was *not* normal, far from it.

"Maia." Nafi's sharp voice made her start.

"What?"

"Maks wants to take us on a Toto factory tour. He wanted to know if you were interested."

"Yes. Yes, of course, I am."

Maia's thoughts drifted again. Just this morning Miir had been his usual self. What happened then? Was it something . . . was it that awkward thing with the bowl? Maia's insides crumpled. Did he guess what was going on with her? No . . . he couldn't have.

Another thought came like a bolt of lightning through her mind.

What if he thought *she* was worried because of what Asiyaah had said? That she feared he would harm her somehow? Could that be why —

"Maia, where are you?" Kusha nudged her elbow. "Pai has been trying to say goodbye."

"Pai?" Maia blinked. "Goodbye?"

"My family got seats on the ark," the boy said. "They called me over, so I'm leaving." Although she was truly, genuinely happy for Pai, tears welled up in Maia's eyes at thinking she would not see the boy's bright face every day. He had become a part of their family, working hard all this time, being Rayan's assistant, helping Maia, and pitching in wherever needed. Maia knew she was going to miss seeing him around. "I have to run now," Pai said. "Hans and Rayan and the rest of the party will be waiting." A quick but fierce hug with Maia later, Pai rushed away.

Pai's departure was a grim reminder of a future that was just around the corner, and an oppressive gloom fell over the group almost instantly. It was as if someone had doused them in a bucket of misery.

"Can't believe it's really coming to this," Nafi said in a grim voice.

Kusha sighed. "Yes, time for the final showdown. We just have a couple of weeks until the Initiative ends, and then who knows what that lunatic prince will do?" He slumped on the bench next to Sana and chuckled wryly. "At least our preparations are going well. We just started working on shelter spaces for everyone in ThulaSu."

"In Appian, they're making shelters in the tunnels in case the worst happens," Maks informed them.

Silence fell over their party once again. It was hard to think that they had so little time left. And knowing she was the only barrier to the deaths of so many people was simply overwhelming. Maia was struggling to shake off the overpowering despair that left her fingers numb, when thankfully, Sana spoke.

"This is why I admire Hans and Rayan. They realized this time is precious and should not be wasted. And look how they scaled mountains to reach each other." She twiddled with the ends of her shiny curls. "We should all be expressing our feelings more. But do we? We are too chicken all the time."

Ren was sprawled on top of the wall behind the bench. He opened his eyes and flashed an impish grin at Sana. "I'm never chicken, Angel. I love you, now and forever."

Nafi groaned and Sana rolled her eyes. "This isn't a joke, Ren," Sana said. "I'm serious. We are always so afraid of consequences. Too afraid. Of being rejected, of being laughed at. But that's not right. We should be bold and fearless. What's the worst that can happen? You might not win, but you'll have tried. Isn't knowing that you didn't give up worth something?"

"Well, if everyone followed that advice, then half of ThulaSu would get married tomorrow," Kusha said. "That'd be scary. I'd have to sign a mountain of marriage permits. No, Sana, I don't approve. Please don't preach boldness around here. Wait until you get back to Miorie."

"Kusha," Dani chided.

"That'll be good business for Totos, though," Maks added with a chuckle. "If we could serve all of the wedding parties at ThulaSu, we'd make plenty of money."

As the chatter went on, Maia's thoughts drifted. Sana was right. There was so little time left. A few more days and then . . . it would all be up to the mad prince of the R'armimon. They could all be dead, just like Zaara had said.

It's foolish, Maia. Realizing you love someone and not telling them that you do? Knowing that in a few days, it might be too late to say anything?

"Hey, Miir!" Nafi's loud voice jolted Maia out of her thoughts. Miir was carrying the last of the boxes away when Nafi called, and he stopped to look. "We're going on a Toto factory tour. Want to come?"

"Thank you, but I have a lot to finish up here. You have fun."

Maia's eyes were glued on him for as long as he spoke to Nafi, and not once did he look anywhere other than Nafi's face. That was just not right. Maia was sure now that her muddle with the flowers had everything to do with it.

Things were past the point where she worried her weird behavior could mess things up. Now it already had. It could not go on like this. She needed the awkwardness to go away. They had too little time to waste. Their friendship was important, too important to be held hostage by unresolved feelings.

And then there was the matter of Asiyaah's message. There was a good chance he thought she was wary around him because of his mother's words. Perhaps he thought she did not trust being around him anymore. That was as far from the truth as could be. And that needed clearing up right now.

Maia took a deep breath and squared her shoulders. She had wasted a lot of time being angry with Miir, and now that she had come to feel something else altogether . . .

No . . . she would not let another day slip past just because she was too scared to face the truth and its consequences.

No!

"Maia, where are you going?" Kusha called. "What about the Toto tour?"

"I'll be back soon," she said simply and headed out through the gates. She had to do this now or it would be too late.

Chapter Thirty-Seven

In Absentia Lucis

Maia walked out of the pavilion, her thoughts a nervous jumble. The closer she came to the storage annex behind the building where she knew Miir would be, the more her feet slowed down. Fear kept creeping into her heart, but every time, Maia resisted. She *had* to put this awkwardness behind them, and the only way to do that was to acknowledge the truth. How they handled it would be the next step, but right now, she had to find the courage to voice the truth she knew she could not change, stifle, or pretend did not exist.

Sana's words kept coming back to her—you might never get a chance to tell someone how much they matter to you. She knew how true that was. She could not remember when she had last told Dada, Emmy, or Herc that she loved them, and now . . . now she never would.

Time was running out for them all. It was not every day that you figured out you cared about someone so much that you could put their happiness before your own. And if you did and when you did, it was every bit worth telling them how much you cared. If for nothing else, she had to do this out of respect for her own feelings. They mattered, and she would not shut them away in a box before they got a chance to see the light.

What was the worst that could happen? He would say he did not feel the same way. But she would have done her part. Besides, once the air was cleared, they could go back to being the way they were. One way or another, this strange, unresolved situation had to end.

Even though she had thought through all of that, Maia's heart thumped furiously, almost as if it wanted to crash out of her chest, as she climbed down the stairs to the annex. A few boxes were still scattered around, which she hoped meant Miir was still there. She had just started to look around when he walked out of the shed to the side, a large crate in his hands.

"Hey!" A tiny smile graced his face. "What are you doing here? No Toto adventure?"

Maia's heart did a wild flip on hearing his voice and a tingle sped up her spine. It was going to be all right, she told herself as she forced a nervous smile.

"Toto adventure is still on. Sana's lecturing now. So . . ."

As he looked at her curiously, Maia clung to the courage that was rapidly slipping out of her. Her fingers were blocks of ice and wild flutters filled her stomach. She threw a glance around, as quickly and as casually as possible. The annex was quiet and it did not seem that anyone else from the Walenveil gang was around. Miir set the crate on a box and balanced himself on the edge.

"Lecturing?"

"Yes. About the importance of time. As in how every moment is important. Especially now, with everything we have going on." Maia thought she caught a glimpse of a frown on his face. Pushing her trepidation aside, she continued. "She says, we need more people like Hans and Rayan. They realize how important every moment is, and fight to make love triumph over all divisions. That we should all be like that. Or try to."

Miir did not say a word, simply crossed his arms and observed her. It was odd how the smile on his face steadily faded, but Maia did not let herself dwell on it, lest it make her stop.

"Sana says if half of us were as brave about expressing our feelings as we are about rushing into battle, the world would be a better place. I think she's right, too. I have never been brave that way. I always worry, I'm afraid of saying what I feel. I realize I should try harder to be more open."

Miir looked away for a moment. Then his gaze, distant and calm, came to rest on her face. "What brings you here?"

"I . . . just wanted to . . . speak with you." Maia suddenly realized she should have thought this through some more, she should have practiced her lines and not rushed out here like an unprepared fool.

"What about?" he said, as she stood drawing lines on the ground with the tip of her toe, tongue-tied in embarrassment.

"About something I've figured out lately." Maia forced the words out. She had to get it out so she could deal with it, and settle it one way or another. She had done enough bumbling around like an idiot. "It's awkward . . . but I think Sana's right, time is running out." Maia paused, just to take a quick breath, before saying it out loud. "So I came to tell you how much I—"

Miir sprang up, his face frozen into taut lines, his hand raised as if he wanted to push her words back inside her. "Stop. Please stop," he said, his voice firm. "Do not say any more."

"But I just want to—"

"If you are here, inspired by Sana's dream of rainbows and candy-colored clouds, to tell me how you feel about me, I do not wish to hear any more." He peered at her face, perhaps to figure out if his guess was correct, and shook his head as he realized it was. The way he sighed, like a person facing an inevitable nightmare they knew was brewing, Maia was sure he had figured it out this morning, if not even earlier. "You should not be thinking of trivial things right now. You have a lot going on, important matters you should be focused on. I did not think *you* would need reminding."

He sounded frustrated, dismayed. Maia stood there, taking in his agitation, wishing the ground would part and swallow her whole. A cloud, dark and terrifying, swirled around her, her fingertips rapidly freezing as she read the disappointment on his face. Her heart screamed for mercy, and her eyes burned. She wanted to turn around and run, away from there, away from everything she knew. Yet she stood rooted to the spot, unable to move, to breathe, to react.

"You should leave now," he said. "Forget you came here. Forget this happened."

Leave? Forget? How could he be so dismissive?

How could she leave just like that? She had done nothing wrong. She had not even asked for anything. She had just come to say a simple thing—that she loved him. Maia's fists curled.

No, I'm not going to run. Not until I've said my piece.

"So you find my feelings so utterly unpleasant that you won't even let me speak about it?"

His eyes widened and Maia thought she could see a hint of sadness in them. What he said next made her think it had just been an illusion.

"I do not want you to have a memory of this misguided moment as more than what it already is, that is all," he said, his voice calm and steady, lacking the slightest emotion. "What you feel is nothing but a distraction, a mistake. A very silly mistake that does not suit you."

Misguided . . .

Silly . . .

His words sank in, one at a time, shredding her insides mercilessly. A blast of emotions—frustration, anger, but most of all, confusion and disbelief—shook Maia.

"A silly mistake that does not suit me?" she repeated his words, slowly, deliberately, needing to truly take them in. When she looked back up at him, the mist in her gaze had vanished. Her intent to deliver the truth faded behind her indignation at his stern pronouncement. "So you mean, I'm condemned to not care about anyone? That I can't have a life, or hopes, or dreams like any other girl? That . . . that I can't love someone?"

He winced as if her words were a whip.

"Not me," he said through gritted teeth. "How could you forget who I am? And who *you* are?"

Those words did what his adamant refusal to hear her had failed to do so far—it crushed Maia's insides, completely, to the core. A pain she had never felt before plunged like a dagger into her heart. She could not breathe, and the world around her turned into a haze. She knew worse was coming, and all of a sudden, she was terrified. Her knees trembled, and she wished she had left when he had asked her to.

Every wall that had ever separated them came crashing like an avalanche. Stone by stone, brick by brick, they rose back up between them. She remembered his words from years ago in Appian, from that night they had met for the first time.

"You're right. How could I forget?" she muttered. "I'm just an ignorant girl with . . . nothing."

For a bit, there was silence. Then he strode up to her, eyes wide, arms outstretched. In that mindless moment, Maia thought he would hold her, comfort her. He drew them back as soon as he came near.

"Please, that is not what I mean," he said, shaking his head. "I am responsible for the death of your family, your Bikele. Or have you forgotten your family, your friends in this wild pursuit of . . . feelings?"

His tone was sharp, his words forceful. They cut and bruised as they sank into her soul. How could she ever forget her Dada, or everyone else she had lost? She would mourn them every day, for the rest of her life. But that did not mean she would blame Miir for his mistakes for as long as she lived. She knew he did not set out to harm anyone, and she knew he had atoned for his sins. The person she fell in love with, the Miir that stood in front of her now, was not the one who followed orders—good or bad—blindly; he was one who had gone against everything he had known, to stand up for a truth that rocked his world. How could he not see that?

"I have not," Maia said, holding his gaze defiantly. "But I don't blame you for my losses anymore. Is it so terrible that I could forgive?"

"This is more than forgiving."

"And that is wrong?"

"Yes, it is. It absolutely is."

"But I don't think that's fair. It is—"

"It does not matter what *you* think. I cannot forgive myself. Not now. Maybe never. And I cannot have you look up to me. I cannot let you make the mistake of choosing me, of all people." He turned away, refusing to let her look at his face.

At that moment, Maia forgot her own pain. All she could hear was the hopelessness in his voice, and she could see the searing guilt that consumed him. Suddenly, it stopped being about her feelings. All she wanted was to help him, heal his tormented heart.

"Miir—"

"Zaara told you to stay away from me. You should listen to her."

"What are you talking about? Zaara is a madwoman who refused to bless Hans and Rayan."

"My own mother told you to stay away." His voice was a whisper, a whisper full of pain.

"We don't even know what she meant."

Miir turned around. "She told you to stay away from her family, from her sons, and that includes me. What else did you need to hear?" he said in a voice so sharp it could cut through stone. "Have we not harmed you enough? What more are you looking for?" Exhaling loudly, he looked away, his head bowed. It almost seemed like he was going to crumble. "Please. Please, leave."

Asiyaah's last words . . . he had changed since hearing those. He had stiffened and pulled back into his shell. She had thought the phase would pass, she had hoped it would. And this morning, she was sure that he had put it behind him. Asiyaah's words were not meaningless, Maia was sure of that, but they could not be taken literally, she knew that also. Why then, why couldn't he see?

"You're hurting . . . over things that might not be real," Maia said, taking a tentative step toward him, hoping her words would get through to him. "We can talk about this. We should — "

He whirled around and shook his head vehemently, his eyes narrowed. "Can you not hear what I am saying? My answer will not change. The future you dream of is not . . . right. And I will not let you talk me into something I know is wrong."

Maia stared, cold to her bones, at his knotted eyebrows, his fisted hands, his hard eyes, and her insides shook. So much anger . . . at her?

His gaze softened a bit as he looked at her. When he spoke again, his voice was gentle, but his words cut her apart. "I promised I would help you in your search for answers. I will. But I promised you nothing more. And there can be nothing more." He turned and took one step away, then another. "There are plenty of good people around who would do anything for you. Pick anyone and you will be happy."

Pick anyone — how carelessly he flung those words at her, as if this was as simple as picking out a dress for an evening. As if . . . Did he think she was that shallow?

Good or bad, friendly or cruel, his words had always mattered to her. Always. Even when she had not knowingly cared about him one way or another. Ever since that night in Appian when she had met Miir, she had spent so much time thinking of things he had said. That would not end anytime soon. Or ever.

Miir turned back a little, his mouth open as if he were about to speak. Maia's insides clenched in fear, of what else he might say, of how else he might wound her heart.

"Don't say any more, please," she said in haste. "I understand clearly. Nothing I say will change how you feel about me. And I won't try to make you." Maia gasped for a breath to fill the cavernous emptiness within her. "I didn't come here to make you think one way or another. I didn't have any expectations or demands. I just wanted to tell you the truth because hiding it didn't feel right. And I *will* tell you my truth." Never had she been surer of herself than in that moment when she let those words pour out. "Nothing you say has changed or will ever change the fact that I . . . I love you." He turned away once more, his shoulders stiffer, his fists curled tighter. "But don't worry. I won't go about repeating these trivial and silly sentiments every chance I get. I promise you."

For how long she stood there, staring blankly at his taut, unyielding form, Maia did not remember. Nor did she know why she kept standing there. It was not that she expected anything more, or different. Yet her feet stayed frozen and heavy, stuck to the ground. Time slipped past in a tedious, lifeless cadence, until he turned back toward her with an inscrutable expression firmly in place.

"Let me walk you back to the pavilion," he said, breaking the hopeless stillness of the moment, his voice calm.

"No," Maia exclaimed. She shrank back and retreated hastily. "I'm fine. I can go by myself."

He did not insist, and Maia trudged away. She had not taken twenty steps before her legs started to give way under her. She did not let them. One step, and then another, she walked on.

Come on, Maia. All that mattered was doing your part, wasn't it? You told yourself it did not matter if he rejected your affections. Where did that spirit go?

That spirit was nowhere to be found. Perhaps it never existed at all. Just the thought of him, that frustrated expression, those words . . . hurt . . . hurt like a knife through her chest. She craved the comforting warmth of a blanket. She wanted to run to her room and hide for a very long time. She could not. She had promised her friends she would come back, and she had to. She had to carry on with a smile on her face. But how? How could she stop her pain from showing? How long could she hold back the tears that were yearning to break free?

Maia plodded along in a vague, meandering walk toward the pavilion, stopping every few steps to fill her lungs with air. Just a little earlier, she had been so blissfully happy. A promising morning had turned into a day just as bright and beautiful. Yet now, even though the warm, golden sunlight streamed around her, Maia shivered.

Gray . . . everything looked so gray.

Chapter Thirty-Eight

Above Everything

As soon as Maia glimpsed the noisy cluster of her friends in the distance, she stopped. Shouts and sounds of laughter drifted through the air. Maia found it hard to believe that not very long ago she was with them, just as happy and carefree as they were now. Now suddenly she was nothing like any one of them. Every laugh tore into her ear and made her shudder, and although she surely did not want to take away their joy, she envied their untroubled happiness. She also realized that she was not ready to join them. She simply did not have the strength to laugh with them.

Maia edged closer to the wall on one side of the pathway and leaned on it, craving support. It only helped so much. Her fingers stayed cold, her legs still wobbled under her, and all she wanted to do was flee to some dark corner and never come out again.

What a fool I've made of myself. What a pathetic fool.

How could she have thought of Miir that way? It was an impossible idea, a stupid idea. No matter where he was now, he was far out of her reach. How could she have forgotten that? People like him were meant to be admired and revered from afar, not considered equals.

His was a different world. That was the truth. That would always be the truth. They must have traditions about such things, norms they followed. And she, barely knowing the basics of her own customs, had simply rushed in like an audacious fool. Not only had she dared to think of him in terms that were obviously impermissible, she had to say it to his face. She must have sounded so impertinent, so uncouth. No wonder he did not even want to hear her.

His was a superior world. That was the truth. He was destined for someone like Amanii — high-born, illustrious, dazzling. Everything she was not. And everything she did today proved how unequal they were . . . they would always be. Shame made Maia's insides shrivel. How could she have made herself so vulnerable to his disgust?

No, stop! Don't think that way. That is not what he said.

What had he said, then? That he could not forgive himself for the things he did to her, that she should not either. Once again, even through the searing pain inside her, Maia yearned to help ease his pain. How could he not let her help him? Why did he have to close himself up like that?

Because he doesn't want your help. He doesn't want you. Or need you.

Mllı had been so close lately, always within reach, always the one she could rely on. She thought that meant something. But she was wrong. Helping her, comforting her, and always being there for her was no more than his way of making amends, working toward his atonement. She had read the signs and interpreted them wrong. She saw it clearly now. For him, it had all been a job.

You're a task to be checked off his list, nothing more. You're work that needs to be finished so he can get his life back.

All along she had thought there was something more between them. All along she had been nothing more than . . . a means to an end? Anything else, even a simple, one-sided expression of emotions, was unacceptable, unbearable to him. Zaara's scowling face flashed in front of her eyes for a moment.

Zaara wins . . .

Maia sucked in a deep lungful of air, but her insides still screamed for more. Tears wanted to gush out, break free from their restraints.

Why did she have to do this? Why now? All her life she had been oblivious, missing clues that everyone else around her seemed to pick up with ease. And now . . . the one time she thought she had figured it out . . . it had to be so miserably, wretchedly wrong.

She had nothing left to treasure anymore . . . neither Miir's friendship nor the hope of having something even more special . . . only the stark truth of what she was to him—a necessary step in his journey to find himself.

Resting her forehead against the rough wall, Maia let the tears fall. One drop at a time, until they came like a flood.

"Maia, there you are."

She froze. She had not heard Ren coming.

"Hey, what's wrong?"

Ren could not see her like this, no one could. What a mess she must look, what a silly, hopeless mess. Maia ran a hand quickly over her face and steadied herself. They could not know. Her heartbreak, her failure, her humiliation were hers, only hers. It *had* to stay that way.

Taking a bracing breath or two, Maia turned. She did not look up at Ren, out of fear that she would start crying again, but she still sensed the shocked look on his face. It took a while for him to take a step closer.

"You've been crying. Did someone hurt you?" His worried gaze was scanning her, looking for telltale signs of injury, even before she could shake her head.

"Someone said something, then?" It took her a moment to decide how to reply, and by then, he was already making his own inferences. He looked over his shoulder at the pathway leading up to the annex behind them, his brows furrowed. "Oh! Let me guess, it has to be—"

Maia clutched at his wrist before he could say any more. "I don't want you to guess. I . . . don't."

He stared at her for a moment, his eyes wide. He did not need to say a word. Maia knew he had guessed right.

"Let's go," Maia said, forcing cheer into her voice, and failing miserably. "They're waiting. We have a Toto factory to visit."

She had not taken two steps before Ren grabbed her arm and turned her around. "No. Let's not," he said.

"What? I promised them."

Ren stepped closer. Cupping her face, he looked into her eyes. "I won't let you go around pretending you're not hurting. I just won't. And I don't think any of them would give a darn about the Totos if they saw you like this."

"I can't just disappear on them."

"Of course you can't." Ren flashed a cheeky smile. "So we both will."

"What?"

"Come on." Before Maia knew what was happening, Ren had dragged her away. Holding tightly to her wrist, he bounded across ThulaSu, not hearing any of her copious protests. He stopped only when they reached the grounds of the Sun Temple.

"What are we doing, Ren?" Maia asked, panting to catch her breath. "Where are you taking me?"

"We are going to catch some happiness, Maia," he said as he led her to the Viperine. "Get in."

Maia did not have a chance to say another word. She was practically shoved inside the craft and strapped into the seat next to Ren's.

"Maia and I will have to miss the tour, guys," he said into the wristband communicator as the Viperine lifted off. "Please tell Maks that we are really, really sorry. We'll visit the factory tomorrow . . . if that works for him."

"What in the—" Nafi's outraged voice drifted in. "Why? Where are you two, anyway?"

"You don't need to know everything, Nafi. See you later." He turned toward Maia and tipped an imaginary hat. "Where to, Princess?"

Maia did not know if it was Ren's crazy antics or the gorgeous view of ThulaSu and the vistas beyond rapidly unfurling before her eyes that did the trick, but her heart was definitely lighter, the humiliation she had just faced hazy for a moment.

"I don't know, Ren," she said, smiling. "Take me anywhere."

"All right, then." He steered the craft around, the world turning under them in a wave of colors and textures. "Would you mind if I took a look at the Dorgashians? I've always heard about them, but never been."

"Mind? Not at all," Maia said. "I'd like that. I'd like it very much."

The Viperine soared through the skies, through golden clouds and over sparkling seas. Maia's eyes picked out landmarks as they went, the excitement of finding themselves so close to her home in Appian making her both forget and remember the current anguish. After admiring the long, curved blade of the Dorgashian Folds, its snow-capped peaks glittering in the sunlight, and after swooping over the verdant plains that cradled Appian, Ren landed the Viperine near the greens around Miorie. It was not near where her house had been, but it was beautiful regardless. They lay on the grass and ate some apples Ren had swiped from Nafi. There were some Totos in his stash too, along with other tidbits. Maia told him stories of her childhood with Sana, and they laughed over forgotten little things. The sun's last rays were fading when Ren started the Viperine back toward ThulaSu.

"How are you feeling?" he asked when they were halfway to ThulaSu. "Better, I hope."

"Yes, very much so," Maia replied, thankful for his company and for his kindness. Ren had saved her, yet again.

The evening had settled deep and dark over ThulaSu when Maia walked up to the living quarters with Ren. Memories barged in, swift and strong. She had not forgotten anything, not that she had expected to. The closer she got to her room, the tighter the stinging thoughts wrapped around her. Even so, spending the day with Ren, far away from every reminder of the afternoon's embarrassing encounter, had helped.

"Thank you," she said earnestly when they reached her door. "I will not forget this day."

Ren grimaced. "Umm . . . that isn't quite the thanks I deserve."

"What do you mean?"

He leaned against the wall and grinned. "Well, the question is . . . why wouldn't you forget this day? What is it you'll remember? The part before me or the part after?"

Maia chuckled. If that was not just like Ren. "I won't lie, Ren. I won't forget either part, before or after. But I'll remember the part after above everything, as the time you brought back joy into my life when I didn't think it was possible anymore. Thank you."

"Aah, you're making me want to cry," Ren grumbled before taking a quick step to close the distance between them. He kissed her forehead and pulled her into a tight embrace. "I won't forget today either." He stood for a moment after that, his gaze lingering on her face. "Well, I have to head to Frauz Point now. See you tomorrow."

Maia walked into her room once Ren left, and as soon as she closed the door behind her, she froze in terror. Someone was sitting on Rayan's bed, and she could not tell who it was. Her hand instinctively moved to Bellator, her senses tightening around her core.

"I'd almost given up on you coming back tonight," said a voice from the shadows.

"Sana!" Maia breathed in relief. "What are you doing here? You scared me."

"What am I doing here? Waiting for you, of course."

"I was out with Ren."

"I know that," Sana replied. She scrambled off the bed and turned on a lamp. Then she walked up to Maia, frowning. "What happened? You two bolted like you'd seen a ghost or something, and disappeared for the rest of the day. Where were you?"

"We were . . . Ren flew me to the Dorgashians. Then to Miorie."

Sana gawked. "Dorgashians? Miorie? You must be joking, right?"

"No, it's—"

"Why?" Sana stepped closer and peered at her face.

"It's nothing. I was just feeling a little off, and Ren—"

"Feeling a little off?" Sana frowned.

"Sana, it's nothing. Really. Ren had never seen the Dorgashians, and we just wanted to—"

"Come on. No one just scampers off like that, and people certainly don't spend a whole day at the Dorgashians at the drop of a hat. Even with Ren in the mix, it's a stretch. What's going on, Maia? What are you up to?"

The thought hit Maia like a sack of rocks. Sana's incessant questions meant something, and it had to do with Ren. Why hadn't she seen that before? Maia flinched at the idea that she could be so blind, over and over.

"Sana, it's not what you think," she exclaimed. "Ren and I . . . we're just friends. You don't need to worry."

"What?" Sana almost shouted. Throwing her arms up in the air, she whirled away. "You think I'm worried about Ren? He can go out with his entire fan club, for all I care. I'm worried about you. I know he didn't fly you all the way to the Dorgashians just because he hadn't seen it before. He took you there because . . ." her words trailed off and for a long while she simply stared at Maia's face.

Looking back at her, Maia knew she was connecting the dots. There was no escaping Sana; she was as sharp as they came. What she did not expect was for Sana to rush over and throw her arms around her as if she were a distressed child who had just woken up from a nightmare. Maia did not know what it was about that hug that made her insides crumble. The tears that she had kept bottled up all day yearned to break free.

I can't let it out. I just can't.

"Sana, we have a long week starting tomorrow with the Initiative," Maia said, in a final attempt to get away from her cousin and her probing. "I need to get some rest now."

Sana drew back, her eyes glistening. "He turned you down, didn't he?"

"What?" It was not unexpected that she'd figure it out, but Maia still did not know how to answer. She dreaded the questions that would follow, and the answers she'd have to give. She could not bear to think . . . those awful moments being looked at, dissected, analyzed. She could not. It was her pain to keep, one she was going to store away in a little box in a corner of her heart.

"He turned you down," Sana repeated. "And it's not Ren I'm talking about."

Once again, Maia did not know what to say to that. She stood, tongue-tied, frozen.

Sana's eyes flashed. "I'm going to have a chat with that guy. I will. Right now."

Maia's hand shot out to catch Sana. "You will not, Sana." Even with all the turmoil inside her, her voice was calm. That was surprising. "This is not a debate to be won or a battle to be fought. What needed to be said has been said. There's no changing anything. I don't need or want to be the subject of a conference now. So please, if you care about me, don't go talking to anyone. Not even to my friends. They don't need to know."

Sana let out a wry chuckle. "You think your friends won't notice? They're all pretty smart, and you're all pretty close. It doesn't take much to put two and two together. They probably already know."

Sana was right. They probably already knew. It was not unexpected, either. Other than Maks and his crew, everyone would have put the pieces together. If not now, they would soon. That was why it was even more important that she put up a facade of normalcy as fast as she could. She had to. She could not show them her tears. If she did, someone surely would bring it up with Miir. She could not let that happen. She had shown him enough of her heart. She could not let him in on the extent of her heartbreak.

Besides, while it was true that Miir's choice had crushed her, he had every right to make it. It was hard to hear, but he was right. He had never promised to fulfill every wish she ever made. He did not deserve punishment—which Maia was sure would be heaped upon him, starting with Sana—for her current misery. That could not happen. She could hurt forever, but blame Miir for the consequences of her choices . . . that she could not.

Maia sucked in a lungful of air. Come tomorrow, everything had to go back to normal, or whatever was left of it.

"Let them. But you're not going to discuss this, Sana. Not now, not ever," Maia said, her fists balled as she slumped onto her bed. She remembered words she had heard not so long ago and repeated them. "We're going to forget this ever happened. We're moving on. All right?"

Sana stared at her for a long while before she sat down next to Maia and slipped an arm around her shoulders. "Maia, I will not talk about it if you don't want me to. I promise. But I'll tell you one thing. You know, it's all right if you feel broken right now. It's perfectly all right to cry."

That did it. All the tears she had dammed up inside her gushed out in a fierce wave at Sana's words. Maia did not try to stop them anymore. She did not have the strength to fight. As she broke into sobs, Sana's arms wrapped around her. It was long past midnight when Maia's tears finally stopped flowing, not because all her pain had washed away, but because she had cried herself to sleep on Sana's shoulder.

CHAPTER THIRTY-NINE

TO THE CURSED MOON

Maia barely noticed the next few days pass. They were a haze, an incessant struggle to keep up a facade of normalcy so no one would notice changes in her. Things altered subtly around her, however. Sana moved in, taking over Rayan's bed, her attention on Maia constant and unwavering. While Maia was with her teammates, Ren took over supervising duties. He did not say a word on the subject, but he did not have to. When Maia was lost in thought, Ren would make conversation. Every time someone brought up Miir, he deflected it with the deftness of a parliamentarian.

For her part, Maia kept trying. She had to get over it and take things back to how they were before. She *had* to. Everyone did it. Sana had moved on from Jez in a matter of moments, and Jez was already seeing another girl. Maks had always been calm and collected after Maia called it off. Maia's fists curled every time her thoughts came to that point. She could not be the exception. She could not be the stupid one that refused to let go.

It's not the end of the world, she kept telling herself. But even though she knew it was not, Miir's words kept ringing in her ears. It was not the rejection of her feelings that stung the most, but the way he did it. The idea that he could not even bear to hear what she had to say, that he found her sentiments so lowly, so disappointing, made Maia's insides crumple in dejection and shame every time.

She reeled, thinking of the indignity she had exposed herself to by baring her heart to him. How could she have not understood? How could she forget all those moments when he clearly said how poorly he thought of her, of her people? How could she imagine he would change enough to think of her as an equal?

The more Maia thought about it, the more she despised herself. Along with the anger came even more pain. It was as if part of her had a vendetta against herself. Despite knowing the truth, despite having been told the truth in no uncertain terms, she missed Miir. She missed the smiles and the laughs, she missed seeing him, talking to him. No matter how many times she told herself those easy days would never come back, her heart kept yearning.

Besides, the fact that their lives had become so intertwined, particularly in recent months, did not help. Miir was everywhere. Every conversation referenced him, every plan involved him, and every other step took them straight to him. How could she avoid someone who was around every turn?

Maia did what she could. She tried reminding herself of the enormity of the upcoming task—winning the Initiative and acquiring Seigvard was critical and the only thing that mattered—and she had to block out every other distraction from her mind. She avoided conversations that led to Miir, and she quietly dropped her sparring session with him that week. But even that did not ensure their paths would not cross.

A day before the trip to Ti, after the final planning report on the task had been submitted, the gang was a little more relaxed. Hadeeyah, impressed by the amount of work everyone, especially Maia, put into the report, had told them to take the evening off. She even dropped off some of the biggest and softest honey cakes Maia had ever eaten.

"You've worked hard," Hadeeyah said. "You deserve a bit of rest."

Maia sat at the far end of the AR with a storybook in one hand and a honey cake in another. Although she stared at the open page, her mind was elsewhere and her thoughts were in a muddle when there was a knock on the door. Nafi was the one to rush to the door, muttering something about Kusha always being late.

"Miir, it's you!" Nafi squealed and Maia's heart just about leaped out of her chest. "Come in. We have honey cakes and they're just . . ."

"Umm . . . not now," he replied. "I am still looking for the books you wanted."

"Thank you."

As they kept talking, Maia wished she could teleport out of the room. She was not facing the door or even near it, so she did not have to see Miir, but just knowing he stood there, so close, left Maia's insides trembling.

"Hey, look at this." A map of Ti fell with a thunk on the table and Ren slipped into the chair next to her, busily tapping the locations marked on it. He talked about one thing after another, and Maia barely heard any of it. But she was happy he had come and grateful for the timely distraction. When the door of the AR finally thudded shut, Maia breathed in relief and whispered a quick thanks to Ren.

"Of course, Maia," Ren whispered back.

"So listen up," Nafi chirped loudly behind them. "According to Miir, the Molligessian Seam is easiest to tackle from the north end, hardest from the east."

Ren turned around. "That's what he came to tell you?"

"Yes," Nafi replied. "That, and we talked about some books he is finding for me."

Nafi dropped next to Dani on the couch, discussing what Miir said.

"Well, I don't know if it's much of a clue, Nafi," Dani said. "We knew that about the Molligessian already. I mean, everyone knows it. I don't understand why he'd take the trouble to come by to mention that."

Nafi nodded thoughtfully. "True, but . . . I'm surprised Miir told us anything at all regarding the challenge. He's usually pretty touchy about cheating and stuff." She tapped her chin as she looked up at Maia. "Don't you find it strange, Maia? You've seen how he shut me down every time I'd bring up Ti."

Maia had planned to shrug and ignore the discussion, but then decided to take a step forward and forced herself to give Nafi an answer. "I don't know. Since it's something everyone knows, maybe he did not consider it cheating."

"Hmmm." Nafi did not look satisfied with her answer. "But then it's just silly. Dani is right. He didn't have to come all this way to tell us something everyone knows." She jumped up and started pacing. "And he wouldn't even come inside. I asked about a hundred times. Something is wrong here."

As Maia looked away from Nafi's worried face, she felt miserable. Something was off, there was no doubt about that. But she could not tell them what it was, because that meant she would have to tell them that she was the one who had messed everything up.

* * *

The trip to Ti started early in the morning. The skies were still dark when the transport, full of sleepy contestants, arbitrators, and assistants, took off from Frauz Point. It docked in Arpasgula for a short time, where they boarded a different, bigger transport, and shortly after that they took off again.

The journey was not long, but it was unsettling as the craft drifted further into space, and the shining orb of Tansi grew steadily smaller. The main chamber of the transport was partitioned off into spacious cubes, and each team had been assigned one. The areas were simple and efficient—two bench seats on two sides of a large rectangular table that sat flush with a long window — but comfortable.

Nafi, after spending a long time fidgeting, had dozed off by the time they crossed the orbit of the fifth planet. Maia sighed a little as Dani rearranged the sleeping girl's blanket. It had to be hard for Nafi, so hard. This was the path her sister Sejya had taken to her unfair and untimely death, and Nafi had to be upset. But Nafi, being the way she was, hardly said a word about it.

"Wish she'd talk a little," Dani whispered to Maia.

Maia wished the same, but talking was a dream. The girl had completely closed down, hardly making a sound or looking at anyone. As much as they hoped, nothing changed even after Nafi woke up from her nap. Soon they were all busy donning suits and masks, and parkas on top of it all.

As their transport orbited the massive striated girth of the sixth planet, there came a sight that stunned everyone into silence. The tiny white moon of Ti shone in the distance, but that was not what everyone stared at, speechless. It was the huddle of gigantic spacecraft that stood out in stark contrast against the reddish-pink surface of the sixth planet.

"The Execution Fleet," Maia whispered, swallowing to ease her parched throat.

Quite some distance separated the transport craft from the fleet, but Maia could see five of them. They were massive, terrifying things, their bulk overwhelming even from so far away.

"Focus, focus," Principal Pomewege's voice boomed across the chamber, and the windows darkened. "Now is not the time for sightseeing. We will be landing on Ti momentarily. You need to be careful out there," Pomewege kept saying, "The weather is ruthless. The atmosphere is not conducive to life. You do not want to be exposed to it. So check your suits and your air supply, make sure everything is working right."

Maia held her breath as their transport drew closer to the surface of the moon. An unending whiteness stretched as far as she could see. The terrain, while mostly flat, seemed to have different textures.

However, it was the barren emptiness that was so intimidating. Soon the transport landed and the teams trooped out one by one. Even though she was wrapped from head to foot in an insulated suit with a parka on top, Maia could sense the coldness of the wind and certainly its strength during the little time she spent walking from the transport to the enormous building that was Base A4. Gusts, strong and sharp, made her sway and she was glad to be inside, even though the building was far from welcoming.

Calling the lobby of the base stark would be an understatement. The cavernous entrance sloped down into the ground, and the curved ceiling rose high above them. There was very little light, inside or out, and everything, even the ice outside, was tinged with gray. There were only about ten people in the lobby, and they surrounded Principal Pomewege like ants around sugar. Zaara and Aerika wandered about the empty lobby on their own, and so did the teams. Core 21 walked over to a large map that showed the various mines in the vicinity, except Nafi, who stayed on the far fringes of the entrance with a dazed look on her face. She joined the rest of the team only after Pomewege called everyone together.

"First, your collection pails," he said. One by one, he handed out small buckets, a different color for each team. Core 21 received a purple one. A long, thick ribbon of the same color was tied to the bucket's handle.

Once all the pails were handed out, Pomewege continued. "Now we are going to take a trip to the mines. The craft you picked are waiting outside." He pointed in the direction of the glass panes. "You still have time to make changes to your travel plans if you want. But the clock is ticking."

Maia walked up to the window and looked out at the gray field. The transport that had carried them to Ti loomed like a giant over a group of Raptors. Seeing them lined up brought back memories of the Seliban Challenge. What a thrill that had been, what a win for them. She remembered the flight through the Draegen fields and —

"Hold on a moment," Maia muttered to herself as a sudden

thought came to her. "Let's not go to the north entrance."

"What?" Ren, who stood next to her, gave her a startled look.

"But, Maia" — Dani peered at her face — "we've practiced keeping the north entrance in mind. We can't change now."

"Yes, but—"

"North is the easiest, too," Kusha interrupted. "We've discussed that."

Nafi held up her hands. "Can we just listen to what Maia has to say?"

Nafi's calm interruption quieted everyone and they all turned toward Maia.

"Well, remember how during the Seliban Challenge everyone was taking the safest route?" Maia said. "And we ended up trying the hardest path? It was tough, but we got there first."

Eager nods greeted Maia. It was difficult to say the next few words, uttering a name she was afraid she would stumble on, but Maia forced herself to continue. "So when . . . Miir came by the other night, perhaps . . . perhaps he mentioned the two entrances to remind us of the choice we made during the Seliban Challenge? Maybe he meant for us not to take the easiest route?"

For a long moment, no one spoke. Then Ren sighed and looked at Dani. "Do you have details of the east entrance? I have no idea what the terrain looks like."

Dani nodded and pulled out a notebook. "I studied all the entrances, so I know some stuff."

Ren and Dani started discussing details and Kusha joined them. Nafi patted Maia's arm. "Good work."

Soon they had amended their plans and started on their way, to the east entrance instead of the north. Their pilot, Eilen, was a short, stocky woman of few words and a stiff smile. But she was supremely efficient. Very quickly, she had their equipment secured and showed them all to their positions.

"We're going to the east entrance," Ren said as he strapped himself into the co-pilot's seat. Maia did not like the sharp look Eilen shot at him, nor the way her mouth twisted.

"Here are the coordinates," Dani said. "We have—"

Eilen waved a hand dismissively. "You don't need to tell me all that. I've flown to every entrance of the Seam thousands of times. I know it all."

"But we're supposed to guide you there," Dani insisted. "We should be navigating and telling you what to do."

"Oh, really?" Eilen slapped a button on the side control panel and spoke into it. "Hello, Principal?"

Pomewege's voice sounded in an instant. "Yes, 2XC?"

"The kids want to teach me how to fly," Eilen said in a tired voice. "Not sure if I can survive that."

Pomewege's laughter drifted in. "Not their fault. That's what they were told. My apologies."

Looks of surprise darted around the Raptor. What did that mean? Were they never expected to guide the pilot? Why then were they made to train—

"So what are we supposed to do, Principal Pomewege?" Ren asked. "Just sit back and enjoy the ride?"

Once again, the principal laughed. If he could have seen the annoyed expressions he produced, he would definitely have thought twice about it.

"Yes, do enjoy it while you can, Ren," Pomewege replied.

"But Principal Pomewege," Dani had flushed a vivid pink, her brows furrowed, "we even trained on those Raptors. And nearly died trying to fly them. Why did you make us do that when you knew we didn't have to?"

"You were trained so you would survive in case your pilot was indisposed. Unexpected situations do occur," the principal said. Dani let out a grunt of dissatisfaction at the answer, making Pomewege chuckle heartily. "Life is like that, Dani," he added in the calm, staid tone of a sage. "You prepare for one thing and then you have to do something else altogether. Consider this a test of your ability to embrace change."

Dani was about to open her mouth to say something when the principal exclaimed, "Oh, I have to go now. Other teams are buzzing in. Same questions, I suppose."

As soon as the communicator fell silent, Ren looked back at the rest of the team. "So what now?"

"As he said, we enjoy the ride," Kusha replied. "The rest we find out once we get there."

That was the only logical option. However, even though the responsibility of flying across Ti was off their shoulders, the thought of a surprise lying in wait made Maia uneasy.

Off they went across the unending whiteness of Ti. Below them, the ground rose and fell. High plateaus gave way to flat plains, solid terrain changed to floes of ice. The Raptor swayed perilously with the winds and Eilen's hands danced incessantly on the controls. No one spoke, and Maia held her breath as the craft went on, pitching and rolling, shuddering and groaning constantly.

"We should be over the Molligessian Seam now," Dani said after what seemed like forever.

"We are," Eilen replied. "See that ice floe coming up? The Seam runs across it."

An endless expanse of flatland strewn with chunks of ice lay in the direction she pointed. The ice floe was like quicksand, only made of ice, Maia recalled, shuddering.

Within moments, Eilen hollered, "Get ready, all of you. Hoods up, masks up. We're here."

The Raptor circled around what seemed from a distance to be nothing more than a large mound of ice, but as the craft sank lower, Maia realized there was a door built into the mound. It was an entrance to the mine. The winds were strong and the craft teetered and wobbled before finally touching the ground.

"Someone will take you in from here," Eilen said before opening the hold. "Remember to take the high road on your way back. Good luck."

"Wait . . . what? Aren't you picking us up?" Maia's words were lost in the howl of the wind. There was no time to find out what Eilen meant, since they, along with their trough of equipment, were pushed out of the hold in a blink. A large figure rushed up to them and herded them away. By the time they neared the large arched entrance that led into the Seam, the Raptor had already taken off.

"Phew! It sure is windy today," the large man who towered over them said. "Be careful on your way back. That is, if you take the high road up to Rogsham Plateau. Now come on inside." He ushered them in through massive metal doors that sealed shut behind them. "We were not expecting anyone here at all. Not many like the east entrance. I hear there's quite a crowd in the north." After passing through the next sealed door, he took off the mask and slipped off his hood, revealing a bearded face and twinkling gray eyes. "I am Gino. Overseer of the East Seam," he said with a smile. "And you can take off your masks in here."

Kusha did not waste another moment. He quickly introduced the team and started asking questions as Gino led them down a long flight of stairs. "So, Gino, how do we get back to the base from here? Will Eilen come back for us?"

"Eilen's not coming back. You drive yourselves." Maia noted that Gino liked to speak in short, broken sentences. "To Poaro's Base. Up on the Rogsham Plateau."

As they walked, the surroundings grew darker and damper around them.

"Poaro's Base? What's that?" Kusha asked.

"That's the next closest landing site. Sort of in the middle of all the entrances. That's where they'll pick you all up. You'll have to drive a buggy back. I'll give you a map. Didn't they tell you all that already?"

Everyone shook their heads. Why this had to be a surprise, Maia had no clue. It did not seem like a good idea. They had no practice driving a buggy, had not researched the ground terrain, and were overall unprepared.

"Oh well. You'll do fine. Now let's get to the heart of the East Seam."

Gino stopped at what looked like the mouth of a well. Above it, a bucket—egg-shaped, the top half completely enclosed in a transparent cover—large enough to fit twenty grown men was suspended from a pulley. As soon as she saw it, Maia's heart thudded. She hoped whatever they did would not involve riding down the well in that bucket. Her hopes were dashed almost instantaneously as Gino reached out and pulled one side of the bucket down toward himself.

"Hop in, everyone," he said. "Your chariot awaits."

This was one chariot Maia had no interest in hopping into. But like it or not, it had to be done. Gritting her teeth, she walked into the bucket and was immediately surprised by how sturdy it felt. Even then, the slow crawl down the dimly lit well after Gino started the contraption was no fun. Maia disliked tight, dark spaces, and being in that well, even though she was surrounded by people, left her sweating. She sat with her eyes closed and only opened them when they stopped moving.

The bucket had finally come to the bottom of the well. From there, a web of tunnels stretched in all directions. Gino marched them out to the one with the largest entrance.

"So anyway, you are"—Gino peered at the purple pail in the equipment box—"Team Purple. Looks like you have all your stuff. Except . . . one thing. You need the most important tool."

Gino marched forward—Core 21 following on his heels—until he came to a wall lined with various apparatus. He pulled out what looked like meters of some sort and handed one to each of them. Then they walked further into the tunnel.

"Those are Calbion detectors. You need them to know where to dig. You're going to the Passive Sprawl, by the way. The deposit is quite shallow there. That is good. You won't have to dig too much. Those people in the north, on the other hand, will have a fun time." He stopped and chuckled. "Not really, no."

Along winding paths they went, and up and down slopes. Chambers, most of them dark, opened up on either side of the tunnel. Some of them—very few, Maia noted, considering the size of the mines—were lighted and had people working in them. Each of the rooms, Maia presumed, was an extraction area for Calbion. Gino stopped at the entrance of a dark chamber and pointed at it.

"This here is 42B. All yours." He marched them inside and turned up some portable lights built into the sides of the chamber. He placed a large red button-like contraption on a hook. "That's the beeper. Press it to call me when you're done. Good luck."

With another smile, he was gone, and the team was left alone in the chamber.

CHAPTER FORTY

THROUGH THE WASTELANDS

C hamber 42B was basically a cavern. The entrance formed an airtight opening into it. Rock surfaces, dark, cold, and forbidding, stretched around and over them. They were far beneath the surface, Maia deduced. She placed a hand on the wall—it was slippery and cold, perhaps from a thin layer of ice over the rocks.

"Time for hard work, guys," Kusha said. "We have to chisel into the rock. Then peel out the Calbion once we find a clump."

"But first"—Ren held up the Calbion detector Gino had handed them—"locate a potential spot with a deposit."

Dani handed out chisels to everyone as Ren went around scanning the rock walls and marking them. Soon they were hacking away at the surface. It was hard work indeed. Despite the cold, beads of sweat soon trickled down Maia's face. Her arms ached and her head throbbed from the constant noise of hammering. Her heart was heavy, thinking of what the miners—many of them younger than herself—had to endure during their captivity here. She would leave here soon, but those poor people had no hopes of seeing their families or their homes again. For most, this was the last place they would ever be.

"I got one!" Dani's excited squeal brought Maia out of her despair. She rushed over to see. It would have looked like a normal piece of rock had it not been for the shiny layer of mineral hugging its lower half. Dani pulled out a thinner chisel and made some dents in the layers before gently pulling them apart. The metal came out in thin strips, one layer at a time, and Dani kept picking at it until none was left. Finding that first piece of Calbion renewed their vigor, and once again, the team chipped away diligently at the rock.

A long and tiring time passed, and everyone was immersed in their work when Maia thought she heard something. It was a soft sound, a whimper. It was odd that she could even hear it over the clatter of the hammers and chisels, yet she did. She spun around and gasped.

"Nafi!"

Nafi was slumped in one corner, her chisel thrown to the ground beside her. As the girl stared at the ground and heaved, Maia and the rest of her teammates stood frozen, barely able to comprehend the situation. Dani was the first to rush to Nafi's side and fling her arms around her shoulders.

"Nafi, what's wrong?" Dani whispered. "Say something."

"What am I doing here, Dani?" Nafi yelped, her voice tripping over every word. "My sister won't ever come back. And my mother will never be herself again. I will never . . . ever have the family I had. Never." She broke into sobs. "And here I am doing this stupid stuff. Why? What's the point of all this?"

As always, seeing Nafi cry left Maia bereft of words. What did one say to console a girl as tough as Nafi? Nothing came to mind, and for a while, it seemed like no one else knew what to say either. Then Ren strode up to Nafi and kneeled next to her.

"You know what the point is, Nafi?" he said. "The point is you are trying to make this world better than it was. So no one else will suffer the way your sister did. So no other family will hurt the way yours has." Nafi kept sobbing, although it seemed to Maia that she had calmed a little. Ren continued in a solemn voice that was very unlike him. "You knew coming here would tear you apart. Yet you came. You know why? Not just because you're brave and strong, but because you want to change the world for others. And I have to tell you, I admire your courage and your selflessness."

Nafi raised a crumpled, tear-stained face to look up at Ren.

"And even though my saying this won't change the past, I want to say it," Ren continued. "I'm truly sorry for what my people did to your sister . . . your family. On behalf of my nation, I apologize."

Silence, breathless yet hopeful, hovered over them for what seemed like forever. Then Ren extended a hand.

"Come on, Nafi. Come and show us how to fight."

Maia had to blink hard to clear her vision when Nafi placed her hand in Ren's. Ren pulled her up, Dani put the chisel back in Nafi's hand, and they all huddled around the youngest of their team. When Nafi finally wiped away her tears and flashed a little smile, Maia's heart soared. It did not matter if they won this task or not. What mattered was whether a friend's broken heart had healed, even a tiny bit.

Nafi was soon scraping away the ice, picking out rocks and peeling out Calbion. The team worked in a peaceful, steady cadence. The purple bucket filled up at a smooth, uniform pace, and soon it was filled to the brim.

"All right, we're done," Ren whooped. "Time to get back."

"Hit that button, Nafi," Kusha said.

Nafi frowned. "Just because I was upset for a bit does not mean you can start treating me like a baby. You push your own button."

Ren groaned and shook his head at Nafi as he slapped the button. "I forgot to tell you one thing back then. You're the most annoying girl I've ever met."

Nafi snorted and broke into loud guffaws. As Ren rolled his eyes, the rest of the team also started laughing. Gino, who arrived promptly, smiled.

"Having fun, eh?" he said. "That's the spirit." He squinted at the bucket and nodded. "You're ready to go. Seal that up and let's hit the road."

Soon they were trooping back to the entrance with Gino. After returning the Calbion detectors, enduring a claustrophobic ride back up in the egg-shaped bucket, and once again securing their masks and hoods, the team walked out into the cold behind Gino as he led them to a row of buggies. He climbed into the first one and drove it out.

"Your chariot back to Poaro's Base," Gino announced. He pulled out a large piece of paper from his pocket next. "And here's your map."

Ren had been circling the buggy. Now he exclaimed loudly. "Guys, do you realize? This is Karhann's prototype."

"What? Really?" Nafi hurried closer, the rest following behind her.

"Yes, I'm sure. This is it. This is *Sejya*."

"You built this?" Gino asked.

"No, not us," Ren said. "But a friend of mine did."

"The best thing to happen to us miners on Ti," Gino informed them. "Solid as a rock. Saved so many lives."

Gino helped them secure the bucket to the rear of the vehicle. He tied the purple ribbon that had come with the bucket to a mount on top of the buggy and hoisted it like a flag.

"The panic button is right there." Gino pointed at the massive red protrusion at the center of the vehicle. "You think you're in trouble, smash it. All right?"

"All right," Ren replied.

"Good luck, Team Purple."

Ren started out slow, taking extra care during the first stretch of the journey where the ground was barely solid. With the ice floe under them, he added a track attachment to the wheels and let the buggy creep forward. Everyone held their breath as they crawled, and not until Kusha declared that they were on solid ground again did anyone dare to speak.

The buggy sped across the unending whiteness, clawing, scrambling, skidding its way across the ice. Ren gained some control over the craft by the time the arched entrance of the eastern mines disappeared from view. Dani was alert as ever, fiddling with controls as needed to assist Ren. Kusha sat behind them and navigated. All the way in the back, Maia and Nafi sat with scopes, scanning the terrain all around to provide as much advance guidance as they could.

Nothing prepared them for the horrendous winds that almost toppled the buggy as they neared the high road. Ren promptly deployed the spike attachments for the wheels, and Dani adjusted the buoyancy canisters to add extra weight, but still, the buggy wobbled like a tiny pebble in the middle of a tornado.

Even that was nothing compared to the situation they faced on reaching the high road across Rogsham Plateau. Quite a few times, the gusts moved the vehicle backward as if it were a toy.

"Anchors," Maia reminded them. "If this vehicle has anchors, deploy them. Perhaps we should wait out the gusts."

"Good idea," Ren muttered.

While the anchors stabilized them and moving only during the lull between the gusts made for steady progress, it was slow. But it was the only way to go, at least until they had crossed the treacherous plateau.

"Don't worry," Kusha tried to reassure them. "The path is downhill after this and we will make up some time there."

If only it were that easy. The path was indeed downhill, but the little dots on the map turned out to be sizable chunks of ice. The buggy rattled and shook and jumped and rattled some more—and on and on it went. Ren added on extra wide tires, but that only helped so much. By the time they had crossed that stretch and reached a flat road, Maia felt as if every bone in her body had been shaken out of place.

The smooth, high plain they zoomed across was a welcome change. Ren did not miss the chance to engage the throttle all the way. Kusha, who was keeping time, had a satisfied look on his face, and

Maia knew they were doing well. Another team might do even better, but the fact that they had handled the unexpected challenges so well brought a proud smile to Maia's face.

"Hey, what's going on down there?" Nafi said suddenly and Maia craned her neck to see.

A long trench ran parallel to the path they were on. Along that trench, two vehicles rushed at breakneck speed. They had Initiative flags flying and were clearly trying to outrun each other.

"I better speed up," Ren said, as soon as he saw them.

"They're going too fast," Dani said with a quick look at the pair of vehicles. "I hope they don't crash."

"Which teams are those?" Kusha asked, then quickly added. "I think that orange flag is Core 7."

"I'm pretty sure the gold one is Core 13," Maia said, remembering who had drawn her favorite color.

"Oh no," Nafi screamed. "They're ramming into each other. No . . . Core 7 is ramming the other one. Have they lost it?"

Maia craned her neck once again, just in time to see the orange-flagged buggy bump into the other. Then as the Core 13 buggy spun around and skidded to a stop, it sped away.

"This is just unbelievable," Nafi said. "This is Karhann's prototype, so Core 7 already has an advantage. And even that's not enough? Now they have to try to kill people to win this?"

"Must have been an accident," Ren said, shaking his head. "Karhann wouldn't do that. He wouldn't."

Maia felt bad for Ren. Karhann was his trusted friend, and to see him behave this way was . . . difficult. Even she had a hard time believing what she had just seen.

"Karhann might not be driving, Ren," Dani said and Ren's face brightened a little.

"Oh no, I think Core 13 has spilled their bucket of Calbion," Nafi announced.

Ren slowed and came to a halt. Immediately everyone leaned over to see. The Core 13 vehicle did not look damaged, only stopped.

The collection bucket—the color matching their flag—was on the ground behind them, its lid open. All the Core 13 members streamed outside and went about picking up what were clearly bits and pieces of Calbion.

"Oh, poor, poor Jiri and his team," Dani said. "This is so unfair."

"Well, at least they're not hurt," Kusha said.

While that was true, seeing them crawl around on their hands and knees searching for pieces was hard to watch.

"We have to go now," Ren reminded shortly. "We're losing time."

"Shouldn't we help them?" Maia asked.

"I wish, Maia," Ren replied. "But we can't get down there. There are no safe roads from here."

Ren was right. A steep, almost impassable slope separated them from Core 13, and trying to negotiate that would surely end in a crash. Sighs filled the buggy, but they had to deal with the fact that they were in no position to help.

"I agree," Kusha said. "Our best option is to get back and tell someone who can help."

"Well, let's just hope they find all their spilled ore," Nafi said in a morose voice as Ren took off once more.

Core 21 soon reached the landing spot at Poaro's Base. Only a single Raptor, one none of the teams had used, sat waiting. Near it was the Core 7 buggy.

"Looks like the brats were the first to get back," Nafi said caustically as Ren parked and they all rushed up the stairs into the Raptor.

"Welcome back, Core 21," Principal Pomewege's bright voice greeted them as soon as they stepped inside. He pointed to where an assistant was collecting the buckets. "Please go to Samal to get your time recorded. Then go inside and pour yourself a cup of soup. It must be cold out there."

As soon as they had finished with Samal, Nafi crossed her arms and looked at each of them. "We need to report what we saw to the principal."

Kusha nodded readily, but Ren raised an eyebrow. "I'm fine with reporting, but shouldn't we talk to Jiri and his team first? It's between those two groups, after all."

"I think we should tell Pomewege now," Maia said.

"Yes. What if Core 13 needs help?" Dani added.

That settled it, and together they marched up to the principal. Nafi had barely started relating the incident when Principal Pomewege waved them off. "No need to worry. It's all under control. Go have yourselves some soup now." He practically pushed them into the inner room of the Raptor.

The inner room was so unbelievably comfortable that it was easy to forget they were inside a Raptor. It was plushly furnished and warm, with the aroma of piping hot soup floating through the air. Maia would have been happily lost in its bliss had it not been for the nagging worry about Jiri and his teammates. However, even before Maia had time to take her first sip of soup, Core 13 arrived.

"Have you reported Core 7?" Nafi pounced on Jiri and gang immediately. "Did you manage to find all your spilled Calbion?"

Jiri nodded solemnly but did not say a word. Anja's face twisted in a grimace, however. "We found all the ore. But we've decided not to file a complaint."

"Why not?"

"What's the point?" Jiri said. "They'd get a penalty. And then they'd do something else."

Nafi's eyes flashed. "Maybe so. But you can't just let them get away with it. That's not right."

Jiri sighed and Anja looked away in a huff. Maia could understand their reluctance, but she had to agree with Nafi. Tolerating injustice was just as bad as committing the injustice itself.

"Well, the principal already seemed to know." Luem broke the uneasy silence. "Did you guys tell him?"

"We tried to," Kusha said. "But he wouldn't even let us start."

Matters remained a mystery until all of the teams returned and Pomewege, cradling a large cup of soup, took his seat next to Zaara and Aerika.

"One more task completed. Well done." He took a long sip and sighed heavily. "I wish I did not have to talk about this, but I do. Once again, I have had reports of behavior that does not belong in the Initiative. I am disappointed."

Clearly, he meant the incident between Core 7 and Core 13. As Pomewege scanned the faces of the contestants, Aerika pursed her lips and shook her head. Zaara kept stabbing at a plateful of bread bits.

"Bakhari, would you like to share anything about today's task?" Pomewege asked.

Bakhari, wearing a disinterested expression, shrugged. "What about it?"

"There was an incident with another group, I believe. Core 13, to be precise." Pomewege walked up to Bakhari, a stern look on his face. His voice was cold and hard, as Maia had never heard it before. "You see, I already know. So you should tell the truth now."

"It was an accident." Bakhari shot a glare at Core 13. "Can't believe you ratted. Is it too much work to clean up after yourselves? Petty little babies."

As Jiri and his team shrank, visibly upset at the open hostility, Maia's fists curled. But before she could say a word, Nafi took a step forward.

"Accident, my foot. We saw how you rammed their buggy. You are lucky no one was hurt."

Bakhari's mouth twisted. "So you're the one who told on us? Loriine was right. You're a troublemaking, attention-seeking, nosy nobody." The boy strode up to Nafi, fists raised and glaring. "One of these days you'll have your face punched in. Or worse."

Maia had already jumped to Nafi's side, but Ren was faster. Fury, its dark blade glistening, was pointed at Bakhari's chest before Maia could blink.

"Back off, Bakhari." Ren's voice was as cold as the frozen wastelands surrounding them.

"Boys, enough!" Pomewege roared. "Step back, both of you."

As Bakhari took a step backward and Ren sheathed Fury, a fragile, grim silence fell in the room. It only lasted a moment.

"She didn't have to tell anyone, Bakhari. I did." Maia's mouth fell open on hearing Karhann's voice, and she was sure even without looking that every contestant was just as stunned. Karhann continued in a tired voice as Bakhari gaped. "I told the principal it was no accident. You rammed them on purpose." Karhann shook his head and sighed. "We could have made the best time overall if not for you and Loriine and your needless drama. But you just couldn't help acting stupid. I'm so tired of this."

The room stayed quiet for long moments after Karhann stopped speaking. Then Pomewege cleared his throat. "Well, Bakhari?"

Bakhari shrugged again. "I still say it was an accident."

"We shall see about that," Pomewege said. He turned toward the rest of the crowd. "Go on, get some rest. You will need your wits about you for the final lap."

"The final lap? B-but . . . we just finished the last task, didn't we?" Jiri said.

A wave of chatter rose across the room until Junko of Core 10 spoke up. "There's really more to it, then? Another step that ties everything together."

Principal Pomewege chuckled. "Yes, Junko's right. The Initiative has not ended yet. However, I sincerely hope all misbehavior ends here."

The teams plunged into animated discussions once more. Although Maia had suspected this since the beginning, the official announcement did change the weight of the matter. With nothing to guide them, tying the tasks together was a seriously challenging enterprise. Everyone was engrossed in conversation all the way back to the base, where they boarded the transport to Tansi.

Maia's heart was heavy as the transport pulled away from the frozen moon. She thought of the many people who had been forced to work here. They must have hoped to get back to Tansi one day. Yet for most of them, that day never came.

Perhaps everyone had weighty thoughts on their minds, because the long trip back to Tansi was exceptionally quiet. The cabin of the transport was faintly lit, and the groups huddled sleepily in their assigned booths. Maia had almost dozed off when Nafi sat up suddenly.

"Do you guys realize something?"

"No. What is it?" Ren said in a gruff voice.

"Miir did give us a valuable piece of advice," Nafi whispered. "It was a subtle and a very roundabout way of telling us, but he did help us."

"Thought we all realized that way back when," Ren said.

"Yes, we did. But that's not the point. The point is, he shouldn't have. That's not like him at all." She slumped forward and scratched her chin. "What is wrong with him?"

"Nothing is wrong," Kusha said. "It was just a little hint."

Nafi sighed loudly. "I know, but it's not like him to blur the lines like that, you know. And that's odd."

"Oh Nafi, get some sleep now," Dani said in a drowsy voice. "We did fine. He is fine. All is well."

Nafi grunted. "Oh well. Guess you're right. I'm happy Maia made the connection." She nudged Maia and giggled playfully. "I'm so glad you get him nowadays, Maia. I really like it when you two are in tune."

"Nafi, can you please pipe down?" Ren said sharply. "Really tired here."

That brought a prompt end to the conversation. Nafi's words, as expected, had once again left Maia's heart twinging. But there was a change, a tiny but distinct change. A small smile slowly curled Maia's lips as she snuggled under her blanket. Conversations about Miir still hurt, but not as much. Could it be that she was finally getting over it?

Maia's fingers curled into a tight ball. She had to put it behind her. And fast!

CHAPTER FORTY-ONE

AN UPHILL RUN

Excitement and frustration were both at the highest level during the last days of the Initiative. News about Core 7 came soon after the trip to Ti. They had been penalized, but Karhann's stand earned them some award points as well.

"I wonder if the whole Karhann business was a setup," Nafi whispered to Maia and Dani when they heard. "They were sure they'd be penalized, so Karhann owned up. Now they've got some award points to offset the penalty."

Although the idea sounded logical, Maia found it hard to believe Karhann would do that. They had been at loggerheads with Karhann a few times, and sometimes Core 21 was to blame for the clashes, but Maia had to admit, Karhann had never been quite like Loriine.

"That's not fair, Nafi," Dani chided, taking an openly vocal position. "You shouldn't accuse people of things with no proof. It only makes your own conscience sink lower."

Nafi rolled her eyes but did not argue anymore. Besides, there was no time to discuss other people and teams with the biggest puzzle facing them.

The day after their return from Ti, Zaara gathered the teams. "Now you know there is a final step to this challenge," she said in a flat voice. "Everything ties together . . . somehow. And your task is to find out how. The Initiative ends in two weeks, or as soon as the first team solves this."

Two weeks! They were so near, yet the final answer eluded them. The Calbion particularly baffled everyone. How was one to use metal—one known mostly for its rigidity—with plants? Nothing in any of the books Nafi extracted from the library gave any clues, but Nafi did not give up hope. She not only got out tomes from the library, but also managed to find some scriptures from the Xinhagyi, and even from the vaults in Kusha's house. Every day they pored over the dusty volumes, hoping to find a link. And every day they had to visit the glass house to keep an eye on their plant specimens.

One such evening, as the three girls headed out of the living quarters, books in hand, Nafi was in a particularly grumpy mood. "Can't believe we're always stuck with the work. Those two boys are useless."

"Kusha tries," Dani protested meekly. "He doesn't have time, but he does try his best."

Nafi scoffed. "At least Kusha has a valid enough excuse. That other one just keeps vanishing on us for no reason. He was supposed to be here by now, but where is he? Must be at Frauz Point. What does he do there, anyway?"

"Maybe he will come, Nafi," Maia said. "Maybe he'll join us at the Glass House."

"Right," Nafi fumed. "He's probably out with one of those fan club girls."

They had just walked down the stairs and were about to turn around the ramparts when they heard voices. They were not very loud, but the evening was quiet and Maia recognized Ren's voice immediately. And so did her friends.

"What in the—" Nafi dashed toward the stairs leading to the top of the ramparts.

"Nafi, stop." Dani grabbed her shirt. "You can't just barge in on people like that," she whispered.

"Why not? He's late and—"

"Wait." Maia stopped both of them and tried to listen. "He sounds really angry. Who is he talking to?"

"Must be some stupid girl," Nafi said, taking another step up the stairs. "Let me check."

"Not our business," Dani chided. "Nafi, we should leave."

Dani had a point, as always, but Maia had to admit she was curious. Ren, boisterous as he was, did not argue with random people out in the open. That job was mostly Nafi's. Still, she decided to listen to Dani's sage advice and turn around. She was just about to yank Nafi away when the other voice drifted in.

"You tricked me, Ren. It was a setup, all of this," someone said.

Nafi's eyes widened. "Isn't that Miir? Ren's arguing with Miir? What about?"

Dani seemed flabbergasted and lost any interest in getting away. Maia, on the other hand, lost all her curiosity at hearing Miir's voice. All she felt was an intense desire to flee. But there was no pulling Nafi away now. The girl had tiptoed halfway up the stairs and was listening intently. Dani, still holding Nafi by the shirt, had followed. Only Maia remained at the base of the stairs, her heart pounding with fear as she listened to the war of words raging above them.

"I couldn't just ask, could I?" Ren replied. "You'd refuse outright if you knew."

"Ren, I trusted you."

"You can still trust me. Why do you think you can't?"

"Because you tricked me," Miir said, the anger in his voice rising another notch.

"That doesn't change anything. I am who I am. And I'm going to see this through."

"You do know what you are putting at risk here. This is not a prank, not another one of your wagers. It means something, do you understand?"

"What makes you think I don't?"

"Because you make it seem like a joke. Tricking me, pulling a fast one on someone else . . . what is this?"

"Oh come on," Ren yelled. "Don't give me that tone. As if you care, as if what happens to . . . anyone . . . matters to you."

There was a moment of absolute silence and Maia held her breath. It was so unlike Ren to be yelling at Miir. Sure, Ren yelled at her plenty and she had shouted back at him just as loudly, but to act that way with Miir? That was unbelievable. And Miir . . . why was he taking this? What did Ren hold over him? Before she could think any further, Miir spoke again.

"So *that* is what this is about?" he said. Anyone who heard him now would call his voice calm, but Maia could easily tell it was not. Not in the least. The way it frayed at the ends, the way it shook almost imperceptibly as he uttered the words—she knew he was distressed and struggling to mask the least sign of it. She could barely hear his next words. "Of course, it matters. I do care."

"You do, huh?" Ren's tone was scathing. "I have my doubts. If you really cared, you would've seen what you've done."

"Enough, Ren. Stop it. I am not going to stand here and listen to this. Or justify to you why—"

"Don't even try, because I don't have time to listen to your lame justifications, all right?" Ren snapped. "Besides, I know what you're doing. You are hiding, that's what it is. What I don't know is why. Why can't you face this one simple truth like every other thing you've faced?"

"You cannot understand. It is *not* simple."

"Of course I don't," Ren shot back. "I don't get you at all. You know, Miir, I have always admired you. Even before I met you, you were my hero, the stuff of legends. I was nothing like you, I could never be like you. You were always so . . . perfect, so right." He stopped, and the silence that followed was scary.

"You thought wrong. I was never that person. I was never perfect, nor always right."

Ren laughed. "Don't worry. I figured that out a while ago, too. You weren't flawless at all. But guess what? I also realized that a real hero is not the one who is perfect, but the one who dares to see their imperfections and tries to fix them. Like you have been doing the last few years. The more I got to know you, the more you truly became the stuff of legends to me." A pause, a long breath, and Ren continued. "But now . . . I don't know what to think anymore. I mean, what are you doing? Destroying everything you've built . . . is that the plan?"

A sudden thought streaked through Maia's mind, making her heart drop to the pit of her stomach. Could Ren be talking about the falling-out between Miir and her? No, it was not possible. Ren would not do anything to disrupt the little peace she was struggling to find. Yet . . . why did it feel like . . .

"Perhaps that is how it should be."

Miir's reply made Maia stir out of her stupor. Ren's subsequent retort, loud and sharp, made her shudder.

"And I'll tell you, it should not. Come on, it's not *that* complicated. All you have to do is take the obvious path in front of you. So take it. What's stopping you?"

"Maybe that path is not for me," Miir said. "Maybe I am quite fine where I am."

For a moment, there was silence. It seemed as if they were done. At that moment, Maia wished that Nafi would relent and leave. Or that she could run away. Or she could at least stop hearing words that sank their talons into her heart and tore it to pieces. None of her wishes came true. Nafi did not give up. And Maia could not run or shut out the words, so she leaned against the stone wall of the ramparts, her fingers cold, her legs frozen, and her thoughts a dizzying whirlpool.

"Oh really? That's your answer?" Ren scoffed so loudly that Maia trembled. She could almost see his irate face, his eyes flashing dangerously. "And I used to think you never lied."

Nafi slunk back to the bottom of the stairs, Dani in tow. "This is weird. I don't understand any of what they're talking about," Nafi whispered. "What does Ren know that I don't?"

"I have no idea. But I think we should leave," Dani whispered back.

"Please, let's go," Maia begged. She could not imagine the situation if they were found. Even the thought of it made her insides clench and freeze in panic.

Thankfully, Nafi agreed. They had only taken a step or two away when Ren's sharp and withering voice came again.

"How can you not see a simple truth? It's clear as daylight, and it has always been. It's beyond all your justifications and all your fears. And don't tell me you don't see it, because you do. You know what you want. You know what you should do, but you'll keep on denying it, you'll keep on building up these walls that have no place here at all."

"For the last time, Ren, it is not that simple. Or easy. I have tried."

"Well, try harder then," Ren snapped.

"What for? All I see are a million ways this can go wrong."

The momentary silence that fell was downright scary. It was still better than the words that came next.

"Can't believe you're saying that, Miir," Ren said. "You're no hero of mine. Not anymore. You're a coward. No . . . you're just plain stupid."

Nafi froze, and even in the dim light, Maia could see the horrified expression on the girl's face. Maia could understand why. Had she not heard it herself, she would not believe it in a million years.

"All right. I'm scared," Nafi whispered, her face downcast.

"Out of here," Dani said. "Now."

Grabbing Maia and Nafi by the arms, she tiptoed away from the ramparts. As soon as they reached the shadows of the buildings, they started off at a brisk pace.

Core 13 and Core 10 were working at the Glass House when they reached it. Maia could hear their voices. They could not see them, however. Since the specimens from Korobieltes arrived, the planting area had been divided into five parts and sections allocated for each of the teams. Then the sections had been blocked off with partitions and gates that were matched to individual auras. Each team was required to stay within their area and allowed access only to their section. Because of the shenanigans pulled by Core 7, they now had to work in cramped quarters.

The girls put on their suits and masks before entering their plot and started tending to their plants, not saying a word to each other. Not long after, Ren walked in, his face dark and stormy, forehead creased in a deep frown. He sat down to the side, a little distance away from the girls, and started poring over a notebook.

"Are you all right?" Dani asked him after they had worked in silence for a long time. The darkness on Ren's face refused to clear.

"I'm fine," came the answer.

Maia would have preferred to leave things at that, but Nafi, who by now had overcome her shock and fear over the argument they had overheard, hopped up to Ren. "What were you arguing with Miir about?" she asked, blunt as usual.

Ren scowled. "How do you know about that?"

"You were going at it so loudly, the whole of ThulaSu must have heard."

"That's not true," Dani corrected hastily. "We were walking past the ramparts and we heard . . . bits and pieces. You weren't that loud."

"Fine, fine," Nafi said. "Question is, what was it about?"

"None of your business," Ren replied coldly. Seeing Nafi continue to stand over him, arms crossed and frowning, he sighed. "Stuff about the Sedara. Happy?"

"What stuff?"

"Can't tell you."

"Really?"

"Really." Nafi was still hovering, and she would have demanded more if Ren had not given her a dead, cold look. "Not in the mood, Nafi. Drop it or I'll leave."

And that was that.

Maia did not venture near Ren or Nafi. First, she tended to the roots of the Spore and the fern, and then sat fiddling with some Calbion flakes. Her thoughts drifted as she tinkered with a small sheet of metal. Such a strange metal it was—so light, so pretty and shiny, yet so tough. The flakes separated at the slightest touch, yet each was the hardest material Maia had ever encountered. Bendable only in the foundries at super high temperatures or by the Tierremorphes, Calbion was almost indestructible. So much happened because of Calbion, and so many lives were lost. Maia sighed, absentmindedly poking the soil with the Calbion flake. She almost screamed when someone grabbed her arm and tugged her backward.

"Be careful, Maia," Ren said.

She had not noticed him rush over to her side and now, suddenly realizing she had leaned too close to the Spore, Maia flushed. Protective gear or not, the Spore was deadly.

Ren tapped his knee distractedly for a while before looking back up at her again. "Maia, I didn't mean to bring this up since I know it upsets you, but"—he started hesitantly in a very low voice—"I need to say this because I care about you and your safety. You're handling the situation, I know. And you're doing great. Just keep your focus, all right? We're working with dangerous stuff, and a moment's distraction can get you hurt or even . . . killed."

Maia flushed with embarrassment. Ren was right. The matter with Miir often made her inattentive. She could not let that happen. She had to stay focused and not let herself be distracted the way she had just been with the Spore. Things had gotten better, but she had to be more in control. She had to remember such things happened. They happened a lot. And she had to forget and move on.

Forget!

But it still hurt so much. And it wasn't for the lack of trying on her part.

Try harder, then!

"What were you doing with the Calbion?" Ren asked, pulling Maia out of her blistering thoughts. His voice, so gentle compared to how he had spoken to Miir and even more recently to Nafi, made Maia stare for a moment before she answered.

"Nothing, really. Just thinking how all this could tie together," Maia replied, keenly aware of the curious glance Nafi shot in their direction. She decided to ignore it and continue her conversation with Ren. "Do you have any ideas?"

Ren shrugged. "Nothing other than they will connect somehow. Hey, look at that!" Ren's excited whisper made Maia look in the direction Ren was pointing.

She immediately gasped out loud. The stem of the Spore looked strange, sort of transparent. Maia had been poking the soil near the Spore with the Calbion sheet and she drew her hand back, startled. Almost immediately, the stem turned normal once more. Maia looked from the Calbion sheet to Ren, her mind racing to make connections. Could the plant be reacting to the Calbion? Or was it just a random event?

Gingerly, Maia extended her hand and placed the Calbion sheet next to the Spore. Almost like magic, the stem turned clear. Ren jumped up and, snatching the sheet of Calbion from Maia's hand, placed it in the soil near the fern. The fern did not turn clear like the Spore, but almost instantly turned a lighter shade of green.

"This could be it, Maia," Ren whispered.

"What's going on?" Nafi was next to them in a blink, followed by Dani.

Hearts thudding, they repeated the motions of putting the Calbion close to each of the plants, and each time they reacted the same way.

"This *is* the link," Nafi whispered as she bobbed up and down a few times, fists curled. "This is the link of the plants to Calbion. It affects them somehow, strengthens them perhaps?"

She rocked back and forth on her feet, and her eyes shone. Then suddenly, she grabbed her satchel. "Come on, let's go. We're done here."

"What?" Before Ren could say any more, Nafi had herded them

all out of their enclosure and then out of the Glass House. She hurried along the pathways and stopped only when they reached the corner of the Sun Temple courtyard. She flung her satchel down on a bench, sat down, and swung her legs vigorously.

"I have an idea, but could not say it out loud in the Glass House with the other teams around. Remember that story we were told about Mindoza the Uniter?" All eyes were on her in an instant.

Maia recalled the tale about the Jueyue. "He plucked out the heart of the moon and swam across the cold, stormy oceans until he reached the broken Jueyue tree. A ribbon out of the plucked heart he fashioned, and then wrapped it around the wounded stalk. The day after, there was a miracle. The Jueyue stood proud and strong once more, healed by the magic touch of Mindoza the Uniter."

"Yes, I remember that," Dani said. "What about it?"

"So . . . what if that story is *the* clue?" Nafi said, her eyes wide. "The Calbion could be the heart we plucked out, and maybe we need to make a ribbon out of it and wrap it around the plants."

Ren started chuckling. "Make a ribbon out of Calbion? Have you noticed it's not exactly ribbon-making material?"

Nafi snorted. "I know that, Prince of Smartness. You have a better idea?"

"Well, these are valuable clues and ideas, but first we need to find out how exactly Calbion affects them," Dani said. "Also, how do we bend Calbion with the resources we have? And then, how does the Challowist task fit into all this?"

Dani was right. As important as their discoveries were, and Maia was sure they were steps in the right direction, the fact remained that there was still much to be solved. This was only the beginning of a long journey.

Chapter Forty-Two

Let There be a Season

Hadeeyah arrived at the AR quite early the next day. Even though they had had a long, tiring evening, the gang was up and about already, poring over information that seemed determined to yield nothing. Even Kusha was present, cradling a thick book, his face stony as he flipped the ancient pages. No one was in the mood to look up at Hadeeyah when she zipped in.

"You're up early," she said approvingly.

Nafi exhaled loudly in response, but Dani returned a smile. "Wish getting up early could solve it all, Hadeeyah. Unfortunately, it doesn't. We're as stuck as ever. But . . . we've made some progress."

Hadeeyah zoomed to her side and sat down next to her. "Progress? Tell me."

Soon they had all taken turns relating the previous evening's discovery and their subsequent investigation.

"That's it, Hadeeyah," Dani concluded. "We're sure Calbion causes a change in the plants. It induces mutations perhaps. But how do we keep the process going? We have ideas but it's taking us nowhere."

"It's all right, Dani. You're all trying hard. You'll figure it out . . . or not. It's all right. I'm proud and thankful to have been your mentor either way."

Everyone snapped around to stare at Hadeeyah. That was unusual, if not completely out of character for her. Never once had she said it would be all right if they failed, and now . . .

Maia's thoughts bounded away to a day years ago on Xif when Miir had surprised them just like that. They had no solution to the Seliban challenge and their faces had been droopy and suddenly he had said it did not matter if they won or lost. Those words had meant so much.

With a shake of her head, Maia drove the memory away. She could not, not for a moment, let him in. Not now. She had to solve this puzzle of a task, win the Initiative, and get Seigvard.

Focus, Maia.

There was something she was missing, Maia was sure. But what it was she could not tell.

You can do it, Maia. Forget the silly and the trivial.

"Are you all right, Hadeeyah?" Nafi was saying, peering at their mentor's face.

"Yes, I am, Nafi," Hadeeyah said, earnestness shining bright in her golden eyes. "I would still love for you to win it, of course, but seeing how far you've come and how hard you're trying" — she placed a hand on Dani's shoulder and smiled — "I am already super proud of you."

"Does that mean you won't buzz around here anymore?" Ren asked.

Hadeeyah frowned. "Why? Don't you like me buzzing around?"

"Umm . . ."

"I have to keep cheering you on until the end, so . . . I will come and go," the mentor said. "Sorry, buzzing's still on." Ren's shoulders slumped but Hadeeyah simply chuckled. "All right, now to the reason I'm here. I came to invite you all as my special guests to my graduation ceremony."

"Graduation ceremony?" Kusha left his perch on the windowsill and walked over. "Since when has there been a ceremony for graduation at ThulaSu? And why don't I know about this?"

"Well, it was just decided. I'm sure you'll hear about it soon," Hadeeyah said. "Usually it's a small affair at the pavilion, with just the graduating class present. But this year they're making it an open event. Guess it's the situation with the R'armimon and stuff," she said grimly. "Anyway, it'll be on the Sun Temple grounds. It's open to all of ThulaSu, but the area closer to the podium is reserved for us, just the graduates and their invitees. So . . . will you come?"

"Of course, we'd love to come," Maia said and heads nodded vigorously around her.

Hadeeyah's face brightened. "It's in three days, and you have to bring your own food. If you'd like, of course. But I think it'll be a nice day for a picnic on the Sun Temple grounds."

"Yes"—Ren's fist shot up in the air—"picnic time!" He smiled sheepishly when he found everyone staring. "I'm just tired. This is the perfect break."

Maia understood exactly what Ren meant. She was just as tired, and the idea of spending some time outside, with their minds off of the fast-approaching deadline for the Initiative, seemed like a dream.

* * *

A bright and beautiful graduation day dawned over ThulaSu three days later. Even though Core 21 had not made any headway on the problem of the final step, they were happy to be doing something different for a change. Their steps were lively, their eyes bright as they trooped down the Sun Temple grounds after a hearty breakfast. The place had taken on a festive look—a podium had been erected overnight, and around it, sections were cordoned off with ropes. In one of the innermost sections near the podium, Maia and her teammates clustered on their blanket.

It was hard to imagine that the sprawling grounds of the Sun Temple could be so full of people so quickly, but soon it was as crowded as a fairground and just as noisy. Maia and her teammates had brought a basket of snacks and time passed happily, the rays of the sun warm on them, the breeze gentle, and the chitchat light and joyful. Sana, looking pretty as ever in a purple dress speckled with yellow, joined them as the monks started setting up for the ceremony.

"You are quite a vision today," Ren commented. "Thank you for gracing us with your lovely presence, Angel."

Nafi groaned and the rest, including Sana, laughed. A bit of normalcy, fleeting as it might be, was back. Soon the ceremony started. The grounds erupted in shouts and cheers as the students went up to the podium one by one to receive their scrolls of merit. When it was Hadeeyah's turn, the gang was up on their feet. They cheered until they were hoarse and clapped until their hands were numb. Hadeeyah was also among the top five graduates, so soon they had to cheer some more. Hadeeyah never missed a chance to wave back. Every time she looked at them, her bright, joyful face said how much she cared. Maia could not have been prouder to cheer for anyone.

Even after the celebrations were over, the grounds stayed just as crowded. Hadeeyah joined them for a while with some of her classmates. Other people—fellow contestants, students of ThulaSu they knew—stopped by to chat as well. Someone brought out string instruments and played lovely tunes, and some others joined in, singing. It was a happy time.

Kusha slipped away for a while and came back with an armful of Toto packs, much to Nafi's annoyance. Kusha, however, was all admiration and praise. "Maks and gang have put up a stall at the walkways. They're raking in some serious money."

A bunch of food vendors had set up booths along the pathways and a spectacularly large variety of edibles was on sale. From the rolled bread-and-eggs stuffed with meat that Maia particularly favored, to the light and crispy honey-glazed wafer cakes that she could not get enough of, to rock candy peppered with sour grape crisps—they were all mouthwatering fare. Of all of them, the Totos seemed to be the most popular.

Ren was the next to wander away, and soon Nafi spotted him with Karhann. The two boys posed happily for a bevy of girls from their fan club. Nafi's nose was wrinkled when Ren returned.

"Cozying up with Karhann again, huh?" Nafi demanded. "And those fan club girls are just . . . so annoying! How you can tolerate them is beyond me."

"The girls are fine," Ren said casually. "And for the millionth time, Nafi, Karhann is a friend, just like you are."

Nafi threw a murderous glare at the boy. "I don't care if he has been wonderful lately. If you compare me to him one more time, Ren, you're dead."

The resolve in Nafi's voice was scary, but Ren simply shook his head and sprawled on the grass.

"Besides, I went to check on their progress," he said.

"And?" Maia asked curiously.

"They have nothing yet."

Maia sighed in relief. One good thing . . . no, the only good thing was, none of the other teams had had a breakthrough yet.

"That's awesome news," Kusha said. Noticing everyone staring at him, he went on to explain. "Well, think about it this way. Assuming we get those special points for Korobieltes and Core 7 has the penalties, we possibly have the best standing among the teams, right? So even if we can't figure out a solution, it doesn't harm us if . . . if none of the other teams get it either."

"But that's only a possibility," Dani said. "Assuming we get enough points for Korobieltes."

Nafi scoffed. "Once again, our valiant Sahiiraan tries to find the laziest way out," she said in a caustic tone. "The forever strategist."

Nafi's comment took Maia back to the XDA once more, and as memories of the final challenge with Miir came crashing back, Maia reeled.

Why did it always have to be like this? Why did every memory have to lead back to him? At this rate, she would never get out of this cycle of pain. For every step she took forward, the memories dragged her back two. She could not let them. She *had* to break out of it.

"Hey, Maia." Dani's soft voice startled her out of her relentless thoughts. "Are you all right? You look . . . upset."

"I'm fine, Dani," Maia assured her, with the brightest smile she could scrape up.

"We'll find a solution, don't worry," Dani said. "We still have a few days left."

"We're all upset," Ren said wisely. "This challenge has worn us out completely. We've always had to work on vague clues, but this one is the worst—it doesn't even have a riddle to go on." He exhaled loudly. "My head's a block of rock these days, seriously. I think we should all go to the shore and take a swim."

"A swim?" Sana's brows shot up. "In the ocean?"

"It's cold," Nafi said, shuddering.

"It's not *that* cold." Ren propped himself up on his elbows to smile at Sana. "Come on, Angel. You just have to frolic around a bit and it'll feel perfect. You wanna go? For me?"

"No," came Sana's resolute reply. "Braving the oceans for you is not on my agenda."

Sana's words stirred up a vague thought in Maia's mind. Something about the ocean . . .

"Maia? You want to come?" Ren asked next. Seeing her befuddled look, he hastily added, "To the shore, for a swim."

Going to the shore meant crossing Walenveil and so many memories . . .

"I don't want to," she said in a hurry, realizing a moment too late that everyone was looking at her curiously because of her hasty reply. "I agree with Nafi, it's too cold."

No one except Kusha showed any interest, and Ren grumbled for a while. The sun rays were slowly losing their intensity, and the crowd thinned around them, yet no one in their gang was willing to leave just yet. The skies were still bright, the air nice and warm, and the misery of the AR did not entice anyone to leave. They opened up their basket and munched on apples, Kusha went to get some more Totos from the Appian trio's stall, and they lingered as the skies started to show shades of purple.

They were all munching on taro-cakes Kusha had brought over along with the Totos, when Dani frowned. "What are you looking around for, Nafi?"

Maia had also noticed the girl's restive looks, but she had not given them much thought. It was all because of the challenge, she thought. Even though they were enjoying the day, they were all stressed, their minds weighed down by the unsolved problem.

"Oh, nothing" — Nafi waved Dani away — "just expecting some books."

"Books?" Ren asked in a grouchy voice. "We've almost set up our own library in the AR. You need more?"

"Just a couple more," Nafi said. "Last year during the Yako Challenge, I noticed some old books on horticulture in the mausoleum at Walenveil. Thought of looking into those . . . just in case."

Kusha looked quizzically at Nafi. "So are you expecting those books to come trotting over to you? That's why you keep looking?"

Nafi's cheeks flushed a bright red as she threw an angry glare at Kusha. "The more Totos you eat, the sillier you get," she snapped. "No, I asked Miir to pick them up for me and I'm looking for him. He should've been here by now."

Maia's heart jumped and she braced herself. It would be the first time she had seen Miir face to face since . . .

Nothing you can't handle, Maia. You've been through so much and this is nothing in comparison. You are stronger than this.

"All right, gang, I'll be back soon," Sana declared. Before anyone could ask where she was going, Sana had disappeared.

"Sana is going crazy too," Ren commented.

Nafi gave him a look. "When has she not? Your idea of braving the oceans didn't help much either." She shuddered a little.

CHAPTER FORTY-TWO

"Swimming in that cold water . . . brrr . . ."

A thought crashed through Maia's mind like a lightning strike and she jumped up.

"Hey, guys! Remember what Nafi said the other night about making a ribbon out of Calbion? I was thinking . . . Mindoza swam through the oceans with the heart. If the Calbion stands for the heart then . . . perhaps we need to put water on it."

"Cold, ocean water, to be precise," Kusha exclaimed. "It's an idea. We should try that."

Suddenly, there was hope. There was a possibility once more. And suddenly Maia felt lighter, happier. It only lasted until Sana marched up and held out a couple of books to Nafi.

"Here, your books."

Nafi frowned as she grabbed them, and looked around. "Did Miir give them to you? Where is he?"

"Yes, he did," Sana said, calmly picking up some bread crisps from the little pile of food at the center of the blanket. "He left. He has work to do."

"Left?" Nafi said. "Just like that? No hellos?"

"You heard her, Nafi," Ren said, in a sharp voice. "You didn't need Miir. You needed those books and you got them. Shouldn't you start reading them now?"

Nafi shot Ren a look, but did not say another word. As they sat on the grounds that warm evening, flipping through the books, Maia felt the air around them change. An odd stiffness descended, and Maia realized they all sort of knew something was wrong. It was evident from the way they drew closer, how every conversation was measured, and why Nafi's eyes suddenly lost their fire. After Sana's noticeable intervention with the books and Ren's equally noticeable interruption, no one mentioned Miir again, not once.

As relieved as Maia was, another thought intruded. Miir did not deserve this. They were all supposed to be his friends. He got them the books and in return, all he received was a cold dismissal. It was not fair. If the falling-out was anyone's responsibility, it was hers. She had known the odds. She had known this could happen, and she had still decided to take a chance.

Maia wanted to tell all her friends that. But courage did not show up for her that afternoon. She feared their questions, and she was not ready to face them. Not yet. So Maia kept her thoughts to herself and went on pretending—forcing smiles, talking far more than necessary, being cheerful when her insides were ashen.

However, that evening, after the boys left for the shore to collect ocean water, and the girls headed back to their rooms, Maia decided to speak with Sana.

"Sana, I know you mean to protect me and I'm grateful for that. But you don't need to be hostile to Miir on my account."

Sana peered at her and for a moment Maia thought she would deny it. Then her right eyebrow shot up. "Hostile? I'm not hostile. I'm just . . . practical. He doesn't need to come near you all that much."

"Sana, you don't need to worry. I'm doing just fine," Maia said bravely. "I won't break in pieces or anything if he does. So . . . go easy on him."

Sana crossed her arms and stared at her for a bit before returning a grudging nod. "All right, I'll be civil," she said. Her tone, however, did not reflect what her words promised. "I will not let him anywhere near you, though. I don't think you're ready for that yet."

"All right, fine. Just don't be unkind to him, please."

Sana sat down on the edge of the bed and tilted her head to peer at Maia's face. "It hurts to think of him in pain?"

Maia did not have to think to answer that. "Yes, it does. His choice is what it is. It's not one I like, but . . . he doesn't deserve to be punished for it." It felt good to say that, comforting and peaceful in a way, even though her heart ached with every word she uttered. "Besides, I have all of you to lean on. He really has no one. Not letting him come near the few friends he has is . . . cruel. Let him be, Sana. I'll be fine."

"Oh, Maia." Sana sighed loudly and flopped onto the bed.

"I sound stupid, don't I?"

Sana shook her head. "Not at all. You sound like . . . you. Kind and caring and . . ." She stared at the ceiling for a while and chuckled. "You know what? I feel bad for your Miir. Poor guy doesn't know what he let go."

Maia laughed. "Well, he's not poor if he doesn't know." She fell back onto the bed and linked her arm through Sana's. "And Sana, let's settle this once and for all. He's not *my* Miir."

She had only wanted to make light of the situation with her comment. But Maia realized her mistake right away. Facing the withering reality still hurt like a knife through her heart. Maybe someday she could make a joke of it. Maybe she would laugh at herself. Maybe. Sana was right. She was not there yet. Right now, she was far from where she wished to be.

But . . . her fists curled with determination. She was going to get there. Sooner or later she would get over this. She had to remember all the pain she had gotten through. This was nothing compared to that. She was going to leave this far behind. Someday . . .

Chapter Forty-Three

Out of Nothing

As much as the team had hoped for a miraculous breakthrough with the seawater, it turned out to be nothing. Pails of water stood lined up against one wall of the AR, thanks to the dedication of the boys. That night, the AR turned into a laboratory. Various samples of Calbion lay all over the place, some sprinkled with water, some dipped and removed, some soaked overnight, and every other combination they could think of. But no instant changes made them jump for joy, and no changes happened overnight either. Once again, spirits dipped.

In the middle of the letdown, there came news of the Nouvus taking off. It was bittersweet to hear that the ark was leaving Tansi. While it brought happiness that so many people would be safe, it also brought back many memories—of Ori, of losing him, of the good times together. Although everyone they knew wanted to see the craft leave, practical challenges prevented hordes from queueing up to witness the event. First, no one was allowed in the vicinity for safety reasons. Second, the Fourth was not right next door, and reaching it was not child's play. Ren, however, was not one to give up easily.

"If we're not allowed on the Fourth, we won't go there," he declared a few nights before the departure date. "We'll camp at the tip of the First Continent instead."

Nafi let out a huge sigh. "What's the point? What will we do there?"

"We'll watch it go up. It'll be fun."

"I like it," Dani chirped. "We've been so stressed lately. Any break I get is fun."

Nafi grunted. "So, who's coming? The five of us? And Sana? And Miir?"

"Not Miir," Ren said as he fiddled endlessly with a piece of Calbion submerged in a pail of water.

"Why not? Doesn't he want to see the ark go up?"

"No, he doesn't." Ren's reply came so promptly that it almost seemed he had been expecting Nafi's question. Nafi immediately frowned, as if she too had been expecting just that response from Ren.

"It's weird how we hardly see Miir nowadays," she observed. "He never comes by. He's not even home. Ever. I went to check on him and he's . . . never there." She looked at the faces surrounding her, and Maia felt as if Nafi's questioning gaze rested longer on her than on anyone else. "I don't like this. Not one bit. Whoever it is that has had a squabble with him better make up."

"Come on, Nafi, you're making too much out of nothing," Dani chided gently.

"He must just be busy, that's all," Kusha added.

"Like I buy that," Nafi said and after looking pointedly at Ren, marched out of the room in a huff.

After Nafi left and Dani followed her, Maia trudged back to her room, miserable to the core. It was wrong, so wrong. She had ruined everything. This was what she had feared. She had known, and yet she had risked it for her own selfish reasons. Now she had managed to destroy all the happiness the team had finally found. Nothing was fun anymore. There was no joy in anything. She hardly had any interest left in watching the Nouvus leave. Maia flopped onto her bed and buried her face in her pillow, wishing Ren had never come up with the idea in the first place. It would have been another distressing evening had it not been for Dusty who strutted up purring loudly and snuggled against Maia. And suddenly, for a while at least, she forgot to be sad.

In the end, however, all of Ren's plans came to naught. Hans somehow got wind of it, and he sent a long note forbidding them from going anywhere close to the Fourth.

"He says it's not worth the risk," Dani summarized his message. "We need to focus on the Initiative and not stray into trouble. The planet's hope rests on us. He promises to send us recordings of the take off."

Ren raised an eyebrow. "Stray into trouble? So, basically, he doesn't trust us."

"In other words, he trusts in our ability to get into trouble far too much," Kusha chimed in with an evil grin.

Perhaps because of Hans's note, or maybe because of Nafi's outburst, Ren let it go completely.

Maia and her teammates barely rested these days. Every day was an endless routine of scouring through books in the hopes of finding clues, and experiments with the Calbion and the pails of water. Nothing worked. That did not stop anyone from spending every waking hour at the AR, reading and tinkering. The only good news was that no other team had made any progress either. As long as that continued to be the case, there was still hope.

One morning, Maia woke up from a fitful night's sleep to the sound of voices. For a while, she was not sure if she was awake or dreaming. Then she realized Sana was not in her bed, the door was ajar, and it was Sana's voice—hushed almost beyond recognition— outside the door. Maia was too tired to investigate, and only a few words drifted in through the haze of sleep that refused to lift.

Sana's voice was low but sharp. "You, of all people, should know that now is not the time for this. But then again, that'd be putting too much faith in you." She stopped and scoffed. "The best thing you can do now is stay away. That is, if you ever cared even a little."

"Who was it, Sana?" Maia asked as soon as Sana slipped back into the room and shut the door.

Sana shrugged. "No one of consequence. Just a boy I used to know."

"A boy?" Maia squinted at the window. There was barely any light outside. "So early in the morning? Couldn't it wait?"

"I know," Sana replied as she slipped under the covers. "He's one of the silliest people I've ever come across."

Sana promptly went back to sleep, but whatever little sleepiness Maia had left had dissipated. She lay in bed and stared at the ceiling. Thoughts poured in. Every step of the final task, every clue formed a huge jumbled web in her head. She kept on looking for ways to piece the puzzle together, but nothing worked. Nothing fit. Maia kept at it, poring over every little detail until she could not take it anymore.

She swung out of bed and, opening a window just a bit, peeked outside. A beautiful dawn, fresh and clean, was breaking over ThulaSu. As Maia looked at the pink swirls in the pale blue sky, a soft, cool breeze blew across her face and made her yearn for the outdoors. It was an off day. She had no lessons to go to, neither at the Xinhagyi's nor with Ruche, so the morning was all hers. Sana was still asleep, so Maia moved quietly as she freshened up and dressed. Then as silently as she could, she grabbed a coat in one hand, Bellator in the other, and tiptoed out of the room.

The ramparts were practically empty. A few Kausakas were on patrol, and even fewer students walked about or sat in small groups. Maia pulled her coat more snugly around her and headed in the direction of the Garaha Gates with quick, forceful steps.

The morning air did its miracle and soon Maia's spirits were soaring again. Hope seeped back into her heart with every step she took. Her fists curled and her spine stiffened. They would find a solution soon. They were going to win the Initiative. She would get Seigvard. And then . . . then everything would be good again. Maia had walked to the Garaha Gates and half the way back again when she saw a familiar figure and slowed. Then, smiling, she walked up to the boy sitting on the wall, his head bent over a book.

"Hey, Maks," she said as softly as she could, careful not to startle him.

He looked up at her, sandy locks blowing across his tanned forehead, his blue eyes smiling as always.

"Maia, what a surprise," he said.

"And why's that?" Maia asked, easing onto the wall next to him.

"It's very early, for one thing. And then, you're alone. That hardly ever happens."

Maia stifled a sigh. "You're right on both counts. My mornings . . . when I'm up this early, anyway . . . belong to training. So no walking the ramparts this early for me. And true, I don't get much time alone." She stayed silent for a moment before letting out a chuckle. "I sort of escaped Sana this morning."

"Really? That's tough, having to escape your own cousin."

"I won't lie, it is," Maia said. "Although I understand they're only trying to help." She stared at the rapidly changing colors of the sky, thoughts crossing her mind at a furious pace. She felt unexpectedly peaceful and at ease, sitting there with Maks, suddenly removed from the worries that always surrounded her. Words came out slowly, but without hesitation. "My life is a mess, Maks. Half the time I'm scared of what will come the next day and . . . and I'm tired of it. I wonder if it will ever end."

Maks patted her hand. "Don't think like that, Maia. Of course, there'll be an end. Everything ends sometime, you know. Every storm clears eventually."

He was right. It was hard to see it that way, but she had to try and remember.

"One day, this will be behind you, Maia," Maks continued, his tone earnest. "One day you'll be back in Appian."

"Appian, huh? You think I'll go back there?"

"Yes, of course. I'm sure of it," Maks replied in a heartbeat. "You have a home to rebuild, don't you?"

The bright and innocent hopefulness in his voice made Maia smile. She had lost that spontaneous optimism such a long time ago that it almost felt alien. She doubted it would ever come back again and her heart twinged.

"To be honest, Maks, I envy you," Maia confessed. "I wish I could be as carefree as you are. But I know it's an impossible ask. I keep coming back to how this will end for Tansi. And how much of it will be my failure? Appian gets lost under that burden."

The soft breeze blowing past them did nothing to alleviate the weight of the silence that fell. Then Maks stirred.

"I'm sorry, Maia. I wish I could help," he said. Maia expected him to say the usual things her friends always told her—that she should take it easy, not fret too much about things she could not control, and not everything was her responsibility. What he said instead took her by surprise. "You remind me of Mindoza the Uniter. You have so much on your shoulders and you carry it so bravely, with a smile on your face. Just like him, you keep your eyes on your goals, not thinking of yourself."

If only that were true. The truth was, she had strayed. She had let herself be drawn to selfish goals. Maia's insides clenched in mortification. Maks and everyone must think so highly of her, when in reality she had been distracted. Falling in love? Chasing her own happiness? How petty was that? Even if her emotions had every right to exist, her actions were utterly disappointing and . . . shameful. Maia's nails dug into her palms.

I have to do better from now on. Put a lid on things and carry on. Keep my eyes on the one goal that really matters — saving Tansi.

"Hey, did I upset you?" Maks peered at her face, his gaze worried.

"No, no, you're fine." Maia shook off her thoughts and forced a smile. "So you're into Mindoza the Uniter as well?"

Maks guffawed. "No, I'm not *into* him. We have a horrible, massive test coming up. That's why I'm up so early, cramming. I thought the morning air and the quiet could help."

"I'm sorry, I interrupted."

"Not at all. I like talking to you," Maks said, flushing brightly as he smiled. "Anyway, we've been slammed with all sorts of crazy reading tasks. Mindoza is part of it. I've read the thirteen fables so many times that I could recite them in my sleep." He yanked a book from the small pile next to him. "Here you go . . . *Fables of the Unsung*."

Maia had read the *Fables of the Unsung* many times since the challenge began, but the version Maks held out for her was different from the ones she had seen. For one thing, it was a very old copy. It was also illustrated. Curious, Maia flipped through the pages, her eyes devouring the lively art that accompanied every story. She went to *The Broken Jueyue of Hanuk Nai* last and read through the tale. The story was almost the same as the one Zaara had narrated, but it was the illustration that captivated Maia. It showed Mindoza swimming across the seas, carrying an open basket on his head that presumably contained the heart of the moon. The waters around him were churning, and waves rose high above him. Dark clouds swirled overhead and lightning bolts tore down on him from the skies.

For a while, Maia looked. Then she sat up as suddenly as a spring uncoiling.

Lightning bolts! That meant electricity.

That is what we are missing. That's where the Challowist task fits in.

She jumped off the wall, book in hand. "Maks, do you mind if I keep this book for a little bit? I will return it this afternoon."

"Keep it, Maia. I told you, I have the whole darned thing memorized anyway."

"Thank you, Maks. I have to go now."

Maia had barely gone a few paces when she stopped and rushed back to the boy, who sat with a perplexed look on his face. She flung her arms around him and held him for a moment.

"You're a hero, Maks," Maia said, releasing him.

"Really? But I did noth —"

"No, seriously. You might have just saved us all. Thank you."

Maia sprinted back to the living quarters, grinning like a crazy person all the way. Nafi peeked out from behind a mountain of books as Maia ran into the AR. Her eyebrows came together almost instantaneously.

"Are you all right?"

Maia dropped into the chair next to her, placed the book of fables on the table, and tapped it. "I think I know what it is."

Very soon, Nafi had been told. Soon after, Dani, along with a drowsy and unwilling Ren, plodded into the room. However grouchy Ren might have been, it did not take long for his face to brighten. In no time, all of them were clustered around a pail of seawater in which a sheet of Calbion was immersed, as Dani tinkered with the Taikorov generator. By the time the modified generator had been securely placed inside the pail, Kusha had arrived also.

The miracle they had been hoping for finally unfurled in front of their eyes. As time passed, the sheet of Calbion softened and curled, until by evening it had turned as pliant as a ribbon. By then Nafi had a proposal for how to use it. The girl had two enormous tomes open on either side of her, and one on her lap from which she read aloud.

"So, this is from the *Secrets of the Ancient Arborists*. Among the many tree-healing practices of the Solianese, the Uniter's knot was one of the most prevalent. This practice started in the fifth century. Jueyue trees, in the Third Continent particularly, were stricken by a virus that destroyed the strength of the trunk. Many trees lay broken, many split down the middle. Arborists devised a method to save the younger ones by putting a fungicide in the middle and tying them back together. They were able to save a considerable number of Jueyue."

"The Uniter's knot?" Kusha said. "As in Mindoza the Uniter?"

Nafi's eyebrows danced. "Sure sounds like it to me."

"But . . ." Maia could not make sense of it. "This is all about one stricken tree. And here we have two, neither of them sick. How do you—"

"I think"—Nafi raised a finger in the air and wagged it wisely—"I think we should tie the two together. It's all a play on unity. It's about bringing the two most unlikely plants together, and . . . who knows what will happen?"

"I hope them killing each other doesn't happen," Kusha said.

"It's very likely," Ren chimed in. "That Spore and the Silverblood . . . can't imagine them together."

"We'll have one more set to test if they do," Dani said. "Anything else, Nafi?"

Nafi picked up the other two books, almost toppling under their weight. "The Uniter's knot is a very specific way of tying and I have sort of figured it out. Need to sketch it, I think."

"Come on, let's do it." Ren was up on his feet in an instant and together with Nafi, he soon had a good drawing prepared.

Plans came together swiftly. Pails were carried over to the Glass House, as was the stash of Calbion. They toiled through the night, carefully wrapping the ribbons of Calbion around the two plants so their stems were one.

"Let's hope for a miracle now," Dani said, clasping her hands in prayer.

Everyone was so excited that night that even though they were bone-tired, they decided to stay at the Glass House to wait and watch.

* * *

Maia had no idea when she had drifted into sleep, but voices and a sharp prodding at her shoulder made her jump up with a start. She found herself in the middle of a sleepy huddle of teammates on one side of the Glass House. Zaara was glaring at them, and behind her, Tessio clutched his belly and laughed silently.

"What is the meaning of this?" Zaara demanded once the team had found their bearings. "In case you did not realize, this is not your living quarters."

"There's no rule against sleeping here," Ren muttered grumpily.

Zaara's eyes flashed but before she could utter another word, Dani spoke. "Sorry. We're very sorry. Didn't mean to break any rules.

CHAPTER FORTY-THREE

We were just tired and —"

"Cut the blabber," Zaara snapped. "I have reports that you worked all night. What for?"

Nafi, who had been twitching with impatience, blurted, "We did something to our plants and . . . can we check now, please?"

Zaara had barely made room before Nafi shot past and peeked into Core 21's enclosure. Then she screamed. And kept on screaming. Maia and the rest of her teammates, as well as Zaara and Tessio, joined her in the next moment. As Maia took in the sight inside their enclosure, she forgot to breathe.

The Spore had disappeared. The Silverblood fern had grown, having clearly absorbed the poisonous plant. Underneath it, the ground looked softer, as if it had been suddenly rejuvenated.

"S-so then, this is really it?" Kusha blurted.

Tessio broke into chortles. "Yes, it is. You have done it. This is how the healing begins."

"And . . . this is how the Alliance Initiative ends," Zaara said before turning away.

Maia could not stop staring incredulously at the plants. It was a miracle that no one could have expected. Yet, obviously, someone — Zaara most likely — had known and planned this. A thought, a memory flashed through her mind. Maia turned on her heel and rushed after Zaara. She found the woman striding out of the Glass House.

"Zaara, wait," Maia shouted.

Zaara turned around, lips pursed. "You will never stop screaming my name, will you?" she said in a voice heavy with disapproval.

Maia hardly registered her annoyance. Her mind was rushing to make connections. "Those ferns in Korobieltes . . . did they somehow have Calbion in them too?"

Zaara stared at her for a moment, her eyes taking on that glazed look Maia knew so well. The woman was drifting into the past.

"It was our experiment," she said in a hushed voice. "Sophie and I managed to get some Calbion from Xif. We had heard stories of its healing properties, and we tried. It was a tiny amount and it took time, but how those ferns grew." Her gaze was clear, her face hard when she looked at Maia. "We requested more Calbion, just enough so we could experiment a little. We dreamed of bringing Korobieltes back to life. But, guess what they told us?"

Maia did not have to guess, she knew. The Xifarians refused.

"They said Tansi was not worth it. That Calbion was precious and there were better uses for every flake of it. That is what your darling friends the Xifarians said."

As Maia flinched at Zaara's biting words, the woman continued. "That's why when they roped me in as arbitrator, I extended the Initiative. That Hilledunn only had three separate tasks for you originally. No creativity at all. I decided to tie the tasks together. I thought . . . I will get some Calbion out of those Xifarians this time." She stopped and chuckled to herself. "Now that all of the materials excavated stay on Tansi, I get to continue the project Sophie and I started."

As Zaara walked away, happy at how she had outsmarted the Xifarians, Maia wondered how much peace that had brought her. And how long would it last? Could Zaara ever have a life unshadowed by her times with Sophie?

Her musings came to a quick end when Nafi bobbed over to her side. "Come on, Maia. We won. It's time to celebrate."'

Indeed, it was. Finally, it was time to be happy.

CHAPTER FORTY-FOUR

THE SENTINELS

The day the Alliance Initiative ended was one of the happiest Maia could remember. For the first time in two weeks, she was eager and excited to get out of bed and get ready for the day. Gloomier thoughts came, but they quickly dispersed, pushed out by the happiness their achievement brought. Her heart ached just as badly from time to time, but again, it was easy to push that away. All she had to do was think of the prize that awaited her and the relief that awaited Tansi.

They had been asked to congregate at the pavilion in the afternoon, yet Maia was ready by midmorning. If she could, she would go there immediately and wait out the time.

Seigvard!

Seigvard will be mine. Ruche will be happy. Tansi will be safe.

"Maia." Sana threw her arms around Maia as she sat on the windowsill, smiling. "It's so good to see you happy."

"We did it, Sana," Maia said. "We did it. We finally did it."

They were soon on the way to the refectory, and after a boisterous breakfast, the gang trooped toward the pavilion.

"Hans and Rayan are coming back today," Dani chirped as they marched happily forward. "Hans says after this is over, we can all go to Zagran for a real vacation. It'll be so much fun. Just like the last time."

Although Maia smiled in response, she was not sure how much fun such a trip would be. It would definitely not be like the last time. Things had changed since then. She was not the same Maia anymore and . . .

Stop it! Get a grip on yourself. Enjoy the day.

Maia firmly banished the gloomy thoughts. Now was not the time to think about anything else. Now she was going to revel in the joy of their win.

However, some things are easier said than done. As soon as the pavilion came into view, gleaming in the sun with its ornate iron columns and its stone-carved balustrade, memories of the last afternoon there flooded Maia's mind. Her feet grew sluggish as every word she had exchanged with Miir that day stomped through her heart and left her shaken.

"Maia!" The excited and unexpected voice instantly yanked Maia out of her melancholy and left her smiling again. A bevy of bright faces surrounded her, their eyes sparkling. They were her dorers, or as Nafi liked to call them, her army. She recognized a few of them right away: the boy Merin, Aiani, and Lonnie, the little girl with long braids.

"You won, you won!" Merin exclaimed and jumped around in circles around Maia. "You won."

Seeing his flushed, jubilant face, Maia wondered if she was half as happy as he was that she won.

"This is for you, Maia." Lonnie pushed a big brown lump at her. Maia realized it was a cloth toy, a lizard to be exact, a replica of the one Lonnie always carried. "We have twin lizards now, only yours is shiny."

"You made this yourself?" As the little girl nodded proudly,

Maia's eyes welled up with tears of gratitude. She had done nothing to deserve this, nothing at all. Clutching the shiny brown lizard tight, she pulled Lonnie into a hug. "Thank you. I will treasure this always."

The pavilion had already gathered a considerable audience. The five top teams were all present, obviously. Other than that, it was mostly filled with students of ThulaSu, and some monks were there as well. Maia spotted the Appian trio on one side—Maks and his friends, Aman and Nisa—along with Jez and some more of their classmates, and they waved at her cheerily.

What a happy day, Maia thought, *with everyone around us to celebrate.* A smile had barely curled her lips when her thoughts screeched to a halt, her heart twinging.

No! Not everyone. She did not have the one person with whom she really wanted to share the joy of this moment. Maia's yearning gaze scanned the pavilion once. Then a wry chuckle made her mouth twist as she realized the futility of the effort.

He's not going to come, Maia. All because of you and your senseless sentiments. You have ruined it all. It was unfair—to Miir who deserved to celebrate with them, to her teammates who undoubtedly missed him.

A gentle touch on her arm made Maia blink and look up with a start. She found Dani staring, her gaze curious . . . concerned. Flashing a quick smile at Dani and hoping she would not ask questions, Maia forced her attention elsewhere.

A small area near the entrance had been cordoned off, and Maia assumed that was where the prizes would be handed out. A few chairs had been placed inside the roped-off section as well as the area right outside, perhaps for the arbitration committee members and visiting dignitaries. Maia wondered if Mahswa Tabrin would be there, if she was well enough to attend.

"Just look at them." Nafi's exasperated voice brought Maia out of her musing. She looked in the direction Nafi was glaring and chuckled immediately. The Silver Wings Fan Club was in action at the far corner of the pavilion. Ren and Karhann, both wearing sparkly garlands, posed for photos and signed autographs. Boys and girls—mostly swooning girls—encircled them.

"It's about time you got used to it, Nafi," Kusha commented.

Nafi returned a glare. "Nafi does not get used to silliness. Ever."

"The K is back," Sana said, and Maia hastily looked away from Ren and Karhann's shenanigans with the fan club. Two men brought Master Kehorkjin in on a carrying chair, Principal Pomewege following the group. Maia placed the lizard toy in Sana's arms and rushed over to Kehorkjin as he eased into one of the chairs in the roped-off area.

"Master Kehorkjin," she cried, ecstatic to see him well. Sinking to her knees next to the master, she threw her arms around him. "So happy to see you again."

The smile Kehorkjin returned as he affectionately patted Maia's head was just as joyful. Soon the whole team, and then every other team, surrounded the master. Seeing the way Kehorkjin laughed and chatted with everyone, no one could have told this was the same grim-faced master who had greeted them at the XDA years ago.

"All right, all right, move back, everyone. The master is not done recovering. Give him some space now." Aerika's sharp voice ended the excited chatter, and the huddle around Kehorkjin fell away in an instant. Aerika's voice had been sharp, but that was where the sternness ended. A warm smile graced her face, and even though she valiantly shooed the youngsters away, there was no hiding the fact that she too, was happy to be with them all.

The only grim one was Zaara. Towering and stiff, she stood to one side clutching a scroll, Monk Tessio and the wall of team mentors behind her. She did not speak with anyone, or even look at anyone. A sigh wafted out of Maia. It was strange indeed that the one person she should have been truly happy to see was the one for whom she could find no feelings, that someone who had been her mother's best friend meant so little to her. It did not have to be this way, yet . . .

A stream of people walking into the pavilion drew Maia out of her musings. All the leaders walked in—Solianese House leaders and their representatives, the Parliamentary council including Uncle Alasdair, Jjordic Premier Oliena and CA Abebe, and finally, Rahina Quemiila and her advisors Taillefei and Lowanabe, Ren's stepfather. Behind the Xifarian group were six chancery guards, all of them carrying boxes.

Maia's eyes searched for Mahswa Tabrin, the woman's absence making her heart sink a little with worry. They had not heard anything about the Mahswa in recent months, and Maia hoped she was well.

One by one, the dignitaries took their seats. Once they were all seated, Zaara started speaking in a flat, bitter voice.

"We are happy to announce that the Alliance Initiative is finally concluded. We thank all the participants for their enthusiasm and their hard work, the team mentors who have supported them despite their own workloads, the teachers who have guided and spearheaded the effort, and every person who has helped to make this project a success. I will now announce the results."

Zaara had unfurled the scroll she was holding when Principal Pomewege raised a hand. "May I, please, say a few words?"

Zaara nodded, and the principal walked to the center. His adoring gaze swept over the huddle of contestants on the side, and his voice shook when he started, "When we began this peace project more than three years ago, it seemed like an audacious dream. I never thought we could come this far. I truly never had the courage to believe that we would. But I loved the idea of it and I decided to give it everything I could give—my complete and steadfast support."

His eyes swept across the contestants' faces once more. "You were all littler then. Little sputters of energy, all disparate, all with their own dreams and aspirations. All of you had promising futures, I could tell from the scouts' accounts of each of you. Some of you, I chanced to find myself." He paused and looked meaningfully at Maia and Kusha.

Maia's mind flew to that day in Shiloh when she had flown Kusha's glider, and then to the night when she had found the

Xifarians in her home. Pomewege had come, along with Miir, to change the life she had known. Forever.

Pomewege's voice boomed again, and Maia forced her attention back to the present.

"I could tell the beginning was not smooth. I could see the differences in you, all struggling to understand, appreciate, and if possible, care for each other. And I look at you now." He stopped and smiled. "I am astounded by the way you have grown. Friends, families, coming together in a bond I did not dare dream of all those years ago. I am also astounded by the way you and your endeavors have touched us all. I know that I have been forever changed. We have come through so many twists and turns, but we have made it to the end, together. And no matter who wins the top prize and who does not, remember that you are all winners to have come this far." He stopped again and bowed a little. "It has been an honor to know you all, generation of the future. Do us proud."

Applause erupted and seemed to go on forever. Principal Pomewege's words had made Maia teary-eyed. Truer words had never been spoken. How far they had all come, from a group of naive little kids to the verge of adulthood, although still bickering just as often. How they had changed, how their closed hearts full of distrust had slowly opened and made room for understanding.

"Now for the results." The cheers and claps died down at Zaara's sharp voice. "I would like to invite Rahina Quemiila to award the prizes to our deserving contestants."

Rahina Quemiila made her way to Zaara's side, and the guards followed, open boxes in their hands. Maia clutched Dani's hand, her heart pounding as Zaara read her scroll.

"In fifth place, we have Core 34," Zaara announced.

Kenan and his teammates walked up to the stage amid applause and cheers, and each of them received a beautiful crystal trophy—a curved stem on top of which was a crystal crown with gold tips.

"Core 10."

The all-Jjord team whooped and bounded up to the stage next.

CHAPTER FORTY-FOUR

"Core 7."

Cheers followed Karhann and his teammates as they walked up to receive their trophies. Karhann looked content, but the rest of his mates were clearly indignant. Loriine had a smile on that looked anything but natural, and the rest did not have a shred of joy on their faces.

"This is surprising," Nafi whispered and immediately received glares from her teammates. She simply shrugged and whispered some more. "What? I didn't expect those fools to come in third. Can't I have opinions anymore?"

Maia had to admit, even though she kept her thoughts to herself, that it was surprising to see Core 7 in third place. Core 7 had always been fierce competitors, and Maia often worried that they would be too hard to beat. Karhann was right; had Loriine and Bakhari behaved better, they would have had a good chance at winning.

Maia did not get to ponder on it any longer since Zaara was about to read the name of the runners-up. Dani's cold, nervous fingers tightened around her. Maia's own heart beat up a storm and she prayed and she prayed —

"Core 13."

A gasp of relief escaped Maia. They had won, they had won after all. Putting her own joy to the side for the moment, she clapped as hard as she could, happy that Core 13 — Jiri, Anja, Luem, Nair, Corin — had come in second. Not only did she have good friendships with every member of that team, especially Anja, who hailed from Shiloh, but she also knew how hard that team always worked, and how they always fought fairly.

"And so, the top honors go to . . . Core 21."

Thunderous did not quite capture the tumultuous applause that rolled across the pavilion. Maia barely felt the ground under her feet as she walked up to the center of the stage along with her teammates.

"Here are the Sentinels of the Tansian Passage," Principal Pomewege shouted.

One by one they received the trophies, bowing, thanking, and laughing all the way. The trophies were even more beautiful up close. As Maia gazed at the one in her hands, she could not have felt happier or prouder of herself, her team, and of every step they had taken together, fearlessly and honestly.

Wish Dada was here. And Herc. And Emmy. They would be so proud.

"Finally, to the special honor for the most valuable member of the winning team. Points and recommendations from teachers and mentors, as well as accounts of team members from each phase, were tallied for every member. And the winner is . . ."

Zaara stopped, a frown growing on her forehead as she read the name. Maia held her breath when the woman looked up and glanced at her, eyes narrowed.

"Maia."

"All right," Ren shouted behind her.

Maia's heart beat like a drum inside her as she walked up to the Xifarian queen once more, her eyes eager to find Seigvard. A guard behind the queen held a box, much bigger than the one that held the trophies for each team. The queen reached inside and pulled out the prize. Maia's heart thudded incessantly. Then it dropped to the pit of her stomach.

It was not Seigvard. It was not a sword at all. It was a replica of Tansi. One just like the others they had seen in the Gallery of Planets at the XDA. Beautiful and perfect down to the last detail.

But not Seigvard.

"Are you going to accept your award?"

The queen's voice jolted Maia back to life. She stepped closer with numbed legs and reached for the replica with cold hands.

"Thank you," her lips whispered.

"Not what you expected, is it?"

In that fleeting moment that Maia held the queen's gaze before retreating to the supportive huddle of her teammates, the facts — as clear as the daylight that streamed around her — stared back at Maia.

Rahina Quemiila knows. She knew I wanted Seigvard, and she deliberately switched the prize.

Maia's mind was blank. People came and went, talking, congratulating them. She responded, unfeeling, unthinking, like an automaton, smiling, thanking, over and over. Her mind was stuck in a ceaseless whirlpool. The idea that they had won the Initiative, and yet Seigvard was not hers, took a long time to settle in her mind.

By the time the consequences sank in, the pavilion was nearly empty. The audience had mostly dispersed, the masters and Aerika had left. Most of the dignitaries were walking out the entrance and down the pathway toward the enclave of buildings to the north.

This cannot be. This is a mistake, and it has to be corrected.

The best chance Tansi had, and Xif too for that matter, was for her to acquire Seigvard. So Ruche had said over and over. And now . . .

"Hold this, Nafi," Maia said, as she placed the replica in Nafi's arms. She knew there was little chance of anything changing, but she had to ask. She had to know. Fists curled, she rushed up to the Xifarian queen.

"One moment please, Rahina Mayen," she called, hoping her voice would carry across the entourage that surrounded the woman.

The queen turned, slowly, her fiery hazel eyes burning on Maia's face as they scanned her.

"Yes, you have a question?"

"I do." Maia braced herself as she gathered up all her courage to mouth her question. "Why did you change the prize? Mahswa Tabrin intended Seigvard—"

The queen's eyes narrowed dangerously. Taillefei's face turned a violent shade of red and his lips parted in a vicious snarl.

"How dare you?" Taillefei spat the words out. "You—"

"Statesman Taillefei, let me handle this. I ask for some privacy," the queen said in a calm, cold voice. Taillefei immediately ushered the rest of the queen's coterie away and Maia's friends stepped back a little as well. Maia's insides trembled as the queen gazed at her. The only thing that stopped her knees from buckling was the presence of all her teammates behind her. It did not lessen the pain of the queen's next words.

"The honorable Mahswa Tabrin is no more with us. We lost her some time ago." The queen closed her eyes and lowered her head for a moment or two before speaking again. "Yes, it was her intent to grant Seigvard to the winning team, but with her passing, Seigvard's fate is mine to decide now. And I do not believe you are a worthy recipient of that legendary sword. That is why I changed the prize."

Words, so many words. They came at Maia's dazed mind like projectile fire, leaving her breathless.

Mahswa Tabrin . . . gone, forever. She had not even known.

A worthy recipient . . . she was not. But she was the one who could use it to help them all.

"But, I-I don't need it for myself. I need it for all of us. To help Tansi, and your Xif as well."

The queen's eyes flashed. "You need not worry about my Xif. I can take care of it. I believe I have told you that before."

"Please, please understand," Maia begged, forgetting how miserable a picture she presented. She did not care what they thought of her; all that mattered was the millions of lives at stake. "Believe me. . . I don't need Seigvard for myself. I need it to stop the R'armimon. There is no other way to end this. I will return it to you when my work is done, I promise."

For a moment that felt like forever, the Rahina stared at her. At that moment, it felt like she would give in to Maia's earnest request. Then her eyes hardened and Maia knew there was no Seigvard to be had.

"Is that so? If that is true, what stopped you from coming to me and telling me the truth? Why the subterfuge?"

"Because I couldn't." Ruche had asked her to go about it by herself, find her own path. Nor would she dare to tell the Xifarian queen anything like that. She could never hope the queen could trust her. "I didn't think—"

"You hid the truth and went about thinking you could get your hands on Seigvard one way or another? You thought no one would notice? You did not think I would have my eye on you?" The queen's sharp gaze scoured Maia's face. "You are no different from your mother. You would say anything, do anything to get your hands on a sacred artifact. You would hide, you would lie, you would betray the people closest to you."

"That's not true," Maia protested. "I wouldn't betray anyone. I—"

"You forget that I can see through your false words. That sweet, innocent face does not fool me for a moment." Maia shuddered as another scathing look swept over her. "You shall never have Seigvard. I will see to that."

She turned and walked away, but Taillefei's sneering face lingered a bit longer. A hand clutched her arm and Maia knew it was Dani.

"Come on, Maia," she said.

Nafi spoke up on her other side. "You tried, Maia. We all tried. It is what it is."

Indeed. She had tried her best, given it her all. For nothing. Maia turned and trudged to a bench near the walls, surrounded by her friends.

It was all over for Tansi. And for all of them.

Maia sat with her eyes closed, unable to think or feel anymore. Then someone nudged her. She found Zaara standing in front of her, her eyes full of mockery.

"You just *had* to beg, didn't you?" Zaara hissed. Somehow, even though she was nowhere near, she must have heard the conversation about Seigvard. "You thought that woman would give you what you wanted just because you asked nicely?"

"Yes, I did. I had to ask."

"I'm ashamed of you, and disappointed. You will never learn." Zaara shook her head. "You should know better than to trust their kind and think they'll do the right thing. They'll trample all over you, girl. And leave you for dead when you're of no use. That's Xifarians for you."

Maia had no strength left in her to fight Zaara. Her insides were crumbling into an abyss of darkness, of hopelessness. Still, she managed to find a few words. "That's not true. There is good everywhere. You can't make me think otherwise."

Zaara had just started to laugh when Ren sprang up. "Do you have anything *useful* to say?" he demanded, crossing his arms as he faced the woman. "If not, leave us alone."

Zaara's fiery gaze snapped onto Ren. "You . . . another one of them. Pretending to be Maia's friend while you plot and plan to betray her."

"You have no idea what friendship is," Ren shot back. "If you were a true friend to Sophie, you'd have been there for her daughter every step of the way, and not try to tear her down every chance you get. You'd be comforting Maia now instead of laughing at her and ridiculing her. Anyway, explanations are clearly wasted on you. So just leave, let Maia be."

A breathless silence descended upon them for a moment or two. Then Zaara hissed.

"Those words would've got you killed, boy. But you are lucky. The world is ending anyway, so I will let you be. Live another day or two. But I know your kind, you are—"

Dani rushed to Ren's side, her gaze matching Zaara's fierce one. "Perhaps you didn't hear clearly enough. Leave now. We don't want to hear another word."

One by one—Kusha, Nafi, Sana—they stood up, forming a wall of collective defiance against Zaara's scorn. Soaking them all with another glare, Zaara stomped away and Maia breathed in relief. Her friends came back to her side and for a while, they stood in a huddle, wordless until Ren broke the silence.

"Hey, guys, I have to catch Principal Pomewege before he leaves for Frauz Point. See you later, all right?" With a reassuring pat on Maia's shoulder, he bounded away.

"We need a place to keep this stupid thing," Nafi said, gesturing at the replica of Tansi she had been cradling.

"Come on, I know just the right place for it," Kusha said. "We'll see you back at the AR." With that, Kusha and Nafi walked away as well.

The three girls stayed there for a while before Dani tugged Maia's arm. "Let's go back and get some rest, Maia. Come on."

Maia had no interest or energy left in her to make it all the way back to the living quarters. Her head was a muddle of thoughts, and she had to clear it first. Rest would come later. But seeing that Dani and Sana were eager to get away from the pavilion, Maia trudged along. They were almost to the entrance when Dani suddenly stopped, her hand clutching Maia's arm.

"Oh no! What is Miir doing?"

Maia's stupor cracked in an instant. She peered in the direction Dani was looking, her heart beating wildly when she saw the scene. Miir stood facing the Xifarian queen and her advisors, Lowanabe and Taillefei. Behind Miir, forming a half-circle, were six chancery guards. Judging by the expressions on everyone's faces, they were not having a cordial conversation.

"What is he doing?" Dani whispered. "Doesn't he realize they'll arrest him?"

"I'm sure he does, Dani," Sana said in a calm voice. "I think he can take care of himself perfectly well. There's no need for us to worry."

Dani stared wide-eyed at Sana before she looked at Maia.

"Maia?"

Maia did not know what to say. She wanted to rush in and pull Miir away, but she knew that was a foolish thought. The reality was that she was in no position to help.

"You think the Rahina will listen to anything we say?" she said in the end. "We surely can't fight all those chancery guards."

Her heart twitched seeing Dani's face fall, but other than watching them argue, there was nothing to be done.

"Maybe we can round up some Kausakas just in case," Dani suggested next.

That sounded like a good plan. Maia had just nodded when the huddle of Xifarians suddenly fell apart. The Rahina waved her hand in dismissal. The guards made way, and Miir, after a hasty bow to the queen, strode away in the direction of the Sun Temple, while the queen and her advisors continued along the pathway.

Dani exhaled loudly. "That was a close one," she said.

Indeed. Maia sighed in relief. Her knees shook a little from pent-up anxiety and tiredness.

"Let's just sit here for a bit, Dani," she said. "I'm too exhausted to walk back right now."

Sinking onto the nearest bench, Maia pulled her knees to her chest and laid her head on them. She had no strength, no hope, and nothing to look forward to.

CHAPTER FORTY-FIVE

A TAINTED INHERITANCE

Maia sat in the corner of the empty pavilion, trying hard to think. Sana and Dani sat on either side of her, both quiet and lost in their own thoughts. No matter how hard she tried, Maia's mind drew a blank. The idea that they had won the Initiative and yet Seigvard was still lost to her felt so unbelievable that Maia could hardly move past it. She was frozen in the moment where the Rahina presented the prize, and it was not what Maia had hoped and fought for so long.

"Mahswa Tabrin might have lived if she'd stayed in Zagran," she said, the loss of something bigger than the sword hitting her suddenly in the gut.

Dani looked up at her, her gaze anxious. "I'm sure she received good care on Xif, Maia."

Maia nodded. "I hope so."

Sana sat up. "Maia, pull yourself together," she said forcefully. "Nothing changes if you don't have Seigvard, does it? Aekken still wouldn't dare destroy Xif because it would harm you, and even if he did, we have the shield. It may not be perfect, but it's enough to avoid complete annihilation."

Sana's words stirred Maia out of her stupor. Although it still seemed to her like wishful thinking, there was a possibility that Sana was right. The basics had not changed. Or at least the fact was that until she spoke with Ruche, she could not be sure about the implications of this setback. There was no reason to be distressed. Yet.

"I need to speak with Ruche," Maia said, jumping to her feet. "He will know what to do next. He must have another plan."

With Dani and Sana behind her, Maia rushed up the side stairs out of the pavilion to the pathway leading up to the Sun Temple. She was focused on the ring that was Ruche's calling card, trying to reach the seer. She screeched to a halt as soon as she turned the corner of the first building, her heart almost leaping out of her chest.

She had missed, barely by a hair's breadth, bumping into Miir as he came in the opposite direction. This was the first time she had come face to face with him since their disastrous last conversation, and as much as Maia wanted to think she had overcome the heartache and embarrassment, she realized she had been lying to herself. She could hardly breathe or even blink, her mind stuck in a strange state of shock and panic. Miir seemed similarly frozen. However, he swiftly recovered.

"Could you please come with me?" he asked Maia, his gaze barely staying on her face.

Before Maia had the chance to consider what he was asking, let alone answer, Sana shot forward, frowning.

"Why? Why should she come with you?" It was clear from her tone that Sana had forgotten all about her promise to be civil toward Miir.

Miir's eyes widened at Sana's openly combative tone. Maia had no idea what he wanted from her, but she expected him to return a forceful answer to Sana's question. He did not.

"So she can speak with the Rahina about Seigvard," he said, his voice low.

"Maia already asked her for Seigvard once," Sana said. "What's the point of asking again? All that arrogant woman will do is refuse, and spew a thousand nasty words while she's at it."

"Maybe not," Miir said. He turned toward Maia. "I might have found something. If you want to give it a try —"

"Stop, stop." Sana held her hands up. "Didn't the queen just drive you away? You expect us to believe she'll speak to you again?"

"Yes," Miir said. "I have no doubt. As I said, I might have a way to make it work."

"What way? What have you found, exactly?" Sana sounded far from convinced.

"I cannot tell you. Not yet. Not until I am sure what I think is correct —"

Sana crossed her arms and fixed a frowning gaze on Miir. "So you're sure and then you're not sure. And you expect Maia to just trust you and follow you wherever you lead her?"

"Wherever?" Miir frowned back. "I am only trying to help her get Seigvard. That is all." He turned toward Maia again. "There is a good chance the Rahina will be harsh to you, but there is also a chance she will give you Seigvard and . . . restore your pendant. If you are willing to take the risk, I will take you to her."

"No!" Sana said.

"It is not your choice to make," Miir replied, quietly but just as firmly.

Looking at Sana's puckered face, her determination to protect her, Maia's heart filled with gratitude. It was not that she did not fear what would come of Miir's plan. But how could she not try, knowing there was still a way to acquire Seigvard? She *had* to try.

She placed a hand on Sana's arm. "Sana, I have to see what this is. I can't just say no because I'm afraid. It's not just about me. So much more depends on this."

"Oh, Maia." Sana shook her head in frustration and finally let out a resigned sigh. "Fine. Then I'll come with you."

Dani, who had been quiet all along, rushed forward and clutched

Maia's hand. "Can we come with her, Miir? Please?"

Miir did not miss the way Dani's arm wrapped around Maia's. He flashed a small, apologetic smile. "I am sorry. No, you cannot come inside," he said. "But I will be with her."

Sana looked away with a huff. By the way Miir's face tightened, the dismissive gesture was not lost on him. He did not say any more, however. He led them further down the pathway and around some turns to where the path led up to a small red building before turning eastward. A pair of chancery guards and some Kausakas flanked the entrance, and Maia deduced that was where the council had convened.

"Wait here," Miir said to Dani and Sana, pointing to some benches on one side of the pathway.

Maia realized how well-planned the venture was by how as soon as they approached, Dorian and a few Black Phantoms appeared at the far end of the path. Someone whistled and after that, things unfolded swiftly. Two of the Kausakas at the door drew their weapons on the chancery guards and moved them aside. Two more Kausakas placed themselves on either side of the entrance. Miir gestured at Dorian and walked up to the door.

"Ready?" he asked Maia. As soon as she nodded, he threw the door open.

A room with a large table at its center met their eyes. Rahina Quemiila and her advisors, Lowanabe and Taillefei, were seated around the table with Sahiiraan Tsininio and CA Abebe. A few other people, assistants, and personnel were scattered around the seated group. A cluster of chancery guards stood along the left wall, and Kausakas were lined up along the other. All the chancery guards drew their weapons and surrounded the queen as soon as they walked in. Taillefei and Lowanabe jumped up.

"What is the meaning of this?" Lowanabe yelled.

"Did you just force your way in here?" Taillefei hissed at Miir.

"I did," Miir replied calmly before nodding at the queen. "I would like to speak with you."

"Again?" Rahina Quemiila's eyes flashed. Her gaze shifted to Maia and her expression changed from anger and frustration to something harder . . . colder. A shiver threatened to speed up Maia's spine, but she did not let it. Fists tight, she squared her shoulders. The queen snapped back toward Miir again.

"Why are you here?" the queen demanded. "Why have you brought *her* here?"

"I am surprised you ask that," Miir said. His voice, cold and sharp, was not one Maia would have expected any Xifarian to use with their queen. The queen's face grew grim as he spoke. "Of all the things that have been whispered about you, there has never been any doubts about your intellect. So you must know why."

"Miir! This is shameful," Taillefei burst out. He shook his head vigorously. "Those words! This behavior does not befit your upbringing. You should know this is not how we speak to Rahina Mayen. Think of your heritage. Have you no respect for it?"

Miir did not even flinch. "Did you not notice that I deserted that heritage a while ago? Besides, someone who tried to steal the ark of Tansi should not be the one boasting of heritage."

Taillefei's face flamed. "How dare you say—"

"Statesman Taillefei," the queen interrupted. "Please. I need some privacy."

She nodded at a bearded guard—Maia recognized him as the leader of the queen's guards from the encounter at Frauz Point—and he immediately led everyone out of the room. Taillefei and Lowanabe, along with Sahiiraan Goren and CA Abebe, were the last ones to leave.

As soon as the door closed behind them, the queen chuckled wryly and shook her head. When she looked at Miir again, her eyes narrowed to slits. "You have the gall to confront me like this. You . . . a fugitive who I can and should drag to prison right now. Are you not afraid of that? I excused you once, but you seem to be bent on getting yourself killed. All for her?"

"For the truth," he replied. "She needs to know it. She deserves it."

Maia looked from Miir's face to the Rahina's, confused by their conversation. What truth could they be talking about? She wished Miir could have told her before they walked in.

"Deserves?" Rahina Quemiila spat the word out so forcefully that Maia almost jumped. "She deserves nothing. She's the daughter of a traitor who destroyed our world. Even so, I have been kind. I was expected to help restore the Sedara, I was expected to champion Phocluus's agenda. Yet I refused. She should be thankful that I did."

So far, their retorts had come at a frenetic pace. Now suddenly, there was silence. The queen looked curiously at Miir when he did not reply right away. Maia saw the horrified look on Miir's face, and she also saw what could only be called mortification in the queen's eyes.

"Do not look at me like that," the woman whispered. "It is not your place to judge me."

Miir replied in a voice as steady as it was sullen. "I cannot believe you could bring up Phocluus, knowing what he wants to do to her. To Phocluus she is just a step toward achieving his goal, but to you . . ."

The queen's eyes narrowed dangerously. "So *that* is the unfounded slander you have come to peddle?"

"Unfounded? A resemblance so striking is hardly my imagination," Miir said.

What resemblance? Maia thought for a few utterly puzzling moments. A resemblance between the queen and herself, she realized slowly. The hazel eyes in the bronzed face, the slightly upturned chin—it looked familiar. It was as if . . . as if she were seeing a trace of herself. Familiar? The pieces fell into place slowly as her dazed mind struggled to cope. Were they related, then? How?

Miir went on. "But that is not all. There are countless other things that make a connection the only possibility."

Maia saw the queen's face freeze, the cold rage in her eyes vivid for a moment. Then she turned away and sighed. "As despicable as this topic is, it would have been bearable if you and I were alone in this conversation. But this girl . . . she should have been left outside, where she belongs."

"She should be outside? You forgive me for barging in like this, for speaking to you as if you were a commoner, and you find her mere presence too much to bear? She is the reason I am here, the reason we are having this conversation in the first place."

"I do not like your tone or your arrogance," the queen said in a voice cold and steely.

"I have heard that before, and I do not care," Miir retorted in a heartbeat. "You want to call someone a traitor, then you should call my mother one first. She was the one who planned it all. Yet you will not. We . . . my mother and I are so easily forgiven."

The Rahina's mouth twisted in a vicious snarl. "If you had a grain of sense left, you would stop fighting for this outsider and mend your ways. You still might be able to scrape yourself a future."

"She, an outsider?" Miir chuckled. "I am a traitor's child, just like she is. You know that. Yet you will speak with me, give me a chance at a future."

"That is because I still consider you one of us, because you come from an exemplary line of people, and because Xif owes your family a lot."

Miir drew a sharp breath. "And what about *her* family? What about the people she comes from? How can you reject . . . your own blood?" He stopped again and sighed. "Is this the heritage we are supposed to be proud of? Is our true heritage celebrating cruelty?"

"You expect me to acknowledge her? You should know, then. She is nothing to me," The queen hissed, anger twisting her face. "Her mother used my family to destroy our nation. Finagled her way into our world, our hearts, and used us like pawns to further her schemes. That girl brings nothing but dishonor and shame to everything I love and respect and hold dear."

Her words were like knives, and they plunged deep into Maia's heart and mind. She tried as hard as she could to put the pieces together. But her mind was racing too fast, and her heart, beating like a hammer inside her, raced even faster. Thoughts refused to coagulate, dissolving into a froth of confusion. She stepped forward nonetheless and forgetting the rules of distance she had decided to put between herself and Miir, her cold fingers reached for him. They did not make it to his arm, only clutched the sleeve of his shirt. He turned his concerned gaze on her in an instant.

"I don't understand," was all she managed to whisper.

"Rahina Quemiila is your grandmother," he said. His voice was gentle. The frigid sharpness from a moment ago had disappeared.

"What? How?"

"Raidyn is her son and . . . your father."

"How do you know?"

"I guessed. It seemed to be the logical conclusion from everything I knew — your pendant, your abilities, Yilosario's response to your touch, my mother's apologies to Raidyn, and yet her continual vagueness about him, the explanation for how they could access the Foundation Chamber. And why" — he gestured at the Rahina — "you are the spitting image of her."

Maia stared at his face, scanning his dark eyes. Was this really the truth? Miir went on, his voice obscured by the deafening sound of her heartbeat.

"I would have told you, but I wanted to be sure. I had no proof. But now . . . well, she just confirmed it."

Do you wonder why the light didn't consume you like it did your mother? Ruche's words streaked through Maia's mind. *This is why . . .* She was descended from Ataii's bloodline. Had Ruche known about Sophie and Raidyn?

"Do not look at me like you have found something," the queen said as Maia looked at her face once again, her eyes seeking out the similarities one more time. All Maia could see was anger, all she could hear was loathing as the queen continued in a low voice. "Raidyn made a mistake. He trusted your mother. And she tricked him into a sham of a marriage. All your mother wanted was to use his privileges as a Royal to get into the Foundation Chamber. All so she could strike at the heart of our world. My poor Raidyn, innocent and unsuspecting. But that is where it will end. I will not be like him. I will not allow you to make a fool out of me." She stepped nearer, eyes flashing with pain and fury. "I am no one to you. Do you understand? You are *nothing* to me, and never will be. You are here to get Seigvard, but you shall never have it. Never! I will not give you anything more than what your mother has already stolen from us."

"She needs that sword to end this situation, not for herself," Miir said.

The queen's eyes stilled for a moment, and Maia thought she saw hesitation ripple across her face. But in the next, anger washed it away. She snapped at Miir, vehemently spitting out words. "I see you have been swayed by her lies, but I will not fall for it."

"It is *not* a lie," Miir shot back with equal fervor. "Besides, Seigvard is her birthright. You cannot deny her that."

The queen scoffed. "Birthright? I accept none of your prattle. It is all just a bagful of falsehoods." Her mouth curled into a hard smile. "What will you do? Challenge me in public?"

"I would if it were up to me. But it is not." He paused and sighed. "This is as far as I can go. The truth is out. My work is done."

"Thank goodness for that. I need this foolish spectacle to be over."

My work is done . . .

It was weird, so ridiculously weird. Of all the things Maia had just heard, out of all the cruel words that pierced her soul, those were the ones that stung the most. The little patches she had put in place to keep her battered heart together fell off in an instant. What the shock of discovery and the queen's savage tirade did not do, those words managed in a moment. Maia's eyes burned.

The truth was out indeed. That *was* what she was to him, had always been . . . a job, a task to be finished.

Why couldn't she see him the same way? As the means to an end?

Miir was speaking, but his voice was faded, distant. "I grew up thinking, believing that we . . . Xifarians uphold and honor truth above everything else. That belief was shattered long ago. But I still hoped. I hoped there was some honor left in us. In you."

Maia took a step backward, away from them.

"I do not hand out honor to all and sundry, and certainly not to a liar whose intent to possess an artifact as sacred and hallowed as Seigvard is responsible for bringing on me the humiliation of this moment."

Shame, dishonor . . .

A mistake . . .

A liar . . .

Yes, she had asked for Seigvard. But not forever and not for herself, but to help Tansi and Xif against the R'armimon. How was that so wrong? Or so hard to believe?

Blinking furiously to keep the tears reined in, Maia turned away. "I want to leave," she said.

Her insides shook, and she feared she would break into pieces. She could not let that happen. Not in front of *them*. She had to get out of this room, out in the sun, and back with her friends. A chill swept up her spine, making her shudder violently as she stepped toward the door. Miir reached for her immediately. His touch on her elbow was warm, and his support so comforting. But Maia would not accept it. She snatched her arm away.

"The door," she said. "Please open the door."

The Rahina's scathing voice drifted to her ears as she left the room. "Do not show me your face again. And you, young man . . . if you dare to harass me one more time, I will set my guards on you and I promise you shall rot in a dungeon for the rest of your miserable life."

Dani and Sana rushed up to Maia as soon as she stepped outside. Their arms were around her, their voices soothing.

"What happened?" Dani asked.

"What did you do to her?" Sana demanded of Miir.

"I can explain now," Miir said. Maia walked away from them and their chatter, breathing in as much of the balmy afternoon air as she could, soaking in the warm rays of the sun. She kept on walking, striding away from everyone as fast as she could.

CHAPTER FORTY-FIVE

"Maia?" Dani called. "Wait."

"Need some time alone, Dani," Maia said. "Please."

They followed her, but kept their distance. Maia continued to walk, her eyes on the paved path ahead of her as her mind whirled with a relentless stream of words.

Sophie . . . Raidyn . . . Foundation Chamber . . . Yilosario . . . dishonor . . . mistake . . . liar . . .

Over and over they circled inside her head.

Maia's steps slowed as soon as she walked past the Sun Temple and her eyes picked out the gray silhouette on the ramparts.

"Ruche," she whispered.

She broke into a run, dashing along the path and up the stairs toward the seer of the R'armimon.

CHAPTER FORTY-SIX

THE END IS NEAR

Maia had rushed in Ruche's direction, wanting to tell him everything that had just happened and cry her heart out. But by the time she reached the seer, scorching anger engulfed her and drowned the ache in her heart. When Ruche placed a hand on her shoulder, she wished to fling it away, and when he gazed kindly at her, she wanted to turn her back on him.

He had known. He had to have known what was coming. And yet he had pushed her on in a direction that only brought her pain. She calmed herself as Ruche led her into the rose garden and sat her down on a bench. A couple of Ruche's Faceless in their silvery-gray uniforms stood guard at the gate.

"How are you, Maia?" Ruche asked.

Terrible, and it's all because of you.

Fists clenched, she stopped herself from uttering the words. She did not know for sure what Ruche had known. Besides, there were more important things than her own situation. Tansi and its people, what would happen to them?

"I failed, Ruche," Maia blurted. "Seigvard won't happen. Mahswa Tabrin is no more, and the Rahina changed the prize. I begged her, but—"

"You tried your best," Ruche said, his hand tightening on her shoulder. "It's *her* failure more than anyone else's. She couldn't move beyond the past."

The fire in Maia's head returned in an instant. Her gaze snapped up toward Ruche and she scanned his face. Her voice was hard when she spoke. "You know what happened. You knew Raidyn was my father, didn't you?"

He did not reply. Maia removed his hand from her shoulder. Her eyes stayed on his face as she whispered, "And yet you let me go to her. Do you know the names she called me?" Maia paused, her heart crumbling when his gaze dropped. "Of course you know. Did you want that to happen? Is my humiliation another part of your grand design?" A sob threatened to choke her but Maia stayed strong. "So you wanted to see me crushed and broken under a mountain of cruel words? Is that it? Your grand plan? Is that how Tansi gets a better future?"

"No, Maia, I did not want that," Ruche exclaimed. "I wanted you to be far from broken. I needed you to be happy and to have your heart healed. That is what my grand plan needed. And believe me, this I could never wish on you." He sighed, his gaze straying to the distance. "I did not know about Raidyn, Maia. Sophie was close to him, so I thought it was a possibility. I knew that for you to have held the light within you, you had to be of a bloodline as powerful as Princess Ataii's. I checked Sophie's family, but there was no one with any supernormal abilities until her. So I figured, even if you got the power to control the light from Sophie, the ability to hold it within you was because of your father. If Raidyn was a Royal, then with them being so close, he seemed the most likely answer to that question."

They sat facing each other, the silence between them prickly and painful, until Ruche spoke again.

"Believe me, I truly did not know about your father. Sophie's last year was a haze. Perhaps it was the force of the light that clouded my vision. I could not see her clearly at all. I did not even see their plan roll into motion. I could've helped them, if not directly, if I had known. I didn't. The fact is, I lost her for about a year, and I only saw her again when she was leaving Zagran with you, two days before she died." Ruche paused, his gaze sad and regretful as it washed over Maia. "When I first saw the queen, I thought I saw a resemblance. So I decided to let destiny take its own course. If what I suspected was true, then she would know. I was happy when you met her. I thought, just maybe, she'd see in you a bit of herself and open her heart to you. I was wrong. Leaving it up to you to piece it together was a mistake. Perhaps the worst one I've made."

There was a pang of sorrow in his tone, so deep that it shook Maia.

"I didn't piece it together, though. Someone else did."

"I know."

"And my father? Raidyn . . . where is he?"

"I don't know, Maia," Ruche said. "I can't see just anyone in the world, you know. I have to bind myself to their essence quite strongly to be able to follow them. Raidyn was never one I followed, so . . . I don't know." He rubbed the bridge of his nose and exhaled. "But seeing how things went with Sophie and her cohort, I would think—"

"He's dead?"

Ruche held Maia's gaze. As much as she wished otherwise, there was no hope in his eyes. A sigh escaped her, leaving her insides cold, utterly empty. She stiffened her spine in the next instant. What was she hoping for? What if Raidyn were alive? He'd probably reject her just as the Rahina had. She forced her wayward thoughts toward more urgent matters.

"So what next, Ruche? Do you have a plan—"

She did not get a chance to say another word because the air behind them shimmered. Ruche's hand clamped on her arm.

"Aekken's here," he whispered as he rose to his feet and pulled

Maia up with him. "Maia, listen to me. You can't show him your distress. Hide it the best you can."

Aekken appeared through the shimmering air, resplendent as always in his red velvet coat, six faceless guards in tow. As soon as they materialized, the guards spread out in an arc around Aekken.

Ruche bowed. "Crown Prince Aekken. I did not expect you here."

"How could I stay away, Seer? I received news that the Initiative has come to an end and the winners have been crowned. That meant felicitations were in order." Aekken turned his smiling face toward Maia. "You won, my starlight. My heartiest compliments." His eyes narrowed as he stared intently at her face. "You do not seem happy. Is this not the outcome you were looking for?"

Maia forced a smile, the brightest she could manage. "I am happy."

His eyes flashed momentarily. "I can see the pain in your eyes, my starlight. Someone must have misjudged your worth once again." He shook his head and let out a long sigh. "You do not belong here. Your place should be among the stars, your every step worshipped. The seer should advise you so."

"I am happy where I am, Prince Aekken," Maia said, hoping that her voice stayed steady enough to camouflage her pain.

"You underestimate your value, my starlight," Aekken said. "Regardless, I came to remind you that the time you asked for, the time I promised you, is over. I have to move forward now."

Maia's mind raced as she faced the near finality of the situation. Their time was up. Xif was as good as gone. There was no guarantee that Tansi would fare much better. The last she had heard, the shield was not immensely stable. Tansi, too, would suffer if Xif blew up next to it. There was still a chance total annihilation would follow. Except for the people in the Nouvus, nothing would be left alive in the Tansian system.

She held her breath as Aekken continued. "It is time I crushed those deadwastes and turned their planet to dust."

"Please," Maia pleaded. "There are so many people in there still.

They'll die, for no fault of their own."

"My starlight, I will not wait anymore. Unless . . . perhaps . . . you can ask the queen. Her head just might satisfy me." The gleeful tone in his voice as he said that made Maia's fingers turn cold. He walked closer and his eyes bored into Maia's face. "I hear you have discovered a special connection with her. Perhaps you could inspire her to lay down her life for her people."

"How in the stars did you—"

Ruche's outburst was cut short by Aekken's sharp, cold voice. "Find out? I have my means, Seer. Just like you have ways to keep track of the goings-on everywhere, I do also."

Ruche's face flamed. "Then you also realize Maia is Princess Ataii's blood. If it is her wish that you stand down, then that should be a command to you. The Crown will want to stand down."

Aekken laughed, the sound shredding the quiet of the late afternoon. "Do you think the Crown will disagree with me if I blast that filthy piece of rock from the sky? If so, you think wrong. I have the Crown's unwavering support, Seer Ruche."

Ruche's face stayed impassive, but Maia did not miss how the light in his eyes dimmed at Aekken's words. This was bad. If the emperor was in favor of Xif's destruction, there was little that could be done.

"I don't believe for a moment that the Crown would let harm come to a Nasfarii," Ruche said firmly. "You can't destroy Xif knowing what that might do to Tansi. So stop the threats and the bluff."

"Bluff?" Aekken snarled. "I'll show you what I can do, Seer!"

His hand snapped around Maia's arm and before Maia could clearly understand what was happening, Aekken had yanked her away from Ruche and toward himself. He pulled Bellator out of its sheath and threw it away.

"Aekken," Ruche yelled and rushed forward.

A lot of things happened next, all in a blur of motion. Aekken's other hand grabbed Ruche by the throat and his fingers curled and dug in.

"Prince Aekken, stop," Maia shrieked as Ruche gasped for breath.

The faceless warriors who had come with Ruche charged forward, but the ones Aekken had brought were swifter. They also far outnumbered the others. Blood flew and splattered as swords slashed through air and flesh. After a few moments of violence, all that remained were the lifeless, mangled bodies of Ruche's Faceless.

"Stop," Maia screamed again, a storm of panic engulfing her insides. She tried to calm herself and focus. She had to bring the light out quickly. But she only managed to stumble inward, her search yielding nothing but a wisp of smoke.

Aekken bared his teeth at her. "I would not try for that weapon if I wished for the seer to live," he said, his menacing voice leaving no doubt about his intentions.

"All right, I won't." Maia hastily submitted to Aekken's demand. "Please let him go. Please."

Aekken shoved Ruche to the ground and placed a foot on the seer's chest. "Seer Ruche, rest assured. I do not mean any harm to the Nasfarii. So please stay calm. I will be very disappointed and annoyed if you try any tricks."

He turned toward Maia and grasped her other arm. Something cold dug into Maia's skin and she felt the world swing in front of her eyes. The bloody scene in front of her, Ruche's helpless face, and the shaded quiet of the bowers started breaking into pieces. A chill, frigid and sharp, spread from the tips of her toes, and as it swept through her, it grew stronger. Maia gasped for air as the light faded and everything around her disappeared.

CHAPTER FORTY-SEVEN

CLEAR CHOICES

Darkness engulfed Maia. Then it passed, followed by a wave of bone-chilling cold. A room painted the color of blood slowly formed around her. It seemed fluid at first, the dark red walls wavering in front of her eyes, the floor, also red, a rolling wave under her feet. The only thing that remained constant through all of it was Aekken's vise-like grip on her arm. It was still there when with a final shudder, the room stabilized.

"Where am I?" A trembling whisper escaped Maia's parched throat. Her heart thudded wildly, and her fingers were cold as ice. Her mind raced endlessly, hopelessly, in search of answers.

"In the Beholding Chamber on my Imperial Battlecruiser," Aekken said.

"I want to go home," she said, her voice a piteous whimper.

Aekken did not appear to hear her. "I hope this ship is worthy of you. Do you approve of this room?"

This room? Maia wished she could sprint away from it as far as she could. But where could she go? She could not even see a door in the seemingly solid walls. She tried to pull her hand away from Aekken's. His fingers only tightened more until Maia winced. "You're hurting me."

"The solution to that is simple, my starlight. Do not fight me."

Fear formed a throbbing lump inside Maia's chest. She reached inside, searching for the light. She found nothing. Not even a flicker, not even a hint of warmth. This room . . . there was something about the room.

"Looking for the light again?" Aekken asked. "You won't find it here. These ships have energy suppressors and this one, in particular, was made stronger than most. Do you know why, my starlight?"

Because he had always planned to bring her here.

"It was specially prepared for you. I had hoped this day would not come, and I still hope we can avoid worse days, but it seems that preparing this was worth the time and the effort." His fingers, cold and hard, slipped down Maia's arm and wrapped around her fingers. He led her to one side of the room. A gigantic chair, high-backed, its metal frame inlaid with ornate designs, its contours sheathed in plush red velvet, sat in front of a gigantic metal frame. Maia recognized the frame—a viewing portal. Aekken gestured at the chair. "Please, sit."

"I'm fine standing."

"No, you are not. Please sit down." The words were polite, but they were an order that one could only defy at one's own peril. Aekken's fingers tightened on her hand and he pushed her backward into the chair.

Maia fell into the red plushness, her insides jolting at the way Aekken shoved her into it. A part of her wanted to fight back, but she stopped herself. She had little to fight with. She did not even have Bellator. She could still resist, and she would, but not yet. It was best to keep her energy for when it might be needed the most.

"There," Aekken said, smiling at her. "Was that too difficult? Please do not make me force you into things, my starlight. Please understand, I only wish the best for you."

A cold shiver sped up Maia's spine as his twisted words steeped in false kindness sank into her mind. She had seen Aekken several times and spoken to him quite a bit, but as much as he unnerved her, she had not realized what it could be like being near him like this, alone. This was the real Aekken, one who would not hesitate to kill Ruche or hurt her. She breathed as deeply as she could, to stop the shivers from coming.

"I hope you realize that you can do nothing against me," Aekken said. He let go of her hand and crossed his arms as he towered over her. "You are helpless, powerless, and all you can do is bend to my wishes. Of course, you could kick me, scratch me and do all sorts of desperate things as an animal would when trapped. But I hope you will not descend to that level. I hope you have more wisdom. Since, usually, such behavior does not bode well for the trapped."

That was a warning, a clear threat. And from the cheer in his chilly voice, Maia knew that not only was it far from an empty threat, it was also one Aekken would enjoy carrying out.

"Do you know why I brought you here? To tell you the truth. It is time you knew, my starlight," Aekken said. "The seer has been lying to you all this time, giving you false hope, making you think you hold power over me. In reality, that power does not exist." He smiled, his eyes glittering in the joy of telling her this and watching her face wilt. "The seer must have said that I cannot harm you, that I could not destroy your planet while you are on it. And it is true that I am honor-bound to the Nasfarii. But as you can also see, I could very easily remove you from your home world. No one could stop us. Our technology is far, far superior. Even those deadwastes, if they cared, do not know enough."

He walked to the giant frame and traced the carvings with his fingers. His lips were twisted into a smile when he turned and walked over to her side.

"I could have brought you up here the very first time we met, and you would have been just as powerless to fight me then as you are now. The seer could have done nothing to stop me, no one could have." He bent down and brushed a lock of hair from her forehead.

His finger traced the outline of her jaw and drew a circle on her cheek. "However, I needed to prepare for our journey home. So I thought I would rather let you be. I humored you when you tried so hard to negotiate. It was tragically amusing watching your eyes light up when you thought you made a point or won a debate. It was quite endearing, too."

Maia's heart twitched repeatedly. So all the hope she had nurtured was nothing at all. All this while, Aekken had been laughing at her, ridiculing her every word, her every move. He had been toying with her. How could she have been so naive? How could she think she stood a chance against the Crown Prince of the R'armimon?

Aekken circled the chair until he stood in front of her. He touched her chin and forced her face up toward him. His soulless eyes stared into her, the darkness pouring into her as he held her gaze.

"Has anyone told you how beautiful you are?" Aekken whispered.

The glint in his eyes made Maia cringe, his smile made her insides squirm, and his voice chilled her bones. She wanted to push him away and run as far from him as she could. She also knew it would be futile. It would only drive him into doing worse. She had to stay calm, so he would let her out of here.

"Do you know why you got these few months to play around? It is because I let you. It is because I did not want to break your heart and rip you from your home world. So I let you fritter away my time playing that useless little game you call the Initiative."

Maia's heart screamed. The Initiative was not useless. She had found her family of friends because of it. Her fists curled. Rage, futile as it was, burned behind her eyes.

"I understand, Prince Aekken. I'm helpless, you're all-powerful. Could we move forward now?" Maia said, unable to contain her anger anymore. "What do you want from me?"

Aekken laughed, the mockery in it loud and clear.

"I like that fire, my starlight," he said when he had finally stopped laughing. He bowed a little. "I believe in respect. And I do not want to force you into anything." He leaned forward to whisper in her ear. "Although I could force you into anything." He chuckled as if impressed by some humor in his crooked words.

"But I will not," he continued. "I will ask you the honorable way. So here is my proposal—I wish to leave this system tomorrow, and I wish to leave *with* you. In return, I will promise safety to your planet. I will not touch the deadwaste scum, and your home world will be safe forever."

Maia blinked, and then blinked again, in a desperate attempt to make sure she had heard right. Aekken went on, oblivious and uncaring of her puzzled state.

"If you agree, a wonderful future will be yours. Your life in the Empire will be peaceful. You will be revered and worshipped. You shall be a legend forever." He turned around, coat swishing, to look into her eyes. "However, if you do not agree to my generous proposal, then perhaps I will take you by force, just as I have now. And I will make sure this system is destroyed when we leave."

"What use am I to you?"

"Oh, my starlight, do not speak like that. You are our Nasfarii, a being so rare and elusive that it is slowly turning into a thing of myths and legends. The Empire is waiting for you to grace us with your presence. You will not be treated like you are here, where no one wants you, where you are a burden to almost everyone."

"I'm not a burden," Maia said.

Aekken bent down to peer at her face. "Are you not? The truth is that you do not even have a place to go, now that the silly game is over." He laughed and the sound tore through Maia's ears and clawed at her heart. He laughed even more as her eyelids drooped with the weight of her pain. Aekken continued, his words cruel and sharp.

"Tansi is my home," Maia whispered.

"Home?" Aekken sniggered. "A home is where you are welcomed. A home is where everyone waits for you to return at the end of the day, every day. After tomorrow, after everyone else returns to where they belong, who will be waiting for you?"

Maia's hands clenched, and she blinked, determined not to let her tears show. The truth could not have been any clearer. Aekken, as vile as he was, was right. She had no home. He was right. Come tomorrow, she had no place to go. Come tomorrow, no one would watch over her, or wait for her to come back to them.

"No one?" The words, steeped in pain, slipped past her lips.

"Yes, no one," Aekken said. He bent down and hissed into her ear. "Then why not come with me? I can give you everything you could ever wish for. You could be Empress, if you so desire." His breath on her face was cold and terrifying, and as Maia turned away in fear, Aekken chuckled. "You want to hide from me, I know. But it would be useless. I will find you. I have the means to find you no matter how far you go. Besides, no one would stand up against us for you, my starlight. No one. Not those spineless people in those puny councils. You know they only care about saving their skins. All you have are a few friends. Only children. Useless and expendable. No one who is anyone cares about you."

He straightened and stared down at her. "What will it be, then? Save your planet or force me to destroy it? I do not think the choice is difficult at all, but, generous as I am, I will not rush you. You have until tomorrow to choose. Until sundown, my starlight. Then, we leave."

"I don't need until tomorrow to decide," Maia said.

The options were tragically simple. No matter what she chose, he would find her and take her with him. But if she did not choose to go willingly, he would destroy Tansi. The choice — it was no real choice at all — was clear.

The words came slowly and unwillingly out of Maia's mouth. "I will come with you." Aekken's mouth stretched with glee, his eyes narrowing slightly when Maia spoke again. "But until sundown tomorrow, I want to be with my friends. And I want to go back to ThulaSu right now."

Maia rose to her feet, her insides churning as she thought of what had just happened, and what was to come in her future. There was no pain, however, only barrenness within her, as if someone had torched her insides until nothing remained.

"I want to go now," Maia repeated. "Please."

For once, Aekken did not ignore her. He grabbed her arm again, the cold touch of the teleportation device tingling her skin. Maia closed her eyes as bitter cold doused her once more.

"Maia!"

She opened her eyes when she heard Ruche's voice. They were back at the bowers. As soon as Aekken let go of her arm, Maia darted away. In an instant, Ruche's arms surrounded her protectively.

"How dare you, Aekken!" the seer fumed. "This is a shame, and an indignity to all we hold sacred."

"The Nasfarii and I needed to hear each other, Seer," Aekken said calmly. "For that, I needed to speak to her in private. There is far too much noise elsewhere."

"You forget who she is. She is a manifestation of Ataii, the one you are here to avenge. And yet you distress her like this."

"No, Seer," Aekken said. "She is certainly not Princess Ataii nor a manifestation of her. She does not even have Seigvard, and she never will. She is just a Nasfarii, Seer. Powerful, no doubt, but not anything I cannot control."

Ruche did not reply, and Maia knew what Aekken had said was true. Not a truth she wanted to hear, but it still was immovable truth. Ruche had nothing to fight Aekken. No one did.

"I will take my leave now, Seer," Aekken said. "I will see you at sundown tomorrow, my starlight."

As soon as his form dissipated, Ruche turned toward Maia. "Are you all right?"

Maia nodded.

"What is this about sundown tomorrow?" he asked next. Ruche sighed and shook his head vehemently when Maia had explained everything. "No, no. That can't happen."

"How can you stop it?"

"If we had that sword . . ."

CHAPTER FORTY-SEVEN

"What if we had the sword, Ruche? What then?"

"I could've tried to obtain a higher power for you that Aekken couldn't have taken lightly. I could've—"

"Try? Even with Seigvard it'd just be trying?"

Ruche looked into the distance. "Yes. Nothing is certain. But we would have a real choice." He held her by the shoulders and turned her to face him. "Kusha is trying to convene a trinational council. I asked him to. If you request them to get you Seigvard, they just might decide to convince the queen."

"No, Ruche. They can't make the queen hand Seigvard to me. She won't. I know that."

"No harm in trying again."

"I'm tired, Ruche," Maia said. She walked away from Ruche and slumped onto a bench. She pulled up her knees to her chest and hugged them tightly. "I'm tired of asking, begging, and . . . being refused. I can't anymore. I just want this to end."

Ruche sat down next to her and slipped an arm around her shoulders. "No, Maia. You can't give up. You can't. You have to keep on trying. As long as you live, you have to try to fight for what you want."

Maia let her head droop to her knees. Try . . . Try to fight. Hadn't she tried enough? And fought enough? Nothing ever seemed to work. Nothing.

"Ruche, have you thought about what will happen if Aekken finds out that I'm still trying to acquire Seigvard?"

Ruche smiled. "He *will* find out. Let him. You just let Kusha do most of the talking, all right?"

Something odd was brewing, but Maia could not tell what. Anyway, she was too tired to think clearly. She looked up at the sound of running feet. Kusha appeared at the gate of the rose garden. "Seer Ruche, I managed to get a council together," he said. "Maia, come on."

She was tired. No, exhausted. Her insides were a crumpled mass of pain, fear, and hopelessness. Yet Kusha's bright face made it impossible to refuse. Then there was Ruche.

"Your friends are trying, Maia. You can't give up just yet." He patted her back. "I will be away for a little while. I need to get some things lined up. In the meantime, be with your friends. Listen to them. Have faith." He peered at her downcast face and smiled. "Remember, Maia, the universe has a way of helping those who do not give up. So don't ever give up."

Even though she knew the effort would be fruitless, Maia forced herself up and trudged with Kusha across ThulaSu.

Chapter Forty-Eight

Let It Go

Back they went, along the path to the house where Miir had taken her to meet with the Rahina. Maia's thoughts were distant and her heart devoid of hope, but Kusha kept talking all the way.

"You don't need to speak unless they ask you a direct question, Maia," he said when they were about to enter. "Let me lead."

Maia had no problem with letting Kusha lead. Her mind was barely in a coherent state to start with, and on top of that, she could not keep herself from feeling hopeless. And that, she knew, was not what needed to come out even before the council began.

The room was emptier than she had seen it some time ago. The people around the large table in the middle had changed. The Xifarian queen had left, and so had CA Abebe. Taillefei sat on one of the chairs along the wall, as did Uncle Alasdair and a few other parliamentarians. In the council chairs on the far end of the table were Premier Oliena, Sahiiraan Goren, and Advisor Lowanabe. The most surprising presence of them all was leaning against the wall behind

Lowanabe—a smirking Ren.

"Sahiiraan Kusha, you may state your appeal," Premier Oliena said as soon as the introductory pleasantries had been exchanged.

Kusha did not waste any time getting to the crux of the matter. After he explained Ruche's request about Seigvard and the changed situation after the Initiative, he stated it plainly. "Maia needs Seigvard. That is the only way to remove the threat of the R'armimon from our system for good. I requested this council to urge you, to beg you to convince Rahina Quemiila to grant Maia this sword. I sincerely hope you will consider my plea."

Kusha had barely finished when Lowanabe shook his head vehemently. "Rahina Mayen has refused it. That is the end of this discussion." He sighed on seeing curious looks from the rest of the council. "Seigvard is her family heirloom, and it is a completely personal affair."

His words lit a fire inside Maia in an instant. Her fists curled, and anger rose like a squall in her mind.

My family heirloom. I'm entitled to Seigvard. I am —

Reality raised its head just as swiftly and cut off Maia's thoughts. Entitled? True, no doubt. But who would believe her claim? No one. Certainly not Lowanabe or Taillefei. Not when it was her word against their queen's. There was no proof she could offer, and Miir, the one who had figured it all out, was not going to challenge the queen publicly. As much as she wanted . . . needed to fight for Seigvard, she had nothing to fight with—that was the truth. Blinking away the hurt, Maia squared her shoulders and forced her attention back on the council.

"My position does not allow me to advise the Rahina about her private matters," Lowanabe said with an air of finality. "I'm only an advisor on affairs related to the governance of our nation."

"This does concern the safety of your nation, Advisor Lowanabe," Premier Oliena said. "That gives you some leeway to act."

Maia stifled a sigh. Lowanabe would not act in this matter, regardless of how sound the reasoning was behind it. Except for Ren, no one in the room knew that Lowanabe would do anything to have her destroyed — killed or exiled — it did not matter how.

"Perhaps," Lowanabe conceded. For a moment he seemed flustered and exchanged a quick look with Taillefei, who simply shook his head in response. Lowanabe was just about to reply when Ren leaned over and whispered something in his ear. Lowanabe smiled. "But even if the girl had the sword, there is no explanation of how it would help, no guarantee of a safe future. Is there?"

"Maia, can you please explain?" Premier Oliena asked.

"There could be a possible solution if I have it," Maia said, a bit rattled by the odd exchange between Ren and Lowanabe.

"A possible solution? What would that be?" Lowanabe asked.

"I don't know for sure," Maia said truthfully.

Once again, Ren leaned to whisper something in Lowanabe's ear. Lowanabe's face brightened.

"Have you spoken to the prince recently?" he asked.

Maia could not answer right away, her mind a whirlpool of confusion at Ren's strange antics. She blinked hard when Sahiiraan Goren cleared his throat.

"Has the prince told you of his plans, Maia? Our time is up. What does he intend to do now?"

As much as Maia hated the prospect of sharing her situation in front of everyone, she could not lie to their faces. Steadying herself, she told them of Aekken's offer.

Maia was not sure what she hoped to hear. Perhaps she had thought they would ask her to reconsider, or someone would say they would take their chances, or the room would erupt in anger at the impossible demand. None of that happened. No one said a word. The room stayed silent when she stopped speaking, and Maia heard nothing other than the drumming of her own heart.

"Maia, you did not accept this proposal, did you?" Uncle Alasdair was the first to speak, and Maia breathed in relief. He rushed over and kneeled next to her chair, his face pale and his eyes wide. "You cannot."

"Do I have a choice?"

"Yes, you do," Kusha burst out. He rose to his feet and looked at each of the council members. "You cannot let this happen. You have to stop Maia from leaving. You *have* to get her Seigvard."

"Sahiiraan Kusha, don't worry. We will discuss this," Premier Oliena said.

"Respectfully, Premier, we need to discuss it now. There is no time to waste," Kusha said.

"Sahiiraan Kusha, this is an agonizing situation," Lowanabe said. "I feel your pain. To have your friend face such a heartbreaking choice . . . I can imagine what you must be going through. But you have to realize that this might be the most rational way forward. We, as adults, must sometimes make difficult choices. You are a child and I will not ask you to understand, but when you grow up, you will —"

"Please," Kusha burst out. "I have taken on responsibilities that adults around me have refused to take. And I am not talking about now. It has been years since I picked up more than my share of duty. So call me unwise, call me sentimental, but please, do not dismiss me by calling me a child. I have not been a child for a while now."

If Maia was taken aback by Kusha's forceful rebuttal, she was not alone. Premier Oliena had a look of admiration on her face, Sahiiraan Goren looked surprised, and Lowanabe's mouth hung open. But Kusha was not finished yet.

"I agree I'm not happy that my friend has to make a choice between her future and this planet's, that even though you have the ability to help her, you refuse. You refuse because it's an easy decision for you. You risk nothing in this choice. The threat that you have brought on us all will disappear because someone else will sacrifice her life for you."

"Please don't make it sound like she is going to be killed, Sahiiraan Kusha," Lowanabe said, a mocking smile on his lips.

"Why shouldn't I? Just because you don't like hearing it?" Kusha argued. "Having to leave a world one has known all their life for the unknown, knowing they will likely never see their home world or their friends and family again, is as good as a death sentence. You think her choice is so easy, maybe you could offer to take her place?"

Lowanabe scowled, but before he could launch a tirade, Kusha spoke again.

"Let's not get into personal sentiments here, Advisor Lowanabe," Kusha said with a smile. "Let us, instead, think of Maia the way you like to think of her, as an object. That object was the reason you were given the extra time that you used to build more shelters and get more of your people out of Xif." He paused and peered at Lowanabe. "Have you considered that once that object is in the hands of the R'armimon, there will be no shield protecting you? No one will be able to buy you time, not even a moment. I do not understand why you would let your shield be taken away when you have the means to stop it."

For a while, there was silence. Then Lowanabe chuckled. "You are persuasive and your logic is sound. I understand the threat we could face, and I am worried. But I will repeat what I have said before. I know Rahina Quemiila is not willing to give away Seigvard, and I have no power to convince her otherwise. She is immovable. My apologies."

Nothing was left to be said after that, and Kusha did not say any more either. With a curt nod, he slumped down on a chair next to Maia's.

"You were awesome," Maia said.

"What's the point?" Kusha said bitterly. "Still couldn't make a difference."

Maia grabbed his hand and smiled, her eyes misty. "But, Kusha, this is what I'll always remember. Your words, this memory of you fighting for me. Even if nothing else goes right, I'll have these moments."

Kusha forced a smile. "Let's go. We've wasted too much time here."

"Maia, one moment." Premier Oliena, her face grim, walked up as Kusha led Maia out.

"Premier Oliena."

"Maia, I will keep trying to convince the Xifarians about that sword. You have my word." She nodded at the council table behind them, where everyone in the room had clustered around Lowanabe. "I know the Sahiiraans and your uncle and his compatriots will support me in the effort."

"Thank you, Premier Oliena." Maia lowered her head in acknowledgment. "I doubt they'll agree, but I appreciate your kindness." A sudden thought came to her and even though embarrassment made her hesitate, Maia decided to say it before she took her leave. "Premier Oliena, I'm being audacious, but may I ask for something?"

"Yes, Maia. Tell me how I can help."

"Please keep the coalition going. Even after the R'armimon are gone and there is no need to support each other the way we are now, it would be good to know Tansi stands united."

Premier Oliena reached for Maia's cold hands, her grip on them firm, her gaze resolute as they locked with hers. "I promise you, Maia. We will be together, for as long as it is within my power to make it happen. I will keep the Trinational Coalition alive."

"Thank you." At that moment, Maia was happy. She forgot all about the future facing her. All she thought about was a happy future for Tansi. Sophie's Tansi . . . peaceful forever.

Ren joined Maia and Kusha as they were exiting the building, after taking leave of Premier Oliena. Kusha immediately frowned at him. "What were you telling Lowanabe back there?"

Ren shrugged. "Nothing much."

"What does that mean?"

"Just that. Nothing much." He walked out ahead of them with a bored look on his face. As soon as the trio walked down the staircase, Sana rushed up. From the leaves and twigs stuck in her hair and dress, it seemed likely that Sana had been hiding in the bushes behind the building.

"Maia, this doesn't mean anything. It's not over, all right?" Clearly, Sana had been eavesdropping. She looked anxious, but determination was etched on her face as she linked her arm through Maia's. "Don't give up yet."

Maia nodded, to satisfy Sana more than anything else. She did not want to give up, but what else could she do?

"Where are you going now?" Sana asked Kusha.

"My house," Kusha said. "Everyone should be there by now. Aren't you coming?"

"Umm . . . no. I have stuff to do. I'll catch up with you later."

Hugging Maia quickly, Sana sprinted away toward the student residences. Her behavior was odd, to say the least, and for a while, Maia stared as Sana's form grew smaller and disappeared. Then they started on a long, quiet walk toward Kusha's mansion.

Chapter Forty-Nine

Unwavering Truths

I t was hard, almost impossible, to remember how that day had begun. The morning seemed like a distant dream from a lifetime ago. How blissfully happy she had been, so hopeful, so sure of success. And now, as a quiet evening drew closer, there was nothing left to cheer about. Maia found her inside hard. A tempest of a day had left it numb. So much had happened—the ceremony of prizes, finding out about Sophie and Raidyn, Aekken's threat, and his subsequent offer. And now, the final truth stared back at Maia—she had a day left to spend on Tansi with her friends.

Her friends had already gathered at Kusha's house, in a large room on the top floor where Maia had never been before. It was spacious and airy, with large windows and a balcony behind, affording sweeping views of ThulaSu and the lands beyond. It was beautiful, but the people in the room had no interest in the beauty. Their gazes, grim and anxious, scoured Maia's face when Kusha led her inside.

Maia told them of Aekken's offer, her decision, the fact that the next day at sundown, she would have to leave forever. She left out the part about how scared she was, how she could still feel Aekken's cold fingers tracing lines on her face, how thinking of it made her shake all over, how her insides were churning, and how she wished there was a place she could hide where Aekken would never find her. She could not tell them all that; it would only compound their misery. She let them be angry instead. She found herself in a strange, dissociated state, as if she were not really there. A wall held her emotions in. Inside it, she was crying soundlessly, screaming for help that was nowhere in sight. Outside, she kept repeating that this was the best path forward for everyone.

Dani's sobs broke the silence in the room after she finished, and Maia realized that she had never been happier to hear anyone cry.

Aekken was wrong. Someone would miss her. Someone would always wait for her to come back at the end of the day. Maia was sure of that.

"We have to find a way," Dani said. "We can't just let him take you away."

"How could you agree to this nonsense, Maia?" Nafi demanded, eyes flashing. "Leaving with that madman? Are you mad yourself?"

Agree to? She had no room to agree to anything. She was given a choice that was no choice at all. There was only one way she could go. But she could not say that to Nafi. Telling Nafi would only worsen her pain.

"I'm sorry to have sprung this on all of you," Maia said. "I didn't have the time to ask for everyone's opinions. It seemed to be the only logical choice left."

"It can't be," Dani wailed. "It can't be the only choice."

Nafi stomped about. "And why is the Council letting you? How stupid can they be?"

Maia did not know what to say. There was no way left to find. She had looked, she had hoped, but nothing she did had worked. The shield was up around Tansi, but they could not pin all their hopes on it. Knowing what she knew of Aekken, the man would not think twice about blasting Xif out of existence, no matter what the fallout. And if the shield did not hold, Tansi would be devastated as well. Sophie's sacrifice would be for naught, along with everyone else's who had fought to keep Tansi alive. She could not let that happen.

Nafi stomped some more. "And Ruche let you do it? Where is that seer guy? I need to have a word with him."

Ruche? The seer was as powerless as anyone else. He had tried his best to arm her, protect her. All his plans had failed, and nothing was left but this path. But she could not tell Nafi that either.

Words Zaara had said a long time ago rang in Maia's ears: Do not rush to sacrifice yourself. Look for other options. People in your life need you too.

Now, looking at her friends' faces, Maia understood what Zaara must have gone through when Sophie decided to give up her life for Tansi. And she wondered if it had been just as hard for Sophie then to take that final step as it was for her now.

Kusha sighed and shook his head. "This should not be. You should not have to do this," he said. "You are not responsible for a woman who won't even acknowledge who you are. You should not have to protect people who would take your life if they got a chance. You should not give up your home for people who won't even ask you to stay."

He meant the Rahina, Phocluus and his goons, and more or less everyone on the Trinational Council.

"I'm not doing it for them, Kusha," Maia said. "I don't care about them. But I care about all my friends, all of you. I'm doing this for those I love."

"Still not exactly an enjoyable thing to do, is it? Hans asked. "You are sacrificing your life."

"Well, it's not as if they'll kill me. I'll live, just not here," Maia countered. The thought of leaving everything she had known and loved for a place so distant and among strangers chilled Maia's bones. Though the words she uttered wrenched her soul, she forced them out, hoping they would bring some comfort to her friends. And some relief to her own aching heart. "I figure that choosing to live my life somewhere else so people I care about get a chance to live their lives in peace isn't that bad a deal."

Her reply did not seem to satisfy Hans, and he looked away, his face shadowed. Maia's heart ached to see Dani's tearful face and Hans's quiet, lightless eyes as he comforted his sister. Nafi paced near the window, her mouth pursed, while Rayan stared outside. Kusha sat on the floor with his eyes closed. Maia's gaze went around the room. Every face was crumpled with despair. The people she truly cared for and everyone that meant something to her were here. Maia's heart filled with gratitude. And her resolve steeled even more. They all had to live, she had to make sure of that.

Arms crossed, Ren stood leaning against the door with a curious expression on his face. Recalling his more curious interactions with Lowanabe at the council, Maia walked up to him. "What's with you? Bored? Angry?"

He sighed and smiled before replying. "Well, I understand. You have no choice."

That was a refreshing and surprising difference in attitude. But then, Ren was always different. Maia looked closely at his face, trying to figure out what could have brought that out. He was not one to give away his intentions so easily or by himself, so Maia continued.

"Everyone else seems to be offended that I decided this on my own."

"I don't think they are. They just wish they could protect you."

Maia sighed. "Yes, I think you're right."

"And no matter what they wish for, they can't help. That's why they're angry. They must all feel . . . useless."

"Not you?"

Ren let out a chuckle. "Well, I haven't given up yet."

Maia peered at him, trying hard to understand what he meant. "There is no Seigvard coming, Ren. You were at the council and you heard that. How else—"

"That ridiculous council was meant to fail," he said in a low, calm voice. "My plan, however . . ."

Maia scanned his face. "Your plan? There is no plan to be made, Ren. I've given Aekken my word, and he has promised me safety for Tansi and Xif in return."

"I know that lunatic won't keep his promise, Maia. I know."

"You know?" How Nafi had caught what Ren had said, Maia could not fathom, but the girl was next to them in a heartbeat. "How do you know?"

Ren put on a bored expression again. "Don't ask how. All right? I just know. He has been preparing an orbiter to send into the sun after they leave the system."

Nafi's eyes were big as saucers. "What's an orbiter?"

Ren shrugged. "Some sort of auto-piloted craft."

"And?"

"And it will do things to our star," Ren said with a casual shrug. "Not good things. Then we all die."

Kusha had come over too and was listening intently. Now he looked up at Maia and frowned. "And you still want to go with this wretched scoundrel?"

"I don't want to. I have to," Maia said. "This information Ren has, I don't even know —"

Nafi glared at Maia. "Maia, I don't know what has come over you. It almost seems like you are happy to go off with this vile, crooked excuse for a living creature. Are you dreaming of being Empress of the Empire R'armimon? Is that it?" She stopped and let out a huge sigh. "I know being called an empress sounds very nice and everything, but you really think you can spend your life with a creepy guy like that?"

Dani's arms were around Maia in a heartbeat. "Nafi, stop it."

"Get some fresh air, Maia." Nafi pulled her away from Dani and shoved her in the direction of the balcony. "Your mind is clearly not on finding an alternative. So leave it to us. Go." Nafi pushed her out and shut the door behind her.

For a moment, Maia stared back through the glass panes,

watching with a sad smile on her face as her friends buzzed around, so hopeful of a solution. She knew it was no use. There was no hope left. She did not know how Ren had found out about the orbiter or whether it was true, but regardless of its existence, there was nothing left to do. It was better to prepare herself for the inevitable.

Sighing, Maia turned her back on the useless optimism swirling in the room behind her. The balcony beckoned her with a promise of escape, and Maia eagerly walked forward. She came to an abrupt halt when she exited the canopy covering the doorway and stepped into the sunlight. Miir stood to one side, hands clutching the railing, staring at the horizon. Maia remembered — he had stood in one corner by himself, silent after she had told them everything, and she had not noticed when he quietly slipped out of the room.

Maia's first instinct was to bolt back inside. Then she steadied herself. Her friends did not need that. Besides, she would be leaving in a day anyway. This might be the last time she would be able to speak to Miir alone.

The thought that come tomorrow, she would never see him again, tore her insides into pieces. She tried hard to rein in her scattered emotions. Yet, her mind went poring over every memory of him, the good, the bad, and everything in between. They swept over her in an unending rush, leaving her gasping for breath.

Miir must have heard her, since he turned. Not fully, but enough to meet her eyes for the briefest moment. He gave her the slightest nod and went back to looking into the distance. Even in that short glance, Maia noticed the wild look in his eyes. She had never seen him look that way before, not once.

Maia hesitated at the threshold, her heart fluttering. Fear made her pause and wonder. There was nothing left to say, so why be afraid, her mind reasoned. Have a conversation, make a final memory, her heart said. Half of her still wanted to turn away, but Maia did not let it take over. That was not how it would end, she decided. She was going to talk to him, say goodbye. Breathing deeply, Maia forced her feet forward until she came to stand next to him. For what seemed like forever, they stood in silence as hurt formed a thick lump inside Maia, choking her.

Was it so hard to spare her a few words of casual conversation? Sure, his work was done, and there was absolutely nothing left between them anymore, but —

It's your memory to make, Maia. So make it.

Maia drew a deep breath. There was one thing she had not told Miir yet, and that had to be said now.

"I don't know if I'll see you again, so . . . thank you for . . . helping me find the truth about my father." She pushed the words out past the lump in her throat. "I searched for it so long, but without your help, I might have never known. I should've said this earlier, but I wasn't quite myself then."

Miir looked up abruptly, eyes narrowed, that wild, lost look still showing. A breeze, light and warm, blew across them. It ruffled his hair a little and softened the lines of his taut face. "Why are you doing this? Why are you leaving with that lunatic?"

Maia blinked. Leave it to Miir to turn a conversation around so swiftly. With him, you never knew what was coming next. It took Maia a moment or two to find the right words.

"It's simple. He offered me the life of millions in exchange for mine. How could I refuse that?"

His hands gripped the railing tightly as if he wanted to strangle it. "There has to be something else. Another way to save the millions."

She had said so many times that there was none. No one seemed to want to hear it. Tired as she was of repeating it, Maia did it one more time.

"There might have been if I could get Seigvard and the pendant. But now there isn't."

"The council could force her to give them to you. You should ask. Did you ask?"

"They already know. And they won't force her to. But this is the logical choice, the right choice for them. There is no clear outcome, no instant solution. What if I did get Seigvard and the pendant? What then? Ruche never says it would make Aekken vanish. He says there will be a chance." Maia paused and took a bracing breath. "So do you take a chance on one and risk millions, or sacrifice one to save them? I won't lie, it would hurt less if the council said they wanted me to stay no matter what. But I understand that emotions have nothing to do with it. I have nothing against anyone."

Maia had not known how much comfort saying those things out loud would bring, but every word she uttered soothed her mind. The fear of an unknown future did not completely ebb, but the more she reasoned, the better she felt.

She looked out, her gaze scanning the misty gray horizon. It was calm everywhere. Peaceful, beautiful, Tansi.

Sophie's Tansi. My Tansi. May you be at peace, forever.

Miir opened his mouth to say something, but not a word came out. Maia could not keep from noticing how his hands gripped the railing even tighter.

"Why do I . . ." He started and stopped. "Why do I get this feeling that you are throwing yourself away?"

His question cracked the wall of serenity she had built around her. A rush of emotions came hurtling through and clawed it down. It crumbled so fast that it left Maia out of breath. Maia tried to gulp away the hurt that swamped her insides, but it did not budge. Images flashed in her mind — Aekken's face so fearfully close, his chilly breath on her face, his soulless eyes boring into hers, his cold, slim fingers tracing circles on her cheek. A shudder swept through her and she had to grab the railing to stop herself from crumpling.

"Throwing myself away?" Maia's words came out trembling with fear. "Truth is . . . I'm terrified. I'm . . . I don't want to be anywhere near Aekken. I want to stay . . . here. I wish someone could help me. I wish there was a place to hide where he wouldn't find me. But . . . there is no one who can help, nowhere to go." Her voice broke and a tear, unruly and adamant, burned its way down her cheek. Maia hastily brushed it away. It grounded her, however, and she fought to build the wall back up again. "Forget I said that, please. I don't want anyone to know. It'll only make them sadder. I'm fine. I'll be all right. This *is* the best way forward for everyone."

She closed her eyes and breathed deeply, letting the cool air settle inside her. Then it hit her, and Maia's eyes flew wide. She turned to take in Miir's tormented face, realizing, in a sudden rush, that he had chalked all this up to his refusal of her wishes. He was still hurting, even more now. It was strange how, even though her heart was shaking like a leaf imagining the abhorrent fate that awaited her, even though she knew there would never be the future she wished for, even knowing she only had one more day left in this world she loved, how dearly she wanted to help him and comfort him.

"You're not blaming yourself for my decision, are you?" she said softly, accepting his questioning look with a calm mind. "Please don't. This is not because of you. I truly don't have any other option, and believe me, I've looked." In her desperation to find some peace for Miir, she went on. "I didn't think I'd ever say this to anyone, certainly not to you." Maia let a wry chuckle escape her mouth. "Cliched as it may sound, I've realized lately . . . when you care about someone, it really doesn't matter what they think about you. You'll always want them to find happiness, watch their joy even if from a distance. So you see, I wouldn't throw myself away into exile because of you, because . . . I couldn't bear the thought of never seeing you again." Swallowing the painful lump in her throat, she forced a hasty, awkward smile. "Please don't think of this as me trying to bring up my silly sentiments again. I'm not. I'm not that pathetic. I do remember the promise I made."

Maia had hardly finished speaking when Nafi's head popped out of the door. "Maia!" Her excited shout cut through the fading golden light of the evening and scattered the melancholy rhythm of the moment.

"Yes, what?" Maia asked.

"The Xinhagyi wants to see you right now," Nafi shouted. "Come on."

"Coming." She started to leave.

CHAPTER FORTY-NINE

"Do not say that," Miir said. "Please."

Startled, she looked back.

"You are not pathetic. You are precious."

As she held his gaze, steady, calm, and painfully inscrutable as always, a small joyful wave inside her flooded her face in a smile. "I'll remember that. Thank you."

"I have to tell you something. I—"

"Maia!" Nafi's head popped out again. "What are you doing? This is urgent."

Miir's gaze left her face, taking with it the momentary warmth.

Nafi careened outside and peered at Miir. "You got any ideas on how to help her?" she demanded, and no sooner had one silent moment passed than she dragged Maia away. "Well then, we've got to get a move on. There's no time to lose."

Maia walked in a daze next to Nafi, her mind repeating what Miir had just said, her heart eager to find something to cling to. She knew those words meant nothing special. He had just said that to cheer her up. It was, as it always had been, a part of his promise to stay by her side, a show of his unwavering loyalty, a necessity for his atonement, but nothing beyond.

Yet she wanted to forget everything else and remember those words. *You are precious.* Forever. In the long, inevitable and arduous life ahead of her, away from everything she knew, it would be her strength, it would keep her going.

Down staircases they went, along the quiet roads of ThulaSu, and across the sprawling grounds that surrounded the Sun Temple. All the way, Nafi talked about plans to outwit Aekken.

"The Xinhagyi is in the inner sanctum," Nafi informed her.

Maia nodded, her mind far, far away from the expansive hallways they trailed across.

CHAPTER FIFTY

OF FAITH . . .

Maia woke to gentle nudges early the next morning. *Early* was an understatement; it was still practically night. The skies were dark beyond the half-open window and the moon was still bright. Maia blinked to clear her tired mind a little, and memories of the previous day hit her like a boulder. The Initiative ending, the award ceremony and then . . . disaster after disaster.

"Maia, wake up." She recognized Sana's voice in the dark.

Maia flipped onto her belly and pressed her face into the pillow. She breathed deeply, hoping to brace her frayed nerves. The session with the Xinhagyi had helped immensely. He had not taught her anything new, nor did he suggest some miraculous plan to escape Aekken. He simply went over the various control techniques he had taught Maia when she had just discovered her powers. When Maia walked out of the Sun Temple that evening, her heart was calmer, her mind steady.

It had not lasted very long, however. The situation was far too grim to ignore, and Maia was not superhuman. Most of her friends had gathered for a dinner Kusha had organized, and as much as Maia enjoyed spending time with everyone, it was a constant reminder of the day that was just a sunrise away. She had retired early, and thankfully, sleep had not denied her that night.

"Maia, get up." Sana's voice and a nudge, both sharper this time, came again.

There was no getting around Sana, so she sat up slowly. "What is it now?"

"Ren is here. You have to go with him."

"Go where? Why?"

"Ren will explain," Sana said, almost dragging her out of bed and pushing a change of clothes into her hands. "Get ready now."

A million questions swarmed Maia's mind as she changed. Ren had a plan, so he had said. Was he trying to hide her? But what was the point? Aekken would find her no matter where she hid. There was no use trying to do anything, as far as Maia could tell.

Sana's arms flew around Maia as soon as she came out. Then things were thrust at her—first a cranky Dusty, whose angry mewling melted into contented purrs as soon as Maia hugged him, then a jacket, finally her belt and Bellator. Then, taking Dusty away, Sana almost pushed her out the door. "I'll see you later."

Ren, who had been standing with his back to the wall, the dark hood of his jacket pulled low over his head, smiled.

"Thanks." He nodded at Sana before turning toward Maia. "Let's go."

They were just about to step away when Sana called, a little hesitantly. "Hey, Ren."

"I'll keep Maia safe, don't worry."

"I know you will," Sana said as she walked up to them. "Keep yourself safe too."

Ren stared at her for a moment before a bright smile flooded his face. "I'll be fine, Angel. It'll all be good. Trust me."

"I trust you plenty." Sana drew a deep breath as if she were bracing herself, and then gave him a quick hug. "Just talk a little less, will you?"

"And . . . what will that get me? More hugs?" Ren cocked an eyebrow. As Sana grimaced, he hastily added, "All right, all right. See you in a bit."

"Ren, where are we going?" Maia asked the moment they exited the building. Ren did not seem to hear or pretended not to, so Maia grabbed his arm as they climbed the stairs leading up to the ramparts.

"Ren—"

He stopped and faced her. "Maia, I have a plan, a very convoluted plan that could help you avoid leaving with Aekken. You want to stay here with us, right?"

"Yes, I do. But I don't see how—"

"Why don't you leave the hows to me?" Ren asked, his eyes scanning her face. "Can you trust me?"

"I do. But that's not the point, Ren." Maia tried to make him see reason. "If this fails and Aekken finds out that I tried it . . . it'll be an excuse for him to go berserk on Xif, and on Tansi."

"It won't fail, Maia. I promise." For a while, they stared at each other. "And for a change, just forget about the consequences for Tansi. Think about yourself, all right?"

If only it were that easy. How could she forget about the millions of lives at stake?

Ren grabbed her shoulders and peered at her face. "Besides, Maia, no matter what you do, Aekken is going to unleash that orbiter and destroy this system when he leaves. That I'm sure of. If there is nothing to lose, why not try to save yourself?"

The orbiter! That was the second time Ren had mentioned it. If that were true—

"What did Ruche tell you, Maia?" Ren asked. "The universe has a way of helping those who do not give up. Remember that?"

Maia blinked. Ren had quoted the exact words Ruche had spoken the previous day. He was not present when Ruche said them. He could not have known. Did that mean . . . that Ruche knew about this plan too? Perhaps—

Maia decided. A leap of faith it would be.

"All right, then. Let's go."

Through the rose garden they went, and down to the side entrance on the ledge into the tunnel inside the ramparts.

"We're going to Frauz Point, Maia," Ren said as they strode through the darkness. "Then we'll take a transport to Xif."

Ren paused a moment or two when they emerged at the mouth of the tunnel, to check for activity. Then he started down the steps to the canyon floor.

"Keep your head down. This way," Ren said as he hurried toward a small shuttle and ushered Maia inside. He got in after her, punched in a code, and the buggy rolled forward soundlessly. They stopped at the edge of the landing field and Ren led Maia out to a spot in the shadows.

"We have to wait for the signal." He pointed at a craft, three airships removed from where they stood. "That should be the one. Keep an eye on it."

For a while they sat in silence, staring at the dark craft in the distance until Maia could not take it anymore. "What do we do in Xif?"

Ren chuckled under his breath. "We'll find out if the spiders take the bait."

"Bait?" Maia's heart jumped as a thought hit her. "You don't mean me, do you?"

"I do. You're bait for Phocluus," Ren said without batting an eyelid. "And Phocluus is bait for Aekken."

Maia did not get a chance to gasp, because a light flashed in the distance. Three times it went . . . blink, blink, blink. Ren immediately tugged her arm and pulled her across the field toward the waiting transport. Maia's mouth fell open when she recognized the three figures standing with a pair of Tokii at the open hold of the transport.

"Hey, you're all set," Karhann said to Ren, and handed him what looked like a silver coin. "Good luck."

"Good luck, Maia," Loriine simpered. "Wish you the very best."

Bakhari, the third person, simply smirked.

Maia watched Karhann, Loriine, and Bakhari hasten away into the darkness. "I can't believe those three plotted with you to help me," she said as they walked into the craft.

Ren exhaled loudly as they settled in a seat in the darkened rear of the transport. "Well, not all of them were here to help you, exactly."

His words, although not unexpected, were hard to hear. They hurt. Maia forced her next words out, hoping to help normalize the hurt a little. "They want Phocluus to get me, of course." Hearing the truth out loud in her own voice hardly helped.

"Maia, did you really expect Loriine or Bakhari to be your friend?"

"No, but I didn't think they'd actually participate in a plot to get me killed." She took a long breath of the cool morning air and let it settle inside her. "Did you *have* to involve Loriine and Bakhari in this?"

"Of course I did. Everything I do is for a reason," Ren said with a chuckle. He slipped an arm around her shoulders and leaned his head against hers. "Don't dwell on your enemies, Maia. Your friends are stronger. We will win."

Moments passed in torturous silence until the transport took off. Ren disappeared somewhere, leaving Maia alone with her weighty thoughts. He reappeared when the craft docked in Arpasgula. Here another transport, this one very small, awaited them. Maia had wondered how they would pass the checkpoints, but it seemed the small token Karhann had handed Ren took care of it all. Even though this time Ren stayed by her side as the smaller craft made its way through Xif's crust, Maia had no urge to talk. She stared outside instead, an unending stream of memories parading through her mind. She recalled how frustrated and angry she was the first time she had been through this tunnel, and how, slowly, she had changed. Oh, how she hated Xif then and —

"Maia, have I ever told you?" Ren said suddenly.

Startled out of her thoughts, Maia turned to look at him, a little taken aback by how serious he looked. "Told me what?"

"Told you how important you are to me," he said, his gaze locked with hers. "Or why?"

As Maia stared, confused by the question, Ren smiled a little. "You changed my life, you know. Just you, without even trying, like no one else before or since," he said.

Once again, Maia stared, unsure of what Ren meant or why he was saying it now. Ren's eyes twinkled as he noticed the expression on her face.

"Don't worry. I'm not about to confess some sort of romantic designs I have on you. I don't think of you that way. I do love you, though. A whole lot." He laughed, noting the small sigh of relief Maia tried so hard to stifle but failed. "It's time I told you this. When I came to the Initiative, I was a lost soul. Home was hell, with a stepfather who never missed a chance to tell me how much of a burden and a trouble I was, a baby brother who took up all my mother's time and attention, and a mother who only cared about the newest things in her life. I had nothing. I was angry and listless, bored and tired of everything around me. I craved something . . . anything that could keep me distracted. Found out taking risks worked the best. Thrills gave me that rush I needed to forget about the realities I faced. I started gambling, and found out I was quite good at it."

Maia recalled how Ren had been into bets and wagers all along, particularly when they first met. Ren chuckled at the amused look on Maia's face. "No, not just the harmless little wagers you caught me making that first day, but serious stuff with . . . dangerous people. I knew what I was doing was bad, and after a bit, I wanted to get out. I was scared really, of things I'd been doing, of what could happen to me if I messed up. But I couldn't let go. I was making money, and I was addicted to the thrills, to the rush. I was hopelessly entangled in this web."

Ren stared at his fingers for a while before speaking again.

"When the Initiative started, I thought the idea of challenges was fun, and being part of it would help me find a path out of my addiction. I was so wrong. Nafi ticked me off, Dani was disgustingly nice, and that Kusha was such a doormat. Just a day into it and I was so darn tired already that I decided to quit the Initiative."

Maia sat up. She had never imagined this. She recalled how Ren had looked a little annoyed in those first days, but she could never have imagined the extent of it. She had never thought he might consider leaving.

"You know what kept me going?" Ren asked. He continued when Maia shook her head. "Your peculiar disinterest in the Initiative. I was so intrigued. I mean, who the heck would want to leave the Initiative unless they were totally, utterly weird like me? And I thought, I had to figure this girl out. It was a challenge. So I stuck around. And before I knew it, I had found myself a family. Slowly, I stopped craving my nightly gambling outings and started wanting to spend more time with you all. Suddenly I had something to look forward to, people I wanted to be with, including that annoying pest Nafi."

Ren reached for Maia's hand. His grip was firm, his face lit with a smile. "I'm happy to be where I am now, Maia. And I wouldn't be here if it weren't for you. So, thank you."

"I'm glad, Ren," Maia said, sighing away the momentary silence. "I'm so glad you didn't leave us. I'm glad we all became a family. I treasure all of you, more than you can imagine."

"We treasure you too, Maia. Remember that." Ren said and patted her hand. He seemed to hesitate for a moment and then looked at her sharply. "Listen, I should tell you something about Miir. Things he said to you—"

The peace of a moment ago disappeared in a blink, and Maia's hands went up like a wall. "No, Ren. Not that," she exclaimed.

"But, Maia—"

"I don't want to talk about it, please. I've said my goodbyes to him and . . . that's where I want to leave it. That's the last thing I want to remember. Please understand."

"Oh . . . all right then."

Maia turned away hastily from Ren's downcast face and looked out of the window, desperately seeking a diversion. It came soon enough as the transport swung out of Aperture 4 and instead of sinking down to a landing site in the cities below, veered upward.

"Ren, aren't we landing?" Maia asked.

"No, we're going to the Seliban Temple."

Maia wondered why. What was Ren's plan? So far, he had only given her bits and pieces of information, and only when prodded. This was not, Maia understood clearly now, some impulsive idea dreamed up by a sixteen-year-old. To have gained access to the Seliban Temple, he had to have plotted long and well, with people influential enough to allow him entry. She looked askance at Ren, who sat with a grim expression. All of the joy that had lit his face moments ago was gone. For a moment Maia considered probing some more, but then she pushed her questions away and looked outside, deciding to accept the inevitability of what was coming. The tunnel of Aperture 15 swallowed their craft and spit them out into the volcanic fields of the Draegen shortly after. The skies were a pale pink when they were dropped off in the cavernous hold of the Seliban Temple.

Another craft—a small one, personal, perhaps—was already there. However, Maia saw no one. While Ren roamed about, clearly looking for the owner of the other craft, Maia walked over to the large staircase at one side. Years ago, they had run up it to find Mahswa Tabrin and win the Seliban Challenge. Memories were everywhere. Memories of pain, joy, triumph . . . heartbreak. Mahswa Tabrin . . . always so kind . . . now lost forever. Maia ran a finger over her firestone wristband, a special prize the Mahswa had given the team. How proud they had been. And then . . . how carelessly Miir had rejected them. Now Maia understood so much better why. He had always known what they were to him—always a task to be completed, with dedication and loyalty no doubt, but nothing more. Some things never changed. How could she have forgotten?

"Ren!" A familiar voice rang across the hold, and Maia was thankful for the interruption. She knew it was Principal Pomewege even before she saw the portly silhouette. He rushed over, his arms outstretched. "Maia, glad to see you again."

Pomewege soon pulled Ren aside and they began an animated discussion. The principal of the XDA had always been an ally, Maia mused as she watched them talk. It was no wonder Ren had found a plotting buddy in him. Her thoughts came to an abrupt halt when Ren drew his sword — Miir's sword, and Asiyaah's before that — and for a breathless moment, Maia did not know what was coming. Her heart calmed as Ren handed it to Pomewege. The principal looked closely at it with a strange expression on his face. Was it amazement, fear, or both? Maia could not tell. Why were they examining a sword now? What —

It came to her in a barrage of fragmented thoughts, ideas, and recollections. They fit together, one by one, parts of a gigantic puzzle in her head, until one conclusion stood out — it was not a sword, it was *the* sword. Asiyaah's sword.

What had Asiyaah said . . . Sophie was caught so soon, so unexpectedly, that Asiyaah had not found the opportunity to hide the chalice where she intended. So she did what she could. Asiyaah had broken down the chalice and merged it with her own sword. And then bound the sword to her child before she left.

The burden . . . this is it!

Asiyaah had thought — rightly so — that no one would think she would put her own child in the middle of all this. No one had, until . . . . Phocluus had somehow figured it out. That was why Remii had come to ThulaSu looking for Miir. Kehorkjin had overheard Remii muttering about something Miir had. It made perfect sense. And then Ren too had found out. Ren must have promised Phocluus he would get the sword. That was why he had reassured her over and over that Miir was safe.

And then . . . all that drama before Korobieltes . . . Ren had staged it all, just to get Miir to give up his sword. Had Miir figured it out in the end? If he did, it would explain the argument between Ren and Miir they had overheard.

"Maia, I will leave now." Principal Pomewege's voice jolted Maia out of her thoughts. "All will be well, I hope," the principal said, smiling. "I will see you when it is all over."

With a pat on her shoulder and a nod at Ren, Pomewege left. Maia walked up to Ren with her questions. She needed to find out for sure.

"That sword, Ren" — she grabbed his arm and made him face her — "that's the chalice, isn't it?"

Ren sighed. "Yes, Maia, it is." He went on to confirm all of Maia's guesses, up until his argument with Miir. "Miir found out, and he was furious that I tricked him. But I had no choice. If he had known, he wouldn't hand over something that could hurt you. Not so easily . . . if at all."

Maia's thoughts drifted. Miir had been so upset when he heard Asiyaah's warning for her. This was what Asiyaah had really meant, for her to stay away from the chalice. Even when he reacted so vehemently to her ill-conceived confession, his mother's words had loomed large in his mind. What did he think when he found out? Would things be any different had he known what Asiyaah had really meant?

Stop it, Maia! His mother's warning was only a small part of everything that he so forcefully opposed that day, yet you still find a way to hope. How pathetic can you be?

With a shake of her head, Maia yanked herself out of her thoughts, forcing herself back into the present and the insurmountable danger facing her. She looked Ren in the eye as she arranged her words. "So Phocluus is planning to use the sword to kill me?"

Ren did not even blink. "Well, he's planning to use it on you. I don't know exactly how. It seems there is a way to encapsulate the light inside you using this sword." Maia could not stop the shudder that raced up her spine and left her shaking. Ren's hands were on her shoulders in a heartbeat. "Maia, I will not let them use the sword on you. It's bound to me, and it can't be used without — "

"You really think Phocluus won't find a way around that?" Maia asked, the hopelessness in her own voice leaving her feeling empty.

This was a scary plan and for once, Ren had probably bitten off more than he could chew.

"Maia, we'll make it," Ren said. "Come on, we're running late. We have to be at the Foundation Chamber soon."

Maia had no doubt something terrifying was about to unfold in the Foundation Chamber, and she had to meet it head-on. There was no other way left to go. So, fists curled, Maia walked with Ren across shadowy hallways and empty chambers and down an enormous stairway. Ren stopped in front of a pair of massive reinforced doors and Maia held her breath. This was the Foundation Chamber. This was where Sophie had changed her own fate and those of so many others for years to come. Now it was time to meet hers.

CHAPTER FIFTY-ONE

. . . COURAGE . . .

Maia had expected the chamber inside to be dark, but it was fairly well-lit compared to the rest of the temple. Maia's steps were slow and she practically dragged herself inside. The chamber was beautiful, with murals depicting stars and galaxies decorating every wall. At the center of the room was a column that rose from the floor to the ceiling. A large, transparent globe surrounded the base of the column where it met the floor. It reminded Maia of the Tyrillic Stabilator they had seen at the Sanctuary of the Stars, only smaller. Brilliant bolts of light flashed inside it in a never-ending rhythm. It dazzled all over, except for one large circular spot that stood out like a smudge in the brightness.

"The receptacle for the heart," Ren said, pointing at the dark spot. "That's where the Verto-balancer Capsule used to be. It's dark because the heart is missing."

"But it will be back there once again, very soon." Maia spun around at the familiar voice, her heart almost jumping out of her chest. Chairman Phocluus of the SDS—flanked by Remii and Amanii on either side—stood at the door, half of his face shriveled like a dried grape, his eyes blazing like the jeweled rings on his fingers.

Maia was thankful when Ren stepped closer. His voice was barely a whisper, his grip on her elbow firm. "And . . . so it begins. Maia, we have only one goal now. We need to buy time."

Phocluus tottered in, leaning on a long stick as he stepped closer to the receptacle, his gaze scouring Maia's face. "My dear Maia, so nice to see you again."

About ten people, most of them in Order of Fyrstell garb—black capes, whip swords in hand—and some in the bodysuits of the SDS, swarmed in behind Phocluus. The massive door closed behind them with a violent thud, making Maia shudder.

"Thank you, Ren," Phocluus said, tearing his eyes off Maia. "You have managed the impossible. You have handed me this elusive creature that is your friend, Maia. So many times . . . so many times she has slipped through my fingers, but finally . . . I'm very proud of you, Ren. You will surely be an apprentice at the SDS, but I see an even brighter future. You have the qualities to lead the SDS, and I think you will lead it well."

Ren lowered his head in acknowledgment and Maia stood, her fists curled into balls as she watched Phocluus's army spread in a ring around them. She had no idea what Ren had planned and how he was going to outwit Phocluus, but this was not looking good. She reached inward, nudging the light to wakefulness. It seemed oddly sluggish, almost uncooperative. Barely a trickle flowed out of the core of her power.

Phocluus cackled. "Can't find your mighty friend, can you?" He cackled some more on seeing her startled look. "This is the Foundation Chamber, my dear. It is sheathed to curb the light, built to contain it. In here, you are just a regular person, Maia. You can still fight and I am sure you will, but it has to be with that sword."

His gaze picked up every trace of fear on Maia's face, and a crooked smile twisted his lips as Maia shifted her feet uneasily. "Impatient, are we? Unfortunately, we have to wait a bit, Maia. I have arranged a very special treat for you. You have strung me along for so long, always, always giving me the slip. Now that I have you alone and cornered, I cannot just rush through it. I have to savor this moment."

He tottered toward the open receptacle and traced its edges lovingly with a bony finger. "Your mother desecrated this room, destroyed the most sacred object on Xif. But you know, Maia, Sophie's betrayal broke my heart in so many ways. It was not just a terrible treachery against my beloved nation, it was also personal. You know why, my dear?"

Maia did not care. All she wanted was to get this over with, but she remembered what Ren had told her, they needed to buy time. Besides, fighting them was not a great prospect, given she only had Bellator to fight with. So Maia simply stared back at Phocluus.

Phocluus walked in circles around Maia. "You learned our history during the Initiative. Tell me then, who came up with the magnificent idea of making Xif fly across the heavens?" He stopped, facing her, and waited, his eyes boring into Maia's. Then he snapped, his voice sharp and vicious, "Come on, come on. Humor me."

"Veiles," Maia blurted.

"Yes, the founder of the SDS, the incomparable, indisputable maker of our nation, the one who should have been king, Veiles."

The reverential voice he used and the adoring look on his face made Maia wonder. A thought came to Maia suddenly, like lightning, and she asked, "Is Veiles your ancestor?"

Phocluus turned toward her, a manic gleam shining in his eyes. "Oh, if only I were that fortunate. I like to think I am, even though there is no means of verifying the ancestry. Veiles purged all records of his family from the databanks, you see, so I will never know," he said with a sigh. "But it does not matter if I am not of his blood, I carry his ideals in my bones, his dreams in my soul. His was an idea so unique, so ingenious, so daring . . ." Phocluus's words trailed away into a dream. "A few inconsequential lives is no comparison to the grandeur of the ideas of Veiles. And to have it broken apart by a girl who came from nowhere?"

Phocluus stumbled closer, his eyes flashing. "Seeing the Sedara's heart destroyed that night tore my heart apart. An unbelievable, unthinkable sacrilege. It had to happen on my watch, too. That girl . . . Sophie. She fooled me. She seemed so dedicated to the SDS, when in reality she was digging around for ways to cripple Xif. She betrayed my faith in her. She could have done so well. All she had to do was ignore the call of the righteous."

Phocluus slammed his stick on the floor with such vehemence that Maia almost jumped. He whirled away, snarling. "Speaking of the righteous . . . Asiyaah . . . what a waste of talent. Always tricky, Always smart, always ten steps ahead of me. And being Miizuken's daughter, so untouchable. But I found her all right and got her in the end. And look who's still standing now."

He jabbed at the dark sword hanging from Ren's belt. "Fusing that special Calbion into her own sword and then handing it over to a child. What a risk, and what an audacious move . . . but found you, I did." Phocluus stopped and chortled like a madman. "So, Remii. Are you happy that your mother did not leave that sword to you? Or are you still moping that your brother got all the attention?"

"I wouldn't have taken that sword if she offered it to me on a platter. I don't take handouts from traitors," Remii growled.

Maia could not help but chuckle to herself. What a lie! Remii would have taken it in a heartbeat. He would have groveled on his knees to have it.

"Good thing you were spared," Phocluus said. "It takes a lot of grit to deal with a Calbion-infused sword, that too the fortified Calbion of the chalice. Not something you could handle." Remii's face twisted into a vicious scowl at Phocluus's casual putdown. Oblivious of Remii's anger, Phocluus went on, "Another waste of talent, that brother of yours. But I will get him back. After all this is settled, I will get him back."

Laughing suddenly, Phocluus walked up to Ren and patted his shoulder. "You did well. Tricking that boy out of his sword . . .

commendable." He threw an annoyed glance in Remii's direction. "When all my trained staff could not even get close to him. I will need you to get Miir back too."

"Of course, Chairman Phocluus," Ren said with a gracious smile. "That would be no trouble at all. In fact, the first chance he gets, he'll be here, I'm sure."

Maia's thoughts stumbled to a halt. Could that be true? Would Miir rush back to serve Phocluus once the Sedara's heart was restored? Her heart twinged as hurtful thoughts swarmed her head, ready to distract her. It only took her a moment to push them away. No, that could not be. Miir would never come back to Phocluus, no matter what the situation. That was the truth, as solid as the ground under her feet.

Phocluus rambled on. "Excellent. Music to my ears. He belongs here, among us. A perfect life he could have had here, a wonderful career, a lovely family." Phocluus shook his head before turning toward Maia. "All ruined because of you." He stepped closer, his eyes boring into Maia's as his gnarly fingers grabbed her chin. "You have caused a lot of grief, Maia. Rattled our world, and upended a lot of lives. You have to pay."

Maia's insides bristled and she could not stay silent anymore. "I upended your lives? What about my life that you destroyed? My family that you murdered? Doesn't that matter?"

Phocluus tittered as if he had heard the best joke of his life. "Your miserable life? No, it does not." He continued without the slightest hesitation. "Your life should not have been at all. Your despicable mother should have died a prisoner, and you along with her." Phocluus's fingers dug into Maia's face as he whispered through gritted teeth. "Then your father had to play the desperate hero. I tried to reason with him, and explain this was a worthless pursuit. All he needed to do was forget Sophie existed and he would be fine. But no . . . he bribed those idiot guards into releasing your mother. Took that boy too long to die."

Maia's head buzzed as Phocluus's cruel rant sunk in, one word at a time. So Raidyn had been the one to get Sophie out. He was the one who sent Zaara the message.

I'm alive because of my father. And he's —

"He's dead? You killed him?" Maia whispered, every word draining her of strength.

Phocluus laughed. "Of course he is dead. I wish I could have killed him. But I could not touch a Royal. He got what he deserved, however, and I could not be happier. They all got the ends they deserved. As will you."

Maia had long known Phocluus, and his unkind words were not unexpected, yet she shuddered at how coldly and remorselessly he spoke. Her insides crumpled into a mass of hurt, her eyes burning from the tears she held back. Sensing her pain, Phocluus smiled. He had just opened his mouth to unleash some new cruelty on Maia when the door of the chamber opened once more and Lowanabe, Ren's stepfather, rolled in a casket.

Ren, who had been calm and smiling for the most part, fidgeted at the sight. Lowanabe however, nodded at Phocluus, placed the casket to one side, and walked up to Ren. "You have made me proud, Ren. I am truly happy today." His gaze turned cold and narrow as it flicked over Maia before he stepped toward Phocluus. He clasped his hands together and lowered his head before speaking. "Chairman, my family's eternal gratitude. I will leave you to conduct your affairs in peace."

"Thank you," Phocluus replied. "This will be a true pleasure to watch." He shot a glance behind him and called, "Amanii. Time to leave."

Amanii dragged her feet as she came forward. "I wish I could see this," she said, shooting a blistering look at Maia.

"I know you want to watch the end, but Amanii, you have to think intelligently. You are being given the gift of deniability. You will need it to resurrect the life you lost, one that you deserve. So take it and go."

As Amanii continued to fidget, Maia fathomed the meaning

behind Phocluus's words. He had plans to restore everything, including Amanii's life, the one she was meant to have with Miir. How very like Phocluus—so calmly pitiless in his planning. How easy it must seem to Phocluus to make things as they were before. All he needed was to use her to restore the Sedara's heart. Then Xif would leave the Tansian system and everything would be . . . back to normal.

"I'm sorry, Chairman Phocluus," Amanii said finally. "I'll find a way to rebuild my life when it comes to that. But right now, I do not want to miss out on the moment of our vengeance. So, pardon my impertinence, I will stay."

Phocluus shook his head but did not try to persuade her. As soon as Lowanabe left with another nod, Phocluus gestured grandly at the casket. "Remii, Amanii, please get this started," he said in a singsong voice.

The duo strode up to the casket and carefully opened the clips that secured the lid. Then he and Amanii, along with two other SDS agents, lifted the lid. Maia had expected them to take out specialized weapons, but nothing could have prepared her for what came out of it. Her heart stilled and she fell back a few steps in panic.

A man—his body the size of a young child's, his head twice the size of an adult's, his eyes fiery in his pale, roundish head—emerged from the casket and stared at Maia from across the room. It was an Innagmen, and if Maia could guess, the same one as in Sophie's memory.

"No!" Ren exclaimed before Maia could catch her breath. "This was not what I agreed to. An Innagmen was—"

"Calm down, Ren," Phocluus said. "Change of plans is a part of life. You have to adapt to it. Only then can you be successful."

"We had a deal, and this was not part of it," Ren shouted. All the while, the Innagmen kept shuffling closer, his steps small and strange just like him. All the while, Maia kept retreating.

"Did you hear what your father said, Ren?" Phocluus asked. "He said he was proud of you. You do not want to let him down, do you?"

"He's the one who let me down," Ren yelled as he fell back in lockstep with Maia. "He's the one who didn't keep his end of the bargain."

"Ren, move away," Remii said. "You have to move away. Leave that girl to us."

"I won't."

"You don't want to be in the middle of this," Amanii cautioned. "I know TEK isn't your thing. You might get badly hurt if you make us take you down."

Ren drew his sword and placed himself between Maia and the SDS duo. Behind him, Maia unsheathed Bellator.

"Wrong choice, Ren," Remii scoffed. His arms went up in the next instant and a TEK wave surged at them. Ren ducked and so did Maia. The long bend in space passed over them, a gust of hot air that only ruffled their hair a little. But evading one was no great achievement, not when faced with two TEKists of the SDS.

Remii and Amanii strode in from two sides, their arms and hands moving nonstop, the air in front of them churning into a whirlwind of energy. One moment a wave lashed out at Maia and Ren, hitting them across the face; the next moment an avalanche of rocks collapsed on them. Remii and Amanii advanced, along with their relentless strikes, and Maia and Ren retreated. Maia tried to slash and cut across the waves, trying her best to find a point of weakness to destabilize the formations. She found a few. Ren, fighting blind for all practical purposes, also fought back valiantly. But their spirit lasted only so long. Soon they were pushed into a corner, with only a few paces left to go before they hit the wall. The TEK waves kept coming, fast and furious, and finding a way to break them up became nearly impossible. They barely managed to keep standing. Maia's arms hurt, her legs ached, and she found little or no hope left in her heart.

"We have to keep fighting, Maia," Ren said. "Help will come, but until then, we have to stay alive. So, focus and fight."

"Who will help? When?"

"I don't know who or when, but I know someone will come. Pomewege needs time to set things up. So —"

Ren's words broke off when the space bent and hurled itself on him. He skidded backward and slammed against the wall, his face contorting in pain at the impact. Maia wanted to rush to his side, but the giant tornado Amanii had flung toward her did not give her a moment's respite. Meanwhile, Remii threw wave after wave at Ren, tossing him across the floor like a twig.

"Go easy on the boy, Remii," Phocluus reminded him calmly. "We'll need him to use that sword on the girl."

Remii laughed. "Of course." The wave he unleashed next was shaped like a snake. It came with the swiftness of a lightning bolt and encircled Ren in a vicious grip. Ren gasped for breath as it lifted him up in the air and then threw him down on the floor. He rolled back, hit the wall, and collapsed in a heap at the edge.

"Ren!" Maia screamed. Ren did not move. In that one moment of inattention, Amanii struck. It was a long whip-like formation that hit Maia across the torso. Then another clawed through her skin, burning its way across the side of her face. Yet another pushed Maia backward. Bellator went flying from her hand and Maia tumbled to the floor.

Towering over her, Amanii laughed. "No one left to save you, is there?" she said, advancing as Maia scrambled backward. "This is how your story ends, Maia. That Innagmen is going to suck the life out of you first, and you're going to scream while he does it, wishing you were dead for every moment you bear his torture. Then, when you're nothing more than a shell, your friend will plunge that sword into your heart. He will be happy to, because you see, it will be the only way to relieve you of your miserable existence." She bared her teeth in a vicious smile. "And you know what, I will be laughing at you all through it."

"Amanii, get back now." Remii's sharp voice made Maia take her eyes off Amanii's scowling face. Her heart dropped to the pit of her stomach the moment she looked toward Remii. He had fallen back, clearing a path for the Innagmen who advanced, his hands slightly raised, his fingers curled, and his burning gaze fixed on her.

Maia's mind raced, as did her heart. She scrambled back desperately until she reached Ren's slumped form. He was breathing, but he did not respond to her nudges. She had to keep fighting. For him, for them. Help will come, Ren had said. But when? How long could she fight twenty people without even a sword? How long could she thwart an Innagmen's assault on her mind?

She had to . . . she had to stay alive. She could not let Sophie's sacrifice go to waste. She had to somehow—

Revsi Sottekaja's training flashed through Maia's mind. Maybe that could help—not forever, but to earn themselves a little time.

Raise the shield!

Maia recalled the words Sottekaja had taught . . .

Arron-meyeh . . . Nison-meyeh . . .

Arron-meyeh . . . Nison-meyeh . . .

The barriers, tiny little coverings over the synapses of her mind, rose up like an invisible army as she exhaled. She felt the warmth of the protective shell around her mind. For a moment, Maia was relieved. For a moment, she relaxed. Then it came—a wave, a deluge, a landslide of sheer pain crashed into her mind and Maia screamed as a dense blackness descended on her senses.

The sound of laughter trickled into her ears. She saw the gloating faces of Amanii and Remii behind the Innagmen before they and the rest of the chamber receded into a fog.

The Innagmen came closer. Maia felt him inside her head, his cold, metal fingers prying into her mind, ripping her senses to shreds. She fell through a rainfall of memories, she floated past long-lost fragments of time. A black fog swirled around her, pulling out every memory inside her, lingering painfully over the worst ones.

Blood-red skies blazing over Appian. Tears forming a clump in her chest. Screams echoing through her empty insides but refusing to come out.

She had to fight . . . she had to get that time Ren needed . . .

So much blood. Ohimet's face turning blue. A laughter so cruel, a face so beautiful, a heart so evil. What was her name again?

Help would come . . . she had to fight . . . But how?

Bikele was gone. A dolphin bobbing inside a cage, its blind eyes wide, fearful, panicked.

Help never came in time.

How could you forget who I am? And who you are?

Because that was what loving someone meant . . . that you forgot the differences, the consequences, the fear of getting hurt.

Green eyes full of hatred blazed like fire. No one cares for the real you. No one. You are just a means to an end.

Zaara . . . something about Zaara . . . she had to remember . . .

You cannot hesitate to do whatever it takes to save yourself. Do you understand? Keep this. Make them pay.

The poison!

Maia's mind clambered out of the cesspool of dark memories. She had one last weapon left . . . the vial of neurotoxin Zaara had given her . . . she still had it. Her hands, weak and slow, fumbled at the container that always hung on her belt. She drifted in and out of patches of darkness, but forced her fingers to keep prying.

Waves of pain racked her head and kept tearing her apart from the inside. Cold sweat streamed down her face, and in the rare moments that the Innagmen's probes relented, her body trembled from the aftershock. Maia did not remember how long it took, but she kept trying. Lupitiali's cold waters were still soaking her senses when she felt the smooth surface of the vial in her hand. Her numb, shaking fingers wrapped around it.

You can do it. Whatever it takes to save yourself.

A plan . . . a moment's respite and . . . with the last bit of energy she had left in her, Maia pushed herself backward as far as she could. The Innagmen, glaring, his teeth gritted, shuffled closer.

He did not expect Maia to reach out and grab him. Maia did not hope to take him by surprise. But it happened. The Innagmen toppled, the fieriness in his eyes momentarily fading. He fell on top of her, and the cloying smell from his perfume-soaked robes inundated Maia's senses, suffocating her as his large, heavy head slammed against her chest. The Innagmen tried to push himself off, but Maia's fingers closed tightly on him. Keeping her grip on his robe, she thrust the vial into his bare neck, pushing it with all the strength she had left and hoping, as she had never hoped before in her life, for him to die.

The Innagmen shuddered in a violent spasm that left Maia shaking under him. Then it came. An avalanche of pain that swept her body in ceaseless waves . . . a serrated sword ripping through her brain and leaving it bloody and torn . . . a fire burning in the mush that remained . . .

Maia gasped for air and found none. Only the stifling smell lingered.

A pit of nothingness opened in the middle of the hacked and scorched remains of her mind. And Maia fell, sucked away into the nothingness until she could not see or hear or feel anymore.

CHAPTER FIFTY-TWO

. . . AND LOYALTY

An endless blanket of snow covered everything. It looked beautiful, but it felt anything but. The heartless cold covered the world above and below, inside and out. It blew against Maia's face in minute pinpricks, it clung to her clothes and clawed through them, through her skin down to her bones. It numbed her, her body, her soul, the core of her being. It made her want to curl up and sleep, even though she knew that if she did, there would be no waking up again. She stared at the snow-covered path ahead—white, barren, and flat. Not a soul stirred. Nothing stood out in that featureless, lifeless whiteness except for the dark, gnarly remains of a gigantic tree on the hillside. The frigid wind blew and Maia's heart pined.

The tree . . . she *had* to get to it. What for? She did not know. But she had to get there. Her legs were stiff, her mouth parched, her vision dim, and a dead weight on her chest crushed her insides. Every few steps, she stumbled and fell. But she picked herself up and soldiered on. Her gaze fixed on the burnt tree that had once held a canopy of nurturing shade over the home she had lost forever, its charred shell all that was left of her existence.

With steps slow and painful, with a heart empty and hopeless, Maia trudged forward. Finally, her trembling fingers touched the scorched surface of the tree. A strange wave, of love and kinship that went far beyond familiarity, swept through Maia's blistered heart. A happy memory — weak and distant — trickled in . . . of golden sunlight warming the face of a girl laughing, her pigtails swaying as she swung on the branches. Another gust of cold slammed Maia, making her totter and sink to her knees, the golden sunlight snuffed out in an instant.

This is how your story ends, Maia.

This is how . . . Maia pulled herself closer to the massive trunk of the burnt-out oak and nestled into it, cherishing the firmness of the dead tree. She drew her knees to her chest and hugged them as tight as she could. Her eyelids drooped. She breathed in the icy, withering air to fill herself before she laid her weary head down on her knees.

This is how my story ends.

* * *

"Maia."

The voice was familiar. It called her name. Her name . . . sounded different, unheard of, as if it were not her own at all.

"Maia," it said again.

The heaviness crushing her fell away and suddenly . . . there was air. Maia breathed as if she had never breathed before.

"Maia, can you hear me?" the voice came again. She wanted to say yes, but there was no sound left in her. So much pain in that voice, so much anguish.

I wish I could help you.

She wanted to open her eyes and look. There was no strength to be found. Darkness pulled her deeper, lower.

Arms lifted her and propped her up against a wall. Hands, gentle and cautious, held her face.

"Maia. Open your eyes. Please."

Do I know you? Are you a friend?

She desperately wanted to see who it was, but . . . the abyss . . . that bottomless pit of restful oblivion called her more strongly.

I don't want to go.

She sank deeper, unable to stop.

"Maia." The voice nudged her again, the warmth of the hands holding her face cut through the murky mist of nothingness. "You have to come back. You *have* to."

I have to.

She forced her eyelids open. Heavy and tight they were, but Maia kept pushing. They opened, fluttering fitfully, to the light and shade in front of her. A face, grainy and faded. Eyes brimming with tears.

I knew you once. But . . .

She searched and she searched. She could not remember his name.

"You are safe now," he said. "You will be fine."

Fine. I will be fine.

If she could only think through this pain. If only she could remember.

"Who are you?" she whispered.

Tears spilled from his eyes and Maia's heart wrenched in pain.

Why are you sad? For me?

She reached for him, to comfort him, to—

Her shaking hand sank before she could touch his arm. He did not let it fall. His fingers wrapped around her hand, steady, resolute. A memory flashed through Maia's mind.

"Miir?"

"Yes." He smiled through his tears.

He placed her hand on his face and closed his eyes as if he were etching this memory within him. His lips rested on her upturned palm for an instant.

"I have to go now," he whispered. "I will be back, I promise." He turned toward someone next to her. "Keep her awake," he said. Then he was gone.

Arms wrapped around Maia. A flash of gold. Eyes . . . shining bright and blue, gazed into hers.

"Maia, it'll be all right," said a kind voice. "We're here now."

"Dani." The name came out of Maia along with a sigh of relief. "Dani."

* * *

Maia leaned on Dani's shoulder and looked around, hearing in pieces, and seeing through the constant ebb and flow of consciousness. Everything was vague and distant. Sights . . . choppy and broken. Sounds . . . fractured bits floating into her ears. Slivers of clarity shone a light in her mind before fading away. Never-ending patches of gray connected it all.

* * *

A bright glow illuminated her wrist. The firestone wristband. Mahswa Tabrin . . . she had given it to them. A tie that would bind them all together, she had said, into a Craedonnen—a circle of trust.

It always glowed during times of trouble. It always helped.

It would help them now.

* * *

A blue disc circled the room at a relentless pace. A mass of people hovered at the far end. More fought at the sides. A girl whirled a set of daggers.

Nafi . . . Kusha . . .

A body slumped at her side . . . the Innagmen.

Maia remembered. She had come to the Foundation Chamber with Ren.

"Ren?" Maia muttered. Her voice was barely a whisper and it took all her strength to get a word out. But . . . Ren was hurt. She needed to know.

"Ren is fine, Maia," Dani replied. "Look."

He was at Dani's other side. Bandages were wrapped around his head and neck. His eyes were closed, but he was breathing. He was alive.

My friend is safe.

* * *

"Kusha, Nafi, get back," Miir yelled. "Stay behind me."

Wild laughter echoed through the chamber. Maia knew that heartless laugh. Phocluus . . . this was his plot, his latest attempt to get to the light inside her.

"Miir, there is still time to choose the right path," Phocluus said. "You can turn this around in a blink, my boy. It does not have to go this way."

"I told you once, Chairman Phocluus, and that was my final word," Miir said. "I have chosen my path. This is the right path, my *only* path."

Another voice, sharp and bitter, cut through Maia's dazed senses. "So you're here to save that girl, is it? Well, you're going to have to go through me first, dear brother."

"Gladly."

A girl took up her stance next to Remii.

"And kill me too while you're at it. Let's see how far you're willing to go to stay on that worthless path of yours."

"Kill you?" Miir chuckled. "No, Amanii, you deserve no such attention."

"Give them hell, Miir," Dani whispered as her arms tightened around Maia. "That Remii and Amanii are just . . . obnoxious."

The chamber erupted in waves. Space crumbled and collapsed, clashed and collided. The air folded into spears and formed barrages of rocks, hail, and boulders. Shockwaves reached the far corners of the room, their force still palpable. Shouts and yells, groans, and grunts filled the air. Every sound, every movement jolted Maia's frayed insides until she could not watch anymore.

Maia hid her face in Dani's shoulder and sobbed quietly.

* * *

"Dani, watch out!" Kusha yelled. "One slipped through."

A flash of metal swished through the air.

"Oh no, you don't." Dani darted away, sword drawn. Metal clashed. Dani lunged and kicked. A body crashed against the wall. "Touch my friends and I'll kill you," Dani screamed.

"Thanks, Dani," Kusha said. "I got it now."

Arms, warm and tender, wrapped around her once more.

* * *

Ren sat up, groaning.

"Maia?" He leaned over to peer at her face.

"She'll be all right, Ren," Dani reassured him. "How's your head?"

"It has seen better days," Ren said with a chuckle. "Ruche's here?"

"Outside."

"Good." Ren squinted at the raging battle at the center of the chamber. "How's the fight coming along?"

"The way Miir's going, there's no hope for Phocluus."

"And this is just the beginning. Phocluus has no idea what's coming."

* * *

Remii lay on the ground. Panting. Bleeding. A large gash tore across his arm up to his shoulder. He could not move if he tried.

"You are a traitor through and through, Miir," he spat. "My righteous and perfect little brother is nothing but a fraud. But that isn't surprising, is it? Our whole family is a fraud. I'm the only one who had any real loyalty to our nation. I'm the only one who did the right thing." He panted some more. "I've always been the one trying to fix the mistakes all of you made. Trying to fix you all. Mother and Father didn't listen when I warned them. They should have. And they paid the price. You should have too."

Silence.

"What do you mean? What price?" Miir asked. "Tell me."

"Tell you?" Remii laughed. "Why should I?"

A blue disc flew out and pressed into his neck.

"Tell him now," Kusha roared. "Or I will cut you to pieces."

Remii yelped. "I suspected what our mother was up to. Could not believe I was born of a traitor. I hated her. I hated myself. I told the Chairman all I knew." He stopped. Gasped for breath. "And Father? Trying to pass a resolution to have the Sedara's lattice reworked? He wanted to disable the heart forever. That coward! The Chairman needed to be apprised, of course."

"And the Chairman had him murdered," Miir said.

"Your father had outlived his purpose," Phocluus said. "He was not only redundant but also being foolish and harmful."

"I pity you, Remii," Miir said. "You always chose wrong."

* * *

The door of the Foundation Chamber opened with a thud. A flood of red swept inside. A swishing cape, the flash of uniforms.

"And here comes the Crown Prince, Aekken the Terrible," Ren said.

Miir fell back in an instant, herding Kusha and Nafi with him.

"Chairman Phocluus?" the prince called. "Chairman Phocluus."

"How dare you set foot on this hallowed ground, you R'armimon filth?" Phocluus roared. "Leave now."

"Hallowed ground?" Aekken scoffed. "This place is tainted with the blood of our princess, and now"—he looked back at their huddle—"you have tried to harm another Nasfarii. I am astounded you dared to try this, when you knew I was here."

"I had to avenge the treachery against my nation. This is a glorious creation of my people, and I will not tolerate assaults against it."

"Are you ready to die for your people, Phocluus?"

Silence.

"Not so brave now, are you Phocluus?" Ren muttered.

Aekken flipped his hand. A wave of red surged toward the ring of black around Phocluus. The room erupted once again in screams, shouts, the clash of weapons, and the crash of bloodied bodies.

Maia's heart thudded wildly, and her head exploded with pain. With a yelp, she curled tighter and closer to Dani.

***

The prince circled a defiant Phocluus.

"You are so proud of this despicable thing"—Aekken spat at the receptacle of the heart—"you will be happy to hear that you carry the blood of Princess Ataii's slayer."

"I do?" Maia's senses were at best unfocussed and faded, but there was no mistaking the joy in Phocluus's voice. "How do you know? There is no record—"

"I had biometrics, thanks to our mutual friend Ren. I matched them with our records of the slayer's sons. You are not closely related, but . . ."

Phocluus laughed like a madman. "I knew . . . I always knew."

"Then you should be prepared to pay for your ancestor's sins."

Maia held her breath.

"It was no sin. It was justice," Phocluus yelled. "You will leave this chamber, R'armimon."

Aekken's face twisted. "I certainly will." He held out his arms. A guard placed a pair of daggers in his hands. "But before that, you shall die."

Phocluus's face wizened and paled.

People held their breaths. Dani whimpered. Maia closed her eyes again, shuddering violently as Aekken struck.

* * *

A regal form strode up. Aekken, Crown Prince of the R'armimon, loomed over them all. Maia's insides shook.

"My starlight," he called.

He meant her. That was what he always called her. How she hated that name . . .

Miir stood in the way. "Please do not come any closer. She is not ready to speak with anyone."

Please, Miir . . . Stop!

Miir had to know how dangerous Aekken was, how he had just shredded Phocluus to pieces. It was foolish to—

"And you are?" Aekken demanded.

"No one of consequence."

"Then move out the way," Aekken snarled. "I need to speak with the only one who matters. I need to see if she is well."

Miir did not budge, not even a hair's width.

Frantic and desperate, Maia searched for every bit of energy within her. She had to intervene before it was too late. She *had* to.

"Prince Aekken, I'm . . . I'm fine," Maia forced the words out with whatever meager strength she could scrounge up.

"My starlight. This"—Aekken pointed at the carnage behind him—"is what you get from the deadwaste scum. This is what you will always get. They will not give you Seigvard, no matter how many times you beg. They will give you *this*." His voice, pitiless and jeering, tore through Maia's mind with its sharp claws. "You have a glorious future, a dazzling future. But not here, not among people who do not need you or respect you."

"Yes, I know," Maia said. She would agree to anything so he would leave.

Aekken extended a hand toward her. "You should leave with me right now."

"Please. You promised me one day with my friends and . . . I'd like to have it, please," Maia begged. "Please grant me that."

Aekken pulled his arm back. His eyes narrowed to slits.

Ren rose to his feet, groaning loudly as he walked over to Aekken. "Well, buddy, I'm coming with you. Isn't that good enough?"

"No, it certainly is not," Aekken scoffed.

Ren was not one who gave up easily. Or ever. "Well, you promised me a tour of your ships. And we're running out of time. You owe me something after I gave you Phocluus and saved your"—he turned and gestured at Maia—"your starlight."

Aekken shook his head and let out a grudging chuckle. "You are quite a fool. But you have been a useful fool." He stopped and sighed. "I will keep my promise. Come. I will be back for you, my starlight. Soon."

Aekken whirled away toward the door.

"Ren!" Maia would have run to him if she had the strength, but calling him was all she could manage.

Ren turned around. He bent down next to her and pulled her into a tight hug. "I'll be fine. We'll all be fine," he whispered into her ear. "Trust me."

He clasped Dani's hands. "Thank you for the thing on the head," he said, grinning.

"You are only visiting my Battlecruiser, Ren," Aekken said as he walked away. "This farewell seems a bit excessive for that."

"Yes, sorry." Ren jumped back to his feet and flashed a sheepish smile. He had scuttled behind Remii, but turned around midway and strode back to Miir. "I made you a promise and I'm keeping it. Find a way to keep yours," he said. Then he hurried away.

Nafi dropped to her knees next to Dani as soon as Aekken and his troops shimmered away. "I saw Ren hand you something. What was that?"

Dani slowly opened her hand. Lying in it was a tiny scrap of paper with six cryptic words.

Ask him to tell me when.

"What does that even mean?" Nafi burst out. "Ask whom? Ruche?"

Silence.

"And Miir? What was that stuff he said to you?" Nafi demanded.

"Not relevant," he replied. "You need to get out of here. All of you. Now."

There was nothing that Maia yearned to do more than to leave that room. If she could run, she would. All she wanted was to leave that chamber of death, blood, and nightmares far behind her.

Chapter Fifty-Three

Around the Bend

A large unit of chancery guards streamed past them and into the Foundation Chamber as Maia trudged out, propped up between Dani on one side and Kusha on the other. Even in her dazed state and even through the unbearable pain that kept coursing through her head, Maia wondered where the guards came from. How did they even know to be here?

"Maia." Ruche's voice, warm and comforting, floated into her ears. As soon as he strode up to them, Maia rushed into his outstretched arms. The seer placed a hand on her head as he led her away. "You'll be fine. You'll be fine," he whispered.

He sat her down on the massive stone steps that wound up to the floors above. Holding her face in his hands, he peered into her eyes. His gaze was worried, his face taut with anxiety.

"How do you feel?"

"It keeps going dark inside. I keep seeing things I don't want to see." Tears coursed down her cheeks, but Maia did not have the strength to wipe them away. "My head hurts like it'll explode."

Ruche placed his hands on her temples. The touch felt comforting, and when he started chanting words she could barely hear, she closed her eyes in immediate relief. The pain eased. Not at once, and not entirely, but bit by bit. The darkness receded, and breathing did not take as much effort anymore. Maia did not know how much time passed before she opened her eyes again, but she knew the tears had finally stopped flowing.

"Somewhat better now?" Ruche asked.

Maia nodded slowly.

Ruche grimaced. "Nasty mind probes. That practice should be banned."

Maia drew a shaky breath. The Innagmen had barely started on her and this was how she felt. How much Sophie must have suffered. And Bikele . . .

"I killed him," she whispered. "That Innagmen."

"I'm happy you did," Ruche said. "I'm glad you didn't hesitate to defend yourself. Dare I say you avenged your mother, and probably many others? Now, don't let a vile man's death cast a shadow on you."

Maia shook her head. "I won't."

Ruche touched the side of her face where a TEK wave had hit her. "You're still bleeding."

"I'll live."

She fell back against the cold wall of the staircase and closed her eyes, relishing the coolness behind her. She looked up again at the sound of footsteps and the touch of something cold on her cheek. Dani's smiling face greeted her, and behind her, Kusha and Nafi hovered. In one hand Dani held a bottle, and with the other, she rubbed something cool and soothing on Maia's cheek.

"Putting some salve on that gouge," Dani explained, reaching for her hand next. "Better?"

"Much. How did you get here?"

"We came with Ruche, of course," Kusha said. "He got us together after you left with Ren. Principal Pomewege had a transport waiting and we came right behind you. Ruche didn't want to be too official about it, for reasons that have stayed unexplained" — Kusha rolled his eyes and shook his head — "but Aihnswothe Feirah had just arrived and refused to listen. So he came with a couple of his people. Hans and Rayan are here too. Sana's army is the largest, though."

Maia blinked in surprise. "Army? Sana?"

"Yes," Dani said with a chuckle. "Some of the Chieftain's Corps are in there, your friends from Appian of course, quite a few of our fellow contestants, Hadeeyah and some of her mates, and . . . you won't believe this, some of the Silver Wings Fan Club. They fought with the Fyrstell people guarding the hold and cleared the way, so we could get to the Foundation Chamber. They're still standing guard down there."

"Funny that Ruche had nothing against that ragtag band," Nafi commented gruffly. "On the other hand, my father, Hans, and Rayan had to beg and argue forever to get included."

Maia chuckled to herself. Ruche and his ways . . . there was, almost always, no explaining why. There had to be some good reason somewhere, though . . . she had come to realize that after all this time.

Nafi chirped in excitement. "Look . . . the chancery guards got all of the Fyrstell scoundrels arrested. Remii and Amanii too."

"How did the chancery guards get here?" Maia asked.

"Ruche brought them. He also brought the queen," Kusha informed her.

Maia winced at the mention of the queen, but her attention, and everyone else's as well, was quickly drawn to the sound of raised voices behind them. All of them turned to look, and Maia's eyes widened when she found Miir glaring at Ruche. Ruche was his usual unflappable self, but she had never seen Miir looking so angry. His eyes blazed like fire, and anyone who saw the expression on his face would be worried about Ruche's well-being.

"Now, now. No need to lose your temper, young man," Ruche said. "Everything is under control."

"Under control?" Miir fumed. "You sent the handful of us in

saying you would send help. Where was that help? You did not send in your people as you promised."

"Yes, that is true. I didn't. But . . ." Ruche shook a finger. "But I did not promise *my* people. I said you would have reinforcements in time. And you had reinforcements. Crown Prince Aekken came himself. You should have been honored by his presence."

"Honored? By the presence of a scheming, murdering maniac?" Miir snapped. "And even that lunatic came late. She could have died. They could have all died."

"She didn't, did she? Neither did anyone else. Seems to me reinforcements were not necessary," Ruche said. "You know why? *You* came through for them. You came together, all of you." He placed a hand on Miir's shoulder. "Be proud of yourself. I am."

Miir was about to say more, but Ruche held up a hand. "There is a method, Miir, and there is always a reason why. You need to have some faith in me." He looked down the hallway and hastily moved away. "You have to excuse me now. Serious matters need my attention."

"That was close. I almost thought Miir would hit Ruche in the face. I would've liked to see that, actually," Nafi muttered. "What's this serious matter, I wonder," she said as she tiptoed to the banisters, Kusha following.

Maia tilted her head to see what Ruche had been looking at, but the banister and Nafi dangling over it blocked her view.

Next to Maia, Dani sighed. "Poor Miir. He's still upset. I never imagined he could get so flustered. I was scared out of my mind too, but he quite lost it seeing you there with the Innagmen."

Dani linked her arm through Maia's and held it tight. Dani's words brought back some faint memories. Maia remembered Miir's face, his voice pulling her out of the pitch blackness in her mind that the Innagmen's probes had created. Next to her, Dani continued, her voice soft and pensive.

"You should have seen him take on Remii and the Fyrstell thugs when we came in, Maia. I've never seen anyone fight so hard. Ruche is right, he did come through. He defended and protected his team the way we kept wishing he would all those years ago."

Sights and sounds of the fight inside the Foundation Chamber kept filtering slowly through the lingering haze of Maia's mind. Her eyes had seen it all and her ears had heard, but like an unfeeling automaton left to observe, her mind had been suspended in the darkness by the Innagmen's probes. Now the memories trickled back, alive and real, but slowly, very slowly.

"Thought I saw Kusha using his chakra," Maia said as more pieces fell in place.

Dani chuckled a little. "He surely did. Kusha and Nafi held off Remii and his gang while Miir and I were checking on you and Ren. Kusha's chakra work was quite scary, actually." Dani's voice swelled with pride. "I'm happy that all that practice was put to good use."

They did not get to talk anymore, since Ruche reappeared with Rahina Quemiila, a chancery guard behind them.

At Ruche's signal, all of Maia's friends slipped away from the staircase. They looked worried, all of them, as they stood in a tight huddle on one side with Miir. As Ruche sat down next to Maia, the Xifarian queen walked up to them. Maia did not glance at her face, she could not make herself, but she sensed concern in the queen's gaze.

"Rahina Quemiila is here to speak with you, Maia," Ruche said. "Do you feel up to it?"

Maia did not want to hear one more word from the woman or even want to be in her presence. The last words the queen had said to her — *do not show me your face again* — rang in her ears and clawed at her heart. Maia found little strength left in her to face the queen again. Every bone in her body ached, the throbbing in her head had subsided, but was not gone, and breathing still felt like a debilitating task. All she craved was some quiet, some rest. But, she deduced, Ruche had to have a good reason for bringing the woman here, so no matter what her emotions or her exhaustion, she had to hear it out.

"I am fine," Maia said, as calmly as she could.

"Seer Ruche" — the queen started hesitantly — "I believe her wound needs attention. My personal healer is in the landing bay and I can have her come here."

Ruche chuckled. "It's the least of our problems right now, Rahina Mayen. All of these kids need attention, but we don't have the time to—"

"I understand. Let us proceed with the important matters, then," Rahina Quemiila said. "Maia, I brought you something that I keep hearing will help you fight the current circumstances. You told me so yourself, but I . . . misjudged you. I am here now, hoping it is not too late to amend that."

She waved at the guard and the man strode over with a long red box. Maia knew right away what it was, and a tempest of emotions rocked her insides. The guard opened the box and the queen took out the most magnificent sword Maia had ever seen, the one she had been hoping to acquire for almost a year now—the legendary Seigvard. Its jeweled hilt caught the light and sparkled, and its long blade shone beguilingly.

As Maia stared, in disbelief and in awe, the queen spoke again. "This is yours. I will initiate the bequest."

"Please wait," Maia said to the queen. She turned to Ruche and searched his face. "Ruche, just this once, will you give me a straight answer? Please?"

Ruche smiled and patted her hand. "Go on. Ask."

"Do you think my having Seigvard will help anything anymore?"

Ruche nodded. "Yes, it will. As you know already, this sword belonged to our Princess Ataii. But Seigvard isn't just any sword, it was made especially for the princess. Seigvard is a super-conduit for energy. I need it to help you transcend to a level where you can wield cosmic power. It's not guaranteed to work, and the state of Arotharan does not last long, but I hope it'll be long enough to handle our dear Aekken." Ruche stopped and sighed. "So, if you want to avoid leaving with the Crown Prince, that sword is your only option."

"And it has to be bequeathed to me?"

Ruche thought for a moment or two, then shook his head. "I don't think so. Given your heritage, it should bind to you just fine."

Relieved, Maia turned to the queen. "Please, then, do not initiate a bequest. I will return Seigvard to you as soon as the . . . procedure is over."

"You do not wish to have Seigvard?" the queen asked, her voice trembling.

The guard who held Seigvard's box was frozen with a look of horror on his face. Maia did not have to look at Miir to know how dismayed and offended he had to be right now. To refuse the bequest of Seigvard must be unheard of and unthinkable. It had to be an offense to every Xifarian. Yet Maia felt no fear, no pain. She had never coveted Seigvard. She only needed it to help Tansi, help Xif, help them all. Why was that so hard for people to understand?

"Please don't say it like that," she said to the queen. "I'm not refusing Seigvard, I'm merely accepting it the way I should. I do not need a sword. I have my mother's and that's fine enough for me. I only need Seigvard to get us out of this situation, and that's all."

"Very well, then," the queen said in a rush, placing Seigvard back into its box.

"Dani," Ruche called. "Can you please take charge of the box?"

As soon as Dani took the box, the queen dismissed the guard. She waited a bit, it seemed to Maia until the guard was out of earshot, before speaking again.

"And there is the other thing I am told you were looking for," Rahina Quemiila said. She parted the collar of her Gambrill and Maia gasped as she saw the sparkle on her neck. It was a pendant, a broken half circle just like the one she wore, only a mirror image of it. She finally realized what restoring the pendant meant—bringing the two parts together. But what did the pendant signify? What would taking it mean?

Bewildered, Maia looked up at Ruche once more. He had been studying her face intently, and he sighed as soon as she looked at him.

"No, I do not need you to have that."

"This is her . . . birthright," the queen said, her brows knit into a tight frown. "Seer Ruche, are you asking her to reject her inheritance?"

"I am suggesting no such thing, Rahina Mayen," Ruche said. "All I'm saying is I don't need it for the purposes of the Arotharan. Maia is free to accept it, of course." He turned toward Maia and smiled. "It's your choice. I wanted you to find it because I thought it would give you the answers you've been seeking all your life. I hoped finding your roots would bring you peace. You'd know where you come from and where you belong. I hoped it would restore your heart a little and prepare you better in case we needed the Arotharan." He stopped and sighed, his eyes scanning Maia's face. "It's too late for all that now. But, as the Rahina said, this is your inheritance, your birthright. She is generously offering it to you so . . ."

Generous? Every name the woman had called Sophie, every insult she had hurled at her, echoed in Maia's mind and wrung her heart dry. No matter what her pain, how badly Sophie had hurt her son, or why, Rahina Quemiila did not have to say the things she said to the child who had no control over the situation fate had put her in. Yet she had. If that was not cruelty, nothing was. Maia did not know why the queen was handing over these objects now, but it surely was not out of generosity. Sophie's pale, smiling face flashed before her eyes, and at that moment Maia knew exactly what she had to do.

"Forgive me," Maia said, squaring her shoulders as she looked into the queen's eyes. "I can't take that. I don't mean to insult you or your family, I truly don't. And Ruche's right, I always searched for and dreamed of finding my father. I've wanted the answers for myself that everyone around me came with. All I ever wished for was to be like everyone else, wished I could be accepted as such." She stopped for a moment to catch her breath and blink away the tears that threatened to burst out. "But I've realized something. I can't change who I am, and I can't be a regular girl. People will find me strange or tainted or cursed and . . . hard to accept. But that doesn't matter. What matters is if *I* can accept myself. And I do now."

A series of memories flashed through Maia's mind, of times when she had been blissfully happy—Dada's face when she made a new turn in her glider, long stories about nothing with Herc during the trips to Shiloh, Emmy fussing for days over the stash of unwashed socks she had discovered under Maia's bed. They brought a smile to her face and made her heart yearn. *That* was home. *That* was where she truly belonged.

"I'm a girl from an unknown corner of a broken planet that no one in the universe cares about. I know that. And I have no shame in it, or regret. I'm content to be just my mother's daughter, Sophie's daughter. I'm proud of Sophie, just as I know she would be proud of me. Unconditionally." She stopped again, relishing the surge of joy that coursed through her as she said that. She felt no anger, no pain uttering the next words. "You've told me I bring you dishonor, and I'm not saying this out of spite, but I feel no happiness in claiming my birthright either. So, as illustrious as it may be, I don't need this inheritance. I hope you can pardon my graceless manner." Her hand reached up to caress the broken half of the pendant at the base of her own throat. "I would give this back to you too, but I can't spurn my mother's last gift to me. So this I will keep."

Maia had expected to be interrupted, to be scolded, to at least be gently imparted some wisdom once she finished. She had not planned to talk for so long. But words had come out of her, like a fountain that had finally found an opening and gushed out, yearning for freedom. It felt good to say it all out loud, but the relief ebbed as soon as she stopped speaking and exhaustion, along with an unbearable silence, encroached upon them.

Rahina Quemiila did not look at her. Mouth pursed, her eyes glistening, the queen stared into the distance. While that did not concern Maia, Dani's tear-stained face and Kusha's sad one next to her certainly did. As did Nafi's hopeless fury, her eyes blazing at the Xifarian queen. And Ruche, his gray eyes dark with anguish. Maia realized that in her quest to free herself, she had brought pain to all of them.

She looked at Miir last of all, and immediately wished she had not. She had not expected to catch him staring, and she did not expect the expression on his face to stick a dagger into her heart. There was an overwhelming sadness in his gaze. And what else? Was it frustration? Disappointment? All of it, most likely.

But what else would there be? Did she expect him to applaud? That would be stupid. As it had always been between them, this was yet another of her offensive tirades against the Xifarian heritage he held dear. Just because he had revolted against Phocluus and his ways did not mean Xif and its traditions were any less important to him than they had been before. Besides, he had risked his freedom, his life, to get her the sword and the pendant, and here she was, casually throwing it all away as if his efforts did not matter.

Maia could not bear to see his dismayed face any longer, so she forced her eyes to the ground. *You did what was right*, she reminded herself, *even if it took you ten more steps away from Miir*. In the end, did it matter what he thought? He was just another traveler she had met on this strange road that was her life. Come tomorrow, he would start to fade away, and in a few years, he would only be a distant memory. Maia stiffened her spine and breathed deeply. She had done right by Sophie and that was all that mattered. She knew that even if she were asked a thousand times, she would not choose any other way.

"If that is what you desire, so it will be," Rahina Quemiila said, finally breaking the quiet and startling Maia out of her thoughts. "I wish you the very best." She turned toward Ruche next. "Seer Ruche, should we discuss the other things now?"

"Ah yes, the other things." Ruche nodded and jumped to his feet. "Miir, could you walk with us, please?"

They strode away, immersed in deep conversation.

Maia had no idea what they needed to discuss, but she did not get a chance to think about it. As soon as Rahina Quemiila left with Ruche and Miir, Dani rushed to Maia's side and flung her arms around Maia's neck. Kusha sat down on Maia's other side and put a hand on her shoulder. "I'm proud of you, Maia. You did the right thing."

Nafi stomped up and down in front of the staircase, her fists curled. "Who the heck called you tainted?" she demanded. "I'll need to have a word with that disgraceful wretch."

Maia chuckled and reached for Nafi's hand. "It's all right, Nafi. Let it go. I really meant it when I said I didn't care. I don't. Not anymore."

"I'm happy that you chose to fight Aekken, Maia," Dani said, her eyes brimming with tears. "I'm not a fan of the Rahina, but I'm glad she offered you Seigvard before it was too late."

"Perhaps I can forgive all her cruel words for that one miracle." Maia forced a little laughter. "Leaving with Aekken just wouldn't work, would it? I'd miss you guys so much, I'd probably have to sneak out of Aekken's ship midway and run back home."

"In case you didn't know, running wouldn't exactly work in the middle of space," Kusha said.

Nafi rolled her eyes. "It's just an expression, Kusha. Seriously, you're getting sillier every day."

"I know, Miss know-it-all. I—"

"Can you two just stop?" Dani interrupted. "Just this once."

Laughter spurted out of Maia at the comforting familiarity of the situation. For that moment, she forgot all the pain she had been through and the fears that loomed over her. She was simply . . . happy. They sat in that little huddle for a long time and Maia wished their time together would never end.

CHAPTER FIFTY-FOUR

THE PATH . . .

R uche came back too soon. Much to Maia's relief, however, he had come back only with Sana, who on seeing Maia streaked ahead and caught her in a fierce hug.

"Maia, are you all right?" she asked, releasing Maia from her long embrace. She did not seem very convinced by Maia's nod in response. "I have to go, and be at the hold with my people, but you be careful." She paused for a moment and looked down at her hands as they held Maia's, her eyes restless. "You are important to all of us, Maia. Please remember that."

"I will, I promise," Maia said, her heart filling to the brim at Sana's earnest words. "Heard you have an army?"

Sana nodded. "Whacked some people real good. Not all on my own, of course, but still." She smiled brightly. "Guess I'm back to being a warrior princess for now."

Happy laughter almost completely lifted the weight of the situation from Maia's shoulders, until Ruche smiled indulgently at their little huddle and sighed.

"I hate to break this up, but we're racing against time. If we're going to do this, the best choice is to get Maia ready before the sun is at its highest, and that isn't too long from now. So . . ."

It did not take long for the group to disperse after that.

"Dani, you're coming upstairs with us. You two," Ruche said to Kusha and Nafi, "wait here. Miir should be back soon. And Sana—"

"I'm already gone," Sana said. Another fierce hug and wishing of luck later, the girl streaked away.

It was a long and tiring climb, four flights up the massive staircase to a room that seemed to be situated directly above the Foundation Chamber. It was almost like the chamber below, but smaller. Also, unlike the Foundation Chamber, this room was filled with light. The reason for that became apparent as soon as Maia entered. The roof was made entirely of glass. Copious sunlight, warm and bright, streamed in.

"This room is above the ground," Dani observed. Indeed it was. The one large glass-covered window in the room looked over an unending expanse of volcano fields.

"This is the Receptor Room," Ruche said. "See that?" He pointed at a large contraption—it reminded Maia of a washbasin mounted on a pedestal—that sat in the middle of the room, directly beneath the crown of the glass dome above them. "That is the Light Portal, which feeds the light outside into the Sedara."

"So that's what senses the light outside so the Sedara can mimic its pattern inside Xif?"

"Yes, Dani, that's it." Ruche led them to a bench on the far side of the room across from the window. "Sit here, Maia." He took out Seigvard and placed it next to her, then drew out a rolled-up master plan from inside his cloak and held it out for Dani. The long climb up had drained Maia, and even though she had a million questions, she did not have the strength to ask any. She simply watched as Dani took the master plan, studied it, and looked questioningly at Ruche.

"What is this?" Dani asked.

"This is the design details of the portal back there. If this goes according to plan and if . . . if we have enough time, we will attempt something. That's what you're in charge of, Dani."

"What, exactly?"

"Well, our wonder-boy had an idea and I think it just might work. We could have Maia restart the Sedara."

"Wonder-boy?" Dani frowned. "You mean Miir?"

Ruche chuckled a little. "He has circled all the circuits you need to switch. Once we reach that point, be prepared to switch them over according to his instructions."

"All right," Dani replied distractedly as her eyes scanned the details. "This looks simple. But I don't understand. Why isn't Miir doing this himself?"

Maia fidgeted and searched for a place to fix her gaze. It was probably because of her, because he would rather not see her face again after everything she said to the queen.

"Because he needs to be somewhere else, and according to him, you're the best person around to handle this," Ruche said. Dani kept frowning so Ruche explained some more. "So here's the plan. We can't have Aekken finding out what we're doing here. If Aekken gets an inkling that Maia is attempting the ascension to Arotharan, he will interrupt because he knows if it works, his scheme has no chance of succeeding. So while we try this here, we need to keep him distracted. We need to buy a little time, and what better to divert him than to give him what he has been waiting for on the other side of the planet?"

"You don't mean they're going to attack the Battlecruiser?" Dani exclaimed. "But . . . but they'll all get killed. Aekken will summon the fleet and . . . the last time the Xifarians faced the fleet, the R'armimon fighters mowed them down."

Maia held her breath as she waited for Ruche to answer. Her eyes scoured his face, eager for telltale signs of honesty. Ruche seemed just like Ruche, calm, his expression unreadable, his intent obscure.

"Don't worry, Dani," Ruche replied. "No one's going about like the last time. This will be different."

"Different how?"

"You'll see," Ruche said. "For now, please study the instructions. That's the best way you can help."

Dani's lips quivered and her eyes glistened, but without another word, she left. Ruche turned toward Maia and frowned immediately.

"What is it, Maia? I have never seen that look on you before," he said. "You're pale. Looks as if you've seen a ghost."

"What are you doing, Ruche?" Maia whispered. "Sending them out to face the R'armimon fleet? Sacrificing them so you can win this war with Aekken?"

Ruche's eyes widened immediately, but after a moment he replied. "You think I could do that? That I would send out those kids to be killed if I didn't have a good enough plan?"

"I don't know." Maia shook her head and turned away. "I don't know anything anymore. I just want this nightmare to be over."

He placed his hands on her shoulders. "Look at me, Maia." His face was hard when she looked up at him. "There is a plan, I swear. However, the fact is, there are risks. Miir and all the flyers who go out to engage Aekken will be taking a risk. But so will you. And you will do it because that is the best way to beat this nightmare once and for all."

Maia breathed in with all her might to fight the dark whirlpool of fears inside her. It did not help at all.

Ruche's grip on her shoulders tightened. "Maia, listen to me. You have to get hold of yourself if you want this to work. You wish everyone to come back safe, yes?" Maia nodded. "Then you have to reach Arotharan as fast as you can, so they are out there for the shortest amount of time. You have to be focused, precise, and in perfect control of your senses. If you can't do that, if your emotions stay scattered the way they are now, you'll take time to get where you need to be, time they can't afford to spend out there. Do you understand?" Maia nodded again. Ruche's voice was sharp when he spoke. "So instead of thinking of what the plan is, do your part and do it well."

She would try. Something told her it would not be easy. But she was going to try and focus and . . . do her part.

Ruche exhaled loudly and placed a hand on her head. "All will be well, Maia," he said in a gentle voice. "Believe in yourself."

They sat in silence, and somehow, the quiet brought Maia some peace, some stability. Ruche was right, she had to believe she could do this.

"Let me explain what we are about to do," Ruche said after a while. "Arotharan is the highest state of consciousness a Nasfarii can achieve. You already wield the light, but this final ascension is more than just wielding the light. It momentarily brings a consciousness that spans the universe. You will be able to see the past, present, and future. You will see near and far." Maia stared in amazement as Ruche continued. "In those moments of supreme awareness, the universe becomes a game board, and everything in it pieces of a game, and you the, lone player."

Seeing Maia's wide, almost disbelieving gaze, Ruche smiled. "Yes, it is possible. You know, Nasfarii like our Princess Ataii were able to ascend to this state whenever they willed. They could move stars if they so chose. That is why they were revered like goddesses and called the star child." He paused and patted her shoulder. "You could do it too if you had her training. You could simply close your eyes and reach Arotharan—it would be that simple. However, you haven't had what she had, so this is a big task for you today. But I have faith in you. I believe you can do it. It won't be easy, but you can."

Ruche picked up Seigvard and placed it gently on Maia's lap. "Hold it," he said. As Maia's cold fingers curled around Seigvard's jeweled hilt, he continued. "As I said, Seigvard is a conduit that harnesses the power of the stars, the cosmic energy. This energy, as you can imagine, is of tremendous magnitude. It is many, many times stronger than what you have within you. When we begin the process of ascension, this energy will come to reside in you. And if you are not careful, you can get hurt."

Maia drew a long breath as her eyes read Ruche's grim

expression.

"Hurt? As in . . . it could kill me?"

"There is a possibility."

Silence drifted in. Maia stared into Ruche's clear gray eyes and saw the truth in them. The seer was trying to ease the facts for her. He knew her death was more than a possibility.

"Scared? Want to change your mind?

Maia did not have to think before answering him. "I *am* scared. But no, I'm not changing my mind. I've decided. I want to do this. I *have* to do this. Aekken won't keep his promise. But more than that, I don't want to leave Tansi. Good or bad, it is my home. I may not be welcome everywhere or dear to everyone, but I don't care. I have a right to be here, just as much as they do. So I will stay. I will fight to keep living here, no matter what the risk."

"Very well then. Let's begin," Ruche said. "We start with binding Seigvard to you. I will tell you that as soon as you and this sword are bonded together, you will feel a shift inside. Your mind and your heart will start thinking and feeling more intensely. It will heighten your emotions."

"So I'll be even more of a mess than I am now?"

Ruche sighed. "You will have to fight them, Maia, and bring them under your control. You have to be in complete possession of your sensibilities before you try Arotharan. If you can't control yourself, you won't be able to control that massive energy. It will take over and possess you instead. And that—"

"Will kill me."

"Yes. It definitely will."

"I will try my best to keep calm."

"You have to," Ruche said. Hesitation was written on his face as he paused. Maia wondered what he was about to say next, how much worse she had to hear. "Maia, after Seigvard is bound to you, I will let you settle down for a bit. When I come back to check on you, if I still find you disoriented, I will call this off. Everything. I am not taking a chance on your life."

Chapter Fifty-Four

"But I can do it. I want to."

"Yes, of course. But I shall decide when I see you."

Maia heard the doubt in his voice, and it crept into her heart and turned it cold. For all that show of confidence in her abilities, Ruche was worried that she would fail.

And what would happen if she failed? She would die, but that was the least of the problems. Nothing would stand between Aekken and his vengeance, and he would surely strike just as he had originally planned. That would be the end of Tansi. And the end of everything she held dear.

"Now, Maia," Ruche said. "Hold Seigvard. Close your eyes and look for it inside you. When you see it, call it. If your request is true, you will have it."

Maia closed her eyes as Ruche began to chant. She tried looking for Seigvard, and for a moment she saw the sword somewhere out there in the distance . . . waiting for her. But then her vision began to muddle. Thoughts came flying in, bombarding her mind with horrific possibilities.

What would happen if she could not complete the ascension quickly enough? What if Aekken found out before she could finish it? All the flyers out there . . . Miir . . . Aekken's full wrath would come down upon them. Maia shuddered. Ren . . . he was with Aekken. He would be killed for sure. And then . . .

CHAPTER FIFTY-FIVE

. . . TO ASCENSION

Ruche's sharp voice tore through her thoughts and Maia opened her eyes with a start. She found Ruche frowning at her.

"What happened, Maia? Where were you?"

Maia looked down at her lap, at Seigvard. Her hand had long slipped off its hilt. In her fear, she had forgotten her task, to look for the sword.

Perhaps this is a sign. Perhaps this is for the best.

"Ruche, I couldn't. I—"

"You didn't even try."

"I'm too messed up, too scattered to do this."

"Are you?"

Maia looked up at the seer through misty eyes. His voice was kind, his gaze kinder.

"Ruche, I couldn't even get across to Seigvard. How do you expect me to get to Arotharan? It will be worth nothing in the end. And all those people you're sending out to distract Aekken, they'll have lost their lives for nothing. This is not going to work. Might as well give up now."

"You want to give up? And go with Aekken?"

"It is the safer way, isn't it? If I go with him, there's a chance he'll keep his promise. But if I do this . . . there are so many ways I could fail, so many ways everyone could suffer. I wanted this, I didn't want to leave but . . . it's too much of a risk."

"My father, Seer of the R'armimon before me, used to say this. Always fight for things you love. Always. You might not win every time, but you'll have tried. Isn't knowing that you didn't give up worth something?"

Maia's insides froze. She had heard those words before. Sana had said them. She had taken them to heart and she had fought. She had stood up for her feelings. And then . . . then she had failed miserably. So miserably that every day was still a struggle. No, every moment since had been a struggle. She could not anymore. She could not try again, knowing that a worse failure could be waiting for her.

"You know what I think? I think you have nothing to fight for," Ruche said sharply, his voice suddenly cold and distant. "If you leave with Aekken tomorrow, your life won't be that bad. Why, it wouldn't be bad at all. Aekken didn't lie when he said they'll cherish you, put you up on a pedestal and worship you. The Empire is rich beyond your imagination, you will never want for anything. Perhaps you'll miss what you'll leave behind, but you're young and with time, the memories will fade. You won't even know if Aekken destroyed this star when he left, so there'll be nothing to mourn." He stopped and peered at her face. "So you see, it's not about the risk. But nothing you have here is worth the fight."

"This is my home. I do want to stay," Maia whispered.

"And I'm telling you that your home, if it survives, will do just fine without you. As for you, your new home will be better. Surely you'll find new friends there. Maybe even better friends than you have now."

Better friends? Maia's eyes searched for Dani. She had walked up behind them, and she stood quietly, clutching the master plan to her chest, her teary blue eyes fixed on Maia's face. Maia remembered the first time they had met, in the Pod to Arpasgula, the bright, sweet girl who had walked across to speak with a couple of awkward, lowly Solianese kids, never thinking of them as anything but friends and equals. She remembered every time Dani's arm had linked through hers, and every time she had come rushing to her side.

And suddenly, Maia knew. She did not want to find better friends. There could not be friends better than the ones she had. She could not leave them behind. And she could not leave their fates in the hands of a bloodthirsty madman. She had to take a chance on herself. She had to fight, fight for everyone she loved and everything she loved, even if there was a chance she would lose.

"I could never have better friends, Ruche. Even if I searched for a thousand lifetimes," she said. "I can't leave knowing there's a chance Aekken will hurt them."

Aekken's face flashed in Maia's mind as she said that, with his dark, soulless eyes, and his charming but mirthless smile. The orbiter, whatever that was, was not just a rumor Ren had heard. It was not a chance, it was a sure thing. It had to be true.

"Sophie gave her life for Tansi. I can't leave, knowing that Aekken might destroy everything she died for. That is not an option." Maia stopped to take a long bracing breath. "And I know — I think you do too — that Aekken's plan is not just a possibility, it will happen." Maia's fingers wrapped around Seigvard so tightly that they hurt. "Try it again, Ruche. I'm ready. I promise."

Ruche did not ask another question. His hands covered Maia's as she held Seigvard. As he began his chants, Maia closed her eyes and searched for a connection to the sword. She looked far and near, hoping and praying it would hear her call and accept her.

For a long time, there was nothing, just the still darkness of her mind. And then it came in a flash so brilliant that Maia jumped a little. She saw it. Seigvard, its beauty so breathtaking and bright that it was almost fearsome. It spun across the spread of countless galaxies behind it. A dazzling beam of light stretched through it to infinity. It was a stunning sight, a vision among an ocean of stars. For an instant, Maia hesitated, unsure of what to do. Then she reached out with her mind. For an instant, nothing happened. And then the sword rushed to her, and along with its beam of light, slammed against Maia.

Maia's eyes opened with a start and she gasped for breath. There was no air anywhere. She screamed for help. Her lips moved, but no sound came out.

"Maia," Ruche called.

She could not see him. All she could see was a wall of white. She looked around frantically, blinking as if her life depended on it. Still, she saw nothing and found nothing. There was no pain, only the panic of being lost. Tears streamed down her face like a river breaching its banks after torrential rains. Then slowly, Maia found a little air. And after she had cried for what seemed like forever, she saw something.

A pair of bright blue eyes, kind and full of love, shining like a beacon in the haze of her mind.

"Dani."

"Maia."

Dani's arms were flung around her neck and Maia sighed in relief, thinking it was over. Little did she know that it was far from over. That the most painful part was just beginning.

Dani's arms were still wrapped around Maia's shoulders when a shudder struck her, sharp and uncontrollable. In an instant, her mind was a blur of blinding brightness and shadowy figures. Her insides burned, and through them came a rush of alertness that turned her mind numb. If she could not see before, now she saw too much. Every crack on the walls became visible, she could count every striation of the stones under their feet, and she could feel every vibration of the volcano under them. The unexpected overload of her senses, the sudden acute awareness overwhelmed, almost smothered her. Maia determinedly fought for breath. It took a long while, but finally, the awareness subsided a little, enough for Maia to open her eyes again.

Ruche was looking at her, his gaze kind and patient. "How are you, Maia?"

Maia barely managed a nod.

"Believe in yourself. Remember what you're fighting for," he said. "The rest doesn't matter. Drive out all distractions from your head. Anger, petty words, sad memories — they can't have a place in you now. They will try to get in, but don't let them." Ruche moved his hand away from her arm, and an unexpected wave of loneliness swamped Maia, making her tremble. "Dani and I will leave for a bit. Take this time to anchor yourself."

Maia nodded, realizing that would not be easy, realizing more clearly than ever before the meaning of Ruche's words. Her insides still shivered and shook. Thoughts and memories streamed past her mind's eye, creating a jumble of emotions in the pit of her stomach. Every single detail was amplified a thousand times. Maia squeezed her eyes shut as another violent shudder coursed up her spine.

"Maia, are you all right?" Dani's voice, her warm touch stabilized Maia for a moment.

"She has to do this on her own, Dani," Ruche said. "She has to find her peace."

Find my peace, find my peace.

Footsteps drifted away. The silence that should have been comforting was anything but. The sunlight burned her skin, and the smell of the volcano field outside was suffocating. Worse was the unending parade of thoughts in her head. Her life, every forgotten moment of it, flashed past in an excruciating rhythm. Sad memories brought tears to her eyes, and even the happy ones left her longing and crying.

After a long time and innumerable failed attempts at finding stability, Maia remembered the Xinhagyi's lessons. After she had discovered the light inside her, she had been just as distraught, just as unstable. The exercises had helped. Maybe they could help again.

Maia closed her eyes and started chanting the words that had brought her peace once, breathing the way the Xinhagyi had taught her. Over and over and over.

How long had passed since she had closed her eyes and begun to practice the Xinhagyi's exercises, Maia did not know. When she opened her eyes again, still waiting in the chamber, on the bench Ruche had led her to, she felt much calmer. She could breathe, her skin no longer felt like it was on fire. Thoughts, sharp and startling, still came, but not in a manic rush. Memories, good and bad, lingered close, but not every little one and not all intent on tearing her apart.

Maia looked around — up at the sunlight streaming in, at the eye-catching carvings that decorated every wall in the room, and finally at the extraordinary sword that rested next to her. Her eyes misted as she remembered the first time she had seen it, when Mahswa Tabrin laid it out in front of them in Zagran. It had been breathtaking, just as it was now.

"I'm sorry, Seigvard," she whispered, placing a finger on the sword's jeweled hilt. "I did not mean to be disrespectful to you when I refused your bequest from the Rahina. It would have been an honor to have you. But I couldn't forget the disgust she showed for Sophie . . . for me. I never meant to possess you, all I ever needed was your help. And she wouldn't believe."

A tear coursed down her cheek, then another. Maia wiped them away forcefully, taking in quick breaths to steady her battered heart.

Don't think like that. Don't lose your calm.

Her gaze drifted to the large window across from her and she found herself walking up to it, her eyes lingering on the shifting smoke plumes rising from the volcano field outside. They were like an ever-shifting screen, only letting in a view of the clear sky beyond once in a while. The skies were a grayish blue, and quickly growing yellower.

So much time had passed since she first came to this temple. A wide-eyed girl she had been, just starting to understand the world outside of the little cocoon she had carefully constructed around herself. She would not be hurt ever again, she had sworn. They had yanked her out of her fortress and, stripped of the right to choose for herself, she went along. Unwillingly, joylessly, she had followed the road laid out for her. She did not know what life had planned for her, how much more hurt she had coming. So much . . . she never would have thought her heart could endure so much.

A pang, sharp and gut-wrenching, tore through her. Her breathing quickened as if by instinct, ready to fight it tooth and nail. Now was not the time to be weak.

It's all right! You'll be fine. Everything will be fine.

She looked back at the door, eyes seeking Ruche. Where was the man? Why was he wasting so much time? He was probably making the diversion plan with Miir.

Miir . . . the look on his face when she refused the pendant flashed through her mind. He must be so disappointed. Maia's eyes burned again, her insides collapsing like a house of sand in the face of a wave. Maia shook her head, desperate to jolt herself out of the thoughts of Miir.

No! Don't. Keep him out of your head. Don't let him in.

And thinking that he would be risking his life trying to keep Aekken distracted —

Just the idea of him in danger . . . yanked her breath away.

Stop thinking like that. All will be well.

Maia wiped her tears and closed her eyes again. She was going to get this under control. She would make it happen. Her fists curled, nails digging deep into her palms. Once again she chanted the words she had learned from the Xinhagyi, once again she restrained her breathing. She would keep on fighting. Over and over and over until she won.

CHAPTER FIFTY-SIX

CATCH YOU LATER

Maia opened her eyes at the sound of footsteps. She looked out of the window before turning back, and exhaled with relief on finding that her gaze was clear. Her heart was beating at a pace she knew, steadfast and steady. The jumbled horde of thoughts and memories had receded almost completely, to the back of her mind where they belonged. She had found her peace, after all. Maia's fingers curled around the windowsill. She was ready now, ready to embrace the light to the fullest, and ready to free her Tansi of the curse that was Aekken. And for once, Ruche had arrived on time.

Maia turned around with a smile on her lips and froze when she realized it was not the seer. Miir walked in, his eyes never leaving her face. Maia's heart jumped again. It thumped faster, in excruciating, numbing beats, as he approached.

Why was he here now? It was all over between them. He had done his part, kept his promise to her. Restored her past, fought to protect her life, and helped her reach here. He was free, his atonement complete. And she? She was free also, beyond the shackles of her wants, her goals clear and vivid before her, prepared to embrace a higher calling.

Nothing was left to be said, to be expected. All that connected them now was this looming disaster, but that would soon be over too. And then, one day soon after, she would wish him all the luck and happiness in the world and they would part ways. It was all good. She had made a plan for herself. After this was over, she would find a place somewhere in the mountains that looked over Appian. Far, far away from everyone . . . everything . . . far from all the memories.

All was settled and done. And yet, her thoughts flitted, captive to some unruly, unreasonable, uncontrollable fancy.

Maia forced her gaze back to the shifting curtains of smoke outside but her mind lingered on the sound of approaching steps, the beats of her heart growing louder with each one.

"Hey."

She turned, as slowly as she could. She wanted to smile and say hello back. Not a sound came out of her mouth, nor a smile.

For a moment or two, they stared at each other. For a moment or two, all she could hear was the thudding of her own heart. Then Maia's fists tightened into balls as she built a wall around herself. She could not let him in, she would not let him disrupt the peace she had found.

"Are you sure you are ready for this?" Miir asked.

"Why would I be here if I wasn't sure?"

Maia's insides shrunk the moment the words left her mouth. He had only asked a simple question, and her answer had to come out all kinds of wrong. Like so many times before with Miir, Maia wished she could take the words back. As always, it was too late. His eyes narrowed a little but his mouth curled into a small, patient smile.

"I've decided. Hard or not, I *have* to do this," Maia blurted, rambling on with pointless reasoning when all she wanted to do was say sorry. "Aekken won't keep his promise, and I don't—"

"You need not explain," Miir interrupted. "I did not come here to stop you or . . . doubt your capabilities. I am happy that you want this because I do not want you to leave." He sighed and a regretful smile played on his lips. "I had only meant to ask if you were feeling up to it after . . . after all you have just been through. I must have used all the wrong words again like I always do with you."

"No, you didn't." Maia rushed to reassure him. "It was me. I . . ." Unable to complete her thought, she turned away in haste.

"I know this is not a good time for me to be here," he said. "You should have had this time for yourself. But . . . but I needed to see you. So, I am the one who is imposing and it is fine by me if you say a thing or two or . . . ten."

She wished he would stop talking like that, being kind and caring and . . . everything she wished for. It only made her pine for a future she could never have. It only made her torment worse.

Desperate to relieve the growing ache in her heart, Maia took a step away. Miir followed. Frustration made Maia's fists clench.

Why did Ruche let him come up here? Why did Miir have to keep following her around? Did he *have* to stand so close? He was done inquiring about her health so . . . why did he not leave?

But even while she wished for the conversation to end, more words tumbled out of her, anxious to break free.

"This *is* harder than I thought it'd be. I'm ready but . . . I'm also afraid. I'm worried I'll fail."

"You will not. I am sure of it."

His words . . . bracing as always, lifted Maia's spirits.

"My head is a pathetic muddle," she confessed.

Miir sighed. "Not that word again." Maia looked up at him, lost for a moment. His gaze, sad but sincere, met hers. "Pathetic is *not* a word that goes with you."

Why, oh why did he keep saying such things?

Maia turned away yet again, eager to hide the misery she knew was written on her face. Her eyes fell on Seigvard and her insides crumpled. Why this kindness when all he felt for her was . . . frustration and disappointment?

Perhaps it was better to just clear the air about Seigvard while she still had the chance. Perhaps it would lessen the turmoil inside her, bring her a bit more of that elusive peace before she embraced the light.

"I couldn't accept the Rahina's offer to bequeath me Seigvard and the pendant," Maia said, her eyes glued on the legendary sword. "I know you risked a lot to convince her to give them to me, and I should have been grateful when the time finally came. But . . . I remembered the loathing on her face when she spoke of Sophie, and I just could not do it. Sophie needed . . . deserved someone to stand up for her. If not me, then who?" She paused to draw a breath, in a futile effort to steady herself. "Sorry I let you down."

"You did not let me down." Miir peered at her face. "Why would you think that?"

"You looked unhappy."

He stepped closer still, his presence filling Maia's consciousness. As much as she wanted to bolt, she stared at his wide and questioning eyes, frozen and wordless as her heart thudded incessantly.

"I was. All the time you spent looking for something and now, after finally finding it, all it brought you was pain. I had hoped it would make you happy and when it did not, I *was* sad. For you. Anyway, that did not last long, because I got busy admiring your courage. It should not surprise me anymore after all these years, but it still does. I wish I had half the strength you have."

Why was it always this way with him? How easily his words wounded her and how easily they healed, how easily they broke her down and how easily they built her back up. How could . . . how could one person's words matter so much?

And why . . . why did the one person who meant so much have to be so near yet so out of her reach?

Maia tore her eyes away from Miir's face and moved away from him once more, hoping to put some distance between them so her thoughts would calm down. She eased onto the bench, thankful for its firm support. Dashing her hopes, he walked over to face her.

"I came here to tell you something," Miir said. "I have been trying to speak with you for the last few days, but I could not get past the wall of people around you. So here I am, at the worst possible moment, being a bother." His gaze was resolute as it locked with hers, and his voice solemn. "I will go away right now if you ask me to, and speak only if you will allow me . . . only if you can put some faith in me. One last time."

It would be a lie to say she was not afraid, thinking of what he could say. It would be a lie to say she did not want to flee while she still had a little bit of stability. But hearing Miir's earnest voice, looking at his anguished face, Maia forgot all about herself. A hopeless fool she would be, but how could she deny his ardent plea?

"Yes," Maia said. "Tell me."

He sat down next to her. Too close, far too close.

"Well then. I came to say that I . . . I realize how unfair I have been, how selfish. That day when you wanted to tell me how you feel about . . . us, I did not even let you start. I only thought of how utterly unworthy of your affection I was. I only thought of all the ways I could cause you harm. I wanted to protect you, and I decided I could not let you choose a path that led to me. No matter how, or how much it pained me, I had to turn you away. I *had* to."

He paused, his eyes scouring her face before he spoke again. Maia's senses hung on to every word he said, all that she could hear over the deafening beats of her heart.

"I forgot to respect your choice. I forgot that your wishes matter as much as mine. All I ended up doing was hurting you. Again. And for that I am sorry."

What did that mean? What was he trying to say? As much as Maia tried to come to a conclusion, she could not. Her mind was racing too fast, along with her heart. So she simply listened, entranced by the gentle cadence of his words.

"Guilt has been my constant companion these years. Never thought I would escape it. Then you came along with your endless generosity and pulled me out from under this crushing mountain. And suddenly, with you by my side, happiness did not feel impossible anymore."

His eyes dimmed and his shoulders stiffened as he plodded through the next words.

"Then came my mother's words. Like a storm, they threw me off my path. All I thought was . . . I could not put you in danger. So back I went, as fast as I could, rebuilding those walls I was used to. I could not explain it to you because I knew you would not listen. You would only want to look ahead, and you would find a way to convince me to come with you. And you would be right, too, just like you were right all along. My mother meant something else altogether."

Maia drew a long, bracing breath. How sure she had been of this, yet he would not believe. So hard she had tried to convince him, but he had closed himself off. Any other time, the vindication of her stand would have brought Maia pleasure, but Miir's heartfelt confession and his remorseful face washed away every misgiving, and all Maia could think of was how he must have hurt.

"I could not see it then," Miir continued, sighing, "because . . . I would not even look. Had I looked, I would have realized what my mother feared. It was all about the sword, one that I did not even have anymore. I could have seen that I was free. But instead, I stayed stuck in the past, poring over every instance of when and how I failed you, afraid that I would do it again."

He placed a hand—cold, just as cold as her own—on hers. Maia's fingers curled, but even though she could have pulled her hand out of his grasp, she let it stay, unable to resist the reassuring comfort of his touch.

"What you came to tell me that day was a dream come true. All I gave you in return was pain and tears. And even after I hurled those cruel words at you, you wanted to help. I should have taken it, grasped it with everything I had. But I had to refuse that too. Because I knew better, right? I could not have been more wrong."

His hand wrapped around her fist and held it tight.

"Forward is the only way to go. You have said that so many times. Stubborn as I am, I have only just begun to accept it. But now I know, I cannot be blind to what is ahead of me because of what has happened in the past. I have to think of what can be, not what has been. I have to believe that I can change. I need to remember that I *have* changed."

His fingers pried her fist open and folded around hers.

"It has taken me longer than you would expect, but I realize now what I really want. I want to see you happy. I want to see you smile and laugh. And most of all, I want to smile with you and laugh with you."

His gaze, wide and glistening, locked with hers. A wild and nervous flutter filled Maia's heart and made it tremble.

"I have made mistakes, and I may make more. But I will not push you away out of fear of hurting you. I will not let my dread of what might happen stop me from accepting the truth."

He dropped to his knees in front of her, his hands cradling hers, the deep amber of his eyes vivid on his upturned face. Maia blinked to counter the rush of emotions inside her.

"Miir—"

"The truth is, every moment I spend with you is a treasure. I cherish you. The truth is, after all this is over, if I have a life, I want to spend it with you by my side. Every moment with you and no one else, for as long as you will have me. The truth is, I love you. I have . . . for a long time now."

She would not show her tears to anyone, she had sworn. Especially not to him. He could not know of her heartbreak. Never! That dam, the carefully-constructed structure she had built to hide her pain . . . it was supposed to be indestructible. How could it collapse like this?

Tears coursed down Maia's face, and as she prepared to fight them, she realized that this time they brought no pain. She did not need that dam anymore. She still found it hard to breathe, but that was because her heart was so full of . . . happiness. Maia's fingers— eager, joyful, content—tightened around his.

What was it that Sana always said? When you find love, the

world erupts in the colors of the rainbow. Everything around you recedes, and you soar into the clear blue skies like a cloud. She had always laughed at the silliness of those words, but now . . . she was that cloud.

The world and its worries faded away into the distance. It did not matter that they were about to walk into a storm. Everything that came before now and all that might come after did not matter either. Nothing mattered except for this moment.

Maia opened her eyes at his touch. He wiped away her tears and brushed the wayward strands of hair from her forehead. His gaze, tender and steady, locked with hers. He looked into her eyes as if wanting to peer into her soul. His hand cupped her face, then slipped into her hair and gently pulled her closer to him.

"If you want me to stop, tell me," Miir whispered.

Stop? Not in this lifetime. Or a thousand more after this.

Their foreheads touched, and for a while, Maia held her breath, caught up in the dream that was the closeness she had wished for so long. She yearned to be closer, to never let go. Her hand found its way around him and pulled him nearer. His lips—cautious, gentle, unwavering—met hers.

Maia wanted that moment to last forever. She also knew that one so perfect rarely lasted long enough. But it did not matter. As long as they had each other, they would create moments like this. Many, many more. Maia was ready, her heart still full of longing yet prepared to let go when Miir drew back. He rose to his feet and tugged her up. She was wrapped in his arms in the next instant, his face sunk in her hair, their hearts beating next to each other.

"Maia," he whispered into her ear, the simplest act of hearing him call her name making Maia's heart flutter and flip. His voice broke as he said it again. "Maia."

The sound rippled through her ears, making her heart swell. Tears filled her eyes once again. Maia clasped him tight and burying her face in his shoulder, she breathed in deeply, wanting to hold on to his rock-steady presence that was so precious to her.

Voices drifted up the stairs. Then came the sound of footsteps. Was it time already?

Miir's arms fell away from her just as Ruche appeared at the door, but his hands held hers firmly. Dani came in after Ruche, clutching the rolled-up master plan, and her eyes lit up on seeing them.

"All well with you two?" Ruche asked as he strode in.

"Yes," Miir replied.

"I wish I could give you more time, but . . ."

Miir smiled. "It is enough for now. Thank you."

He let go of Maia's hand, one finger at a time until all that was touching were their fingertips. "Be careful. Try not to rush into things," he said.

"I won't," Maia declared with a bright smile and an emphatic shake of her head. "I'll take my time and consult with Ruche and think through every step twice and —"

Miir burst into chuckles. "You know all that is quite impossible given the situation. Just be careful."

"And you too."

"I will. I have to see you again," he said, his voice soft and wistful. "I have so much to tell you."

Yes, there was much to talk about, much to share. She would need a lifetime or more.

"Catch you later."

Maia smiled. "Yes, I'll find you."

There was no pain inside her anymore. All the darkness had washed away. She would come back to make another memory like this again. Soon. She had to.

As Miir walked away, Dani rushed over to him, the master plan open in her hands. Maia turned to look at Ruche. The seer had taken a seat on the bench, a smile hovering at the corners of his mouth as he peered at her.

"You look better," he said. "Still want to do this, yes?"

There was no doubt, not even a shred.

"More than ever."

CHAPTER FIFTY-SEVEN

ENDGAME

Ruche sat Maia down under the glass dome of the Receptor Room. Sunlight flooded her and held her in its warm embrace, calming and soothing her. Ruche sat facing her, Seigvard unsheathed and placed on the ground between them. His eyes were closed, his lips murmuring words Maia could not even hear. When he opened his eyes, they had taken on a dark sheen.

"Maia, I will begin the process of ascension now. After I start you on the path, I won't be able to reach you again. You will have to navigate on your own while in that state. And you will have to come back to us once you are finished."

"I will. I will come back."

Ruche's lips curled a little. "I do not know exactly what you will encounter in that state, but you will face choices. Hard choices they will be, and I can only wish you luck in making the right ones."

The right choices? It was difficult thinking of choices when she did not even know what would happen when she got there . . . And what did *there* even mean?

"And then, once you're done with the fleet and the prince, you have to try to get to the Light Portal."

Maia slowly nodded. That would probably be the easiest part. If she had any energy left. If she survived whatever situation it was that she was going to face. Maia took a deep breath and squared her shoulders. Worries and fears had no place in this. She was going to get it all done, she had to. She had to come back here again, to Tansi, to all her friends, to a future she wanted.

"Let's get started, Ruche," she urged.

Ruche chuckled a little. "I can't just yet, Maia. The pieces are still not in place. The assault on the Imperial Battlecruiser has to begin first. Aekken needs to be distracted enough so he won't notice the surge in energy when you begin ascension."

As if on cue, Dani scuttled over. "Ruche, Ren says it's in place."

Ruche's face lit up with a smile. "Good kid. He managed it after all." Maia did not get a chance to ask what Ren had put in place, since Ruche started directing Dani. "Tell Miir they are cleared to begin. But take it slow."

Ruche turned his attention back to Maia as soon as Dani turned away. "We begin now, Maia. Things are going as planned. Let us make good use of the time we have." He placed his upturned palms in front of her. Then he sighed and looked at her, his gaze clouded.

"I have to tell you, there is a chance you will lose your powers after this, Maia," he said.

It was strange how worried he looked, but it was stranger how empty Maia felt as his words sank in. She had endured so much because of this strange power inside her. So often she had wished it would not be, and so many times it had come to help her. Now it was part of her, an extension of herself. And losing it would be like . . . losing a part of herself.

"Are you all right with that?"

It was weird that she had to think about it. What was having special powers compared to the lives of everyone she loved? What was it next to the futures of millions at stake? Yet, cringing inwardly at her selfishness for a moment, Maia thought. Then her fists curled.

What was the point of having special abilities if you could not use them to help someone?

"I am perfectly fine with it, Ruche," she said, her voice hard with conviction. "Let's begin."

Ruche returned a small nod. "Place your hands in mine. Try to clear your thoughts and focus on Seigvard." He closed his eyes and began chanting once again, as did Maia. Thoughts flew across her mind, and Maia forced them to settle down, her eyes on the glinting form of Seigvard in front of her. By the time Ruche opened his eyes once more and placed Seigvard on her lap, she was calm, her mind clear.

"Repeat after me," Ruche said. "*Pariyuttaha brikkashti aroyahan.*"

She knew those words. They were the ones that she had said to release the light inside her.

"*Pariyuttaha brikkashti aroyahan.*"

They came out soft and light at first. Then, as Maia kept on repeating them, they grew stronger and louder and they echoed in her head, through her mind and her consciousness. Her fingers wrapped around Seigvard's hilt as she let the words carry her away.

The pull came from the pit of her stomach. Sharp, somewhat painful, and utterly unnerving. For a moment and by instinct, Maia resisted. Then as she let herself go, she found herself pulled in.

* * *

For the longest time, there was darkness. Then a brilliant wave engulfed Maia. She found herself swirling through a sea of endless light, golden and bright. She rose and she fell, and the brightness seeped into her and rose and fell inside her. She felt no pain, only the endless rush of energy sweeping her out in every possible direction. And then, all of a sudden, it stopped. Maia found her spirit seeping out of herself. She became the light and she soared.

* * *

For a moment or two, Maia's senses hovered in the Receptor Room. She saw herself, eyes closed as she sat stiff and erect, Seigvard on her lap. Ruche, as he stared worriedly at her.

"Ruche, the Battlecruiser has released its fighters." Dani's voice was sharp.

Maia rose higher. Below her, the Seliban Temple floated in a sea of volcanoes. In the distance, the Imperial Battlecruiser hovered. An endless stream of craft sped out of it. They swarmed around another melee of craft—Xifarian fighters—near the surface of Xif. They dove, they ducked, and they chased each other, in a never-ending game of cat-and-mouse.

A voice, irate and fearsome, drifted to her ears. "What is wrong? Why is it taking so long to destroy the pests?"

"The weapons systems are malfunctioning, Crown Prince Aekken."

"What? How is that possible? Rectify it. Now!"

Maia rose higher. Above the barren, ashy surface of Xif she soared. A glimpse of Tansi, so blue and pretty, like a shiny marble. More planets, then the star in the middle, so bright and warm.

Higher still.

Farther out she went, across a sea of stars, until the galaxy lay beneath her in a never-ending spread of lights.

As she floated over it, eyes eager to locate Tansi in the vastness, scenes flashed past. They were not ones from her own memories. There were not her own at all. A girl, tall and willowy, a sweet smile on her face, walking through the snow. A man and a boy next to her. They looked familiar. She knew them . . . Dada, Uncle Alasdair when they were young. Sophie!

Another flash and she saw the girl again. She was older now, her smile just as sweet as she gazed fondly at a young man. The smile on his face was as bright and happy as hers. Raidyn and Sophie . . . lost in love.

Maia wished to linger, but she rose once more. Past galaxies and their unending ocean of lights shining all around her until she went so far that they all receded. Their distant glowing forms turned small and paltry, and Maia was left alone in the endless emptiness of dark space.

*　*　*

A light, as bright as a star, dazzled in the darkness. Maia squinted, and then, recognizing a human figure within the light, she squinted some more.

It was a woman. Red hair flew like a lion's mane behind her. Her dress, white and gold, shone just as brightly as her face. She was smiling, but there was something in that smile that scared Maia. She wanted to get closer, to find out who the woman was, but her steps were slow. Unwilling.

Maia knew there was no avoiding this woman. Her own path lay through her. Good or bad, she had to face this dazzling vision. So she went, one step at a time, striding through endless empty space until she could see the woman's shimmery presence clearly. The light swirled closer as she approached. The tall and slender figure of the woman, radiant and beautiful, cloaked in her cocoon of brilliant light, was clear. She smiled, her gaze at once tender and defiant.

"Greetings, Maia," the woman said.

Maia's insides shook as she recognized the voice. She had heard it many times before, and she had always wondered. It was right after Ruche had given her the words to set the light free that she had heard it the first time. It had been a cry of pain. She had glimpsed a being in chains, surrounded by walls of fire, a being in terrible agony . . . this was who it was. She had heard it again and again, every time she was faced with grave danger. It had offered her paths of escape, and thoughts of retribution. Sometimes she had taken them, other times she had refused. But the voice had always been strong, insistent, and wrathful.

Now Maia had no doubt the woman was part of the light she had come to possess. Perhaps she was the manifestation of the light? Or was it . . .

Maia looked at her face, her attire, and the regal way she carried herself. Slowly, a realization came to her.

"Princess Ataii?" Maia whispered, her voice full of trepidation.

The woman smiled, but her face hardened. "No," she replied. "Ataii, Queen of Xif."

As Maia slowly fathomed the implications of the statement, Ataii spoke again.

"I have been waiting for centuries to speak with someone and now, finally, I have you. I have a story to tell you, Maia."

"I would be honored to hear it, but . . . we don't have time. If Aekken realizes —"

"Where we are, Maia, time stands still. In the time the people outside take a single breath, we can spend a lifetime here. So do not worry, your world will be fine."

"Oh . . ." Maia breathed in relief. "If I may ask, where am I?"

"You are physically still in the Receptor Room in the Seliban Temple," Ataii explained. "This is your spirit form, also called the Roohe-Sama. It is a form you can split into once you have reached Arotharan."

A wave of joy swept through Maia. "I have reached Arotharan?"

"Not fully, not yet. But you are well on the path."

Maia had no doubt she was going to make it. Relieved and confident, she lowered her head. "I would like to hear your story, Ataii, Queen of Xif."

Ataii smiled and flicked her fingers, and the world changed around them. A city, the largest Maia could imagine, stretched in front of her eyes. Innumerable lights flickered across it in a breathtaking view.

"This is where I was born, Maia," Ataii said. "Ragamallor, the capital of the Empire R'armimon. Come, let me show you."

CHAPTER FIFTY-EIGHT

TEARS OF A DISTANT STAR

Ragamallor was a stunning amalgamation of beauty and opulence. Shining buildings, tall and imposing, stretched endlessly in all directions. Boulevards, wide and straight, cut through them like a finely-woven web. People, dressed in finery, thronged the streets. Maia passed them by, alongside Ataii, toward the highlands in the distance. Ataii's life as the princess of the R'armimon unfurled around them as they went and Ataii's voice streamed over Maia.

"When I was born, lighted candles decorated Ragamallor for a week. My arrival was a blessing, the Empire was grateful, and it spared no effort in showing its gratitude to the heavens. Ataii—a name bestowed on no one else before me—meant splendor of the stars. A girl child was rare in my family, and a child so gifted was even rarer. If only I truly knew what my gifts were then. If only I understood sooner why my birth was celebrated as if I were a manifestation of the stars themselves.

"My life was wrapped in luxury and love, and also unending

training. My days were busy, my education went far beyond what the princes—my brothers and cousins—had to go through, and differently. As I grew older, I sometimes wondered. Why did I have to take lessons from the head priest of the Star Temple three systems away? Why was I sent to the Xienotaph system to spend time with the Roohe-Lenkkei? Sometimes I asked, and the reply was always the same: I was special."

The Imperial palace, beautiful and lavish, covered a verdant hill, the buildings rising in tandem with the natural slopes they were built on. If the rest of the palace was breathtaking, it was nothing compared to the splendor of Ataii's private living quarters. Guards surrounded the opulently appointed rooms, maids waited in droves around the young princess. Maia watched as time flowed past, and Ataii grew from a child to an elegant woman with grace and poise that would make anyone bow their heads in respect.

"So I was. Special. A blessing from the stars. Everyone treated me like the princess I was, but I felt there was something more. Something separated me from everyone else. Even my father, the Emperor, was a mortal, but I was above everything. I was worshipped and revered, I was looked at with different eyes. It was as if I were a goddess.

"I wished, oh how I wished I could have a friend, but who would dare to be friends with a goddess? I wished I could love someone, but who could see the girl I was when all they saw was a deity to be worshipped? I was treasured and revered, my every wish granted, and every demand promptly fulfilled. Yet I was alone, forever lonely, always seeking a connection to someone, but never finding it.

"Then one day, the Centennial Gala was upon us. As I drifted from one ball to another, I chanced upon a dreamy-eyed man with a smile that could touch your soul, with words that could make your heart soar in rapture. He was Afriel, the prince of the renegade nation of Xif.

"I was warned. He was beneath us, his presence only tolerated for the Empire's gain. But little did anyone know that the princess had finally found a friend, a companion, a connection. For the first time in my life, someone saw the human in me. When Afriel looked at me, he saw the person in me seeking a friend, he saw the girl in me seeking a future of happiness. It only took me a day to realize that my only future could be with him."

Maia had no doubt as she watched them dance through the night among a whirlpool of colors and sparkles. Their affection for each other shone in their eyes, and all the splendor around them paled in comparison. Maia also knew the troubles that were coming for the young couple. Soon, the R'armimon would hold hostage Afriel's younger brothers, Minhaas and Lenetto, and Veiles's young son, Castien. Ataii would flee to Xif with Afriel, but Veiles would be swallowed by the grief of losing his child. At the moment, however, Ataii's eyes sparkled and her smile was as bright as the sun.

"What a future it turned out to be. Even though the beginning of our story was written in the tears of those we had to leave behind, we had a love like no other. I came to Xif, fearing I would be considered an enemy. They took me in, with open arms and kindness. What a wondrous place Xif was, miraculous, sparkling, and happy."

A young Xif unfurled before Maia's eyes as Ataii led her through her own journey. So small it was compared to the grand cities of today, and so fresh. The Sedara was smaller, and although everything was not perfect—the skies were not blue all over, patches of the planet's insides still showed, the settlements were clumps on the ground, different from the sea of shiny buildings that left anyone overwhelmed now—Xif looked . . . warm and inviting. Maia realized why Ataii would have fallen in love.

"Shadows lurked in our hearts, however. King Arka was a broken man, a part of his heart destroyed by the grief of losing Minhaas and Lenetto. And Veiles, that kind man who had introduced me to Afriel . . . I never saw him again. All I saw was a shell, the joyful brightness in his eyes now a manic gleam. I tried so hard to find a way to get my brother, the Emperor, to release the boys. My efforts took me nowhere. I was told that the only way I could help Xif was if I severed my ties to Afriel and returned to Ragamallor.

"Then one day, I found out about my curse. I was a Shimugien. I saw the fear in Veiles's eyes when he told me of it. My own fear was even greater. I knew what being a Shimugien meant on Xif. It meant I could lose everything dear to me — my home, my love, and my life. I begged Veiles to keep it a secret, I begged and begged until he relented. But every day after that was filled with dread, every moment was filled with anxiety. Veiles offered to cure me, and I hoped and prayed that he would find a way.

"My hope for a cure only lasted so long. Until I heard the truth from the Emperor, my brother Ondeiir, the truth that had been hidden from the world out of fear that I could be used as a weapon. Now, finally, my own was ready to use me as one. Ondeiir told me that I was what the legends spoke of, a Nasfarii, a star child. That I could use the energy of the stars and wield it. Now it finally became clear. I was not just another princess, I *was* a goddess. All the training I had received since my childhood was to prepare me to use my powers. The clearest truth of all was — there was no cure in my future. I would always be a Shimugien, feared and despised on Xif. That was my fate."

Maia could see the dark clouds gathering. She could also see the fears and worries filling Ataii's sparkling eyes. The vibrance in the young queen's face swiftly faded as time passed, her steps lost their liveliness. Terrible times were upon Ataii and her family, and Maia knew there would be no happy ending.

Ataii sighed, her anguish filling Maia's heart and making it droop.

"Ondeiir knew my fears. Once the truth came out, Afriel would shun me, he said. On Xif, I would be deemed a threat worse than a Shimugien. I would be held captive. Wouldn't it be better if I struck them instead? He offered me help to learn full control of my powers, and if I used them to help subjugate Xif, he would let the hostages go.

"I agreed. I had a different plan, however. To my brother, I said I would vanquish Xif, while in my mind, I was preparing for a siege against Ragamallor to free the hostages. If I could free them, Afriel would not shun me for my powers, and the people of Xif would still love me. So I believed and so I trained. The priest of the Star Temple gave me words, and I invoked them. My lifelong training had already prepared me, and it was easy. One word at a time, a little step at a time, I came closer and closer to the final ascension.

"It was like a dream. One moment I was a young woman, a minuscule object in the immensity of the universe. In the next, the universe was my plaything. I played . . . in the ocean that was space, my fingers touching a galaxy, my breath moving a planet. I was intoxicated by the power, addicted to rising to the pinnacles of strength, too distracted to notice that Veiles had observed the changes in me, to realize what was coming before it was too late."

Maia's insides quaked, thinking about what was coming next. She had shed tears after listening to Ataii's story from the Origin Scrolls, and now, hearing it from the one who suffered through it all was a pain hard to endure.

"Veiles had me imprisoned for treason. No matter how hard I tried, I could not convince him of my innocence. He put me in a cage I could not break out of. The Empire tried to show its power, but it did not envision the thoughts of a man turned mad by grief. When they butchered Castien, Veiles revealed the mightiest, the worst of his plans. Nothing could stop him, nothing. Not my pleas, not my tears, and not even my promises to bring him justice. And when he struck down the love of my life, Afriel, I stopped trying.

"Veiles had found a path to avenging his son, and that path lay through my destruction. He brought in the light. It was beautiful. Pouring over me, within me, through me. My soul surged with the light. And then it took over, tearing me apart, assimilating me in its immense power . . . until I was no more."

The pain in her words made Maia's core crumble. It was wrong, so wrong. Just as she had not asked for the powers that had come to her, Ataii had not asked for them either. And yet Ataii had been sacrificed, her life destroyed. Ataii's thoughts, wracked with despair, told her just that.

"But what about my future? My happiness? I had not wished to be a princess or an all-powerful goddess. I had only dreamed of a life filled with love and happiness, like every other girl. A simple wish — was it too much to ask?

"They got their revenge. The Empire, with the execution of those innocent boys. Veiles, with his sacrifice of my life and my family.

"What about my vengeance?"

Maia shuddered as understanding finally dawned on her. This was why she had heard the voice time and again when she was blind with rage. The time she had struck down Miir, the time she had almost strangled Remii, and many other times in between. It was because Ataii was in pain, desperate for revenge.

"As my spirit lingered within the cage Veiles had built, my heart cried for retribution as never before. It demanded blood and death. As my trapped soul traveled from system to system, leaving millions, billions, perhaps even more dead in our wake, I laughed. Let them understand what losing everything meant. It did not matter that they had done me no harm, it did not matter that they were just as innocent as I was. I simply wanted someone to feel the pain I was made to feel.

"I was going to leave it all dead. Nothing would survive me."

Anger, fierce and pitiless, flashed in Ataii's eyes. Maia recognized that urge to destroy, to take from people what she had been denied herself. She also knew that it brought no peace in the end. She was startled when she heard Ataii once more, her voice calmer and softer.

"And then, one day, someone released me from my cage. And suddenly, once more, I lived. Not in the same way as before, but still, I was a girl again. A small planet was my new home and on it, a little farmhouse was my palace. For the first time in ages, I felt happiness touch my heart."

Around them, familiar scenes unfolded. Maia watched herself grow up through the carefree days of Miorie, then after she came to Appian. Days passed before her eyes, in a steady, peaceful rhythm.

"I lived through you. I dreamed your dreams, I surged with your joys and sank with your sorrows. And I knew, this time I was not going to accept my fate . . . our fate quietly. I would wield my powers and wreak vengeance on anyone who came to hurt you.

"And they came in droves to hurt you. Some were jealous of your powers, others were hungry to use them for their own benefit. Different faces, but the same old greed. But this time would be different. This time, I will fight with you, for you. Your dreams of life and love and happiness will come true."

The scenes swirled continuously around them as Ataii gazed at Maia and smiled. "I am ready to destroy anyone who stands in your path, Maia."

As much as Maia was thankful to have Ataii's formidable spirit pledging her support, all she felt was fear. Every time Ataii had helped her, she had found herself teetering on the edge of darkness. The taste of unbridled power, intoxicating as it was in the moment, always left her soul tormented. And using Ataii to destroy everything—even the Execution Fleet—was not something Maia wanted to do unless provoked. She had to make that clear, even though the chances were that Ataii would not take her choice happily. Still, Maia knew she had to hold on to her own choice and stand her ground.

"I want to save my world. But I don't want to destroy anything unless I'm left with no other choice." Just as she had expected, Ataii's eyes narrowed and her jaw hardened. Maia did not relent. "Please, is there any way to get rid of the fleet other than destroying it?"

"Your enemies won't hesitate to harm you or your friends," Ataii said, her voice harsh. "Do you realize that?"

"I can only hope to be faster than them, and smarter," Maia said. "But I cannot simply destroy the entire fleet without even a warning. There are people in those ships who must not even want to be here. I have to give them a chance. If I don't, how will I be any different from the people who want to destroy everyone in Xif, knowing well that most Xifarians don't even know of their terrible history?"

Ataii studied her face for a while. "As you wish," Ataii said finally. "Remember, I am with you. All you have to do is ask."

Maia had just breathed in relief when she noticed a change in Ataii. In an instant, her expression had turned severe.

"The prince knows the seer's plan," Ataii said.

Maia's heart skipped a beat. "I need to get back there," Maia said. "How do I—"

Even before Maia could finish her sentence, she found herself receding. Everything she had seen sped backward. Maia flew past galaxies and stars, back to the Tansian system, past the bright blue marble that was her Tansi, to the ashy surface of Xif, and back into the sunlit Receptor Room where Ruche was still chanting in front of her. Her body shuddered violently as her spirit fused back into it, and her eyes flew open.

Chapter Fifty-Nine

Birth of a Legend

The meshing of body and spirit was neither easy nor instantaneous. The world swung in front of Maia's eyes for a moment before she could move. She could hear sounds, much more than normal. She could sense things far, far out. She felt Aekken's arrival two stories down, and heard the shouts and screams of people as he made his way through them. She felt the anger bubbling in Aekken's heart, and the wrath flowing through his veins. She knew he would tear through anyone who stood in his way. There was no time to lose.

She reached inside for the light and it flowed out before her lips could whisper, "*Yoteh.*"

Ruche almost jumped as Maia tried to rise to her feet.

"Maia, what are you doing? We aren't there yet."

"We don't have time to finish this, Ruche," Maia said. "Aekken's here already."

"What? How do you know?"

"I do. I hear him, I see him." Maia reeled as she heard more, and felt more. "Ruche, call back the flyers. Aekken has summoned all his motherships."

Ruche stared at her, his eyes wide. Dani, who had been hunched near the Light Portal, looked just as flabbergasted.

"Now, Ruche. Call them back, now," Maia said as she strode toward the door. "And you stay behind me."

"But Maia, you're not ready yet. You can't —"

"It is what it is, Ruche," Maia said. "I have to fight with what I have." A scream drifted up from the floors below. "Aekken is hurting people. I can't just sit here while he does that."

A huge brawl was already underway when Maia rushed to the hallway outside. Aekken and ten or so of his Faceless were trying to make their way up the stairs to the Receptor Room. A group of chancery guards and some of Ruche's ragtag army blocked their way, but Maia could tell they were no match for the Faceless with far superior skills. By the time Maia made it to the head of the stairs, Aekken had broken through the barricade. He rushed up brandishing a huge sword, dragging a bleeding Ren by his collar, his guards in tow.

Maia considered her options. Ren was barely conscious, his face bloodied. Aekken had tortured him already, and Maia could only hope that none of the wounds were deadly. As much as Maia wanted to rush out and snatch Ren out of Aekken's clutches, she knew she would not be fast enough. One slip and Aekken would not hesitate to use that sword on Ren. She had to wait until they got closer. But that meant having to quietly watch Aekken mow down the other fighters as he made his way up. Bracing herself, Maia took position right behind the massive doorframe, so she could look out but keep herself out of Aekken's line of sight.

It was hard to watch such an unequal fight. The Faceless used TEK and swords, and they were all trained fighters. Most on the opposing side were blind to TEK, and could do little other than be thrashed by the prince's army. The only exception was the few chancery guards. Then there was Principal Pomewege and, to Maia's utter surprise, Karhann, the only real challenges to Aekken's steady progress up to the Receptor Room. Whether Karhann had come as part of Sana's army or as Pomewege's assistant, Maia had no idea, but she could see the distress and desperation as he fought Aekken. Every time Ren's barely conscious form bumped against a stair, he winced just the way Maia did herself. Karhann, without a doubt, was Ren's true friend.

Heart beating like a hammer in her chest, Maia waited until Aekken and his Faceless reached the top of the stairs. Ren collapsed, and Aekken's face twisted in rage when he tried and failed to yank Ren to his feet. Maia held her breath and gritted her teeth as Aekken raised his foot and took aim at the unconscious boy. His kick landed on Ren's chin and Dani yelped as Ren flew backward, blood spurting out of his mouth as he fell in a crumpled heap.

Karhann lunged at Aekken in a desperate bid to grab Ren, and Aekken jumped backward. A pair of Faceless rushed between the two, their arms swishing up a blockade with TEK, but Karhann crushed it without much trouble. Aekken fell back once more, dragging Ren with him, and seeing a clear line of attack, Maia took her first step forward.

"*Yoteh.*"

The light swirled to her hands in an instant, curling into a pair of whips at her fingertips. She strode forward, her steps long to quickly bridge the distance between them. She had a plan. But she had not expected Karhann to make a mad dash at Aekken at that very instant, nor the Faceless to throw a TEK spiral at Karhann that made him topple in front of Aekken. The prince advanced, grinning maniacally as he raised his sword over the boy, a pitiless look on his face.

Many things happened at the same time. Aekken struck. Principal Pomewege threw himself between Aekken and Karhann. Light erupted from Maia's hands and streamed forward, making its way toward Aekken. And Aekken turned around and spotted her.

Maia kept going, barely knowing what she was doing, only aware of Ataii's presence growing stronger inside her. The light flowing from her was different, more complex than she had ever managed herself. It streamed out of her hands in different textures, one a gentle wave that scooped up Ren and carefully deposited the boy on the ground next to her, and the other a scorcher toward Aekken and his guards that pushed them back.

But even then, it was too late to help Pomewege. The principal had pulled Karhann away, but he could not get out of the way himself. Aekken's sword slashed across his body, and a shower of blood erupted in its wake. As Principal Pomewege toppled down the stairs, his eyes wide in the throes of pain and shock, Maia screamed. She screamed and screamed, in grief and in rage. It was not her voice at all, but the pain was all hers. The rage was all her own too. The sound, almost animalistic, echoed through the chambers.

"I will burn you, Aekken," she shouted, advancing on Aekken and his guards. Maia knew it was Ataii giving her those words, and she happily let her. "I will kill you all."

Aekken tittered. "You do not have it in you, my starlight. You cannot kill people. You should know that threats are only as good as the people making them."

At his signal, his Faceless—all except two—charged, their swords raised. Half of them came toward Maia, and the rest bounded down the stairs.

"Wrong move, Aekken," Maia hissed.

Fire burst out of her, a violent inferno that rushed like the tongues of a dragon and swirled around the faceless guards. It picked them all up and threw them on the ground around Aekken.

"Burn," she whispered.

Heat flooded the area, its raw power singeing Maia's skin as it swept over her. One moment the Faceless were in the middle of a whirlpool, like insects in the middle of an open flame, and in the next, nothing remained.

Aekken's horror-stricken face was a treat to watch, but Maia did not bask in joy for too long. The motherships were on the way and she had to stop them.

"Call the ships off, Aekken, or I will do the same to you," she said, taking another step toward the prince. "Call them off and I may still spare your life."

"You tricked me," Aekken snarled. He threw an enraged glare at Ren behind her. "That boy tricked me. I should have chopped his head off."

"Be glad that he's still breathing, Aekken, or I'd have burned you alive by now," Maia said. The vortex of flames encircled Aekken, growing hotter, larger, and tighter around him with every passing moment. "Now call off the motherships."

"And you . . ." Aekken's lips twisted into a vicious scowl. He was looking at Ruche behind her, Maia realized. "You betrayed the Empire. I will have you flogged and flayed, you filthy traitor."

"You will never touch him." Maia stepped closer to the prince as she tightened the tumultuous ring of light around him even more. Aekken winced, his face red with the heat.

"The motherships, Aekken," Maia reminded him, her voice rising a notch. "Call them off."

"You expect me to listen to you after you deceived me?" Aekken shouted. "You gave me your word. You promised you would come with me."

"And after I had come with you, you'd unleash the orbiter to destroy our star and everything else in this system along with it. So you would have me and your vengeance on Xif too?"

Aekken did not bat an eyelid, he did not even flinch. But Aekken did not know the state of mind Maia was in, that she heard his thoughts, that she had the confirmation she needed.

"I hear you, Aekken," Maia let Ataii speak for her, and let out a wicked, spine-chilling chortle. "I see all your plans. The orbiter is real. You lied to me. Aren't *you* ashamed of that?"

"Some lies are meant to be told," Aekken snapped.

Maia yanked on the light and the vortex of fire closed like a noose around Aekken, making him howl in pain. She felt pure pleasure when she uttered the next words. "And some promises are meant to be broken."

For the longest time, they stared at each other through the fire. Aekken's face was flaming red, and his eyes were pits of darkness in it. Malice, open and uninhibited, shone back at Maia. A ripple of fear passed across his face and Maia thought he would relent. Then a small smile curled his lips and in a blink, he shimmered and disappeared.

Maia had never had any intention of holding the prince captive, and she had wanted him to leave. But not so soon, and not before she could be sure he had called off the motherships. Now that he was gone and she had no way to reach him, Maia felt lost.

What was she to do now? How was she going to force him to yield?

Ataii's voice, clear and sharp in her head, brought her out of the haze of panic.

"He will attack with the motherships. Xif's deflector shield is too weak to hold off a combined attack from all of them."

"Take me to him, please," Maia said. "I have to stop him."

"I will. Are you ready?"

"A moment."

Maia strode back into the Receptor Room. She had to be near the Light Portal once Aekken had been dealt with, so she kneeled in front of it. She was about to call Ataii once more when Ruche bent next to her and grabbed her wrist.

"You are still on the rise," he murmured. "I do not understand. I stopped the process of ascension but you are still growing in strength."

"I haven't reached the highest point yet, have I?"

"I don't believe so." Ruche shook his head. "Whatever you're planning to do, Maia, it'll be dangerous. You are not there yet, and Aekken—"

"Now that Aekken knows, there's only one way to go from here, Ruche," Maia said. "Don't worry, I have Ataii guiding me. I have faith in her. I will be fine."

How much her words convinced Ruche was doubtful, since his

eyes filled with tears as he placed a hand on her head. His voice was calm and steady when he spoke momentarily. "Go then."

Maia cast a quick look at Ren's limp form, cradled in Dani's arms. Rivulets of blood streamed down from his head and streaked his pale face. "Please help him. And Principal Pomewege."

"I will, I promise."

Maia just had to close her eyes and call Ataii, and once again, she was sucked in. It was not unexpected, but the pull was just as sharp and unnerving. Maia went, her senses churning, through expanses of dark and light, heat and cold, until she was thrown out in the open. Dizziness swarmed her senses, and her vision stayed grainy for a long while before it finally cleared.

She was back over Xif, beyond its thin atmosphere, the darkness of space stretching before and behind her. A transparent suit of sorts, its surface pliant and cool, surrounded her form, and Maia quickly realized it was a shield.

Ataii's voice came from inside her. *"You can shoot through it."*

That was good to know. But shoot at what? Where were the motherships? Where was Aekken's Imperial Battlecruiser? Maia's eyes scanned the darkness in front of her for the fleet. For a moment, she hoped. Perhaps Aekken had called them off after all. Her joy only lasted until she turned around.

Then her heart sank like a stone in water. Five spaceships stared at her, their enormous presence looming over her like mountains over a minuscule ant. The sight was overwhelming and panic rose in a cold rush up her spine. There was not a chance in this world that she could win against one monster like that, let alone five of those. This was it . . . the end.

Ataii's voice, kind and firm, came to her. *"Do not be afraid, Maia. Right now, you are more powerful than you think."*

"More powerful than those things?" Maia said, her voice shaking. "They are each a million times larger than I am. How . . ."

Ataii laughed. *"Your thoughts alone can move them. You only have to believe."*

The power of Arotharan! But she had not completely reached there. How then could she take on these behemoths?

"They are charging up, Maia. Preparing to blast Xif."

Indeed. This was battle formation. The Imperial Battlecruiser had been taken inside one of the five motherships. The five now formed an arc, their front ends aiming at a point on the surface of Xif, ready to shoot their missiles.

"Do you want a life after this, Maia?" Ataii's voice came again.

Maia nodded. She wished to live. She wanted peace, happiness, and days without fear. She hoped for this nightmare to be over. She yearned for a life filled with little joys and love and laughter.

"Then you have to fight for it, Maia. I cannot help you if you refuse to help yourself."

She had to fight this fear and panic. She *had* to. No one else could stand up against the R'armimon fleet. No one but her.

"How do I get in front of them? How do I talk to them?"

"As I said, it's all in your mind. Will for it to happen."

She had to focus. For her friends, her world, for everyone Aekken had taken, and for everything else he would take if she did not fight back.

Maia felt wrath sweep through her consciousness, lighting fire in her veins as it went. It washed away her doubts and fears. As she thought of facing the combined cannons of the behemoth fleet, she found herself speeding forward toward them. She stopped and balanced herself when she was at the center of their target.

Innumerable voices—fearful, indignant, panicked—trickled through her mind. Those were the voices of the people in the ships. Then there was Aekken.

"Shoot at her when you are ready, you hear me?" he screamed.

Another voice, doubtful, perhaps of a general, came back at him. "But Crown Prince Aekken, we do not know what will be the aftermath of—"

"I will deal with the aftermath," Aekken shouted. "You follow my orders."

The energy was growing inside the behemoths, their cannons were charging. Maia did not know what the aftermath would be either, but she was not going to move out of their way.

"Destroy them before they strike, Maia," Ataii advised.

"I have to give them one last chance. Ask them to leave."

"You will not remain in this state for very long. Use your time wisely."

Wisely, yes. But first, she had to warn them all.

"Fleet of the R'armimon," Maia said, projecting as much power as she could into her voice. All conversations stilled inside the ships as soon as she spoke. "This is my warning to you. Leave now or risk destruction." As a wave of murmurs came in the wake of stunned silence, Maia followed Ataii's advice and focused her will on the ships.

She nudged them. Nothing happened. She nudged them again, harder this time.

For another moment, nothing changed. Then they moved back, sluggish and awkward, like boulders unused to being shifted. A cacophony of voices rose inside them. Maia felt their fear, their doubts, their desperation.

Laughter broke out of her, loud, almost raucous. And she knew that laughter was not hers. The voice that came after was not all hers either, yet she let it be.

"Leave while you can," she roared. "Or I will destroy you. If you attack, I will burn you down, every one of you."

The blast came out of the rightmost ship before Maia could finish. The fire, an enormous ball of molten heat, slammed against her with the intensity of an avalanche of boulders and disintegrated in a shower of meteors around her. Even with the surrounding shield, Maia reeled. She flew backward, the impact leaving her senses in a painful daze.

As she balanced herself once again, she realized a few things. She had blocked most of the blast, and it had drained her energy. Her mind flickered like a flame in the wind, almost turning dark for a moment before turning back on again. Her time was indeed limited, and Tansi's chances were dwindling with every passing moment. She had to end this quickly. She had to decide, fast, what to do. For sure, the next time, she was not going to take it quietly.

She had not completely thought through it when she felt the surge of energy ahead of her. The ships were about to fire on her again. Anger rose through her like a tempest, flowing through her consciousness and overwhelming her in its burning rage.

She had given them a chance. She had warned them. She had done enough.

Now it was time to think of her own people, of herself. Maia felt her spirit kindle at the thought, brighter than the sun in that instant, as she braced for impact and prepared to strike back.

The attack came like a hailstorm, sharp, painful, and incessant. Missiles shot out of the two ships on the right. Maia ducked and swerved and dodged, until she could not anymore. They were too numerous and they came too fast. The next wave struck and flung her backward. Like a little straw doll, she fell, swept away by the sheer intensity of the bombardment.

Ataii's sharp voice tore through her hopeless thoughts. *"It is all in your mind, Maia. Deflect them."*

It was all in her mind. This was not even really her, but a manifestation of her. Then what was holding her back?

I am. My fear is.

Maia steeled herself and focused her thoughts. Then she picked herself up and willed her way to face the rain of missiles. It came again. But this time, Maia had a plan.

"Yoteh."

Out came the light, in her favorite whip formation. She flicked it as the missiles came, up and down and round and round. Not a single one touched Maia, and when the rain of fire stopped, her heart swelled with pride. She also thought they had given up.

Maia realized her naiveté soon enough. This was only the beginning. This was the time the other ships needed to prepare their weapons. The effort of dodging those missiles had drained her. She barely found the time to turn to face the three ships on the right when three torpedoes hit from three sides, almost at the same instant. They exploded and formed a gigantic ball of fire rushing toward her. Maia was sure she was no match for it, certainly not with her own powers rapidly depleting. When the shield around her collapsed in the heat of the fire around her, Maia braced for the end. Instead, she felt a surge within.

"I will show you." The voice that came from her lips was unrecognizable to her own ears.

The fire outside coagulated around Maia and the light inside her flowed out to join it. Her hands weaved them in a motion she hardly recognized, fiery balls bouncing on her fingertips. She swirled and flicked and kicked. One by one, the balls flew out, striking the ships and tearing them wherever they struck.

"Crown Prince, we should leave," someone said. "We are taking massive hits. We can't sustain this."

"No," Aekken growled. "Get the Executor out."

"But—"

"Get it out."

Maia was sure this was the weapon meant to break Xif apart.

"Xif's deflectors do not have the strength to withstand the Executor, Maia." Ataii's voice came in an urgent rush, confirming her fears.

"Don't worry," Maia replied. "I won't let it get past me."

She was going to stand in the way. But what if she could not resist it? One option was to attack the fleet before it released the weapon, but seeing how quickly her energy was depleting, the chance she would be able to take down all five was remote. She had to wait for her power to recharge a little, but that meant giving them time to attack. Until then, she could try to scare them and make them leave.

"Go away, Aekken," Maia said. "You can't beat me. So go away now."

"I will have my revenge," Aekken hissed. "I will destroy it all. My win over you will be a legend. Forever."

"Do not let them destroy my Xif, Maia." The plea in Ataii's voice was

urgent, throbbing.

"I won't," Maia replied. "I promise you."

The ships lined up for the strike momentarily, all falling back except for one in the middle. Maia could only imagine the strength of the weapon that was coming. All she could do was strengthen her will to beat it. So she went looking inside her mind for every happy memory she could find, for every reason that could give her the strength to end this terror. She did not have to search long. They came in a flood, days of brightness and laughter, moments of happiness and hope, and reasons, numerous and strong, to win over the Execution Fleet. As determination surged within Maia, the shield grew back around her. While she waited and watched the ship, she realized a change in her. Fear and doubt were in her no more, not even a trace.

I'm going to defeat Aekken and I'm going to live free.

That was the one thought in Maia's mind when the gargantuan beam of light shot out of the ship facing her. It impinged on her, and at that moment, she was blinded by its intensity. By instinct, she let it soak into her. The stream of energy filled her consciousness and lifted her. Her life flashed before her eyes, memories, good and bad, tinkling through her mind until in a manic rush Maia found herself back in the present. The beam was gone, she had taken it in.

"Yoteh."

A massive wave of energy swept out of Maia, a near-invisible ripple in space that went surging toward the Execution Fleet. Maia felt Aekken's panic, the horror in the heart of every soul watching.

The ship that had fired the Executor took the backlash right on the nose. It was a given that the consequences could not be good, but Maia did not expect the ship to crumble the way it did. It almost looked like a sand sculpture in the face of a wave. The edges collapsed first, and then the inside, until all that remained was a ball of fire.

The rebound caught up with the rest of the fleet a moment or two later, in a massive wave of energy. Maia watched as the ships were tossed and tumbled and swept away like pieces of straw in a storm.

"This, Aekken," Maia said as the last of the Execution Fleet vanished into the darkness of space, "will be a legend. The legend of Tansi."

As the words faded from her lips, her vision flickered, and warmth seeped out of her along with her strength. Silence returned, along with the dark loneliness of space. Below her lay the ashen surface of Xif, and beyond it, the sparkling blue Tansi and their star.

Safe.

Free forever.

"Home," Maia whispered. "I want to go home."

"Let us go, Maia," Ataii said. *"You did well."*

"And you, Rahina Mayen."

Maia felt the pull at her core and in a blink, she was speeding backward. When her Roohe-Sama slammed back into her body this time, Maia could barely see anything. The world, dark and hazy, wavered in front of her. Maia held on to her dwindling senses, desperate to follow the last of Ruche's instructions.

The portal . . . she had to guide the light into it.

But there was no strength left in Maia's arms to lift Seigvard, or in her legs to stand. Her insides were parched and empty. From time to time, a flood of nothingness swept over her and pushed her fading senses to near oblivion. She heard voices, but she could not tell what they were saying. She blinked to clear her rapidly fading vision, barely discerning the outline of the portal.

Maia reached out, her arms shaking, and grabbed its cold surface. The slightest movement tapped into her scant energy, and a blur descended over her eyes and threatened to spiral her out of consciousness. Drawing a breath, and then another, she somehow pieced together strength. Somehow, she laid Seigvard across the basin of the Light Portal and said a silent prayer. Then she whispered, *"Yoteh."*

Maia felt the warmth drain out of her. The frigid chill started in her toes and spread upward. Up her legs it came, flooding her torso, and then it shot further up and engulfed her heart.

Chapter Sixty

Home

She opened her eyes to a blur of light. Shapes, a muddle of grays, moved in jumbled patches beyond the haze. Voices, a mix of many, drifted in from beyond the fog. She blinked hard. Slowly but steadily, the mist cleared and she found herself staring at a bright ceiling. She was lying in a bed. She could barely even move a finger. Across the room from where she lay, windows rose from floor to ceiling. A gossamer curtain stretched over them and beyond that, something sparkled.

She could not remember. Who she was, where she was, how she could have got there . . . nothing. She closed her eyes and searched.

Nothing!

She looked again inside her mind, up and down and round and round.

Still nothing.

Her head hurt. She wanted to sink into the comfort of the white nothingness.

But I want to know who I am.

She held on, desperate, adamant.

Then something came. A faint whisper . . .

Maia . . . Maia . . .

"I . . . I'm . . . Maia," she muttered. The relief of being able to pull out that one memory brought tears to her eyes.

To her left, someone stirred. Maia turned to look, pain all over her making her movement slow. A man—his face pallid, his ashen hair long and straight, and his eyes a frosted white—smiled at her. He looked happy but . . . tired.

"Welcome back, Maia," he said. His voice was steeped in kindness. Maia knew he was a friend, and she had known him. If only she could remember his name.

She closed her eyes and tried to think. Nothing came back to her. All she could see was white, a sea of blankness surrounding her.

"I can't remember," she whispered, terror making her voice break. "I-I can't . . . don't know your name."

"Don't push yourself, Maia. Let it come to you. It will."

"It will?"

"Yes, I promise," the man said, placing a hand on her head. "Sleep now."

As Maia closed her eyes, the haze swept over her again, and she sank deep into it.

* * *

Maia remembered seeing the room before. White ceilings, huge windows with delicate curtains, the sparkle beyond it.

"Hello there," said a voice.

That man . . . he was still here.

"Ruche." The name slipped out of her mouth as she turned to look at his pale, smiling face. His smile grew wider, the weary look on his face disappearing in an instant.

"There . . . you found my name," he said, the relief in his voice loud and clear.

"Where am I?"

"At a hospital. You've been here since . . ."

It all rushed in: memories, a flood of faces, times, words, places. It did not hurt. It simply swept over her, filling her to the brim.

"I remember. I remember everything," she whispered. "How long has it been?"

"About a week now."

"I've been sleeping for a week?"

Ruche chuckled. "You'll have to sleep a while longer before you can get back to being yourself again."

"Is this Zagran?" she asked.

"No. Why do you say that?"

"The window. That sparkle outside."

Ruche left his chair and parted the sheer curtains that held back the view outside. Maia gasped at the sight of the luminous ball in the distance. In her excitement, she tried to sit up, but her back gave out and with a piteous moan, she fell back onto the bed. Ruche was next to her in a heartbeat, patting her shoulder as she tried to catch her breath.

"Don't try to sit up just yet, Maia. Not just yet."

"The Sedara," Maia whispered. "It's back."

"Yes, it is. Miir's plan worked."

Indeed. At long last, after much anguish, Miir had found a solution. She was happy, happy that this dream came true for him.

"Is everyone all right, Ruche?" Maia asked, remembering all her friends and the last time she had seen them, heading out to divert Aekken while she tried Arotharan.

"Well . . ."

"Principal Pomewege?"

Ruche shook his head slowly and Maia's insides crumbled. Tears spurted out of her in a never-ending rush. So many times the principal had helped her. A true believer in unity and in the power of the Initiative, he had not even hesitated to come to Appian. How hard it must have been for him to travel so far, how difficult it must have been to be greeted by her impertinence. Yet the smile never left his face, and his support for her never wavered. He loved his students, and now he had sacrificed himself for them.

For a long time, Maia let the tears fall. Ruche did not say a word. Then, finally, she scraped up enough courage to ask more.

"Everyone else?"

"It'll be a while before Karhann walks again. He had a nasty fall down those stairs trying to help the principal." Tears coursed down Maia's cheeks once again. Karhann's laughing face flashed before her eyes. He did not deserve this. Ruche patted her hand gently. "Pray for him, Maia. That's the best we can do."

"And . . . the rest?" she whispered.

"The rest are all right. Some bumps and bruises, cuts and scrapes. Nothing they won't survive. Ren was a little worse off than most and we were worried about him for a while, but he's pulling through." Ruche handed her a glass of water and settled back down in his chair. "All your friends have been coming and going," he informed. "One of these days they'll catch you awake."

Maia let out a sigh. They had suffered numerous losses, but they had made it, finally made it to the other side.

So many questions hovered in her mind, so much she needed to find out. But the haze came once more and her eyelids drooped.

"Ruche, I . . ."

"Sleep now. We will talk later."

* * *

"The healers released Ren today," Ruche informed Maia. He had pulled up a chair next to her bed and sat wrapped in a blanket, a cup of soup in his hands. "I wished they would keep him here for a few more days. That's the best way to keep *that* boy down."

Maia chuckled a little. So true. Ren . . . the wild one. It was hard to pin him down.

"So you put him up to all this?"

Ruche's eyes widened. He sat up and put the cup down before shaking his head. "No, I absolutely did not. I simply provided expert guidance. He was already engaged in some spectacular planning of his own."

"He had been trying to get back at Phocluus for a while." Maia recalled how angry Ren had been that even after Lowanabe had forced him into helping Phocluus, he had been left out of the plot on Queen's Honor.

Ruche closed his eyes and placed his chin on steepled fingers. "That was his main plan. I had a vague impression of it, but I did not pay much attention until . . . until he started making friends with our dear prince. His actions startled me, scared me. And I had to look into him, very closely."

Ruche fell back in his chair, his gaze on the ceiling as an indulgent smile formed on his lips. "I was both impressed and worried by what I saw, Maia. I could not believe the audacity of a sixteen-year-old." He sighed and his eyes twinkled. "But as bold as he was, he needed a guide and a confidant to teach him and to make this plan work. So I offered myself."

"And you've been planning and plotting ever since?"

"I knew we could never match Aekken and his fleet in sheer force, there had to be some sort of sneak attack to take him down. Or at least to hold him up until I could empower you. I just did not know how until Ren showed up. He was just the perfect fit, the final piece I needed to solve this puzzle."

"Would it have killed you to tell me?"

"Aah, Maia. There is power in the element of surprise. We needed that," Ruche said, flashing one of his infuriating smiles.

"Right."

"So . . . back to Ren. When I cornered him and confronted him, he quite unhappily spilled his secrets. He had a lot on his agenda. First, he had to eliminate Phocluus so you didn't have to live with him looming over you all your life. He had been entrenching himself in their midst. And now, with Aekken bothering you, he had yet another problem to solve. I realized it was far too much for this young lad to handle. He would try, but he would get himself killed in the process."

"He's crazy. I told him not to, but he wouldn't listen."

"He cares for you very deeply, Maia. You turned his life around. You're not only his best friend but the foundation on which he stands. He has to protect you at all costs."

A sigh coursed out of Maia. At all costs . . . it almost cost him his life.

"It was a good thing I took him under my wing when I did," Ruche continued. "Ren had just found out about Fury. He had promised Phocluus he'd get them this sword. That was a dangerous pledge. I had hoped that sword would never come into play. But Phocluus had found out and Ren was adamant. Not only would acquiring the sword get him the leverage and standing he needed with Phocluus, he also wanted Miir safe and out of the cross-hairs of the SDS. He had a plan. It was not half bad. But I still worried, mostly about what Fury could do to Ren once he possessed it."

"It didn't make any difference," Maia said when Ruche paused. When Miir had passed on Fury to Ren, she had not known of the sword's significance. But she could clearly remember that Ren had stayed the same. Just as wild and cheeky and fun. Just Ren.

"Yes, I thank the stars for that. I hoped it wouldn't, but I wasn't sure until it was done. I was prepared to interfere if he posed a threat to you. But his bond with you, his loyalty was already too deep to be swayed by the artifact he came to bear. It was a relief, a great relief." Ruche left his seat and walked over to the window. He stared at the glistening orb of the Sedara for a long while. "Phocluus was pleased beyond expectations, and he went on with his plans to entrap you. Ren carried those plans to his *buddy* Aekken and got our prince all riled up. Then, as luck would have it, it turned out Phocluus was distantly related to Veiles. Aekken fell for it with the zeal of a shortsighted boar. Killing Phocluus was just the kind of vengeance he craved, and now he had every reason to do it."

"So the plan was to get me to Phocluus and then call for Aekken while I was being tortured?"

"Yes. Although the Innagmen convoluted matters a little. Aekken came in a little late. But it still worked. Seeing a descendant of Veiles try to capture a Nasfarii again was the last thing Aekken needed to see. Nothing could hold back his wrath." Maia shuddered, thinking of the moment Aekken had faced Phocluus. She had been in a haze then, but she had seen enough. It would give her nightmares for years to come. Ruche continued. "Now all Ren had to do was beg his way onto the Imperial Battlecruiser. If he could thwart the fighters for a while, we would have all the time we needed to get you prepared."

"Aekken could have killed Ren if he suspected," Maia said. Her lids drooped as a wave of dread and exhaustion swept through her.

"Aekken had no reason to think Ren could do anything to the Battlecruiser," Ruche said. "Because Ren couldn't have. Not if I hadn't supplied him with the exact steps to sabotage the weapons systems. And Aekken had little reason to suspect a connection between him and me."

Maia had to admit that she had not suspected a connection either, until the very end. Ren showed scant respect for Ruche, if any. She could never have guessed they had the patience for each other, let alone plotted together.

"That is why when Aekken came for Phocluus, I had to hide in the temple's hold," Ruche said. "Aekken needed to think it was all Ren's idea, the antics of a silly, reckless boy. He needed to think that he was the wiser one, the smarter one. He had to feel overconfident and not see my hand behind Ren's moves. That's why I couldn't get my guards or the chancery guards involved. I could only have a small, outwardly unorganized band of people to fight the SDS thugs."

"Sana's army?" Maia said. "That was your solution?"

Ruche nodded and smiled indulgently. "That girl has pluck. She recruited quite a handful of people in the little time she had. Those were good eggs, every one of them."

* * *

"Have you heard from Aekken?"

"Why? Do you miss him?" Ruche chuckled as Maia grimaced. "He's fine, just cranky. I told him he should be thankful you saved them so much of the journey back home. Didn't seem happy, that ungrateful brat."

"Do you think he will come back?"

Ruche sighed. "Aekken being Aekken, he is raring to go again. But I think the emperor realizes the truth. They just got beaten badly. They know you wielded the full power of the Nasfarii. They are not going to challenge you. Not yet, anyway. I also think the emperor has other plans. Right now, he wishes to have cordial relations with Tansi, revive the old alliance."

"And Xif?"

"Forgiven for now. The emperor says that since they have changed their ways, there is nothing more to be done. The fact is, the stories about Tansi have spread and they don't paint the Empire in a favorable light. The Empire cannot afford another offensive, not after this grand debacle." Ruche twiddled his fingers and laughed. "However, the emperor is very annoyed with me. I've been disowned, forever."

"No. I'm sure he'll take you back. You can't lose your home like that. Whatever you did was for everyone's good."

"Aah, Maia. Don't worry about me. I don't mind his anger." Ruche looked back at the sparkling Sedara outside. "I had to do this for Tansi."

"Why?" The question, likely inappropriate, tumbled out of Maia. "Why do you care so much for Tansi?"

"That's another story for another day, Maia," Ruche said, his eyes twinkling. "Let's leave it at . . . I owed Tansi a debt."

The mysterious expression that was so typical of him descended again, and Maia knew he was not going to say any more on the subject. Not at the moment, anyway.

"You lost your chance to go back home."

Ruche chuckled heartily as he settled back in the chair with his cup of soup. "Well, you know what? I don't feel like I've lost anything. Tansi is home, and has been for a long time now."

Chapter Sixty-One

Happiness is . . .

Maia had been eagerly looking forward to the day Ruche would finally declare she was strong enough to see her friends. More than two weeks had passed since the day of the face-off with Aekken, and she had slept through most of that time. Things were improving steadily, however. So one afternoon, once Ruche had left after extracting a promise not to stress her still tired senses too much, Maia awaited the arrival of her friends.

Dani, Hans, and Rayan were the first to arrive. After a long and welcoming session of fierce, tearful hugs, they settled down around Maia's bed.

"Maia, I have something to ask you," Dani said suddenly, hesitation rippling in her bright blue eyes. She shot a nervous look at Hans, who returned a quick, sincere nod. "I . . . we want you to come live with us when you get better. We will go to school at the UAAS together and it'll be perfect." She stopped, her hopeful yet anxious gaze scanning Maia's face. "I really hope you'll agree."

Maia could not find a single word to say in response. *After I get better* . . . she had thought of it so much since consciousness returned to her, realizing that finally, once and for all, the Initiative was truly over. And she had to face the worst truth of all—that she had no home. There was nowhere for her to go. She had to walk out of this hospital someday. But where would she walk to?

In the end, she had decided. She would go back to Appian and find a place to work and live. And then, someday . . . she would slowly rebuild the house.

Dani's unexpected offer came like a gust of wind through her well-settled thoughts and left her choked with pain. It took her a long time to think up a reply, and even longer to whisper it. "Thank you, Dani. But I couldn't. I've decided to go back to Appian."

Rayan frowned. "Appian? You cannot be on your own yet. You are too young for that."

"I'll be fine, Rayan. Young I may be, but I'm not a baby."

"What's wrong with living in Zagran for a few years?" Dani asked, her wide eyes glistening.

"There's nothing wrong with it, but I can't impose—"

"Maia." Hans peered at her face, his kind gaze holding her moist one. His warm hand wrapped around Maia's. "Maia, 'impose' is not a word you use with family," he said. "I told you this once and I meant it. To me, you are just like Dani. And if I haven't been able to make you think of me as your own, I'm a total, utter failure."

Maia shook her head vehemently. "Please don't say that, Hans. I've always considered you family," she said. "Always. But . . ."

Rayan placed a firm hand on her shoulder. "There is no but, Maia. You are coming, that is final." There was nothing but certainty in those blazing brown eyes, and Rayan's kind yet resolute tone brought a smile to Maia's face.

Dani jumped to her side in an instant. "So it's a yes, right?" she said, hands clasped as if in prayer. "You're coming, right?"

"Of course, she is," Rayan declared even before Maia could nod.

Dani squealed and threw her arms around Maia, and Hans laughed. Maia had not even fully rejoiced in their generosity when the door fell open and a noisy whirlwind careened in. The rest of the gang — Nafi leading the way, Sana and Ren in between, Kusha behind them all, carrying a basket — had arrived. A loud, boisterous conversation followed. For a while, Maia was worried the hospital staff might come to remind them of appropriate behavior. But things did not get *that* rowdy, and even though it took a while, a semblance of calm soon returned to the room.

Nafi marched up to Dani and gave her a meaningful look. "And?"

"It's all settled," Dani replied with a brilliant smile. "She's coming with me to Zagran."

The room erupted in shouts once more, and Maia suddenly realized they had all been in it together. While she had been searching for a way to handle her future, her friends had already plotted to find a path through it for her.

"Now, we need to celebrate," Nafi said. She opened up the basket Kusha had carried in and out came apples. She handed the first to Maia. "Try it, Maia. Fresh apples from ThulaSu. They will do you good."

"Don't force her, Nafi," chided Dani, who sat next to Maia, their arms linked, but it was a useless effort. Nafi did not relent until Maia had taken two whole bites. "She has been bringing apples for Karhann too," Dani added with a giggle.

Ren chortled. "Karhann almost wishes Nafi had kept hating him."

"Not fair. I bring people nutritious stuff and this is the thanks I get?" Nafi huffed. She crossed her arms and turned her nose up in the air. "Even so, Nafi refuses to give up. She will keep fighting the good fight."

Maia chuckled heartily before taking another bite of her apple. It was good to have them all together in the room. Hans and Rayan looked cozy on the sofa, Kusha, Ren, and Sana were at the window, and Nafi buzzed around. It was also the first time she had sat up for any length of time. Propped up by pillows, of course, but it was still an improvement.

"Have to say, Maia, this view is just awesome," Sana said. She had been looking out at the Sedara, which was dimming into the colors of sunset. "The queen is certainly trying to make up for her earlier lapses. This is probably the best room in the hospital, reserved just for the Royals."

"She'd better," Nafi snapped. "Can't believe anyone could torment their own grandchild like that. That heartless woman."

"Nafi, please," Hans cautioned. "It's easy to slip back into memories that distress us, but let's not. Let's look forward, all right?"

"Easy for you to say," Nafi grumbled. "You didn't see how she treated—"

"No, Nafi. That's not true at all." Hans was not one to give in. "It's not easy for me to say. I do understand. I may not have seen how the queen treated Maia, but I have seen my share of cruel, wicked behavior. But I've also come to realize that the more you linger on the pain, the more you hurt yourself. Learn from the situation and move on. Forward is the only way to go."

Nafi groaned and muttered grumpily to Dani, "I don't like it one bit when your brother switches his lecturing mode on."

"I heard that, Nafi," Hans said, chuckling loudly. "Unfortunately for you, you're not getting rid of me anytime soon."

Nafi had just slumped into a chair. Now she sat up, eyes wide. "Why is that?"

"I'm working on setting up a base on the Third. We're going to work on reviving the land. It's the first revitalization project of the Trinational Coalition."

"That's still a thing, then?" Ren asked. "They're keeping the Trinational Coalition even after everything is back to normal?"

Hans nodded. "Yes, seems like it. Everyone is eager to work together and rebuild. I pitched this idea and guess what? There was no opposition, none at all."

"The revitalization projects already have quite a following," Kusha said. "There was a council of House leaders last week, and even Leeam seemed all excited about it. It was weird seeing *him* agree with everyone else for a change."

"Can't believe they let that stupid Leeam in again," Nafi said.

"Moving forward, Nafi," Kusha said and promptly received a snort in response.

"Well, it's good that the revitalization projects are coming along," Maia said when the chuckles died down. "No, actually, it's great." After all the strife they had been through, this amity was well-deserved. Even though she knew there would always be some forces that would try to undermine the unity of the three nations, this was a beginning. A good one, too.

"It is," Hans said. "I'm really excited about this."

Maia did not miss the adoring look Rayan shot at Hans. Her heart swelled with happiness for the duo. They had found each other after all.

"So wait." Nafi held up a hand. "How is it that I can't be rid of you? The Third is a big continent, in case you didn't know."

"The base will be in Contes," Rayan said.

"Oh, I see," Nafi said and sighed loudly. "Well, guess I'll have to endure Hans's lectures, then. But I'm happy that you have not chosen to set up camp near Korobieltes out of some heroic desire to impress Zaara. The farther you two stay from her, the better. That woman's a nut. And after the hell she gave you—"

"Nafi, what did we just say about moving on?" Hans said in an exasperated tone.

Nafi raised her hands in submission. "All right, all right. You're correct. We are lucky to be here today. All of us, together, happy. We should keep our eyes on the good."

"Well, that's a great sentiment, but . . ." Ren walked over and cocked an eyebrow at Nafi. "Luck has nothing to do with why we're all here safe and sound. It was all about meticulous planning, courtesy of . . . me."

Maia had to admit that Ren had pulled it off. She had been scared and at times things got downright unpredictable, but Ren and his audacity had made it through. He had pretended to be Phocluus's mole, then pitted Aekken against Phocluus, and finally tricked

Aekken into believing Maia was within his grasp. Maia shuddered, thinking how close they had come to getting killed in the process. But, in the end, they made it.

Nafi, however, was not about to admit any such thing. She stared at Ren for a moment and then broke into guffaws. "Meticulous planning? You almost got Maia killed. You still have a bandage wrapped around your head. It was more like the crazy antics of a hyperactive monkey."

Ren crossed his arms and glared. "Seriously? A monkey? That's what I get?"

"Yes. You're lucky you've got a thick skull. Anyone else would still be in the hospital."

"You are so ungrateful, Nafi. I did all this and you say . . . You're just . . . You know what? I'm happy I don't have to see you every day anymore."

Nafi made a face. "Feeling's mutual, winsome prince of the skies. I'm glad the Initiative's over and we all head back to our own schools and everything."

"Seriously, you guys," Sana chimed in. "You're going to miss each other like crazy but it kills you to admit it."

Ren gave Sana a dejected look. "Sana, my angel, why do you always have to go against me?"

Nafi rolled her eyes. "Oh, please. Not that stupid angel stuff again."

Ren arched an eyebrow. "Why? Jealous much?"

"Some of you should be sent to a circus," Rayan quipped. "You make a good act."

At that point, a cacophony broke out. Hans repeatedly asked them to quiet down so as not to tire Maia out, but to no avail. Exhausted as she was, Maia enjoyed seeing them all like this. This had been her life for close to four years, and she treasured every moment of it. She had no hesitation in admitting that she would miss this— Nafi bickering with Kusha and Ren, Dani desperately trying to calm them down, everyone else praying for some quiet. Not having them around would leave a big void in her heart.

Sana walked over and slumped on Maia's other side. She shook her head at the squabbling duo at the center of the commotion. "I just don't get it. Where do they find the energy?"

Dani's arm tightened around Maia's. "We're a hopeless bunch, aren't we?" she said with a sigh. "But there's no other bunch I'd rather be around."

So true. One of the few things in her life that Maia would never wish to be different was this—her friends. Always opinionated, sometimes annoying, and at other times downright aggravating—her friends, her family.

"I'm happy, Maia," Dani said, laying her head on Maia's shoulder. "I only wish Miir could be here with us now."

Maia looked at Dani, startled, fearful, caught unawares by the sudden mention of Miir. Over the past couple of days that she had finally spent a little time awake, she had thought of him constantly. That he did not come to visit her was strange, and the fact that Ruche kept dodging talking about Miir was even stranger. A worry had started in her mind, and it grew bigger every day. Now that Dani brought him up, she stared, wide-eyed at her friend.

Catching her glance, Dani sat up. "Oh, you don't know. Oh, dear."

Maia's fingers turned numb in an instant, her heart freezing in terror. She barely had the strength to push the words out of her mouth. "What is it, Dani? Has something happened to him?"

"What? No, he's fine. He's busy rearranging the lattice of the Sedara's receptor. It's being modified so the Sedara can sustain itself from the ambient sunlight. You can't be restarting it every other day, you know. It'd kill you. Obviously, this needs to be finished quickly, in case the Sedara falls apart again. So Miir and a team of engineers have been working day and night to get it completed as fast as possible. We've been volunteering too."

Maia released the breath she had been holding. Miir was fine. She did not care if he did not visit, she did not care if she had to wait a long time before she saw him again. He was safe and well, and that was all that mattered.

Next to her, Dani continued. "He has been here to check on you, but mostly in the dead of night after the work is done at the receptor site. Of course, there's no chance he'd catch you awake then. I'm surprised Ruche didn't tell you that. He knows." Dani stopped and squeezed Maia's arm. "Anyway, now you know. Happy?"

Sana had been watching Maia's face intently. As soon as Dani stopped speaking, she nudged Maia's arm and flashed an impish grin.

"All right, this I need to settle right here, right now," Sana declared. "Do I have permission to call him *your* Miir now, dear cousin?"

Dani giggled, making Maia flush to the tips of her ears. She was about to protest as she always had at Sana's calling him that, but paused.

"You may," Maia said with a bashful smile while Dani broke into fresh giggles.

Chapter Sixty-two

Never Too Late

Over the next few days, Maia's strength quickly returned. Every day she felt better, stronger. Ruche allowed her to walk to the window and urged her to do more, but Maia did not venture any farther. Even those ten steps exhausted her. However, she kept at it and her stamina, nonexistent at first, improved at a steady pace.

Ruche had been leaving her alone more and more as time passed, and Maia did not mind that at all. She welcomed the quiet and relished the peace. Most days, Ruche came in the afternoon and then again in the evening to join her during mealtimes. The rest of the day was hers, except for when her friends dropped by.

One morning, Maia was curled up on the sofa with a blanket, a book in hand, Keiki clutched to her chest, when the chamber door opened. She had not expected anyone, so Maia craned her neck to look. When she saw who it was, she hastened to sit up, and in her haste, she almost fell off the sofa.

Rahina Quemiila rushed to her side. "Please, be careful. There is no need to get up. Stay where you are."

Maia relaxed a little, but it was difficult with the Xifarian queen staring down at her.

"Are you feeling better now?" Rahina Quemiila asked after she had pulled up a chair next to Maia.

Maia nodded. It was not appropriate behavior, but words refused to come out of her mouth. Her mind kept slipping back to the last few times they had spoken. The resentment inside her was still fresh, although, Maia realized, there was a bit of embarrassment as well. Her conviction did not change at all, she still wanted no part of her inheritance, but she decided to keep things civil.

Dada would want me to be polite at least. And Sophie too . . .

"You are a brave girl," the queen said, breaking the prickly silence in the room. "What you did the other day —"

"It's nothing," Maia said. "Anyone in my place would do the same."

"That is *not* true."

A flush crept up Maia's face and she fidgeted. Kind words from the queen were not something she was used to. It felt strange, uncomfortable. Maia wanted the meeting to end as fast as possible.

"Oh, I need to return Seigvard to you," she said in a rush, suddenly remembering. "It's in that closet. I asked Ruche to take it to you, but he always seems to forget. I'm sorry. I —"

"Please, Maia. Do not worry yourself. I will take it back, just as you wish."

"Thank you."

It was a good thing she did not have to fight or argue about it. It did not feel right to be refusing something as precious as the legendary Seigvard again and again. It felt like she was slighting the Mahswa who had held it before her, and Ataii, the one whose sword it was to begin with.

"However, I have one request that I hope you will not turn down," the Rahina said.

Maia held her breath and stared as the Rahina started to unfasten the other half of the pendant from her neck.

"No. Please, no," Maia started to protest. "I told you once, and I still mean it. I do not want it. Please don't think I'm lingering here to stake my claim to your legacy. I promise I will leave here as soon as I am strong enough to walk. I-I truly do not wish to be a bother to you."

The queen did not appear to hear her fervent pleas. She took off the pendant and, holding it in her palms, gazed wistfully at it. The pendant—a mesh of crystal, veins of minerals in a myriad of hues running through the dark, shimmering blackness of the rock—sparkled and shone as the Rahina cradled it.

"My Raidyn, your father, would have wanted you to have this, Maia." The queen's mournful gaze held hers, and in that instant, Maia could see the intensity of the woman's pain. "Please do not turn him down. Please do not punish him for the sins I have committed against you." Maia could not find an answer quickly enough, so she stared, dumbfounded as the queen continued. "I do not expect you to forgive me after the way I have treated you, and I shall not ask for kindness I do not deserve. But Raidyn . . . he would have treasured you."

Maia blinked at the sudden rush of tears. The face of a young boy in a photograph from long ago flashed before her eyes—a face with laughing eyes—of a father she would never know. Her heart ached, and she wanted to curl up and cry.

"My Raidyn loved your mother, Maia. He loved her with all his heart and soul. He could have been with anyone he wanted, but he wanted Sophie. Sophie was his world, his beginning, and his end. And to Sophie . . . he was the sun."

Maia sat up, frowning, struggling to understand what she had just heard. "But . . . but you said . . . you said Sophie did not care. All she wanted was to use him to get to the Foundation Chamber."

The queen looked up at her and smiled sadly. "Sophie . . . so innocent and honest . . . so much strength in that fragile slip of a girl." She sighed and closed her eyes. When she opened them again, they were brimming with tears. "I never knew a kinder, sweeter person. Sophie did not have a mean bone in her body. Using people? Using

Raidyn? Not Sophie. That is something this wicked old grief-stricken woman made up so she would have someone to blame for the disaster that unfolded on her family. And who could be a better scapegoat than the outsider who had no one to defend her?

"I still remember the evening when Phocluus came to me with the news about the Sedara being broken. They knew Raidyn's key had been used to get into the Foundation Chamber, and now they needed more. I was furious at Phocluus. How dare he slander our family? How dare he? Phocluus did not bat an eyelid. He was so certain, so collected, so utterly . . . cold. He wanted to speak with Raidyn, but Raidyn was nowhere to be found. I did not understand. How could my son be capable of this heinous crime? Impossible. It could not be."

Tears streamed down the Xifarian queen's face.

"Raidyn came back a week later, distraught, with a wild look in his eyes that I will never forget. They had taken his Sophie away, he said. I had to help him free her, he said. She was family, his wife, I had to. He begged, how he begged for help. I turned him away. I called him a traitor, a disappointment, a failure. And I turned him away. I refused to help my boy."

Rahina Quemiila bent over and erupted in violent sobs. For a while, Maia did not know what to do, what to say. What could she say to a mother grieving for her child, the child she had turned her back on when he needed her the most? Then she wiped away her own tears and placed a hand on the queen's shoulder, hoping to comfort her, knowing it was a futile effort.

After a while, the queen sat up again. "I found Raidyn a few days later in a hovel in the Gnelexian Sector. He was sick, delirious. He barely recognized me. Something inside him had snapped. All the while he kept saying "Sorry, Soph, I couldn't help. Wish you had told me, Soph." And the next day, he was gone. My boy died of heartbreak. He could not live knowing there was nothing he could do to save the love of his life."

"But Phocluus said Raidyn was the one who bribed the prison guards. He did help Sophie in the end. He was why I survived."

Rahina Quemiila sighed. "He must have tried everything he could. He never found out that Sophie got out, and he probably never knew about you either. My darling boy died, hopeless, his heart shattered to pieces. If only I had helped. I could have helped."

They sat in silence, connected by their shared grief for the dear ones lost forever. Time passed in slow, protracted beats until the Rahina lifted her upturned palms that cradled the pendant.

"So, Maia . . . please, please accept this. Let Raidyn be part of you."

Maia did not need to be asked again. After hearing Sophie and Raidyn's story, there was nothing she wanted more than to have a part of her father with her, always.

The Rahina smiled in relief as soon as Maia nodded. "Thank you, thank you. Ideally, this should have been done in a formal setting, but I do not want to wait another moment." Soon she had unfastened Maia's half of the pendant as well, and she placed the two halves side by side on Maia's lap. "Do you know how the Navioneki works?" she asked. She continued when Maia shook her head. "This is another one of those secrets we Royals keep close to the vest. They are made of the heart stone or Navione, a very precious mineral, and carved with powerful and ancient magic." She looked up and smiled at Maia, who had been listening with rapt attention. "As you can tell, these two are parts of a whole."

"But it's broken."

"No, not broken, only separated. I will put them together now, as they ought to have been since the moment you were born."

"I-I don't understand," Maia said. "I thought it was just an heirloom Raidyn gave Sophie. What does my birth have to do with it? And how can you put them together?"

"The Navioneki is not just another heirloom, Maia. This is what we call the Promised Heart. It is passed down through generations. It only comes apart once in a generation, when an heir chooses a partner for life. It is part of our marriage vows: *I give a piece of my heart to you.* That is where it is now, separate."

CHAPTER SIXTY-TWO

"So Raidyn gave a half to Sophie when they married?"

"Yes. Surely," the queen replied. "Sophie must have taken it off and passed it to someone before they caught her. I am so glad she did that. Had it fallen into Phocluus's hands, it might have been lost forever."

Quemiila ran a finger over the two pieces, tenderly, reverently. "You might laugh, but I feel the yearning in them. They want to come together. They would have, sixteen years ago, if things had gone right. You see, when the firstborn arrives, the parents bring their pieces together and the heart becomes whole again. Then it stays with the child until they are ready to begin the giving cycle once more."

As Maia held her breath and stared, excited and enthralled, the queen brought the two pieces close, setting them side by side so the edges matched. Then as she chanted words that Maia could tell were born in an ancient past, the pieces meshed together with a soft, subdued flash.

Rahina Quemiila picked up the pendant, now whole and sparkling even more, or so it seemed to Maia, and gently tied the strings around Maia's neck.

"There, as it should be. I wish your parents were here to see this." The queen sighed, her melancholy gaze lingering on Maia's face for a long time. "It is all yours now," she said. "From now until you are ready to spend your life with someone you treasure, when you will have to separate them yourself. I will show you how."

Maia touched the pendant as it rested at the base of her throat, her fingers caressing its smooth surface, taking in the feeling of having it whole. It brought her an unexpected calm, just thinking of her parents, smiling just like they did in that photograph. Happy. Content.

"Sophie and Raidyn . . . together at last," she whispered.

"Well, that is not wholly true. They have always been together in you," the queen said. She stayed silent for a moment before she looked up, her gaze questioning. "I am curious, do you always call your mother by her name?"

Maia flushed violently. It was a long, convoluted story. She had not known Sophie was her mother until she was eight, until that evening in Miorie when she overheard Uncle Alasdair. Then, in a desperate bid to keep her distance from the traitor she wrongly believed her mother to be, Maia had decided to keep calling Sophie by her name. Dada had tried to correct her a few times, but had given in to her persistence. Later, even after Maia had found out the truth about her mother, she kept calling her Sophie. It felt right, somehow. Dada did not mind anymore. Perhaps he liked to hear Sophie's name being spoken, his only remaining reminder of her existence when all other memories had to be destroyed.

"Yes, I do. I know it's strange and sounds . . . disrespectful, but I think I . . . kind of like to hear her name."

Quemiila let out a small laugh. "Such are the ways. Raidyn always, always referred to us as Quemiila and Rynolde. How many times did I take him to task for his insolence? It never worked. We remained Quemiila and Rynolde no matter what I said or did. You do not understand, he would say, I feel happy when I say your name." The queen stopped and sighed. "I never understood."

Once again, a breathless silence fell in the room and Maia bristled in discomfort. She wished she could alleviate the woman's pain a little, but she did not know how. So she prayed for peace, however little was possible, to heal the queen's splintered heart. She searched for words, something, anything that could distract her, if only for a moment. She found one question at long last.

"I'm curious, Rahina Mayen."

The queen flinched. "Oh, do not call me that, please. You need not call me anything, but . . . not that."

"All right, I won't."

"Thank you." The queen gave her a small, relieved smile and bowed her head. "You wanted to ask something?"

"Yes. I wondered . . . what made you change your mind about Seigvard and the Navioneki that day? Did Ruche tell you something?"

Rahina Quemiila shook her head. "Seer Ruche did visit that day, but by then I had already decided. I knew I could not make the same mistake all over again." She stopped, and a soft, happy smile played on her lips. "That boy came before Ruche did, broke into my house to be accurate. I was certain he deserved to be thrown in prison, but then I saw him. His face, his eyes . . . the anguish, the helplessness, how he begged me to help. He reminded me of my Raidyn. And I knew if I did not help him, if I turned him away, I would have killed my son all over again."

Maia stared in utter bewilderment when the queen paused. The only person she knew to be capable of a break-in was Ren, but Ren was with her that day.

"Boy?" she asked. "What boy?"

An amused look came over Quemiila's face. "The same one who keeps risking everything for your sake." She shook her head again. "Breaking into the Royal compound . . . who knew that was possible? He has too much of his mother in him."

Maia blinked a few times before understanding sank in, and a few times more before she managed to utter another word. "You mean . . . Miir? Miir broke in?"

"Yes, he certainly did."

As Maia sat open-mouthed, trying to put the pieces together, the queen rose, "I will leave now, Maia, I do not wish to exhaust you any more. I thank you for all you have done for Xif. And thank you also for your kindness to me, for letting me finally confess my sins." She retrieved the case containing Seigvard and gave Maia a reassuring smile. "Here, I am taking this away, as promised." She started to walk out but turned around at the door. "Be well, Maia. Always know that your parents would have been very proud of you. I will stay away, do not worry. I know you do not wish to see me again, and I understand."

"Actually . . ." Maia blurted. "I would like it if you visit again. I-I would like it very much."

Maia had no idea where those words came from, but on seeing how the queen's pallid face lit up, she was happy that they did.

"Then I will. I most certainly will," Rahina Quemiila said, wiping the corners of her eyes. "Thank you. You have your mother's heart. And I am glad you do. So glad."

After the queen left, Maia sank back into the blankets, and clutching the Navioneki, she wept. She cried for the lives that were lost, for the loves that were doomed, but most of all she cried because she sorely missed her parents.

CHAPTER SIXTY-THREE

SKIES SO BLUE

The Sedara was sparkling in the vivid blue sky. The buildings of Xif were an unending wave of silver, white, and gray that glittered and stretched to the horizon. Maia gazed spellbound at the sight as she stood at the window of her hospital room.

"Are you sure you feel strong enough?" Ruche asked for the third time that morning. He wanted to take her somewhere—Maia did not know exactly where because Ruche would not tell—but he kept hesitating.

Maia chuckled before replying. "I won't know until I've tried, Ruche," she said. "But I think, unless you ask me to climb mountains all day, I'll be fine."

She had regained most of her strength. Although sudden fatigue often came over her, it was not as bad anymore. She spent more time awake during the day, which was certainly a change for the better.

Ruche's eyes lingered on the pendant around her neck when Maia turned toward him. "Are you happy about that?"

Maia's hand flew up to clutch the restored Navioneki. "Yes. I am. They're together now. And close to me."

Thinking of her parents always brought tears to Maia's eyes. This time was no different, but she blinked them away. *They wouldn't want me to be sad,* she thought and smiled.

"All right, then," Ruche said. "Let's go."

He led the way out of the hospital, down its wide, gleaming stairs, and toward a waiting transport. Maia breathed deeply before getting in. For almost four whole weeks she had been inside a room, sleeping for the most part. Being out in the open again was wonderful. Her eyes lingered on the Sedara for a while, admiring its bright, luminous form.

She wondered . . .

"Ruche, has the light left me?"

Ruche shook his head. "Not entirely, Maia. No matter what, a part of it will always remain within you."

"It's odd. I don't feel it inside me anymore," Maia confessed with a little sadness. She had tried to nudge it, and finding nothing, she had tried harder. And still, she had found nothing.

"You will find it," Ruche said in a comforting tone. "Right now, you have expended a lot of energy. First when you were in Arotharan and then when you rekindled the Sedara. Just as you are trying to regain your strength, it is as well." He paused and peered into her eyes. "You miss it already?"

Maia returned a shy grin. The light had become a part of her indeed, and it was true, the thought of not having it anymore was not a happy one.

Ruche placed a hand on her shoulder. "Aah . . . don't fret. We talked about this. There was a possibility that you'd lose it all. That was the chance you took."

All that was true. But it hurt to not have it. All these years she had spent wishing it did not exist within her, and now . . . now that she had just begun to accept herself as who she was, she had changed again? Maia suppressed a sigh. It was a just punishment for having hated it so long. Amid the aching sadness rose a fear, and she grabbed the seer's arm.

"Ruche, if the only thing that the R'armimon fear is the full power of the Nasfarii, then with it gone . . ."

She could not finish the sentence, but Ruche understood and patted her hand.

"Maia, what they do not know is our weapon. Besides, who knows? Perhaps along with your strength, the light will come back to you in its full glory. We shall see. Now, let's enjoy the peace while we have it."

Soon they were cruising across Armezai in the transport. Maia recognized the sprawling Boulevard Central, the blooming Sakoro trees lining the grand avenue. The view of the magnificent Xifarian Chancery building brought back memories.

"We are going to the Chancery Annex, Maia," Ruche explained. "That should be to our left now."

Sure enough, the transport started to veer left.

"You know your way around here, Ruche," Maia said, a bit surprised at the seer's knowledge.

"Well, the queen has bestowed a lot of favors on me. I'm now an honorary member of the Royal Circle, and that includes unrestricted access to Xif. So I've been walking about, sightseeing." He chuckled to himself a little before speaking again. "I did not think it would end this way for me. That night when I came to beg her for Seigvard and if need be, force her into giving it to me, I half expected to be thrown into prison. Instead, I found her welcoming me with open arms, yearning to help you in any way possible."

Maia recalled what Rahina Quemiila had told her, about how seeing Miir beg for Seigvard had changed her mind.

"Miir's pleas touched her in a miraculous way," Ruche continued. "I couldn't have done anything without him. Although I had no idea he was going to break in, and I wouldn't have approved it. That was a bit too reckless."

'Reckless' was an understatement, Maia mused. That sort of

shenanigan was usually the kind of thing she and her teammates pulled. Who would have thought of the forever righteous Miir breaking into the Royal compound on Xif?

"Apparently, wild behavior has its rewards too. Who knew?" Smiling at Maia's confused look, Ruche continued. "Since Miir is missing a proper sword, the Rahina offered him Seigvard. I think she couldn't have chosen a better person to bequeath it to. He won't accept it until you agree, but I think you approve. Don't you?" He broke into laughter in the next moment. "Aah, young love . . . the way you blush. It makes me happy."

"You've known about us for a while, haven't you?" Maia asked. Seeing his smug face, she shook her head a little. "Why am I even surprised?"

Ruche chuckled heartily. "Indeed, why are you? Laugh all you want, Maia, but you've become like a daughter to me, and I know that heart that beats inside you. So yes, of course I knew." His kind gaze swept over Maia's face once. "Besides, that pocket-sized dragon confronted me and demanded advice on the matter a few months ago. When I said 'leave them be', it did not make her happy."

"Nafi? A few months ago?"

"Yes, this was sometime after your last adventure here. You fought off an army of SDS goons together, so the reports said."

Maia sighed. Nafi had figured it out even before Maia had realized the depth of her own feelings. That meant . . . her friends— some of them, at least—had known it all along. To think she had assumed everything was under wraps.

Next to her Ruche spoke again. "Truth be told, I've watched that boy for just as long as I've watched you. He was the bearer of the chalice, so I had to, for your protection. The chalice and the light, it's a tricky balance of opposites. One yearns to contain and the other wants to break free. Had you known each other and cared for each other before you came to carry your bequests, it would be one thing. Your personal bonds would've been strong enough to counter the influence of the loads you bore. But there you were, both already bearing your respective charges, being unknowingly shaped by them, long before you came to know each other. In such a case, it would have been safest if your paths hadn't crossed at all. And for a while it was going fine, you were separated by a great distance. And then . . ." A curious look came over Ruche's face and he paused. "Your flight in Shiloh came out of nowhere. Here I was, quite certain that the little girl had a firm grip on temptation, and suddenly . . ."

Embarrassed laughter spurted out of Maia. "I was so happy that day. I finally had permission to go to ThulaSu. I was going to leave in a couple of days anyway, and Kusha's gliders were so, so beautiful. I couldn't resist. I did not know of the Initiative or the scouts until later. If I had, I wouldn't have done it."

Ruche let out a long sigh. "I rushed to Shiloh, but it was already too late. You had been spotted and, as destiny would have it, by the bearer of the chalice. Now, it could only go one of two ways—he would be the one to take your life, or in the rare case that he was able to see through the differences, he could be an ally and protect you." Ruche's eyes had taken a frosted look, as if he were looking back upon a far-off time. "For a while, it was hard to tell. Things were . . . uncertain. I even considered intervention at one point. But . . . he chose right. When I finally spoke with Miir in that tunnel at Frauz Point, I had no doubts about which side he was on. He was ready to do anything for you. He was in control of his destiny. I suspect"— Ruche tapped the firestone wristband on Maia's arm—"this might have had something to do with bridging your differences." Ruche stared at the band thoughtfully for a while before he looked up at Maia, his eyes twinkling. "Just so you know . . . that boy doted on you long before you were even willing to consider him a friend."

Maia's thoughts had already flown back to Frauz Point. That was ages ago. She had not even fully trusted Miir then. Her heart twinged. How it must have hurt him when she doubted his intentions so many times. So long he had cared for her deeply, quietly, and she had not even known. Then he was ready to sacrifice it all just so she could be safe, while she kept thinking he had never cared. Surely, she could not have known everything then, but thinking of it now made Maia's insides shrivel in regret.

She stifled a sigh and turned toward Ruche. "You knew all that and yet . . ." A wave of frustration made her words trail away. "I thought healing my heart was important."

"Oh sure, I could have saved you some tears if I had told you. But I would have taken away your thrill of discovery, that joy of finding each other after everything. Would you really have preferred that?"

Maia could not help but smile a little. Ruche and his ways.

"I was surprised you let Miir talk to me that day at the Seliban Temple. Didn't you think it'd unsettle me even more?"

"I can be many things, but I'm not heartless, Maia." Ruche shook his head in mock anger. "I did not need special vision to see his mind was not on the planning of the air siege. So I told him to be where he wanted to be. He took off for you as if his life depended on it. I didn't have the heart to stop him. Besides, the possible rewards outweighed the risks."

"Aah! You saw the pawns could benefit your hand in the game, so you let them play."

Maia had only meant to tease him, but Ruche's eyes darkened.

"The ability to see the future is not always a gift, you know. Most times it's a burden. Knowing that you have the power to achieve the end you desire . . . it's a terrible temptation." Ruche closed his eyes and fell back in his seat. Then he laughed a little. "Aekken once called me a failure because I declined to shape the future the way he wanted. The fact is, I don't like to change the course of events, Maia. I believe in people, and I believe in the power of the choices they make. I try very hard not to think of them as pawns. Things would be so much simpler if I did."

Silence fell between them for a moment or two.

"I know it always annoyed you when I refused to tell you things that could cloud your thinking," Ruche said with a teasing smile. "When I look at you now, I know I did right. You've made your choices, some good, some not so great, but look . . . you've come to the right place in the end. You've found all the right people on your own."

"Thank you for letting me be." Maia linked her arm through Ruche's and leaned her head on his shoulder. "You do make a good father figure, Ruche," she added with a chuckle.

It was indeed good to know that she had not been shown a predetermined path. Her life—mistakes and triumphs included—was of her own making. Annoying as Ruche's riddles had been, they had served a purpose.

Maia's musings came to an end as the transport stopped in front of a rectangular pale-pink and yellow building. When they got out, Ruche gestured at the structure.

"This, Maia, is the new Trinational Council building on Xif."

"That's wonderful," Maia said. The coalition between the nations had been going strong two weeks ago, and she was happy that even with the threat of the R'armimon now gone, the council had not been disbanded. By the looks of it, not only was the coalition alive, it had grown even stronger. Premier Oliena had kept her promise. "Why are we here now?"

"Today is a momentous day, Maia. A day you have dreamed of for a long time is finally here. Many agreements are being ratified, and all the treaties from before are being rewritten. New coalition statements are being prepared." He peered at her, a bright smile lighting up his face. "The Exchange has been voided. The Jjord have lifted all the sanctions they had on the Solianese as well."

Maia's heart did a somersault. "Really? We're free now?"

"Yes, certainly. The new treaties will have guidelines on future technology and the path forward from here, but they're not punitive the way they were before."

That was truly wonderful. Finally, the Solianese would have a chance.

Finally!

"Come on now." Ruche nudged her elbow as Maia stood caught up in happy thoughts. "Your friends are waiting."

They walked into the lobby and Maia's gaze stilled on a gigantic door. It was not the size of the door that stopped her, but the curious emblem that was etched on it. A large tree with a canopy full of tiny leaves stood at the center, a mighty dragon encircled its wide trunk, and an ethereal mermaid floated gracefully at the base. A circle of flames ringed them all.

"That, Maia, is the emblem of the Trinational Coalition," Ruche said. "Like it?"

Maia nodded. What was not to like? It was the union of the emblems of the three nations. So apt, so perfect.

"Come this way." Ruche led her to one side of the lobby and into a small elevator that after some strange twists and turns, spiraled right into a viewing gallery.

"Maia!" Joyful shouts erupted as soon as Ruche walked her in. Nafi instantly bounded up to her side. Even before Ruche left, Maia was surrounded by all her teammates and Sana, everyone chirping in excitement. After a lot of telling and repeating and chiding and arguing, Dani pulled her toward the open side of the gallery that overlooked the expansive chamber below.

"Just so you know, this gallery was kindly offered to us by the queen. It's quite fantastic, I have to say, with its private elevator and everything," Dani informed her. Maia cast a glance around. That explained the opulence—the plush carpet under her feet, the fancy upholstery on the seats, that table to the side laden with refreshments that were surely worthy of Nafi's approval. "We've been watching the sessions since this morning," Dani added, pointing at the gigantic hall beneath them. "There's a break now. They'll start again soon."

Seats, a thousand or more of them, formed a semicircle around a large, elevated stage in the council room below. People thronged the space. Maia could tell there were representatives from all nations. She spotted Sahiiraan Goren, Premier Oliena, and Rahina Quemiila conversing on one side. Uncle Alasdair was there too, speaking with a woman in Jjordic garb.

"Hans and Rayan are down there. Their revitalization project on

Korobieltes is on the discussion docket." Dani linked her arm through Maia's. "This has been a good day, Maia. Things are going well, finally."

Yes, finally!

Maia's heart twinged, and her eyes filled with tears. So many people were lost on the way. Brave, selfless souls all of them. Maia pictured the thousands of nameless people—miners, the resistance fighters, the ones who died when the Damoclian fell. She remembered every supporter and believer—Principal Pomewege's bright smiling face flashed before Maia's eyes—who deserved to be here. Then there was family, both her own and her friends', taken too soon. They had all lost much. This day had not come easily. This day was to be treasured, honored, and cherished. Forever.

"We kept hoping you could join us," Dani continued. "Ruche did not give us one straight answer when we asked if you could come. But then, that's him."

"Seriously, that Ruche," Nafi grumbled. "He had to bring you late so you missed Miir's big presentation."

Seeing the questioning look on Maia's face, Dani rushed to explain. "Well, this morning they finally finished the reworking of the Sedara's lattice, and Miir announced the successful completion. The Sedara and the other systems are self-sustaining on ambient starlight now. Also, the—"

"Dani, don't give everything away," Sana reminded sharply.

Dani stopped and flashed a sheepish grin, but Kusha frowned. "But Maia should know. She should've been the one to hear it first. This news was—"

"I agree, she should've," Sana interrupted once more. "But telling her now will take away from someone's big reveal to darling Maia."

"Ohhhhh . . ." Kusha said, grinning.

Laughs and giggles erupted at that point. As curious as Maia was about this big news, her attention was soon diverted by a familiar, but unexpected face in the crowd below. It was Ren's stepfather Lowanabe, the advisor to the queen. He had plotted the attack on her along with Phocluus, and as far as Maia had understood, he was supposed to be under arrest. But there he was, mixing and mingling with everyone as if he had done nothing. Ren was next to her, watching the people below, and he sighed the moment she looked at him.

"Lowanabe, right? He's gotten away with it again," he said. "There's no proof he was working with Phocluus. On the other hand, I have been disowned. My mother won't speak to me."

"Oh, I'm so sorry, Ren," Maia said. Her heart twitched at the unfairness of it all. Ren had risked everything to do the right thing, and to be punished for it was not fair. "I wish I could help."

Ren slipped an arm around her shoulders and leaned his head against hers. "Don't worry, Maia. Your being there for me is all I ever need. I'll be fine. Trust me. It's about time all those ventures of mine came in useful."

They stood in thoughtful silence for a while until behind them, the elevator thudded. The door opened and Miir strode in. He looked somber in his black Gambrill, his neurogenic interface covering the left half of his face, his closely-trimmed hair making his sharp features stand out. His keen eyes scanned the room, and Maia suddenly remembered the boy she had met so many years ago in Appian.

Then, as his intense gaze came to rest on Maia and softened, and his face broke into a bright smile, Maia held her breath.

That same boy, yet so different.

As was she, and the way she looked back at him. So different.

Nafi cleared her throat loudly. "Well? Are you two going to stand there looking at each other and ignore all of us?"

"I need to take Maia," Miir blurted.

Nafi crossed her arms and smirked. "You do, do you?"

A flush crept up his face but he nodded at Maia. "Yes. Ruche is waiting downstairs. So if you will excuse us, Nafi . . ."

Maia had just started to walk up to him when Sana sprang up from her seat.

"Hey! Not so fast." She wagged a finger severely at Maia before turning toward Miir. Squinting at him, she jabbed his shoulder with her finger. "You be good. Or I'll have to be very bad. You hear?"

Miir exhaled loudly. "Yes, I do."

Sana slowly moved aside and smiled at Maia. "All right, you may go now."

As they walked into the elevator, Nafi's exasperated voice boomed. "Seriously, guys? After everything those two have put us through over the years, that's all the grief we could give them? You disappoint me."

Ren chortled. "They're not going anywhere. We're not going anywhere either. There's all the time in the world to give them grief."

"Relax Nafi," Sana said, her voice determined. "Sana is not going easy on those two. Sana will make them pay for every bit of trouble they've caused."

As she watched the door of the elevator swivel and shut, Maia chuckled. She had to admit, they had put everyone through a lot. But her friends had never given up. Every time she had strayed — and she had, many times — they had found her and brought her back. Her friends were the reason today was happening.

Miir's voice brought Maia out of her thoughts.

"Your Sana is scary," he said, busily punching buttons on a panel.

"*My* Sana?"

"Well, I know her because of you, so . . ."

That was how it was going to be, then, Maia mused as the elevator whirled downward. All this while it had been "your Miir", and now it would also be "your Sana." She was still absorbed in her thoughts when Miir walked up to her.

"We finished re-latticing the Sedara," he said.

"Yes, I heard."

"Did you hear about the flight mechanism that fed off the heart?" He continued when Maia shook her head. "It has been permanently disabled."

"Oh!" Maia blurted. So *that* was what Sana had interrupted.

"Now you have nothing to worry about. Ever."

"Thank you." A smile, happy and relieved, flooded Maia's face. She was free. *Finally!* And that was why Miir had been working relentlessly for weeks. "I hear you've hardly had any rest."

"Rest was the last thing on my mind. But I did wish I could talk to you sooner," Miir said with a small chuckle. Another step bridged the space between them. His hand came to the side of Maia's face, tucking a runaway lock of hair gently behind her ear. His fingers, warm and tender, brushed over her cheek, making her tremble. Cupping her jaw, he tilted her face upward, and Maia stared, lost in the deep amber of his eyes as he leaned closer. "I have missed you, Maia."

Maia had never thought such simple words could make her heart flip so wildly. But then, the deepest truths were often just as simple, just as moving. Laughing as a wave of joy swept through her, Maia threw her arms around his neck and held him tight. Never, ever was she going to let this happiness slip away. The way Miir's arms wrapped around her, instantly and without hesitation, and pulled her even closer, Maia knew her happiness would last forever.

Ruche was waiting outside when the elevator door opened again.

"There you are," he said, smiling. "Come, Maia, they're waiting for you."

"What do you mean? Who's waiting for me?"

Ruche stopped outside the gigantic door with the emblem of the Trinational Coalition. "The whole council, obviously. Everyone wants to thank you for all you've done for them. Go on."

She looked curiously at Ruche and Miir as they fell back a step or two. "You're coming with me, right?

Ruche shook his head. "The floor is yours. But we'll be right behind you."

"What do I do in there?"

"Just be yourself," Miir said. "Be happy."

Be happy . . . could it be that simple?

Maia's steps were slow as she walked through the open doors into that massive room, her heart beating like a hammer in her chest. So many times she had walked into a council, and each time she had come back hurting. Could this really be any different?

A sea of faces stared at her and Maia could not tell one from another. Were they glad to see her? Not all, not likely. Some would not approve of her being on this stage, being alive at all. Did she even belong—

I do. I do belong.

Maia's stiffened her spine and stood taller, steadier. She had made this day possible. She had to remember that.

Someone clapped. As Maia's eyes grew wide, someone else joined in. And then there was a rumble. It soon grew into thunder as the entire council broke into applause. Tears welled up in Maia's eyes, and a smile, nervous and shy, broke on her face as her heart soared, freely, fearlessly, and full of hope.

. . . AND . . .

Chapter Sixty-Four

Beyond

The skies were the deepest azure, and soft golden sunlight lit up the grassy slopes around the little village of Appian in a luminous glow. A young man lay on a gray rock platform nestled cozily on a hillside full of bright yellow blooms. Next to him, a little girl sat with her arms wrapped tightly around her knees. She listened with rapt attention as he told her tales of years past, stories of the people who had rebuilt the world and brought everyone together. Her dreamy brown eyes widened slightly when the story ended.

"So the XDA opened up for everyone after the R'armimon left?" she asked, tilting her head inquisitively.

"Yes. Thirteen years ago, the XDA became a part of the Trinational University Systems of today—the old academy building now houses the largest and the best of them, the one you will go to in a few years."

The girl's face clouded at his last words and she looked away abruptly into the distance; her eyes rested on the dark patch of trees standing behind them.

"Vivi, what is it?" the man asked softly as he sat up to face her.

"They won't . . . take me," she said as she fidgeted with the ends of her tiny pigtails. "I can't hold a stick right and I can't even take off straight on a glider. Why will the best place in the world want someone like me?"

"I can think of several reasons why they would," he said, tenderly brushing at the strands of dark hair that had spilled onto her forehead. "For one, you will get better; you have years before you turn eleven. By then we will learn to hold the stick right. And you know what?"

"What?"

"Who needs a glider anyway? We will learn to fly a Raptor."

Little Vivi's eyes sparkled brightly for a moment before she whispered, "Mama?"

"Hmm . . . maybe Mama does not need to know," the man whispered back, a mischievous smile playing on his lips. "This will be our little secret."

"And maybe she means that I'm standing right behind you," said a woman, chuckling. Her hazel-green eyes caught the sunlight and sparkled, and a bright smile made her face luminous.

"Oof . . . that one is stealthy. Sneaks up like a cat." The man shuddered and cowered in pretend fear and as the little girl burst into giggles, he whispered, "Run and hide."

"Rawr!" the woman growled, swaying her arms in the air as Vivi shrieked and giggled some more. "You can't hide from me. I will find you." She kneeled next to the duo, laughing before speaking to the man. "She's barely five, Miir. Even you didn't fly a Raptor until you were ten."

Miir turned a little to peer at her face. "She will be fine, Maia." His voice was a gentle whisper. "I will be with her . . . we will be with her."

Maia had just started to protest when the child sighed.

"It doesn't matter. I won't be any good at it anyway," she said.

"Vivinah" —Maia's arms wrapped around the little girl in a blink and drew her close— "don't say that."

"But, Mama, I'm not as brave as you were or smart as you were." Vivinah curled up in Maia's lap, her little fingers nervously clutching a filigreed pendant that hung at her neck. "You were all heroes . . . and special . . . and I'm not."

Maia pulled Vivinah tighter into her bosom and kissed the top of her head. "Let me tell you a secret. We were not brave all the time. Or smart. Most of the time, we were just plain silly. And when I was your age, I was so, so silly. This one time, Herc showed me a complicated move, a circle-parry-strike. He told me not to try it, just about a hundred times. Guess what I did?"

"You tried?" Vivinah asked.

"Of course. I had to. I had to show him I could do it better. I fell over my wooden sword and scratched my arm so badly that Emmy refused to let me train for a month. Even Dada couldn't make her change her mind."

The little girl laughed and the sadness in her eyes faded, but only a little. "But you got better," she said. "What if I don't?"

"Shhhh . . . no more talking." Miir peered at his daughter's face and said with mock sternness, "Now show me your hands."

As Vivinah extended her hands, he held them together and placed a fistful of dust on her upturned palms.

"Go on," he said, smiling indulgently, "play with it the way you do."

The girl's face lit up with unexplainable joy—her tiny fingers started to tremble, slowly at first, and then faster and faster they danced in a silent mystical rhythm.

In the space above her hand, the dust spun and twirled into stunning shapes—it briefly took the form of a dragon, complete with tiny scales, morphed into an ethereal mermaid before turning into an enormous tree, its million leaves quivering expectantly. Then it all merged: the tree stood at the center, the dragon encircled its wide trunk and the mermaid floated gracefully at the base.

As the exquisite form dissolved and crumbled into powder again, Vivinah's fists closed possessively over it. Miir smiled and reached out to cup her small hands in his.

"You have a gift, Vivi. A gift that we have waited and prayed for over the centuries. You are a part of the hope, the dream that one day this scarred planet will be healed again and another one up in that sky will continue to thrive. You are more special than any one of us ever was, always remember that."

A soft sigh of relief escaped Maia's lips at the words that soothed and calmed. And when he stopped speaking, little Vivinah rested her head contentedly on Maia's cradling arms.

"And maybe . . ." Maia started. She chuckled as Miir looked at her knowingly even before she could say a word. "Maybe, just for a day . . . we can take Shadow out for a spin."

"Really, Mama?" Vivinah jumped up in excitement, and her eyes sparkled.

"Really."

The little girl took off with a whoop of joy; Maia smiled as Miir edged closer and laced his fingers through hers. On the luxuriant carpet of grass that stretched in front of them, Vivinah pranced and skipped and laughed with delight.

The soft sounds of the child's happy laughter filled the light morning air as it wafted gleefully across the hillside. Weaving through the flowers, down the slopes, and towards the wave of lush green that stretched outward assertively beyond the Penning Woods, it carried the young dreams of a world that was whole again.

— THE END —

APPENDIX

THE SOLIANESE

In order of appearance

Maia – girl from Appian, Core 21

Dorian – chieftain of Walenveil, leader of the Black Phantoms

Sana – Maia's cousin

Rayan – member of the Desert's Watch

Niyani – wife of Ori Pistado

Commander Hiso – leader of the Parliamentary Guards

Alasdair – parliamentarian, Sana's father, Maia's uncle

Steward Lok – steward of the House of the Sun, Kusha's father

Nahlo – younger son of Ori Pistado and Niyani

Nafi – girl from the Third Continent, Core 21

Sahiiraan Tsininio – Leader, unnamed Solianese House

Kusha – boy from the First Continent, Core 21

Monk Konnae – teacher at ThulaSu

The Xinhagyi – Chief of the Kausakas

Hadeeyah – student at ThulaSu, mentor to Core 21

Monk Tessio – teacher at ThulaSu

I

THE SOLIANESE (CONTD.)

Zaara – Sophie's friend, Leader of the Inception colony #4, Chief Arbitrator for the Initiative

Jiri – boy from the Second Continent, Core 13

Jez — student at ThulaSu

Monk Atriss — librarian at ThulaSu

Sahiiraan Goren – leader of a Solianese House

Pai – apprentice of the Desert's Watch

Anja — girl from Shiloh, Core 13

Maks — boy from Appian, student at ThulaSu

Enzo — attendant, House of the Sun

Aman — boy from Appian, student at ThulaSu

Nisa — girl from Appian, student at ThulaSu

Kenan — boy, Core 34

Lonnie — student at ThulaSu

Aunt Rowyena – Maia's aunt, Sana's mother, Alasdair's wife

Iriana – housemaid at Uncle Alasdair's

Hozzy — assistant at Inception Colony #4

Kam — assistant at Inception Colony #4

Nahsemi — older son of Ori Pistado and Niyani

THE SOLIANESE (CONTD.)

Aiani – student at ThulaSu

Merin – student at ThulaSu

THE JJORD

In order of appearance

Dani – girl from T'ra (Coloni Centrei), Core 21

Bikele – Sophie's friend

Aerika – Training Supervisor, UAAS

Luem – boy, Core 13

Junko — boy, Core 10

Hans – Dani's older brother

Oliena – Premier, Jjordic Council

Vin — engineer

Abebe — Chief Advisor to Premier Oliena

Joolsae – assistant trainer, UAAS, former mentor to Core 21

THE XIFARIANS

In order of appearance

Miir – former apprentice at the SDS, son of Asiyaah and the late Xifarian Chancellor, former mentor to Core 21

Ren – boy from Ixiil, Core 21

Asiyaah – mother of Remii and Miir, wife of the late Xifarian Chancellor, former Master at the XDA

Kehorkjin – Resident Master at the XDA

Baecca – girl from Armezai, Core 7

Loriine – girl from Armezai, Core 7

Karhann – boy from Armezai, Miir's cousin, Core 7

Bakhari – boy, Core 7 Geir-Sei – Vice Principal at the XDA

Demissie – Flight Master at the XDA

Remii – operative at the SDS, older son of Asiyaah and the late Xifarian Chancellor

Rahina Quemiila – Queen of the Xifarian Republic

Statesman Orano Taillefei – Xifarian statesman, Amanii's father

Amanii – apprentice at the SDS

Damone – apprentice at the SDS

Pomewege – Principal of the XDA

THE XIFARIANS (CONTD.)

Adi — boy, Core 7

Eilen — pilot on Ti

Gino — Overseer, East Seam

Samal — assistant to the principal of the XDA

Neiran Komus Lowanabe – advisor to the Supreme Ruler on Xif, Ren's stepfather

Phocluus – Emeritus Master of the XDA; Chairman of the SDS

THE R'ARMIMON

In order of appearance

Aekken – Crown Prince, heir-in-waiting of the R'armimon Throne

The Emperor – emperor of the R'armimon Empire

Ruche – Seer of the R'armimon

ABOUT THE AUTHOR

S. G. Basu is a telecommunications professional with a passion for writing. The first ideas for this story came to her on a blustery winter's evening while watching the setting sun and realizing how vital it is to our existence. As she dwelled on the central premise, characters joined the fray, each with a voice that would not be denied. Therefore, their stories grew, unfolding over several episodes. Their adventures continue as they mature and flourish.

Ms. Basu resides in Maryland with her husband and daughter.

There's more to come. Find out about upcoming books at
www.sgbasu.com.